THE JACKAL OF NAR

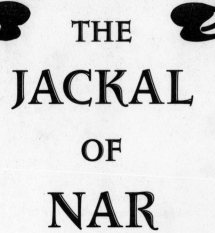

THE
JACKAL
OF
NAR

BOOK ONE OF
Tyrants and Kings

JOHN MARCO

BANTAM BOOKS
NEW YORK TORONTO LONDON SYDNEY AUCKLAND

THE JACKAL OF NAR
A Bantam Spectra Book / March 1999

SPECTRA and the portrayal of a boxed "s" are trademarks of Bantam Books,
a division of Random House, Inc.

Library of Congress Cataloging-in-Publication Data
Marco, John.
The jackal of Nar / John Marco.
p.   cm.—(A Bantam spectra book) (Tyrants and kings ; bk. 1)
ISBN 0-553-37984-4
I. Title. II. Series: Marco, John. Tyrants and kings ; bk. 1.
PS3563.A63628J3   1999
813'.54—dc21   98-36117
CIP

Published simultaneously in the United States and Canada

Bantam Books are published by Bantam Books, a division of Random House, Inc. Its trademark,
consisting of the words "Bantam Books" and the portrayal of a rooster, is Registered in U.S. Patent
and Trademark Office and in other countries. Marca Registrada. Bantam Books, 1540 Broadway,
New York, New York 10036.

PRINTED IN THE UNITED STATES OF AMERICA

FFG   10 9 8 7 6 5 4 3 2 1

For Deborah,
the light of my life

ACKNOWLEDGMENTS

Like all first novels, this one was completed with the help and encouragement of some very special people. I would like to express my enormous appreciation to them all.

First, to my wife Deborah, to whom this book is dedicated. She is my greatest inspiration and my truest love.

To my family—Mom, Dad, Christine, Donna, and Grampa—for always being there and for always believing in me. Thanks, gang.

To my editor Anne Lesley Groell, for her insight and guidance, and for just being open to new writers.

To Russell Galen and Danny Baror, for sharing my vision of this book and for helping to make it a reality.

To Kristin Lindstrom, for being there at the beginning.

To Douglas Beekman, for his magnificent cover art.

Lastly, to my dear friend and fellow writer Ted Xidas, for convincing me it could be done. This book simply would not exist without him.

Many thanks to you all. I am tremendously grateful.

Visit John Marco on the web at www.tyrantsandkings.com

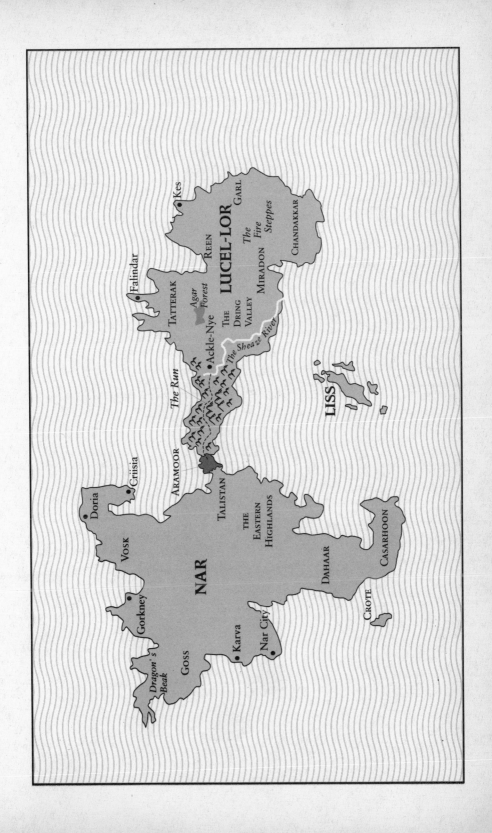

KES

GARL

LUCEL-LOR

REEN

The Fire

Steppes

MIRADON

CHANDAKKAR

FALINDAR

TATTERAK

Agar Forest

Ackle-Nye

THE DRING VALLEY

The Sheaze River

The Run

ARAMOOR

CRÜSIA

TALISTAN

LISS

DORIA

THE EASTERN HIGHLANDS

VOSK

DAHAAR

CASARHOON

NAR

GORKNEY

CROTE

KARVA

Nar City

GOSS

Dragon's Beak

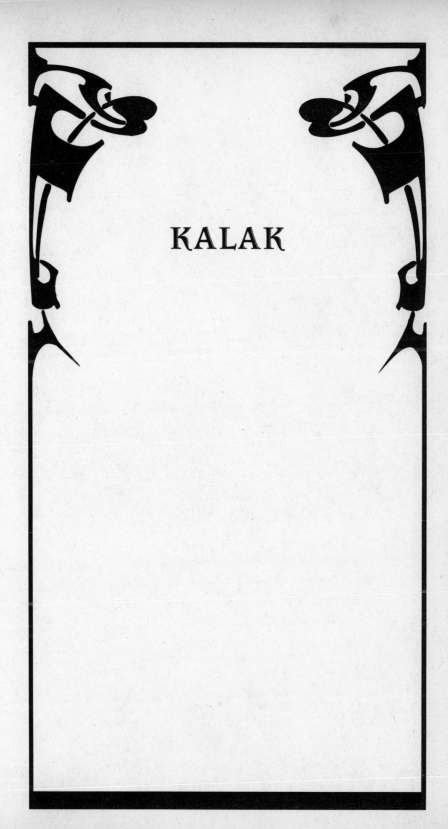

KALAK

From the Journal of Richius Vantran:

I have been dreaming of wolves.

Sleep has become too precious for us now. The war wolves come almost every night, and we are all afraid to sleep for fear of waking to that terrible sound. I've had the men take turns on the flame cannons so that some of them may rest. We've already lost our best cannoneers to the beasts. It's odd how they know how to hurt us. But the cannons are still working, and we have enough kerosene to keep them going for a few more days. Perhaps Gayle's horsemen will arrive by then.

It seems Voris doesn't care how many of his people die. These Drol are not like other Triin. They are zealots and die too easily. Even the cannons don't frighten them. Their bodies are piling up outside the trenches, beginning to stink. If the wind doesn't shift soon we shall all be sick from it. We've taken to burying our own dead in the back trenches so they don't rot here next to us. I don't think the Drol are so concerned about their fallen. I've watched them leave their comrades to die when they could have easily pulled them to safety. They don't cry out when wounded, but crawl away alone while we pick at them with arrows. And when they die they do it silently. Lucyler says they are madmen, and sometimes I cannot doubt it. It is hard for us from Nar to understand these Triin and their ways, even with Lucyler's help. He is not very religious, but there are times when he is as inscrutable as any Drol. Still, I am always thankful for him. He has taught me much about his strange people. He has helped me see them less as monsters. If I ever get home, if this damn civil war ever ends, I will tell my father about Lucyler and his folk. I will tell him that we of Nar have always been wrong about the Triin, that they love their children just as we do, and that they bleed red blood despite their pale skin. Even the Drol.

This valley has become a trap for us. I haven't told the men yet, but I don't think we can keep the Drol from Ackle-Nye much longer. Voris has been pushing hard. He knows we are weak. If more men don't come soon we will certainly be overrun. I've sent a message to Father but have yet to hear a reply, and I don't think one will be forthcoming. We haven't had supplies from home for weeks, so we've started hunting for our own food. Even the hard army bread has spoiled from keeping too long. We've been throwing it out of the trenches to keep the rats away. Spoiled meat and bread doesn't seem to bother vermin, and while they feed we are free of them. But we are also slowly starving, for even in this valley we can't hunt enough meat to keep us all fed. Perhaps Father doesn't know how bad it is for us, or perhaps he no longer cares. Either way, if help doesn't come soon we'll be fighting our final battle in Ackle-Nye and then it will be done. And Voris will have beaten me.

The Drol of the valley have taken to calling me Kalak. Lucyler told me it's Triin for "The Jackal." They are bold about it, too. I can hear them shouting it in the woods, taunting me, hoping to lure us out of the trenches. When they attack they yell it like a battle cry, swinging their jiiktars and screaming Kalak as they fall upon us. But I prefer this battle cry to the one they always yelled before. To hear them cry the name of Voris reminds me of his loyal wolves and the long nights ahead.

Lonal died in this morning's raid. No one seems to know how the Drol who killed him got so close to the cannon, but by the time I saw him it was hopeless. I had to take the cannon myself, so quickly I couldn't even help him. He lived for a bit after he was struck, but his arm had been taken off and the men who dragged him away had left it there, and I didn't notice it until the raid was over. Dinadin and I buried Lonal in the back trench, and Lucyler said some words neither of us understood. Lonal liked Lucyler, and I doubt a Triin prayer would have bothered him. But we are bothered that our friend has been buried like a dead horse in the corner of this foreign valley. When I return home I'll have to tell Lonal's parents how he died, but I won't tell them how his body is moldering in a mass grave, and I won't tell them that a Triin who was his friend said a prayer over him. Any Triin prayer, Drol or not Drol, would be an insult to them. It is Triin prayers that have caused all this. We are dying because of their prayers.

Dinadin is quiet now. I've never known him to be so damaged by the death of a friend. Back home he was always the loud one, but things here have made him thoughtful. After we buried Lonal, he told me that we should leave the valley, leave these Triin to slaughter themselves. We've all done things we're not proud of, things we won't tell our parents when we return home. Maybe even things we'll have to answer for to our own God. Tonight I'll let Dinadin mourn, but tomorrow I must have him back. He must again be the one who makes our regiment want to fight. He must hate the Drol again, hate Voris and his warriors.

Still, I can't help but wonder if Dinadin is right. I hear the men talking, and I fear I am losing them all. Worse, there is nothing I can say to them. Even I don't know why we're fighting. We're propping up an evil man, only so another evil man can extend his overgrown empire. Father is right about the emperor. He wants something here. But what he seeks is a mystery, and while he waits comfortably in his palace, we die. None of the men believe our cause is just, and even Lucyler has doubts about his Daegog. He knows the royal line of Lucel-Lor is doomed, that the Drol and their revolution will sweep away the old order eventually. Yet he and the other loyalists fight on for their fat king, and we of Nar fight with them, just to make our own despot richer. I hate the Drol, but they are right about one thing. The emperor will suck the blood out of the Triin.

But, Journal, I should be quiet about such things. And tonight I need to rest. This evening is peaceful. I can hear the sounds of the valley creatures and the stray calls of my name in the woods, but they don't frighten me. Only thoughts of the wolves that might come keep me from sleeping. Today's dead are all buried, and I can smell the fatty grease of the roasting wild birds we've caught. A pipe would be welcome now, or the wines of Ackle-Nye. If my sleep is peaceful I may dream of them both.

And tomorrow we'll begin again, maybe for the last time. If the Wolf of the valley knows how weak we are, he'll surely come in force enough to crush us. We'll do our best to stand, and hope the horsemen promised by Gayle will arrive in time to save us. We hear little in the valley, and the horsemen can't travel quickly here. I only wish it were my own horsemen coming to our rescue rather than those of that rogue. It would indeed be a tale for him to tell that he had saved me.

If we make it through the fight tomorrow, I'll send another message to Father. I'll tell him that we've come to depend on the House of Gayle for survival. I can think of nothing else that will rouse him to our aid. I know he doesn't want this war, but I'm here and he must help me. If no more troops are sent, all the valley will fall back into the hands of the Wolf. We'll lose this war and Father's argument with the emperor will be our deaths. If we are to survive, I must convince Father this war is worth fighting.

ONE

Richius awoke to the smell of kerosene. A familiar cry sounded in the distance. He knew what it was before his eyes snapped open. *Oh, God, no . . .*

He was on his feet in an instant. Around him the trench bloomed big and black. The yellow fingers of a new day's sun had barely begun to scratch at the horizon. He squinted hard, struggling to see down the earthen corridor. Dying torches tossed their light onto men in muddy uniforms, a group of soldiers huddling at the trench's other end. Richius slogged toward them.

"Lucyler, what's happening?" he called, sighting his bone-colored friend.

"It is Jimsin," said Lucyler. "Got him while he slept."

Richius pushed his way into the armored circle. At the center writhed what only vaguely resembled a man. Though the band of soldiers tried to pin his flailing limbs, Jimsin's body pitched to the ugly cadence of his screams. Beside him, lying in a great unmoving heap, was the body of a wolf, its hide punctured with a hundred stab wounds.

"Took it in the throat," said one of the group, a big ruddy man with the face of a boy. As Richius bent over Jimsin, the big man knelt beside him.

"Careful," warned another. "It's bad."

The war wolf's teeth had ravaged Jimsin's throat, leaving a wound that ran all the way up to the jaw. A mangled windpipe blew on tattered flesh. Jimsin's eyes widened hopefully as he recognized Richius.

"Don't move, Jimsin," ordered Richius. "Lucyler, what the hell happened?"

"My fault," confessed Lucyler. "It was so dark. It was in the trench before I saw it. Let me help—"

"Get back to the deck," snapped Richius. "Keep an eye out for them. All of you, get back to the deck!"

The big man passed Richius a soiled cloth. He wrapped it gingerly around the oozing wound. The muffled echo of a scream escaped the ruined throat and Jimsin's hands shot up, seizing Richius' wrists. Richius started to pull his hands free then stopped himself, unwilling to release the pressure from the wound.

"No, Jimsin," he said. "Dinadin, help me with him!"

Dinadin quickly pulled Jimsin's hands away, holding them down while Richius worked to secure the bandage. The awful half-scream kept coming, muffled now by the dirty rag. From the corner of his eye Richius noticed Dinadin's blond head begin to turn.

"Are they coming?" Richius asked, already beginning to work more quickly.

"Not yet," said Dinadin. There was a note of mourning in his voice. By the end of the day Jimsin would be lying next to Lonal.

"God," Richius moaned. "He's suffocating."

Dinadin still had Jimsin's wrists. He fought to hold his comrade down as blood gushed from the wound. Jimsin tried to scream again, each cry sending another bloom of crimson into the bandage. The high-pitched gurgles grew in urgency. Jimsin closed his eyes. A stream of tears burst from beneath the lids.

"Help him, Richius!"

"I'm trying!" said Richius desperately. If he removed the rag, Jimsin would surely bleed to death. Leave the bandage, and he would suffocate. At last Richius reached out and lightly touched Jimsin's tear-streaked face.

"Jimsin," he whispered gently, unsure if the man could hear him. "I'm sorry, my friend. I don't know how to save you."

"What are you doing?" shouted Dinadin, releasing his grip on Jimsin. "Can't you see he's dying? Do something!"

"Stop!" cried Richius, dropping down across the wounded man to hold him still. Dinadin made to undo the bloody bandage, but Richius pushed him aside.

"Damn it, Richius, he can't breathe!"

"Leave it!" Richius ordered. The sharpness in his voice made Dinadin recoil. "I know he's dying. So let him die. If you take away the rag he'll live a lot longer. Do you really want that?"

Dinadin's eyes were glassy and mute, like a doll's eyes. He sat stupefied as Richius motioned him closer.

"You want to help him?" asked Richius. "Then hold him still. Be with him when he dies."

"Richius . . ."

"That's it, Dinadin. That's all you can do. All right?"

Dinadin slowly nodded. He drew Jimsin into his arms and held him, hugging him tightly. Richius turned away to find Lucyler, leaving the two soldiers in their dismal embrace.

The Triin was easy to spot in the dim trench. His white skin was a beacon; his white hair waved like a flag of surrender. He stood upon the observation deck built into the trench wall, fascinated with the silent forest of birch trees in the distance. He hardly stirred as Richius climbed onto the deck.

"Is he dead?" asked Lucyler.

"Almost."

Lucyler's chin fell to his chest. "I am sorry," he said wearily.

"Blame the rebels," said Richius. "Not yourself."

"I should have seen it coming."

"A single wolf in the night? No one could have seen that, Lucyler. Not even you."

Lucyler closed his eyes. "Why only one?" he muttered. "Voris never sends only one. . . ."

"To break us. We're not up against honorable men, Lucyler, you know that. Hell, you're the one who told me that. They're Drol. They're snakes."

"Voris does not lay siege, Richius. It has never been his way. They are out there. They will be coming."

Richius nodded. When it came to figuring out his rebellious adversary, he always deferred to Lucyler's judgment. Lucyler wasn't Drol, but he was a Triin, and there was a perplexing chemistry in all Triin brains, a singleness of thought that even the most intelligent Naren couldn't decipher. Call it instinct or breeding, call it the "touch of heaven" as the Drol did; the Triin did indeed seem more than human sometimes. And Lucyler's mind was like a razor blade. When this particular Triin smelled fear, Richius never argued.

Lucyler had been somewhat of a gift, an aide sent by the worried Daegog to make sure the valley war went right. Of them all, Lucyler was the only Triin in the company, and he did not hail from Dring but from Tatterak, the rugged region of Lucel-Lor to which the Daegog had been exiled. As a sworn servant of the Triin leader, Lucyler had one mission—to ensure Richius was victorious. Though they didn't always agree, Richius was forever grateful to the Daegog for sending him Lucyler. He was the fastest bowman in the company, and he could spot a red-robed Drol faster than a hawk.

Richius looked out over the trenches behind them. Barret gave them a wave from the one his men were stationed in, some ten yards to the rear. Behind Barret's trench he saw that of Gilliam, and behind Gilliam's the least-seasoned men in the company sat in their own trench, commanded by Ennadon.

There were those in the company who had quarreled with Richius about the way he had posted the new recruits. Lucyler had argued that only battle could teach the new men the things they needed to know. Richius saw no use in such a tactic. He remembered with painful clarity his first days in Lucel-Lor, when Colonel Okyle had been in charge of the valley war. Okyle had ordered Richius and a dozen other "virgins" into a forest on a scouting mission. Like Lucyler, Okyle believed battle to be a soldier's best teacher, and it only made things worse for Richius that he was the king's son. Favoritism, Okyle had told him sternly, was not to be expected. Only when Richius returned from the forest alone did Okyle start rethinking the way he handled new recruits. But Okyle was dead now, and Richius had taken over. He was determined to do everything he could to spare his new men the horrors that would be upon them too soon anyway.

Keep them in the back and they'll be safe, he told himself as he signaled to Ennadon. *Let Ennadon teach them what they need to know first. Time enough for fighting.*

Still . . .

If Voris came at them fully it would do the new men no good to be in the back trenches. There would be no haven in the Dring Valley for any of them. He supposed that he had three hundred men left, yet he had no idea how many Voris still had. A thousand? More? Even Lucyler couldn't guess at the numbers of their enemy. They knew only one thing for sure; the master of the valley had enough warriors to destroy them.

Only the cannons can save us now, thought Richius fretfully. *If the fuel lasts . . .*

At both ends of the trench, where men gathered in little bunches to talk and worry, the flame cannons were heated and poised. Wisps of smoke rose from their tapered noses, their igniters glowing red against the coming dawn. The sight of their two-man teams forced an uneasy smile from Richius. These machines had been their salvation. Though a dearth of fuel had forced him to ration their use, he was grateful to have even a few of the weapons. The scientists who tinkered in the war labs of Nar had outdone themselves when they created them.

To the men in the trenches the cannons were worthy of worship. Like the soldiers of Aramoor, the Triin of the valley had arrows and spears and their own odd-looking swords, but they had nothing so powerful as the cannons. Even their magic—the dread of which had long deterred invaders from their land—had yet to prove a threat. Though many said otherwise, swore in fact that the Drol leader Tharn was a sorcerer, none of the men had seen Triin magic, and Lucyler had been vocal in his skepticism. The belief in the touch of heaven was the one great division that separated the Drol from the rest of the Triin. It was part of what made the Drol fanatics.

"Richius?" asked Lucyler. "Should I have Dinadin take a cannon?"

"Kally and Crodin can handle them."

"Dinadin's the best cannoneer left. What if . . ."

"Lord, Lucyler," interrupted Richius. "Look at him." He pointed down the trench to where Dinadin sat, cradling the limp body of Jimsin. "You want to tell him?"

Lucyler said nothing. Of the three close friends that remained, Lucyler was the hardest of the trio. Perhaps it was his Triin blood that made him so callous, or perhaps it was because he had seen more of the war than any of them. Whatever its origin, Lucyler's severity was always evident. It was only at times like these, however, when he had a mind to question decisions, that Lucyler's hard-heartedness irritated Richius.

And Dinadin had changed. He still followed orders, but there was a reluctance in his eyes, a kind of sad maturity that had never been there before. Richius had promised Dinadin's father he would look out for the man, that he would bring him home alive from this hellish place, and that one day they would sit again around the hearth in the House of Lotts and laugh about better days.

"He'll be ready," said Richius with feigned confidence.

"I hope so. We're going to need him if . . ."

Lucyler stopped, his gray eyes widening. Richius let his own gaze slip back to the birch grove. There, among the twisted limbs, something stirred. From behind the trees and rocks came a torrent of crimson. Spots of charcoal with shining eyes dotted the forefront of the flood.

A knot of terror tied itself in Richius' stomach.

"Ignite the cannons!" he cried.

Far down the trench Kally fired up his weapon. The cannon screamed as it came alive, belching a cloud of spent kerosene into the air. Within seconds a red funnel of flame poured from its orifice. Next Crodin ignited his own cannon, trimming its fiery plume into a spear-shaped stream. Other cannons ignited in the trenches behind them, kerosene pumping into their long noses and being spit out again as fire. Even in the cold morning, Richius could feel the heat of the bursts beneath his armor.

"Protect the cannons!" Richius barked. "They're coming!"

What had looked at first like a flood of scarlet water was now plainly a wave of red-robed men breaking toward them. Wolves were running before the wave. Dozens of them.

"Lorris and Pris," whispered Lucyler. "We are finished."

Behind the beasts came swarms of warriors, each one shouting and brandishing a dual-bladed jiiktar. Lucyler gritted his teeth and snarled.

"Come then, damned Drol!" he cried, and gave the center of his own jiiktar a powerful twist. The weapon came apart in his hands, forming two light, long-bladed swords.

Along the deck the soldiers steeled themselves. There was the snapping of bowstrings as the air filled with arrows. The missiles landed among the wolves, puncturing their thick black hides. An arrow caught one of them in the snout, lodging itself between flaring nostrils. Undeterred, the wolf raced on, homing for the cannons—just as Voris had trained it to do.

At once the archers at the trench's left flank focused on the pack. Kally aimed his cannon, his face streaked with black smudges from the weapon's backblast.

"More fuel!" he barked.

His lineman twisted the valve on the feed hose. Kally squeezed the trigger. Red lightning erupted. The bolt blew the wolves backward, their coats torn by the impact of the fire. An unearthly shriek rose above the bellow of the cannons. To Richius, the sound was like music.

Dinadin climbed onto the deck and peered out into the distance. His face was flushed from weeping.

"Bloody gogs," he spat, fumbling an arrow to his bow.

"No," said Richius. "Not here. I want you near a cannon."

"They're already manned. . . ."

"By a cannon!"

Dinadin grumbled and started off down the deck, squeezing his big body past the others. In wolf attacks, cannoneers were always the first to fall.

A shout from Lucyler galvanized the deck. The Triin stretched out one of his swords, pointing at a black mass closing quickly in on them. The wolf with the arrow in its snout had somehow made it through the cross fire of the cannons. Little blazes glowed and smoldered in its coat, sending bits of burning hair drizzling down in its wake.

The beast leapt, a howl tearing from its mouth, its nostrils snorting bloody mucus. Lucyler cried out. He dropped to one knee and swung his curved blade in a blazing arc. Richius stumbled backward, falling off the deck into the trench below. He felt the shock of pain as his armor was driven into his back and rib cage. The head with the arrow splashed into the mud beside him.

Quickly Richius got to his feet and dashed to the nearest ladder. But before he could place his foot on a rung another scream stopped him. He looked left and saw a wolf on top of Kally. The beast had knocked the cannoneer into the trench. Already Dinadin had leapt into the ditch after it, smashing his bow against the wolf's head. Yet it wasn't the sight of Kally being savaged that frightened Richius; it was the sight of the unmanned cannon. The wolf had toppled the cannon from its base so that the weapon pointed skyward, spewing flame upward like a huge orange fountain. And though he was no longer on the deck to see it, Richius knew the wolves had already sensed the hole in the Narens' defenses.

"Dinadin!" Richius shouted. "Get the cannon!"

Dinadin glanced at Richius, a horrified expression on his face. Kally was still alive.

"Get the bloody cannon!" Richius repeated, his voice cracking. He was sure Dinadin could hear him, even over the roar of the fallen weapon. Yet Dinadin ignored him, continuing instead to land blow after useless blow on the wolf. When at last Richius reached them he pushed Dinadin aside and brought his sword down upon the creature's neck. There was a spray of blood as the head fell forward, held to the torso by a hinge of skin. The wolf fell upon Kally, lifeless. Kally too was still. Richius turned and glared at Dinadin. The young man stared back at him, his face twisted in confusion. Richius grabbed Dinadin's breastplate and shook him.

"What's wrong with you?" he screamed, ignoring the storm of sparks coming down and biting them like bee stings. "You heard me ordering you to the cannon!"

Dinadin said nothing. Tears ran down his face, leaving clean rivulets on his sooty skin. Richius stopped shaking him.

"Dinadin?"

Dinadin was silent.

"Come on, Dinadin. We have to get the cannon."

At last Dinadin's eyes flared to life. He pulled away from Richius, roaring, "To hell with your cannon! What did you want me to do, leave him to die?"

"God's death!" cursed Richius, pushing past Dinadin. "The cannon is more important! You know that." He stooped to avoid the flames and grabbed for the weapon, shielding his face with his forearm.

"Richius, stop!"

The voice was Lucyler's. Richius released the cannon at once, unable to loose the jammed trigger. The Triin was waving at him frantically.

"All right, let's get out of here," said Richius, turning away from the cannon. "The trench is lost."

Dinadin looked helpless. "Richius . . ."

"Forget it," Richius snapped, waving for Dinadin to follow. Lucyler jumped into the trench ahead of them.

"Too many," the Triin called out. "And the warriors are coming."

"Signal the second trench to cover our retreat," Richius called back. "Dinadin, get everyone out of here."

At the other end of the trench, Crodin was struggling to hold back the onslaught of wolves and warriors with his cannon. When Richius barked retreat, Crodin beamed with relief. Richius and Lucyler made their way to him, climbing onto the deck beside him and his lineman, Ellis. All around them men hurried out of the trench. Drol warriors were pouring out of the woods. Only a few precious moments remained.

"One last blast, Cro, then we move," said Richius, his hand already poised to undo the fuel line. "Lucyler, you and Ellis take the tank. We'll get the cannon."

Lucyler put his hands around the fuel tank. Ellis did the same, his back stooped for lifting. A chorus of *Kalak* broke from the ranks of the running Drol.

"Get ready, Crodin," whispered Richius. "Ellis, give us all you can."

"Here's everything," Ellis answered, loosening the valve that fed the cannon its combustible fuel. There was a hiss as the liquid swam through the line.

Crodin squeezed the trigger, coaxing a blast from the cannon like none Richius had ever seen. It exploded all around them with a concussive boom. Richius fell to his knees, gasping and clasping his ears. Beside him Lucyler and Ellis were running for the rear trenches, the fuel tank in their hands.

"Richius!" cried Lucyler, dropping the tank.

Richius waved him onward. "Get moving!"

He staggered to his feet as Lucyler and Ellis hurried away, the heavy tank dangling between them. A volley of arrows rose from the rear trenches to cover their escape.

"Let's go, Richius," said Crodin, wrapping the hot metal cannon in a swaddling of rags. He had already loosened the fittings that kept the cannon secured to the deck. Richius had yet to remove the weapon's feed line. Cursing, he fumbled to find the metal collar that fixed the line. Crodin shook his end of the cannon.

"Forget the line," he shouted. "We'll drag it!"

Richius grabbed the cannon and lifted. He tucked the heavy weapon beneath his arm and ran for the next trench, Crodin and the still-fastened fuel line in tow. Barret was on its deck, waving and shouting. Behind them, the cover provided by the last blast had dissipated. There was another shower of arrows from Barret's men.

They were only yards from safety now. Soldiers scrambled out of the trench to meet them. Richius gratefully let the others carry the cannon the few remaining feet. Exhausted, he collapsed onto the deck next to Lucyler.

"You all right?" Lucyler asked quickly.

"Set up the cannon in the center of the trench," Richius gasped. "Have Dinadin and Ellis man it."

Crodin was already working to settle the cannon into its new home, propping the weapon into a makeshift stand Ellis had built from two swords. The swords had been driven into the deck and fashioned into a "V," so that now the cannon rested uneasily in the notch. Dinadin was beside them, cracking the knuckles of his trigger hand.

Richius looked out over the battlefield. Ten yards away, Drol warriors were climbing into the forward trench, digging themselves in for protection. Already Drol archers were sending their own arrows skyward. Fires flickered about the field, some of them as small as the corpses they consumed, others as large as battle wagons. Clouds of bluish smoke floated above them, bearing aloft the stink of flesh and kerosene. And past the smoke, past the infernos and the flying arrows, the birch grove was crimson with Drol.

Crodin erected the cannon in its unsteady cradle. Lucyler stepped back and looked at their handiwork as Dinadin slipped his finger into the weapon's trigger guard. The cannon swayed without toppling.

"It will work," Lucyler called to Richius. "Not for long, though."

"Good enough," said Richius impatiently. "With three cannons we should be able to hold them off awhile."

And then what? wondered Richius. *Throw rocks at them? We're running out of fuel. Without the cannons . . .*

He stopped himself. *Not now. Work to do.*

"Dinadin," he called. "Get ready. Give them a big blast first, then ease up on the trigger."

Dinadin had turned an unpleasant shade of gray. He tucked himself behind the flame cannon.

"Take it slow," encouraged Richius. "That cannon isn't stable and we're running out of fuel. If—"

A shout from the rear trenches made Richius stop. He turned and looked behind him. Another shout rose up, high and strangely gleeful.

"What . . . ?"

From out of the distance a mass of galloping horsemen was riding toward them. At their forefront, barely visible against the horizon, flew a banner of green. Though he couldn't see it, Richius knew that a golden, charging horse was embroidered on the banner. It was the banner of Talistan, the crest of the House of Gayle.

"The horsemen!" cried Crodin.

Richius grimaced, a name coming to his lips like a sickness. "Gayle."

"Look, Richius," exclaimed Dinadin. "We're saved!"

"Seems so," replied Richius dully.

There were scores of horsemen, enough to best even this many Drol. From his place on the deck Richius could see the Drol already reacting to the coming cavalry. The tide of red robes ebbed a little.

"We should attack," said Dinadin anxiously. "We could crush them with so many horsemen!"

Richius shot Dinadin a pointed stare. "We'll hold our position." He turned to Lucyler and added, "I want everyone ready to defend the trenches. Let's avoid a fight if we can."

"Unlikely," said Lucyler. "Look."

Across the valley, a cloud of dust rose up. The horsemen were charging.

"Oh, God," Richius groaned. "They're going to attack." He quickly raised his arms over his head and signaled to his men, shouting to get their attention.

"Listen to me!" he called. "The horsemen are attacking. But we still have a position to defend. Nobody gets out of the trenches unless I order it. Barret, make sure all of your men stay put. In the other trenches, too. Dinadin, I want you ready on that cannon. As soon as the Drol see what's happening they might make a run for us."

"I'll be ready," Dinadin replied, settling himself behind the weapon.

The horsemen were closing the gap quickly. In the forward trench Drol warriors squatted on the deck, gibbering and pointing toward the coming cavalry. The banner of the horsemen was clearer now, shining green and gold in the growing light, carried forward by a charging, armored gelding. Richius grinned. Rivals or not, the sight of so many fine animals was beautiful. These were among the finest horses in the Empire, and the men that rode them rivaled his own kinsmen in skill. But these were not the horsemen of Aramoor.

The riders drew their swords. Ugly, serrated blades. On their heads were helmets forged into the likenesses of demons.

These were the horsemen of Talistan.

"You were right," Lucyler whispered. "Impressive."

Dinadin scowled. "Not as impressive as the Aramoor Guard, right, Richius?"

"Hardly," Richius quipped.

The horsemen galloped faster, shaking the air with the thunder of their attack. Splitting into two groups, they began to flank the trenches. Not even when they reached the bodies did they slow their hellish charge. With a trained sureness they trampled over the loose earth of the graves, and where unburied bodies lay supine, the chargers simply jumped over them. Soon the two teams were galloping past the trenches, hurrying across the battlefield toward the Drol.

Richius had fought from horseback before. He knew the power a man could will into a weapon from the back of a speeding steed. The Drol, however, seemed stunned by the attack. Despite their numbers, the warriors of the valley were helpless beside the horses. They had come out into the open. And the beasts they faced were bred for war. They showed none of the respect for people that their parade-ground brethren felt. Unless the tug of a rein came to stop it, a warhorse paid little attention to the barrier posed by a living being. Within moments dozens of the warriors were crushed beneath hooves.

From atop their armored mounts, where the white heads of the Drol floated at the level of their waists, the horsemen lowered their weapons. Jiiktars collided with broadswords and bare fists with armor, and Richius watched it all with a feeling of utter impotence. He longed to run out of the trench, to join in the bloodletting and his own liberation. But as Dinadin and the others eyed him hopefully, he barked only one command. "Hold your position!"

A single horseman rode toward the trench. He was grander than the rest, his warhorse gilded with silver, his demon-faced helmet polished and bejeweled. Upon his breastplate pranced an embossed horse of gold, and at his side dangled an unblemished blade. Lucyler pointed his chin at the rider as he drew near.

"Richius, is that Gayle?"

Richius straightened. "It is."

The rider stopped his horse just shy of the trench. He raised the visor of his helmet and looked down into the trench and the men there watching him. Finally, his black beard parted.

"Vantran?"

Richius raised a filthy hand. "Here."

Blackwood Gayle laughed. "The valley has been hard on you, Vantran. I scarcely recognized you."

Richius forced a smile. "You were easy to recognize, Baron."

"How many gogs are there?"

"As many as you see and more," answered Richius. "Voris has been pushing us hard."

"Indeed. Well, we're here now, Vantran. We'll take care of them for you." He lowered his helmet and began to turn his horse back to the battle, calling over his shoulder, "Clear that forward trench, why don't you?"

Richius cringed in hot anger. He wanted to yell back at Gayle, to hurl an obscenity at him, but he only swore under his breath. To his surprise, he heard Dinadin cursing with him.

"What scum," Dinadin hissed. "He can't talk to you that way, Richius."

"He doesn't care who we are, Dinadin, you know that. We're Aramoor and he's Talistan, and that's all he sees when he looks at us."

"What now?" asked Lucyler carefully.

Richius tightened his hand around his sword and sighed. "Now we clear the forward trench."

TWO

It was his father who had taught Richius the value of trenches in warfare. The older Vantran, a veteran of numerous battles, had used the ditches and catacombs in his war against Talistan. Though not impregnable, a trench was like a fortress to the men inside it. With a wall of archers on its deck, a trench was difficult to reach and nearly impossible to overrun. They had kept Richius' company alive during countless Drol raids. Until now, the Drol had never breached them.

The job of clearing the forward trench had been sickening. Refusing to flee or surrender, the Drol who had seized it had chosen to fight, leaving Richius with one dismal option—to go into the ditch after them. So, with shield and sword in hand, he led a brigade into the trench. And the Drol were summarily slaughtered.

The sun was high overhead when the gruesome work was finally finished. Slick with Triin gore, Richius emerged from the trench in a stupor. The field, once teeming with men and wolves and horses, was now awash with bodies. Drol bodies. They were everywhere, some whole, some in pieces, some so trampled by horse hooves as to be only pulp. The mud of the field had turned a ruddy purple. Things that had been men and wolves burned in stinking pockets of fire, and the air was rank with the smell of kerosene. Except for the buzzards, only one thing moved amidst the astonishing carnage.

Blackwood Gayle sat astride his horse, surveying the damage his troops had occasioned. His demon-faced helmet gleamed in the smoky sunlight. At his side hung his still-unblemished sword. His head turned toward the trenches as he noticed Richius.

"Vantran," he cried, spurring his horse forward. Beneath the helmet's faceplate the big voice rang like metal.

Richius ignored the baron. He got to his feet and stooped to help Lucyler out of the trench. Behind the Triin came Dinadin, who whistled when he saw the battlefield. Blackwood Gayle reached them just as Dinadin's boot came off the ladder.

"You see, Vantran?" said Gayle proudly. "Nothing to worry about. You make too much of these valley Drol, I think."

"Really?" asked Richius angrily. "How would you know? You look . . . uninjured."

Gayle stiffened. His eyes flashed through the slits in his metal mask. "I killed my share," he assured Richius. "And I will kill more when we find them. Most of the gog cowards fled. I've already sent my troops into the forest after them."

"What? I didn't order that!"

"You don't order my men, Vantran," said Gayle. The demon helmet bobbed as he looked Richius up and down. "And from the looks of you, I didn't think you up to chasing them."

"I don't want to chase them!" thundered Richius. "Especially not on horseback. If you had bothered to ask I would have told you how stupid that is. There's hardly enough room for a horse to move on those forest paths. Your men will be lucky not to be ambushed."

"I waited until you were done to tell you what I'd planned," said Gayle. "That's all the courtesy I intend to show you. I will not defer to you more."

"I'm in command here, Gayle," insisted Richius. "The valley's under my authority."

Blackwood Gayle scoffed. "I brought my horsemen here to fight, and fight they will. You may sit in your holes if you like, letting the real men do battle."

"You arrogant ass. You can't fight from horseback in the forest. Those woods are crawling with Drol. If you ride in there they'll be on top of you before you can draw your sword."

"Enough," ordered Gayle. He reined his horse around, turning away from Richius. "You have no dominion over me, Vantran." Then, spurring his horse into a gallop, Gayle rode back toward the forest.

"That fool," seethed Richius. "He doesn't even know his way around the valley. We'll have to go after him."

"Why bother?" asked Dinadin bitterly. "Why not just leave him to the Drol?"

"No. I don't want him stirring up any more trouble."

The company's horses were kept on the other side of the camp, just outside the confining catacombs of the trenches. There were not many of them now, but the horse master did have three geldings for the trio. Ignoring his exhaustion, Richius climbed into the saddle.

"Let's keep it quiet," he ordered the others. "There's no sense in telling the Drol we're coming." Then, with a snap of the reins, Richius led Lucyler and Dinadin across the reeking battlefield and into the forest. Though he knew the horsemen had gotten a healthy lead on them, he was hopeful they would find the Talistanians quickly.

The part of the valley through which they traveled was less overgrown than the rest of the land, and its earth was level enough for a horse to tread on. Still, the forest paths were treacherous and narrow, and the trio had to struggle to keep their mounts from stumbling. More than one of their horses had broken a leg in these woods, and Richius was determined not to cause any more of the precious animals to be killed.

To their relief, they found the horsemen easy to track. The rich soil of the valley did a fine job of showing hoofprints, and it was a simple matter for Lucyler to trace the path of the heavily armored horses through the woodlands. They rode slowly, wary of every sound, their eyes constantly in search of crimson robes or the gleam of a jiiktar. But all they saw were the creatures of the forest, the bucks and the birds and the small furry things that shot across their path. So they continued, and it wasn't until an hour had slipped by that Richius began to worry.

"We should have reached them by now," he said. "I wouldn't have thought it possible they could get so far."

"They waste their time," scoffed Lucyler. "The Drol have disappeared back into the deep forest. Gayle's men will never find them by staying on the path."

"Still," replied Richius, "we have to find them. It isn't safe to leave them alone here."

"It is less safe for us," said Lucyler, peering around the forest. The woodlands had thickened, the path they followed on becoming less defined. "We should head back now, Richius. We're too far from camp."

Richius shook his head. "We continue. We must if we're going to catch up to Gayle."

"Why?" pressed Lucyler. "The horsemen can look after themselves."

"I'm not worried about the horsemen, Lucyler."

Lucyler looked surprised, but said nothing. He merely nodded and continued following Richius through the woods. Dinadin was also quiet, a blessing for which Richius was enormously grateful. They rode like this for long minutes, until finally Richius spoke. A faint, mysterious odor was becoming evident. The aroma, mingled as it was with the perfumes of the forest, was almost undetectable. But it was there, and it clung to the inside of his nostrils with a woodsy sweetness.

"What's that smell?"

Lucyler and Dinadin both breathed deeply.

"I don't smell anything," said Dinadin quickly.

"No," Lucyler countered, taking another breath through his sharp nose. "I smell it. Like smoke."

Richius was still sniffing the air. "Are there any villages around here, Lucyler?"

"There could be. There are villages throughout the valley." Lucyler paused and sniffed again. "But the smell is too strong for cooking fires."

Richius agreed. The smell was almost acrid. Dinadin could smell it now, too. The young man turned his head away with a jerk when he noticed it.

"Lord!" he exclaimed, bringing his forearm to his nose. "What is *that*?"

Richius gave Lucyler a pointed stare. "You know what it smells like to me, Lucyler?"

"What?"

"Gayle."

The trio moved with urgency now. Richius forced his horse into a gallop, hoping his mount could negotiate the dangerous ground. Lucyler and Dinadin galloped after him. Before long the smell became a stench. Richius' eyes began to water. By the time the horses had taken ten more strides, a noise rippled through the forest like the breaking of ocean surf. But Richius knew he wasn't hearing water. The noise was the dull roar of fire. He continued to charge, his imagination reeling with dismal visions.

They emerged quite abruptly into a clearing. Beneath them was farmland, the soil sprinkled with red tubers. The garden was pitted with hoofprints. Before him, across the torn-up field, was a small village. The place was typically Triin, simple and unadorned, with houses of wood and paper, wet clothing hung to dry on linen lines. Narrow avenues with paving stones ran between the homes. And amidst all this were the horsemen of Talistan.

Richius could see the horsemen clearly, some setting torches to the homes, most gathering the Triin of the village into small groups, gleefully dragging them out of their dwellings while they stripped them of any belongings. At the outskirts of the village, where the stonework ended and the field began, an inferno was coughing black smoke into the air. Horsemen were tossing all manner of items onto the fire. Furnishings and clothing, weapons and farm tools—all going to ashes in the blaze.

"God," Richius gasped.

Lucyler looked stricken. "We must stop them," he said quickly, and without waiting for Richius' order galloped off toward the village. Richius and Dinadin raced across the garden after him. They reached the pyre quickly and flung themselves off their horses. The soldiers gathered there goggled at them.

"What's going on here?" Richius demanded.

One of the horsemen stepped forward. In his arms was cradled a squealing pig.

"Who are you?" he asked, glaring at Richius over the struggling sow.

"I am Richius Vantran of Aramoor," declared Richius. "And I asked you a question, soldier."

The man rolled his eyes.

"Well?" pressed Richius. Other horsemen were beginning to gather around them now, some mounted, some on foot.

"This isn't your concern," answered the man at last. "We take our orders from Baron Gayle."

Richius stepped closer. "Everything in this valley is my concern, Talistanian. I give the orders here, not Blackwood Gayle. Now talk."

"We're looking for Drol," the soldier answered stiffly. "We followed them into the forest but they scattered. Baron Gayle ordered the village searched."

"And did he order the place burned?"

"This village is full of rebels," the soldier insisted. "It's got to be destroyed."

Lucyler stepped up before Richius could answer. "There are no Drol here. This is just butchery. These people have done nothing."

"And the pig?" continued Richius, nodding toward the sow in the man's arms. "Were you going to burn that, too?"

"We're taking the animals back with us," said the man. "And any other food the gogs have. Baron Gayle says we're to bring it all back to the trenches, share it with you."

"Forget it," snapped Richius. "These Triin aren't our enemies. And they're going to need their animals and food for the coming winter."

"Any one of these gogs could be a Drol," said the soldier. "If we let them go they'll be back at our throats in an hour. Baron Gayle says—"

Richius raised a hand. "Let me explain something to you. I know you're only a stupid Talistanian, but try hard to understand. See these people in this village? They're farmers. That means they grow food and tend livestock all damn day. They don't make weapons for the Drol, and they probably don't give a hang who wins this bloody war. So now we're all going to turn around and leave quietly. All right?"

The soldier scoffed. "All the Triin in this valley are under Voris' control. That makes them all Drol."

"No," said Richius angrily. "That makes them all victims. And I won't have any massacres under my command." Over his shoulder he called, "Lucyler, you and Dinadin put a stop to this mess."

The soldier looked shocked. "What are you doing? You can't just . . ."

"Quiet, fool. The emperor has given me the power to do as I wish here. Now you order your people to stop their killing at once or I'll make sure you're sent back to Nar in chains. Do you understand?"

The emperor's title made the soldier swallow hard. He stooped and lowered the pig to the ground. The animal scrambled from his arms and ran off into the field.

"I understand, Vantran."

"Prince," corrected Richius as he began walking into the village.

"What?"

"Prince Vantran to you."

He didn't care to hear the man's reply. He only wanted the soldier to obey him, to put an end to the carnage his countrymen were causing. And he wanted to find Gayle.

Richius quickly discovered that the villagers were as afraid of him as they were of the horsemen. Most looked away as he strode by, and some of them ran. These were mostly women, doubtlessly afraid of being ravaged by the pillagers. Those whose houses were not yet burning sought refuge in them. All around him Richius could hear the slamming of doors. There were screams, too, and the wailing of children.

As he searched the burning village, Richius could see his companions trying to calm the more distraught villagers. He saw Dinadin fall to one knee to console a small girl. She was hysterical, repeating something again and again in the throaty language of the Triin. Like Richius, Dinadin knew almost nothing of the odd language. He stammered an unintelligible mix of broken Triin phrases as he tried to quiet the girl. And though he silently applauded the efforts of his comrades, Richius didn't join them in trying to calm the panicked villagers. He walked with determination through the chaos, ignoring the incomprehensible pleas of the children that gathered at his boots. He shooed them away when they came to him. But every child he saw hammered home his outrage.

Outside one of the still-undamaged houses, a single Talistanian stood with his arms folded across his chest. No one else was around, and there was nothing about the dwelling that Richius could imagine being of interest. From within the house he could hear the unmistakable sound of a woman's screams.

"What are you doing here?" he asked, approaching the man with his sword held at belt level. The man's cocky expression evaporated at the sight of him.

"Prince Vantran," the man stammered. "I am under orders to guard this house."

"Orders? From who?"

The man hesitated before answering. "Baron Gayle."

"Is he inside?"

"He is. But Prince Vantran, I'm not to let anyone disturb him."

"Why? So he can rape some old woman? Step away."

"Please . . ." the man implored, but Richius shoved him aside and gave the door a kick. It splintered open, revealing a small, dimly lit room. In the corner of the room, under the chamber's single torch, a polished mound of silver armor moved on the floor.

"Gayle!"

Blackwood Gayle twisted around to face the doorway. An ugly blend of anger and lust flashed in his eyes. He cursed when he recognized Richius. The girl underneath him squirmed to free herself but Gayle pushed her down again.

"Get out of here!" Gayle roared, then added with a laugh, "Get your own."

The baron turned back to the girl and put his lips to her throat. She roared at the unwanted touch. It was only when he felt the blade at the nape of his neck that Gayle realized Richius was behind him.

"Get up," said Richius coldly. He pressed the edge of the weapon into the big man's skin. Gayle froze.

"Vantran," he hissed. "Remove that sword. *Now.*"

Richius grabbed the man by the hair and pulled. "Arise, Baron!" he said, his sword still kissing Gayle's skin.

As Richius yanked, Gayle rose to his knees with a howl. The girl scrambled out from beneath him. She balled herself up in the corner, drawing her ruined garments over her breasts.

"I knew you would do something like this," whispered Richius, bending over Gayle's shoulder. "You animal."

"You idiot," Gayle sneered. He was still on his knees with the sword at his throat. "What do you think you're here for? This is a war, boy!"

"In this valley I run the war," said Richius, moving the blade off the baron's throat. "Now go."

Gayle rose and turned to glare at Richius. He towered over him by more than a foot, but Richius didn't back away. Instead, he walked past Gayle to the corner where the girl waited, watching them both with red-hot contempt.

"Are you all right?" he asked gently.

"I didn't hurt her," Gayle insisted, straightening his uniform. "And what would you care if I did? You're a bigger gog-lover than your father!"

Richius glowered. "Go, Baron. Leave my valley."

"Your valley? You've been trying to take this place for months. Voris will eat you up in a day if we leave—"

A sudden screech tore from the corner of the room. Richius turned to see the girl lunging forward, a sharp stiletto in her fist. She barreled past

Richius and collided with Gayle, bringing the stiletto down with a scream. Gayle howled as the knife skidded off his armor and across his arm, tearing open the leather and the skin beneath.

"Bitch!" he swore, batting her away. She fell back, dazed from the blow, and the stiletto dropped to the floor. Gayle stalked after her and she rose again, hissing and lunging at him with clawed hands. Richius hurried over and pulled her away, dragging her from the enraged baron.

"Get out, Gayle!" he ordered, fighting to hold her back. It was like holding one of Voris' war wolves. She spat a string of Triin curses at the baron. Blackwood Gayle's face contorted with rage.

"You little tramp," he snarled. "You're dead. . . ."

She kicked at him, driving her foot into his thigh. Richius hauled her backward, tossing her against the wall to get between them.

"Go!" he snapped. "Get out now!"

"Gog-lover," Gayle countered. "You bloody little bastard . . ."

"I'm ordering you to leave, Baron."

"If I leave, you'll lose here, Vantran," said Gayle. "I swear it, you'll lose."

"I'd rather lose with honor than win with your help."

Gayle smiled sardonically. "Then lose," he said, and left the room.

Richius looked back at the girl. She had sunk down, exhausted and dazed, and he could see her clearly at last. She was young. Barely eighteen, he guessed. Her hair was long and the bone-white of all the Triin. Almond-shaped eyes looked back at him, ripe with loathing, and around her left eye a purplish swelling was beginning to rise.

"Are you all right?" Richius asked again, reaching out to inspect her bruised face. She swatted his hand away.

"Ee sassa ma!" she yelled, pulling away from Richius' probing hand and drawing her torn dress tighter around herself. "Sassa ma! Sassa ma!"

Richius fell back, startled. "No," he said, holding his open palms out before him. "I don't want to hurt you. I want to help."

With the quickness of a cat she dove for her stiletto. But Richius was closer and brought his foot down on it.

"No!" he directed, reaching down to pick up the weapon. She inched backward, regarding him. She swore at him, but all Richius could decipher from the jumble was that she wanted no part of him. Yet something about the girl kept him from leaving.

"Stop," he begged. "You're safe. I won't hurt you."

As if she understood him, the girl grew suddenly still. Her breathing slowed and her gray eyes narrowed as she watched him suspiciously. Richius forced a thin smile.

"Good," he said. He let the hand with the stiletto drop to his side. "That's better. Nothing's going to happen to you now. We're here to help."

The girl looked at him blankly, the shade of shock drawing over her eyes. Richius had seen the look before, but seeing it on this young girl sickened him. He went to reach out for her again, but before he could he heard his name being called. The voice sounded far away. Richius recognized it immediately as Dinadin's.

"They're looking for me," he said, half to himself. He knew she had no comprehension of his words, yet he didn't want to stop talking for fear of losing her tenuous trust. "Can you hear it? That's my name—Richius."

The girl didn't move, just stared at Richius fearlessly. He continued to smile at her.

"Richius," he repeated, pointing to himself. "I'm Richius."

For a moment the girl continued her empty silence, then suddenly her eyes widened with recognition.

"Kalak?"

Richius was horrified. "No!" he exclaimed, springing to his feet. "Don't call me that! I'm not your enemy. We're here to help you. We . . ."

He stopped himself. She was still staring at him, her eyes blazing with pain and confusion.

"That *is* why we're here," he said mournfully. "But you'll never believe it."

Still the girl said nothing. Behind Richius, the sunlight streaming into the room was blocked by a figure in the doorway.

"Richius?" called Dinadin.

Richius kept his frown fixed on the girl at his feet. "Yes?"

"Gayle and his men have gone, but the fires have gotten out of control. I think we should leave."

Richius nodded. "Find Lucyler."

"He's already waiting outside with the horses," Dinadin answered, stepping into the room. "Who's that?"

Richius turned from the girl and walked toward the door, dropping the stiletto on his way. "No one."

Dyana waited for Kalak to leave before daring to stir. Her body had become a frigid corpse. Dirt seemed to cover her. Her garments hung open and she clamped them shut with a fist, gritting her teeth against the tears.

Breathe, she told herself. *Kalak is gone.*

Or was he? Outside she could still hear shouting, but they were all Triin voices. Smoke seeped into the tiny home and fire crackled beyond the walls. She examined herself quickly. Her face hurt where the big one had struck her. She tested the bruise with her fingertip and winced. The contusion was swelling, closing off her eye and blurring her vision. She heard herself moan like a girl, angry and frightened.

And then she thought of her uncle. Where was he? Why wasn't he looking for her? She stumbled to her feet, grabbing for the wall to hold herself up. Nausea washed over her so that she thought she would vomit, and she wondered if her cheekbones had been fractured. Carefully she inched along the wall toward the door, steeled herself, and peered out.

Smoke blotted out the sun. The horrible sounds of screaming assailed her. Children rushed by, wailing, and the sobs of the elderly poured through the streets. It seemed to her that the whole world was burning, that only her uncle's modest house still stood unscathed. She staggered out of the doorway and onto the street, appalled at the devastation.

"Jaspin?" she called, peering down the avenue. "Jaspin? Where are you?"

An older woman she didn't know spotted her. The woman took a pitying look at her battered face and ruined garb and slid an arm around her.

"Child?" asked the woman. "Are you all right?"

Dyana nodded, unconcerned for herself. "I need to find my uncle. And my cousin . . ."

"Your face is bleeding," said the woman. She smiled gently and tried to ease Dyana down. "Lie down. I will get something for your face."

"No," said Dyana. "Shani. Where is she?" Her words seem to come from an enormous distance, and she heard how slurred her voice sounded. "Take me to her, please. I need to find her, make sure she is all right. She is little. . . ."

The woman blanched. "You are the one that lives with Jaspin."

"Yes, yes," said Dyana impatiently. She pointed toward her uncle's house. "I live here with them. Have you seen them?"

"Oh, child," groaned the woman, her face collapsing. She took hold of Dyana's hand and squeezed.

"What is it?" asked Dyana. "Take me to them."

"I . . . I will," the old woman managed. "Come with me."

She led Dyana through the frenzied streets, past the burning buildings and the hollow-eyed children, and past the huddled families. Dyana followed, all the tangles of emotion choking her so that she could hardly think. At last they came to another huddle, not far away from Jaspin's home. Here she saw a few familiar faces, all long and drawn in misery. She heard the agonized groans of something at the group's center. It sounded vaguely like a man. The old woman stopped and looked at her. She couldn't speak but pointed toward the huddle.

Dyana pushed herself toward the group of people. She recognized Eamok, Jaspin's neighbor. He glanced up at her as her torn dress brushed past his cheek. Angry recognition dawned on his face, and very slowly he moved aside to reveal the shaking thing at the center of the mass. As she had known, as she had dreaded, it was Jaspin, his body racked with sobs. Cradled in his arms was a tiny, pulverized body.

"Trampled," she heard someone whisper.

Dyana peered down at the small figure, at the red-stained clothes pitted with horseshoe-shaped markings. The face was bloodied but intact—except for one eye that had popped out whole from its socket and now stared obscenely in an impossible direction. All the strength in her evaporated. She slumped down next to her weeping uncle.

Little Shani was limp, a broken doll with disjointed, dangling limbs. Jaspin was moaning, rocking back and forth with his daughter cradled lifelessly in his arms. Dyana slipped an arm around him and squeezed him tight.

"My poor cousin," she murmured. "My poor child . . ."

Jaspin tore away from her. Dyana toppled, hitting the ground with her palms.

"Get away from me!" cried Jaspin. "Devil!"

"Jaspin," Dyana said. "What?"

Her uncle scooped the dead baby away from her, rising from his knees and towering above her. "Get away!" he roared. He picked up his booted foot and pushed it into her chest. Dyana toppled again.

"Stop!" she shouted. "Jaspin, what is it?"

"This is your fault! You cursed little witch!" He raised a fist, threatening to strike her. Dyana held her ground, and Jaspin's anger imploded. "Damn you, Dyana," he wailed, lowering his hand. "Damn you for doing this!"

"Me?" Dyana said. "It was not!"

"Look at my baby!" Jaspin screamed, holding out the child for her to inspect. "This is Tharn's revenge on you."

"You should never have let her come," said Eamok, Jaspin's friend and neighbor. He was crying, too, and wore the same crazed expression as her uncle. "This is what she has brought on us, Jaspin. I told you she would!"

"It is not me!" declared Dyana. Her head was swimming. The stench of smoke polluted her lungs. "And it is not Tharn. They were Kalak's men!"

Jaspin clutched his dead daughter closer to his chest. "Tharn is punishing you. He knows where you are!"

"He will come for us all now," added Eamok, shouting to the crowd. "We are not safe."

"Jaspin, please . . ." She reached out, but her uncle turned his back on her. "Please!"

"Do not speak to me anymore, Dyana. You are cursed. And, oh, I knew you were! I knew it! This is my fault!" His head dropped and he began to sob again over Shani's body, and his words ran together in a garbled blubbering. "You are not family to me anymore, girl."

Stupefied, Dyana let her hands drop to her side. "It was not me. Kalak did this."

"You brought them here," growled Eamok. "You did because you are cursed like your father. It is Drol anger that brought them here, Tharn's anger!" He grabbed at her torn lapel and shook her. "We should send you back to him ourselves."

Dyana wrenched free and struck Eamok hard across the face. "Do not touch me!" she flared. "I will never go to him. Never! I would die first."

Eamok stalked toward her. "And I would like to kill you. See what you have done? It is your defiance of your master that brings this death to Jaspin. He is too good to tell you this, but he never wanted you here!"

"Stop!" cried Jaspin. He turned slowly to face Dyana, walking over to her and showing her the tiny, fractured body. "Look at my daughter, Dyana. Look how they have killed her."

Dyana could not look. Shani had been her uncle's world. She had been the sun and the moon. Now he was alone, not only a widower but childless. What Jaspin had been was gone, probably forever.

"You're a foolish girl, Dyana," said Jaspin. "Tharn has learned of you." He gestured broadly at the destruction around them. "All of this is a sign. He wants you. He does, and you cannot fight it."

"And he is Drol!" thundered Eamok. "He can call the gods. He can destroy us. And if Tharn knows you are here he will tell Voris. The warlord will punish us." He turned toward his friend. "Jaspin, send her away! Send her back to him now. Do not let her hide here anymore. He will come for her again!"

"You are all mad!" cried Dyana. She knew it was useless to argue with them, that they were all convinced that the Drol had powers. But all the rage in her was boiling over and she could not contain it. "Tharn is a cunning-man, nothing else. You fear nothing!"

"Listen to her, Jaspin. She loves the Narens like her father. Send her away!"

Jaspin came very close to her, and they stared into each other's bloodshot eyes. Dyana's expression was hard. She grieved for the little girl, and it pained her that no one wanted her grief.

"Uncle," she said evenly, tempering her ire. "Do not send me away."

She had nowhere to go, and he knew it. She could never go to Tharn. And yet she could not beg her uncle. Not with the hatred she saw in his eyes.

"Some others are talking about going to Ackle-Nye," said Jaspin. "Go with them, or go to Tharn, I do not care which. Just leave me."

"Ackle-Nye? Jaspin . . ."

"They are leaving in the morning, Dyana. They don't want to live here when Tharn takes over. I had thought you should go with them, and now I am sure. Dring is not the place for you. This is Voris' land. We are his people. Go to Ackle-Nye. Go with the other Nar lovers."

"But there is nothing there!" she said hotly. "Just refugees. Is that what you want to happen to me?"

Jaspin shrugged dispassionately. "I don't care what happens to you, Dyana. I swear, you are just like your father, hardly Triin at all."

Then he turned his back on her and left, still holding his child. He disappeared into the crowds and smoke. Eamok leered at her, tasting the victory he had sought since she had come to the village. And as Dyana watched her uncle leave, she realized he was the last family member she would ever see. Now she was truly alone. She put her arms around her shoulders and sank to the ground, letting the tears come.

THREE

The poppies that grew in the Dring Valley were enormous. In all his young life, Richius had never seen anything like them. Big and lush, the valley was overgrown with them, an oasis of color beside the bleakness of the trenches. Aramoor had poppy fields, too, but the crimson flowers of his home were not comparable to the variety that sprang out of the earth here. The sight of the white and violet blooms made him sigh. The last few days had been wonderfully good.

Richius lowered his quill into the hinge of his journal. He was grateful to be free of the confines of the trenches, to feel the fickle sunlight of Lucel-Lor on his face. Unperturbed by the rough bark of the tree at his back, he smiled up at the sun. Its warmth caressed him, as welcome as the touch of any woman.

Across the mountains, they never spoke of Lucel-Lor's beauty. This place was a mystery, a puzzlement to be shunned. Richius had never even seen a Triin before coming here. But like all children of the Empire, he had heard the tales of the white-faced vampires, the magicians who were quick as a breeze and as inscrutable. When he had reached an age to understand, he had asked his father about Lucel-Lor. Darius Vantran, ever pragmatic, had told his son that the Triin were different from other humans, that they enslaved their women and were more violent even than Nar's princes.

"Like Talistan?" the young Richius had asked. The question had troubled his father.

Since then, Richius had learned about the Triin. They were not the beasts the Empire portrayed, nor were they cannibals. Even the Drol, zealots though they were, showed moments of humanity. They did not torture their prisoners as did the Narens in the Black City, and they did not enslave their women—not precisely. Richius had seen far worse in the brothels of Nar, where an impoverished woman's only sustenance came from the sale of her body.

A slight breeze stirred the poppies, tickling the underside of Richius' bare feet. The sensation forced a schoolgirl giggle from his lips. Embarrassed, he looked to where Dinadin and Lucyler sat close by, a game board on the grass between them. Dinadin was studying the ornate wooden pieces intently, but he raised an eyebrow at the sudden sound of Richius' mirth.

"Happy?"

"Yes," said Richius. "For the first time in a long time."

A yawn welled up in him and he let it out, stretching like a cat. The bright warmth was making him sleepy, and his thoughts turned lazily to a nap. He chuckled again, amused at the idea. It had been almost a week since the raid on the village, and all they had done since returning was sleep and eat. The respite provided by Gayle had been put to good use, and the fair weather had cooperated in their hunting. There had been no wolves or warriors to bother them, and each man who left in search of game had come back with a stout bird or even a buck with which to feed the company. Richius patted his stomach. The heaviness in it felt fine.

"Who's winning?" he asked. Dinadin had taken a red peg from its hole and was chewing on its end while he contemplated the board.

"Who do you think?" he replied. "I can never win this damn game." Quickly he placed the piece into a new hole. Lucyler groaned.

"Because you do not concentrate," said the Triin, pulling the piece from the board. He shoved the peg under Dinadin's nose. "The red pieces are your footmen. You cannot jump with footmen."

Dinadin snatched the game piece from the Triin.

"All right," he snapped, and without even glancing at the board stuffed it into another hole. "Better?"

"Play correctly," replied Lucyler, his anger thickening his accent, "or not at all."

"It's just a game, Lucyler."

Lucyler scoffed, already starting to pull the game pieces from the board. "You could learn from Ejai, boy," he said. "It is about strategy and wits. A game like this could help keep you alive."

"We do a fair job of keeping ourselves alive without *Triin* help," replied Dinadin. "Why, you're the only Triin I've ever seen fight alongside us. All the rest of you are Drol, I think."

"If you believe that, you are a fool, Dinadin," said Lucyler, getting to his feet. "We have lost more people than all the nations of your Empire together. You are trapped here in the valley and you think this is the entire war. But I have seen Kronin's warriors fighting in the north. I have been to Tatterak and I was there when Falindar fell." He jabbed a finger into Dinadin's face. "Where were *you?*"

"Enough," ordered Richius. "I want to rest, not fight. Sit down, Lucyler."

Lucyler hesitated for a moment, then finally lowered himself back onto the grass, muttering. Richius turned to Dinadin.

"You should know better than to say such things, Dinadin. Edgard has told me about the fighting in Tatterak. If you want to see Triin fighting for the Daegog, that's the place to go."

"I know," Dinadin conceded. "I'd just like to see some of those warriors here. We could use their help, especially with Gayle's horsemen gone." He gestured broadly at the serenity around them. "This won't last, you know."

Richius grimaced. What Dinadin said was true, but he had no wish to think of it. He could scarcely remember the last time they had been able to doff their armor and escape the trenches for even a few hours, but he didn't want to squander the precious tranquillity with talk of war.

"Kronin cannot help us," said Lucyler. "He would send warriors if he could. He hates Voris as much as any of us."

"I've heard that," said Richius. "Edgard told me about it once. They've been feuding for years."

"Years on top of years, since before I was born. Kronin is not Drol, and never was. And he supported the Daegog from the start. But Voris was born Drol, one of Tharn's own clan. That alone makes them hate each other."

"Like us and Gayle, Dinadin," said Richius with a grin. He had always found the animosity between the warlords of Lucel-Lor intriguing. Just as political rivalries had brought the Houses of Vantran and Gayle to war, those same bitter feelings were now tearing the Triin apart. In the end, though, the Vantrans and the Gayles had put aside their malice, forming an uneasy alliance under the banner of Nar. And though he knew his ruthless emperor had designs to bring Lucel-Lor under his rule, Richius still thought it unlikely that the Triin warlords would ever be at peace again.

"It's that kind of thinking that started this war, you know," said Richius. "In the Empire we don't fight among ourselves."

"No," said Lucyler. "Your emperor would not allow that."

"The emperor has kept the peace in Nar for nearly twenty years," replied Richius coolly.

"By attacking other lands? Nar is at war throughout the world. How can you say Arkus has kept the peace when you are sitting here?"

Dinadin jumped in before Richius could answer. "You don't seem to mind us being here, though, do you, Lucyler? If it wasn't for Nar, you and your Daegog would be in a Drol prison camp."

"Your emperor only helps the Daegog because he wants something from him," countered Lucyler. "You are like these game pieces, being moved around by a master player."

Richius stifled an angry reply, mostly because his comrade was right. No one knew for certain why Arkus was so eager to help the Daegog of Lucel-Lor. The emperor and his vast appetites were a mystery to everyone in Nar. He supposed that not even the Daegog himself knew why Nar was here. But it was the same question that had vexed Naren kings for decades. Arkus was never satisfied. He was a machine, a devourer of nations. And no one really questioned the emperor's motives anymore; they simply did his bidding.

"And what about you, Lucyler?" asked Dinadin hotly. "Do you think it's not the same for you? When your Daegog pulls a string, you dance. Arkus may be a bastard, but the Daegog's no better."

Lucyler started to his feet again then stopped himself. "You are probably right."

"Don't let it bother you," said Richius. "It's just the way it is for us all. And we won't need Kronin's help anyway. Patwin should be back from Aramoor with word soon. If he's told my father how grave we have it, we'll be sent the troops we need."

"Really?" asked Dinadin. "Do you think so? Or are you just telling us what you think we want to hear?"

"What's this?" said Richius. "Is some homesickness making you doubt me?"

Dinadin looked away. "I'm sick for home, that's true enough."

"Is it my father you doubt, then?" Richius pressed.

"I'm honor bound to our king, and I won't speak ill of him," answered Dinadin. "Especially not to you. It's just that we . . ." He stopped and thought for a moment, choosing his words with care. "We hear things."

"What things?"

"Perhaps it's nothing," said Dinadin. "Or just the same things you've heard yourself. We all know how badly the war's going. But we're not all privy to the messages your father sends you. It makes me wonder what you write in that book of yours." He pointed his chin toward the journal in Richius' lap.

"My journal? There's nothing worth your knowing here, believe me. I tell this book the same things I tell you, and nothing more terrible than what you already know." Richius lifted the book and offered it to Dinadin. "Read for yourself if you like."

Dinadin smiled weakly. "Just a learned man's ramblings, huh? Maybe you should be back in Aramoor, Richius, writing war croons for us on the line. If you say there's nothing I should know in that book, I believe you."

Relieved, Richius set the journal back in his lap. "So? Tell me. I know something's bothering you. What is it?" He watched Dinadin closely, his eyes narrowing into slivers. "Do you think the king has forsaken us?"

"Maybe," answered Dinadin. "It's been a long time, and you've asked for troops before and not gotten them. Why should this request be so different?"

"Because we've never been so close to losing," said Richius. "My father has too much faith in me, I fear. He probably thinks we can take this valley with the trickle of men he sends us. But now that I've made it plain to him . . ."

He stopped suddenly, seeing Dinadin glance sideways at Lucyler.

"What?" asked Richius.

"Let us change this talk," said Lucyler, fidgeting with the game pieces he had gathered from the board. "You are right, Richius. We should be enjoying the peace, not arguing."

"No," Richius insisted. "You're sharing some secret. What is it?"

"Richius," said Lucyler calmly. "It is no secret your father sent you here against his will. And why should it be? No one thinks poorly of him for wanting to keep Aramoor out of our war."

"Oh, come now," said Richius. "I know my father wasn't eager to send us here, but he listens to the emperor. He's sent hundreds of men into Lucel-Lor."

"True," agreed Dinadin grudgingly. "But he hasn't been so forthcoming with the men and supplies lately."

"If your father has heard how badly the war is going he may think it lost," Lucyler added. "The news from the north is not good, and if we have heard that here in the valley, then surely your father has also."

Dinadin agreed. "I've heard Tharn has Kronin's warriors on the run. Even some of our own kinsmen are talking about retreating."

Richius laughed. "Oh, sure. Where did you hear that, Dinadin? From Gayle's men?"

"Yes," said Dinadin sheepishly.

"And you believed them? Think about that for a moment. If any Aramoorians were retreating, I'm sure I would have heard of it myself. It may be true that Tharn and his Drol are doing well, but winning? I doubt it. And Kronin's land is big, bigger even than Voris'. We can't expect him to keep it all free of Drol."

Dinadin shook his head. "Tharn is gaining, Richius. If Tatterak falls we'll be stuck in this valley with Tharn above us and Voris all around us. We'll be trapped. We have to do something. *You* have to do something!"

"Kronin's men can hold off Tharn," insisted Richius. "Don't you think, Lucyler?"

Lucyler shrugged. "Kronin has many warriors," he admitted. "But so does Tharn. Voris is not the only warlord to pledge himself to Tharn, you know. There is Nang and Shohar and Gavros. . . ." He hesitated, wrinkling his brow and counting on his fingers. "All the warlords of the east, I think. Since Falindar fell there has been little of the east that Tharn has not taken."

"He doesn't have the Dring Valley yet," boasted Richius. "And he won't as long as we hold on, whether Voris the Wolf has pledged himself to Tharn or not."

"You know what I think?" said Dinadin. "I think Tharn is planning a final assault on us, all the Naren troops and loyalists. Now that we're weak he can finish us." Dinadin's voice became hushed. "Now he can use his magic."

"Magic," Lucyler scoffed. "Do you know how foolish you sound, Dinadin?"

"Why foolish?" Dinadin fired back. "I know the stories, Lucyler. They say Tharn's a sorcerer. Hell, he's a Drol. He's just been waiting for his chance to crush us."

"Tharn is no sorcerer," said Lucyler. "He is a Drol holy man. You Narens should stop believing everything you hear. To you, all the Drol are sorcerers."

"They worship evil gods," said Dinadin. "I know these things, Lucyler. I'm not as stupid as you think. They believe their gods grant them powers."

"Yes, and they are as stupid as you for believing that." Lucyler shook his head in disbelief. "Do you know why the Drol believe they are touched by heaven? Because they are fools. They believe in myths. They are devoted to an ancient religion of nonsense."

"That's not what I've heard," countered Dinadin.

"Tales to frighten you, Dinadin. It is the same thing the Drol want the Daegog's followers to believe. But even if Tharn does have some great magic, which he does not, he would never use it to kill."

"Oh?" Richius asked indignantly. He was unaccustomed to his men defending his enemies, and it irritated him. "Why not? What makes you think that mad devil wouldn't use sorcery if he could?"

"Because no Drol would," said Lucyler flatly. "They believe their magic is divine. Magic or sorcery—or whatever you call the touch of heaven—the Drol say all these things must be used to heal, not harm. The Drol may be zealots, but they hold the old ways of our people sacred. They, above all Triin, know the price of misusing the favors of their gods. Whatever his cause, Tharn would be damned if he used his blessing to destroy."

"But he took Falindar," said Richius.

"True. But by blade, not by sorcery. Understand me, Richius. Tharn is a demon. I saw his butchery at Falindar. But he is also a Drol. No Drol, no matter how evil, would use the touch of heaven to kill. If he is pushing troops back to Ackle-Nye, he is doing it with men and jiiktars only."

"That doesn't sound so bad," said Dinadin. "I wouldn't mind retreating to Ackle-Nye, would you, Richius?"

"Maybe not," said Richius. "But I'd rather not fight Tharn to get there." He looked to Lucyler.

Lucyler glanced away. He had been there the night the revolution had begun, the night Drol rebels attacked Falindar to free their enigmatic leader. Like his father and grandfather before him, Lucyler was in the service of the Daegog, a warrior of the royal caste sworn to protect the Triin lord. Tharn was only a prisoner then, rotting in the catacombs beneath the Daegog's palace.

Until that bloody night.

Drol warriors, mostly Voris' red-robed fanatics, attacked the palace on a moonless evening. They were merciless, as the Drol always were, and they spared no one in their efforts to rescue Tharn. But Lucyler had been lucky that night, lucky enough to steal away from the palace without being seen, and had smuggled his Daegog to safety. Falindar fell to Tharn, and the Daegog was in exile. And for his great loyalty and courage, Lucyler was given the unenviable assignment of helping secure the Dring Valley, and of keeping an eye on Richius.

Together they had shared many horrors since the fall of Falindar, but of the trio only Lucyler had faced the Drol leader in battle. Even Voris, pledged as he was to do the bidding of his master, could not lay claim to Tharn's dreadfulness. The warlord of the valley had jiiktars and war wolves and warriors sworn to die for him, but these were things comprehensible and natural. The bloodlust Tharn could conjure in his men was legendary. It was, in a sense, magical.

Dinadin reclined on the grass, for once ignoring an opportunity to pester Lucyler as he gazed into the cloudless sky. "Perhaps Patwin will have news of the war in Tatterak when he returns. No doubt he will stop in Ackle-Nye on his way back."

"No doubt," agreed Richius with a grin. "Patwin likes the ladies as much as you do."

"You know," said Dinadin, rolling onto his stomach and resting his chin on his fists, "Ackle-Nye is only two days' ride from here."

"Forget it," said Richius.

"But why? Why not now, when there's a break in the fighting?"

Richius groaned, regretting the promise he had made to Dinadin that they would ride to Ackle-Nye when and if there was a good lull in the fighting. Now, it seemed, that lull had come.

"We can't go, Dinadin. Voris could attack at any time."

"After the routing Gayle gave him?" said Dinadin. "Not likely."

"No?" asked Richius. "I'm sure Voris knows by now that Gayle and his horsemen are gone."

"So? He still can't have his men ready for another attack so soon. Right, Lucyler?"

"Who can say?" replied Lucyler dully. "The Wolf thinks like no other warlord. He is unpredictable."

"And strong," added Richius. "The Dring Valley's big, Dinadin, and Voris still has scores of warriors. It wouldn't be wise to think him so damaged by the last fight."

Dinadin frowned and looked away. "All right," he conceded, getting to his feet and wiping the grass from his backside. "But you should at least think about it. The way Tharn and the Drol are gaining ground, this chance might not come again."

"Sorry," said Richius. "We simply can't risk it."

Dinadin made a slight, unhappy sound, then turned and left his comrades. A feeling of melancholy washed over Richius. He hadn't enjoyed breaking his promise to his friend, nor had he taken any solace in Dinadin's explanations as to why he had become so distrustful. He felt Lucyler press one of the wooden game pegs into his foot.

"He is young," said Lucyler. "All he can see is the chance to lie with a woman."

"No," said Richius sadly. "It's more than that. He hasn't been the same for weeks now. He doubts me, Lucyler. He doesn't trust me anymore."

"He is angry, that is all. He feels trapped here, and he blames you for not doing more."

"What can I do? Lord, I've done everything I know how to. It's not my fault my father won't send more troops. I didn't ask for any of this!" Richius folded his arms and lowered his chin to his chest. "Lucyler, tell me something, will you? How widespread is this talk of my father?"

Lucyler cast his somber eyes on Richius. "The truth?"

"Of course."

Lucyler smiled one of his rare, friendly smiles. "I do not believe your father will be sending any more troops here to fight. You've told me yourself how reluctant he was to send you. Were it not for the will of your emperor, you and Dinadin and all of your company would be safe at home in Aramoor."

"But . . ."

"I think this war is lost, Richius," Lucyler continued mercilessly. "And I think you think so, too. Dinadin is probably right. By now Tharn is planning a final assault. It might be a month or more away, but it is coming. There isn't much time left for any of us."

Richius was silent, letting the pain of Lucyler's words echo in his mind.

Lucyler was looking at him, his gray eyes drinking in all the truths Richius' expression betrayed, all the things he had tried so hard to conceal. He looked back at Lucyler, his own eyes filled with apology.

"It wasn't really a lie, you know," he said.

"No."

"In the Black City there are theatres where men can act to entertain. I've never been there, but I hear they're paid quite handsomely." Richius groaned, resting his head against the gnarled tree trunk. "I tried to be as good an actor, but I see now that no one believes me."

"Do not say that. It is not you they doubt, Richius. Every man here knows you have kept them alive."

"Dinadin doesn't think that," said Richius. "And maybe he's right, maybe he should be angry. I've kept us alive only to be trapped here, and I'm too damned afraid of the emperor to retreat. We're alone now."

Lucyler shrugged. "There is still Talistan. They might send more troops."

"Not into the valley they won't," countered Richius. "They have already sent in twice the troops my father has, and even if they could send more they would go to Tatterak to save the Daegog. The Gayles would see us lose the whole valley before they sent more horsemen here to help us."

The shadow of a frown crossed Lucyler's face, and Richius began again to regret his angry words. Feud or no, he should have let the horsemen remain in the valley. Now the valley might be lost, and all for the sake of family pride.

"I'm sorry," he said. "I know it was wrong to send Gayle away."

Lucyler waved the remark away. "No. You have told me about that one. We are better off without him, I am sure."

"Then what?" asked Richius. The Triin's jaw was set in the same tight way it always was when he was angry, and he looked distracted, as if arranging his thoughts in just the right way to spare Richius the worst.

"I have been here with you for nearly a year now, Richius. Yet still you keep such secrets from me. I have tried to help you, but still you do not trust me."

The bitterness in Lucyler's voice startled Richius. Never in the many long months of their efforts had he heard his comrade talk like this. Now that the words hung in the air, Richius didn't know what to do with them.

"Lucyler, don't mistake my secrecy for mistrust. You've been a greater help to me than you know, but I'm the leader here. I can't tell my men everything I know."

"But I am not one of your men, Richius. I do not need to be protected as they do. You forget that I am the Daegog's man here. There is nothing about this war I do not know, even if I do not hear it from you."

Richius bit back an insult. Lucyler hadn't seen the Daegog of Lucel-Lor in months. As far as any of them knew, the Triin leader was in Tatterak with the loyalist warlord Kronin, and probably too preoccupied with the invading Drol to give much thought to his man in the Dring Valley. To Richius' thinking, it was self-importance at best that made Lucyler believe he was still of concern to the Daegog.

"Even I don't know everything that goes on outside the valley, Lucyler. And as for my father, he is an even bigger mystery to me."

As soon as he had spoken the words, Richius regretted them. His father wasn't a subject he cared to discuss with anyone, even with a friend as close as Lucyler. But Lucyler's eyebrows rose, and Richius knew he couldn't avoid the turn their conversation was about to take.

"That surprises me," said Lucyler. "Only you see the messages your father sends you. The men can only imagine what he writes."

"My father is a man of few words. If you'd read the messages he's sent me, you wouldn't think me in possession of great secrets. The king tells me precious little, and what I think matters I share with you."

"But it all matters. How can I help you if I do not know what is happening? If I am to continue with you here I must know everything. I demand it."

Richius knew Lucyler was neither bluffing nor lying. He would hear everything, or he would leave them. And without Lucyler's guidance, the loss of the Dring Valley was certain.

"So," said Richius dully. "You would leave us here to deal with the Wolf ourselves, huh?"

"I would."

"What can I tell you that you don't know already? That the war is lost? Perhaps my father will still send us more troops, but I don't think so. He's never taken so long in sending us word. My guess is that he's decided to end it."

"I had feared as much," said Lucyler. "But can your father really decide the war for himself? What of the emperor?"

"Arkus and my father have never been friends. You said it yourself. If it weren't for the emperor, my father wouldn't have sent us here at all. Only Talistan sent troops here willingly, and that's only because the House of Gayle is the emperor's boot rag." Richius shook his head. "My father wanted to keep Aramoor out of this war."

"But you are already here. Why would your father forsake you?"

"Because he still believes Aramoor is his to rule," said Richius. "He only let Aramoor become part of the Empire to save his people from a war with Nar." He sighed, seeing the bitter irony of his father's predicament. "And then the emperor thrust this war on him. God, we are lost."

"Perhaps," Lucyler said. "But we should not lose hope. Not yet. Patwin has still to return. Maybe we are wrong about your father. Maybe Patwin will bring us good news."

"You're more hopeful than you should be, my friend. I know my father has already sent more troops here than he ever intended to. He won't re-call us. Even he knows the emperor would crush Aramoor if he did. But he may think that Arkus will spare Aramoor if he simply lets the war be lost."

"But his own son . . ."

"It doesn't matter," Richius snapped. "Even I don't expect him to risk more lives for my sake. Scores of us have died already, maybe more. For all we hear, the fights in Tatterak and the Sheaze have already cost Ara-moor hundreds of men. I know my father. He's just foolish enough to stand against the emperor. He's going to end it here, and we will all be trapped."

Richius caught himself then, seeing his own black mood settle over Lucyler. For months he had done his best to keep his true beliefs from his men, and now he was droning on about how little chance they had of vic-tory. He cursed himself, sure that Lucyler's mind was mulling over the consequences. Even if they should lose, he and Dinadin and all the others could still return home. But Lucyler was home already, and would have to live with whatever government Tharn and his Drol revolutionaries im-posed on Lucel-Lor. The weight of that knowledge must be heavy indeed.

"Then you should go," said Lucyler. "Listen to Dinadin. Do not let yourself be trapped here. Just leave."

"I can't do that," said Richius. "I wish I could, but it's impossible. If we retreat, the emperor will kill us as surely as the Drol would. And then he would take Aramoor away from us, maybe even give it to the Gayles to rule. Dinadin is too blind to see the politics of things. But I'm sorry for you, my friend. If we lose we'll just be dead. But it's your country that will really suffer."

Lucyler smiled sadly. "I have already lost, Richius. You and I are not so different. You are here to serve an emperor you hate. I am here to serve my Daegog."

"Who you hate?"

"Not hate exactly. But it is hard to ignore what Tharn and his follow-ers say about the Daegog. I lived in Falindar, remember. We were less than perfect. There were excesses. And the Daegog can be very cruel. They say he was merciless when he tortured Tharn, and I believe it. He knows your emperor means us no good. He simply does not care. Just as Arkus wants something from Lucel-Lor, so too does the Daegog want something from Nar, something more than protection from the Drol."

"What?"

"Weapons, perhaps. The warlords have followed him only because he has the title. But he is weak, and he knows his time would end soon even without Tharn to hurry it. I have no doubt he would risk our lives to get the power he wants. And your emperor was very obliging."

"They're both bastards," said Richius. "Power mad. But how can you follow him?"

"Why do you obey your emperor?" Lucyler countered.

"Because I must. Aramoor would be crushed if I didn't."

"It is like that for me, too. I know what I have in the Daegog. I lived well in Falindar. Maybe too well, but it was a fine life. I do not know what Tharn and his Drol would bring to Lucel-Lor, but I am certain it would be worse. The time for Tharn's dead religion is past."

"It sounds like you'd just be trading one despot for another," said Richius.

"Maybe. But it is what I am. My father served the Daegog, and his father before him. I am sworn to the Daegog. I cannot explain the oath, but it defines me."

Richius sighed. "Then we are both doomed. If, as you say, Tharn is gaining ground in Tatterak . . ."

"They claim so, but it may only be a rumor."

Richius frowned. Rumors were the bane of all military men. Somehow he had to find out what was really going on.

"We're blind here," he said bitterly. "This war could end tomorrow and it would be a week before we would even hear about it. We have to get the truth."

Lucyler raised his eyebrows at Richius and smiled. "Like Dinadin said, it is only a two-day ride to Ackle-Nye."

FOUR

Tucked away in a corner of the Dring Valley, veiled from the world by a tangle of vines and a forest of birch trees, stood a dilapidated castle. It was an ancient, unremarkable place, decorated with drooping catwalks and bordered in the rear by a crystalline stream. From many of its clouded windows one could see the overgrown sculpture garden rambling across its front yard, a graveyard of neglected statues chewed to ruins by lichens. In its spiderwebbed halls hung crooked portraits of the long dead, and its high, cracked ceilings were ornamented with vast candelabras of tarnished brass. At sunfall the place was lit by a network of torches and oil lamps, a ritual always followed by the baying of distant wolves.

Yet despite the castle's disrepair, it was far from deserted. Castle Dring was the stronghold of Voris the Wolf, warlord of the Dring Valley. It was where he orchestrated his war against the invading Narens and the weak, traitorous Daegog who had invited them in. And it was where he raised his three daughters with his dutiful wife, Najjir. Even in the smallest hours of the night the castle hummed with the familiar sounds of life: restless children crying for comfort and the earnest whispering of the red-robed guardians pacing along the catwalks. The primeval music of the forest permeated every hall and bedchamber, and any with a mind to sleep in Castle Dring learned quickly to accept the noise of the valley's nocturnal inhabitants.

Of all the rooms in the meandering structure, only one was dedicated wholly to silence. It was a tiny chamber buried near the back of the place, windowless except for a metal grate that let in divided shafts of sunlight at dawn and let out the cloying smoke of the perpetually burning incense. The chamber was almost entirely bare. Strewn along its wooden floor was a scarlet carpet, a weave plush enough for kneeling on, and beside one wall was a gold-trimmed altar. On the altar was a statue of a man and woman, deified mortals both. Incense burned on either side of them, sending up thin, mystical signals to heaven.

Outside, the night was dying. Tharn opened an eye and spied the grate in the eastern wall. The tiniest spark of infant sunlight glinted on the metal. He closed his eye and lowered his head again. His back ached. His knees burned from genuflecting too long. But his mind was clear and open as the sky, inviting in the answers he had prayed for throughout the night. He had come to Castle Dring hoping to find solace in the company of his adopted family, to seek counsel from the Wolf, and to beg his patron god for guidance. He was rested now and well fed on Najjir's fine cooking. His body was ready. But it was his mind that troubled him, and it was the loss of his soul that terrified him.

Lorris, he called out soundlessly. *Guide me. I am your tool. I will do your bidding. Just tell me what to do.*

His silent voice had taken on the frail tone of a child. He had started out at sundown calling upon the Drol god, hoping to ease the guilt over what he was planning. But Drol gods were fickle. Sometimes Lorris spoke to him, and at other times the deity was as silent as stone. And it was only he that spoke, never his adoring sister, Pris. Pris was a good Drol woman, devoted like a fine wife to her brother Lorris, and she never spoke to anyone save the most pious of Triin females. But they cared for all Triin who sought their divine guidance and were willing to endure the difficult life of a Drol. The Drol favored them and worshiped them above all others, and for this worship the immortal siblings granted enlightenment and courage and love. And, on rare occasions, the touch of heaven. What they had granted Tharn had been beyond his comprehension. It had shattered and astounded him.

I grow stronger, Lorris, Tharn went on. *Your touch in me is fire. I beg you, end your silence. Speak to me, before I do this dreadful thing.*

He waited quietly, but there was no answer, and he thought for a moment, as he had thought throughout the night, that his god's silence was the answer, and that the answer was approval. It had to be, he reasoned. The touch of heaven was strong in him, stronger than in any Drol he had ever heard of. Far stronger, even, than in any of his own priests. Lorris and Pris had gifted him, and he was more than just a man now. He was part of nature, a force like the ocean and the moon. The pattern of every leaf foretold the tree's demise. He could hear the drone of a cricket and know if it was hungry or ready to breed. Dreams had become living entities that he could touch and walk through, so that every night's sleep was a spectral journey.

And the air obeyed him. It trembled when he bid it to, and if he thought of clouds he could slay the brightest sun. He could summon the rains and the winds and the fog, could squeeze water from a rock with the viselike focus of his brain. He couldn't fly, but he could open his consciousness so that his mind could soar untethered and let him feel the iciness of mountaintops and the suffocating depths of the sea. All these things he could do, and he was so terrified by them that he spent long hours in prayer, begging for an explanation.

I will do this thing if you wish it, Lorris, he prayed. *Do you? Tell me, please. Please.*

All his new abilities had a purpose. The other cunning-men, priests like him, had told him so. Voris too seemed to believe it. They had all been at war with the Daegog for years, and with the Daegog's powerful protector, the warlord Kronin. And they were weary. Certainly Lorris had touched him for a reason. But it was not they who would bear the guilt of the crime they were considering. Tharn alone would endure that burden, and in a way he hated them for it. If they were all wrong, then Lorris would punish him alone.

I have been so loyal to you. And you have given me so much. Will you not tell me why? Am I not your favored? Shall I do this thing for you, or are these gifts for something else?

Tharn unclasped his palms and let them fall to his sides. There was only a little time left. He had told Voris he would leave Castle Dring at dawn, and Voris was always punctual. But he still had no answer, and the night of prayer had weakened him so that he wanted only to crawl into one of the castle's many beds, and sleep until the war was over. Lorris had his reasons, Tharn was sure, but he felt abandoned anyway.

"Let me rest," he whispered. "When this is over, be finished with me. Let me sleep in peace. No dreams."

He started to rise, but his knees would not let him. They burned with such fierceness that for a moment he thought he would cry out. But then he thought of the Daegog again, and how the fat Triin leader was to blame for this misery, too, and the resolve to do the evil deed came to him in a violent flash. His knees had been like water since his torture. The Daegog's jailors enjoyed their work.

In his heart, Tharn knew he was not an evil man, though the world now thought him so. His name was infamous among the Triin, and he dreamed of a day when he could change that, and prove to his people that the gods still existed and that they had expectations of their children. Lorris and Pris wanted the best for the Triin, and the Triin had shunned them, turning instead to the devils of Nar for enlightenment. Like the Daegog, the Triin had gotten fat on Naren pleasures. They had forgotten their place in creation, their service to heaven, and they had become sinful. They needed cleansing, they needed the fire that only he could bring.

Like Dyana, the cunning-man thought blackly. She was the worst of them, defiant and offensive to Pris herself. She too would have to be cleansed, and learn her place as a good Triin woman. A current of passion rushed through him. He would reeducate her.

A knock came on the chamber door, soft but intrusive. Tharn ignored it. He heard the door slip open, and Voris' familiar footfalls on the wooden floor. His friend's voice was apologetic.

"Am I interrupting your prayers?" asked the warlord.

"Nothing interrupts my prayers," said the Drol. "Come in. You can help me."

Voris stepped into the chamber. "Your knees again?"

"My knees," replied Tharn. He took Voris' huge, outstretched hand and let the warlord pull him to his feet. Pain shot through his legs and he winced. Voris watched him dutifully, waiting for him to work the stiffness out of his body.

"It is dawn," said the warlord. "Your cunning-men are outside, waiting."

"I am ready."

Voris grimaced. "You do not look ready," he remarked. "You have been awake too long, and so much praying wearies you. You should rest first."

Tharn shook his head. "No time. There is too much to do. And I am as ready now as I ever will be."

"What happened?"

"Nothing," said Tharn bitterly. "Lorris is silent."

"Then you have not changed your decision?"

"I have not," said Tharn, heading toward the chamber door. "There is no other way I can see."

Voris smiled. "It is the right decision, my friend. We will all honor you for this. And it is what Lorris wants, I know it."

"Do you?" asked Tharn sharply. He had stopped at the door and turned to glower at the warlord. "How would you know that? How would any of you? This is a crime, what I go to do."

"It is not a crime if it is Lorris' will," replied Voris. "You have been chosen to do this. He would not have granted you these powers if he did not intend you to use them."

"His intent is lost on me!" flared Tharn. "He ignores me. He gives me only silence, now. This may only be a curse, Voris. You and I have done some terrible things."

"For good reasons," interrupted Voris. It was the argument Tharn expected. "We kill with jiiktars, we kill with hands. Has not heaven given us these things, too? Then why not use these other gifts?" He snorted in disgust and folded his arms across his chest. "To kill our enemies is no crime at all."

Tharn drew a deep breath and went over to his friend. Voris was a good deal older than he, more like a father than a follower sometimes, but he was not a Drol priest.

"It is written in the texts of Lorris that the touch of heaven is for the benefit of all Triin, and that those who are selfish with it or who use it for death will be themselves forever damned."

"I know all this," said Voris impatiently. "But what do the texts say of the Daegog? What would Lorris think of a man who deals with devils from Nar? Lorris was a warrior, Tharn. Like us."

Tharn's face cracked with a melancholy smile. He was no warrior, just a holy man who had picked a fight with royalty. "Lorris was also a man of peace," he corrected. "Let us not forget that. Remember the story of the oak and the lion? Lorris risked his sister's life for peace."

"Peace is all I pray for, Tharn. And when you do this thing we will have peace at last. You crush Kronin and his Daegog, and I will deal with the Jackal."

Tharn put up a warning hand. "The Naren is not to be harmed," he insisted. "Do what you must, but take him alive. He must witness what I have planned for the Daegog. All my enemies must be there, particularly the Jackal. He must believe in my powers, so that his emperor fears us."

"As you say," agreed Voris. "But you should know that the horsemen of Talistan have left the valley. They will probably return to Tatterak to fight with Kronin and the Daegog again."

Tharn's eyebrows went up. "Left the valley? Why?"

Voris shrugged. "The Jackal is an arrogant one. Perhaps he thinks he no longer needs them. But be on guard for them. They are surprisingly vicious."

"We have fought them before," said Tharn. "They will be a small matter. If I can, I will try to capture their leader along with Kronin. If I cannot, I will kill him or let him escape. The Baron Gayle is not of interest to me. He does not have the mind to grasp what I have planned. I want the man from Aramoor."

"You will have him," said Voris. The warlord's eyes burned with laughter. "I will capture the Jackal for you, and you will capture Kronin for me."

Tharn's expression hardened. "You take too much pleasure in this, my friend. Remember who our real enemy is."

"I do remember. Too well."

"Do you?" asked Tharn. "I wonder. Kronin is a good man. He serves that bastard Daegog out of loyalty and because he has taken an oath. I will not let your hatred of him taint what we are doing. I will not kill Kronin if I do not have to."

"That is fine with me, Tharn," said Voris. "His humiliation will please me just as well."

Tharn sighed. The warlords of Lucel-Lor had bickered and warred for centuries, and some of their rivalries had gone on so long that they no longer had any real meaning. Hate was like that, Tharn knew. And hate had blinded his friend Voris for decades. The Dring Valley and Kronin's land of Tatterak fought now over the pretense of the Agar Forest, a useless tract of land that had come to symbolize bloodshed. And though Voris was a devout Drol who did Tharn's bidding unquestioningly, his hatred of Kronin was a vice he simply would not renounce.

"There is something else, Tharn," said Voris evasively. "Something we should talk about . . ."

"Yes, I know," replied Tharn. "The woman." He sighed heavily and fell back against the wall, staring up at the ceiling. "I have looked for her. I had thought she was in your valley, but . . ."

"What?"

Tharn shrugged. "I do not know where, exactly. This thing I do, it works poorly. I see her, and yet I do not. I glimpsed her in a village somewhere, and now I cannot see her there. She is somewhere else, I think."

"Where? Tell me and I will get her for you."

"I cannot. She may still be in Dring, maybe in a different village, maybe somewhere where I cannot find her. I am not strong enough yet to use this 'sight.' "

Voris frowned. "That is not much good. There are many villages in Dring. You have to tell me more if I am to find her for you."

"There is no more, not yet." Tharn looked straight into his comrade's eyes. "But you will try, will you not?"

"If I can," replied Voris. "It might not be possible—"

"You must," Tharn insisted. "Dyana is mine. She was pledged to me and I will have her." The anger rushed through him, sickening him. Again he fell back against the wall and wiped a palm across his forehead. He found a slick of perspiration there and groaned. "I am too tired for this. But when I am stronger I will find her, and I will capture her myself if necessary."

"*That,*" insisted Voris, "is not why Lorris has given you power. Just find her if you can. I will take her for you."

Tharn nodded but said nothing. He knew Voris was right, that his new abilities were certainly not meant for abducting a woman, yet he was still beguiled by her. He had been since their parents betrothed them. And every day she defied him, every time a Drol asked him where his woman was, he seethed. It was not her place to break the promise of their parents. She was a woman. This female independence was just one more dirty Naren influence left unchecked. When he and his revolution were victorious, they would turn back the clock on this obscenity as well.

"She is mine," Tharn whispered darkly. "I will have her, my friend. And then I will teach her what it means to be a woman."

Voris laughed. "Is she so fair? She must be to have you so entranced. She is just a girl, Tharn. And from what you have told me, a wildcat. You might be better off without her. There are women enough in Dring, good Drol women. I will find one for you if you wish."

Tharn shook his head. "No. You do not know her. You have not seen her. She is . . ." The Drol master closed his eyes. "A dream."

"A dream," scoffed Voris. "You have been bitten by a snake, Tharn. This Dyana is the daughter of a heretic. She would make you a very poor wife. Forget her father's pledge." The warlord's tone softened. "I know you. A woman like this will not make you happy."

"There is no other woman for me," said Tharn softly. "She is part of my curse. I want no one else."

"She can never love you. If that is what you want—"

"She is mine," Tharn railed. "She was betrothed to me, and I will have her!"

"I say again—she will not love you. Ever. She runs because she fears you. She saw what you did to her father."

Tharn's dark eyes smoldered. "Her father broke his word to me."

"You were pledged at twelve, Tharn. He did not know the man you would become. If you were Drol then, he would never have offered you his daughter."

"And is that how followers of the Daegog keep their word? When it is convenient to remember the giving? Her father deserved his death. I would behead him again if I could."

"This is why she hates you, my friend. This is why she will always hate you. Whatever you believe you had is dead. Find another."

"I cannot," admitted Tharn. "When you see her, you will know why I am so possessed."

Voris looked profoundly sad. "Then I will find her for you, if I can. Now come. Your men are packed and ready."

Voris opened the door for the Drol master, and the two of them stepped out into the quiet hallway. A pair of Voris' warriors were waiting there for them, their red robes perfect against their hard bodies, their twin-bladed jiiktars slung ready over their backs. They fell into step behind Tharn and the lord of the valley, following them through the dark hall, past the main entrance to the castle and out into the courtyard where five horses waited for them among the broken statues. Atop two of the horses were cunning-men, Tharn's Drol priests dressed in the saffron robes of their station. They were silent as their master approached, not even tilting up their heads to regard him. Voris' warriors went directly to their own horses, mounting them quickly and leaving the warlord and Tharn room for a private farewell.

"It is a long way," said Voris. His expression had softened with concern. "You take care of yourself, my friend. And do not fret. What you are doing is right."

Tharn tried to smile but couldn't quite manage it. "Right or wrong, I expect to be damned for it." He went to his own horse and started to mount when he heard a cry echoing from inside the castle.

"Bhapo! Wait!"

Tharn pulled his foot out of the stirrup and looked toward the castle gate. From out of the darkness came Pris, Voris' youngest daughter. She was running toward them, her arms outstretched.

"Do not leave yet, Bhapo," she cried. She tried to run past her father but Voris caught her by the collar.

"Daughter," he scolded. "Get back to bed."

Pris tried to squirm free of her father's hand, but Voris held her tight. "I want to say good-bye," she pleaded. "I saw Bhapo leaving from my window. Please . . ."

"All right," agreed Voris. "But be quick. Bhapo has to leave."

Tharn went over to the little girl and dropped to his knees. The pain of the gesture blew through him but he ignored it, staring into the girl's face with a smile. "I am not going to be gone forever, Pris," he said gently. "Do not worry. I will come back as soon as I can. I have things to do first, though."

"What things, Bhapo?" asked the girl. "War things?"

Tharn loved to hear her call him Bhapo. It was a term of endearment meaning "uncle," and Tharn always smiled when he heard it. "I have to go and stop a bad man, Pris. I have to go help some people. But I will be back, I promise. And things will be good then. All right?"

Pris nodded. "Yes, Bhapo. Will you bring me back another book when you come?"

"I will try. But here, let me show you something. You will like this."

With Pris and her father watching, Tharn picked up a stick from the ground, a gnarled, dry branch that had fallen from one of the courtyard's birch trees. Quickly he pulled off the twigs studding it, then began to crack the stick into pieces. Each piece he laid on the ground in turn, until he had formed what looked like a figure, a wooden man with a branch for a torso and tiny sticks for legs and arms.

"There," said Tharn. "Do you know what that is?"

Pris didn't hide her disappointment. "Nothing," she said sourly.

"Not nothing. That is a man."

The girl cocked her head inquisitively and studied the stick figure. "It is?"

"Yes!" Tharn waved his hand over the twigs. "Look."

The sticks quivered for a moment, and then the little wooden man stood up, teetered on his blunt feet, and began to move. Pris squealed with delight, clapping her hands. Tharn laughed and looked up at Voris, whose eyes were wide with a sort of horrified fascination. As Pris clapped, the little wooden man began to dance, and soon even the cunning-men, who had slowly been growing accustomed to their master's bizarre abilities, began to chuckle.

"Keep clapping, Pris," directed Tharn. He got up from his knees and headed back to his horse. "He will dance for you a little longer."

So enthralled was the girl with her new toy that she hardly noticed her beloved Bhapo leaving. Voris walked past her and helped Tharn onto his horse. His white face still bore a look of utter shock.

"What was that?" asked the warlord.

Tharn shrugged. "Ask Lorris," he replied, then snapped the reins of his horse and rode away. Moments later, when he had disappeared into the green forest, the little man he had made of sticks stopped dancing and fell broken to the ground.

FIVE

His name was Nebarazar Gorandarr, but no one ever called him that. He had a royal pedigree longer than most Naren kings, save for perhaps the emperor himself, and he could trace his bloodline back a thousand generations, to the time when the Triin were gatherers of plants and the first troublesome Drol had yet to worship a mythical god. Because of his lineage and the twistedness of his name, his people had long ago settled on a title for those of his once-powerful clan.

They called him Daegog.

It was an ancient word meaning "leader," and the Daegog of Lucel-Lor took pride in the title. He was not Daegog Nebarazar Gorandarr, he was simply the Daegog. His wife called him thus, as did his dozen children, and to speak his full name while in his presence was to commit the highest heresy. Those who served him did so not out of love, but the deepest, inbred loyalty. His family had been revered throughout Triin history, and though he had been the weakest of his clan, he still commanded honor, at least among those who had not fallen under the spell of the Drol.

Some thought him petty. He knew this and generally did not mind the insult. He was vastly wealthy, or at least he had been before losing his citadel to Tharn, and he always considered it mere jealousy that those with less should call him mean or tight with his riches. In his mind he had earned every bauble simply by virtue of who he was, the latest descendant of a venerable family.

Today the Daegog of Lucel-Lor was in a particularly foul mood, and he intended everyone to know it. He drummed his pudgy fingers on the meeting table, so that his stout rings rubbed together. Of all the things the Daegog hated, he despised waiting above all else. In better days, keeping a Daegog waiting would have been a crime. But those days had passed, and even he knew he couldn't expect the Naren savages to understand such complicated etiquette. So he waited, seething, on pillows of less than quality silk. A servingwoman placed a bowl of dates before him and he batted it away, spilling the fruit to the floor.

"Get out," he snapped at the woman, who quickly obeyed. Next to him he could feel the warlord Kronin bristle, but he didn't care. He was tired of living in this hovel of a castle, tired of being the warlord's guest. He wanted to go home, and he blamed the others in the room for keeping him away from his beloved Falindar. One-armed Edgard, the Aramoorian war duke, rubbed the stump of his shoulder distractedly and gave Kronin a furtive wink. The Daegog cringed inwardly, sure that they thought him an idiot.

"I want to start," he said to Kronin. "Where is this fool baron? Go and find him."

Kronin, warlord of Tatterak, stifled a grunt and got up from the floor. Mildly annoyed, he started toward the open archway before noticing Baron Blackwood Gayle. The baron pushed past him without regard, strode into the chamber, and bowed deeply to the Triin leader. He was a giant man, the epitome of a Naren barbarian, and when he moved, his leather armor stretched and groaned. Behind him followed another Talistanian, the ubiquitous, weasel-faced Colonel Trosk, who never removed his feathered hat for anyone, not even the Daegog.

"Daegog," said the baron with a flourish. "Forgive my lateness. Matters of weight occupied me, and I only just arrived."

"It is a disservice you do me, Baron, to keep me waiting. What do you think I do all day that I have such time to waste? Sit."

Gayle cocked his head deferentially, and he and his colonel sat crosslegged on the floor, fighting to maneuver the silk pillows under their buttocks. They made no attempt to speak to Duke Edgard, nor did the Aramoorian pay them any attention. Kronin returned to his place beside the Daegog without a word.

"Woman!" cried the Daegog in his own tongue, directing his voice out into the hall. "Bring us some food. More dates, and drink."

Seconds later the servingwoman returned, bearing with her a tray of fruits and a tall silver decanter. She placed the tray on the table and nervously poured some tokka, the Daegog's favorite liquor, into her master's outstretched glass. When it was filled, she attended to the others.

"Now," said the Daegog haughtily, "may we begin?"

"Of course, wise one," said the baron through one of his insincere smiles. "If the others are ready . . ."

"We were waiting for you," said Edgard. The war duke looked contemptuously at Gayle. "I think you do this on purpose, Baron."

"Just like an Aramoorian to speak out of turn," countered Gayle. "You talk boldly for a man with one arm, War Duke. Reconsider your tone." His eyes flicked toward his silent colonel, who was stroking the handle of his saber. "It's not just a jiiktar that can take off an arm."

Edgard started to rise. The Daegog brought a fist down on the table. "Enough!" he cried. "Sit, Duke Edgard. And do not bicker around me again. I am tired of you all!"

The Aramoorian sat back down. The Daegog knitted his fingers and rested his elbows on the table, glaring at each of them in turn. Gayle and Colonel Trosk merely grinned.

"I warn you, I have no patience for this," said the Daegog. "Baron Gayle, Kronin tells me the rebels are gaining ground in the south. He says that soon they may even be able to reach us here on Mount Godon. You are supposed to be securing that land, yes?"

"Yes, Daegog," replied Gayle. "And I am doing so, to the best of my ability."

"Your best is very poor, Baron."

Gayle made a face. "I have been away in the Dring Valley, Daegog. Young Vantran needed my assistance." The baron glanced at Edgard. "He had to be pulled from the fire. We arrived just in time."

"And he is strong again?" asked the Daegog.

"Strong? Oh, no, Daegog, he's never been strong. He is a whelp, and it is all too much for him. As I've always said, the valley war should be mine to conduct." He sighed. "Frankly, I sometimes wonder why the Aramoorians are here at all."

The Daegog watched unhappily as Edgard swallowed the insult. Of the two, he preferred the mild Aramoorian to the brassy baron. Edgard was certainly honest, even if he wasn't as bold as Gayle, and his counsel had always proved useful. But he did wonder, as he watched Edgard shifting, if the baron was correct. The Talistanians were crude but rugged, and they obeyed their emperor without question, something the Aramoorians did only grudgingly. In fact, the only man the Daegog trusted at all was Kronin. Kronin was Triin. A fool, of course, like all the warlords, but more than a match for any Naren.

"Tell me about Dring first," directed the Daegog. "What is happening there?"

"It goes poorly, wise one," replied Gayle. "The boy doesn't know what he's doing."

"That is not what I have heard from my man there," countered the Daegog. "Go on."

"Well, what can I say? He is not a good military strategist. He lacks experience and will. You should see his men! They look half-starved.

They're dressed in rags and they're running out of everything." Gayle shook his head ruefully. "I really don't know how much longer they can last."

"To be honest, though," added Colonel Trosk, "we are not doing much better. We lack for everything, too."

"Yes," agreed Gayle, "but it's more than that. They're becoming demoralized, and it's Vantran's fault."

"I'm sure Richius is doing his best," rumbled Edgard.

"I'm not talking about your precious prince, Edgard. I mean Darius Vantran, his father. He's not sending in any fresh troops or supplies. You haven't had any yourself, have you? Your king has abandoned you."

Edgard didn't respond to the charge, and his silence piqued the Daegog's interest. "That is the other matter," said the Triin leader. "Duke Edgard, why no word from your king? Where are the troops the emperor promised me?"

"It's not the emperor's fault, Daegog," offered Gayle.

The Daegog silenced Gayle with a wave. "Duke Edgard? An explanation?"

"Aramoor is a small country, Daegog," said Edgard calmly. "We don't have the resources needed to fight this war. I'm sure my king is sending in everything he can."

"A lie," snarled Gayle. "Your king is a coward. He could send more men and supplies if he wanted to, but he's like a child who can't stand the sight of blood. Why, as we speak he's letting his own son starve to death in Dring! Aramoor controls the Saccenne Run. He is the reason no supplies are getting through. He is a single-minded renegade who has always been trouble for the emperor."

"You speak very highly of your emperor," said the Daegog. He sat back and popped a date into his mouth, examining Gayle as he chewed. "Tell me, Baron. Do you like being under Nar's boot?"

"You mean protection, Daegog," corrected Gayle. "And yes, I appreciate it. As I'm sure you do."

"And you do not mind that your emperor is a conqueror, or that he and his underlings kill for pleasure?"

"Your pardon, Daegog, but the emperor wants only to help you. He fears for you, for all Triin. . . ."

The Daegog closed his eyes and tried to quell his burning temper. "He is a madman, Baron. All the world knows that."

"Oh?" asked Gayle indignantly. "If he is such a threat, why then do you accept his help so readily, Daegog? May I ask you that?"

"No, Baron, you may not. That business is mine and Arkus' alone. But know this—I speak your language and I know the truth of things, more than you do. I am not a savage you can outwit."

"Wise one, I never suggested—"

"Be still!" thundered the Daegog. "And listen to me, both of you. I know the king of Aramoor plays games with me. And I know the emperor's mind, too. So you may tell Arkus for me that if he wants the thing he seeks from me, he had better start sending in the troops he promised. And not Talistanians or more weaklings from Aramoor. I want Naren soldiers, from the Black City. Because if I fall, he will never get what he wants from Tharn. Never!"

Blackwood Gayle was finally at a loss. He glanced at his colonel for support, but the lanky Trosk merely shrugged and tried hard not to seem concerned, a ruse the Daegog saw through easily.

"No?" pressed the Daegog. "You will not tell him that?"

"Daegog, it is not that simple. The emperor is pressed for men just as we are. He is still at war with Liss, and there are rebellions in the north of the Empire. I swear to you, he would send his legions if he could. . . ."

"I do not care about Liss or rebellions," hissed the Daegog. "I have my own rebels to deal with! Tharn and his Drol could be at the gates of this castle any day. I need men to fight them off!"

"We need support, too, Daegog," said Gayle. "It is not our fault that the king of Aramoor leaves us to fight alone. Why, Dring itself might fall in days. The warlord Voris may be victorious."

Kronin perked up at the mention of his enemy. "Voris?" he asked the Daegog in their shared language. "What did the baron say?"

The Daegog laughed ruefully. "You see?" he said to Gayle. "Do you see what I am surrounded by? This fool protector of mine thinks of nothing but Voris. He should be defending *me*, yet all he talks of is killing Voris. Would that be better, Baron? Should I let Kronin loose in Dring to help Vantran?"

"No, Daegog," said Gayle coldly. "That's not what I'm suggesting."

"Then offer me something useful!"

"Daegog," said Edgard calmly. "It is time for us to talk truthfully."

There was so much seriousness in the war duke's tone that the Daegog was stunned. He turned to Edgard and said, "Truthfully? Yes, that would be a good change, Duke. Please . . ."

"Now I will speak your language," growled Edgard in Triin, "because Kronin is my friend and he deserves to hear my words."

"What? What is that you're saying?" asked Gayle.

Edgard ignored him.

"Plain talk, Daegog. The war is lost, not only in Dring but here in Tatterak, too. You know it. We all do." Edgard eyed the warlord Kronin, who looked suitably shocked. "Aramoor is not sending any more troops. Maybe they cannot. Maybe they will not. I do not really know or care. But it is not our war anymore. If you have business with the emperor, then let him send his own men to die." He got up slowly, then turned to address Kronin. "Kronin, my friend, may your gods look after you."

"Where will you go, Edgard?" asked the warlord.

"Back home, to Aramoor."

"You will be hung!" exclaimed the Daegog. "You cannot retreat. The emperor will kill you if you do."

"Probably," replied Edgard. "But I would rather die with honor at home than die here in your defense. You are a cruel and miserable man, Daegog. I am sorry so many of my countrymen have perished for you."

Kronin stood up, smiled at the war duke, then embraced him. "You have always been my friend," said the warlord. "Fighting with you has been my honor."

Incensed, the Daegog stood up and shook a fat fist at Edgard. "You are a fool!" he raged. "Your emperor will ruin Aramoor for this!"

But Edgard ignored the Daegog's barb. He turned and walked away, stopping and looking down at the astonished Blackwood Gayle, who had remained seated throughout the entire exchange. "Blackwood Gayle, it's your war now. You may not believe this, but I wish you and your men well."

"What?" sputtered the baron. "Daegog, what is this?"

The Daegog snorted with contempt. "It is as you have always said, Baron Gayle. The Aramoorians are cowards. He is retreating."

Gayle and Trosk both sprang to their feet. "Retreating? Edgard, you cannot! Your troops are needed, now more than ever. What will become of the rest of us?"

Edgard laughed. "You'll probably fare better than I, Gayle. Don't worry. You'll always have a place in the emperor's heart. If you live, that is."

"War Duke," called the Daegog. Then he softened his expression and said, "Edgard, please. Do not do this. We do need you. We can win still, if you stay. If you go . . ." The Triin's round face wrinkled. "Tharn will kill me."

The war duke of Aramoor smiled sadly at the Daegog. "Every man dies, Daegog. And if I may say so, you deserve it." Then he turned his back on them all and strode out of the chamber, saying, "I leave in the morning, with my men."

That evening, the Daegog of Lucel-Lor sat brooding on a balcony, overlooking the rough terrain of Tatterak. He sipped absently at a cup of steaming tea and ate sparingly from a tray of sweet biscuits, both Naren affectations he had learned to love. The moon was full and red behind Mount Godon. Kronin's granite stronghold cast its dentate shadow across the plain, while moonbeams splashed on the stones and the carved mahogany of the balcony, setting them alight. The Daegog licked at the rim of his cup, mopping up the honey there with his tongue. In the distance he could see the tattered dragon banner of Edgard's troops, huddled around torches that stirred in the evening breeze. It was late. There was very little movement among the Aramoorians now. The war duke would have them sleeping, the Daegog surmised, resting for their long march back home.

"Coward," muttered the Daegog. He had always liked Edgard, and the duke's betrayal was a bitter blow. Now he had only Gayle to protect him, plus whatever warriors Kronin had left. There was still young Vantran in Dring, but he would no doubt be leaving, too, once he heard that his war duke had retreated.

The Daegog let out a little whimper. It had been a long, protracted war, and his allies were dwindling. Every day it seemed more of the Triin warlords sided with Tharn. He was a sorcerer, that one. He could turn men's minds to slush. Now only Kronin and a handful of others still followed the Daegog, and if the Drol pushed hard enough, they could probably topple them all right into the ocean.

The Daegog poured himself another cup of tea, dashed it liberally with honey from a silver spoon, and sat back to stare at the Aramoorians. They were going home, and he hated them for it. He ached for his own home, the dazzling spires of his usurped Falindar. Kronin was a loyal man but a middling host, and in these days of shortages Mount Godon could only provide modest hospitality. He was accustomed to stretching out each night on a bed of ivory inlaid with rubies, but here he slept on a mattress of scratchy fabric stuffed with straw. In Falindar, there had been scores of servants to attend him, beautiful young women trained to be perfectly servile, who bathed him and rubbed his feet with oil. But here in austere Mount Godon, every woman was engaged in the same bloody business as the men, trying to win the war. There were weapons to sharpen and clothes to mend and food to be harvested. There were shortages of everything now that the Drol had started burning the eastern fields. Day by day, he was becoming less royal, and he despised it.

He was sure Arkus of Nar was having no such problems. Arkus, his Naren benefactor, was comfortable in his black palace. Arkus the puppeteer, who never showed the world his face but let his golden count— the strange one called Biagio—be his voice. He would send a message to Biagio at once, he decided, to tell him of Edgard's treachery. He would demand the emperor send his own legionnaires into Lucel-Lor to put down the rebellion. The Daegog ran a chubby finger over the rim of his cup and grinned. He admired Arkus, but age had dulled the old man's reason, and his obsession with magic had made him reckless.

"Magic!" The Daegog snorted. The Narens were such passionate

fools. They had all the science of the world in their hands, had built cities
and weapons the Triin could only dream of, yet they were still as supersti-
tious as any Drol. Now only he, the Daegog of all Triin, could pretend to
give Arkus what he wanted, and the price was steep indeed.

"Go home, then, Edgard," whispered the Daegog. "Go home to your
death."

He lowered his glass to the rickety table next to him and let out a giant
yawn. It was very late, and he was weary. In the morning he would meet
with Baron Gayle again to discuss the defense of Mount Godon, and
speaking to the Talistanian always taxed him. It was time for sleep.

Retreating from the balcony, he entered his bedchamber, the plushest
one in the entire castle and still smaller than his own in Falindar by at
least half. Miserably appointed, the room reminded the Daegog more of
his citadel's dungeon than its bedchambers. But he was too exhausted to
dwell on his plight, and as he shut the twin doors leading to the balcony,
he took one last breath of the night air and turned to his bed. There was a
candle near the bedside and he blew it out, satisfied with the moonlight
coming through the glass. He was already in his satiny bedclothes, and as
he slid into the bed and drew the sheets over his bulk, his eyelids drooped.
It took only a moment for sleep to come.

But it shattered just as quickly.

The Daegog sat up in bed, hearing a noise at the balcony doors. Startled, he pulled the sheets close to his face and peered out toward the balcony. Past midnight, he recalled, past the hour of decent folk. Something
outside shimmered, twinkling darkly in the moonlight. A white and man-
sized shadow hovered just beyond the doors. The Daegog made to
scream, but lost his voice in terror as the thing moved wraithlike through
the glass.

It was a man and yet it was not. It was white and thin and without sub-
stance, but it had form and it had eyes, and it watched the Daegog with a
wicked humor. The Daegog's heart seized. His breath came to him in
short, painful bursts. And the thing that was not quite alive floated closer
on its legless torso and stopped at the foot of his bed.

"Do you recognize me, fat one?" asked the spectre. Its voice was hollow, and it rang in the Daegog's head like a broken bell. The Daegog studied the thing, examined its determined face and saffron robes, and knew
with horrible certainty what the visitation was. His dry lips pursed and a
name dribbled out.

"Tharn."

The ghostly face grinned. "How nice to be remembered. I, of course,
remember you, Daegog. I remember you every time it rains and I cannot
walk."

The Daegog backed up against the headboard. "What are you, demon?"

"I have become the sword of Lorris," declared the Drol, and as he spoke his body shimmered. "The touch of heaven is within me. I am the air and the water. Look upon me, fat one. Look and fear me."

"I do fear you," chittered the Daegog. "Spare me, monster. Take what you want but let me live. . . ."

The Drol laughed. "I go to make your end, Nebarazar Gorandarr. Tonight you are undone."

"No!" wailed the Daegog. "Tharn, forgive me. I never meant for you to be harmed. It was not my doing, I swear to you."

"Liar. I remember seeing your face through the blood in my eyes. I remember you there."

The Daegog held up his palms. "I thought you were a criminal. I . . . I was wrong. Please, we can talk. . . ."

"You are the one with crimes to answer for, and I do not talk with devils." The ghost gestured with his transparent hand toward the balcony and the darkness beyond. "Look to the skies tonight. Wait for the purple mist. Tonight I am Storm Maker."

And then the image of the Drol faded and dissolved, leaving the Daegog shivering, alone. It was long moments before he could move, but at last he slid out of his bed and tiptoed toward the doors. He flung them open and stepped onto the balcony. The steam had stopped rising from the teapot on the table. It was colder now, almost wintry. He looked to the bloodred moon hanging like a death's-head in the sky. A purple cloud floated across the horizon.

SIX

Even before the war with Nar, the Dring Valley had never been a peaceful place. Voris the Wolf had done his best to live up to his title of warlord, and so the people of his land endured many hardships for his sake, losing sons in battles with their neighbors from Tatterak, the largest of all the Triin territories. Voris was iron-fisted, and his feud with Kronin had dragged on for years, never coming to any conclusion, and never winning the ostensible prize of the Agar Forest. This attrition had drained the coffers of Voris' castle and had made his people pariahs among the rest of Lucel-Lor, who looked upon the Drol of the valley with suspicion and disquietude.

And yet the Wolf was beloved in Dring, a mystery Dyana puzzled over as she walked with her ragged company along the winding Sheaze River. They were refugees now, these people she traveled with, the meager handful of the valley's populace who saw the Wolf as something less than deified. With their shabby clothes and dirty faces, they no longer looked Triin at all. They were ghosts now, thin and pale, and Dyana muttered bitterly as she trudged alongside the wagon, for she knew that they all had Tharn and his henchman Voris to thank for their misery, and she wondered at the stupidity of people who would follow such men.

People like her uncle, Jaspin.

She didn't miss the Dring Valley, not like she missed Tatterak. Dring had merely been a home of necessity, a place to flee when no others would accept her. Jaspin had opened his home to her, but had never made her feel welcome or called her "niece" with any affection. He had feared her, like her mother and sisters before him. And he had discarded her with the rest of the outcasts, labeling them as dangerous heretics. But they were not heretics. They were survivors and fighters, and Dyana was glad to be among them.

Each day for them was much the same. By Falger's reckoning, they had journeyed halfway to Ackle-Nye so far, crawling along at a snail's pace. Because there were only two riding horses, most of the group walked, except for the children and the infirm, who were allowed to ride in the mule-drawn wagon along with the few possessions they had brought with them. Falger walked in front of them all, leading his horse over the rugged landscape and letting the weary take turns on its back. Only on rare occasions did he ride his horse himself, and only then when he was just too tired to continue walking.

Falger was an older man, with a well-earned reputation for eccentricity. If there was a heretic among this dismal lot, it was he. A self-proclaimed hater of the gods, he was quick to denounce those who prayed and quicker still to laugh in the faces of the village's devout. And like Dyana, he despised the Drol and their revolution with a fervor she had thought no one else shared. This mutual disdain had fostered an unusual kinship between them, and Falger quickly became her one defender, for even these folk were nervous to have Tharn's betrothed among them. But they showed her respect, and that was all Dyana wanted. That and to find her way, somehow, to Nar.

None of them knew precisely what they would find in Ackle-Nye, but they hoped it would be freedom and a willingness to take them into the Empire. They would be outcasts there, too, of course, but they would be free of Drol tyranny. For Dyana, Nar might mean a new life. Perhaps in Nar she could fulfill her father's dreams and become a woman with dignity, and not a lapdog of the kind she so despised, the type of woman a Drol society demanded. In Nar, she could choose her own husband, and not be sold to a man. She hoped that not all Narens were like Kalak and his murderers.

The noon sun beat down on her uncovered head, and as she trudged along she considered this again, letting her imagination ease the drudgery of the endless trek. These days, her thoughts often turned to Nar and the marvels she might find there. Her father had told her that the Empire was a vast and powerful place, with machines and high buildings made of sweeping stonework. He had said that in the Black City there was a palace as beautiful as Falindar itself, and that Emperor Arkus sat in that palace upon a throne of iron and ruled his many kingdoms with wisdom.

Dyana laughed lightly as she recalled this memory and her father's bright face. He had never even been to Nar. He was one of the richest men in Tatterak, but he had never once purchased passage through the

Run. Too busy, he always used to claim. Busy raising a family and caring for a wife who betrayed him. Busy helping the Daegog deal with the Naren representatives who poured in from the Black City. Too busy for himself. Dyana's smile evaporated. She missed him, and sometimes the pain of it was unendurable. Worse, she still heard his screams at night, and when she dreamed of him her visions always ended the same way—with his severed head looking up at her vacantly, and Tharn standing over his decapitated body. Years had passed, but the memory was still vivid. That vision would haunt her forever, she knew, and she was resigned to such nightmares. Just as she was resigned to her solitude.

They went on like this for hours more, silently plodding along, until at last the sun began to dip and Falger called a halt. Gratefully they all dropped down at the riverbank and took their fill of the fresh water, careful that all their skins were filled in case of emergency. According to Falger, the Sheaze would take them straight to Ackle-Nye, but none of them had ever been to the infamous city of beggars and so they took no chances with their water supply. Food, however, was another problem entirely. What little they had taken was dwindling fast, and they collected what they could from the brush and forests, gathering nuts and berries and any wild roots they were lucky enough to find. Falger was in charge of rationing the food, and each time they rested he doled out a meager allowance of bread, barely enough to keep the children from crying. Since Tharn had started burning the croplands, food was scarce nearly everywhere in Lucel-Lor. It was just one more of the Drol leader's obscenities, one more brutality he performed in heaven's name.

Exhausted, Dyana collapsed at the riverside and pulled off her doeskin boots, dipping her burning feet in the blessedly cool water of the Sheaze. She let out a sigh of pleasure at the sensation, letting her eyelids droop. Around her the men started making camp, going off into the brush to gather firewood and spreading out blankets to sleep on, while the women fussed over the restless children, who splashed happily into the river to play. Dyana smiled as she watched them. There were six boys and three girls. She noticed the way they played together. At this age, they were still equal. The girls had yet to know the sting of male domination, and the boys could still see their playmates as more than just objects. Too bad they would grow up.

"Dyana?"

She looked up to see Falger hovering over her, a small chunk of bread in his hands. She smiled up at him gratefully.

"Thank you," she said, taking the food. She tore off a small wedge and began to eat, slowly so that it would last. The taste of it was wonderful. Falger remained above her, staring down at her with his peculiar grin.

"Can I join you?" he asked.

Dyana chuckled. "You do not need to ask that, Falger. Sit." She patted the ground beside her, urging him down.

Falger dropped to the earth and stretched, letting the muscles in his neck pop and yawning like a lion. He had no food for himself, just a blade of grass between his teeth.

"You are not eating?" asked Dyana.

Falger shook his head. "I thought I would wait until the morning, let the children have some more."

Dyana looked down guiltily at her meager portion.

"Eat," Falger urged. "I am not trying to be a hero. I just want there to be enough. Who knows what we will find when we get to Ackle-Nye?"

"There will be food there," said Dyana. "Will there not?"

"Hopefully. From what I have heard there are many like us, Dyana. And the Narens are not doing so well themselves, remember. We may need to conserve what we have."

What they had was ridiculously little, and would barely last them all the way to Ackle-Nye. Dyana bit into her bread pensively. How could she make such a smattering last?

"You did not come to talk to me today," said Falger. "I missed you."

"I was thinking," said Dyana.

"About what?"

Dyana shrugged. "About everything. About Ackle-Nye, and Nar. I was thinking about what it will be like there."

"Hard," said Falger. "And it is a long road through the Run. And we will need the Narens to guide us, give us food." Falger's expression became forlorn. "Do not get too hopeful, Dyana. We will make it to Ackle-Nye. More than that . . . who knows?"

"*I* know," said Dyana. "We will make it to Nar. I swear it. I will get there if it kills me."

Falger laughed. "Oh, yes? Better to die in the Run than here in Lucel-Lor, eh?"

"Better to die free than be Tharn's wife," corrected Dyana.

"He will not find you now, Dyana," Falger assured her. "We are too far from Dring for that. Even Voris will not send warriors looking for you now." He looked up into the darkening sky and smiled. "We are all safe here."

Safe. It was a wonderful word, but Dyana couldn't believe it. The night he killed her father, Tharn had made it clear she would never be safe again. He was obsessed with her, he always had been. They had both come from prominent families, and the union had seemed the perfect pairing to their misguided parents. Now she could scarcely remember the man he had been, the Tharn that he was before the call of the Drol. He had been kind once. If her memory wasn't wrong, he might have even been shy. She laughed silently to herself. It was hard to reconcile those memories with the revolutionary.

"There is no safety from Tharn," said Dyana bleakly. "And I do not like being driven from my home."

"Nor I," said Falger indignantly. "But show me a choice. Tharn will win this whole thing soon enough, and there will be no place for us who are not Drol. Once Kronin falls, the rest of us are dead. We must leave."

"I know," said Dyana. "But would it not be better to go with our heads high, and not as rats? Would it not be so much better?"

Falger fell silent, and Dyana quickly regretted her words. She could see the hurt on the older man's face, and knew she had insulted him.

"Sorry," she offered. "That was wrong of me to say. We are not rats."

"But we are running," admitted Falger. "That bastard Tharn has beaten us."

"Oh, no. He will never beat us, Falger. Not while we live and escape him. Once we get to Nar, we will have beaten Tharn."

A boy splashed out of the river and fell to his knees in front of them, panting and giggling. "I can beat Tharn," he declared proudly. "I can fight!"

"Can you?" said Falger. "Well, all right then. Let us get you a jiiktar and send you off!"

"Yes!" cried the boy excitedly. "Dyana, I can beat him."

Dyana smiled ruefully. "You stay here and protect us, Luken. You can fight him off if he comes."

"I will," said the boy adamantly. "I wish he would come. I am not afraid."

None of the boys claimed fear. They all clambered out of the river, wringing the water from their clothes and declaring their defiance of Tharn. The girls came ashore, too, sitting down with Dyana and Falger and giggling at the boys' boasts.

"Tell us more about him, Dyana," urged Luken. "Tell us again what he is like."

Dyana laughed. "It was a long time ago, Luken."

"Is he ugly?"

"Is he fat?"

Dyana started to answer, but a little girl whose name she didn't know plopped down next to her and asked the most disquieting question.

"Why does he hate us?"

And no one asked another thing. They just stared at Dyana, waiting for her sage response, and Dyana found herself at a loss.

"I don't know," she said sadly. She took the little girl's hand and pulled her closer, hugging her wet body and not minding the soaking at all. "Maybe it is not really hate," she said. "Maybe it is like what happened in the Agar Forest. You all know that story, right?"

The children were wide-eyed.

"No? None of you knows what happened in the Agar Forest? Luken, you do not know?"

She could tell Luken wanted to lie, but instead he simply frowned.

"Well then, let me tell you. There are giant birch trees in the forest, you all know that. But the story of how they got so tall, that is the good part." Dyana's tone took on drama. "This was a long time ago, long before any of us were born."

"Before Falger was born?" asked one of the boys.

They all chuckled. "Well?" Falger kidded. "Was it?"

"Oh, yes," said Dyana. "It was much longer ago than that. This was before Voris and the Drol, before everything. This was when there was nothing but trees in the forest, no animals, no people, nothing. Just the birch trees, and the redwoods."

Luken wrinkled his nose. "Redwoods? There are no redwoods in Agar."

"Right," said Dyana. "Not anymore. Because they lost their war with the birches. Trees can fight, did you know that? Well, that is what they used to do. They used to fight, talk, everything just like people. Only they did not get along with the redwoods, because the redwoods were cruel to them. Just like the Drol are to us."

"What happened?" asked the girl in Dyana's lap.

"You all know how tall a redwood is. Really, really tall." Dyana raised her hands and knitted her fingers together. "So tall they block out the sun. There were thousands of them in Agar, too, so many that the poor birch trees had no light! They were in the dark, because the redwoods were selfish, and wanted all the sunlight for themselves. And when the birch trees complained, the redwoods got angry. They told the birches that they were the most powerful of all trees, that the gods had made them that way and that the gods liked them best."

"Like the Drol!" Luken echoed.

"Exactly. But those birch trees were tough, like us. They would not let the redwoods suffocate them, so they fought back. Even though the redwoods were taller and stronger, the little birch trees got together and decided to make their roots go even deeper into the earth. Well, the redwoods were so tall and proud they did not even bother looking to see what the little birches were doing. And the birch trees dug deeper and deeper, until their roots were stronger than the redwood roots, and they took all the water from the ground, and did not let the redwoods have any."

Dyana paused and looked at the children.

"Then what?" pressed Luken.

"Then?" Dyana shrugged. "Do you see any more redwoods in Agar?"

All the children laughed, and even Falger gave a chuckle. Dyana laughed, too, recalling the time her father had told her that story. She had been about Luken's age then, and Voris and Kronin had already been at war over the Agar for years. But that wasn't the moral of her tale.

"You see?" she asked them all. "Those birch trees are like us. They were small, but now look at them. They are tall and strong, and they did not give in to the redwoods. And we will not give in to the Drol. We are leaving now, but we will return someday to take back what is ours."

The children loved this, and so did the mothers who had overheard Dyana's story. Falger's smile was wide and proud, and he slipped a hand into Dyana's and gave it a thankful squeeze. Dyana smiled. After months of being a shadow, it was good to suddenly be a light.

They all ate sparingly that night, picking up Falger's lead, and eventually retired to their own corners of the camp, to talk around fires or just to sleep and ready their bodies for the next day's march. Dyana always slept alone, not too far from Falger, not too close to the other men. She still preferred her solitude. The quiet coolness of night always calmed her, and she enjoyed the music of the river while the others slept. Tonight the moon was full. It was very late, yet despite her exhaustion Dyana found sleep impossible. Soon they would arrive in Ackle-Nye, and the excitement of it rippled through her, setting her imagination aflame. There would be Narens there. Her father had trusted the Narens. Soon she might be free.

Dyana sat up and looked around. Nearby, Falger was asleep, his blanket tangled around his body. A fire crackled at the riverside, waning in the moonlight and sending up smoldering wisps. Crickets chirped and the river babbled over the rocks, and all at once a great feeling of melancholy seized Dyana. This was still her home, no matter what she found in Ackle-Nye. She would miss this land. Unable to sleep, she slipped on her boots and tiptoed away from the camp, following the river in the moonlight until she could barely see the campfires. She found a rock on the bank and sat down on it, dipping her hand into the muddy earth and fishing up a collection of stones. One by one she pitched them into the moving water, listening to their splashes, and when she finished each handful she gathered another and did the same. It was a pleasant sound, regular and therapeutic, and Dyana lost herself in the simple act.

"Dyana . . ."

Dyana jumped at the call of her name, springing from the rock and turning to look behind her. For a moment she thought she saw the smoke of the campfire hanging in the air before her, but then she realized it was not smoke at all, but a shimmering aerial figure, half there and half not, its body a loose vapor, its torso false and legless. Dyana gasped and backed away. The thing drifted toward her.

"I have found you," said the apparition. "I told you I would."

It was a purple mist, a shroud of murkiness shaped like a man. Dyana stared at it, and knew in a dread-filled instant what it was.

"Tharn . . ."

"It has been many years, girl. I am pleased you recognize me."

"Tharn," she whispered, gesturing at him. "What are you?"

He smiled at her. He did not seem evil at all, only vastly pleased with himself. "Look at me," he said, brushing his vaporous hands over his body. "I am the touch of heaven. I am what I wanted to be."

Appalled, Dyana moved in closer, not hiding her disgust. "Tharn, what is this magic? What have you done?"

"I have done what I am meant to do, what heaven has chosen me to do."

Dyana stared at him and through him. He had left his family to find the science of Nar, then later to search for truth among the Drol. He had become a cunning-man and a revolutionary. But this, his latest incarnation, this astounded her. This was incomprehensible.

"But is this you?"

"This is me and not me. This is my mind without a body. I cannot explain it, Dyana. It is just . . ." The ghost shrugged. "Me."

"But why?" she pressed. "What are you?"

"No questions," flared Tharn, his body breaking for a moment in his anger. "I have no answers. I am the sword of Lorris. I am his herald. Just as I told you I would be."

Dyana looked at him sadly. "You are mad. And now you play with these arts, and make a monster of yourself. Tharn, you are . . ."

"I know what I am!" roared the ghost. His image swelled. "I am touched by heaven! I have searched for this all my life, and now I have found it. And I will not be called mad by heretics like you! Can you look at me and say that I am wrong about the gods?"

Dyana didn't answer.

"Can you?"

"I cannot," she admitted. "But you were not this way always, Tharn. You were not always a killer. I remember what you used to be. I remember you when you were kind."

A veil of sadness fell over the ghost. "I am still kind, girl."

"No," Dyana argued. "You are not. You have harmed countless people for your cause. You claim you are Drol, and now you break their highest rule. Touched by heaven, you say? Is it not your way to use these gifts for peace?"

"It is," Tharn admitted. "Or so I always thought."

"Then why do you kill? Why all this brutality?"

"It is what Lorris wishes, I think. Dyana, I am not such a villain. I have reasons for this bloody work, things that are beyond you, beyond even me. I have prayed mightily for answers, and I am trusting Lorris to guide me. It is the will of heaven. In time you will see the right in it."

"I will not," Dyana insisted. "Because I will be gone. Where I am going, even you cannot follow."

Tharn shook his head. "I have come to warn you, Dyana. I have almost won this wretched war. When I am done, I am coming for you. You will not resist me."

"Resist you?" Dyana laughed. "I spit on you! I am no man's slave."

"You are my betrothed. Your father's word binds you. And I am laying claim to you."

"Your laws mean nothing to me, Drol. Or the bargain of our parents. You were not Drol when we were young. My father would never have promised me to you if he knew the devil you were becoming. I am a free woman."

"And you go to Nar to be free? Then you are a fool, girl. Like your father. There is nothing for you there. Nar is evil."

"Liar!" she cried. "I will get to Nar, and I will marry someone else. And I will have children who are not Drol and we will all laugh at your sick revolution!"

Tharn sighed, but there was no breath from the apparition. "Run then, Dyana. But hurry. This thing you see is only the beginning. I grow stronger, and when I am strong enough I will reach out my hand and take you, wherever you are."

"And you will continue to kill? And children will starve because you burn the grain fields? Is this the love of Lorris and Pris?"

"This is the way of things in our ugly world. There are dangers to us that you do not know, and I doubt could ever understand. When we are together, you will see all the truth."

"I will never be yours, Tharn."

"You will be. And listen closely to what I say. When you are mine, I will not seem such a monster to you. I will be kind to you and you will be happy."

Dyana scoffed. "Is this some Drol prophecy?"

"Not a prophecy. A promise. From me to you. I will not harm you, Dyana. You have nothing to fear from me. I have always loved you."

"More madness," said Dyana. Suddenly Tharn seemed like a lovesick boy again, climbing a tree to impress her. "You do not know me. You are in love with a dream. I am not the person you think. Let me go."

"I cannot. I am a Drol cunning-man, and you are my betrothed. I will not bear that disgrace. I say again—I love you. When I am victorious, I will have this whole nation to give you, and you will see how much I care for you."

Dyana shook her head. "I do not want a nation, and I do not want you. I will fight you."

Tharn smiled sadly. "Run, then," he warned. "Like the wind . . ."

He was gone as quickly as he had come, vanishing into the darkness until the only shimmering was from the moonlight on the water. Dyana stood staring at the emptiness, at the place where his invisible feet had left no impressions in the soil. He was powerful now. Soon he might be able to take her. She needed to hurry, she needed to get to Ackle-Nye before he was done with his grisly war. And that meant leaving her friends behind.

Silently, she walked back to the camp where the others were sleeping. Careful not to wake them, she collected her few possessions—her bag of clothing, her waterskin, and some of the bread she had saved from supper. Lastly she took up the little silver stiletto her father had given her. This she tucked into its place in her boot. She was almost out of the camp when Falger awakened.

"Dyana?"

"Shhh," she cautioned, going over to him.

"Where are you going? What is wrong?"

"I am going to Ackle-Nye, Falger. But I have to hurry. There is no time for wasting, and I cannot go slowly."

"We will be there in a few days," said Falger, not understanding.

"No," said Dyana gently. "I cannot wait." She wanted to explain it to him, but thought better of it. She was dangerous to them now, and that she couldn't live with. "Please," she implored. "Just let me go."

"Dyana, this is crazy. You cannot make it alone. It is too far, too dangerous."

"I can do it. I will just follow the river."

"But what about food? What will you eat?"

"I have some bread in my bag. And I should get to Ackle-Nye in a day or so. They will have food for me there."

"You cannot go now," said Falger. "It is too dark!"

"I have the moon. I can see. Please, do not worry about me." Then she kissed his cheek. "But thank you. Thank you for everything."

"But how will you get to Nar?" Falger asked. "What will you do?"

"Whatever I have to," Dyana answered, then started off into the darkness.

SEVEN

When Richius told Dinadin about the trip to Ackle-Nye, Dinadin took the news like a small boy who has been told a holiday was coming. Unlike most of the Naren troops, Dinadin had known where he was going even before he arrived in Ackle-Nye, and so had no opportunity to enjoy the many pleasures the city offered most men before they went into the war. He had always regretted this, a fact he reminded Richius of nearly every time the subject arose. It seemed to Richius that Dinadin thought he was owed something for missing out on this rite of passage, and Richius took as much glee in the telling of the news as Dinadin took in the receiving. In a small way Richius was excited by the trip, too. Though he had told Lucyler and Dinadin that there were important reasons for making the journey, the idea of leaving the trenches and camps for even a little while pleased him. It had been nearly a full year since he had arrived in the Dring Valley, and almost two years since he had left home. If there were any Aramoorians in Ackle-Nye, he would be grateful to see them.

Over Lucyler's objections, Richius decided that only he and Dinadin should make the trip. Lucyler himself didn't want to go, for even he was too pious a Triin to go to Ackle-Nye, but he made the point that his comrades would be more secure if they traveled in greater numbers. Richius had considered this, but finally decided that the security of the men he was leaving was more important than their own, and he wanted every body, should Voris choose to attack again. He explained this to Lucyler, after telling the Triin that he would be in charge of the company. The Triin didn't argue his leader's reasoning. But Lucyler wasn't beyond mothering the men, and before they set out the next morning he had made sure they had packed enough of the dried meat and hard army bread that had been their sustenance for months now to last them well past the two-day ride. Richius allowed this indulgence. Though he was the leader of the men, he knew that Lucyler was more like a father to them even in his sternness, and Richius himself wasn't unaffected by Lucyler's almost parental concern.

The morning was as clear as the night and day before. It was, as Dinadin had cheerfully remarked, the perfect day for riding. In the depths of the valley there were thorn patches and choke weeds and mud traps to break a horse's legs, but where they were going the valley thinned and became passable, and when the horse master had handed the reins of two fine geldings over to Richius, the man had eyed his leader jealously. Being in the valley was a chore for any who had been in the Aramoorian Guard, and the chance to take a horse out was a privilege for which they always vied.

"Be careful with them," the horse master had insisted. "If the word comes, we'll need them to escape."

Richius had let the man chide him. Whatever else he felt for Feldon, the horse master had kept their handful of mounts alive in the fickle weather of the valley, had seen the beasts through disease and hunger. Unlike the men under Richius' charge, the horses seemed neither ill nor starved. Richius gave Feldon a courteous smile and his assurance that the horses would be well cared for.

The sun had barely risen when Richius and Dinadin left camp. Lucyler was somber as they wished him good-bye.

"Keep a sentry posted in each trench," said Richius. "And send out scouts in pairs. If any wolves come, make ready for an attack. And start waking the men up. Voris could hit us. . . ."

"Stop," said Lucyler impatiently. "I know what to do. Just come back when you can. We will still be here."

"Five days, no later," Richius assured him. "Take care of my men."

Lucyler nodded but said nothing, and Richius took a long last look at the camp. The thought of staying occurred to him briefly, but an artless nudge from Dinadin shoved the idea aside.

"Let's go," crowed the young man anxiously. "I want to get there before the war ends and all the wenches go back home!"

Lucyler rolled his eyes. "Do not bring me back anything incurable," he remarked.

"We'll be careful," laughed Richius, giving the reins of his horse a snap. He waved farewell to Lucyler and was off, disappearing into the woods with Dinadin behind him.

The path on which they traveled was passable, though not well worn, for the recent cessation of supply trips from Aramoor had allowed the prolific brush of the valley to narrow it somewhat. Still, the horses handled the path precisely, and it wasn't long before both Richius and Dinadin relaxed and let their old instincts take over. Richius felt a familiar peace draw over him and in his hands the reins quickly turned to comforting friends. His stint in the valley had not taken his horsemanship from him. Dinadin was riding smoothly beside him, his own face beaming. It felt to Richius like a lifetime had passed since he had last experienced the powerful sensation of a horse beneath him. In the trenches he was only a soldier, often so muddied he couldn't recognize his own reflection in a pool. But when he rode, borne up tall by a proud Aramoorian steed, he was a Guardsman again.

They rode in silence for a time, content to listen to the creatures of the valley, alert for any unusual or threatening sound. This area of the valley was secure but they knew also that Voris was prone to sending spies into their midst. They could not let the lulling calls of birds make them unwitting. Still, the day was so fair that some peace of mind couldn't be helped, and both men settled in for the long ride, the light breeze cool but not so cold as to prick under their leather surcoats. It was the kind of weather they were accustomed to in Aramoor—a hearty, rugged morning.

"Oh, I've missed this," said Dinadin with a sigh. "If we were not such friends I would desert you, I think."

Richius laughed. "Edgard's men have been using horses in Tatterak, and they have not fared so much better than us."

"That's not the point. They can be the soldiers they were trained to be, but we have to crawl around in the mud like pigs." Dinadin shook his head ruefully. "Someone should put an arrow in Voris' head and be done with it."

"And you would like that honor, would you?" asked Richius. They had spent many nights fantasizing about killing the warlord, had dreamed up a hundred ways for their nemesis to die. But it was always a faceless head they severed in their dreams, for none of them had ever seen the Wolf.

"I would kill him in his sleep if I had to," replied Dinadin with a smile. "And I would not feel the smallest bit of guilt for it."

"Not me. I would rather face him on the field and see if he is as good with a jiiktar as I am with my sword."

The boast made Dinadin chuckle. "If you want to kill him yourself, that's fine with me. Just so I see him dead. Maybe then we could get out of here."

"If we weren't here we'd be in Tatterak," said Richius flatly. "And then we'd be facing Tharn."

"So? He's the reason we're here at all. If he were dead the war would be over and I'd be home with my brothers. Perhaps we should be helping Edgard in Tatterak, and stop bothering with this little warlord."

Richius made to laugh, then stopped himself. He was accustomed to the young man's outbursts, and so decided not to say what had popped into his mind—that the "little warlord" had been more than a match for them for almost a year, had in fact almost rid his valley of them without the aid of his master, Tharn. Whatever else their unseen enemy was, he wasn't little.

"I've known Edgard since I was a boy," remarked Richius, trying to sway the talk from Voris. "He's too proud to ask for help. My father has told me many times of how they fought together in the war with Talistan. God, the tales. One would think the old man was immortal."

"Edgard got the best of it, if you ask me," muttered Dinadin. "He's the duke of war. He should be trying to take the valley, not you."

"My father believed me up to the job, I suppose. And Edgard is too old to be crawling around with the rest of us. Better that he should secure the territory we have than try and take the valley."

"The warlord Kronin already had his land secure," said Dinadin. "And he's the Daegog's man. We all should have ridden against Falindar the moment Tharn seized it. The war would have been over long ago."

"Maybe," said Richius. They had a long trip ahead of them, and he had no desire to spend the journey arguing over things that couldn't be changed. Moreover, the unpleasant idea that his father valued Edgard's life over his had occurred to him, and he wished to bury this painful theory as quickly as he could. He, not Edgard, had been charged with taking the Dring Valley, the "gateway to Lucel-Lor." He would do it if he could.

By late morning they were out of the valley, in the part of Lucel-Lor that no warlord claimed as his own. These were the drier, less arable parts of the Triin nation, and the trees thinned out here, the path disappearing into a rocky terrain. They stopped here for a time, watering their horses beside what they figured to be the last stream they would see for a while. The horses drank thirstily, as grateful as their riders for the chance to stop and rest. Richius, in the old habit of a Guardsman, took the time to check his bags and assure himself that they had everything they needed. Night would fall hard upon them here, and he made sure that he still had the fire rocks Lucyler had given him. These, plus the cloaks they had wrapped and ready in their packs, should see them warmly through the night. He checked his weapons, too, though there were few Triin to threaten them here, and ran his fingers gently over the stock of the crossbow slung at his horse's side. He was a good shot with it, far better than he was with a bow, and any Drol who meant to harm them while they slept might well find a bolt in his chest before he could reach them.

Dinadin had long since become cheerful again, and had been going on about the women he intended to bed when they reached Ackle-Nye. Now, through bites of a small bread loaf, he continued to entertain Richius with his fantasies. Richius only half listened, grateful that his friend had dropped his political talk for a while.

"I want to find a Triin wench," said Dinadin, sighing as he reclined against a tree trunk. "Then I'd really have something to tell Lucyler!"

"Not much chance of that," said Richius, checking his bags and relieved to find his journal still nestled safely in the leather sack. "There isn't a Triin alive who's not more holy than both of us. You'll just have to settle for a broad-hipped Talistan whore."

"You're wrong, Richius," said Dinadin earnestly. "Some of Gayle's men were talking about it. They said they saw Triin women selling in the city." He paused, then added with a laugh, "Their gods haven't been so good to them lately."

As he mounted his horse, Richius turned to Dinadin with a frown. "I don't believe it. Most Triin women are as fanatical as Drol. They could teach our own priests a thing or two about chastity. Why, they won't even look at a man who isn't their master."

"You really have been in the valley too long! What do you think happens to all those people when their houses are burned or the Drol take their village? They have to survive, you know."

"Lord," hissed Richius, giving the reins a sharp snap. "And you want to add to some woman's misery? We're here to help these people, Dinadin, don't forget that."

To Richius' relief, Dinadin ignored him. Instead, the younger man simply snapped the reins of his own horse and followed his leader once again toward Ackle-Nye. They were silent as they rode, leaving Richius free to ponder the ugliness of what Dinadin had just told him. He was more eager than ever to reach the city and see if the rumors were true.

It was afternoon of the next day when they caught up with the Sheaze. They had seen no water since the day before, and the night had been harsher than they had feared. Winter was drawing its mantle back over Lucel-Lor, and the mere sight of the river soothed them, for it told them how near they were to reaching their journey's end.

"We'll follow the river northwest from here," said Richius, hearing the weariness in his voice. He saw that Dinadin too looked haggard, all the bluster of the previous day taken out of him. Richius smiled at his companion and said, "It's not much further now."

Dinadin's face brightened at the news. "Do you think we can make it by nightfall? I wouldn't mind getting a night's sleep this time."

Richius looked carefully around them, surveying the terrain. He didn't recognize this part of Lucel-Lor, but he wasn't troubled. For all the time he had spent in the Triin nation he had seen little of it. He knew only that the river would lead them to its origin in the Iron Mountains, where they would find Ackle-Nye.

"I don't know," he confessed, seeing Dinadin's face darken a little. "It's hard to tell how far west we've come. The Sheaze winds a lot in these parts."

"Then we should be moving. I don't want to spend another night out here if we can help it."

Richius agreed and, after stopping a short time to rest and water their horses, they set out alongside the river. The land here was moist, with patches of moss and water-softened earth where the river bubbled over its banks, and though they wanted to hurry their horses, they knew that to do so would be risky. So they plodded along, navigating the rocky shore of the river with care, and contented themselves in the knowledge that their trek would soon be over.

By late afternoon the western sky finally revealed the landmark Richius was seeking. Past the trees, where the river wound out of sight, towered the Iron Mountains. Though obscured in a blue-gray haze, the range was nonetheless a welcome sight.

"Look there!" cried Richius, thrusting out a finger toward the mountains.

"Oh, thank God," Dinadin said. "I thought we'd never make it."

"You may yet get your wish, Dinadin. If we hurry we can probably make it before dark. The city should be in sight within an hour."

They quickened their pace a little, still careful not to move too swiftly, and watched as the rugged forms that were the Iron Mountains cleared and defined themselves. Behind the mountains the sun was just beginning to mellow, painting the western horizon a hazy crimson. It would not be long, Richius knew, before that pleasant hue vanished into blackness. Richius hadn't seen the Iron Mountains or Ackle-Nye since arriving in Lucel-Lor, and a vision of his home suddenly struck him. On the other side of those monoliths, nestled safely from the war, lay Aramoor.

I could just keep riding, he thought to himself. *Another five-day ride through the mountains and I'd be home.* He caught himself then, shaking his head to rid himself of the idea. It was insane to think that he could simply leave his men behind and return home. He could never return to Aramoor until his work here was done.

Dinadin was in the lead now, running his horse impatiently along the riverbank, and Richius knew that his friend's mind was filling with thoughts of a warm bed and an equally warm maiden to share it with. Richius realized that he had given no thought to how he would spend the night. He had been so preoccupied with finding out where Aramoor stood in the war that the idea of sharing his bed hadn't even occurred to him. He chuckled to himself, musing over just how old the war had made him.

Before an hour had fallen and the pink of the sun had vanished completely, Richius heard Dinadin cry out.

"There it is! Do you see it, Richius? That must be it!"

Richius did indeed see it. Ackle-Nye, the city of beggars, was like a sparkling pinpoint in the failing daylight. Positioned at the visible end of the Sheaze River, it shimmered with the combined fire of a thousand torches, pulsing and beckoning them forward.

Much of Ackle-Nye was as Richius remembered it. And much of it was worse. Two years ago, when he had first laid eyes on the city of beggars, he had been stunned by it. Weary from his long ride through the Iron Mountains, Ackle-Nye had seemed like paradise. The city was an oasis for a rider from the Saccenne Run, a gateway from the austere wastes of the mountains into the fertile land of Lucel-Lor. This was where the Empire and the Triin nation had met, and their union had fostered a wholly fascinating, if unusual, offspring. Before that time there had been only the traditional Triin woodwork, the subtle curves and soft earth-tones of a simple people. To this the Narens added power. Not content with what their Triin hosts had created, the craftsmen of the Empire came with chisels and hammers to forge a place worthy of Nar. And the Triin said nothing.

In time, Ackle-Nye swelled. The curious people from the Empire, eager to meet their long-silent neighbors, poured through the Saccenne Run. Merchants came, lured by the prospect of new markets and inspired by the city's proximity to the Sheaze. From here, all the southern lands of Lucel-Lor were opened to them, and all the folk who lived there could be sold the goods the merchants hawked. And still the Triin said nothing.

The priests were next. Sure that this was a pagan land, the holy men of the Empire sought to bring the Triin under the dominion of their own vengeful god. In this they were unsuccessful, and it was the priests, more than the merchants or the curious, who brought the Drol back to life.

Such was the history of this place as Richius understood it. The revolution was in its infancy when he had first come here, and Ackle-Nye had yet to suffer under the heel of war. He had left the city then as he had found it, confident in the talk that it would only take a month to subdue the Drol. Tharn, and his warlords like Voris, had shattered that dream, and the hoped-for month had since bloated into two long years. Now, finally returning to Ackle-Nye, Richius could see that something had gone vastly wrong in his absence. There was a conspicuous shroud of misery about the place, and the city now seemed garish and grotesque.

Richius and Dinadin trotted their horses through this malformation. Darkness had fallen hard, and only the lamps in the windows above let them navigate the narrow avenues. The city seemed deserted. They could hear the occasional sounds of merrymaking echoing through the streets, the slurred voices of merchants and Naren workers as they staggered between taverns. They could smell the earthy odor of beer, the sickly sweetness of wine, and the foulness of vomit. They could almost taste the unmistakable stench of urine.

It was among this filth that Richius saw the beggars. They huddled in every corner of every building. The lucky ones had small fires to warm them. As he watched them he recalled seeing beggars when he had first come to Ackle-Nye, but he hadn't been alarmed by the sight of them then. All Naren provinces had beggars. It was said that the Black City was overrun with them. Yet now, seeing them massed together, Richius felt oddly alarmed. There was an absurd amount of them, but that alone didn't disturb him. It was something else about them, something that he had never seen before. Yet he couldn't place the oddness of it until a form came shambling toward them.

Richius could scarcely see in the dimness, but it seemed that this beggar was small and stooped, like an old man. Yes, he remarked silently, an old man with white hair. But then the man was before them, lifting his face and revealing his almond-shaped eyes, and Richius realized that it was blood that had colored the man's hair: Triin blood. Richius and Dinadin brought their horses to a sudden stop.

"Plaey guin min!"

Richius shook his head, regarding the man's grimy, outstretched arm. Even through the heavy dialect the entreaty was plain.

"No," said Richius. "Move away."

The Triin fell to his knees. He clasped his bony hands together and, as if praying to them, repeated his plea more earnestly.

"Guin min, plaey guin min!"

Richius groaned. He wasn't without sympathy, but he had almost no coinage on him, and he knew from past experiences that they would be overrun by the other beggars if he gave to this one.

"Please," said Richius. "We have nothing for you. I'm sorry."

Dinadin unsheathed his sword. "Are you deaf?" he shouted, brandishing the blade above his head. "Out of the way, or I'll cut your ugly white head off!"

The Triin fell back, startled, and in a moment scampered away more quickly than Richius would have thought possible. Other eyes were regarding them now, all Triin, and all from the dirty piles of people.

"Stupid gogs," spat Dinadin, returning his weapon to its sheath. "I come here to find a woman and I have to be pestered by this filth."

Richius looked at Dinadin in disbelief. "What was that about? For God's sake, Dinadin, he's only a beggar. Why threaten him like that?"

Dinadin didn't respond, but Richius could read his drawn expression. A bitterness etched his face, all the terror and anger of life in the trenches. They sat there, unmoving, until at last Dinadin spoke.

"Damn it all, look at all these bloody gogs. You know what this means, don't you?"

Richius said nothing. He knew well what the sight of so many refugees meant, but he couldn't force himself to voice the revelation. Unlike Dinadin, Richius had hoped that the tales of Triin beggars in Ackle-Nye had been exaggerated. Now, seeing so many, all the words Dinadin had ever spoken were washing back over him. He felt trapped, frozen like a mouse seeing the falling shadow of a hawk.

"Well?" Dinadin urged. "Say something."

Richius lowered his head. "What do you want me to say? That you were right? Fine, you're right. Happy?"

Dinadin brought his horse alongside Richius'. "Is that it? Don't you see, Richius? The war's lost. All these people know it. Why don't you?"

"But there are no troops here, Dinadin. Do you see any?"

"Richius . . ."

"No troops! No one's retreating. It was all a lie, a rumor. Would it make any difference if there were a million Triin here? No, it wouldn't. Not to the emperor." Richius put his hands to his pounding head, as if to keep it from exploding. He had ridden miles for an answer, and there was none. All he had now was the long ride back.

"I want to rest," he said weakly. "Let's go into one of these taverns. We'll get a bed for the night. In the morning we will head back to Dring."

He turned from his comrade and snapped the reins, guiding his horse farther down the dirty road. He wanted to say something more to Dinadin, to convince the man that they had no choice but to remain in Lucel-Lor and fight. Yet now, seeing so many devastated Triin, it was hard to convince even himself to continue. Again the sensation of imprisonment seized him, leaving him speechless as he passed the clusters of white-haired beggars.

They rode past several boarded-up inns before coming to one still open for business. This one, on the corner of a particularly well-lit avenue, was big and brass-leafed, and the huge oak door had been left open to accommodate the trickle of patrons.

"We'll try this one," he said to Dinadin. Then, with an almost imperceptible movement, he slipped off his ring and dropped it into the pocket of his tunic. Dinadin shot his companion a troubled look.

"What are you doing?"

"I don't want anyone to know who we are," said Richius. "If anyone asks, make up something. Tell them we're merchants from Aramoor or Talistan." He knew their clothes would do a good job of concealing them, and he could only hope that he had enough of a beard to hide his well-known face.

Quickly agreeing to keep their identities secret, Dinadin dismounted along with Richius. There were horses outside the inn, most of them gaunt from lack of feed, and Richius noticed a small Triin boy tending them. He dug back into his pocket and fished out a coin.

"Do you speak the tongue of Nar?" Richius asked, crouching to face the boy. The boy looked at him in puzzlement, then uttered something unintelligible. Richius turned to Dinadin. "Do you know what he said?"

"No, but it doesn't matter," explained Dinadin. "Give him the coin. He'll look after the horses."

Richius turned back to the boy. "You'll take care of our horses, right?"

The boy nodded eagerly. Certain the boy didn't know what he was agreeing to, Richius placed the coin in the small outstretched hand.

"Don't worry," insisted Dinadin, bobbing his head to peer into the tavern. "The horses will be safe. Let's go inside."

Richius agreed, tying the reins of the horses to a post on the curb. When he was done securing the reins he straightened to find Dinadin. His companion was in the doorway of the inn, beckoning him forward. Richius followed Dinadin through the giant oak portal and into the almost-empty tavern. As they entered, a pudgy man greeted them.

"Welcome, welcome!" he cried, forcing his hand into Richius' and giving a vigorous shake. "Come in and warm yourselves."

Richius pulled his hand from the sweaty grip. "Are you the proprietor here?" he asked.

"Yes, I am," the man replied. "My name is Tendrik and I am at your service. What can I do for you? We have wines from all over the Empire and good beer from Aramoor. . . ."

Already weary of the merchant's pitch, Richius stared down at him coldly. "Look, we only want to have a drink and, if you have one, a room to rent for the night. All right?"

"Whatever you want," said Tendrik congenially. "I have some nice clean rooms upstairs. Cheap, too." He paused, then laughed and winked at Richius. "But if you want to share them with one of my ladies that'll be extra."

Richius made to speak, then felt Dinadin nudge him gently from behind. He groaned, then said, "Get us two good beds, separate rooms. We'll take care of the rest ourselves."

"If that's what you want," said the man. "But I have some fine women. Young, too. You might want to think about it."

"Just the rooms," said Richius tersely. "Get them ready. We'll wait for you down here."

He brushed past the innkeeper and headed for the bar. There was a brick hearth beside it, ablaze with a roaring fire. Richius welcomed the heat, letting it work itself into his joints. The comfortable odor of burning cedar filled the room. He looked around at the other patrons, a uniformly seedy lot. Down-at-their-luck merchants sat around one table, noisily playing cards. Several other men caroused in a corner, poking at the prostitutes that passed them by. Dinadin spied the girls and growled. They weren't young as the innkeeper had promised, but they certainly looked experienced.

"Barman!" shouted Dinadin. Another man, not unlike Tendrik in size, looked at him from behind the bar. Dinadin tossed him some coins and ordered, "Get us two beers. And from Aramoor, not that Talistanian swill."

Richius put his lips near Dinadin's ear. "Damn it, Dinadin," he whispered. "What are you thinking? I told you, I don't want to attract attention. Now just shut up and listen to what you can hear."

"Sorry," said Dinadin. The barman was placing two long glasses of beer before them. Dinadin reached for his glass thirstily and began to drink it down. But before Richius could taste his own beer, a gasp from Dinadin stopped him. "Oh, God, look at that, Richius!"

Alarmed, Richius lowered his glass onto the bar. He followed Dinadin's gaze, but saw nothing. His pulse slowed to normal again and he shrugged.

"What?"

Dinadin stretched out a finger. "There, by the minstrel. Don't you see her?"

Richius let his eyes rest for a moment on the man playing the lute. Then, as if a curtain had parted, he saw her. Her skin, bone-white and brilliant, was set off by a green silk dress. Milk-colored hair framed a porcelain face painted with ruby lips. Eyes the shape of almonds shone an ocean-gray. Thin and fragile arms tapered into thin and fragile fingers, and her legs were long and exquisite. She sat on the lap of a card-playing merchant, letting the brute toy with her as if she were a doll. The smile on her face was the frightened, forced grin of a prostitute.

"She's beautiful," crooned Dinadin, his big voice softer than Richius had ever heard—softer even than the minstrel's.

"And Triin," Richius added in amazement.

Dinadin nodded. "I told you they were selling here." He bit his lip and a low growl rumbled out of his throat. "Oh, that's the one for me."

"Easy," said Richius sharply. "We've got business here first. And I don't like the idea of you taking a Triin wench. I told you, we're here to help these people."

"Sorry," said Dinadin. "She's the one I want."

Richius too was captivated by the woman, by the curve of her hips and the frightened way her eyes darted about the room. She seemed so out of place. The man laughed, nuzzling her neck, and Richius watched in a sort of embarrassed agony as the woman closed her eyes against the unwanted touch of his lips. And then he noticed something more. The porcelain face that had captivated him was blemished, for around one of her eyes was a purplish bruise. He considered this, at first dismissing the injury as the rough treatment of one of the louts she was forced to sleep with. But then he remembered Gayle, and how he had pulled the baron off a girl not a week before. And then he remembered her.

"What do you think, Richius?" asked Dinadin. "Should I go for the whole night or just an hour?"

"Not her, Dinadin," said Richius firmly.

Dinadin slapped Richius on the shoulder. "Don't worry. I brought my brother's silver dagger with me. That should be enough to buy a girl for both of us."

"That's not what I mean. I don't want you taking her to your bed, not even for an hour. She's a Triin, and she should be treated with some respect. My God, what are we here for? To see how many Triin whores we can bed?"

"What difference does it make?" asked Dinadin angrily. "Look at her, Richius. If it's not me it's just going to be somebody else."

"Then let it be somebody else. Let it be one of these drunks. Or better still one of Gayle's cowards. Maybe the damage is already done, but I don't want one of my men adding to the misery of these people." He paused, then added, "Please, Dinadin."

Dinadin grunted and lowered his glass. "If you wish it."

"I do. Just find yourself a girl from the Empire. I'm sure that little underwit who greeted us has a whole gaggle of Talistanian whores."

"All right," conceded Dinadin. "But if Lucyler asks, I'm going to tell him that I had ten of his breed!"

Richius tasted his beer, letting the cool liquid slosh over his tongue and into his belly. It had been more than six months since he had tasted the heady brew of his homeland, and the delicious sting of the beer on his lips made him moan like a rutting dog.

"Oh, that's good," he sighed. "I had almost forgotten how good our beer is back home."

The word "home" made Dinadin wince. Richius took a good look at his friend in the firelight and smiled. He loved Dinadin. They had grown up together, had become Guardsmen together, and had even endured the hell of Dring together. Side by side is where they had always been, from the time they were toddlers. For Richius, his friend's pain was unbearable.

"Dinadin," said Richius carefully. "I want to talk to you."

Dinadin turned evasively to stare at the Triin girl. "She's really something, huh?"

"Forget the girl. Listen to me."

"What is it?"

Richius grinned. "You're not going to make this easy for me, are you?"

"No."

"Fine. Then I'll give it to you straight. I know you want to go home. But look around. There's no one else here. No troops, not from Aramoor or Talistan. Just a bunch of Triin beggars."

"Not beggars," Dinadin corrected. "Refugees. And they're here for a reason. They already know the war's over. Don't blame them if they're smarter than you."

"The war isn't over until Arkus says it is," argued Richius. "And I don't like it, but there's nothing I can do about it. You have to understand that. None of us can go home, not if we want Aramoor to survive. The emperor—"

"Oh, burn the emperor!" rumbled Dinadin. "Sure, it's easy for him. He's not here. He's not sleeping in filth every goddamn night with bugs crawling over him. You know what I think of the emperor, Richius? I think he's an old bastard that's gotten what he's wanted for too long. I think Aramoor should stand up to him. Let him roll in his legions! Better that than to live as slaves."

Richius reached out to touch his friend's arm. "Dinadin, listen to yourself."

"No," flared Dinadin, shaking off the grasp. "Stop talking to me like I'm an idiot. God, I'm sick of it. And I'm sick of your reasoning, Richius. First your father abandons us, and then you tell me we still can't leave? Well, why not? The hell with your father. The hell with the emperor, too. I want to go home!"

The few patrons in the bar were staring at them now. Even the lovely Triin prostitute was watching them. Richius turned away, embarrassed, putting his elbows on the bar and dropping his head.

"Thanks for not making a scene," he said sourly, and closed his eyes against the anger welling up inside him. "It's getting late. Why don't you find yourself a whore and go to bed?"

"Richius . . ."

"Stop," Richius said. "We're not retreating, and that's the end of it. I won't discuss it with you anymore."

Dinadin said nothing for a long moment. Richius could almost see the waspish frown on his companion's face.

"All right," said Dinadin at last. "Are you coming, too?"

"No. I want to stay here a little while longer, see what I can find out."

He waited until he heard Dinadin's gruff good-night before opening his eyes again. It was late, well past midnight, he supposed. His vision was a little misted, and he fought back a yawn. The thought of a soft straw mattress popped into his head, making him smile. It would be warm upstairs, and dry. If there was any to be had, he would bribe the innkeeper out of some good bread and honey in the morning. Then, after they had breakfasted, they would set out again for the valley.

A sudden churn of his guts told Richius what he already knew. He was afraid. The notion of returning to that hellish place sickened him and made the glass he held tremble. They would be alone now, save for any troops that Talistan might send them. His father, for reasons he couldn't fathom, had forsaken them all. He was trapped, forced by an emperor he didn't know to fight for a mystery he knew nothing about.

An hour and several beers later, the room's population thinned. Only the drunkest of patrons remained behind, still carrying on like schoolboys as they leered and poked at the prostitutes.

Richius surveyed the room, searching for the beautiful Triin girl. She wasn't around. His mood soured a little more. She had been the only thing worth looking at in this filthy place, and now she too was gone. He drained his glass, remembering her perfect skin against the emerald dress. It had been months since he had been with a woman.

He stopped himself, cursing. She was Triin, and he had sworn to protect these people.

God save me. Am I no better than Blackwood Gayle?

And then Richius recalled what Dinadin had said. Whatever else they did, she was already a prostitute. Surely someone would share her bed tonight. Why shouldn't it be him? He had endured everything the valley could conjure against him. He had gone without food and without clean clothes, and he had slept in mud while rats nibbled at his ears. But he was still a man. Of all the human traits Voris had taken from him, this the Wolf could never steal.

Not far away, the innkeeper Tendrik was mopping beer up off the floor. Richius went over to the man and took the mop away from him.

"There was a woman here tonight," he said evenly. "A Triin."

"A Triin? Oh, you mean Dyana!"

"She's one of yours?" asked Richius.

"She is," said the man proudly. "New to it, but I'm sure she'll please."

Richius put a gold coin into Tendrik's hand. "I want her."

Alone at last in her dismal chamber, Dyana collapsed onto her threadbare mattress. Exhaustion had drained her, so that even the simple act of standing seemed impossible. She didn't bother to peel off the dress, not caring if it got soiled or stained. There was only one thing on her mind now, the precious release of sleep.

I did it, she told herself as she shut her eyes. *I made it through the day.*

But only barely. The other girls she shared the chamber with were off to other beds. She lifted her hand listlessly to her face and fingered the ripe bruise about her eye. It was probably the injury that had kept her from being taken. How bad was it? All she knew was that it hurt. It had throbbed the entire day, sending a knife blade through her temple. It had made even the greedy innkeeper question her value. Dyana closed her eyes again and chuckled. How odd that she had that Naren beast to thank for her spared virginity.

As the silence of her chamber wrapped around her, Dyana's thought turned again to Falger and the others. They were still probably plodding their way to this dismal city. They would be heartbroken when they arrived. There was nothing here for any of them, no food or freedom, and no passage to Nar. Unless the women were willing to sell themselves, which Dyana doubted. Falger might even lead them back to Dring. He was a proud man, and wouldn't take to begging lightly. He would probably die before joining in that chorus of the damned that had greeted her.

Dyana sighed. Whenever she closed her eyes those huddled forms haunted her. She had arrived in Ackle-Nye exhausted and starving, and the first faces she had seen were theirs, vacant and cold and filthy, pained from exposure and mute from frustration. And Triin. They were everywhere in Ackle-Nye, an army of refugees from every province in Lucel-Lor. And they had all come in search of the same impossible dream—freedom from Drol oppression. What they found instead—what Dyana had found herself—was scorn. The Narens here had their own troubles, and simply couldn't be bothered. Not unless the Triin had something to barter. And besides her stiletto, there was only one thing Dyana had been able to offer.

She rolled over pensively, surveying the room. She was grateful to have it to herself, at least for a little while. The two women she shared it with had hardly given her more than a disgusted stare when she'd arrived this morning. The big one, was Carlina her name? She had insisted Dyana take the dingiest mattress. Tendrik seemed afraid of her. But why shouldn't he be? Carlina was Naren. She had rights. All Naren women had rights, that's what Dyana's father had told her. It was why Nar was better for women.

"And when I am a Naren, I will have rights, too," she seethed. "She-wolf."

Dyana nestled her head into the pillow. Tonight she would dream of Nar. Tomorrow, perhaps, she would lose the only thing she had left, but tonight she was intact and she would think on better days.

"I wish you were with me, Father," she whispered to the darkness. "You would understand why I am doing this. Forgive me."

She almost heard her father's answer in her mind. He would have been proud of her, she was sure. Not of this filthy act, of course. He could never approve of that. But he had taught her to take care of herself, to not depend on the whims of men. Men had stripped her of everything, but she still had one weapon, one way to buy her freedom from Tharn. They were hardly Triin at all, she and her father, that's what everyone had always said. They were heretics, declared so by the Drol. Now she was selling her body for passage through the Run. She would never be able to return home. Never.

Of all her father's daughters she had been his favorite. Only she had believed in his visions of unity with Nar. Only she had let him teach her the Empire's twisted language. If her sisters were still alive she neither knew nor cared. They hadn't even bothered to seek her out when their father was murdered. And she hadn't sought their aid. She had survived the last months on her own, sneaking from one relative to another, always hoping she was one step ahead of Tharn. Today she had reached Ackle-Nye. She had outrun him at last.

"I will beat you," she whispered to the darkness. "I will be free."

A sudden knock jolted Dyana out of her reverie. She sat up, tossing her legs over the side of the mattress. Tendrik the grubby innkeeper pushed the door open and peered inside. He noticed her on the bed and beamed.

"Dyana," he said excitedly. "You're still dressed. Good." He entered the room without shutting the door and urged her to her feet. "Hurry. I have someone for you."

Dyana's mood shattered. "What? You want me? But it is so late . . ."

Tendrik grabbed her arm and pulled her toward the door. There was a greedy gleam in his eyes, the same look he'd had when she'd come to him earlier, begging to be let in.

"There's a merchant waiting for you down the hall," he directed. "A man from Aramoor. He doesn't seem like a rough customer, so don't worry. Just do as he asks and make him happy. Close your eyes if you want."

Dyana wrenched away. "No. Not tonight. I am . . . not ready."

The proprietor laughed. "No one's ever ready the first time, girl. But it'll be over before you know it. He's so piss drunk he may not even manage it."

"No," declared Dyana. She suddenly regretted ever having come here. "I cannot. Tomorrow, please. Not now."

Tendrik's humor evaporated. "Listen," he said roughly, clamping his hand around her wrist. "He gave me a full golden for you. He paid for the whole night and I'm not giving it back. Now you get the hell in there and do it. And if he comes back with any complaints . . ."

Dyana tried to pull her wrist free, but the fat man's grip was like iron. "Let me go," she growled.

He clamped down harder and pulled her toward him, reaching for her hair with his other hand. The manhandling brought the wildcat out in her and she cried out, lashing at his face.

"Let go!" she railed as her nails raked across his cheek. Tendrik roared in frustrated pain but did not loose her. He dragged her against the wall and pinned her there until his face was flush with her own.

"You little bitch," he hissed. "You will do as I say!"

Dyana gritted her teeth. "Get your dirty hands off me, you Naren pig!" She brought up her knee and drove it into his groin—the greatest mistake she had made since coming here. Tendrik's eyes bulged and he let out a string of loud obscenities. Dyana bolted for the door, but he was on her, snatching a fistful of hair and dragging her back against the wall. She hit the hard surface with a jolt, knocking the air from her lungs. The next thing she felt was the innkeeper's sweaty hand around her throat.

"You Triin tramp," he seethed, tightening his grip. "You will do this!"

She spat at him. Tendrik laughed.

"No? That's fine then, girl. You go back and eat garbage with the rest of your kind. Live in the streets. I don't need you if you won't perform." He pushed her roughly toward the door. "Get out. Find your own way to Nar."

"You bastard," seethed Dyana. "I have nowhere else to go."

"So what is that to me, girl? I run a business, not a charity. You said you would do as I asked. That's the only reason I took you in. If you won't do it, you're no use to me."

"I can do other things," Dyana offered. "I can cook for you, mend clothes. I will serve downstairs if you want. . . ."

"I don't need a kitchen wench, girl. I need bodies. You have all I need without opening your mouth. Now either go to him or get out. My place isn't a home for runaways, not unless they can work for their keep. That's the job. Take it or leave it."

He had trapped her. Without him, there would be no passage to Nar, no escape from Tharn. Worse, he was right. She had agreed to do this vile thing. If she didn't, he would abandon her. Like all the others. And she would be trapped here when the Drol came.

"Do it," ordered Tendrik. He jabbed a finger toward the hall outside. "He's waiting for you."

Dyana poked her head out into the hall. Down the dark corridor there were several rooms with closed doors. Carlina was in one of them. She could hear the girl's indifferent moans. A sickening feeling lurched in Dyana's stomach. But she managed to suppress it, burying it under an instinct to survive.

"Which room?"

"The yellow door. Just knock and he'll let you in."

"The whole night?"

"That's what he paid for. Don't worry. It won't be more than once. Just sleep when it's over. You can leave in the morning before he wakes up."

Small consolation. Dyana hovered in the doorway. She wanted to ask the fat man if it would hurt, if she would be with child in the morning or polluted like Carlina. But this sweaty, cruel man wasn't her father. He didn't dispense advice to frightened girls. To him, she was merely a shiny gold coin. She survived the first shaky step into the hall, then let her rubbery legs convey her down the corridor. She passed the red door where Carlina's throaty cries echoed, and passed the silent blue door where the other girl had obviously finished her work. The yellow door was at the end. Dyana stood outside it and listened. She cocked her head back toward her own room and saw Tendrik encourage her with a wave. Inside the chamber she could hear nothing.

Asleep, she supposed, and considered turning back. But Tendrik squashed the notion.

"Knock," the innkeeper insisted.

Dyana tapped lightly on the door. A sprinkle of yellow paint peeled away. Something inside the chamber stirred. She backed away as the door creaked open. A disheveled young man stood in the threshold, teetering to one side as his bleary eyes washed over her. He was dark, maybe even handsome by foreign standards. His face was thin and haggard and his clothes were filthy, like his breath. A spark of interest lit his eyes.

But he said nothing. He merely regarded her with his wild gaze. Sudden fear rushed through Dyana and she faltered. His hand was there to catch her. A rough hand, calloused and hot against her soft skin. The faint hint of a smile stirred on his lips. Very gently he drew her into the chamber and closed the door.

EIGHT

In the Dring Valley, rain had been falling steadily for more than a day. It was an unexpected cloudburst, and the men in the trenches were ill prepared for it. The homes they had dug for themselves in the earth were unstable even in the driest weather, and in the copious rains of the valley the trench walls seemed to melt away on top of them, covering them each in an inescapable slick of mud. But storms in Dring were not uncommon, and the men did their best to fight away the damp with cloaks, and the rats with shovel backs. The rats always seemed to multiply in the rain. Worse, it was necessary now to keep the igniters of the flame cannons lit continuously, for it would be impossible to fire up the weapons in such weather. So, when the first raindrops began to fall, Lucyler had ordered that the cannons be kept warm and ready, expending more of the precious kerosene fuel.

The unanticipated rains had ruined much of the food stores, and what little had been left untouched by water had been gotten at by rats. Unlike the men, the rats were plump now. Already two men were lying near death, and Lucyler thought it likely they had consumed some bread or meat that the rats had crawled over and diseased.

Lucyler had taken his charge over the company with grave seriousness. Yet he alone couldn't provide for so many men, and he had already sent a dozen of the soldiers out of the trenches to hunt for game. But Lucyler wasn't one to shrink from duty, and while he had sent the others into the relative calm of the plains, he had given himself a more difficult task. The plains did have game, but it was the lush forests that were teeming with life. That the birch forests might also be teeming with Drol was of little consequence. They would need meat if they were to survive, and lots of it. Lucyler knew that only the forest could provide game in such abundance.

He had started out alone, his bow and jiiktar on his back, when Crodin had decided to join him. Crodin wasn't the best of hunters. Unlike Lucyler, he preferred the devouring blast of a flame cannon to the precision of an arrow. But he was as good as any other at slogging through a muddy forest, and Crodin had decided it best that Lucyler not go alone.

They had disappeared into the birch grove at the first gray light of morning. Lucyler was grateful for Crodin's company, but he was more grateful for the serenity he found in the forest. To his great relief, there were no signs of Voris' warriors, and although they spent their first hours mindful of every sound, they soon settled in to the peaceful rhythms of the forest, and by midday even Crodin had two wild birds slung over his back. Lucyler, more skillful with a bow than his comrade, had been able to land four birds, and after a time they began stowing the fowl under a blanket in a small clearing they had made for themselves.

The rest of the day was much the same. The hunting was good despite the poor weather, and they had seen no evidence of warriors or spies. Since they had landed more game than they could comfortably carry, at dusk they settled down in the tiny clearing. Nighttime in the valley could be treacherous, and both men thought it best to wait until morning before attempting the journey back.

Crodin was asleep long before Lucyler. Of all the men in the company, it seemed that only Crodin was capable of sleeping anywhere. He had drawn his cloak about his body, rested his head on a particularly smooth stone, and was sleeping before Lucyler had finished storing the last of the birds. When at last Lucyler turned to lie beside his friend, he couldn't help but chuckle at the snoring. Still, feeling the thousand aches of his own body, he could easily understand Crodin's weariness. They had hunted almost without rest today, and Lucyler guessed that they were a good distance from camp. At dawn they would return to the others, and they would need all their strength to haul so much game.

But Lucyler's sleep was not as sound as Crodin's. When he was a boy, there had been a Daegog who was the leader of all the Triin, even the warlords, and Lucyler had slept under trees that no man claimed to own. Time and the revolution had changed that. Now, though his blood was still Triin, there were many parts of his homeland in which he was no longer safe. Tonight, under the constant, melancholy rain, these thoughts tormented him. Despite the heaviness of his eyelids, Lucyler lay suspended in that strange state between wakefulness and dreams, listening to the lulling calls of night creatures. He heard them in the canopy of trees above and saw their eyes twinkling like stars. Yet they did not disturb him. Lost as he was in his own troubled thoughts, he paid them only slight regard. Finally, he fell into a fractured sleep of visions and remembrances. . . .

And then he awoke. It seemed to him that nothing in particular had roused him, yet he couldn't understand why his eyes had opened. He listened, unmoving, to the croaking of wild things, and waited for whatever had disturbed him to come again. But he heard nothing. He glanced over at Crodin. The man lay in a deep slumber, his mouth slung open to the incoming rain. The familiar sight put Lucyler at ease. He sighed, and rolled over onto his side.

The moment his eyes closed he heard the sound again. He was awake now, and so could hear it clearly this time, shrouded though it was in the noises of the forest and the storm. Lucyler sat up and cocked his head to listen. It was a cracking sound, like that of a great animal moving over sticks. A familiar sound. All day long Lucyler had heard that sound as they themselves moved through the woods.

Lucyler leaned over and put his lips to Crodin's ear. "Crodin, wake up!" he whispered, giving the sleeping man a jab in the ribs. Crodin only rolled away from him. "Damn it, Crodin, wake up," Lucyler repeated.

Still Crodin did not awaken. Furious, Lucyler pinched Crodin's jaw between his thumb and forefinger and squeezed, shaking Crodin's head until the man's eyes suddenly opened.

"What the . . . ?"

Lucyler quickly put his hand over Crodin's mouth. "Be still," he ordered, then dragged his hand away so his friend could breathe. Crodin looked about fearfully.

"What is it?" he asked, watching as Lucyler slowly retrieved his jiiktar from the mud. Lucyler ignored the question, putting up his hand to silence Crodin as he scanned the murky forest. "God, Lucyler," Crodin repeated. "What's going on?"

"Quiet!" Lucyler ordered, then cursed himself for his loudness. If he was right, whatever was out there hadn't noticed them yet. Slowly, soundlessly, Lucyler got to his knees, all the while focusing his eyes in the darkness, watching intently for any signs of movement. Again he listened, holding his breath so that only the din of rain on leaves could be heard. At last he heard the sound again. Much nearer.

"What's that?" asked Crodin, scrambling to his feet. Lucyler grabbed hold of the man's cloak and pulled him back down into the mud.

"Get down!" he ordered.

Crodin fell into the mud, then looked about in a terrified daze. To Lucyler's great relief, though, the man was finally silent.

For almost a minute the two stayed like this, kneeling in muck with their eyes fastened on the woods. At last a spot of crimson appeared in the dark maze of trees. Lucyler narrowed his eyes to confirm his worst suspicions—warriors. Even in the blackness of the forest, their scarlet robes betrayed them.

"Oh, Lord," moaned Crodin. "Do you think they've seen us?"

Lucyler shook his head. "No, not yet. I am sure they do not expect us here."

"How many of them are there? Can you tell?"

"I cannot see," admitted Lucyler. "Pick up your sword. We have to warn the others."

"What? We can't move. They'll skin us alive if they discover us!"

Lucyler turned and glared at Crodin. "Those warriors are heading for our camp. They may all be killed!"

Crodin protested, getting to his feet. "How are we going to get back to camp? We can't even see!"

"Just follow me," called Lucyler over his shoulder. He was already moving through the rain. After a moment he heard Crodin's boots squishing in the mud after him.

The moon, nearly invisible behind a thick blanket of clouds, lent almost no light to the forest, but as Lucyler ran he kept his jiiktar stretched out before him, letting the weapon guide him. He could feel the jiiktar's twin blades cutting through the foliage, breaking the branches that strove to pluck out his eyes. Already the branches had torn great rents in his sleeves, so that now they bit into his flesh as he dashed past them. He felt the warm sensation of blood running down his arms. He ignored the pain as he ran, reminding himself that he was a Triin. Like the warriors he raced against, he did not need the light of the sun to run through a forest.

"Slow down," came Crodin's sudden plea from behind. Lucyler slowed just long enough to glimpse his comrade. Barely visible in the darkness, Crodin's face was red with effort.

"No," answered Lucyler quickly. "Keep up!"

"I can't," insisted Crodin. His voice was little more than a wheeze. "I'm not a goddamned Triin!"

Cursing, Lucyler stopped and turned to Crodin. Crodin was stooped, his hands on his knees. He looked about to vomit.

"Listen, Crodin," Lucyler demanded. "Those warriors are headed for our camp. We must warn the others to be ready for an attack. If you cannot keep up with me . . ."

"Just go," Crodin interrupted, panting. "I will follow as closely as I can."

Without a word, Lucyler turned from Crodin and continued on his dash through the forest. He wanted to say something, to call back some apology over his shoulder, but there was no leisure for that. Already Voris' warriors had a lead on him, and if he was to reach the camp before his enemies he would have to run as quickly as he could.

He moved as if in a dream. The calls of the night creatures, the scratching limbs, the rain and the mud: all these things were lost to him. He didn't care what noise he made or if his fellow Triin could hear him. He moved with feline sureness, like a leopard or one of the giant lions of Chandakkar, leaping over fallen trees and ducking under the vines that stretched out to strangle him. Faster and faster he raced, his jiiktar brandished before him, until the world became a dark and manic blur.

Lucyler ran like this unceasingly, unknowing of time.

And then he was out of the birch grove, in the clearing where burnt bodies littered the earth. Exhausted, he fell to his knees, and the delicious madness of the run left him as quickly as it had come. Not far away, he could see the sparkling pinpoints of the campfires, the glowing igniters of the flame cannons. Shaking with exhaustion, he rose unsteadily to his feet and, ignoring the burning and pleading of his muscles, ran toward the camp. He could see the trenches clearly now, the huddled men within them oblivious to his approach. The sentries hadn't sighted him.

"Awake!" he cried madly. "Barret! Gilliam! Awake!"

At his cry he saw the stirring of the sentries on the trench deck. They raised their bows as they spotted him. Lucyler put up his hands, flailing them wildly as he ran toward the trenches. Still the sentries drew their bowstrings back, and still Lucyler ran to them. Though he half expected an arrow to slam into his chest, he continued on at full speed, shouting his name and waving to the sentries.

"Hold! It is me, Lucyler!"

Now he was only yards from the first trench. On the deck, he could see the sentries murmuring to themselves, clearly confused as they tried to discern who or what white-skinned Triin charged toward them. Then the man lowered his bow.

"Lucyler?" shouted the man. "Is it you?"

Lucyler at once recognized the gruff voice of Gilliam. "Yes, Gilliam!" he yelled back. "Wake the men. There are warriors behind me!"

Immediately the other sentries dropped their weapons and peered out into the blackness. Lucyler threw himself onto the deck and skidded across the rain-slicked wood. Before he could fall into the trench beyond, Gilliam caught hold of him. Gasping, Lucyler let the other man support him.

"Warriors," Lucyler said. "Following me. We have to wake the others, be ready for them. . . ."

Gilliam nodded, then turned to the others in the trench, barking at them to wake the men and make ready for an attack. Soon the air was filled with the ringing of drawing steel and the hot burst of flame cannons coming alive. The deck shook with the heavy load of armored bodies as the men took their positions. When he was finally satisfied with the activity in the trenches, Gilliam turned back to Lucyler.

"Lucyler," Gilliam asked. "Where's Crodin?"

"I do not know," admitted Lucyler. "Behind me, I think. He could not keep up with me, and I had to warn you. I had to leave him."

"It's all right," said Gilliam calmly, putting a hand on Lucyler's shoulder. "Crodin's a good woodsman. He'll find his way back safely. How many Drol are there?"

"I saw maybe a dozen," said Lucyler. "But they wore the red of warriors, Gilliam. More of them are coming."

"You're probably right," said Gilliam. "Spies wouldn't wear the scarlet." Gilliam looked Lucyler over, inspecting his bloody arms. "What about you? You are injured."

Lucyler was about to tell Gilliam that he was well enough when a cry from the deck stopped him.

"Here they come!"

Together Lucyler and Gilliam twisted their heads to look out over the clearing. There, barely illuminated by the meager moonlight, they could see someone running toward them. Gilliam raised his bow again, but Lucyler reached out and pushed the weapon down.

"No! Nobody fire. It is Crodin!"

Crodin was running like a man being chased by wolves. Again and again he stumbled, looking over his shoulder for whatever terror was trailing him. Even through the darkness Lucyler could see the look of panic on Crodin's face. Worse, the noise of the wind kept him from hearing what Crodin was yelling.

And then Crodin stopped running. He stopped so suddenly that Lucyler didn't know what had happened until he caught a flashing glimpse of red in the forest. Crodin dropped to his knees, hung there for a moment, then fell facedown in the mud. From out of his back a dozen feathered arrows protruded. Behind him the white birch grove turned scarlet with Drol.

Every dark crevice of the forest was oozing red-robed warriors. They emerged as if from a fog, silent and purposeful, their jiiktars and bows in hand. With them were packs of war wolves. The beasts snarled and fought against their chains, their red eyes glowing. Lucyler watched in horror as the tide of men poured from the woods. He could see them plainly now, some with torches and brands, and in moments all the white of the birches was lost behind a curtain of crimson robes. Yet they didn't run for the trenches or shoot a single arrow. They merely stood there, letting their numbers swell.

"We're done for," whispered Gilliam. He lowered his bow at the unbelievable sight. Already a defeated moan was rising from the trenches.

Lucyler's mind raced, groping desperately for a strategy to save them. But he could find none. His men were sick from starvation and hopelessly outnumbered. Even the flame cannons would do them little good now.

The rain would cut the range of the weapons in half, and he was sure there wasn't enough fuel for a prolonged battle. He turned and glanced out over the trenches. Everywhere his soldiers were frozen with fear, their faces drawn in fright and as white as his own. Like him, they understood the impossibility of victory.

Richius, Lucyler thought remorsefully. *I am sorry, my friend. I have ruined us.*

"What are they waiting for?" said Gilliam anxiously. "Why don't they attack?"

Lucyler knew why. "They know they have us. They want us to surrender."

Gilliam sneered. "In hell. I'd slit my own throat before submitting."

Lucyler focused his attention on the milling warriors beyond. A single man was walking slowly toward them. He was shouting something in Triin, but Lucyler couldn't decipher the words over the noise of the rain.

"Look at that," said Gilliam. A thin, evil smile crossed his lips. He raised his bow again, drawing back on the string so that the arrow aimed straight at the approaching warrior. "Good night, gog!"

"No," insisted Lucyler. "Do not kill him. He is coming to tell us something."

"What's he saying?"

"It's Triin," another soldier on the deck answered. "Lucyler, what is it?"

Lucyler shrugged. The words were still lost under the storm. Then, when the Drol was only yards from the deck, Lucyler understood.

"Kalak! Oonal ni Kalak?"

A shudder went through Lucyler at the words. *The Jackal! Where is the Jackal?*

"Lucyler?" pressed the soldier.

"Richius," he said coldly. "They are calling for Richius."

"My God," said Gilliam. "Praise the Almighty Richius isn't here." Turning to Lucyler he said, "Please, Lucyler. Let me kill him. Let me kill him before he speaks another word."

"No," answered Lucyler stiffly. "We will see what else they want of us."

"Why? You know what they want. If we surrender . . ."

"Quiet!" snapped Lucyler

The Drol was just outside the trench now. He stood there fearlessly, uncaring about the score of arrows pointed at him, an expression of contempt on his pale face. His body was draped in the same brilliant scarlet robes as all Voris' warriors. When the Drol stopped outside the deck, Lucyler stepped forward. Only then did the Drol's expression change. He looked at Lucyler in disbelief.

"Triin?"

Lucyler answered the man in their shared tongue. "I am."

The warrior sneered. "Traitor."

For a moment Lucyler said nothing, frozen into silence by the insult. That this Drol, this zealot who had sided with Tharn against the royal line of Lucyler, should call him traitor . . .

"You have a message for us," said Lucyler coldly. "Speak it."

The warrior smiled at Lucyler, looking him over with arrogant humor. His gray eyes seemed to laugh.

"I bear the words of Voris, warlord of Dring and counsel of Tharn. My master demands that Richius the Jackal present himself for judgment. In return, my master will allow the lives of the imperial invaders to continue."

Lucyler silently thanked the gods Richius was safe in Ackle-Nye. "You are too late to take your vengeance, Drol," he laughed. "Richius is dead."

All at once the humor left the warrior's face. "Who leads here, then? Who among you stands in the Jackal's place?"

Now Lucyler smiled. "I do," he said proudly.

The warrior considered this for a moment, then said, "Voris is merciful. You may satisfy him, traitor."

"And these men will be spared?"

"One of you must answer for the crimes against the people of Dring. If my master finds you suitable, he will spare the lives of the other cowards."

"Back then, Drol," said Lucyler. "Tell your master that Lucyler of Falindar will gladly die in the Daegog's cause. Tell him also that if I am not enough for him, he will have to come and kill us, and we will die to a man trying to destroy him."

This made the warrior's eyebrows rise. He looked at Lucyler oddly, then turned and strode back through the clearing. Lucyler walked back to the trench. On the deck, Gilliam and the other soldiers were staring at him.

"Well?" asked Gilliam. "What do they want of us? Surrender?"

Slowly Lucyler shook his head. "Not all of us. Just me. If I surrender myself to Voris the rest of you will be spared."

Gilliam's face was ashen. "No, Lucyler. Don't think it. You can't. They'll kill you, torture you. . . ."

"Stop," interrupted Lucyler. He had already considered the unsavory end Voris had planned for him. It changed nothing. "Please, say no more. I must do this. All of you will live if I surrender."

"And you believe them?" asked Gilliam. "How can you trust their words? They are snakes, Lucyler."

Lucyler put a hand on Gilliam's shoulder. In a gentle, reassuring voice he said, "They are Drol. Whatever else I think of them, I know they do not lie. Please, Gilliam, follow this last order. Do not fight them."

Gilliam smiled grimly. "You ask the impossible of us," he said. Then, under the silent gaze of a hundred mournful eyes, he took Lucyler in a strong embrace. "Go with God, my friend."

"And you."

Before Gilliam had released his hold on Lucyler, a cry from one of the men on the deck shattered the moment.

"Look there!"

From out of the darkness a party of warriors approached. They walked with the erect arrogance of conquerors, clearly visible in the light of the torches they bore. Lucyler quickly counted five men, all in scarlet, all with jiiktars in their hands. The group seemed wholly unremarkable, save for the one who walked in the center. That one was taller than the rest, his robes more splendid and trimmed in gold. Atop his head, the usual mane of white Triin hair was gone. Only a bare scalp could be seen shimmering in the torchlight and the paleness of the moon. Two white wolves walked beside him. Unchained, the beasts moved with the perfect poise of house dogs. Lucyler felt his breath catch. A name slipped from his lips.

"Voris."

Voris the Wolf, Warlord of Dring, stopped some ten yards from the trench, near enough for an arrow to pierce his heart. Almost absently he raised a hand. The small gesture brought his party to a halt.

"Lucyler of Falindar!"

The voice boomed like the thunder of the rainstorm. Lucyler lifted his head at the sound of his name. Ignoring the pleas and outstretched hands of his men, he strode from the deck and into the clearing toward Voris.

"I am Lucyler," he called out. He saw Voris give a look of utter disbelief.

"Remarkable," said Voris. "As often as I see it I am amazed by it. How did it happen to you, traitor? How have you come to side with these barbarians who rape us?"

Lucyler willed his lips into a grin. "I have come for your judgment, butcher. Your words are meaningless, and I do not hear them."

Voris reddened with rage. "Dare you call me butcher? You, a traitor to your people?"

"And you are a traitor to your Daegog," said Lucyler. "You have brought this ruin to our land, not I. It is you who have betrayed the royal line of Lucel-Lor."

"The Daegog is the biggest of traitors, and those who follow him are the biggest of fools. Tharn will show you the truth of things."

"You are Tharn's lapdog, Voris. The toy of a usurper." From some mad corner of Lucyler's mind, a laugh erupted. "Give me your justice, dog. I am ready for it. But please, spare me your lies."

Unable to control his anger, Voris lashed out at Lucyler, striking him on the cheek with the palm of his hand. The blow sent Lucyler reeling. He stumbled, falling backward into the mud. Lucyler shook his head, felt the sting of a crushed lip, then rose unsteadily to his feet. He glared back at the trembling Voris.

"Your judgment, warlord," he said calmly. "Your judgment for these men."

"I will spare the dogs of Nar," said Voris. "Because I have said I would, and because Tharn wishes it. But it is not my judgment you will face, traitor. It is his."

"Take me, then," said Lucyler. "Take me to this 'Storm Maker.' I welcome death now that he has won."

Voris grinned. "Not Storm Maker," he corrected. "Peace maker. But if you live long enough, you will see the storm he brings."

NINE

Morning came to the dingy room as a single ribbon of light. Richius watched it pass through the cloudy window, illuminate a fleet of dust motes, and gently strike the white, unmoving face of the woman in his bed. The light did not disturb her. She stayed asleep, lost in the exhausted slumber she had fallen into after their coupling. Richius was careful not to stir though he had been awake for nearly an hour, lying still and naked beneath the covers. He wanted her to go on sleeping, after what he had done to her.

He reached out a finger and barely touched her cheek. She was beautiful—more lovely than any woman he had ever seen, Naren or Triin. But she was less than perfect now. Her face was still bruised, but that wasn't all. Blackwood Gayle had done that, not he. What he'd done was more despicable. Worse, it was irreversible. A bruise on the face would purple, swell, and then be gone. A small nastiness, completely forgettable. But maidenhood, once given or taken, would never return.

These thoughts needled him. It did him no good to try and convince himself he wasn't responsible. He hadn't been drunk enough for that. Lust was the only true answer, and the realization disgusted him. She was a Triin, one of those he had sworn to protect, and he had forsaken her. He couldn't even remember her name, though he was sure the innkeeper had told him. And now, with the heat of passion expelled, it all struck him as absurd. He vaguely recalled his ecstatic convulsion, then the awful stab of guilt. But he was tired, so tired . . .

And she hadn't protested. He had paid the innkeeper for a whole night with her, and she, like he, must have been weary beyond words. Now she slept, amazingly still and silent and, he hoped, peaceful.

"I'm sorry," he whispered, tracing his finger around her eye, not quite touching the skin. "Poor girl."

Richius let his finger drop. His eyes fell on the red stain on the sheet.

She must remember me, he thought. *Why else would she have endured it? She has rewarded me with the only thing she had to give. And like a Talistanian dog I took it.*

He bent his head and pressed his lips lightly to her cheek. Her eyes sprang open. For a moment she lay still, half-asleep and dazed. But then she noticed him and the dingy room and she jumped out of bed with a cry, dragging the sheet with her as she tried to cover her naked body. Forgetting his own nakedness, Richius leapt out of the bed after her.

"Wait," he cried. She ignored him, her eyes darting around the room. Quickly finding her dress, she retrieved it from the floor.

"No," he begged, going to her and grabbing her hand. "Please . . ."

The girl pulled her hand away. She dropped the sheet and scurried toward the door, then noticed he was blocking it. Motionless, she stood and watched him, her eyes burning, her dress held up like a curtain over her bosom.

"Please," Richius said. "I won't hurt you. Really, no more. I'm sorry about what happened. But I can help you." He pulled his trousers closer with a foot, then squatted and dug his fingers into the pocket, pulling out several silver coins. Standing, he held out the coins. "Money."

The woman looked at the coins for a moment, then spat into Richius' face. "No more money!"

Richius' hand dropped, the coins tumbling out of his palm onto the floor. Slowly he wiped the spittle from his face. "You understand me."

"I speak the tongue of Nar," she said, still clutching the dress.

"Then you heard what I told you. I won't hurt you." He stooped and picked the coins off the floor. "Please, take this money. I want you to have it."

"No," she said angrily. "Unless Tendrik orders me, we are finished."

"The innkeeper? Oh, no. You misunderstand. I want nothing more from you. This money is . . ." He grimaced. "An apology."

The girl's gray eyes turned a shade darker.

"I've taken something irreplaceable from you," Richius continued. He gestured toward the sheet on the floor, the stain of her blood. "I'm sorry. I didn't notice until this morning. Had I known . . ." He hesitated, considering how best to explain the awkwardness he felt. "Had I known you were a maiden I wouldn't have done it. Forgive me. I'm no better a man than that savage I saved you from."

"Saved me?"

"Don't you remember me?"

"I don't know you. I am not a whore. You are the first man I have been with since coming here."

"No, you don't understand," he said, stepping closer. "I'm not a *customer*. I only just arrived here. I'm Richius. From the village, remember? You were being attacked by a soldier. I pulled him off you."

A look of horror froze the young woman's face. "No. Oh, no, no." She slumped to her knees and the dress fell away, but she seemed not to notice as she cried, "You are Kalak!"

Richius was thunderstruck. How had she not known? He went to her, falling to one knee before her. "Don't worry. I promise I won't hurt you. You're safe."

"You are Kalak!" she said again, the shock of it reddening her face.

"Why won't you listen?" pressed Richius. "I'm not your enemy."

"You are!" she flared, fumbling with the dress and drawing it back over herself. "You are the greatest of them. Kalak. Jackal. Murderer!"

Richius drew back. "How can you say that? All I've ever tried to do is help your people."

The girl stormed toward Richius and tried to push him aside, but he wouldn't move.

"Stop," he pleaded. "Nothing's going to happen to you, I swear. I'm here to help you."

"Help?" said the girl. "I know you. I know what you have done. I have seen it! And now I have diseased myself with you."

"I'm sorry about that," said Richius. "But you're wrong to think I'm your enemy. Only Drol should believe that." He looked into her eyes. She looked away. "I'm telling you the truth. What I did to you last night I will regret for the rest of my life."

The girl scoffed and Richius went over to her. But as he leaned close she lashed out, clawing him across the face. Her painted nails dug deep into his cheek and he staggered backward with a shout.

It was all the chance she needed. She sprang to her feet and headed for the door, still clutching her dress. Richius tried to snare her wrist but she was too quick. The door opened and she darted out of the chamber.

"Wait!" Richius called. He went out into the hallway and watched her disappear down the rickety stairs. A bold breeze stirred down the corridor, reminding him that he was naked also. His face burning, he went back to his dingy room and closed the door. Blood trickled down his cheek and he wiped it away with the back of his hand. Her green slippers lay on the floor where she had kicked them off last night. He closed his eyes and cursed. The bed still smelled like her. He let her scent climb up his nostrils. Unbearably sweet. Her hair had been like that. Fine and soft, he had buried his face in it. His skin still tingled where it had touched her, so raw that it burned. It was all like a flood coming back to him; the way she had lain back and let his clumsy hands do the work, the way she had whimpered just at that moment. Then darkness, and utter, complete exhaustion.

"Oh, God," he moaned, burying his filthy face in his hands. "Why does she hate me so?"

Because I am Kalak, he told himself. *And because I don't belong here.*

But he wasn't her enemy. How, he wondered, could he make her see that?

He retrieved his own clothes from the floor and pulled them on. Dinadin would be awake by now. Hopefully he would be alone. Still barefoot, Richius went back out into the hall. The red door to Dinadin's room was closed. Richius put his ear to it and listened. Dinadin's familiar snores rumbled through the wood. Very carefully he pushed open the door and peered inside. There, tangled in the wrinkled sheets, was his friend, blessedly alone in the small bed. Richius tiptoed inside and shut the door behind him.

"Dinadin," Richius said lightly. "Wake up."

Dinadin grumbled and rolled over, turning his back to Richius.

"Dinadin," Richius repeated, a bit more sharply.

"What?" his friend moaned.

Richius sat down on the bed and shook the bigger man's shoulder. "Come on, get up. I need to talk to you."

Dinadin reached up a hand and pushed Richius away. "Lord, Richius. Let me sleep. I'm tired!"

Richius slid back onto the bed. "Sleep later. I need to talk to you."

"How early is it?"

"I don't know," said Richius. He glanced at the dirty window and noticed the feeble rays of sunlight struggling through. "Dawn?"

"Dawn? Too early. Get out."

"No," insisted Richius. "Wake up. I want to tell you something." He took Dinadin's shoulder again and tried to roll him over.

"What is it?" Dinadin grumbled. "Tell me fast so I can get back to sleep. I want to rest before we have to leave."

Richius smiled weakly. "Don't worry about leaving. We're not going just yet."

This snagged Dinadin's attention. "We're not? Why?"

Richius could hardly answer. "I . . . I've met someone."

"Oh, Lord!" crowed Dinadin. "And Lucyler thought it would be me!" He sat up, gesturing for Richius to go on. "Tell me everything. Did you spend all your money in one place?"

"Dinadin . . ."

"You know, we talk to you young soldiers about this but you never listen. I just wonder what your father's going to say."

"Dinadin, stop. Really, I'm serious."

"Oh, serious," said Dinadin. "All right, tell me. Who is she? Not that pig Carlina, I hope. Did she crawl into your room after she did me?"

"No," said Richius sharply. "No, it wasn't anyone like that. This one is beautiful. She is . . ." He stopped himself then, remembering suddenly how Dinadin had noticed the girl. "She's Triin," he said carefully.

Dinadin stared at him. "Triin? The one we saw last night?"

Richius nodded dully.

"The one I wanted?" Dinadin thundered. "How could you?"

"I don't know why," Richius fumbled. "I saw her and I was kind of drunk and, well, then I was asking the innkeeper for her. I'm sorry, Dinadin. I know I was wrong. But you were right about her. She was incredible."

"Tell me about it," said Dinadin sourly. He pointed his chin toward Richius' scratched face. "And wild, too, huh?"

Richius touched his cheek. The bleeding had stopped. "This? No, this isn't from last night. She did this to me before she left."

"Yes, I can see she really fell for you." Dinadin looked away. "Richius," he said rigidly. "I'm angry."

"I know you are. And I'm sorry. I don't know what came over me."

"Lust came over you," said Dinadin. "The same thing you chided me about. So fine, you proved you're just a regular fellow. But now that she's used to Naren men I want a try at her. Then we'll be even. Agreed?"

Richius sat back. "Dinadin, you don't understand. This girl . . . she's something special. I don't want . . ."

He stopped. Dinadin was staring at him in utter disbelief.

"All right," said Richius easily. "Let me explain. It's not you, Dinadin. It's just that I don't want anything to happen to her. She'd never been with a man before. I was the first."

"But you won't be the last. She might as well get used to it."

"No," cried Richius, getting up from the bed. "I don't want her to get used to it. Don't you see what I'm saying?"

"What are you telling me?" Dinadin fired back. "That you're in love with this girl after just a night? Come on, Richius, use your head. Do you have any idea how many men come here and think they've found the perfect woman?" He tossed his legs over the side of the bed and stared down his comrade. "Listen to me. You're not thinking clearly. And maybe I'm to blame for some of that. Just forget about what I said to you last night. I didn't mean it. I know you're doing the best you can. So we'll go back to Dring, I'll stop arguing with you, and you'll see how fast you forget this whore."

"She's no whore," said Richius. "And we're not going back to the valley, not yet. I want to see her again. Tonight."

"Richius, the others are waiting for us. Lucyler will be worried."

"I told him five days. If we leave in the morning maybe we can still make it back in time."

"Just so you can bed this girl again? Lord, Richius, I wish you could hear yourself. What's wrong with you? We have to get back."

Richius sat back down on the bed next to Dinadin and gazed down at the floor. "I don't know if I can explain this, but I have to see her again. She knows who I am. Remember when we chased Gayle out of that village? She was there. I found her in one of the houses. Gayle was trying to rape her and I pulled him off her."

"And that's why she hit you?"

"I don't really know why she hit me. But she called me Kalak. You had to see her, the rage in her eyes. She hates me, Dinadin. And I don't want her to."

"She's from the valley, Richius. They all hate us."

"But they shouldn't," said Richius. "She should know the truth."

Dinadin's face crinkled. "You know what it sounds like to me?"

"What?"

"It sounds like you want to rescue her."

Richius made a face, but Dinadin held up his hands. "No, really. I know what you're thinking. You're wondering how you can take care of her. But you can't, Richius. She's here because she's trying to survive, and unless you're going to rebuild all of Lucel-Lor for her, there's nothing you can do. She's doomed."

"Please, don't say that."

"It's true. You were right about what you told me last night. We're just adding to these people's misery. The faster Nar gets out of Lucel-Lor, the faster the Triin can start building a new country for themselves."

"Even if it's under Tharn?"

"Yes, even then. You and Lucyler don't think I'm smart about these things, but I see clearly enough. And I know that you're being foolish over nothing. This girl hates you for a reason. To her you're just Kalak. You're the Jackal who kills people in her valley. Don't think for a second that you're going to change that, because it won't work."

"I have to try," Richius sighed. "I have to see her again. And I need a favor from you."

"What?"

"I want to do something special for her tonight to make up for what I did to her."

"And you need money, right?"

"Yes," admitted Richius sheepishly. "Do you have any? All I have is a few coins. But you, well . . ."

"I still have the dagger," said Dinadin. "Carlina wasn't worth a tenth of it, so I gave the innkeeper a silver instead. You can have the dagger if you want it."

Richius beamed at his comrade. "Thanks. I'll give you back whatever I don't spend, I promise. I'll make a good bargain with the innkeeper."

"Don't expect there to be much left over," said Dinadin. "We'll need these rooms another night, and once the innkeeper knows you're soft on the Triin girl he'll hike up her price."

"I'll do my best," said Richius. "If there's anything left it's yours."

"Actually it's all mine," said Dinadin. He got out of bed, yawned like a lion, and went to the window. "It's bright out. It must be past dawn by now. The innkeeper . . ." His voice trailed off and he pressed his nose up against the murky glass. Richius watched him curiously.

"What is it, Dinadin?"

"Richius, come here."

Dinadin stepped aside and let Richius have the window. The panes were caked with years of filth but Richius could see the barren horizon that stretched to the east of the city. And there, off in the distance near the Sheaze, was a huge mass of men and horses. There were tents and giant pavilions, smoke from cooking fires and the distinct sight of a tattered blue banner flying high above the assembly. Richius blinked and looked again. There was a crest embroidered into the banner, the streaking symbol of a yellow dragon.

Richius stepped away from the window. Dinadin was staring at him in amazement.

"Richius," said Dinadin softly. "Do you know whose flag that is?"

Richius said nothing. Of all the flags he thought he might see when he came to Ackle-Nye, it had never occurred to him that this one might be flying here. It was the flag of Aramoor's duke of war. It was Edgard's flag.

With the morning light breaking through the hazy sky, Richius and Dinadin trotted their horses through the camp of the Dragon Flag. They moved slowly through the host of men and animals and, just as Richius didn't recognize the young horsemen under the charge of the duke, so too did they not realize that their prince rode among them. Busy with the work of setting up camp, few of the soldiers turned to look at the strangers, and those who did glanced at them without interest before returning their vacuous eyes to their work. Despite their numbers, the men made little sound, and it seemed to Richius that they rode through an encampment of ghosts. Only the uniforms of black and gold lent the horde any resemblance to Aramoor Guardsmen, and even these were tattered and grimy. The garments, now too big to fit their malnourished bodies, gave them the look of children playing in their father's wardrobe.

Battered tents and pavilions were strewn throughout the camp, each marked and weathered by the harsh climate of Tatterak. The air was stale, acrid with the filth of men and animals and ripe with the scent of distant Ackle-Nye.

"Lord," exclaimed Richius. "What the hell happened?"

Dinadin said nothing, but Richius could see from his expression that his companion shared his shock. Whatever misfortunes Edgard's men had met in Tatterak had left them ragged and defeated, no longer proud enough to even care for themselves. Their beards were overgrown, their uniforms threadbare and filthy, their cheeks pale and sunken. Of all these things, it was the sight of so many bony faces that distressed Richius the most. Even his own men in the valley had not fared so badly. When their supplies had dwindled to nothing and Aramoor's caravans had ceased coming to their aid, they had the lushness of Dring with which to fill their stomachs. But Tatterak had no such bounty for its people. Unlike the valley of his adversary Voris, the warlord Kronin's land was a rocky, unforgiving place, and the Triin who lived there had to be hardy and frugal to survive. Without the aid of the Empire, Richius knew, none of the troops could last. Richius frowned. Clearly, they hadn't lasted.

"This is absurd," he said angrily. "We ride in here and nobody even challenges us or asks who we are. Are these Guardsmen or not?"

He grunted in disgust, then noticed a single man walking past them. The soldier walked as if in a fog, his shoulders slumped with weariness. He shuffled past Richius and Dinadin without a glance, his expression apathetic, his gait so slow that he seemed on his way to nowhere. He was just as unkempt as the others, and Richius would not have noticed him at all if not for the golden tassels of a captain that he bore on his right sleeve.

"You there," cried Richius, bringing his horse to a stop. "You're a captain in this army?"

The man looked up quickly, startled by Richius' tone.

"What's that?" he asked, blinking, and Richius saw the yellowness of hunger staining his eyes.

"Who are you, soldier?" asked Richius.

The man reared back belatedly. "I should ask you that, stranger. No one from the city is allowed in this camp. You'll have to leave at once." He began walking around Richius' horse and added quietly, "We don't have the gold for whatever you're trading."

Richius realized suddenly that the casual garb he and Dinadin wore gave no hint of who they were, or even that they were soldiers at all. With their leathers and their horses smeared with grime, he supposed they could have easily been mistaken for traders from the Empire.

"Captain," Richius shouted after the man, turning his horse to follow alongside him. "We're not merchants. I'm Richius Vantran."

The man stopped and looked up again at Richius, his jaw falling open. Richius reached into his pocket and fished out his ring, the ring bearing the crest of the House of Vantran. Only those of the royal blood of Aramoor possessed the bands of gold and onyx, and Richius had always found the ring a useful tool in places like this that made all men anonymous.

"Sir?" the man asked cautiously, taking careful study of the ring. After a moment he inclined his head and said, "Forgive me, my prince, I didn't know you were here. There was no news of your arrival."

"We only arrived in Ackle-Nye yesterday. We saw your encampment from the windows of our rooms in the city. You must have gotten here yourself last night, yes?"

"Late last night," said the captain wearily. "Closer to the morning, really."

"And you're Edgard's troops?"

"Yes, Prince Richius. The duke is here. Have you word from home, my lord?"

Richius smiled sadly at the hopefulness in the man's voice. "I think I'm more in the dark about home than you are, Captain . . . ?"

"Captain Conal, sir," the soldier answered. "I've been Duke Edgard's captain of cannons since old Sinius died."

"Sinius was killed?" asked Richius, remembering the bald man who was always at Edgard's side. "When was that?"

Captain Conal cocked his head and recollected for a moment, then said finally, "Two months now, maybe three. He was killed in the battle for the Dead Hills, near Falindar. A bad battle, that. Even the duke took a wound there. Nearly wiped out a third of us. That was the start of the worst of it. Didn't you hear about it in Dring?"

Richius spared a look at Dinadin and, seeing his companion's slight shake of his head, said, "We don't hear much in the valley, Captain, but from the looks of things here, all the bad news we've heard is true. You arrived here last night, you say?"

"We left Tatterak four days ago. Things went wrong there, my lord. But I think the duke should be telling you all this. I can take you to him if you want."

"That would be best," answered Richius.

"I'll see to your horses, my lord," said Conal. "Follow me, sirs."

Richius and Dinadin dismounted, and Conal quickly took the reins of their mounts and led the procession through the smoky camp. When he found a young horsekeeper, brushing the coats of two other beasts, the captain gave over the horses with an order to find a good place to shelter the animals. The younger man protested at first, arguing that there wasn't enough feed for the horses they had already, and that any riders from the city should find their own stable lodgings. Without revealing Richius' identity, Conal merely lowered his voice in the stern, trained tone of a leader and ordered that the two new horses be well looked after. After this the young soldier complied, however reluctantly, and led the two horses into the crowd, leaving Conal free to escort Richius and Dinadin to the duke.

"I'm sorry, Prince Richius," Conal apologized. "The boy is strained and things are a bit desperate. He'll take care of your horses, though, don't worry."

Richius waved the remark away. He had seen what desperation could do to military courtesies. They walked quietly through the camp, while a flock of homeward-bound starlings dotted the bright sky. To Richius, the birds looked more like bats or vultures soaring over a graveyard. Winter was drawing near. It was time for the birds to abandon their summer nests in search of warmer climes. If he and his men were still here when the season closed, Richius knew, the coming winter would be desperate.

Edgard's pavilion was on the other side of the encampment, the side farthest from the stink of Ackle-Nye. Despite his rank, the duke's place was no more splendid than those of his underlings. It was as ragged as all the others, and only a tiny flag thrust into the dirt marked it as his residence, bearing as it did the crest of the dragon. Inside the pavilion, Richius could see several figures moving about, their silhouettes cast through the thin fabric by the light of the rising sun. Voices passed through the fabric, too, and one of them Richius recognized at once as Edgard's.

Conal put up a hand to slow them. "Come in with me, my lords. I'll tell the duke you're here."

The tent was unguarded, and the three men slipped quietly through its entry flap. As they did so, the others in the tent gave a brief glance in their direction, then looked away and continued their conversation. They were standing around a table, empty glasses in their hands, talking in voices too loud for sober men.

Richius recognized Edgard at once. The heavy skin, the long legs, the gray beard, the booming voice that still sang in his ears as it did when he was a child. But Richius' smile melted away when he saw that where a left arm should have been there hung only a uniform sleeve, pinned up at his shoulder.

Conal wasn't lying, thought Richius sadly. Edgard really had taken a wound, and a bad one. But how, he wondered? His duty was to plan battles, not fight them. That the Drol had forced the war duke of Aramoor into combat was remarkable, and Richius was surprised he wasn't dead from such a wound.

Conal moved away from Richius and Dinadin, going over to Edgard and telling him something in a voice too low for them to decipher. Richius saw Edgard glance in his direction, and he tried to force the smile back onto his lips. Edgard did not return the gesture, and Richius wasn't surprised that the duke's face didn't spark with recognition. This war had changed him, too, and it couldn't be expected that any friend, even one as close as Edgard, should recognize Richius after what the valley had done to him.

Without taking his puzzled eyes off Richius, Edgard leaned closer to the man at his side. He took his arm in a friendly way, pulling him near and asking him, Richius supposed, to excuse them. The man, whom Richius didn't recognize, looked at him suspiciously, then nodded in compliance and left the tent. Edgard looked hard at Richius.

"Richius?" asked Edgard cautiously, his eyes narrowed. "Is it you, my boy?"

Now the smile returned to Richius' face, and he went toward the duke without awaiting permission, his arm outstretched.

"Yes, Edgard," he said. "It's me."

"Oh, my boy," said the old man, wrapping his single arm about Richius and kissing his cheek. "You've changed so much! I scarcely recognized you. And what is this?" He put his hand to Richius' face and playfully rubbed the short beard there. "Do you wear your beard like a Talistanian now?"

"You mean like yourself?" asked Richius, gesturing toward the man's own unshaven face. Edgard chuckled. All the puzzlement was gone from his old face now, and he glowed with real warmth. It was the kind of welcome Richius expected from this man who had been more like a father to him than his own blood father had ever been.

"Oh, it's good to see you here, Richius," said Edgard. Richius didn't know if it was the dim light in the tent or the liquor making his host emotional, but it seemed that Edgard's eyes were sparkling with tears. "I thought you might be dead by now. Gayle was telling me stories of the valley war. Have you come for retreat, my boy?"

"No," Richius responded gently, sure that Edgard wanted him to say differently. Then, lying to spare the old man worry, he said, "But we are all well enough, Uncle. We have Voris on the run for the first time in months." He gestured over to where Dinadin was standing, still in the doorway, silently watching. "May my companion come inside?"

"Of course," said Edgard. "And who is this young man?"

Richius made to answer the duke, but Dinadin stepped quickly forward, saying, "Dinadin of the House of Lotts, my duke." He bowed.

"Dinadin!" the duke cried. He went to him and kissed him, too. "Oh, I'm sorry. I must be going blind not to have recognized you!"

Dinadin laughed. "We're all a little dull these days, my duke."

"Dinadin's turned out to be my best cannoneer, Uncle," said Richius. "I'd have taken the valley months ago if I had twenty more like him."

Dinadin seemed to shrink away from the compliment, his cheeks flushing. "Richius exaggerates."

"Nonsense," said Edgard cheerfully. "You were both fine pupils. Now sit, and let's have some talk!"

The duke motioned them to the few rickety chairs strewn around the small table. A map had been laid on the table, its edges tattered and its ink blotched by the moisture of glasses. Wine stains streaked its old parchment, but Richius could still see clearly that the map was of Lucel-Lor. There was a decanter on the table, too, filled now with only the scarlet residue of its previous contents. As the three men took their seats, Edgard lifted the decanter and thrust it toward Captain Conal.

"Conal," said Edgard. "See if you can hunt down more of this wine."

Conal, who had dutifully remained standing, quickly took the decanter from the duke, then left the pavilion.

"It's all we've been doing since we arrived last night," the duke said. "I sent some men into Ackle-Nye for supplies and they came back with nothing but wine and beer."

Richius frowned. Trying to keep his tone congenial, he said, "It's a bit early for drink, Uncle. Besides, it looks to me like your men need food more than wine. Some of them can hardly stand."

"True," agreed Edgard ruefully. "But there's just not enough food to go around. Even the poorest peasant won't sell us any. You should see them starving in Tatterak." He paused, shaking his head. "I tell you, Richius, you've never seen anything like it. Tharn's been setting fires to the croplands. Even Kronin's own warriors are starving. He is a bastard, that one. He'd see his own people starve just for his bloody revolution."

"Is that why you're here?" asked Richius. "No food?"

"No food, no troops, no anything. I sent word to your father months ago, telling him Tharn was on the move, but I didn't get an answer back."

"But what about the city?" pressed Richius. "Surely there's at least one merchant there with some food for you."

"Not from what my men told me. There's not one of them left that's not selling whores or wine. They're all just waiting to head back through the Run."

The "Run," Richius knew, was the Saccenne Run, the passage linking Lucel-Lor to Aramoor and the rest of Nar through the Iron Mountains. It wasn't an easy trip, and there was no way that any merchant who had tied up all his money in wine could get it through the Run. A sardonic smile began to play on Richius' lips. To his reckoning, these merchants had been the cause of the war, them and the priests. The Daegog had let them in, and it was their greed and zealousness that had fostered Tharn and his revolution to turn back Lucel-Lor's clock, and now they were paying for their vices. They had been given the grim choice of returning to Nar penniless or taking the chance of being trapped here like the rest of them. Good for them, thought Richius dryly.

"So," said Richius slowly, trying to approach his questions gently. "You have no word from Aramoor, then?"

Edgard frowned, but before he could answer Conal returned, a freshly filled decanter of wine in his hands. Without a word the captain placed the wine on the table and, obviously conscious that his presence had broken the conversation, quickly left the tent. Edgard watched him go before speaking again.

"You're fortunate to have loyal men like Dinadin around you, Richius," said Edgard. He had picked up the decanter and was pouring the thickly colored wine into Richius' glass. "I haven't trusted a man so much since Sinius."

"Yes," said Richius sadly, remembering Edgard's old companion. "Your captain told us that he was killed. A fine man."

"The best," Edgard agreed. "Conal's a good man, too, but not like Sinius."

"What happened to him?" asked Dinadin.

"Caught an arrow in the back at Dead Hills. That's where I got this." Edgard pointed to the ugly stump that was left at his shoulder.

"Jiiktar?" asked Richius.

"Yes. And God damn all of 'em. Those things are too fast for men to fight against. The wound was so clean I didn't even know I'd lost my arm until I saw it laying next to me. That's when Sinius found me, and the arrow found him."

Edgard stopped and took a deep pull from his glass. Richius could see that the memory still pained the old war duke. What other things had he seen, Richius wondered? What was so horrible as to make Edgard of Aramoor retreat?

"Edgard," said Richius gently. "What of Aramoor? Has retreat been called?"

"No," said Edgard bitterly. "At least not by your father. I called retreat myself. Didn't you hear of it in Dring?"

Richius shook his head. "No. All we heard was from Blackwood Gayle's men, that things were going badly in Tatterak. But I had no idea . . ." He broke off, the shock of what he was hearing hammering into his mind. "Edgard, what's happened to you?"

"Oh, my boy," Edgard said gravely, lowering his glass onto the map and staring into it blankly. "The war in Tatterak is over. Tharn and his warlords had been breaking through for weeks. Kronin's castle might not even be standing anymore. We left while the Drol were laying siege to it. They were trying to get to the Daegog." Edgard laughed and took another drink. "I hope they got him, too."

"How can that be?" asked Dinadin. "Kronin has more warriors than even Voris does, plus all of you to help him. Even Talistan has its troops based there."

"It's like I said. Tharn was gaining ground for months. He's like a king to the peasants in the countryside. Why, some of Kronin's own villages started to take his side. And as for Talistan, Gayle's bastards always left the real fighting to us. Most of them had retreated to safer places in Tatterak. Gayle himself even went down to help you in the valley, didn't he?"

"Yes, we had his help," said Richius. "For as long as I would take it. I'd rather lose the whole damn war than win it with Gayle's aid. But to retreat, Edgard! How can you, without even a word from home?"

"It was retreat or die, Richius. The night we left Mount Godon . . ." Edgard put up a hand to silence himself. "I'd better start from the beginning, or you'll never believe a word of it. I sent word to your father months ago, begging him for help. He never answered me. My guess is that the king wants to end the war without actually calling for retreat. Maybe he thinks losing the war legitimately will keep the emperor from being too angry with him. Either way, I'm running things my own way now, friendship or no."

"Oh?" challenged Richius. "And what about the emperor?"

"Same answer," said Edgard defiantly. "If he wants Lucel-Lor so badly, let him come and take it himself. Or Talistan can win it for him. Let the House of Gayle have their people slaughtered. I won't fight a hopeless battle for the Daegog, and certainly not for the emperor. Anyway, it doesn't matter. Mount Godon has fallen. Tharn has the Daegog, and it's just a matter of time until the rest of Lucel-Lor falls."

Richius gave Edgard a surprised look, shocked at the notion of his withdrawing without the emperor's consent. But the duke's expression didn't soften under the accusing stare. Not that Richius expected it to. This was, after all, Aramoor's duke of war, and despite outward appearances, he was as proud as a lion. There would be no apology from him.

"Retreat," said Richius finally. "I wouldn't have thought it of you, Edgard."

"Don't judge me too harshly, Richius. I haven't told you the worst of it yet. I called retreat just in time. It wasn't just Drol warriors that attacked Mount Godon. It was magic."

"Magic?" blurted Dinadin. "You've seen Tharn, then?"

"No, but I've seen what he can do. My God, I thought all the talk was just a legend." He wrapped his single hand tightly around his glass, as if some great chill had come over him and only the glass could warm him. "Unbelievable."

Richius put his own hand over the old man's and gave it a reassuring squeeze. "Tell me," he coaxed.

"I cannot. There aren't words. He's got powers, Richius. To command the sky, the lightning. He's from hell, I swear it."

It seemed to Richius that Edgard was raving. Suddenly sure that it was the drink that was unbalancing the duke, Richius pried the glass

forcefully from the old man's hand. "Enough," he snapped, pushing the
glass to the other end of the table. "Tell me what you saw."

Edgard sat back, and Richius could see his eyes glaze over in recollection. His breathing slowed, and he let out a weary sigh. "It's much as I
have told you. Tharn's warriors had been gaining ground for months in
Tatterak. My men were being slaughtered. Gayle's and Kronin's, too.
Gayle didn't call retreat, but he had his men hidden where the fighting
was light. Kronin and I were taking the brunt of it."

"No surprise there," quipped Richius. "Go on."

"Well, I'd had enough. I'd asked your father for help and not gotten
any. The Drol were handing us our heads in every battle. They were overwhelming us, there were so many. I knew Mount Godon would fall soon,
so I told the Daegog I was taking my men out of Tatterak. That was a
week ago, before the storm came."

"Storm?" asked Richius. "What storm?"

"Nothing like you've ever seen. Like the winter gales in Aramoor, but
so much worse. It came over the horizon the night before we were going
to leave. Winds so strong we couldn't stand against them. I thought the
whole of Mount Godon was going to be picked up and dropped into the
ocean."

Edgard's voice was growing shrill, but Richius made no effort to calm
him. The war duke's face was white and terrible.

"Is that it?" asked Dinadin. "Just wind?"

"If only," said Edgard. "The winds were just the start. It was as if he
knew the winds alone weren't enough to crush us. That's when he sent
the lightning."

"Who?" asked Richius, suddenly confused. "Who sent the lightning?"

"Tharn," growled the duke. "It was all his doing, I'm sure of it. The
Triin in Tatterak call him 'Storm Maker' now, or something like that. He
can control the skies!"

Richius saw Dinadin's brow crease in disbelief, and felt his own doing
the same. Even in the valley they had heard the legends about Drol magic,
but the stories had always been no more than a way to amuse themselves
around a campfire.

Richius put on a gentle face. "Uncle, surely it was no more than a rainstorm. Maybe the change of season . . ."

"No!" cried Edgard, pounding his fist on the table so that the glasses
shook and spilled. "Don't tell me what I saw! I lost a third of my men in
one bloody hour. Tharn brought the lightning down on us, and the
winds. The storm thought for itself, and never did the lightning strike an
empty place. It always felled a man or a horse or a wagon when it struck.
Always."

"All right," conceded Richius, still unconvinced. "But how can you explain that? I've never seen a Triin do magic, and neither has anyone else I

know. Even if Tharn is some great holy man, no man can command the elements."

"Tharn can."

Neither Richius nor Dinadin spoke a word as they watched the weird grin twisting Edgard's face. In the soft light he looked like a madman. Certainly the tale he was regaling them with was mad. If Tharn was such a wizard, why would he have waited until now to show what he could do? No, Richius reasoned. A man as powerful as that would have ended this war long ago.

"You know I can't believe you," said Richius finally.

Edgard nodded. "I know. But I'm not lying. And I'm not as drunk as you think I am. I called retreat that very night. The storm was dissipating, and we spotted Tharn's warriors on the horizon. There were hundreds of them, maybe thousands. I didn't wait around to find out how many."

"My God, Edgard. You left Kronin and the Daegog alone?"

"And Gayle," said Edgard. "And they're all probably dead by now, God save 'em. And you know what else? I'm not a damn bit sorry."

Richius got up from his seat. "No? Well, you should be. What kind of war duke are you? Kronin needed you. He trusted you."

Now Edgard rose and towered over the table. "Kronin knew why I did it. I think he even agreed with me. And how dare you tell me what's best for my men? You don't even know what we were up against."

"What do you expect me to say? You come to Ackle-Nye with some crazy story about Drol magic, and you expect me to believe it? Do you think Arkus will believe it? Kronin trusted you, damn it. And now he's probably dead. The Daegog, too. Without Tatterak, only the Sheaze and the southern lands will be left."

"And you in the valley," said Edgard gravely. "You say you have Voris on the run there?"

"Probably not for long. When word reaches Voris that Tharn has taken Tatterak, he'll attack again. And likely in numbers strong enough to defeat us."

"Then you must leave now," Edgard insisted. "Escape while you can. Otherwise you'll be trapped in the valley with no way home."

"Retreat without the emperor's word? I can't."

Edgard looked at him sharply. "The war is over, Richius. The Daegog's dead."

"Maybe," said Richius. "But maybe not. If you had stayed with him we'd know for sure."

"And then I'd be dead, too. Is that what you would have preferred?"

"Of course not."

Edgard's expression softened. "I've sent word to the king that I'm retreating from Lucel-Lor. Now you must do the same. Don't be like Gayle, doing the emperor's bidding at all costs. Save yourself."

"And then what?" Richius asked. "Be hanged for a traitor? Haven't you thought of what Arkus will do to you? Arkus would never agree to us leaving. It won't matter to him if the Daegog's dead. He's got us here for something else. And what about Aramoor? He'll take Aramoor completely if we retreat." He shook his head, exasperated. "You're so like my father, Edgard. When will you realize Aramoor isn't ours anymore?"

Edgard seemed unperturbed. "I have a responsibility to my men, Richius. Just like Darius has a responsibility to the people back home."

"My father? How can you say my father is prepared for any responsibility? This mess is his fault. We might be winning the war if not for him."

"You think so?" asked Edgard. "Would you really have your father send still more men into this hell? Haven't you seen enough death?"

"You and my father live in the same dreamworld," cried Richius. "It doesn't matter what I want. All that matters is the emperor's will. He's running Aramoor now, whether you know it or not. By defying him, you and my father will bring about its destruction."

"Your father is trying to save Aramoor," insisted Edgard. "You are right to say Arkus will crush Aramoor if the king calls for retreat. That's why he's not sending more troops. He wants to lose the war without declaring it lost." Edgard gave Richius an imploring look. "If I'm right, then your father's willing to die to keep more of us from coming here. Can't you see that, Richius? He's trying to save lives."

"Don't talk to me about saving lives!" Richius shouted. "That's all I've been doing since I got here, no thanks to my father. I'm up to my knees in blood every day while he sits in Aramoor and waits for the war to end itself."

"No," argued Edgard. "I've known your father since I was a boy, and I know how he thinks. If Darius calls retreat, the emperor will crush Aramoor. But if he simply lets the war be lost, then maybe he can keep our country whole."

Richius laughed sourly. "Surely Arkus is not as dumb as that. He'll know why the war's been lost, and he'll have all of us answering for it."

"Not all of us," said Edgard. "Just the king."

Richius frowned. "That seems like a dangerous gamble to me. To let us all die like this . . ."

"Why die?" thundered Edgard. He towered a good head over Richius and the sight of the angry man gave Richius a start. "Haven't you been listening to me? If you pull out now maybe you can save yourself. If not, you'll only be dying for pride, because I swear to you this war is over."

Richius lowered his eyes. He could feel Dinadin's nervous stare burning into him, begging him for an answer he didn't have. All that his mind was filled with now was a string of fractured questions. How could he leave without the emperor's order? Edgard was being too kind in his assessment of Arkus' mercy. His father would certainly hang, but if they pulled out without the emperor's consent, he and Edgard would hang with him.

"What's to consider?" asked Edgard easily, putting his hand on Richius' shoulder. "Death on the gallows might be in store for us, but if you stay here Tharn or Voris will certainly kill you. Take your chances with me and you may yet live."

Richius sighed ruefully. "So it's a choice of deaths now, is it?" He let his eyes fall on Dinadin's. "What do you think, Dinadin? Shall I die a traitor's death? Or would a jiiktar in the back suit me better?"

Dinadin shifted awkwardly. He stammered something meaningless, then fell silent.

"We're not as tired as your men, Edgard," concluded Richius. "We can last awhile longer, maybe long enough for aid to arrive from the Black City. When Arkus hears of this he'll probably send his own troops in, and then we'll be able to fight Tharn, magic or no."

"You can't win, Richius."

"Neither can you, Edgard. But at least this way Aramoor may be spared the worst of the emperor's wrath. You're wrong to think Arkus will only blame my father if we pull out. If we retreat there won't be an Aramoor anymore, and there won't be any dukes or princes, either."

Edgard seemed astonished. "I can't believe you'd die for Arkus, Richius. Why would you give your life for a man that has a boot on the throat of your homeland?"

"Not for Arkus," Richius corrected. "For Aramoor. Get your men home safely, Uncle. And when you see my father tell him I will go on without his help."

Edgard's face was like granite. "I will tell him."

"Let's go, Dinadin."

Dinadin sprang to his feet and went to Richius' side. As they turned to leave the pavilion Edgard's voice called softly after them.

"There's a reason he's doing it, Richius," said the duke. "You have to try and understand."

Richius stopped. He closed his eyes. "I don't care why he's doing it," he said bitterly. "I'm his goddamned son."

Then, without waiting for the duke's reply, Richius stepped out of the pavilion, Dinadin on his heels. He looked around for Conal, and when he didn't see the captain he headed directly for the stable where he knew their horses were boarded. Will alone kept him from breaking into tears. Edgard had been his mentor and friend and uncle. Now that old friend, like so many old friends, was leaving him. Dinadin grabbed at his shoulder. Richius shrugged it off.

"Richius," Dinadin said sharply. "Wait."

Richius stopped. He turned to face his comrade and saw Dinadin's face twisted and confused.

"Say it," he ordered. "I know you want to."

Dinadin swallowed hard. "Edgard's right, Richius. You know he is. And . . ."

"And what?"

"I want to go with him."

The grief Richius had tried so hard to check overtook him. "Are you going to leave me, Dinadin? Is that what you're saying?"

"God, Richius, open your eyes. The war's over. It's like Edgard said. The Daegog's dead."

"Edgard doesn't know that. Nobody knows that! We're not done here."

Dinadin shook his head. "I am. I'm done helping the emperor get richer. I'm not going back to Dring with you, Richius. I'm going home."

"You'll abandon all of us, just like that?"

Dinadin grabbed hold of Richius' lapel. "We've already been abandoned by your own father! Lord, isn't that enough for you? Or won't you be satisfied until all of us are dead? Lonal's gone, Jimsin's gone. Almost half our company is gone! And it's your goddamned fault!"

"It's not!" cried Richius, shaking off Dinadin's grip. "It's not my fault. I've done my best."

"Well, your best stinks. And I'm not going to be your next victim." He reached into his belt and pulled out his silver dagger, the one he'd promised to Richius earlier. Roughly he shoved it into Richius' hand. "Here. Take this and pay for your precious whore. Have a good time tonight. Because when you go back to the valley, you're going to die." Dinadin's lower lip began to tremble. "And I don't want to be there to see it."

"Don't, Dinadin, please . . ."

But Dinadin was already walking away. Richius started after him, then stopped himself as his friend put up a hand. He could tell Dinadin was weeping.

"I'm going home," the big man choked. "I'm going."

Richius let him go.

TEN

The noonday sun was high overhead when Richius returned, alone, to Ackle-Nye. The city of beggars was awake now, and stirring up a noxious smell. Triin refugees lined the streets like living garbage, and in the sky above a family of buzzards coasted on the thermals, looking down on the starving with cool anticipation. In the light of day Richius could see the city for what it was, and the former glory of what it had been. Urine stained the pretty cobblestones. Fire had gutted some of the works of the Naren architects. Broken mosaic windows hung in the unused church, the only house of worship in the city, and everywhere the desperate Triin huddled with their hands out, politely hassling the few Narens still in the city.

Richius hurried past it all, driving his mount back toward the little tavern. He arrived and found the same little boy from the night before, patiently waiting for a horse to tend. The boy beamed when Richius handed him a small coin. He took hold of the horse's reins and carefully tied them to the post. Then he smiled reassuringly at Richius.

"Look after him," said Richius, "and I'll have another coin for you in the morning."

Inside the tavern, Richius immediately sighted the innkeeper, Tendrik. The place was deserted but Tendrik was behind the bar anyway, stacking up a row of cloudy glasses. He brightened when he saw Richius.

"Afternoon, sir," he said cheerfully. "Welcome back."

Richius approached the bar, trying to smile. "Can I speak to you a moment?" he asked. "I need something from you."

"I'm here to please," said the innkeeper. "Especially for you, Prince Vantran."

"You know who I am?"

"I do," said the man secretively. "Dyana told me, the girl you spent the night with. She was very upset to have been deflowered by Kalak!" The man broke into a hearty laugh. "I didn't know they called you that in Dring, Prince. She said it means 'jackal.' Frankly, I'm not sure it suits you."

"It's not something I care for," said Richius sharply. He watched with satisfaction as the humor on Tendrik's fat face drained away. "And there's no need for anyone else to know who I am, understand?"

"Perfectly," said the innkeeper. "Now what is it you need? The room again?"

"The room and the girl. And I want her for the whole night again. No one else is to be with her before me."

The innkeeper grimaced. "Ah, well, that could be a problem. You see, I think she'd rather slit your throat than sleep with you. She has a grudge against you, after all. Rather understandable under the circumstances, don't you think?"

Richius remembered suddenly what Dinadin had told him. "Your price has gone up?"

"Prince Vantran, it's not the money. Dyana is fiery, and not easy for me to control." Tendrik gestured to the scar on Richius' face, then traced his own. "You see? My little cat likes to use her claws, and I don't care to try for a matching pair. I really don't think even you have enough money to make her do it with you again."

"I don't want to 'do it,' " said Richius angrily. "I just want to see her, talk to her. Tell her that if you have to, but get her to agree."

Tendrik looked puzzled. "You just want to talk to her?" he asked. "May I ask why?"

"No."

"Fine. But the price is the same for talking or touching. And with those soldiers camped outside I'm sure I could line up a busy night for her." The innkeeper grinned. "It's a good thing you're a prince."

"How much?" asked Richius. "And before you answer, I should tell you I want something special tonight."

"Special? I thought you said you just wanted to talk."

"I do. That's not what I mean. I want some special arrangements made."

The innkeeper laughed. "Royalty is strange. Very well. I'm sure I can make whatever arrangements you want."

"Don't agree until you know what I'm asking," said Richius. "How hard is it to get some food around here? I mean real food, something good?"

"Food? That's a tough one," Tendrik admitted. "You have to know where to go, and it's expensive. I can get it, but it'll cost you."

Richius pulled out Dinadin's silver dagger and showed it to the innkeeper. Tendrik's eyes bulged.

"Will this cover it?"

Dyana had slept the entire day. The trip to Ackle-Nye had exhausted her, and then there had been Kalak. Both had been enough to put her out for a week. Even in the noisy, filthy room she shared with the Naren women, sleep came easily. But when she had finally awakened she was still in Ackle-Nye, and what Kalak had done to her was still sore in her mind and between her legs. She awoke staring into Tendrik's sweaty face. The innkeeper had shaken her. She remembered hearing her name called as if from a great distance. In slumber she had thought it was her father's voice, but now Dyana recognized her captor.

"Wake up," said the grubby man. "It's night. I need you."

Dyana sat up. The satiny green dress was still wrapped around her. "Night?" She glanced toward the window, and saw that it was indeed dark. A solitary star twinkled on the horizon.

"I am not ready," she said, hoping to stall the inevitable. "I am not clean and I have nothing to wear." She realized suddenly that she was alone. "Where are the others? Working already?"

Tendrik showed her his stained teeth. "No, not exactly. I sent them away. They'll be working elsewhere tonight."

"Away?" asked Dyana suspiciously. "Away where?"

"Don't worry, I'm not sending you away. I've got a special customer for you tonight." The innkeeper's face grew dark. She knew what he was about to say.

"No!" she railed. "I will not! Do not think it!"

"Girl . . ."

"I will not be his again!" she cried, jumping out of the bed and stalking toward him. "You cannot make me!"

Tendrik put up his hands to calm her. "Easy. Let me explain. It's not what you think. You're right, it is Vantran. He wants to see you again. But he doesn't want you to sleep with him. He just wants to talk."

"Talk? I have nothing to say to him. I said it all this morning."

Tendrik got off the bed and came close to her. He could be quite menacing when he wanted to be. "You're not listening. He went through a lot of trouble to see you again. He's even set up a sort of surprise for you. I can't tell you what, but believe me, it's something you'll like. And he promised me he wouldn't touch you. He wanted me to tell you that."

"I do not believe it," spat Dyana. "Kalak is a beast. He lies."

"It's not a lie," said Tendrik. They were face to face now, and his breath was hot against her cheeks. "I know. I saw him. You're making too much out of this. He's a whelp, a boy. There's nothing for you to be afraid of."

"I will not do it."

"Yes you will." Tendrik seized her wrists and pinned her hands up against the wall. Dyana beat at him, but so much fat bearing down on her thin wrists threatened to crack them. She turned her face away as he whispered his familiar threat into her ear.

"In three days' time I am leaving for Talistan. Carlina and the others are going with me. If you want to be with us, you will do as I tell you. If not, I will be more than glad to leave you here for the Drol to find. And the Drol don't much like Triin whores."

Dyana cringed, wanting to argue but knowing the man was right. He owned her now. He was her only passage to Nar. Still, she had to try.

"Offer him another girl. Give him that wretch Carlina."

"Don't ask me what he sees in you, little one. I saw that mark you gave him. If I were him, I would buy a night just to beat you. But he won't do that because he's soft. And for some reason he's taken with you, enough to pay all our passage back through the Run. I'm not giving it back, girl. I'd kill you first."

"Let me go," commanded Dyana. "Now."

"Will you go to him?" asked Tendrik, pressing down harder.

"Yes!" Dyana cried. He was crushing her. "I will! Let me go!"

He finally released her and she fell forward, panting. Two stout red marks circled her wrists. She rubbed at them distractedly.

"Where is he?"

"Downstairs. He wants to see you in an hour."

"I have nothing to wear." Dyana pulled at her dirty dress. "This will have to be good enough for him."

"Pretty yourself up!" the innkeeper rumbled. "He's not paying for a night with a kitchen wench. Borrow a dress from one of the others, something clean. And brush your hair. It looks like a rat's nest!"

He stomped out of the room and slammed the door behind him. Dyana picked up a shoe and hurled it against the door.

The sun was down, the stars were up, and Tendrik's dirty little beer hall had been turned into the perfect romantic venue. Richius lifted his glass and tested the wine. It was a strong red from the south of Gorkney, and he smiled to himself as he tasted it. The little table in the corner of the room had been set with Tendrik's own stoneware, a collection the innkeeper proudly explained had been "acquired" from a Naren nobleman who had traveled to Ackle-Nye and developed a nasty lung infection on the way. The infection had killed him, and Tendrik had done the rest. Richius guessed that the ornate candlesticks were also the nobleman's, since they bore the crest of Criisia, a minor but wealthy province of the Empire. There was fine flatware on the table, too, and the crystal goblets were worthy of any royal banquet. Richius grinned as he inspected the table. Tendrik was unbearable, but he was certainly resourceful. He was sure Dyana would be impressed.

It had cost Richius more than just Dinadin's dagger to make the arrangements. He wanted the place to himself for the night, and that meant a severe loss of business for the innkeeper, a fact that could only be corrected by Richius' emptying his pockets and providing the innkeeper with a note. Actually more like a bill, one he could present to the king of Aramoor upon his safe passage through the Run. Richius knew his father wouldn't be pleased, but he also knew he would pay the innkeeper. And if it was an annoyance to the old man, well, to Richius that was just an added benefit.

Now only he and the lute player occupied the room. The musician, a Naren vagabond with an overly friendly smile, had agreed to play for them. His name was Po, and his services had come much cheaper than the food. As Richius sat back, anxiously waiting for Dyana, Po plucked absently at the strings of his instrument.

"So who is she?" the musician asked. He leaned back on his seat, his long legs propped comfortably on another chair. "Some sort of princess?"

"No, not a princess," said Richius. "Just a girl."

"Oh, not just a girl! Not for all this trouble." Po leaned in closer and winked. "She must really be something, eh?"

"Yes, she is. But do me a favor, Po. You're going to notice when she comes down that I think a lot more of her than she does of me. Just ignore it, all right?"

"Lovers' spat, huh?"

"Not exactly."

Po took the evasive hint and nodded. "Not a problem. You won't even know I'm here." He went back to playing his lute, stroking a soft and easy melody from the strings. Richius leaned back to listen. He heard a sound and thought for a moment it was Dyana, but it was only the serving boy returning from the kitchen. When he noticed Richius was alone he stopped halfway to the table.

"She's not here yet?" asked the boy awkwardly. "Your pheasant . . ."

"It's all right," said Richius, waving the boy closer. "Just leave them on the table. She'll be down soon."

The boy did as Richius bade, taking the time to breathe deep of the sweet odor of the roasted birds. An excited giddiness rippled through

Richius. She *would* be impressed, he was sure of it. Po took a glance at the plates, too, and his smile widened.

"Nice," he commented. "Where did you find those?"

"Tendrik," said Richius. The answer made the musician laugh.

"That explains it. That man could find a baked ham in the middle of a desert. But I don't know about that wine. Are you sure it goes?"

"It's fine."

Po shrugged, then added, "You should think of a white."

"It's fine!" said Richius. "Come on, fellow. Can't you see I'm nervous? Just play."

"It's going to get cold," said the boy.

Richius sighed. "So what if it does? The last fresh meal she had was probably still moving. You think she's going to mind cold pheasant?"

"I could take it back to the kitchen. . . ."

"It's not necessary. Please, just be quiet. All right?"

The serving boy started to apologize, but Richius ignored him. Over the boy's shoulder he could see Dyana descending the stairway. A quiver of anticipation moved through him as he rose to greet her. She was splendid. Her white face was colored lightly by a dusting of makeup across her cheeks, a mellow pink that complemented the dazzling scarlet of her dress. There was a resentment in her eyes that made them sparkle. She moved like a wraith down the staircase, soundless, and she did not look at him until she reached the lower level. Richius heard Po give a small, impressed whistle. The lute player's smile was as wide as his face.

Dyana wore no such smile, and her face held no exuberance. She looked defiant. Cold and unapproachable, she raised her eyes to look at him. And when she saw the splendid table he had set for her, an expression of utter shock passed over her.

"Hello," said Richius, offering his hand. "Thank you for coming."

The music, the smell of the pheasants and the candle wax; all of it rushed at her senses just as he knew it would. She stood dumbfounded, spying the servant boy waiting to push her chair in, and what looked almost like a smile passed her lips.

"What is this?" she asked. She did not take Richius' hand, but she did not pull away from him, either. Richius took a breath.

"This is an apology," he replied.

"It will take more than all this to make up for what you have done, Kalak. I am only here because Tendrik said I must. He said you want to speak to me. Why?"

"We can talk about that," said Richius easily. He gestured toward the table and the serving boy waiting to seat her. "Will you sit with me?"

Without a word she went to the table. She saw the exquisite food and her mouth twisted hungrily. Richius tried to hide his smile. It was like setting an elaborate trap. He would have to speak like an angel and move like a serpent. Dyana's eyes flicked up to him as he took his own seat. He could almost hear her stomach rumbling over the lute. Then the girl's expression hardened, and she pushed the dish away.

"I am not hungry," she declared.

A lie, Richius knew. He feigned agreement. "No? Me, either. I really just wanted to talk to you. We don't have to eat all this."

Dyana's face fell. "This is a bribe. You should know I cannot be bought like this. I may be a whore, but I am not a fool."

"I don't like that word," said Richius. "Don't call yourself that."

For a moment it seemed she would get up and leave. She looked down at the table and let out a sigh. "Why am I here?" she asked. "Tendrik told you I will not go to your bed again, yes?"

"He told me," replied Richius. "That's not why I wanted to see you."

"Why then?"

"To talk. To tell you how sorry I am for what I did." He touched his face to remind himself of the stinging bruise she had given him. "This morning, when you ran from me, I told you I was sorry for taking your maidenhood. I was wrong to abuse you so. But I truly didn't know. I swear to you, if I had I would never have done it."

"Then it would have been someone else," she said simply.

"Why?" asked Richius. "Why are you even here?"

"You ask too many questions," said the girl sharply.

Richius shrugged. "I'm curious about you. I want to know why you hate me so much. You call me a jackal but you don't know me. I'm not your enemy."

"You *are*," she corrected harshly. "You destroy. I knew people in that village. Now some of them are dead. Your men killed them. This is why I hate you. This is why you are Kalak."

"You have me wrong. Those weren't my men who burned that village. And it wasn't my order. No one from my company would ever hurt you or your people."

"I saw you there," countered the girl. "And Kalak is the supreme Naren in Dring. Even the Drol say that."

"But it wasn't me," insisted Richius. "I was the one that stopped the burning. I saved you from that brute, remember? He's the one you should hate, not me."

"You kill Triin. I know you do."

"I kill Drol," said Richius. "I'm not proud of it, but I kill people who are trying to kill me. Don't think I enjoy it. Whatever your people say about me, they're wrong to think I'm a butcher. I'm not." The thought of Dinadin ripened in his mind and his smile melted away. "I'm just stuck here."

The girl stared at him skeptically. "You have made your apology. Can I go now?"

Richius didn't know how to answer. Finally he nodded and said, "Yes, if you want. But I wish you wouldn't. I would rather not be alone tonight."

There was a definite softening in her harshness. She looked down at her food, then back up at Richius.

"We don't have to talk if you don't want to," said Richius hopefully. He felt on the verge of tears, but he didn't know why. "We don't have to do anything, just listen to the music."

The girl's face was miserable. "I am hungry."

Richius looked at her. "Me, too."

It was all the encouragement she needed. She pulled back her plate, then waited for Richius to do the same before picking up her fork and tearing off a piece of pheasant. Together they tasted the poultry, perfectly prepared by Tendrik's woman in the kitchen. The girl's eyes glazed with satisfaction. Food was painfully scarce in Ackle-Nye, and she was so thin. Richius had known the symptoms of hunger too well not to be able to recognize them. Dinadin had been right. He did want to rescue her.

Not far from the table, Po strummed his lute, playing a soft ballad. He tossed Richius an encouraging wink.

They ate in silence, and Richius was content just to have her close. Then suddenly she stopped eating. She lowered her fork to the table and looked up at him. He was sipping his wine and noticed her staring at him through the bottom of the glass.

"What's wrong?" he asked.

"You are right," she said. "You did save me. I know that." She seemed to be struggling as she added, "Thank you."

"You're welcome. And thank you for staying with me. I meant what I said. I won't hurt you anymore. If I hurt you last night, well . . . As I said, I'm sorry."

"It only hurt a little. I am better now."

"Would you like some wine?" Richius asked, to keep her talking. "It's a good one."

Her defenses rose up instantly. "No. No drink."

"Tendrik told me your name is Dyana. That's a very pretty name. Where I come from lots of women are called that. Is it a Triin name, too?"

"My father named me," said Dyana, and didn't elaborate.

"You told me you arrived in Ackle-Nye yesterday. Did you come from Dring?"

Her lips twitched evasively. "Yes, from Dring."

"Why? Was the village badly damaged?"

Suddenly the misery on her face changed to a hard anger. She got up from the table. "I have to go."

"Wait," Richius cried, jumping up after her. "Don't go, please."

"I must." The girl was almost at the stairs when Richius caught up with her. She turned on him, her eyes wild. "Do not follow me. Leave me alone. I cannot be with you."

"I don't want to hurt you, I swear. I don't want anything from you tonight. Just some company."

There was something in his words that stopped her from retreating. Maybe it was the aching loneliness in his voice, or maybe it was simply the allure of the food. Richius didn't know why, but when he opened his eyes again she was still standing before him.

"My cousin was in that village. My little cousin, just a baby." She wrapped her arms about her shoulders. "She is dead."

And in that instant Richius understood all the venom she had dealt him. He felt filthy, dirtier than the lowest dog. The music stopped. Dyana stood there, smoldering. Richius moved toward her and reached out a hand, barely grazing her naked arm.

"I'm sorry," he said weakly.

"She was trampled," Dyana went on. She looked away. "Just a baby . . ."

"Dyana, I swear to God it wasn't me. I grieve for you but it wasn't me. Blame the Talistanians. They're butchers, and they're nothing like my people from Aramoor. You have to believe me."

"I do. But I still must go. I have said too much already."

"Don't. I want to help you. It doesn't have to be this way for you."

She shook her head and said, "It will not be for long. Tendrik will look after me."

"Tendrik?" asked Richius. An ugly idea was occurring to him. "What do you mean?"

"It is my business, Kalak. Do not ask me of it."

"I'm not Kalak," he growled. "Don't ever call me that. I'm Richius Vantran. Call me Vantran or Prince, I don't care. But don't call me a jackal."

She bit her lip. "I do not know what to call you. To me you are Kalak."

"Call me Richius. That's my name."

"I cannot."

"The innkeeper. What do you mean, he looks after you?"

"Please," she implored. "If I am wrong about you, I am sorry. But let me go now. I have nothing for you."

"I can't do that. I can't let you go until you tell me what hold Tendrik has over you. I know merchants like him. And I bet I know what he's got planned for you. If you think you're going to escape the war or hunger or anything else by working for him, you're wrong. You'll be nothing but a slave, especially if he takes you back to the Empire. Is that it? Is that what he's promised you?"

"You do not understand. I must go with him."

"Where's he going to take you?" pressured Richius. "The Black City?"

"No," she said simply. "Talistan."

Richius started, struck by her terrible innocence. She might speak the tongue of Nar, but it was clear she had never been anywhere in the Empire, especially not to Talistan. No woman, no matter how desperate, would agree to such a fate.

"Dyana, come back to the table. We have all night, and I really have to talk to you." He held out his hand. She regarded it suspiciously. "Trust me."

Amazingly, she took his hand. He led her back to her seat and sat her down, gestured for Po to continue playing, then took his seat.

"You said you have to go with him. Why? Because of the war? If so then you should stay in Lucel-Lor. From what I've seen lately, the war is almost over anyway. Going to Talistan would be worse for you than living under Tharn, I'm sure."

"You are wrong about that," said Dyana. "Very wrong."

"No," continued Richius. "*You* are wrong if you think your life would be better in Talistan. I know Talistan, Dyana. You would regret that the rest of your life. Triin have no rights there."

"But women have rights there," said Dyana. "My father told me so."

"Your father was wrong. I'm sure he didn't mean Talistan when he spoke of Nar. In some parts of the Empire women are treated no better than here in Lucel-Lor. And Talistan's the worst of them. You would be Tendrik's property if you went with him. He'd sell you to every man with a gold coin."

"That's not true," she protested. He could see her frustration welling up. "Do not say so. My father would never have lied to me. Tendrik will let me go when we get to Talistan. He promised he would."

"Sometimes fathers don't know everything. Believe me, I know. If you go to Talistan you'll be this cretin's slave forever. He'll never let you leave, because he won't have to. Do you really think that's better than staying here?"

"I have no life here!" she flared. "You do not know me. You do not know why I am here, why I have done this to myself."

"You'd better tell me, then. Because I can think of no reason worth your taking this innkeeper's offer. What's in Talistan that's so important?"

"It is what is *not* in Talistan that is important."

"Oh? And what's that?"

"Tharn."

"Tharn?" repeated Richius. "I don't understand. Why should you be afraid of him?"

She looked at him, her eyes filled with despair. "Let me go. You are not Triin. You cannot know what I have been through, and I cannot explain it to you."

"Try, at least."

She shook her head. "No."

"I can't let you leave until you do," said Richius firmly. "I know it doesn't make much sense to you, but I can't."

The girl shut her eyes. "It is difficult. So much has happened to me, so much . . ."

"If I'm going to help you, you'll have to try and trust me."

"Help me?" asked the girl. "Why should you do that? You have already gotten what you want from me."

The words stung but Richius tried not to show it. "Please," he coaxed. "It's not as hard as you think. Why don't you tell me about your name again? Why did your father give you a Naren name?"

The woman's lips twisted in hesitation, and it seemed to Richius she was considering his inquiry with unnecessary care. Finally she answered, "My father believed Nar and Lucel-Lor would be allies one day. He gave all his children names that would be acceptable in the Empire, so we could live among them and not be different."

"Really? Then he was a supporter of the Daegog." Richius chuckled. "You see? You and I aren't so different. Where's your father now?"

"Dead."

Richius' smile vanished. "I'm sorry."

"Do not be. It was Tharn who killed my father, not Narens."

"Is that why you want to leave?" asked Richius. "Because you're afraid of Tharn?"

"I have been on the run from him since the revolution started. That is when he killed my father. You know about the Drol, yes?"

"Not a lot. I know they're zealots. And I know they hate Nar and the Daegog. That's why they fight, to rid Lucel-Lor of Naren influence."

"You are mostly right. The Drol are zealots. And anyone who disagrees with them is their enemy. My father was loyal to the Daegog. He helped the Daegog open up our country to your Empire."

"And for that Tharn killed him?"

"There is more," said Dyana gravely. "My father was a very powerful man. So too was Tharn's father. We were both very young when our parents pledged us to each other."

"Your father betrothed you to Tharn? How could he do that?"

Dyana shrugged. "As I said, it was long ago. No one knew what Tharn would become. He was not Drol then. My father thought he was making a good marriage for me. He thought Tharn would be a leader someday, someone who could help Nar and Lucel-Lor come together. But later, when the revolution started, my father stayed loyal to the Daegog. He and Tharn became enemies. That is when he broke his pledge to give me to Tharn."

"And that's when Tharn murdered your father."

Dyana nodded. "I have been running from him ever since. He still believes my father's vow binds me to him. If he finds me, he will kill me or force me to marry him. Now do you see why I must get to Nar? I have heard that the Daegog has already fallen. If that is true then Tharn will rule Lucel-Lor. There will be nowhere here for me to hide." She looked down at herself, at her scantily covered legs, and a shadow of disgust passed over her face. "I have not done this to myself because I am hungry or afraid. I am still Triin. But I have no other way to escape him."

"But why are you alone? Don't you have any other family? What about your mother?"

"My mother left my father years ago. She was devout. She believed like the Drol that Nar was evil. One day I woke up and she was gone. I have three sisters that she took with her. I have not seen any of them since." Her expression soured more. "They might be dead, or they might be living among the Drol now, I do not know. But they will not help. And I do not want their help. Only Tendrik can save me."

"No," said Richius. "I have something better for you." He held up his hand, pulled off his ring, and showed it to Dyana. She eyed it curiously.

"What is it?"

"This ring bears the crest of the House of Vantran," he said proudly. "The Vantrans are the rulers of Aramoor. I'm a Vantran."

Dyana was unimpressed. "So?"

Richius reached for her hand. To his surprise she didn't pull away, but let him place the ring in her palm. "My father is the king of Aramoor. If you show him this ring, he'll know I've sent you to him." He gave her hand a gentle squeeze. "There are men from Aramoor camped just outside the city, friends of mine. They'll be going home soon. I can bring you to them. They'll take you back to Aramoor, protect you on the journey. You'll be safe in my homeland, Dyana. Far safer than you would ever be in Talistan."

Dyana's gray eyes slanted with suspicion. "Why would you do this for me? You don't even know me."

"I know you're alone," said Richius. "I know you need my help."

And I know you're beautiful, he added silently. She was staring at him, looking at him with her astonishing gray eyes, and the same fire that had seized him the night before flared up again. He had felt it when he'd rescued her from Gayle, and again when he saw her in the tavern. Somehow he knew he would never be the same again. And the thought of her leaving the room was unbearable.

"You could go to Aramoor and start a new life there," he said. "Someplace Tharn would never find you."

Dyana's hand closed tightly around the ring. "Aramoor," she echoed. "I do not know that place."

"You don't know Talistan, either," said Richius. "But believe me, mine's the better choice."

"Are you going there, too?"

"No," said Richius sadly. "I can't. I still have men in the valley who need me."

Dyana frowned.

"Don't worry," he assured her. "I'll return home when I can."

"If you can," she corrected. "You are going back to Dring, yes?"

"Yes."

"Then you may not return. I know of the war there. It is not safe for you. You should leave with your friends."

"I wish I could," said Richius. "It's too much to explain, but there are reasons I can't go home yet. But you'll see me again."

"And what will become of me in Aramoor?"

"My father will look after you, if you wish it. I admit there's little else for you there, but at least you'll be safe and no one will make demands on you." He looked at her, suddenly understanding the fear she was voicing. "You won't be a slave, Dyana. Not mine or anyone else's. Trust me, please."

"I want to," she said with a hesitant smile. "And it is like my father told me there? Women are free in Aramoor?"

"In Aramoor, yes. But not everywhere in Nar. Your father was both right and wrong about the Empire. There are beautiful places, but there are places you must stay away from. If you ever leave Aramoor, you could be in danger. Triin are not welcome everywhere."

Dyana seemed stunned by this. "No? But your emperor helps the Daegog. He sent you all here. Father told me he was good."

"Your father meant well, but there was a lot about Nar he didn't know. It's true that we of Aramoor are here to help the Daegog, but I think the emperor wants something more from your people, Dyana. He can be a devil."

"You confuse me," said Dyana. "You speak like a Drol now. Do you say Tharn is right?"

"Never," said Richius adamantly. "Tharn is also a devil, to be sure. It's just that the world outside of Lucel-Lor may not be what you expect. Nar can be difficult. But life in Aramoor is good. You'll be safe there. And happy, I hope."

"Then I want to go to Aramoor," declared Dyana. "You are not like Tendrik. I . . . I will trust you."

Richius had an overwhelming urge to touch her, but he fought the impulse. Instead he watched Dyana examine the ring. Even in the weak light it twinkled, and he could tell she was enthralled by it. Small wonder, he thought. That ring was her passage to freedom.

"I will take you to Edgard in the morning," said Richius. "He'll probably be leaving for Aramoor soon."

Dyana frowned. "What will I tell Tendrik?"

"Don't tell him anything. He's already been well paid for you, Dyana. I don't think he would dare come after you. Now, you should finish your dinner. And when you're done we can go upstairs."

"Upstairs? Why?"

"Just to talk," he assured her. "And so you can get a good night's sleep. You'll need it. It's a long way through the Run."

"But there is only one bed," she protested. "A small one."

"There's also a chair," said Richius. "I'll sit there all night and watch over you."

Dyana laughed, and the sound of it was musical. "You are a strange man, Richius Vantran."

ELEVEN

"I'm not a coward, Edgard," said Dinadin thickly. "I never have been."

He looked at the old man's face, scarred now from the things he had seen, and remembered a time when the war duke of Aramoor was vital and invincible. Dinadin and Richius had both been boys then, playing around Edgard's legs and dreaming of the day they could be like him. But he had changed. They had all changed, because war had a way of destroying more than just bodies and buildings. War made men ugly and atrophied courage. War could turn friends into enemies.

Edgard leaned back on his chair and held his glass under his chin. Outside his tent, the camp had quieted to a breezy murmur. It would be dawn soon, but the moon still hung in the sky and shone through the threadbare fabric of the pavilion. The beams mingled with the orange torchlight, making the wine look black and Edgard's visage ancient. Dinadin had drained his glass more times than he could count, and his head swam on his shoulders. But the last decanter was empty, and all that was left of the stuff was the few mouthfuls still left in Edgard's goblet.

"I know you're not a coward," said Edgard. "It takes a brave pair to do what we're doing."

"Then why do I feel like one?" asked Dinadin. "I know it's the right thing to do. The war in Dring is lost, surely. We would be fools to stay. Richius is a fool to stay."

"We've been through this," Edgard said. "You're abandoning a friend.

That's never easy. I left Kronin at Mount Godon. And I regret that. But it had to be that way. Blackwood Gayle couldn't see it, and neither can Richius. But that doesn't make Richius a fool, Dinadin. Be careful."

"I'm sorry," replied Dinadin sadly. "I shouldn't have said that."

He got up from his seat and strode over to the tent flap. Pulling it aside, he peered out into the darkness. The night was cool on his face and the fresh air felt good. A million stars burned in the sky. Off in the distance, the city of beggars was asleep, a graveyard of neglected buildings, while throughout the camp Edgard's exhausted horsemen slumbered on bulging saddlebags and mumbled to themselves as they dreamed dark dreams.

Exhausted and a little drunk, Dinadin's mind began to wander. He thought of his father and of Alain, his little brother, both back at home and wondering what had become of him. His father had warned him about the Triin, that they were inscrutable devils who deserved to be shunned by the Empire, and who would very likely bring even Arkus to ruin. This was a place of magic and evil, his father had claimed, and as Dinadin traced his gaze over the horizon he puzzled over those words and over his place in the emperor's scheme. When he was a boy, he had been fascinated by this land of mystery. He had thought that one day he and Richius would come here together as adventurers or fortune-seekers, and learn its sorcery for themselves. But he was older now, and no longer saw magic here, only blackness and death. In an odd sense, his father had been right about the Triin. This whole bloody business had been ruinous.

"I'm tired," Dinadin said, mostly to himself. "I'm going now."

"Get some rest," said Edgard. He stretched his neck with a popping sound. "I think I should do the same."

"Good night, Edgard," said Dinadin, but before he could leave the duke called after him.

"Dinadin, wait."

"Yes?"

"I've known you a long time," said the old man. "And I've known your family. There's not a coward among you."

Dinadin forced a smile. "Thanks," he said weakly, then turned and left the tent.

He wandered through the camp, tiptoeing past the sleeping men and the sentries posted haphazardly on the grounds. He was hungry, and the lack of food had caused the wine to ricochet straight into his brain so that he tottered a bit as he walked. A cold breeze stirred through the camp, making him shiver, and he suddenly realized he had nowhere to go. All that he had was his horse, so he headed toward the makeshift stable. There, across the camp, he found the tending boy asleep against a crate full of feed. There were blankets and bridles strewn about, making it easy to trip, so he walked as carefully as his wine-soaked brain would allow.

His horse was there, droopy-eyed and waiting for him. He passed the boy soundlessly and undid the horse's reins.

"Hello, my friend," he whispered into the gelding's ear. The horse perked up at the sound of his voice, cheering Dinadin a bit. The House of Lotts were the finest horse breeders in Aramoor, perhaps the finest in all of northern Nar. It would be good to be home again, if only to see the rolling hills of his father's estate. There would be a banquet when he came home; his father had promised him that when he left. His brothers would be there, and his mother would cook for them and invite all their relatives and friends.

Dinadin's mood abruptly shattered. Not all his friends would be there. Some were dead. Others were still in Dring. And of course Richius couldn't attend. It occurred to him suddenly that he might never see that particular friend again. They would never again ride through Aramoor's exquisite forests or argue about horses. There would be no more hunting, no more roasting the venison they had caught. Aramoor wouldn't be the same without Richius. It wouldn't really be home at all.

"Oh, God," he groaned softly. "What shall I do?"

Dinadin led the horse out of the stable. There was no saddle on the beast but the rest of the tack was in place, and as he passed by the sleeping stableboy he stole a dingy blanket from the ground and draped it over the horse's back. He could ride bareback for a time, just long enough to get some air and think. He wanted to get away from the stink of the camp, to be alone with the dying moonlight before he left the horrid place forever. So he mounted his horse and rode, heading south toward the Sheaze River, and the horse quickly broke into a gallop, letting the camp drop away behind them.

Soon the ebbing night enveloped them, and all the majesty of heaven broke out above them. Dinadin slowed the horse to a trot. He gazed up at the roof of the world, feeling dwarfed by its vastness. The stars were brilliant here, floating magically like distant fireflies. Crimson splashes speckled the east, heralding the coming dawn. Dinadin felt weightless, bodiless. Free at last. He thought of heading west without Edgard, of going through the Run without the old duke and his wretched brigade. He didn't want to wait, he wanted to see his family now.

"I'm alive!" he shouted to the endless sky, and laughed. He loved Richius but he loved life more, and now that it was his again he would never give it up. Let Arkus come for him, he would be ready. The emperor would have to find him first.

For long moments he sat there atop his silent steed, all alone in the universe. He wasn't a coward. He knew he'd done his best. It just wasn't his war anymore.

"We're going home," he said to the horse. "When we get there we're going to ride and be free and—"

A burst of lightning froze his words. He scanned the horizon; the sun was coming up. There was another blast, silent but shocking, a blue flash that lit up the sky. He squinted into the burning crimson at the world's edge, and saw what looked like a purple mist crawling out of the east.

"Lord Almighty," he whispered, and a memory came slamming back into his mind. Dinadin spun his horse around and kicked his heels into the beast's side. He didn't head for the camp of the Dragon Flag, but instead flew westward, toward the city of beggars and Richius.

At dawn, Richius' eyes popped open. His back ached from sleeping in the chair, but when he saw Dyana still asleep in the bed, resting like a beautiful child, the pain in his body melted away. The room's ratty curtains were drawn, but she was no less lovely in the darkness. And she had not left him, but had stayed safe under his watchful gaze.

True to his word, he had not touched her. He hadn't even given into the impulse to brush by her. Her trust in him was tenuous, and he knew the slightest violation would destroy it forever. So they had retired to his room and simply talked, and it was the most romantic evening of Richius' life. She told him more about her father, and how he had taught her to speak Naren. In return he told her how his own father had abandoned him in Lucel-Lor.

Not long past midnight she had drifted off to sleep, just as Richius was telling her about Dinadin. Since it was not a particularly comfortable subject, it hadn't bothered him to lose his audience. Dyana slept peacefully, except for a brief, episodic nightmare that made her cry out. But the nightmare had been blessedly brief, and Dyana had quickly fallen back into a deep slumber. Richius, exhausted himself, found the little chair suitable enough for a doze. It had taken him hours to stop looking at her, but when he finally did, he slept, and had only awakened when the first rays of ragged sunlight wandered into their little hideaway.

My father will love her, he thought. *He'll look after her, and she'll be happy there.*

Happy and safe. It was all he wanted for her. She was the one thing here he could do right, the one person he could save. Jimsin and Lonal and all the others had died on his watch. But not her. In time, she might even love him, but that was hoping too much. He still had a war to fight, and if he came back at all he might be maimed like Edgard, or mad like Blackwood Gayle. If he wasn't careful, the war would smother what was left of his humanity.

He yawned, louder than he wanted to, and the sound of it awakened her. Her gray eyes opened.

"Morning," he said cheerfully. It was her turn to yawn.

"Is it?" she asked. "The night went fast. Did you sleep?"

"A bit."

Dyana sat up and swung her legs over the side of the bed. Her dress had hiked up during the night. Richius politely looked away.

"I'll take you to Edgard today," he said. "This morning, after we eat something. Do you think Tendrik has anything for breakfast?"

Before she could answer, there was a wild thundering at the door. They both jumped at the sound. Richius spied his sword and belt under the bed. He was halfway to it when he heard Dinadin's familiar voice.

"Richius! Are you in there?"

"Who is that?" asked Dyana. Richius laughed.

"Don't worry. That's Dinadin!"

"Richius, open up!" Dinadin clamored. He tried the knob, but the door was locked. He started pounding on the door. Richius hurried to the door and undid the latch. When he opened it Dinadin stumbled into the chamber. He was sweating profusely and reeked of liquor. Richius put a hand to his nose.

"Lord, Dinadin," he exclaimed. "What's wrong?"

Dinadin paid Dyana no attention, but doubled over, panting and pointing toward the window. "Outside," he wheezed. "Haven't you seen?"

"Seen what?" asked Richius.

Dinadin rushed to the window and pulled aside the ragged curtain. "Look!"

Outside, dawn had darkened into dusk. No more strands of sunlight seeped through the filthy glass. A canopy of sable clouds hung over the earth, smothering the morning and the rising sun. Confused, Richius went to the window and looked down at the outskirts of the city. In the streets below he saw Triin beggars looking skyward.

A massive thunderhead, larger than any he had ever seen, was crawling over the eastern horizon, rolling toward them on a churning fog, obscuring the whole of the landscape beyond. The storm cloud towered to the heavens, reaching into the dark sky as it spewed upward in a fountain of purple vapor. Bursts of electric-blue lightning snaked around its anvil-shaped crown, and all through the living body of the thing blasts of hazy, orange fire erupted. It boiled and exploded as it slid closer to the city, pulsing with a strange, unearthly aura. The dull roar of thunder made the panes in the window tremble.

"My God," he exclaimed, backing up from the window for Dinadin and Dyana to see. "What is *that*?"

Dyana raced to the window, pressing her cheek against the glass as she strained to look eastward. She paled when she saw the cloud and backed away from the window. Richius caught her just as she collided with him.

"Dyana?"

"I dreamt of this," she said. "Last night, I dreamt of this. It is Tharn."

"Tharn? Dyana—"

"He spoke to me in the dream," Dyana went on. "I remember it now. He said he was coming for me."

Richius felt a stab of terror. All at once, all the unbelievable things Edgard had told him about their enemy rushed back into his memory. Shocked, he peered back out the window. Surely what they were seeing could be nothing more than a storm cloud. There was simply no other reasonable explanation for it.

"How can it be? No one can conjure the weather. It's impossible."

"It is Tharn," insisted Dyana. "He is coming for me!"

"Be still," said Richius. "No one's going to harm you, I promise. I won't let them."

"It's like Edgard told us, Richius," said Dinadin. "Just like he said! It's Tharn."

"It's not Tharn!" roared Richius. "I don't know what it is, but it's not Tharn."

Dinadin stepped up to Richius, his expression furious. "Get your things together. We have to get out of here, leave the city before the storm comes."

"We'll head for the Run," agreed Richius. "There are caverns in the mountains that will shelter us. Dinadin, hurry downstairs and get our horses. Mine should be there waiting with the Triin boy. We have to move quickly."

"What about Edgard?"

"Don't worry about him. I'm sure he's already seen that thing coming. He'll know enough to ride for the Run, too. Hurry now!"

Without another word Dinadin bolted out of the room, and soon Richius could hear his heavy boots hammering against the stairs. Outside the sky continued to darken. Richius released Dyana and picked his boots off the floor.

"Come on, Dyana," he said as he slid his feet into his boots. "If we hurry we'll be able to beat the storm to the mountains. We can wait it out there until . . ."

Richius turned to see Dyana frozen in place, staring out the window in disbelief.

"It is too late," said Dyana bitterly. "Lorris and Pris, that bastard has found me."

Richius snatched her hand and pulled her to the doorway. "Come on!"

He dragged her out into the hall. "I won't argue with you," he said as he raced down the steps. "I told you, I'm not going to let anything happen to you."

"Richius, stop," said Dyana. She had paused halfway down the stair-case and would not follow him further. "It is Drol magic! He is using it to look for me. I cannot get away. You must leave me or he will kill you, too!"

Richius looked at her hard. "Dyana, stop this rubbish. You've run this far. So keep on running. Don't let this bastard get you."

Dyana gritted her teeth, and her eyes flared with new determination.

At the bottom of the stairs they found the tavern empty. Even Tendrik was gone. The door to the place was flung open and a stiff wind was blowing in. Outside they could hear the roar of the approaching storm and the voices of those gathered in the streets to watch it.

"Listen to me now," said Richius. "The place I know of in the mountains will keep us safe until the storm passes. It's well hidden and no one will find us there. Not even Tharn. But we have to move fast."

Before she could answer Dinadin ran into the tavern. "The horses are ready."

"Let's go," said Richius, coaxing Dyana toward the door. Outside he saw the two horses waiting. Dinadin was already climbing on his horse.

"The storm's getting closer," said Dinadin. "We have to leave now."

Richius nodded. He could see the gray-black crown of the thunderhead over the roofs of Ackle-Nye. The thing was already much closer than it had been a minute ago, and fog was just beginning to roll through the streets. He could feel the cobblestones beneath him vibrating with the storm's extraordinary power. Beside him, Dyana watched as the storm extended its reach over the city. Gently, Richius' hands encircled her waist.

"Don't worry," he said. "We'll be able to outrun it with these horses." Richius tossed himself onto the horse and took hold of the reins. "Come on," he ordered, stretching out a hand for Dyana. She took his hand and swung herself onto the beast's back. Dyana's arms closed about Richius' waist. The horse came to attention immediately, snorting and eager to be commanded. In a moment they were off, racing through the narrow streets of Ackle-Nye, the hooves of their mounts echoing off the ancient stonework. They rode past throngs of worried merchants and Triin beggars, all with their eyes fixed on the mysterious giant rolling out of the east. But Richius did not look back as they galloped westward. They were already on the outskirts of the city. It would take them only minutes to reach the Run and the safety of the Iron Mountains. No storm, magicborn or otherwise, could move as quickly as they were.

Soon they came to where the streets of the city ended. They could see the mountains clearly now, unobstructed by the looming towers of Ackle-Nye. Richius grinned. They had only to cross the bridge over the Sheaze before they reached the Saccenne Run.

"Richius!" cried Dinadin suddenly. "Edgard's camp!"

Richius glanced over his left shoulder. He could see the war duke's encampment far off in the distance. Unlike before, however, he could only see it through a haze. The fog of the coming storm had enshrouded the camp in a glistening mist. Though he thought he saw movement in the fog, Richius knew with sudden alarm that Edgard's men were trapped.

"My God!" he exclaimed, reining his horse to a stop. "What's happening?"

Dinadin brought his horse to a stop beside Richius. All through the camp the lights of unnatural fires twinkled in the fog. Men and horses darted through the mist, scrambling aimlessly under the shadow of the looming thunderhead. The whole of the cloud was visible now, and its anvil-like crown seemed to swell and darken as it rolled on legs of smoke toward the camp of the war duke.

"What should we do?" asked Dinadin anxiously.

Richius bit his lip. A sickening feeling of impotence seized him. "There's nothing we can do."

"But Edgard—"

"I know!" cried Richius. "God help them."

The storm was just above the camp. The glowing fog thickened, obscuring the camp behind a vaporous curtain. Richius ignored Dyana's insistent tugging at his shirt, ignored too the fog that was creeping over the grasses toward them. He was frozen, torn between fleeing and rushing headlong into a vain attempt to rescue his countrymen. Yet in his heart he knew the doom that faced them. So he stayed, refusing to turn his back on them, and watched as the sky cracked like an eggshell.

A sound like a thousand detonating flame cannons ruptured the air. Fingers of blue lightning discharged from the thunderhead's crown, exploding into the camp and sending clumps of earth and shards of wood and fabric shooting skyward. Dyana flinched at the burst, taking her hands from Richius' hips and cupping them over her ears. Richius and Dinadin did the same, but though the flash was blinding, neither man was able to look away. Soon another, more intense blast arrived. Richius felt the jolt of a shock wave blow by them as countless bolts of electricity showered out of the thunderhead, igniting the earth behind the foggy veil.

"Go, Richius!" Dyana urged. "Hurry!"

Richius could scarcely move. He knew he had to get them to safety, but all he could think of was Edgard. He was almost sobbing when Dinadin called to him.

"Richius, come on! The fog's getting closer. We have to move now!"

Richius slowly turned his back on the war duke's camp. "Forgive me, my friend," he said softly, then spurred his horse back to a gallop. Beneath him, the cobblestones of the city had given way to sandy earth and he raced across a well-worn path toward the bridge, Dinadin charging behind him. Within moments the bridge was in view, its long, Naren-built stringers forging the wide river. Richius could hear the racing waters of the Sheaze over the rumbling thunder and noticed at once that the concussive booms of lightning had stopped. Curious, he glanced over his shoulder to where Edgard's camp had been. The bizarre fog still clung to the earth, but now he could see the eerie glow of fires burning in the haze. Ghostly wisps of black smoke struggled skyward. Nothing moved within the mists, and a frightening calm blanketed the ruined camp. And over it all, buoyed forward by ever-growing winds, the storm was moving toward them.

Richius cursed and spurred his horse again. The bridge was only yards away. He glanced over his shoulder at the behemoth stalking them. The thunderhead had turned a dusky burgundy. It shimmered and shifted as it rolled onward, reaching out for them with fingers of purple fog. Already the hooves of their mounts were hidden in a shallow lake of vapor.

"We'll make it!" he cried. "God damn it, you nag! Run!"

But as the thunderhead spread out over them, Richius knew they couldn't outrun it. They reached the bridge just as it descended, ensnaring them in its mists. There was a thick, smoky stench and a rush of air. Dyana gripped his waist tighter. Behind him, Dinadin was shouting something that sounded like his name. He turned to find his friend but saw only the foamy, purple mists around them. Unable to go farther in the fog, his mount reared and whinnied. Richius fought to still the horse, snapping and tugging on its bridle to make it obey, but another rush of air knocked him from the saddle. He only barely saw Dyana ripped from the saddle after him. She fell into the fog and disappeared.

"Dyana!" Richius screamed, stretching out his arms like a blind man. He heard a cry and scrambled after it, groping wildly for any signs of the girl. Again she cried out his name and he knew that she was close, but the winds had stiffened so that he could barely stand against them. He moved as if in a nightmare, his feet leaden, his breath short, his muscles straining. At last he caught a glimpse of her. She lay stomach-down on the bridge, her hands scraping and scratching to get a grip between the bridge's wooden planks. It looked as if some giant hand had seized her legs, pulling her into the abyss.

"Help me, Richius! Something has me!"

Richius lunged for her, landing on the deck with a crash. He caught hold of her fingers just as they slipped out of the groove.

"Hold on!" he shouted. "I've got you!"

"I cannot!" she cried, struggling to maintain her grip.

Richius wrapped his leg around a trestle, anchoring himself and stretching out his other hand. She reached for it, straining to make contact. He tried to stretch out more but couldn't. Cursing, he closed his grip tighter around her fingers. The fragile bones within popped but he ignored the ugly sound and Dyana's shriek of pain, fighting to free her. Again she tried to reach his other hand, but always the breadth of a hair separated them. The storm surged and gave a violent bellow. Richius could feel the sweaty oil of their hands forcing them apart. He had only her fingertips now.

"Richius!"

"No!"

The grip broke and Dyana slipped into the mists. Richius screamed and stumbled to his feet. Amazingly, the storm was already lifting. He watched it roll off the bridge and into the sky. Panicked, he blundered after it, sure that somehow Dyana still lived within it. But the thing moved too quickly for him, and at last he fell to his knees, exhausted and weeping as the thunderhead disappeared into the sky. Behind him Dinadin was shouting his name. Richius ignored him.

Dyana was gone.

TWELVE

The tickle of a spider startled Lucyler awake. His eyes flicked open just before the insect entered his mouth. Cursing, he sat up and batted the thing away. It scurried across his lumpy mattress, but Lucyler's palm thudded down on it with an unpleasant splat. He looked at its creamy remains before wiping the residue on the side of the bed. In the catacombs beneath Falindar, spiders were a plague.

Lucyler looked up at the filth-encrusted ceiling of his cell, at the myriad of webs burdened with egg sacks. He had already been here long enough to see an entire family of the pests born. He had even studied them, idling away the hours as he watched the young pull themselves free. Their plump mother hadn't assisted them, but had instead busied herself wrapping a centipede for their first meal. She was a big thing, probably the terror of her tiny world. With broad yellow stripes, she looked to Lucyler like some sort of eight-legged tiger, and when she moved, which was seldom, she danced gracefully across her dewy web, racing in to kill the unlucky things that fell into her domain. Oddly, Lucyler had grown accustomed to her. She was the only constant company he had.

Lucyler had served in Falindar all his adult life, ever since he could wield a jiiktar with some skill, but he had never seen the catacombs. He was one of the Daegog's warriors: proud, clean, and above the deeds that went on beneath the citadel. For that the Daegog had others. They were men with dark minds, and they went unseen by the people in the palace, going about their work in secrecy. The Daegog's warriors saw only what they chose to see, and though he had known that a sprawling prison existed beneath the home of his royal master, Lucyler never cared to learn the sordid details. It was simply not his place to question.

But now, caught in its depths, time had lost all meaning. From his beard growth he could tell that it had been days since Voris imprisoned him, but exactly how many he didn't know. It might have been a week, or it might have been more. He could only gauge time's passing by the occasional meal slipped between the bars, but these seemed so irregular as to have little or no timekeeping value. The little spiders had been born in the morning, that he knew for certain. He had overheard one of his Drol captors remarking about the sunrise. Lucyler remembered Falindar's sunrises. They were magnificent.

But there was no sun down here, and no moon or stars, either. There was only the feeble light of a torch hung on a wall just out of reach. Sometimes his jailers extinguished the torch, leaving him alone in the deepest, maddening blackness. The cell became smaller then, the darkness oppressive and suffocating. There were others down in the catacombs. Lucyler could hear their distant mumbles, but they were far off in the twisting labyrinth, and they didn't answer when he called. So he had only the mother spider to converse with, and she watched him back with cold curiosity, her multifaceted eyes black and omniscient. Unlike Lucyler, she could easily leave the cell but she never did. She was wholly satisfied with her squalid home.

It had been a long ride from the Dring Valley. Lucyler had only seen Voris that once. Afterward he had been blindfolded, bound, and stuffed into the back of a wagon for the long and rocky ride to Falindar. They had not even undone his blindfold long enough for him to see the spires of his former home, but it hadn't mattered. He knew the smell of the citadel. The air here had a unique taste, ripe with the salt of the nearby ocean. And he had known he was being taken to Tharn.

"But why?" he wondered aloud, absently asking the spider. She didn't answer him, nor did any of the Drol guards that attended him. They all wore the scarlet robes of Voris' clan, and only spoke to him enough to order him awake, or to spit "traitor" at him under their breath. Everything else was a mystery, and if there had been a rope or a sharp object in his cell, he would have been dead a week ago.

He sat staring at the ceiling for long moments, counting the spiders and their elaborate webs, and remembering how life had been for him in Falindar. Everything had been plentiful then: food, female company, all the things a man could want. The Daegog had been generous to those who served him. Lucyler closed his eyes and imagined a fine meal. He was eating a delicate pomegranate when he heard a sound out in the corridor. Hoping it was one of his occasional meals, he rose groggily from the mattress and went to the rusted bars. Down the labyrinth, someone was shuffling toward him.

It was a cunning-man, one of the Drol priests. Easily recognizable from his simple saffron robe, the man moved with his head high and his long hair running loose against his back. He walked with an uncertain gait, as if he were in pain or intoxicated, but his eyes were clear and youthful, younger than most of his calling. When he reached Lucyler's cell he stopped. There was a trace of regret in his smile.

"I do not need a priest," Lucyler growled. "Go away."

The cunning-man came closer to the bars. "The Jackal is dead?" His voice was strong and melodious, with an almost instrumental beauty. When he spoke, his eyes glowed hypnotically.

"Yes," answered Lucyler, then began to cough. The cunning-man waited for him to stop.

"When?" asked the priest. "And how?"

Lucyler laughed. "Are you my interrogator? If so, Tharn will have to do better."

"I am Tharn," said the man.

It took a moment for the words to register, but when they did Lucyler exploded toward the bars. He reached out an arm, trying to snare the grinning Drol, but Tharn was just out of reach. There was barely an inch between them, yet Tharn did not flinch.

"Pig!" snarled Lucyler, balling his hand into a fist and shaking it in the Drol's face. "What do you want from me?"

"You call yourself Lucyler of Falindar, yes?"

Lucyler spit at Tharn. "I do."

Tharn very calmly wiped at the spittle with his sleeve, studying Lucyler as he did so. "One of my jailors," said the Drol. "But I do not remember you."

"I am a warrior," declared Lucyler. "Not a jailor." He turned from Tharn and went back to his mattress, sitting down on it and ignoring his captor.

"But you are one of the Daegog's," said Tharn. "Good. Then you will be even more privileged to see what happens to him."

Lucyler sat up. "What do you mean?"

"Listen closely to what I tell you. It is not only the Dring Valley that has fallen. My revolution has taken Mount Godon. Like you, the Daegog is my prisoner. So too is the warlord Kronin, and the other warlords that opposed me. You are here to answer for Kalak."

"I answer only to the Daegog, Drol," said Lucyler.

"The Daegog?" said Tharn viciously. "And why would that be? Why would you ever give your loyalty to such a man? He is a traitor to the Triin people. Do you not know that?"

Lucyler chuckled. "*You* are the traitor, Tharn. You can hide behind your dead religion, but all Triin know what you really are."

"Oh? And what is that?"

"A madman," said Lucyler.

All the pleasantness disappeared from the cunning-man's face. "In Nar, they think we are all madmen. Did you know that? Did you know that the talk of us in Nar spreads like a disease, and that little children are told tales of us as monsters? We are so white because we are vampires they say, and the little ones believe. Do you know what you would be in Nar, Lucyler of Falindar? A freak."

Lucyler grimaced.

"Yes, you know I am right. I have lived among them, and I have seen their shocked faces at the color of my skin. To be sure, they have built some dazzling things, but they are weak-minded and cruel, and the one who leads them is insatiable." Tharn stepped closer. "I wonder what you truly know of their emperor. You speak of madmen so casually. If you really wish to know one, study Arkus of Nar."

"Interesting," said Lucyler. "Perhaps you are twins."

"My insanity is a misconception I expected. That is why you are here, so that I may convince you otherwise. Come closer, let me show you something."

At first Lucyler stayed seated on his mattress, but when he saw what Tharn was doing he got up and approached the bars. The cunning-man had undone the belt cinched around his waist and was pulling his saffron robes down around his shoulders.

"Let me show you the good cause you fight for," said Tharn. When his upper body was completely naked, he turned his back toward the cell for Lucyler to see. "This is how good your Daegog is."

Tharn's back was a collection of crisscrossing scars. Stripes of whitened flesh ran along every inch of skin, the telltale remnants of a whip. Still red after all this time, the skin had knitted into a giant, coagulated cicatrix, more like the hide of a reptile than the flesh of a man.

"Beautiful, am I not?" said Tharn. He pulled up his robe and turned to stare at Lucyler. "The Daegog's jailors were very thorough. And the Daegog watched every moment of it. They even took a rattan cane to my knees. When it rains I am as crippled as an old man."

Lucyler was horrified.

"This is what happened to those who spoke out against your Daegog, Lucyler of Falindar." Tharn gestured to the catacombs around him. "This lovely place was my only home for months. How long have you been here? A week? A bit more? And you are ready to go mad, are you not?"

"He did you wrong," Lucyler admitted.

"He did all Triin wrong!" thundered Tharn. "He brought in the Naren devils for his own selfish gain. He thought only of gold and weapons. He lived like a king while others starved. You know all this!"

"He was flawed, I know," said Lucyler. "But you have been unspeakable. You are an atrocity, Tharn. Your Drol are demons."

Tharn sighed. "If you believe that, you are more ignorant about my people than I feared."

"Your people are fools. Their devotion to your religion is pathetic."

"You are here to learn otherwise, Lucyler of Falindar. The Jackal was to be here, but now you must witness for him."

"Witness what?"

"I am not the man you think I am," said Tharn. "Now I must prove that to you all."

"That," said Lucyler pointedly, "will be difficult."

Tharn smiled effortlessly. It was a beautiful smile, innocent, like a child's. "I wanted Kalak to see what I have planned for the Daegog. I wanted him to see what I have planned for Lucel-Lor. Will you stand in his place?"

"Do I have a choice?" asked Lucyler bitterly. "I am your prisoner. You can do to me what you wish."

"That is not what I want. True, you are imprisoned. So are the warlords that opposed me. But it was not to torture you. It was to teach you. I wanted you to know what it was like for me here in the Daegog's play pit. I wanted you to feel at least a little of my pain, to help you see the truth about this man you follow."

Lucyler couldn't help but look away. It was atrocious what had been done to Tharn, and it had not been a secret. Some said it was why the Drol master hated the Daegog so very much. Seeing Tharn's flayed skin, Lucyler could almost understand his ire.

"Do not expect me to denounce my Daegog," said Lucyler wearily. "You have won. Be glad in your victory."

"It is not a victory for me alone. It is a great day for all Triin. And I will prove it to you." Tharn came closer to the bars. "Do you know why the Daegog dealt so closely with the Naren devils?"

Lucyler started to reply, but stopped when he knew his answer would be a lie. Publicly, the Daegog claimed he was trying to better the lives of all Triin by dealing with the Narens, but the truth was evident enough. The Daegog was as power-hungry as Nar's own emperor.

"His reasons are not important," replied Lucyler. "And I do not need to be reminded of them."

"Oh, but you are very wrong. His reasons are as black as his heart. He has confessed them to me."

"Confessed?" asked Lucyler. "So now it is you who are the torturer, eh?"

Tharn said nothing, but his eyes betrayed the truth of things.

"Is vengeance a Drol virtue?" pressed Lucyler. "Was not your own god Lorris called the forgiving one?"

"Do not task me," warned Tharn. "Lorris was also the sword of heaven. Now he has touched me so that I may do his bidding. I will not be questioned by a heretic."

Lucyler snorted contemptuously. "Do you really believe that nonsense? Or is it just your means to make others follow you? I have heard the tales of your sect since I was a tiny boy. They made fine stories, but they are for children, not grown men."

"You do not believe in the touch of heaven?" asked Tharn.

"No, I do not. It is the stuff of fools."

Tharn's smile widened. "Can you be so sure? Have you never been curious?"

"Curious?" countered Lucyler. "How can you use that word? Do you kill simply from curiosity, to see how it is to watch people suffer?"

Tharn sighed. "Do not be obtuse. Listen, I will tell you a story."

"Spare me, please."

But Tharn went on anyway. "When I was a boy, I was privileged. I was like you, content to be on the side of the Daegog and to eat my fill of good food. I was as sure and arrogant as you are now, but as I got older I changed. I began to seek meaning in my life. That is why I went to Nar, to study science and the things of the future."

Lucyler scowled. "I am not interested."

"You will listen!" commanded the Drol. "You will because it is important. In Nar I found the science and knowledge I craved, but I also found a heartlessness I never knew existed. I went there seeking answers from the world's great minds, and all I discovered was misery and hatred. They hated me because I did not look like them, and I knew that all their grand talk of peace and alliance with Lucel-Lor was a lie. I did not know why then, but I know now. And when I returned home I was a changed man. I heard the call of Lorris."

"The call of Lorris," Lucyler scoffed. "Ridiculous."

Tharn gave a bitter laugh. "I see you may be the most difficult of my foes to convince, Lucyler of Falindar. Very well. I accept the challenge."

The cunning-man called down the corridor, and in a moment a warrior appeared, one of Voris' wearing the scarlet of the valley Drol. The warrior produced a key from his vestments and handed it to Tharn, who placed it in the cage's lock and twisted. The lock gave way with a rusty groan.

"Come with me," said Tharn. He opened the shrieking gate so that Lucyler could follow, then proceeded back down the corridor. Astonished, Lucyler scrambled after him. He caught up with the cunning-man, and was surprised when the Drol warrior made no attempt to keep them apart.

"Where are we going?" Lucyler asked.

"Up. Protect your eyes. It will be bright for you."

The catacombs beneath the citadel seemed to snake on endlessly. Lucyler followed Tharn as quickly as he could, but he was weak and the walking winded him quickly. But the cunning-man moved slowly also, hindered by his ruined knees. When they came at last to a mossy stairway built into the side of a stone wall, Tharn took the first step then held out his hand to Lucyler.

"Take my hand," he directed. "It is a long climb, and the stairs are slippery."

"I do not need your help," said Lucyler. He knew he did, but he would rather fall than accept his enemy's aid. Tharn shrugged and headed up the stairs, leaving Lucyler panting near the bottom. The Drol warrior stood behind him, waiting impatiently. Lucyler's head began to spin with each step. He tried to find a grip on the stony wall, but the rocks were as wet and slippery as the stairs, and at last he begrudgingly let the warrior pull him up the staircase. There was brightness at the top of the stairs, partially blocked by Tharn's body. The cunning-man stepped aside and let Lucyler tumble out of the dungeon.

"Welcome home," said Tharn.

Lucyler surveyed his surroundings, and knew at once that he was indeed in Falindar. Even the hall he had spilled into, so close to the torturous catacombs, was splendid. The walls were of a bleached white stone, radiant and perfect. And the hall was gigantic, too grand for a mortal's dwelling. The ceiling reached up into a roof of crystal glass that let in all the powerful light of the sun. Lucyler put a hand to his eyes and closed them tightly. Sunlight pierced his eyes.

"Can you walk?" asked Tharn. Lucyler felt the Drol's hand on his shoulder.

"A moment," replied Lucyler. "My eyes . . ."

"They will adjust," said Tharn, and without waiting took hold of Lucyler's hand. "Come. We are expected."

Lucyler let Tharn guide him through his former home, uncomfortable with the Drol's assistance but unable to continue without it. His eyes became slivers, and the sunlight made them tear. They moved slowly through the giant halls, passing by Drol warriors who stared at them in disbelief. Some even offered to help their master, but Tharn refused their services, guiding Lucyler carefully down the splendid corridors. Then at last they stopped. Lucyler forced his eyes open a bit more, and found that they had reached the throne room.

"Come," directed Tharn, guiding him into the grand chamber. A hundred triumphant Drol faces turned to regard them. They had all lined up for this moment, flanking the path to the glass throne. Voris of Dring was there, a massive white wolf sitting dutifully at his side. There was also Gavros of Garl, and the wondrously cruel Shohar, the warlord of Jhool who had sided with Tharn early in the Drol crusade. The fanged warlord Nang had come from the Fire Steppes with a trio of his bare-chested warriors. And there were some Lucyler didn't recognize, all splendidly garbed for this long-awaited moment, when their master would ascend the throne of Lucel-Lor.

But Lucyler's heart sank when he noticed the other warlords, those who had stayed loyal to the Daegog. He recognized the long-haired, long-faced Kronin at once, his head bowed in defeat, his wrists manacled to his ankles. The other warlords, maybe five in all, were similarly chained, and shared with Kronin the same lost and ruined expression. They were all closest to the throne, kneeling at the foot of the golden dais. Drol warriors flanked them with drawn jiiktars, waiting to sever their heads from their shoulders.

"Is this your mercy, butcher?" spat Lucyler as Tharn led him toward the throne. "Will you make a display of us?"

Tharn leaned into Lucyler's ear and pointed toward the throne, whispering, "Do you see him?"

Lucyler followed Tharn's finger. Behind the kneeling warlords, a large, round object squirmed on the dais. The Triin leader was trussed up like a prize turkey, his arms bound behind his back and roped to his tethered ankles. He lay on his side, sweat beading on his forehead, a huge knot of fabric stuffed between his teeth.

Lucyler groaned, pulling free of Tharn's grip and stopping halfway to the dais. "What have you done?"

The Daegog had been badly beaten. There were scars on his neck from a garrote, and his cheeks were puffed out with bluish bruises. One eye was closed, forced shut by an oozing contusion, and his white hair was plastered to his forehead by a crust of dried blood.

"You bastard!" cried Lucyler, backing away from the dais. "Is this Drol justice?"

"Hold!" ordered Tharn. Voris stepped out from the line to assist his master, but Tharn raised a hand to stop him. "Choose where you stand, Lucyler of Falindar. You must witness this. Do you stand with your Daegog?"

Lucyler straightened. "I do," he declared.

"Then come with me to the dais. Stand with Kronin and the others."

Tharn turned and went toward the dais. Lucyler, unsure what he should do, followed the cunning-man to the throne. When he reached the dais he stopped beside the bound Kronin and stood there, watching as Tharn climbed the dais and hovered over the Daegog. The Daegog whimpered as Tharn put a booted foot onto his chest.

"Warlords of Lucel-Lor," he cried. "I am Tharn, the Storm Maker. I bear the touch of heaven within me." He pointed down at the man beneath him. "This thing at my feet is the former Daegog of Lucel-Lor. He is a criminal. He has confessed his crimes to me, and now he will confess them before you all."

Tharn stooped and pulled the knot of material from the Daegog's mouth. No sooner had it popped out than the Daegog screamed.

"Help me!" he shouted through the mucus clogging his throat. "He means to kill me!"

"Indeed I do," said Tharn with all seriousness. "But not before you speak again of your crimes." He pressed down on the Daegog's chest with his boot, forcing the air from the fat man's lungs. "Confess! Confess and get the merciful death you do not deserve!"

"Help," wheezed the Daegog. He was crying now, fighting against the ropes. Tharn's face twisted with fierce disgust. He ground his foot harder against the man's chest.

"Confess, fat one! Tell these good men who followed you how you meant to betray them!"

A hush fell upon the gathering. The warlords and their warriors stood and listened with grave anticipation.

"Speak, Nebarazar Gorandarr!" commanded Tharn. "Is it true that you only wanted Nar's science to defeat the men gathered here?"

The Daegog wouldn't answer. He turned his head toward the bound warlords at the foot of the dais, gibbering at them for help. Lucyler felt a rush of nausea at the spectacle, hoping Tharn would end it quickly. Instead the Drol leader stepped off the Daegog's chest and leaned down. His words were soft, nearly inaudible, but Lucyler's proximity to his fallen king let him hear every violent word.

"Tell them, Daegog," whispered Tharn. "Or you will spend the rest of your days in those catacombs, and I will have the rats eat out your eyes."

"No!" the Daegog wailed. "Spare me, monster, I beg you! Please . . ."

"Be still!" roared Tharn, standing up again to tower over the prone man. "Be a man in death at least. Nebarazar Gorandarr, is it true that you cared nothing for the people of Lucel-Lor?"

"Yes, all right," blubbered the Daegog. "Now, spare me, please. . . ."

"Is it true that you are a weak and useless ruler, and that you envy and hate these men who honored you?"

"No, no, I cannot say it, do not make me—"

"Confess!" roared Tharn, and kicked the Daegog's face so hard that several teeth flew from his mouth. Lucyler felt a spray of blood strike his face. The Daegog let out an agonized sob. Unable to stand another cry, Lucyler ran up onto the dais.

"Stop it!" he ordered, dropping down over the Daegog and shielding him from Tharn's blows. "You are killing him! Is that what your revolution is for?"

Voris sprang out of the crowd, his tame white wolf on his heels. He reached the dais in an instant and grabbed hold of Lucyler, dragging him off the Daegog. He was a giant man, and the snapping jaws of his pet made Lucyler relent. He pulled free of Voris' grip, cursing.

"Beast!" he spat at Tharn. "Do not torture him like this!"

"You must learn the truth of this man, Lucyler of Falindar. You must hear his confession." He looked down at the writhing thing at his feet. "Nebarazar Gorandarr, I put it to you again. Speak truthfully, and you will die quickly and without pain. Tell these men why you invited in the devils of Nar. I know the truth already, traitor. You cannot change that. Now speak it and be free."

Horrified, Lucyler watched as the Daegog turned to regard the gathered warlords. There was the most unholy expression on his face. Disregard, contempt, avarice, and spite: all the worst of emotions glowed in his defeated eyes. A trickle of blood fell from his bulging lips, and when he spoke his voice was a hollow, diseased rasp.

"He says you honored me, but that was never so," croaked the Daegog. "Dogs, every one of you. I am the Daegog of Lucel-Lor. I am supreme."

Voris growled and made to strike the groveling man, but Tharn's quick hand on his shoulder stayed the blow. Kronin was staring up into his Daegog's eyes, his face stricken, and Delgar of Miradon began to weep. But the Daegog laughed horribly at seeing his loyal warlord's tears, and spat a wad of saliva and blood at him.

"All of you are fools," continued the Daegog. "Nar was not for gold or trade or knowledge. Nar was for weapons. Had none of you the brains to see that?"

"He meant to crush us all with the weaponry of Nar," said Tharn. "He dealt with their evil emperor so that he could have the means of gaining all your lands."

"They are my lands!" said the Daegog. "I am the Daegog of Lucel-Lor. Only my blood is fit to rule!"

Lucyler backed away from the Daegog, horrified and hating himself. He was almost off the dais when he backed into Tharn. The cunning-man took hold of his arm and kept him from leaving.

"No," whispered Tharn. "You must hear this."

"I cannot," said Lucyler weakly.

The Daegog fought one last time against his bonds, then hurled an inhuman cry into the air. "I die," he bellowed. "And I leave you all to the Drol!"

Tharn stepped closer to the Daegog. "Nebarazar Gorandarr," he said softly. "Your time is ended."

The cunning-man held a hand over the Daegog's face, merely inches from his nose. And all at once Nebarazar Gorandarr fell silent, and the cruelty of his expression vanished as the muscles in his face slackened. His breathing slowed, ebbed, then suddenly stopped.

The Daegog was dead.

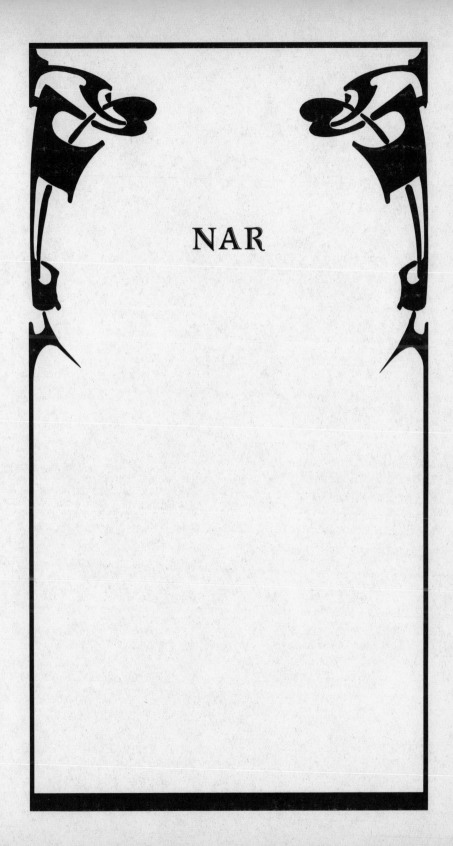

NAR

From the Journal of Richius Vantran:

Father is dead.

Nearly a month has passed, and I have hardly said these words at all. They are so strange to me. Until now I have avoided writing them just to keep them from being real. But truly he is gone and I must at last accept it.

The last month has gone by in a dream, a nightmare from which I am finally awakening. Jojustin has been a blessing. Were it not for him my anguish would have crushed me. He has nursed the sickness in my soul better than any mother could have. It is easy to see why Father always cherished him. He claims that I am to be king now. If so, I can think of no better a steward. It is for his sake that I am trying to be myself again. Aramoor will need a leader when the emperor takes his vengeance on us. Edgard is gone. Only I am left to carry that burden.

Jojustin has been taking Father's murder with real mettle. While I have been useless and despondent these weeks, he has ignored his own grief and continues to tend to the needs of the castle. I know he does not want to worry me, but I can tell how concerned he is for my safety. He tries to keep me indoors and out of the gardens. It is as if we are living in a prison. Through my chamber window I can see the sentries he has posted at the gates, and an uneasy mood has settled over the servants. There is none of their happy chattering in the hallways that I remember so vividly and so looked forward to hearing again. Most of them knew Father since their childhoods, and have been as stricken as I by the news of his death. Still, they were not his kin. There is a part of me I fear may never mend.

The thought of a Triin killing Father still shocks me. Before the fall of Ackle-Nye I would not have believed them capable of such evil. Never have the Drol seemed quite so wicked. They have shown me a spitefulness to rival that of Nar's. But they never knew the truth about Father. If they had, Tharn himself would have thought him a hero. Instead we are left with the curse of being enemies, and wait for more assassins to crawl into our gardens and murder us. We are even deprived the satisfaction of justice. I have tried to tell Jojustin that no one could have captured the assassin, but he has never lived among Triin and so does not know how agile and cunning they can be. If only Lucyler were here to convince him. He could scale the garden wall like the assassin and show Jojustin the uselessness of guilt.

The lands around the castle are finally quiet again. At last the parade of well-wishers has stopped. I know they mean no harm, but their questions about the war are lurid and bothersome to me. They cannot possibly know what we have been through. Even the old veterans of the Talistan war trouble me, they are so curious. I am sick of their stories and comparisons. They are all experts, yet none of them has ever faced a Drol or seen the handiwork of a jiiktar. I listen to their tales, and doubt the House of Gayle was ever as fierce as the Drol of the valley.

Thankfully, not all the talk has been of war. Sometimes, when they are drunk and melancholy enough, they speak to me of Father. Everyone seems to know something new about him, something he hid or simply never told me. And all of them say how proud he was of me. They leave me with ideas to struggle with. How can a father abandon a son he loved so sweetly? Edgard said it first, and I think Dinadin thought it likely. Now Jojustin says it is true, but I still cannot accept it. Father would never have left me to die, not even to save Aramoor.

I have had Father's letter since Patwin gave it to me in the mountains. Jojustin has been urging me to read it. He seems to believe it will solve this riddle for me, but perhaps I do not want it solved. If Father's own words say he abandoned me, my memory of him will be forever tainted.

I have been grateful for Patwin's company since the others returned home. It is good to share time with someone who understands. But he is mending well from his long trip, and it is likely that he too will be leaving. I do not welcome the loneliness his absence will bring. Things are too quiet without Father around. The castle never seemed so large before, and winter is coming. We will have snow soon, and then none of my men will want to journey to the castle. How I wish Lucyler was here. I had always thought he would return with me to Aramoor when the war ended, and he and Dinadin and I would eat and drink like we never could in the valley and let our own tales get taller like the old veterans do. But he is gone, like Father and Edgard, killed for nothing but the vengeance of Voris.

I suppose I will never know what horrible end he faced in my stead. Gilliam and the others were kind about it, but I know Voris must have had an unholy death planned for me. What a cruel creature he must be. Now we all live with Lucyler's death in our hearts, and Voris has killed us even so. But if I can I will take my own vengeance some day, and in Lucyler's name will cut out the Wolf's heart and feed it to the rats in his damned valley. Dinadin would like that. Were it not for so many Drol in the valley I think Dinadin would yet be there, overturning every rock to find Voris. I never knew how fond he was of Lucyler until now.

Dinadin has changed since returning home. Maybe it is simply what war does to young men, but we hardly spoke at all during the long ride back with Patwin. I know he bears me ill will, and I suppose it should be that way. Lucyler died because of me, and Dinadin is right to say so. Voris wanted Kalak, but Lucyler suffered his revenge. Dinadin and Lucyler had a strange friendship, and I doubt I can ever make this up to him. He has not been back to the castle since returning home, and I miss him. I need him to stand with me now, to help me face the days ahead. We will all need to stand together if the emperor comes to challenge us. I only hope the grudge he holds softens soon. So many have gone now, that even my memories seem unfamiliar to me.

And she is gone, too.

It is as if I have known this girl for years. There is nothing else that quickens love like war. Each night I lie awake to visions of her. I lull myself to sleep with whispered prayers for her. I pray she is not in the mad devil's hands. I pray she can forgive me for not keeping her safe. But I think God is deaf and does not hear me. Or maybe it is as the emperor's priests say, that God only answers the prayers of true Narens. If that is so, I will be in His hell forever.

The storm that took Dyana was a magic, evil thing. Even Dinadin told me I could not have fought against it. Yet regrets still haunt me. I lost so many. Like Jimsin. Like Lucyler.

What a bloody list I have.

Tonight is eerily quiet. The servants have all gone to their beds, and Jojustin has long since come by to say his good-nights. Nights like these unnerve me. Through my window I can see the watchful glow of torches and the sentries at the gate, yet they do not comfort me. Home is not what I remembered. Outside the world has turned a watery gray. Winter is coming too fast. I had hoped to see color here, but the autumn leaves have died and fallen away. In the gardens only thorns grow on Father's roses. And Jojustin says I am to be king of this place.

By now the emperor has heard of Father's death. No doubt he does not grieve for him as we in Aramoor do. Only Arkus wanted war with Lucel-Lor, and now I suppose I'll never know what grand designs he had for the Triin, or why he had us fight their bloody war. Whatever Arkus sought from them, we have lost it for him, and so it is likely he will punish us for that. Perhaps his legions are already on their way. Or maybe it is the Drol who want more vengeance and are planning to come at us through the mountains. I say let them all come. Nothing is as it was anymore, and I see no way to be even a shadow of the king that Father was. Peace escapes me even here. At night I hear wolves howling and see white faces in my dreams. Home still seems so very far away.

THIRTEEN

It was nearly noon when Richius awoke and found that an early snow had fallen. In this part of the Empire, snow was as ordinary as the changing of seasons, but autumn hadn't gone yet and winter was still weeks away. He quickly splashed his face with the cool water from his washbasin and went to the window, pushing it open. The old iron frame screeched and flecks of rust tumbled down the tower, caught up in a stiff northern breeze. Richius took a long, sweet breath. He could taste the morning, and the brightness of the day forced his eyes into slivers. It was only a light snowfall, more like a sheet than a blanket, but it covered the courtyard and the hills beyond the castle in a brilliant mantle of white. On the horizon, Aramoor's giant green fir trees were dressed in coats of frost and topped with hats of ice. Below him Richius could see the castle garden and its frozen, dormant rosebushes, and past the place where the courtyard ended, stable hands were milling tracks in the snow and grooming the coats of warhorses. Richius sighed. He had not seen snow for almost two years, and the perfect picture through his window made the word *home* ring in his head like a church bell.

Aramoor in late autumn. Home. He smiled and turned from the window just as a snowball clipped the back of his head. The sudden explosion of frost in his hair made him jump and he whirled around.

"Patwin!"

Far below, Patwin was doubled over with laughter, his guffaws echoing through the courtyard, catching the attention of the stable hands and workers. His face was purple with glee.

"I'm sorry!" he managed between chortles. "You moved."

Richius squirmed as the melting ice trickled under his nightshirt. "Idiot!" he called back, more startled than angry. At least Patwin hadn't packed the snowball too tightly.

Patwin got unsteadily to his feet, little rivers of tears running down his face. "Sorry. I just wanted to frighten you, really. I didn't even think I could reach!"

"Well you can. And what are you doing back here anyway? I thought you were going riding with Jojustin."

"It's almost noon, Richius. We just got back. Have you been sleeping all this time?"

Richius nodded and looked up into the sky. Somewhere above him the sun was glowing dimly behind a shroud of clouds. He had guessed right about the time.

"Well, come down for breakfast. Jenna's fixing some eggs and honey bread for Jojustin and me." He winked up at Richius. "I'm sure she'll make you some if you ask her nicely."

"Stop," Richius said, lowering his voice so no one else could hear. "I told you I'm not interested in her. Did you check the fences by the east ridge?"

"They're fine, except for some holes where wolves got through. Not big enough for the horses, though, don't worry. Jojustin told some of the houseboys to see to the fences, and Terril said he'd keep a look out for the wolves. You coming down?"

"Wolves? Maybe Terril should have some of the mastiffs with him."

Patwin's expression filled with sympathy. "Don't worry, Richius. They're far away on the north acres, probably looking for food. You know the first snow makes them crazy. I'll take some of the dogs over to Terril later if you like, but it's nothing to be concerned about. What about breakfast? I'm starved."

"Let me get dressed and I'll meet you downstairs. Start without me if you want."

"We'll wait. Jojustin wants to talk to you, and Jenna won't serve us if she thinks your food will get cold. Just try to hurry."

"I will," said Richius and closed the window, shutting out the draft. The thought of breakfast hadn't occurred to him until Patwin mentioned it, but now that it did it set his stomach rumbling. He had only picked at his suppers the last few nights, leaving Jojustin to think that a fever had caught hold of him. But Richius knew it wasn't a fever that kept him from eating. What had suppressed his appetite was more like apathy. Since coming home, food no longer had the importance it did in the valley, and there were no more dreams or long talks of it. Yet this morning, perhaps through the intangible power of snow, his appetite had returned, and it pleased him.

He hurriedly finished washing, and dressed himself in a finely tailored pair of trousers and a shirt. Jenna had made the shirt for him. She had said it would keep him warm on just such a morning and she'd been right, but as he put it on he began to dread the look of satisfaction she would give him when she noticed him wearing it. Everybody knew how Jenna felt about him, and it was becoming irritating. Worse, there was nothing he could do but endure it. Jenna was far too sweet to explain things to, and Richius guessed she would be mortified if he even tried. So he would wear the warm, well-made shirt and that would be the end of it. Unless Patwin started gibing him again.

When he was done smoothing down the wrinkles on his pants, he slipped his feet into a stout pair of riding boots and went to the door, careful to check himself in the mirror one last time. Jojustin had been fussing like a mother over his appearance lately, and he didn't want to give his steward any more reasons to worry. He would eat a hearty breakfast this morning, do his best to be cheerful, and put this talk of fevers and depressions away for good. Today there was important work to do.

He followed the smell of honey and eggs down the twisting, granite staircase past the kitchen to the small dining chamber where he always took his meals, careful not to let Jenna see or hear him. The young woman, busily occupied with the pans and ovens, took no notice of him as he slipped past. In the dining chamber he found Patwin and Jojustin, both still dressed in their riding gear and sipping mugs of barley beer.

"Good morning," said Jojustin sunnily, pouring Richius a mug of the beer and handing it to him. Richius accepted the drink gratefully and sat down. The table was set with stoneware, and at its center sat a small bouquet of winter lilies. Richius eyed the flowers suspiciously.

"Jenna?"

Jojustin smiled. "She's just trying to make you feel comfortable, lad. Ignore it if you want but don't say anything. It'd only hurt her."

"Of course I won't. I just wish everyone would stop worrying so much about me. I admit the last few weeks were a little tough but I'm fine now, really."

"You are looking better today," admitted Jojustin. "Sleep well?"

"Very well, thank you," answered Richius, taking a sip from his mug.

"We got snow last night. Did you see it?"

Richius turned an admonishing stare on Patwin. "I saw it. Felt it, too."

Patwin chuckled. "Are you all right, Richius? The side of your face looks a little red."

"What's this?" asked Jojustin, inspecting Richius' face from across the table. Richius waved away the old man's concern.

"It's nothing. Just a little accident. Pass the bread, will you please?"

Jojustin passed a plateful of warm honey bread to Richius. The scent of the steaming grains and honey was intoxicating. Richius stuffed a piece of the bread into his mouth and passed the plate on to Patwin, who greedily snatched up two slices.

"Richius," said Patwin between bites. "Remember how Dinadin used to always talk about food before going to sleep?" He turned to Jojustin and went on, "Every night he'd tell us about some new specialty of his mother's. Maybe one night would be roast goose, the next leg of veal. And he'd always tell us just before we turned in. God, it was impossible to sleep after talking to him!"

"And we'd have nothing but stale army bread to satisfy us," said Richius, shaking his head. "I remember."

"Stale bread?" came a young, shining voice. "That bread's as fresh as the snow outside. What's wrong with it?"

Richius looked up into Jenna's brown eyes. "The bread's fine, Jenna, really. It's wonderful." He peered up into the plates of steaming eggs and sausage she was carrying. "That looks pretty good, too."

She smiled and gave Richius his breakfast first, setting the plate down before him with a flourish. "I know how fond you are of sweet sausage, Richius. I had Elena make some up for you special. The way you like it— not too hot." She put Patwin's plate down next. "We have to get you back on your feet, fatten you up like this one here."

Patwin sat up indignantly. "It's fine for you, Jenna. You didn't spend three weeks riding through Lucel-Lor looking for Richius. I went almost four days once without eating. Why, I was half dead when I finally found him and Dinadin." Patwin pointed his fork at Richius. "Tell her, Richius."

Richius glared at Patwin slyly. "I can't recall."

"I thought not," said Jenna, at last serving Jojustin. "Just more of your tall tales, eh, Patwin? Sometimes I think the only reason you stay around here is to get more of my cooking. You look fit enough to me."

Patwin reached out and lightly slapped Jenna's rump. "Fit enough for you and more, girl. Why don't you go warm up some spice wine for us? Richius has his appetite back today. What do you say, Richius?"

Richius shrugged. "Fine."

When Jenna had gone, Patwin leaned forward to Richius. "What did you say that for? Now she thinks I've been lying to her. You know I was telling the truth."

"Don't exaggerate," said Richius lazily. "Of course I know it's the truth. Jenna knows it, too. She's just playing with you." Then, grinning, he added, "Maybe she's a little sweet on *you*."

Patwin sat back, coloring at the suggestion.

"Personally, I think she'd be good for either of you," said Jojustin. "And she comes from a hardworking family, so there's nothing for you to turn your nose up at, Richius."

Richius grimaced. "I haven't given it much thought."

"Well you should. Pretty girl like that. She'd make you a fine wife. You have to start thinking about these things, start thinking like a king."

The word *king* made Richius drop his fork. "I'm not the king, Jojustin. The only king of Aramoor is my father, and he's dead." He retrieved his fork and started toying with his eggs, drawing little patterns in the yolks. "Please stop calling me that."

"Richius, listen to me," said Jojustin easily. "I've been avoiding this lately, but you have to face it. You were king the moment Darius was slain. You have responsibilities."

"Right now my responsibility is to make sure we're ready to defend ourselves against Arkus. We have horses to train, supplies to gather. . . ."

"Enough," interrupted Jojustin. "No more talk of war with Arkus. I sent word to him after your father died. If he was going to send his legions he would have done so by now. Really, Richius, why do you think such thoughts?"

"We may be talking about treason, Jojustin. Do you really think the emperor is so forgiving? Don't you think he knows why we lost the war?"

Jojustin looked at him sharply. "What do you think?"

Richius sat back. "I don't know."

"Why don't you read your father's letter and find out?"

There was an expectant silence. Richius felt Jojustin's eyes burning into him. Patwin had stopped eating. At last he said quietly, "I can't." He lowered his fork again and stared down into his plate. The eggs had cooled into rubbery lumps. "Why did he do this to me?"

Jojustin slid his hand onto Richius'. "He did it to save Aramoor, lad. Maybe it was misguided, but that was his reason. You know how much he loved you. He didn't abandon you easily. Believe me, I know."

"Do *you* think his reasons were misguided?"

"Ah, well now . . ." Jojustin leaned back, choosing his words with care. "Your father was always at odds with the emperor. I don't think he really weighed everything fairly. Aramoor stood to gain considerable favor with Arkus if we'd won the war." His expression soured. "It would have been nice to unseat Talistan as Arkus' favorite in this part of the Empire."

"Now we're Arkus' enemy," said Richius sullenly.

"No," Jojustin assured him. "I think your father's death is good enough for Arkus. And I don't think he wants any more wars, not within the Empire. He's far too busy fighting Liss to bother with us. He needs a king here. Someone he can depend on to take care of the land. Someone the people will follow."

"Someone like you, Richius," said Patwin past a mouthful of sausage. "Think of it," he added theatrically. "King Richius!"

Richius frowned. He thought of Edgard's final words to him, remembered how the old war duke had tried to convince him that Arkus might simply be satisfied by his father's death. Somehow a Triin assassin had stolen that pleasure from the emperor, but the result was the same. Darius, the thorn in Arkus' side, the man who had cost him all the untold riches of Lucel-Lor, was out of the way. It was an ugly notion, but conceivable.

"I can't believe it," concluded Richius finally. "If Arkus is planning to make me king, why haven't we heard anything?"

"These decisions aren't made quickly, lad. Arkus has politics to consider. There are a lot of ambitious nations in Nar, countries with kings less honorable than your father. Like the Gayles." A shadow of disgust darkened his face. "You can bet they've been whispering in the emperor's ear."

Patwin perked up. "Did you hear about Blackwood Gayle, Richius?"

"What about him?"

"He's not dead. Terril talked to someone who's seen him."

"Not dead?" blurted Richius. They had all assumed Blackwood Gayle had perished with his horsemen at Mount Godon. It was the only bright spot in the whole sordid ordeal. "How can that be? Did you know about this, Jojustin?"

Jojustin nodded. "I knew," he said glumly. "I can't say I'm glad about it."

"He's wearing a mask now," Patwin went on. "Remember that fire you saw? Well, Edgard wasn't the only one attacked by it. Gayle's horsemen got it, too, all the way in Tatterak. They say it took half Gayle's face off."

"Only half?" growled Jojustin. "The bastard should be happy. He was luckier than Edgard."

"Alive," Richius said incredulously. "How could the horsemen have survived it?"

"That's just it," said Patwin. "They didn't survive. Just Blackwood Gayle."

"You mean he left his men behind?"

"Left them to die like pigs in a slaughterhouse. Almost everyone else was killed except for Colonel Trosk. I heard he made it out, too."

"Trosk," sneered Jojustin. "Now there's a wretched man. Every bit the butcher Gayle is. I'm surprised they're not brothers."

"I can't believe it," said Richius. "To let his men be massacred like that. It's incredible."

"It's despicable," corrected Jojustin. "Even for a Gayle." He shrugged in disbelief. "But fools still follow them, and the emperor still listens to their advice."

"They've probably told Arkus about my father, then," said Richius.

Jojustin nodded. "Probably."

"Well, if the Gayles know it then the emperor does, too. Why would he even consider letting me rule here if he thinks my father betrayed him?"

"Arkus has no quarrel with you, lad. As far as he's concerned you were in Lucel-Lor trying to win the war for him. He may suspect Darius betrayed him, but he has no proof. All he has is the word of those cutthroat Gayles." Jojustin smiled slyly. "And we all know what liars they are, right?"

"Right," declared Patwin with a conspiratorial wink. "Don't worry, Richius. None of us knows anything."

"We're just going to deny it?" asked Richius. "Pretend it didn't happen?"

Jojustin's face hardened. "Of course. Arkus can't prove anything, and that's the end of it. It doesn't matter what he might suspect. You are of the royal blood of Aramoor. No one else alive can claim that, and Arkus knows it. Who else would the people follow? Some puppet of the emperor's? No, Richius. You are king here, like it or not."

"Well, I don't like it. Even when I was a boy I dreaded this day. I'm no king."

"Why do you say that?" asked Patwin. "You led us into battle, kept us all alive."

"It's not the same," Richius interrupted. "And I didn't keep everyone alive, did I?"

"Men die in war," said Jojustin. "That's the way it is. How many men did you have under your command? Almost five hundred, right?"

"Only three hundred came back."

"After almost a year of brutal battle," Jojustin countered. "And you were fighting *Triin*." He spat out the word with disgust. "The devil's own."

"That's ridiculous," said Richius. "They're not devils, Jojustin. They're men, like you and me."

"Not like me," said Jojustin defensively. "I know what they are. They're all sorcerers. And they don't worship God."

"They have gods," said Richius. "Just not our God."

"Oh, yes. What do they worship? Snakes? And the Drol are the worst of them. You're best rid of that place, lad. We should get a priest in here to bless the lot of you." Again he slipped his hand onto Richius'. "I'm proud of you, Richius. God would be proud of you, too. You're more of a king than you think. Read the letter. Read it and put all this bad business behind you. You have a kingdom to rule."

Jenna suddenly returned to the room carrying a decanter of wine. When he saw her come in Richius quickly jerked his hand back. She gave him a long, insufferably sympathetic look.

"Your glass," she said lightly. Richius held out his glass and let the girl pour some of the mahogany liquor into it. He thanked her and she went on to the others, all the while keeping an eye on him as she poured. She finished quickly and left the room, but the silence she left in her wake was palpable.

Lord, thought Richius. *She probably thinks I've gone mad.* He lifted his glass to his lips. *Maybe I have.*

He drank. The spiced wine was hot, almost unbearably so, yet he kept swallowing until his glass was drained. He was still hungry, but since he had raked his eggs into unappetizing streaks, he reached for another slice of bread.

"After breakfast I'm riding for Gilliam's," he said. "I have to start readying the men if there is to be war again."

"Don't go chasing phantoms, Richius," said Jojustin. "You're only going to scare everyone over nothing."

"If I'm to be king I have to start looking after my people. And you can't guarantee me that Arkus isn't sitting in Nar right now thinking of ways to destroy us. We have to be ready if his legions come."

"All right, then," conceded Jojustin. "Go. Maybe the fresh air will clear your head, get you thinking straight again. But take Patwin with you."

Patwin looked up from his plate. "Me? I just got back from riding. Why do I have to go?"

"Because I want you to look after Richius. There's no telling how many more of those Triin dogs are lurking around."

"It's not necessary," said Richius. "I can take care of myself."

"I would feel better if there was someone with you. Oh, and another thing. Jenna tells me she saw you in the garden last night."

"So?"

"At night? You know how dangerous that is. How can we protect you if you go wandering off? You could have been killed."

"The sentries were close enough to protect me. And I like to get out of the castle sometimes."

"That's fine," said Jojustin. "You should get out more. But why the garden of all places?" He looked down broodingly at his own breakfast. "The stain's not even gone yet."

Richius didn't answer. Despite the garden's recent history, he felt a closeness to the place he could not explain. Perhaps the bloodstain was the very thing that drew him there. Like Jojustin had said, the blemish was still quite visible, clinging to the flagstones like spilled wine on a carpet.

"I'm comfortable there," said Richius at last. "Besides, I really don't think an assassin would try to get me there, not with all the guards around now."

"I promised your father I'd look after you," said Jojustin. "I can't let you take such chances. Please, stay out of the garden. At least at night?"

"I'll try," said Richius, hoping the halfhearted answer would satisfy his steward. These constant, loving concerns for his welfare were becoming a burden.

Jojustin smiled at him, genuinely pleased. "Thank you, lad. I don't want to make a prisoner of you. Just a few more weeks, till things settle." He shuddered. "So much killing. Why—"

There was a sudden, jarring silence. The old man went rigid with surprise, his eyes locked on Richius' hand, following it as it lowered his glass to the table.

"Jojustin?" asked Richius, alarmed. "What's wrong?"

"Your ring. Your royal ring. Where is it?"

Richius swallowed hard. He'd been trying to hide the loss of the ring from Jojustin since returning home. Panicked, he grabbed the first response that bloomed in his mind. "Upstairs. I forgot it when I woke up."

"Forgot it? That's not like you, Richius. That's your king's ring. You have to wear it all the time. You can't just take it off whenever you want to, you know that. You . . ."

Their eyes met squarely.

"You lost it."

Richius could hardly find his voice. "Yes."

"Lord, Richius. How could you? Where did you lose it, do you know?"

"I don't know," Richius lied. He could never explain to Jojustin how he had given the ring to Dyana. "It probably fell off when we were fleeing Ackle-Nye. I had it when Patwin found us; after that I can't recall."

"I don't think so, Richius," Patwin interjected. "I was going to ask you about that. You weren't wearing your ring when we met up in the Run."

"Well, maybe I lost it in the valley," said Richius impatiently. "There was a war going on, you know. Anyway it's gone."

"But that ring was your seal of kingship," said Jojustin. "You have to wear it."

"Why? Aren't I king without it?"

"It's tradition. It marks you as the royal line of Aramoor. You're supposed to wear it until you die, be buried with it like your father was. The people must see it."

"I'm sorry," said Richius. "But it's gone. And anyway it was only a ring. Can't we just have another made?"

"Of course we can, but that's not the point. Your father gave you that ring. You have to bear something of his with you always. Something more than just the crown."

Before Richius could answer, Jojustin was up and snapping his fingers.

"Wait," he said, pushing back his chair. "I have just the thing for you, lad. Something that wasn't buried with your father. Don't go anywhere, I'll be back in a moment."

Jojustin turned and left the dining chamber, leaving Richius and Patwin behind to exchange confused looks.

"What was that about?" asked Patwin.

Richius shrugged. "He took that better than I thought. The way it was going, I was beginning to think he'd never notice."

"He notices everything, Richius. Like how odd you've been lately. Give him a little room. He's just worried about you." Patwin pinched another sausage between his fingers, popping it into his mouth and saying, "We're all worried about you."

"Patwin," said Richius affably. "You're all making it so hard to be angry with you. But you can stop worrying now, I'm fine."

"Really?"

"Of course."

"Then why don't you read your father's letter?"

"Oh, no. Not you, too."

"Well, I carried the damned thing around for almost a month. The least you could do is read it."

"Why should I?" Richius shot back. "Why is it any of your business? My father wrote that letter to me, not you or Jojustin or Dinadin. It's my concern, not yours."

"Easy," Patwin interrupted. "We already know what the letter says. We guessed it a long time ago. Now *you* have to know it. You won't be able to go on until you do." Patwin's expression softened. "Jojustin's right, Richius. Read the letter and put all this madness to an end. Be king."

Richius could hardly speak. "Maybe," he said, the word emerging in a whisper.

"I'll help you all I can. We all will. Dinadin, too, I'm sure."

"That," said Richius pointedly, "I'm not so sure of."

"Richius, he's just angry. It'll pass. In his heart I'm sure he knows the truth of things. And if he doesn't, I intend to help him remember. You had nothing to do with Lucyler's death, or anyone else's. So don't go believing Dinadin's nonsense, because it will only make you crazy."

"You're a good friend, Patwin, but you don't have to spare me. Dinadin's mad at me for a hundred reasons, and at least half of them are true. My father did abandon us. I did keep us all in Dring longer than I should have. And Voris took Lucyler away because I wasn't there for him. Dinadin's right."

"He's not right!" said Patwin angrily. "You were our leader. *You* had to make the tough decisions, not Dinadin. And wasn't it his idea to go to Ackle-Nye in the first place?"

Richius leaned back in his chair and peered through the dining-chamber door. Jenna was in the kitchen. He could hear her insistent scrubbing of the pots and knew she couldn't hear them, but he had no idea when Jojustin would return.

"Listen, Patwin," he said almost soundlessly. "I'm not riding for Gilliam's, not today at least. I'm going to the House of Lotts."

"Dinadin's?"

Richius nodded. "I want to talk to him, see if we can put this ugly mess behind us. You're right to say I'm going to need him. We all have to stay together to protect Aramoor from Arkus."

Patwin looked stricken. "Do you really think the legions are coming?"

"Maybe. If they do we'll have to be ready for them. Don't misunderstand me, Patwin. I hope to God Jojustin's right, but if he's not . . ."

"Then it is war again," said Patwin solemnly. "I'll ride with you to the House of Lotts. Gilliam's, too, if you wish."

Richius put his hand on Patwin's shoulder. "You're always welcome."

At that instant Jojustin burst into the chamber, a giant broadsword in his fists. The suddenness of the old man's entry made Richius spring from his seat, startled beyond words.

"Here it is!" Jojustin cried.

Richius recognized the weapon at once. He had seen it strapped across his father's back countless times. In all the castle, loaded though it was with swords of every design, there was none so large and ominous as this. With its chipped blade and battered hilt, it looked like a relic from a bygone time. It didn't gleam like other swords, for its metal had long since turned a lusterless gray. But it had a glow all its own, a kind of aura that only those intimate with its past could see.

"Jessicane," Richius said softly, reaching out to take the sword from Jojustin. He let his fingers caress the blade, feeling the cool, imperfect metal against his skin. Jessicane. The name of a wife and a mother, a woman all but unknown to Richius, after whom this weapon had been called. "Jessicane," he repeated, speaking directly to the sword. "I thought for sure you'd been buried with Father."

"It's yours now," said Jojustin. "So everyone will know you are king."

Richius hefted the weapon to the level of his chest. It was far larger than he was used to, at least a full foot longer than his own sword. But his father had been a giant of a man, easily capable of swinging such a huge weapon. Even when he had grown to manhood, Richius looked like little more than a schoolboy next to his father, and since his two years in Lucel-Lor had only weakened him, he found the sword difficult to lift with one hand. He managed, though, despite the small ache it sent coursing through his wrist, and held the sword out for the wide-eyed Patwin to inspect.

"The sword that won the war," said Patwin dramatically. "I never thought to see it so close. Can I hold it?"

"I suppose so," said Richius, gingerly passing the sword over to his comrade. Patwin quickly wiped his oily hands over his tunic and took Jessicane as though it were something holy, careful not to soil the weapon's already well-worn hilt.

"Ooohh, heavy." He twisted the sword in his grip and scanned every inch of it, every nick and blemish, hardly breathing as he did so. At last he handed the sword back to Richius, saying, "It's beautiful. But you can't carry it, Richius. It's too old."

"Nonsense," said Jojustin. "You just run your hand over its edge and then tell me how old it is. That sword's as sharp as the day it cut Gayle's heart out."

Gayle, Richius knew, was Angiss Gayle, the long-dead uncle of Blackwood Gayle and the brother of Talistan's present king. At the drop of his name, Richius braced himself for the story he was sure would follow.

"Your father was only twenty-seven when he killed Gayle, Richius," Jojustin continued. "Not much older than you are now." The old man's eyes glassed over as his mind skipped back through the years. "The three of us were all so young then, your father and Edgard and I. I'll never forget the moment he plunged that sword into Gayle. We were both there with him, fighting alongside him. Lord, that was a day!" Jojustin sighed. "But I must have told you that story a thousand times."

Richius chuckled. "You and my father both. But I don't mind. It was a great day. It should be remembered." He paused, regarding the sword with a distant reverence. "I only wish I'd been there to see it."

"Be glad you weren't," said Jojustin. "Your father had enough sense to want his children to live in a free nation. That's why we went to war with Talistan, and that's the only reason we're all still around to talk about it. Now you remember that, Richius. Keep that thought with you always and you'll be as good a king as Darius was."

"I'll do my best," Richius said, and knew in that instant that he meant it. He would do his best to fill the empty throne his father had left him, even if it meant battling all the legions of Nar. He smiled grimly. Darius Vantran had Angiss Gayle to struggle with for Aramoor's independence. Now, twenty-five years later, his son had Arkus of Nar to fight.

"I know you will, lad," said Jojustin. "You and Patwin and all the other lads are fine replacements for us older soldiers. Now, finish your breakfasts. I've got work to tend to." He turned, stepped halfway out of the dining chamber, then called back over his shoulder, "Do me a small favor, would you, Richius? Don't make too much of a noise at Gilliam's. There's no sense in getting everyone all stirred up over something that probably won't happen."

"Don't worry," answered Richius. "I'll be . . . discreet."

"That's all I ask," said Jojustin, turning and leaving the room. When he had gone Richius stared back at the sword. Patwin was right. It was old, but there was something timeless about it. He felt a kinship with the weapon, felt the spirit of his parents forged into its metal. Jessicane was all he had left of either of them.

"Lord, that's big," said Patwin. "Are you really going to carry it with you?"

Richius shrugged. "I might as well. I lost my sword in Lucel-Lor, too."

Richius and Patwin set off for the House of Lotts shortly after breakfast. Unlike most of Aramoor's noble houses, the House of Lotts was on the sea, far from the uneasy border the tiny nation shared with its neighbor, Talistan. It was, Richius remembered, a considerable distance from his own home. But the road leading north from the castle was a good one, and the wind had abated into a calm, almost mild breeze. Above them hung a cooperative sky, a passive, mother-of-pearl canopy of clouds that Richius guessed was empty of snow. With luck and a steady pace, he was sure they could reach Dinadin's and return before nightfall.

Within an hour they came to the end of the sprawling Vantran property, past the horse yards and farms to the place where the path narrowed and the trees stood thickly abreast like sentries along the roadside. A hood of evergreen branches closed over them and dripped melting snow onto their uncovered heads. Richius welcomed the cold tickle of the drops. It was good to be outside again, to have a horse beneath him, to be with a friend, to comment on things of small matter. Here, under the perfume of fir trees, it was easy to forget his burdens.

As a boy Richius had ridden these paths countless times, first sharing the back of his father's mount, then later on his own. He often came this very way, taking the winding road to the little bit of ocean that Aramoor claimed as its coast, and watching the white-capped waters pitch the tiny boats of the fishermen. It was here, amid the ancient trees, that he learned to be a horseman—the goal of every Aramoorian male. Here was where his father first raced him home to the castle, and where Edgard showed him how to swing a sword from horseback. And not far away, on a ridge too steep for a young, aspiring Guardsman, Jojustin had bandaged his arm after a particularly bad fall. The recollection made Richius flex his elbow. It still twinged when the weather was damp. He smiled. Darius Vantran had been an only child, but he had given his son uncles just the same. Now only one of them remained, and that made Richius cherish the officious white-haired Jojustin more than ever.

An unexpected wind gusted through the tunnel of trees, shaking loose cakes of snow from the branches above. Richius shivered slightly beneath his long riding coat, silently thanking Jenna for the shirt she had made him. He glanced over at Patwin and watched him turn his face from the wind. His cheeks had gone an unhealthy-looking crimson. A patch of fallen snow landed on his shoulder and he cursed.

"Are you all right?" Richius asked. "You don't look well."

Patwin coughed before answering. "I'm fine," he replied, brushing the snow from his coat. "I'm just not used to riding so much yet."

"I should have made the trip myself. It's silly for you to be out again so soon."

"No, Jojustin's right. You shouldn't travel alone, not yet. Don't worry about me. I'm just tired."

Richius frowned. *Tired* was the least that Patwin looked. Even at this distance he could see the little red specks staining Patwin's periwinkle eyes. At just over five feet, Patwin was a small man, thin-boned and slightly-muscled, and the time he had spent traveling through Lucel-Lor had almost killed him. It was true what Patwin had said over breakfast. He really *had* nearly died trying to get Richius his father's last letter. But even Richius believed his friend had recuperated over the last month, fattening up on sleep and Jenna's good cooking. Now, seeing Patwin sway in his saddle, Richius knew he'd been wrong.

"This is fever weather, Patwin," said Richius. "We should go back. You need rest."

"I'll be fine," Patwin insisted. He pointed his chin toward Richius' horse. "As long as that old nag can keep pace. I don't want to still be out here when the sun goes down."

Richius leaned over and patted his horse's neck. "Don't listen to him, boy. He's just mad because you're prettier than he is."

"Why do you still ride him, Richius? He can't do half the things the war-horses can. You should find yourself a new horse. One that's not so . . ."

"Old?"

"Well, yes. You're a Guardsman. You need a horse that fits your station. Like this one." Patwin gestured to the horse beneath him. Dragonfly was one of Jojustin's own horses, a fine dapple-gray beast with a perfectly arched back and impeccable gait. A horse befitting a Guardsman of Aramoor.

"Thunder's good enough for me," said Richius. "We've been together too long for me to just get rid of him." He gave the horse's ear an affectionate scratch. "Haven't we, boy?"

"Thunder," Patwin scoffed. "Looks to me like Thunder's lost some of his rumble. How old is he, anyway?"

Richius quickly counted the years. His father had given him Thunder on his sixteenth birthday, the best gift a boy of Aramoor could hope for. That made the horse about . . .

"Fourteen, I think," Richius answered, fairly certain of his figure.

"Fourteen? And you don't think you should have another horse?" Patwin shook his head in disbelief. "We should ask Dinadin to pick out one of his for you, Richius. If war does come, you don't want to be riding that old bone bag into battle."

"True enough," said Richius amiably. The average stable hand could tell with a glance that Thunder was indeed past his prime. But he was still an able-enough runner, and the thought of retiring the old horse for one of the Lotts' choice geldings simply held no appeal. As an Aramoor Guardsman he had saddled many horses, horses that were faster and stronger than Thunder had ever been. None, though, had claimed the place in his heart that this sweet-tempered gelding had. Thunder was precious to him, an old friend who, unlike too many old friends, was still around to comfort him.

"If the time comes for war I'll have Jojustin find me another horse," Richius said finally. "He'll probably let you keep Dragonfly if you want him. Maybe I'll take Shadow or one of the others." He shrugged, knowing it would be difficult to find a suitable horse for him. He disliked the disposition of most warhorses. Though not as aggressive as the sort Talistan bred—a stock well known for biting even their masters—Aramoorian horses were often fiery and difficult to control, requiring more whip than kindness. Worse, the long conflict in Lucel-Lor had depleted their stables so that now most of them stood empty. If war did come, finding mounts for battle would be their first problem.

"Let's ask Dinadin to see some of their horses anyway," said Patwin. "You can't keep riding Thunder if you're going to be king."

"Maybe not," said Richius. "But I really don't think there's much chance of that, do you? Jojustin's wishing for too much."

"I don't know, Richius," said Patwin. "Jojustin has an ear for these things. If he says you're going to be king . . ."

Richius chuckled. "He does seem to believe it, doesn't he? Still, it would be a miracle. My father hated Arkus and the emperor knows it. And with the Gayles telling him things . . ." He shook his head. "No chance."

"And how do you feel about it?" Patwin asked. "Don't you want to be king?"

Richius shrugged. "It's preferable to war, I suppose."

"Oh, come now," Patwin admonished. "I don't believe you really feel that way."

"You're not a prince," said Richius sharply. "If you were you'd know how hard it can be. I can just imagine what being king would be like. Everyone would want something from me, expect me to do things. Particularly Arkus. If he does make me king, he'll want something for it."

"You don't know that. Maybe Jojustin's right. Maybe Arkus just wants a king here he can depend on, someone who won't cause trouble for him. He's still at war with Liss, after all. He can't afford any strife within the Empire."

"Maybe," said Richius. The war between Arkus and the islands of Liss had been going on for almost a decade, and no one expected Arkus to divert any of his forces away from that cause. Liss was too important to the emperor, more important than even Lucel-Lor had been. Whatever designs Arkus still had for Lucel-Lor were a mystery, but everyone in Nar knew the emperor intended to take Liss, whatever the cost. It was more than just greed now. It was a matter of personal honor. Somehow Liss had managed to keep the machines of Nar from swallowing them up, a feat none of the conquered nations of the Empire had accomplished. Aramoor hadn't done it, nor had Talistan nor Gorkney nor a dozen other states. Only Liss had been able to stare into the eyes of the dragon without being devoured. It was a circumstance Arkus could neither fathom nor allow. To Nar and all its ugly ideals, that kind of boldness was an intolerable cancer.

"We have to be ready," Richius concluded. "I can't imagine that Arkus is afraid of us, the condition we're in. With Talistan on our border his legions could roll over us in a week."

"All the more reason for you to hope Jojustin's right," said Patwin.

Richius nodded. Despite his opposition to being king, it was a far better choice than the possibility of war with Arkus.

"How are you feeling?" he asked, eager to change the subject. "It's not too late to turn back."

"And have Jenna think I'm still ill? Forget it. I don't want her fussing over me anymore. All she ever does is ask me about *you*."

"Oh?" asked Richius casually. "Does that bother you?"

"Why should it? She's your problem, not mine."

"Maybe you should take another look at her," said Richius. "She's a pretty girl."

Patwin shook his head. "She's not interested in me. It's you she's got in her blood."

"That could change. Maybe if I talked to her, told her what a fine fellow you are ..."

"You think I'm sweet on her, is that it?" asked Patwin defensively.

"You're certainly acting like it. Are you?"

Patwin's face colored. He looked away, a thin, embarrassed grin on his lips.

"A little, maybe," he confessed. "But it doesn't matter. She's in love with you, Richius. And if Jojustin's going to marry her to either of us, it'll be you."

"That's not for Jojustin to decide," said Richius. "King or not, I won't marry. Not Jenna, not anyone. I intend to make that very clear to Jojustin."

"But you must marry, Richius. You must have an heir if you're to be king. It's expected of you." Patwin chuckled wryly. "I'm not sure you have a choice in it. Even kings have their orders, I suppose."

"I won't marry, Patwin," said Richius. "Be certain of it."

"But why? I'm just teasing you about Jenna. It doesn't have to be her.

When you're king you can marry anyone you want. You have only to name her and she will be yours; the emperor will see to it."

Richius looked away. "If only it were so easy. Even Arkus can't grant me the woman I want."

"What's this?" asked Patwin. "Have you a sweetling I don't know about?" He winked at Richius playfully. "Confess now, Richius, who is she? Is it Terril's daughter? She's a beauty that one. Every lad in court must be after her, I swear. But you've got nothing to worry about. As king—"

"It's not Terril's daughter," said Richius flatly. "I haven't even seen the girl since coming home."

"Who then? Someone in the court?"

"No, she's not from Aramoor," said Richius. "She's from . . ." He paused, considering his words. "Someplace far away."

"Someplace I've heard of?"

"Oh, yes."

"Well, where then? Come on, Richius, tell me. It's not Talistan, is it?"

"Of course not," said Richius indignantly.

"Thank God for that. Jojustin would have your head on a pike if you told him you were in love with one of their wenches. So where's she from? I've been just about every place you've been and I've never . . ."

He stopped, turning suddenly to face Richius. "Oh, no. She's not a Triin, is she?"

Richius was silent, long enough to convince Patwin he was right.

"Richius! You can't mean it! A Triin? How did that happen? I mean, there wasn't even time for it!"

"It wasn't in the valley, Patwin. I saw her first in Dring, but I really met her in Ackle-Nye."

"Well, who is she? What's her name?"

Richius smiled bleakly. "Dyana," he said. He had not spoken her name to another since coming home. "And before you ask, yes, she was a prostitute."

At once all the interest on Patwin's face fell away. "Lord, Richius. Is that all? I thought this was something serious. We've all fallen in love with a whore before. Forget about it. It'll pass."

"You don't understand. This *is* serious. You weren't there, you didn't see her. She was . . ." He sighed. "Incredible. More beautiful than anyone I've ever seen."

Patwin looked at him curiously. "Are you in love with her?"

"Perhaps. I think about her all the time, when I'm alone in my chamber or in the garden. She's impossible to forget. I've tried, God knows, but her memory is always there with me." He glanced over at Patwin. "Would you call such a fate love, Patwin?"

"Love or some other disease," Patwin gibed. "But where is she now? Why didn't you bring her back with you if you care so much for her?"

Richius started to answer, then abruptly stopped. Except for himself, only Dinadin and his journal knew the ugly story of how he had lost Dyana. Now, though part of him yearned to talk about it, he wasn't sure he could.

"Well?" Patwin pressed. "What happened to her?"

"I don't know," said Richius gloomily. "That's the worst of it. She was carried off by the storm, the one that killed Edgard. I tried to save her but I couldn't." He glanced away. "We ran from it, tried to make it into the mountains, but it was too strong . . ."

He paused, unable to continue. The sky above seemed suddenly darker. The horses had slowed to a snail's pace, as if they themselves were listening to his confession.

"Richius," said Patwin sternly. "Don't start thinking such nonsense. Dinadin told me about that storm, and from what he described no one could have lived through it."

Richius smiled grimly. "I did."

"A miracle," said Patwin.

"Oh, yes," snapped Richius. "I always have that kind of luck, don't I? It was never me that was attacked by a wolf, it was always someone else. I failed her, Patwin, just like I failed Lucyler."

"You did not," insisted his friend. "You did the best you could, I'm sure. So don't berate yourself. It's a horrible thing to live with, but you have to learn to move on. She's dead and that's the end of it."

"If only I could know that for sure. She was running from Tharn. That's why she went to Ackle-Nye, to escape him. But somehow he found her. That storm was his doing, Patwin. She told me it was him, looking for her."

Patwin sat back in his saddle. "Richius, think about what you're saying. It's preposterous."

"I know it sounds absurd. I don't expect you to believe me. I didn't believe Edgard myself when he told me about it, but it's the truth. Somehow Tharn made that storm happen, and somehow he knew Dyana was in Ackle-Nye."

"And you think she's still alive? Not likely. If as you say the storm carried her off, then surely it must have killed her. I'm sorry, Richius, but she is certainly dead."

Richius closed his eyes. "Please, God, let it be so," he murmured, meaning every word. The alternative was unthinkable. He remembered Dyana's small hand slipping out of his. Slipping, slipping, slipping, and all the while trying to hold on, his grip so strong he could feel her bones cracking. But it wasn't enough. She slipped away from him, maybe to her death, maybe into the hands of Tharn. Silently he cursed himself. He truly had failed her, and nothing Patwin could say would convince him otherwise.

At last he opened his eyes. "Patwin, did Dinadin tell you anything about Dyana?"

"No," answered Patwin. "Nothing. He just said that you two left the city in time to escape the storm. He didn't say anything about the girl." Patwin shrugged, clearly confused. "I don't know why. I guess he just didn't want to. You know how private he can be sometimes."

Richius chuckled. He knew indeed how tight-lipped Dinadin could be about such things, but he also felt a surprising pang of respect for his friend. He had expected Dinadin to tell the world how Dyana had been stolen from him, but to Richius' surprise that was still their own, shameful secret.

"I took her from him, Patwin," said Richius. "We were in a tavern and he wanted her. I told him not to, because she was a Triin. You know how I feel about that."

Patwin said nothing, waiting for Richius to continue.

"Well, he listened to me. He wasn't happy about it but he didn't argue with me, either, just went upstairs to find another wench. But I couldn't do the same. She was too beautiful, and I was drunk and lonely. Before I knew what was happening I had paid the innkeeper for her and we were in bed together."

"And Dinadin found out about it?"

"I told him about it the next morning. God, I was so stupid. He was already mad at me for not letting us leave the valley, but when I explained to him about Dyana, do you know what he did?"

"Broke your nose?" quipped Patwin.

"No. He gave me his brother's silver dagger so I could buy another night with her."

Patwin's face collapsed. "Oh, Richius . . ."

"I know. Believe me, I'm not proud of what I did. But she was so special, Patwin. And Dinadin didn't really know her at all. He just wanted to have his way with her."

"Oh?" asked Patwin scornfully. "And you didn't? How do you know Dinadin didn't think she was special, too?"

"Patwin, he only saw her for a moment."

"Sometimes a moment is all it takes to fall in love. Especially in a war. You said she was beautiful. Maybe Dinadin was as taken with her as you were."

"Maybe," said Richius sadly. Until now it hadn't occurred to him that Dinadin had felt anything but lust for Dyana. Somehow, he had forgotten he wasn't the only one lonely and afraid that night.

"I feel like I've betrayed him," Richius concluded. "First my father, now me. But I don't want this to go on. We can keep arguing about Lucyler's death, about the things I did wrong, but what good will it do? I—"

Richius broke off, startled by a movement in the road up ahead. Five doglike figures waited there, their tongues lolling lazily out of their mouths as they spied the approaching horsemen. The horses stopped at once. Richius felt Thunder bristle. Dragonfly gave an angry snort. All five of the beasts bore the common markings of their breed, recognizable to both men and horses alike.

Mountain wolves.

"Richius . . ."

"I see them," Richius whispered. "Don't move. And don't let Dragonfly run."

Patwin pulled back on the reins. The big warhorse obeyed, remaining perfectly still as it stared into the eyes of its foes. The beasts had a lean and hungry look about them, a wildness that made Richius shudder. He recalled with growing dread what Patwin had said that morning. *The first snow makes them crazy.*

Not war wolves, he told himself. *Don't be afraid.*

But he was. His stomach pitched the same way it always did before a battle. He had faced wolves before, creatures far larger and more malevolent than these, but that was in Lucel-Lor, a place where he expected wolves to hunt him. He found himself wishing for a flame cannon.

"What should we do?" Patwin asked.

"Be still," said Richius. They had been riding for almost an hour, and Terril's home on the north acres was too far to hope for. If they bolted and the wolves gave chase, they would be overrun before they even came close to reaching it. He glanced over his shoulder. The road behind them was empty. He listened for a voice or the squeak of a wagon wheel, but heard only the snowy silence. They were alone. Slowly he pulled the big blade off his back. It was time to see what Jessicane could do.

"We're going to turn around," he said softly. "Slowly."

Patwin nodded, almost casually placing his hand on the hilt of his own sword. With his other hand he gingerly tugged at the reins, ordering Dragonfly around. There was a brief hesitation before the steed obeyed. Richius did the same, turning Thunder about. As they began trotting slowly away, he glanced behind them. The wolves were following.

"Damn," he hissed, sure now that the wolves meant to attack. He had heard that wolves could smell fear, and knew they must reek of it. He pulled Jessicane from its scabbard. The huge battle blade felt heavy in his grip, a good weapon for what he needed to do. Patwin pulled out his sword, too. They looked at each other for a moment.

"Ready?" Richius asked.

Patwin nodded weakly.

"All right then."

With a cry Richius kicked his heels into Thunder's side. As if the old horse had been waiting for the order he bolted forward, digging his hooves into the snow-slick road and tearing out clods of frozen earth.

Amazingly, Dragonfly was already ahead of them. Richius felt the gray wake strike his face like a shower of knives. He lowered himself in the saddle, tucked his head against Thunder's neck, and glanced behind them. The wolves were running after them, gaining quickly.

"They're coming!" Richius shouted over the crash of hooves.

"Faster!" cried Patwin.

"I can't," Richius called back. Patwin cursed and twitched his wrist, slowing Dragonfly to a less enviable gallop. Thunder was soon running alongside the bigger horse, his old legs pumping furiously to keep up.

"No!" yelled Richius. "Get going, Patwin! Don't wait for me."

"We can't outrun them. We have to fight!"

Dragonfly slowed a little more. There was a snapping of jaws close behind, then a hollow crack and a yelping as the warhorse's iron hooves connected with a skull. The blow sent the wolf reeling backward. Yet still its brothers came ahead, driven on by the maddening hunger for meat. In a moment the four remaining wolves were alongside them, two flanking Thunder and two Dragonfly. Richius could hear them closing in around Thunder's legs, the quick, insistent patter of their paws, the clashing of their jaws. He raised Jessicane.

Just a little more, you bastards.

At his right a wolf was closing in, readying to make its leap. Richius knew that Thunder was tiring, that exhaustion would overtake the old horse at any moment. When that moment came the wolf would jump. He pulled back on the reins with a practiced smoothness. Thunder slowed and the wolf leapt—and Richius lowered the sword. Jessicane's heavy edge buried itself in the wolf's snout, cutting through its muzzle and sending teeth crashing backward down its throat. At once Richius turned to face the other wolf. The beast was already in the air. It caught Richius' forearm in its jaws, tearing through the thick wool of his riding coat and piercing the flesh beneath it as it yanked him from the saddle. He tumbled from Thunder's back, pulling the horse down with him. Both he and Thunder collapsed into the roadway. The horse gave an agonized whinny as one front leg snapped.

Richius still had Jessicane. He lifted his face out of the mud, struggling to see past the blood and filth covering his eyes. He heard Patwin gallop past him, crying out his name, heard too the inhuman rattle of Thunder's wail. He whirled, expecting to find the wolf behind him, ready to pounce. But the wolf had no interest in him. Its teeth were already in the neck of the fallen horse. Thunder's insane cry grew as he tried to rise to his broken legs, but each time the wolf dragged him down again. The horse's neck erupted in a fountain of blood.

"Patwin!" Richius cried, slogging through the snow toward his fallen horse. He tossed himself onto the wolf, pulling the thrashing beast from Thunder and driving his heavy boot into its ribs. Before the wolf could leap again, Richius swung the sword, catching the beast in the side of its head, slicing past its ear and eye. The wolf fell back, howling, its broken face twisting in pain. Again Jessicane came down, silencing it.

Richius turned back to Thunder. Already the two remaining wolves had broken off their chase and had begun feeding on the still-living horse. Patwin galloped up to Richius, stretching down a hand.

"Come on!" he barked.

"No!"

Richius dashed to the closest wolf. He brought the giant sword down, breaking the wolf's back in an instant. There was only one more left. It lifted its nose out of Thunder's neck and stared at Richius, a low growl rumbling from its throat. Slowly it drew closer, its head low, its eyes black and furious. Richius was still, his own rage blinding him to fear.

"This is my land, wolf!" he hissed. The wolf seemed not to hear him. It growled again and tensed, its haunches poised to leap.

"I have killed your brothers!" said Richius, gripping Jessicane's hilt with his fists. "Now try and kill me!" He was shouting, his voice clear and powerful. Patwin rode up close on Dragonfly, the giant warhorse whinnying and snorting.

"Back, wolf!" yelled Patwin, shaking his sword and drawing Dragonfly up on its hind legs. "Back to the mountains!"

Still the wolf did not withdraw. It was between the men and the dying horse now, jealously guarding the meal it had worked so hard for. Thunder's hellish rattle went on. Richius screamed and rushed toward the wolf, his sword stretched out above his head. Dragonfly was on his heels in an instant. The wolf reared back, hesitating, then leapt for Richius. It was in the air when Jessicane came swinging down, swift and heavy and alive with vengeance. Metal and flesh collided, and for a moment Richius saw only a gray wall of fur pressing toward him. But he felt Jessicane dig deep, the blade biting into the wolf's lean breast. Staggering backward, he heard the clap of jaws near his face and he fell to the ground, kicking and cursing and driving the sword deeper through the beast's rib cage. At last the wolf yelped, falling lifeless upon Richius as the sword pierced its heart.

Richius twisted out from under the beast. His body ached and blood pulsed from his bitten forearm, yet his concern was only for Thunder. The horse was still barely alive, its broken legs trembling as its life ebbed. Richius stumbled through the snow and dropped onto the horse's belly.

"Oh, my beautiful boy," he moaned. He didn't bother to look more closely at the horse's wounds. They would kill Thunder for sure. He only rested his head on the horse's belly, feeling the rise and fall of the gelding's last breaths. "My sweet friend."

"Richius," said Patwin lightly. He had dismounted and was standing over Richius. "You're hurt. We have to get you help."

"Listen to him," said Richius. The horse's cries went on. Richius turned to Patwin. "Do it for me, Patwin," he said softly. "I cannot."

Patwin was ashen. "He'll die soon, Richius. I—"

"Please," Richius begged. He handed Patwin Jessicane. "Do it with this."

Patwin took the sword uneasily. "Don't look, all right?"

Richius nodded.

"Forgive me," he said, and walked over to where Dragonfly stood. The big horse was still, as if aware of the solemness around him. Richius closed his eyes.

Good-bye, old friend.

And then it was over. Richius opened his eyes. Patwin was running his sleeve over Jessicane. The small man looked at Richius weakly.

"It's done," he said. "God, what unholy work that was."

Slowly Richius walked over to Thunder, looking down at the corpse. Patwin had severed the horse's head, so that now the body lay in a thick pool of crimson. Little wisps of steam rose from the pool and the horse. The sight sent a wave of nausea rushing over Richius, buckling his knees.

"Oh, God," he groaned past a mouthful of bile.

"Look away," Patwin ordered, taking hold of Richius' shoulder. "I'm sorry, Richius, but he's gone. That's it."

Richius shook off Patwin's grip. "No," he said, sinking his face into his hands. "Why did this happen? Why here? I'm supposed to be *home*."

Patwin dropped to his knees beside Richius. Carefully he pulled Richius' hands away from his face and stared at him hard. "Listen to me, Richius. You're hurt. Look at your arm. I've got to get you help."

Richius nodded silently, letting Patwin inspect his wounded forearm. The pain was intense, yet he was scarcely aware of it. As if from a great distance he heard Patwin muttering.

"How far are we from Dinadin's, Richius? Do you know?"

Richius glanced down at his bloodied arm, then looked back at Patwin. "Take me home," he said softly. "Please."

FOURTEEN

The ride back to the castle was dreary and sullen. Richius, his fore-arm bandaged in a swaddling of rags torn from his ruined coat, said almost nothing. He was in a kind of shocked stupor, a fog of which he was only scarcely aware, and even the fiery pain of his punc-tured arm hardly reached his mind.

It took only minutes for Dragonfly to reach the castle. Even with two grown men on his back, the young gelding made the trip effortlessly. The castle came into view just as a rain cloud opened up above them.

"There it is," said Patwin. "You'll be all right now, Richius."

Richius lifted his head, heartened a little by the sight of his home. Past the high stone wall surrounding the castle he could see the three towers reaching skyward, striking in the ebbing light. Already tiny points of candlelight glowed in the castle's many windows. Richius shivered, once again feeling the cold. He welcomed the idea of his warm bed and Jenna bringing him porridge. She would make a fuss over him, he knew, and suddenly the thought of her attention didn't bother him. Just now he wanted to be mothered.

Dragonfly got them up the steep tor quickly and came to a stop at the wall's iron gate. Since the murder of Richius' father, Jojustin had ordered the gate locked and guarded at all times, and even Patwin didn't have free access to the castle. He cursed when he reached it, shouting for the sentry. As if out of nowhere the guard appeared, a giant, twin-bladed axe in his fists.

"Who is it?" he asked gruffly, peering at them through the metal shafts.

"Open up!" Patwin demanded. "Richius is hurt!"

"Richius?" The guard's small eyes narrowed as he looked past Patwin. "Is it you, Prince Richius?"

"It's me," Richius called back. "Do as he says, Faren."

The man dropped his axe and produced a key tethered to his armor by a thin chain. Hurriedly he fumbled with the lock and pulled open the portal.

"Sorry, my lord," he said. "Jojustin told me to be careful tonight. We've had some strange visitors."

"Visitors?" Richius asked. "Who?"

The sentry gave a furtive glance toward the courtyard. "From Nar, my lord."

When they were through the gate Richius noticed the strangers. Two horsemen, both wearing the green and gold uniforms of Talistan, leaned lazily against their horses, unmindful of the drizzling rain. A third horseman was with them, still atop his horse, bearing a standard instantly recognizable by its bleakness. It was a plain field of black fabric without crest or embroidering. It was the flag of Nar, the Black City. As Richius and Patwin rode into the courtyard the two Talistanians looked at them, wry smiles on their faces. The rider from Nar never moved. Richius noticed now that a fourth horse was behind him. Its flanks also bore the black banners of Nar, but its saddle was empty.

"What's this?" asked Richius, sliding down from Dragonfly's back. "Who are they, Faren?"

Faren bid Richius closer and, putting his lips near his prince's ear, whispered, "Biagio."

Richius' eyes widened. In good company, the name Biagio was always followed by a respectable silence. It was a name that had a unique power within the Empire. Richius glanced over at the trio of horsemen. The two Talistanians were still watching him. Quickly he pulled his wounded arm under the folds of his tattered coat.

"What does he want? Do you know?"

"He wanted to talk to you, my lord. I don't know why."

"Did you take him to see Jojustin?"

"Almost an hour ago. He told the others to wait outside."

"Thank God for that," said Richius. At least Biagio had shown the good sense not to let the Talistanians join him inside the castle. It was enough of an insult that they were in Aramoor at all. As for the other man, whom Richius supposed was a bodyguard, Biagio must have thought himself safe without him. Richius grimaced. Aramoor wasn't much of a threat to anyone these days.

"Biagio," spat Patwin. "What's that dog doing so far from home?"

"I wonder," said Richius. As head of the Roshann, Biagio was one of Arkus' closest advisers, a member of his so-called "iron circle." In the tongue of High Nar the term *Roshann* meant "The Order," and that was exactly what Biagio was charged with maintaining. Every prison, every labor camp, every trial of sedition fell under his jurisdiction, and every public hanging in the Black City happened because he said so. It was rumored that the Roshann had spies in every court of the Empire, even Aramoor's, and as absurd as that claim sounded to some, Richius secretly admitted to himself that no one really knew for sure. He was certain of only one thing about the Roshann—they were everywhere.

"Faren, take the horse back to the stables," said Richius. "Patwin, you come with me."

"Richius, your arm," Patwin protested. "It has to be tended to. Let Biagio wait."

"Yes, my lord," agreed Faren, taking Dragonfly's reins from Patwin. "I'll tell Jojustin you've returned."

"No. I don't want to be announced. And don't tell Jojustin I'm hurt, either. Don't tell anyone, Faren. I don't want a lot of fussing."

The big man nodded. "I understand, my lord."

"Damn it, Richius," grumbled Patwin, mindful of the nearby soldiers. "Biagio came all the way from Nar City. He can wait a little longer while you get a proper bandage."

"No," said Richius. "Biagio doesn't ever have good news for anyone, Patwin. He probably wants to talk about my father. If so, I don't want Jojustin to have to explain it all. That's *my* business." He turned and strode toward the castle. "Are you coming?"

"Yes," said Patwin reluctantly, following Richius across the courtyard. The Talistanians were still watching them. They both gave a slight, mocking bow to Richius.

"Good evening, Prince Richius," said one of the soldiers.

Richius said nothing, only glared at the arrogant duo. It had been over twenty years since Talistanian soldiers had stepped on the soil of Aramoor, and Richius reasoned that these two villains were proud of their accomplishment. As for the other horseman, whom Richius could see clearly now, he seemed to feel no such glee. He was perfectly erect in his saddle, his black armor dazzling. A cape of black with crimson lining was draped over his giant shoulders, clasped around his neck by a golden chain. He only turned his head toward Richius for a moment, long enough to display the death's-mask helmet he wore. It was the absolute likeness of a skull. Richius gasped. This silent, beautiful spectre was a Shadow Angel.

Bodyguard indeed, thought Richius. The Shadow Angels were Arkus' personal protectors, an elite group of soldiers famous for their skill and loyalty. They were the best fighters in the Empire, a hand-picked regiment of zealots, and they never spoke to anyone unless their masters bid it. In all his life, Richius had only seen one of them before, and that was so long ago he could scarcely remember it. Now, face to face with this soldier, he wondered just how long Aramoor really could stand against Nar.

"Come on, Richius," said Patwin, pulling at his sleeve. "Let's get inside."

Richius let Patwin lead him out of the courtyard and into the castle's foyer, a small room where a traveler could knock the mud off his boots before entering the palace's more elegant rooms. Patwin looked Richius over carefully, inspecting Richius' arm again. The bandage was filthy, drenched with rain and stained with earth and blood. Richius flinched as Patwin probed it with his finger.

"Ouch," he snapped. "That hurts!"

"I'll bet," Patwin muttered. "Not too long, all right? You have to get a clean bandage on that."

Richius snatched his arm back. "Enough. It'll be fine, believe me." He slipped the scabbard from his back, then started taking off his coat, peeling the sleeve gently from around his arm. "Give me your coat," he said to Patwin.

"My coat? Why?"

"Because I don't want anyone to see my arm. If Jenna knows I'm hurt . . ."

"Richius!" came a sudden cry.

Richius' face fell as he recognized the voice. Jenna came rushing up to him, her expression almost comically fretful. She took one look at his bandaged arm and put her hands to her face.

"Lord!" she exclaimed. "What happened to you?"

"Wolves," said Patwin. "They got us on the north passage. Richius took a pretty bad bite."

"And that's your idea of a bandage?" she asked Patwin sharply. "It's filthy! You need a fresh dressing fast, and a washing."

"No!" said Richius. "I need to find Jojustin. Where is he, Jenna? With Biagio?"

Jenna nodded, reaching out for Richius' arm. "Yes," she said, carefully examining the wound. "This is bad, Richius. Come with me and—"

"Are they in the council chamber?" said Richius impatiently.

"Yes, but you can't go in there like this."

"I have to," said Richius. "I have to know what's going on. Patwin?" He put out his hand for Patwin's coat. Patwin reluctantly handed it to him, and Richius slid it on. It was a snug fit, particularly around the bulk of his bandage. He brushed some of the mud from his knees, grateful that the long coat covered most of his body, then started off down the hallway. Jenna was calling after him, but he ignored her. He could deal with his wounds later.

"Shouldn't I announce you or something?" asked Patwin anxiously. "I don't want to just break in on them."

"This is our house, Patwin, not Biagio's. We don't stand on court ceremony here. If Biagio wants courtesy he can go back to Nar City."

The council chamber was on the ground floor of the castle, down a long, quiet corridor. Like the throne room, the council chamber was seldom used. Darius Vantran had been an unpretentious king, and most of the matters he decided upon could be settled without the need for meetings or grand designs. He had governed a land of horse breeders and farmers, and so the trappings of state had little consequence or interest to him. Though he did have a throne, it was a small one and he rarely sat upon it. It was mostly an object of show, an affectation he could exercise to impress dignitaries on important occasions. There were very few important occasions this far north in the Empire.

When they reached the council chamber they found the door tightly shut. Richius put his ear to the door. He could hear voices coming from behind it. Soft voices, mannered and disciplined. He breathed a little easier, pleased not to hear any of Jojustin's hot-tempered shouting.

"They're in there," he whispered to Patwin. "Ready?"

Patwin nodded nervously. "Yes."

Richius gave his friend a reassuring smile. "Don't worry," he said, barely audibly, and lightly pushed open the door.

". . . will retain full rulership over Aramoor, right?"

The voice was Jojustin's. Startled, the old man turned to the door, at once forgetting his guest across the table. "Richius! I'm glad you're back. We have a visitor."

Count Biagio was out of his chair in an instant, staring back at Richius with a pair of brilliant sapphire eyes. He crossed the room in a few quick strides.

"Prince Vantran," said the count, putting out his hand. "I am honored to meet you at last."

Richius took the count's hand and gave it a wary shake. Biagio's many rings bit into his flesh. "Thank you," he answered awkwardly.

"I am Count Renato Biagio," said the count through a dazzling smile. "You have heard of me, I'm sure."

"Yes," said Richius, releasing the man's hand at once. There was an icy coldness to it.

"Forgive my hands, Prince Richius," said Biagio. "It's a bitter day, and I have a condition that makes it worse for me. These rugged climes are not kind to us from Crote."

Richius nodded. Biagio's homeland of Crote was in the south of the Empire. Like all Crotans, Biagio had rich, satiny skin and an obvious aversion to rugged weather. Long days in the sun had turned his hair the color of amber. Even the way he spoke hinted of somewhere very far away. There was a faint foppishness to his tone, an overfriendliness that made Richius uneasy. And then there were the eyes, like two multifaceted gems—sparkling and pure, like a child's or a cat's.

"You are very far from home, Count," said Richius. The tone of his voice spoke the question for him. Why? Jojustin lifted himself out of his chair and strode over to Biagio. There was an unmistakable look of excitement on the old steward's face.

"The count has news for you, Richius," said Jojustin. "Why don't we all sit down so you can tell him? Count?"

"Of course," said Biagio. "And the prince looks absolutely miserable. He should sit down, perhaps have some wine. Allow me, please." Biagio walked over to the table and retrieved the decanter of wine resting there. He took his own glass, filled it liberally, and handed it to Richius. "For you, Prince Richius. And we should have a glass for your companion, too. Who is this young man?"

Richius took the glass and waved Patwin forward. "This is Patwin, Count. A friend."

Biagio beamed as Patwin bowed to him. "A soldier?"

"Yes, my lord," said Patwin. "An Aramoor Guardsman."

Biagio sighed knowingly. "Ah, one of the heroes of Lucel-Lor. The emperor wanted me to express his gratitude for all you did there. He's very proud of each of you."

"He is?" asked Patwin.

"Certainly. You all fought gallantly. The emperor knows that." Biagio leveled his alien eyes on Richius. "He knows you did your very best for him."

"Indeed they did," said Jojustin. "It's good to hear the emperor honors their sacrifice."

"Oh, he does," said Biagio. "And he has a special reward for you, Prince Richius. Sit and I will tell you."

Richius glanced at Jojustin. The old man was still wearing an "I told you so" grin. Biagio went to the table and held out a chair for him, and as he took his seat Richius realized Jojustin had been correct. Impossible, but true. Soon there would be a new king in Aramoor. When they were all finally seated, Biagio took his own chair across the table from Richius. He leaned forward and rested his chin on his hands.

"I have something very special for you, Prince Richius. A priceless gift from the emperor himself."

"Oh?" said Richius casually. "What is it?"

Biagio reached beneath his cape and pulled out a thin yellow parchment. "This."

Richius took the parchment carefully, breaking the wax seal with a fingernail. It was good, heavy paper, the kind treaties were written on. He unfolded it and began to read.

> To Richius Vantran,
> The death of your great father saddens me. You are to come to
> Nar City on the thirtieth day of winter for your coronation as
> King of Aramoor.

It was signed very simply *Arkus*.

Richius sat staring at the summons. It wasn't what he had expected, particularly the complimentary way it spoke of his father. The emperor and his father had been bitter enemies, had argued about every small matter of Aramoor's governing. Though the king had always lost those arguments, that had never stopped him from having them. It puzzled Richius that the emperor should now be so magnanimous as to call his father "great." There was also the queer matter of the signature. Arkus had signed his name, nothing more. It was almost friendly.

Too friendly, thought Richius suspiciously. *Like Biagio.* He passed the letter on to Patwin, who accepted it eagerly.

"Well, my boy?" asked Jojustin. "What do you think of that?"

"I'm honored," lied Richius. Some quick figuring told him that the thirtieth day of winter was only two months away. Time enough to reach the Black City.

"It's a pity that it had to happen under such sad circumstances," said Biagio. "Your father was a great king. All in Nar feel his death keenly, I assure you. The emperor is particularly heartsick about it."

Richius flinched. Biagio was obscenely comfortable with lying. "You must thank the emperor for his kind offer, Count," he said. "It was unexpected."

"Oh?" asked Biagio coyly. "Why is that? Surely you must have thought yourself in line for the throne, Prince Richius."

"No doubt Richius is just surprised by the suddenness of everything," Jojustin inserted. "After all, such news would surprise anyone." Jojustin gave Richius a furtive glance. "Isn't that right, Richius?"

"Yes, surprised," agreed Richius quickly. "And as I said, you must express my gratitude to the emperor for his generous offer."

"You may tell him yourself when you see him. The emperor is greatly looking forward to meeting you. There is much he would like to discuss. But please, do not say that this is an offer. The emperor prefers to call it a gift." For one brief moment Biagio's eyes flashed. "One that I'm afraid you have no choice but to accept."

There was a sudden silence in the chamber. At last Richius said, looking straight into the count's intense gaze, "Why would I do otherwise, Count? As I said, it is an honor for me to take my father's place."

"I am pleased to hear you say so, Prince Richius. There are men who are shy about following the ways of Nar. Such men do not do well in the Empire. It takes courage to be a good king."

"Richius has courage enough," piped up Patwin. "You wouldn't wonder about it if you had served with him in Lucel-Lor, my lord. All of us are sure he'll make a fine king."

Biagio raised his eyebrows at Patwin. "My, such loyalty. It does you well to have such complimentary subjects, Prince Richius. But truly, I do not question your mettle. We have all heard the tales from Lucel-Lor, how brutal it was for you there." Biagio's tongue darted out to lick his lips. "It was quite brutal, wasn't it, Prince Richius?"

"Yes," said Richius, his voice toneless. "Brutal."

"And that fire that swept through Ackle-Nye. Tell me of that."

"There isn't much to tell."

"Some say it was a magical storm. Do you think it was magic, Prince Richius?"

Richius couldn't answer. He was convinced that it was indeed a magical storm that had destroyed Edgard and his troops and stolen away Dyana, but what should he tell Biagio? He wasn't even sure why the count was probing.

"Lucel-Lor is full of strange things, my lord. Even their weather is unlike ours in the Empire. Perhaps it was only a thunderstorm I saw."

Biagio shrugged, unconvinced. "It wasn't only you that saw it, Prince Richius. There are some from Talistan who told of great, unusual storms, storms unlike anything ever seen before." He leaned back in his chair and watched Richius carefully. "Unnatural, ungodly storms. What do you think could have created such powerful things?"

"I have no idea," replied Richius coolly.

"Did you serve with any Triin?" asked Biagio.

"Only one."

"Did you ever see him use sorcery?"

"Never," Richius said adamantly. "Why do you ask?"

"It's not unreasonable for the emperor to wonder why the war was lost," said Biagio. "If, as you say, the Drol used no sorcery . . ." Biagio let his voice trail away, all the while keeping his unearthly stare on Richius. Again Richius' stomach churned. He had thought to avoid this, but he had blundered into it the way a rabbit does a snare. It was becoming very clear to him why Arkus had sent this man to him. An errand boy could have delivered a letter, but only Biagio could deliver this kind of message.

"My mission was to take the Dring Valley, Count," said Richius, returning Biagio's dubious gaze. "I saw no sorcery there. It may be that there was magic used in Tatterak, I cannot say. The Talistanians were charged with securing that land. Perhaps you should ask them your questions."

"Most of them died at Mount Godon, defending the Daegog," said Biagio. "And those that did survive swear to me that sorcery was used. Even your own war duke died in this strange storm. Was he not also part of the Tatterak campaign?"

"He was."

"And you saw him die, did you not?"

Richius nodded.

"Well, then," said Biagio, leaning back comfortably in his chair. "I can't explain it. Can you?"

"No."

Biagio smiled, and in that instant Richius felt the count's invisible fingers running over his mind. *Jojustin's right,* he thought. *They know about Father.* It all came rushing over him like a waterfall, the anger, the betrayal, the abandonment, and for a single, shameful moment Richius hated his father for making him sit here and face this madman. But he couldn't stop it now, for there it was on the table between them, plain and naked for everyone to see. The truth. He dropped his hand to his arm and gave it a slight, surreptitious massage. The wolf bite was throbbing furiously now.

"We did our best," he said at last. "Aramoor is only a small nation. It was almost impossible to fight with so few troops, even with the help of Talistan. Perhaps if we had gotten more support from the Black City we could have kept the Drol from taking Lucel-Lor." He spoke slowly, measuring every word carefully. "Still, I'm sure the Empire would have sent us troops if they could have. The war with Liss must be quite a strain on even Nar's resources."

The mere mention of Liss erased Biagio's arrogant grin. Jojustin seized the opportunity.

"How does the war with Liss go, Count?" he asked. His voice had the perfect politeness of a diplomat. "Tell us, please. We hear so little of it in Aramoor. What is happening?"

Biagio smiled again. "Liss is being dealt with."

"They're a pack of devils, to be sure," Jojustin went on. "None of us ever thought it would go on this long. Is it true that their fleets have begun to raid the south coast? I had heard that from a traveling merchant."

"A lie," said Biagio emphatically. "Our navies have complete control over those waters. I myself would never allow such a thing."

Richius sighed knowingly. "Crote *would* be in danger if that were true. I've heard that Liss' ships are even finer than the imperial dreadnoughts. And there are more of them, too."

"More nonsense. Really, Prince Richius, where does your news come from? The emperor thinks Liss will crumble within the year. Then we shall see whose ships are finer."

Richius was silent for a moment, considering that valiant collection of islands called Liss. It was certain Liss would fall to Nar's might eventually, for despite their courage and superior navy, there was no way that Liss could hold out forever against the weapons Arkus had arrayed against them. Amazingly, they had withstood the siege for nearly a decade, drowning the warships of the Empire in the thousand mazelike waterways that only they could travel. They had resisted flame cannons and blockades, had survived being isolated from their trading partners in the Empire; they had even had the beautiful audacity to proclaim themselves "the world's last free nation." Richius didn't know how they were thought about in Talistan, but in Aramoor the folk of Liss were revered. When the dark day of their defeat came, he knew Aramoor would mourn for them.

"So much talk of war," said Jojustin. "This is a happy occasion. We should be celebrating."

"Yes," agreed Patwin, slapping Richius on the shoulder warmly. "It's a great day for Aramoor. And for you, Richius. It will be my highest honor to call you my king."

"And mine," added Jojustin. "I will try to serve you as well as I served your father, lad."

"And you will serve the emperor well," said Biagio soberly. "I am sure of it."

"I will do my best," said Richius.

There was a sudden knock at the door. Richius, relieved at the interruption, rose at once to answer it. He opened the door and found Jenna standing in the hallway, a nervous look on her face. She dared one small step into the chamber.

"I'm sorry, my lords," she said softly, her head bowed to the floor. "I thought you might be getting hungry. It's past mealtime, and I know the count has had a long journey." There was a slight quaver in her voice. "I could bring you something, perhaps?"

"Yes, Count," said Jojustin. "Why don't you dine with us this evening? We'll have chambers prepared for you and your man. You can stay the night."

Biagio raised his jeweled hands. "No, thank you. Your offer is most kind, but I really must be on my way."

"What?" said Jojustin amiably. "You shouldn't be traveling on a night like this. I won't hear of it. The emperor would think us the poorest hosts in the Empire. Really, you must stay, at least for the night."

Biagio rose from his chair. "Forgive me, but I cannot. I have business elsewhere, and I have already made arrangements for the evening. The Gayles of Talistan are expecting me back soon. They will be worried if I do not return."

"Why need they worry?" pressed Jojustin. He hadn't yet risen as the count had. "Just send those two horsemen back to tell them you're staying the night. It's a long ride back to Talistan, Count. And this weather . . ."

"Really, no," said Biagio. "I would feel more comfortable in Talistan."

Jojustin's face hardened. "I see," he said icily, getting to his feet. "Very well. Perhaps we will see you in Nar, then."

"Most certainly. The emperor intends this to be an event. He's inviting all the kings of the Empire to attend."

"Really?" asked Richius, also rising. "Why so many people? I thought it would be a private ceremony, just close comrades."

"Oh, no, Prince Richius. Perhaps you do not understand what an honor this is for you. You will be the first new king in Nar in almost six years. The emperor wants this to be an occasion for the whole Empire. There will be royalty from all over Nar in attendance. There will be foods and wines fit for your king-making, and music the likes of which you've never heard. It will be glorious, and it will all be for you."

"It sounds like a great deal of trouble," said Richius. "Perhaps the emperor is being too generous. Such extravagance—"

"No, no," interrupted Biagio. "It is what the emperor wants for you."

Richius held back a frown. "I am honored," he said simply. "I shall be in Nar on the appointed day."

"Excellent. The emperor will be very pleased. I will dispatch a messenger to him at once informing him of your coming. Remember, Prince Richius, the thirtieth day of winter."

"I will be there," said Richius, showing Biagio to the door. "May I bring some attendants with me? It's a long journey, and I will need advisement."

"Of course," said Biagio. "It's to be a celebration! Bring as many as you wish. The palace has room enough for all of you. And I can arrange transport for you, if you like. Talistan has a port. I can call for a ship of the Black Fleet."

Richius considered the offer. A ship would certainly be the fastest way, but he rather liked the idea of riding and seeing the rest of the Empire. More, he had no wish to set foot in Talistan.

"Thank you, no, Count," he replied. "I think we can ride it. We'll take our time, get to know some of the Empire." He turned to Patwin. "What do you say, Patwin? You up for it?"

Patwin smiled. "If you'll have me."

"Wonderful," beamed Biagio. He looked over at Jojustin. "I expect you will be there, Sir Jojustin?"

Jojustin was indifferent. "It is difficult to get away, Count. The castle does not run itself and, as Richius said, it is a long trip. I will come if I can."

"You really must come," Biagio insisted. "The emperor is expecting you. He would be very disappointed if you were not there."

"We shall see," said Jojustin. He led Biagio out into the corridor and silently walked him to the castle's muddy foyer, Richius and Patwin close behind. The door to the place was open, and a shrill wind was blowing in, making the torches on the wall flicker and sending their shadows dancing. Outside, the rain had built to a steady drizzle, and the men from

Talistan stood awkwardly in the downpour, their uniforms drenched, their faces no longer bearing the arrogant humor they had before. Only the Shadow Angel seemed unperturbed. He watched as his master approached, but he didn't speak a word nor stir a single muscle. Biagio drew his fine cape closer about his shoulders as he spied the inclement night.

"You should reconsider, Count," said Jojustin. "We have warm beds for both of you."

"No, thank you," barked Biagio. Then, as if catching the insult, he added more genially, "It's a kind offer, but I really cannot stay the night here. I must return to Talistan. Matters of weight require me."

"Then be well," said Jojustin stiffly.

"I will," said Biagio. He turned to Richius and gave a slight bow. "Prince Richius, it was an honor to meet you. I look forward to your coronation."

"Safe journey, Count," said Richius, and watched Biagio step out into the rain. The count mounted his own horse and smiled one last time before turning away and riding off into the night, the Shadow Angel and the Talistanians close behind. When they were almost out of sight Jojustin gave a great, brooding sigh.

"It's good to see those Talistanian pigs leaving," he said. "When I saw them ride up with him I nearly died."

Patwin laughed and gave Richius another slap on the back. "My God! That went well, don't you think, Richius?"

"I suppose."

"What?" said Jojustin. "Of course it went well, lad. It's like I told you. You're going to be king! So stop wearing the long face. This has been a great day. A great day indeed!"

"No," said Richius softly. "It hasn't been." He put his hand to his wounded arm. The punctures in it burned savagely, and he knew the filth of his bandage was working its way into his wounds. Yet still he didn't care to tend to it. Something else was puzzling him.

"Why would Biagio not spend the night?" he asked Jojustin. "Or even have a meal with us?"

"Or drink his wine?"

Richius looked at the old man oddly. "He didn't drink with you, either?" Jojustin shook his head.

"I don't understand," said Richius. "Why not?"

Jojustin's old face softened. "Make no mistake, lad. Biagio's coming here was a warning. The emperor knows about your father. He wanted us to know that he'll be watching Aramoor from now on."

"And still he wants to make me king?"

"It's as I told you. Arkus must make you king, whether he wishes to or not. You saw how Biagio looked when we spoke of Liss. The war with them must be going worse than we thought." Jojustin grinned. "I was right. I knew Arkus couldn't risk a war within the Empire. He's as anxious as the rest of us to keep your father's secret."

Richius nodded dully. "You were right," he conceded. "But why would he not sup with us? And to travel on such a night . . ."

Jojustin laughed. "You are the son of a traitor, Richius," he said. Then, taking Richius in a light embrace, he said, "Be proud of it."

A knot of emotion clenched in Richius' throat. "I am."

"Richius," said Patwin, stepping up to him. "Are you ready?"

"Ready?" asked Jojustin. "For what?"

Richius was silent, refusing to look at either of them.

"Come on, Richius," said Patwin sternly. "You have to be looked after."

Jojustin's face went from cheerful to concerned in a heartbeat. "Tell me what's going on," he demanded. "Richius, is something wrong?"

"A pack of wolves attacked us on the way to the House of Lotts," said Patwin. "Richius was bitten."

"Bitten? Lord, Richius, why didn't you say something? Where were you bitten? Let me see."

"No," said Richius flatly. "Not yet."

He took the torch from the sconce on the wall and, without even glancing at Jojustin or Patwin, stepped out of the foyer and into the night.

"Richius!" called Jojustin. "Where are you going?"

"I have something to do," Richius called back over his shoulder. "Don't worry, I'll be back soon."

The night encircled him, and to his relief they did not follow. By the light of the torch he made his way across the courtyard, his boots sinking deep into the mud, letting the cool rain trickle down his face and soothe the burning of his arm. He went quickly past the castle gardens, past its walls overhung with dormant roses, and past its locked, finely wrought gate. Soon he came to the stables, where only the quiet sound of horses could be heard, and these he walked past, too. His movements were heavy, purposeful, and as he went by the stables the thing he sought came into view.

It was a tomb.

It was not very large, and it was not excessive or garish. It was a simple tomb, built by a grieving king for a woman who had been a simple queen. Darius Vantran had found parting with his beloved Jessicane nearly impossible, and so the tomb had been constructed close to the castle, built on a hill so that one could easily see it from any of the castle's three towers. For nearly twenty years the tomb had housed but one corpse. Now it housed two.

Richius slowed as he neared the tomb, measuring his steps, watching the structure take focus in the torchlight. Two stone faces stared back at him, rising in relief off the doorway. They smiled at him. He stopped.

"Father," he said to one of them, the one with the steely eyes. And then he looked at the other face, the one whose eyes seemed to be laughing, and he smiled lightly back and said, "Mother."

He paused for a moment, alone in the rain, as if waiting for an answer he knew would never come. Then he sighed, and reached under his coat to his shirt. His shirt was soaked with rain and stained with blood and dirt, but it was the thick shirt that Jenna had made him, and so it kept him warm and dry and protected the things he put in its pockets. Quickly he found what he was seeking, folded neatly against his breast.

His hand trembled a little as he pulled it out. He had had this letter for over a month, and despite what he had told everyone, he had carried it with him most of that time, occasionally feeling his breast for it, but never reading it. He regarded it in the torchlight. Its careful creases were worn and frayed. Already raindrops were making tiny water stains on it. He swallowed hard and unfolded it, immediately recognizing his father's broad, elaborate penmanship.

My Dear Son,

By now you know what I have done to you. I will not try to persuade you of the rightness of it. Of all the duties my kingship has forced upon me, none has been so hard as leaving you to fight alone. But the war does not go well, and far too many men have already given up their lives. I can be the emperor's puppet no longer.

Patwin has told me how desperate the valley struggle has become. So far I have been able to keep this from the emperor. The war with Liss yet preoccupies him, and what little I do tell him does not include the truth of things. Unless the Gayles tell him otherwise, I believe I can go on convincing Arkus of my commitment until the war is lost. By then it will be too late for him to send his legions, and no more of our people need die. I alone will have to answer for the loss, and I will tell the emperor that no one had knowledge of my treachery. My only hope now is that you will survive and return home before I am discovered.

Perhaps a day will come when you are king and can see the correctness of my actions. The burdens of the crown are many and heavy, and sometimes inconceivable to those unencumbered by them. By the time you read this many rumors will have reached you, but I hope none will tempt you to believe that I have forsaken you for any reason but the saving of lives. I have never cowered from a just war, but this conflict has no graces worth its ruinous toll and so it must be ended. I can think of no other way to end the war and still save Aramoor.

The emperor's priests tell us that God looks after heroes. If

so, He is surely with you. May He bring you safely home, my
son, and grant you the charity to forgive me.

With love and regrets,
Father

Richius folded the letter back carefully and replaced it in the pocket of
his shirt. The steely-eyed relief was watching him.

"I'll try, Father," he said softly, then turned and walked slowly back to
the castle.

FIFTEEN

Alain was only ten, but he already had the family's love for hunting, and Dinadin knew his brother would someday be a fine bowman. The bow he was using had been specifically tailored to his diminutive stature, a gift from his father on his recently passed birthday. It was made of hardwood, like a real bow, and just like a real bow it fired arrows precisely where an archer aimed. If the archer was any good, the target was hit. If not, then lessons were needed. Alain needed lessons desperately.

"I can pull it back myself!" insisted the boy. He tried to pull loose of his brother's embrace, but Dinadin stood firmly behind him, helping him draw back the string.

"No," directed Dinadin easily. "You're holding the string wrong again. Don't use your whole hand. Here . . ."

Dinadin let the tension out of the string, then folded his brother's little hand around the arrow shaft, using just the top two fingers. He guided Alain's hand back to the string, positioning it and carefully drawing it back.

"It hurts that way," complained the boy. "I like my way better."

"You'll lose control over the arrow your way," said Dinadin. "That's why you can't hit the target."

Alain grimaced as he took stock of his marksmanship, inspecting the target yards away. It was a round bale of hay with a sloppily painted red circle at its center. The center hadn't been hit once, nor had any other part of the bale. The ground around the target was littered with arrows.

"I can't get it," Alain sighed. "I'm just no good. Not like you."

"It takes practice, Alain," Dinadin consoled him. "I didn't get good quickly, either. I had to work at it. Del, too. Father taught us both when we were your age. Now it's your turn to learn."

"I can't," said Alain, tossing his bow to the ground. "And I don't want to practice. I want to be good. *Now.*"

Dinadin laughed. Alain had always been impatient, even before Dinadin had left for Lucel-Lor. He was glad the boy hadn't changed. Nothing had really changed since coming home, and that helped to quiet Dinadin's restless heart. And whenever he spent time with his brothers or rode with his father, he silently swore he would never leave this place again. He picked Alain's bow up from the ground and offered it to him, but his brother shook his head.

"I don't want it," said the boy sourly. "It doesn't work."

"Don't blame the bow, Alain," said Dinadin. "That won't help."

"It's too small, I can't reach the target."

"Of course you can. Here, let me show you."

He pulled another arrow out of the quiver on the ground, notched it into the string of the small bow, and drew back with one eye closed. The red circle took focus immediately, like a Drol's robes, and the world closed around him until all he saw was the target and the distortedly large arrowhead. When he released the string the arrow whistled away and slammed into the bale, just inches off center. Alain screeched happily and clapped his hands together.

"You see?" said Dinadin, handing the weapon back to his brother. "It's not the bow. It's you. You just have to practice."

Alain took the bow cheerfully. "You're better than Del. Better than Father, even. Maybe you're the best in Nar!"

"I'm not," said Dinadin, embarrassed by his brother's praise but nonetheless loving it. He could still make Alain smile. "There's a lot better than me."

"I don't know any," said Alain.

"Well, I do. Like Triin. They're the best bowmen in the world. Fast. And always on target."

Alain stared up at him inquisitively. "Did you know a lot of Triin?"

"Not a lot," said Dinadin. All at once his mood deflated. "Just one really."

"Was he a good bowman?"

"Oh, yes," replied Dinadin. "Come here, I want to tell you about him."

He took his brother's hand and led him to the shade of a nearby sycamore. Beneath the tree were pillows of fallen leaves that had been kicked into neat piles. The snow that had come earlier in the week had disappeared, and the weather was seasonable again, ripe with autumn dampness. Alain plopped down into one leaf pile and Dinadin into another. Alain's green eyes were wide with anticipation.

"His name was Lucyler," began Dinadin dramatically. "He was my friend." Then he thought again and said, "No, that's not right. He was more than just a friend. He was like a brother."

"Like me?"

"A little taller," joked Dinadin. "But yes, like you and Del."

"And Richius?"

Dinadin's smile evaporated. "Let me tell the story, all right? Anyway, he was a great bowman, really the best I've ever seen. I mean better than me, better than Father, just the best. He could notch an arrow, shoot, and have another ready to go before you could even pull an arrow from your quiver." Dinadin sighed. "Lord, he was something else."

"Father says the gogs are fast because they're part animal," said Alain. "Is that right, Dinadin? Are they like animals?"

"No, they're not animals, they're people. And don't call them gogs."

Alain's eyebrows went up. "You called them gogs all the time! I remember."

"Not anymore I don't," said Dinadin. "And you shouldn't, either. Father doesn't know what he's talking about, so just forget what he tells you about Triin. If you want to know anything, ask me. I'll tell it straight."

"What happened to your friend?" asked Alain. "Did he die?"

Dinadin nodded. "Yes."

"What happened?"

"Alain," said Dinadin gravely, "I can't really tell you that. If I told you the truth it might upset you, change the way you feel about things. And I don't want that."

Alain didn't hide his disappointment. "Dinadin, come on. Tell me."

"I can't," said Dinadin. "Not all of it, anyway. Let's just say he was left behind, and because someone left him behind he was captured by the Drol. They took him away, and . . . I guess they killed him."

Alain slid closer to his brother, dragging his rump across the grass. "You miss him?" asked the boy.

"Yes," said Dinadin sadly. "I miss him. I miss a lot of people."

He reached out his long arm then and snatched up his little brother, squeezing him with one hand and mussing up his hair with the other. Alain cried out comically and tried to wiggle free, but wound up just dragging his brother over into the patch of leaves. They both laughed and pulled twigs from their hair, and would have broken into a chase if not for a sudden shout from the castle yard. Dinadin heard his name being called and looked up to see a slight, blond-haired figure waving at him from the stone railing of the courtyard. He recognized the small man at once, but Alain squealed the name first.

"Patwin!" cried the boy, jumping to his feet. "Look, Dinadin!"

"I see," said Dinadin dully.

Patwin was waiting to be waved down. Dinadin sighed and put up a hand, gesturing for his friend to come. A certain dread surged inside him. It had been such a bright day. Now a cloud was coming. Patwin sauntered over to them casually, a beaming smile on his face. Alain ran up to him and wrapped his arms around Patwin's legs, dragging him toward his brother. As his friend approached, Dinadin leaned back against the sycamore.

"Hello," said Patwin. He peeled Alain off his thigh and took the boy's hand.

"Patwin," acknowledged Dinadin with a nod. "I didn't expect to see you. Is something wrong?"

"Nothing," said Patwin. "Just a visit."

"Of course," said Dinadin heavily. "Well, I'm glad you came."

"Yes, you look it," quipped Patwin. He smiled wryly then looked Alain up and down. "Lord, Alain, you're almost as tall as your brother!"

"I'm ten now," declared Alain proudly. "And I'm learning to shoot." He picked up his bow excitedly and handed it to Patwin. "Father got me my own bow, and Dinadin's showing me how to use it."

"Very nice," remarked Patwin, inspecting the weapon. There was the old, characteristic twinkle to his voice, the same magic lilt Richius always had with Alain. "I'll bet you're getting really good, huh? Like your brother."

Alain shrugged. "Not really," he admitted. "My hands still get in the way."

Patwin looked to Dinadin. "What?"

"He uses his whole hand instead of just his fingers," Dinadin explained. "But he's getting better."

"I'm sure he is," said Patwin, handing the bow back to Alain. "Your brother's a good teacher, Alain. He was one of the best archers in our company. You listen to what he tells you."

Alain smiled up at Patwin. "Will you stay for dinner? I'll tell Mother you're here."

"She already knows. And she already invited me. I saw her and Del on my way here. They told me you were around back, so I thought I'd come and have a talk with you."

"So?" asked Dinadin. "You going to stay?"

Patwin was careful to hide his face from Alain. "That depends," he said seriously. "I have to talk to you, Dinadin."

"Stay, Patwin," begged Alain. "Father won't mind. I'll go tell him."

"Good idea," agreed Dinadin. "Alain, go tell Father Patwin's staying for dinner. Give us a chance to talk, all right?"

The boy agreed eagerly and darted off toward the house. When he was gone, Dinadin patted the ground beside him, bidding Patwin to sit. Somewhat haltingly, Patwin folded himself down on the pile of leaves. They stared at each other for an awkward moment.

"I really am glad you're here," Dinadin began. "But I don't want to argue."

"I'm not here to argue, Dinadin," said Patwin. "I have news."

"Good news?"

"Yes. At least I think so."

Dinadin folded his arms over his chest and gestured with his chin for Patwin to continue. He could already tell from his comrade's tone that the subject would be Richius. "Go on."

"Richius has had news from Nar City," said Patwin. "The emperor wants to make him king." He waited for Dinadin's hard expression to change. When it didn't, he went on. "He's supposed to be in Nar on the thirtieth day of winter. That's about two months from now."

"King," remarked Dinadin absently. "Nice."

Patwin strained to smile. "He's taking some people with him on the trip. We're going to have a fine time, take it real easy and see some of the sights. I'm going, and of course he thought of you right away. I think you should come with us."

"I can't," said Dinadin. He picked a dead leaf from the ground and studied it, twirling it around in his fingers. "I have things around here to do."

"Dinadin, that's a lie."

Dinadin shrugged. "I suppose it is." He evaded Patwin's probing eyes, inspecting the leaf with interest. "But I still can't go."

"Can't? Or won't?"

"Either."

"Damn it, Dinadin," exclaimed Patwin. "Stop fooling and talk to me!"

Dinadin crumpled the leaf and glared at Patwin. "About what? Richius? I told you already that's a dead subject. What did you think? Did you think you were going to come here with this great news about him being made king, and I was going to forget about everything?" Dinadin tossed the leaf away. "Some king he'll make."

"I think he'll make a fine king. And I think you're being a pigheaded fool, Dinadin. How long are you going to hold this grudge? Richius is going to be our king. Are you going to ignore him forever?"

"If I can," said Dinadin honestly. "Unlike you, I remember what happened."

Patwin laughed bitterly. "Do you? It seems to me your memory is a little vague. You're the one who badgered Richius about going to Ackle-Nye, remember? If there is blame to go around for Lucyler's death, you're as much at fault as Richius."

"Voris didn't come looking for me," said Dinadin coldly. "He wanted Richius. And because Richius wasn't there Lucyler got killed. Hell, we were all about to die anyway. But did Richius care? Hardly. He just let us go on dying, while his damn father abandoned us!"

"Dinadin, he did his best. . . ."

"If that's his best, then Aramoor's in real trouble. Lord, I can't imagine him as king after the way he let us die like flies in Dring."

Patwin's expression was stricken. "Dinadin, I know you don't believe that. You're just mad. It's all right to be angry. We're all angry about being left behind. But you have to get over it. Even Richius is trying, and it was his own father. How do you think he feels about it?"

Dinadin couldn't answer. At one point he had thought Patwin was right, that he was just bitter and would get over it. But there were just too many deaths to forget. And Lucyler's capture kept coming back to him, gnawing at him, demanding to be remembered. If only Richius had been there, Lucyler might still be alive. He didn't want Richius to be dead, either, of course, but it was just another twist of Richius' weird luck, letting people die in his stead. If they had left a month earlier, there were at least a dozen more who would have come home. But Richius hadn't let them leave.

"I'm sure he feels badly," said Dinadin at last. "But don't you think he should? If we had retreated, Lucyler would still be alive. Jimsin and Lonal, too."

"It doesn't work that way, Dinadin. We had a job to do. Richius knew that. He didn't want to be there, but he had to be. And you're right, he does feel badly. Badly enough to try and come here and apologize to you."

"He tried to come here? When?"

"The day before yesterday," said Patwin. "He wanted to talk to you, say he was sorry and try to put all this business in the past. We didn't make it, though."

"What happened?" asked Dinadin. He couldn't keep the alarm from his voice.

"Wolves," said Patwin. "They attacked us on the road. We tried to outrun them but they were too fast. Thunder couldn't make it."

"Oh, no . . ."

"There were five of them," continued Patwin ruthlessly. "They got hold of Thunder. Killed him."

Dinadin closed his eyes and took an unsteady breath. "I'm sorry," he said carefully. "I really am. How's Richius?"

THE JACKAL OF NAR 201

"He took it about as hard as you'd expect," said Patwin. "But one of the wolves got him, too. Bit him in the arm, not too bad. He's resting now and should be fine in a few days. That's why I'm here, Dinadin. Since he can't get around, I'm helping him make the plans for the trip to Nar." Patwin paused and locked eyes with Dinadin. "You should come see him, Dinadin. He'd like that."

Dinadin shook his head. "I . . . I can't," he stammered. "Sorry, Patwin. I just can't."

"But why? Look, he told me all about the girl in the tavern. He's even sorry about that."

"It's not about the girl," said Dinadin. "Haven't you been listening? Lord, where's your memory gone? He could have gotten all of us killed! His father abandoned us and he still wouldn't let us come home. He's got a lot of blood on his hands, Patwin. An apology just isn't enough."

Patwin's eyes narrowed, studying him. "So that's it? You won't come with us to Nar?"

"No," said Dinadin. "I won't."

Patwin got to his feet. "Fine," he snapped. "I won't beg you to do the right thing. I'm sure you know in your heart how wrong you are. But he's going to be your king, Dinadin. You can't avoid him forever. If you wait too long your friendship may never recover."

Dinadin said nothing, merely gazing off into the distance. He let Patwin hover over him for a few moments, staring down at him with barely disguised contempt. The fleeting idea of agreeing came to him, but vanished just as quickly. He was bitter, like an old man, and he wondered if he would ever be the same again.

"Well?" pressed Patwin. "What do you say?"

"Alain's much bigger, isn't he? I'm glad you had the chance to see him again. If you're staying for supper maybe we can play some cards after."

Patwin's expression was like ice. "No, I won't be staying. Tell your father I'll see him when he comes around the castle, to honor his new king."

Patwin turned to go, but before he had taken three paces Dinadin called after him.

"Patwin, stop. You're still my friend. You're welcome here anytime. But don't ever try to convince me I'm wrong again."

"You are wrong, Dinadin," replied Patwin. "You just don't see it yet."

Dinadin watched him go, wondering bleakly if he had severed more than one old friendship.

SIXTEEN

Five days after Biagio's visit, Richius set out on the long journey to Nar City.

There had not been much time for preparation. Richius wanted to enjoy the trip, and to take it easy on the way so as not to tax the horses too much. There was only time enough for him to pack some essential items, nurse his wounded arm, and invite a select few to join him on his journey.

Dinadin had been the first to decline the invitation, and when Patwin returned to the castle with the news, Richius had been devastated. He knew then for certain what he already felt in his heart, that he would probably never see Dinadin again. Richius felt as though he had lost a brother.

Jojustin too declined to make the trip. Were they to travel by ship, Jojustin had explained, he might have considered it, but his days of long rides were behind him. This Richius understood and tried to accept graciously, for he hadn't really expected the old man to accompany him. Jojustin was almost sixty, and though he prided himself on his fitness and horsemanship, even he admitted that such a long trip was for younger men. Moreover, Richius knew, Jojustin didn't relish the prospect of meeting the emperor. Like Edgard, Jojustin was a symbol of a time when a rebellious king sat on Aramoor's throne.

Though disappointed that Jojustin would not be there to see him made king, Richius was also somewhat grateful that the old steward had declined to join him. It was true what Jojustin had told Biagio. The castle needed someone to tend to it, and only Jojustin had the knowledge to make sure things ran smoothly in Richius' absence. To leave both the castle and Aramoor unattended for so long would have been unthinkable. Since Darius' death, Jojustin had seen to almost every aspect of Aramoor's governing, giving Richius ample room in which to grow into the responsibilities he had inherited. There were times, in fact, when Richius himself deferred to Jojustin's authority, for his long tenure in Lucel-Lor had left him ignorant of many of his nation's affairs, especially those that hadn't existed before the Triin conflict. It was a far better thing, Richius reasoned, that Jojustin should stay behind. Aramoor needed him.

There was too the ugly possibility that the Drol revolution might spill over the Iron Mountains and find its way to Aramoor. Though that had once seemed an impossibility, Darius' recent murder made the chance of it appear much more likely. Since returning home, Richius had spent more than one sleepless night considering how to deal with this invisible threat. He had ordered regular patrols to keep a watch on the Saccenne Run, and to his great relief he had found that the Iron Mountains remained blessedly quiet. Still, it was an unnerving thought that Aramoor was so defenseless, its troops and weapons woefully depleted by the war, and Richius didn't want to leave his homeland wholly unprotected. If the Drol did come, Richius knew, they might well find Aramoor easy prey, and it was unlikely that Talistan would come to their aid in any way. It heartened Richius to know that he was leaving Aramoor in Jojustin's capable care, for although Jojustin was too old to ride into battle himself, his mind worked in subtle and dangerous ways, and his long experience with war made him a canny foe.

There were, however, several of Richius' companions who did accept their new king's invitation. The first of these was Patwin. Like Dinadin and Lucyler, Patwin had been one of Richius' most trusted comrades while in Lucel-Lor, and the thought of not having him present at his coronation was simply inconceivable.

Because of Richius' wound, Patwin had taken on the responsibility of preparing for the journey, leaving Richius time to recuperate. It had also given Jenna and Jojustin something to fret about, for they both treated Richius like a child. The bite had left some nasty scars, but by the morning of his departure Richius was sure his arm had healed enough to make riding at least passably easy.

While Richius convalesced, Patwin set upon gathering the things they would need for their journey. First, of course, was fellow travelers, men that Richius wanted to accompany him. Not long after Biagio's departure, it had become commonly known throughout Aramoor that Richius was to be made king, and every man who could ride a horse seemed to

want to go with him to Nar for his coronation. Most of these were soldiers who had returned alive from the Dring Valley, some three hundred
in all. The outpouring of adoration made Richius forget about Dinadin,
at least for a moment. But he knew that there was simply no way so many
men could accompany him. Aramoor had neither the horses nor man-
power to spare, and with the very real threat of a Drol attack looming,
every able-bodied soldier was needed at home. When Richius realized
that only a handful of men would be able to join him, the choices became
obvious.

Of all the men he had served with in the valley, there were three whom
Richius had trusted with the vital and demanding task of commanding a
trench brigade. They were men who had proven their loyalty and courage
innumerable times, who had borne the awesome responsibilities given
them with distinction and with selflessness. Though Richius truly believed that all his men had fought bravely, he knew that Barret, Ennadon,
and Gilliam had served with the highest calibre of courage. He could
think of no others who so richly deserved the reward of going to Nar and
partaking in the great feasting that awaited them there. It was a small reward, not really more than a token when compared with the horrors they
had endured, but it was at least something that Richius could do.

As Richius had expected, all three of the men had accepted the invitation. Ennadon, the oldest of the trio, had even agreed to find Richius a
new horse, for by this time almost everyone had heard of the gruesome
fate that had befallen Thunder. Ennadon was a sensitive man, who had
been a breeder of livestock before being pressed into service in Lucel-Lor,
and so he shared with Richius that strange, intangible love that binds a
man and a horse. Richius was grateful for the offer, but in the end he had
told Ennadon not to bother. There were horses enough in the castle's stables, he had said, and replacing Thunder wasn't possible anyway. Ennadon didn't push the point, but he had promised Richius that he would
not stop trying to find the perfect horse for him.

Barret and Gilliam had come to the castle together. Both were only
slightly younger than Richius, not quite twenty-five, and both of their
faces glowed as they thanked Richius for the chance to go to Nar. Like
most Aramoorians, Barret and Gilliam were somewhat provincial and
not really knowledgeable about the world outside their narrow borders.
But they had heard the tales of the Black City, and were anxious to see
what truth there was to the talk. They were Guardsmen, after all. Like all
Guardsmen, they ached for the chance to be on horseback and travel to
places they had never been before. They were entranced with the notion
of seeing Nar, and even Richius found their enthusiasm contagious. He
too began to look on the coming journey with favor. It would be a long
trip, maybe difficult at times, but they would be together, five compan-

ions riding without the threat of a Drol arrow finding their backs. They would be free.

It was a bright, late autumn morning when Richius and his comrades finally set out for Nar. Ennadon, ignoring Richius' protests, had found a beautiful gelding for Richius to ride, a sandy-coated, pleasant-tempered horse that bore an almost eerie resemblance to Thunder. Though Ennadon claimed it was from his home stables, Patwin and the others knew the truth, and told Richius that Ennadon had purchased the gelding with his own gold from a horse breeder he knew. Richius was overjoyed with the gift, and on the advice of Patwin said nothing to Ennadon about how he had acquired it. Upon seeing the horse, Richius promptly named the beast Lightning.

At last they rode away from Aramoor Castle, heading west across the continent toward the Dhoon Sea. Patwin had devised a simple course for them, and kept a trove of maps stuffed in his saddlebags. They would not really need them, for wherever they went they could always ask the locals to direct them toward the Black City, but it made Patwin feel better to have them. There was a saying in the Empire, that "all roads lead to Nar." One needed only to know the general direction of the Black City to find it. Whatever else the conquering soldiers of the Empire had done, they had constructed a network of roads that was without peer. Even in the far northern reaches of the Empire, in places such as Gorkney and Criisia, there were roads. They were well-traveled roads, too, for the tax collectors of the emperor made good use of them.

Richius was pleased with the route Patwin had planned for them. They would take the Naren roads west until they reached the western coast, where the port city of Karva lay. From there they would travel south, perhaps for no more than a week, over the hills of Locwala and finally to the Black City. By Patwin's closest guess they would reach Nar within seven weeks, and they would not hurry. They would spare the horses that misery, and enjoy the trip. For food and shelter they would stop at any of the hundreds of towns and villages that lined the roads to Nar, and make good use of the hospitality of farmhouses. Each of them had some gold, and whatever they couldn't buy they would simply do without. Doing without had been a way of life for them in the valley, and none of them particularly feared it.

The first few days of the trip were blithe and carefree. Aramoor was behind them, and the great open fields and forests of central Nar were yet to come. The weather was mild for so late in the year, and they passed the time regaling each other with stories of what they might find in the fabled Black City. None of them had ever been to Nar, but they had all heard the

tales, some bizarre, others flatly unbelievable, and every time they spoke
of them it made them coax their horses on a little faster. Richius told
them that Biagio had promised them a feast beyond imagining, with
beautiful women and heavenly music and all of the emperor's palace at
their feet. It was only a half-truth, Richius knew, but it made for great
conversation, and after telling his tales a dozen times he started to believe
them himself. He was, he reasoned, going to be a king. It only seemed fair
that he and his men should be treated as such.

Richius enjoyed the journey. These were days like those of his boyhood, before he had learned what being a prince really meant. Here, lost
in the rolling vastness of the Empire, he wasn't a prince or a king or even
an Aramoorian. He was just a man, and he had no concerns greater than
where he should spend the night or how much beer he should let his comrades buy him. He loved being outside, loved being with his friends and
sleeping under the stars when a bed could not be found. He cherished the
talks about little things, about women and horses and wars that didn't in-
volve them in the least. They sharpened their swords around campfires
and never spoke of using them. And never once did any of them slip and
say the word "Drol" or "Lucel-Lor" or "Tharn."

The days passed quickly. Seven weeks after leaving Aramoor behind,
they reached the port city of Karva. From here they would follow the
coast south to Nar, a ride of perhaps six more days, according to Patwin.
But they stopped in Karva for a time, for they were making good progress
despite their leisurely pace. Karva was a small, salt-stained merchant city,
old and decrepit and more than willing to take the gold of weary travelers. It was night when they reached the city. A cold rain had just begun to
fall. It was the beginning of a storm that lasted three days, and so they
spent their time in Karva gambling and sleeping and stuffing themselves
in Karva's bakeries. When at last the storm abated, they rode out of the
port city on a road that was flooded and muddied by the rains. They had
four days left to reach Nar.

"Four days until you're made king," said Patwin to a melancholy
Richius. "Excited?"

"A little," said Richius, looking up into the gray sky. The rains had
gone, but clouds still canopied the horizon. "I just hope we make it. We
still have a long way to go."

"Not as far as you think," said Patwin with a chuckle. He leaned in his
saddle a little closer to Richius. Ennadon, Barret, and Gilliam were several paces behind them. "I knew the others wouldn't be able to pass up
the taverns of Karva so easily, so I exaggerated the time a bit." He smiled.
"We should be in Nar in three days."

Richius stared in amazement at Patwin. "Three days? Are you sure?"

"I can show you the maps if you like," said Patwin. Then he sighed,
saying, "But no, you wouldn't be interested in my maps, would you?"

Richius couldn't help but laugh. Since leaving Aramoor only Patwin had been truly concerned with the roads, poring over his maps each night to make sure they selected the best route in the morning. The others had made sport of Patwin's studious interest, gibing him that a real Guardsman could find his way with only the sun and stars to guide him. Now, it seemed, it was Patwin who was laughing.

"Lord, Patwin, you know how worried I was. Why didn't you tell me?"

"You've been known to stay in a beer house too long yourself, my friend. This way I could be certain we'd make it. It's a good thing I did lie about it, too, what with all the rain we've had."

"We'll still need to keep up a good pace," said Richius, glancing down into the churned-up soil of the roadway. His horse's hooves were caked with soggy earth. "It's going to be slow going in this mud. I just hope none of the roads are flooded."

An hour later, they discovered to their dismay that the roads were indeed flooded. The rains that had forced them to enjoy Karva's hospitality had been worse in some parts than in others, and even the wide Naren highway they were following had turned into a bog. The floods slowed their progress to a crawl.

"Damn," said Ennadon. "We'll have to rest the horses soon. This muck is tiring them too quickly."

Richius reluctantly agreed. It was well past noon now and they had hardly gone a fraction of the distance he had hoped to cover. But the labored breathing of his horse told him that Ennadon was right and he reined his mount to a stop, thankful that they were out of the thick woods they had traversed that morning. At least here the roadside afforded them room to rest. But just as he brought his horse to a halt, Richius heard something in the distance. He cocked his head to listen, raising his hand to halt his party.

"Shhh," he said. "Listen. Do you hear something?"

Each man inclined his ear to listen, and all at once they heard the distinct sound of a whinnying horse. Punctuated between the strains was the equally discordant sound of a man swearing.

"Well," said Barret. "It sounds like we're not the only ones stupid enough to be riding in this swamp."

"Whoever he is, it sounds like he's in trouble," added Patwin.

"Probably stuck," said Richius. "We should help if we can."

In a few moments they rounded a bend and found a carriage, its tall, spoked wheels stuck fast in the mud. The carriage driver was yelling at his team, a weary-looking pair of horses that seemed about to drop from exhaustion. He made good use of his whip as he swore at them.

"You there!" cried Richius angrily. "Easy on that whip, fellow! You're not going to get out that way!"

The carriage driver turned, obviously startled by the unexpected order.

Then, from within the shadowy recesses of the carriage, Richius caught a glimmer of blond hair. The glimmer became a striking yellow mane as a young woman poked her head out of the carriage window.

"Oh!" she cried excitedly, waving at them as they approached. "Could you please help us? We're stuck and can't get out!"

A low murmur passed between the men as they sighted the girl. Even from a distance she was beautiful. Like the carriage she rode in she was unspeakably elegant, her shoulders draped in a richly brocaded dress of scarlet. Two stout hoops of gold hung loosely from her ears, and around her neck dangled a pendant of azure gems. She was very young, perhaps no more than sixteen, yet she still looked every bit a woman in her expensive ensemble. Richius glanced at the carriage, hoping to notice a banner or insignia that marked it. Yet if there was one, it was splattered with mud and invisible. Still, he already knew one thing for certain—she was a *lady*. He waved back, trying not to smile too broadly.

"We'll help you," Richius said. "Tell your man to stop beating those horses!"

The man sat up indignantly. "I know what I'm doing." His voice cracked with a harsh northern accent. But the girl pulled herself further out of the carriage, and in a low, deliberate tone ordered the man to lower his whip. The man did so, muttering.

"Damn fool," Ennadon hissed. "He'll kill those beasts before he gets that carriage out."

"It's a good thing we showed up when we did," said Richius. "Patwin, we'll need a rope. Any chance that you packed one along with all those maps?"

Patwin shook his head. "Sorry, Richius. I didn't think we'd need one."

"I've got a rope," the surly driver called. "This isn't the first time I've gotten stuck. I knew these damn southern roads would be a nuisance."

"Good," answered Richius, relieved that they would not have to push the vehicle out of the mud themselves. The carriage looked to be at least three feet under, deep enough to get a man well soiled. "We'll tie the saddle rings together. Between all our horses we should be able to get you out." Richius glanced over at the girl in the carriage. "Don't fret, my lady. We'll get you along safely."

"Thank you so much," she said. "You don't know what trouble we've had trying to get out. Why, it's probably been near an hour."

"Not much longer," said Richius. "But first we've got to get you out of there. The less weight we have to pull, the easier it'll be to get the carriage out. Do you think you can open that door?"

The girl looked down thoughtfully at the mud and grimaced.

"Don't worry," said Richius quickly. "I'll bring my horse over to you. All you'll have to do is slide on. All right?"

"All right," she responded dubiously. Richius smiled. She was obviously unaccustomed to getting dirty. He would do what he could to spare her that misery. The driver, who had been fumbling with a chest behind his seat, now stood up and tossed a long coil of rope to Richius. The rope was oily and ragged, obviously used many times before. Richius tested its strength with a snap before deciding it would do. He handed the coil to Patwin.

"Start getting the horses tethered together, Patwin," he said. "Use the cantle rings on the saddles to bind them to the carriage riggings."

Patwin took the rope and tossed one end of it back to the carriage driver. "Do you think you can reach the riggings?" he asked.

"I can do it," the man rumbled. While he began to secure the rope to his carriage, Richius trotted his horse into the mud. At once the hooves disappeared, and in two more paces half the gelding's legs were mired. He gently coaxed the horse over to the side of the carriage where the girl awaited him, her knuckles white as she clung to the small door of the vehicle.

"Hold on," said Richius. "Not much further."

"I don't know how to ride a horse," she said nervously.

"All you have to do is hold on," said Richius. "Leave the riding to me."

After a moment he had reached her, his horse's legs well buried in the sticky ooze. He put out his hand.

"Easy," he said. "Just slide on."

The woman took Richius' hand, breathed deeply, then let go of the door. Richius grabbed her firmly around the waist and slid her onto the horse in front of him, sidesaddle.

"I have you," he assured her. "Don't be nervous."

Once upon the horse the young woman's face relaxed and she smiled broadly at Richius. He noticed at once what a perfect smile she had. He could smell her heady perfume, feel the firm ripeness of her body beneath the scarlet dress. Carefully, he adjusted his grip, making sure he neither crushed her nor let her slip from the horse.

"Thank you," she said lightly. Like her driver, her voice had the pronounced brogue of the northern lands. "I was afraid we'd never get out."

"It seems the roads around Karva aren't as good as the others in Nar," said Richius as he steered them out of the bog. "But you're not from around here, are you?"

"Oh, my," said the girl sheepishly. "Is my accent so plain?"

"A little," admitted Richius. "You're from Criisia, maybe?"

"From Gorkney," she corrected. "We were on our way to Nar City when we fell into this hole."

"Nar? Then we are traveling the same way, my lady. We too are heading to the Black City."

"Are you going for the coronation?" she asked.

Richius laughed. "Oh, yes," he said. "We will be there. The emperor has said we are to be his special guests."

"Ooohh, how wonderful! Are you coming from very far?"

"Indeed, my lady. From almost as far away as you yourself. We're from Aramoor."

"Aramoor? Then it is your prince I go to see crowned king. Tell me of him, please. Do you know him?"

"I do," said Richius. "For you see, my lady, I am he."

The girl's face did a remarkable trick of contortion. "*You're* Prince Richius?"

"Soon to be King Richius, I fear. And may I ask who you are, my lady? You're obviously of royal blood, yes?"

The girl didn't answer. She sat transfixed, scrutinizing Richius.

"My lady?" Richius prodded. "Is there some trouble?"

"No," she said at last. "Forgive me. I was considering something." She looked away from him, catching her breath. "This is awkward for me. To be rescued from a mud pit by a king is, well, embarrassing."

"It's your driver who should be ashamed, my lady, not you. He shouldn't have had you out on such roads. But may I at least know the name of the woman I've rescued? I must be able to brag properly."

She smiled again. "I am Sabrina, daughter of the duke of Gorkney."

"Well then, Lady Sabrina, it is an honor to meet you. I'm pleased you've come so far just for my king-making. But did you come all this way by yourself? Where are your guardians?"

She laughed, and Richius could feel her relax. "Gorkney has no Guardsmen, my lord. We are too small for that. Have you never been there? Aramoor is not so far from Gorkney, you know."

"I have never been there," said Richius. He had just about taken her all the way out of the bog. "But I have heard that it is quite beautiful."

The girl looked away, a pensive shade drawing over her face. "Yes, very beautiful," she said sadly. "More beautiful than any of the lands I have had to ride through to get here." She smiled at Richius with a visible effort. "Perhaps one day you will see it for yourself."

"I would like that," replied Richius. They were out of the mud completely now. Patwin had already rigged the other horses to the carriage and was waiting for Richius to join them. Reluctantly Richius lowered the Lady Sabrina to the ground, in a place not too muddy for her fine shoes. She let her hand linger a moment in his before letting go.

"Thank you," she said. "You are very kind."

"It was my pleasure."

He turned from her and steered his horse toward Patwin, who quickly tied the last bit of rope to the ring on his saddle's cantle. When they were both satisfied that the knots that bound them all together were sound, Richius signaled to the carriage driver.

"Are you ready?"

"Yes," said the man, taking hold of his reins again. "Not too fast, now."

"We'll take it slow," answered Richius. He waited for each of his men to signal their readiness. Gilliam, the first man on the rope, gave him a curt nod.

"All right then," said Richius. They each gave their horses a gentle nudge, and almost effortlessly the carriage began to move out of the mud.

"It's coming!" said the carriage driver. "Give it a little more and she'll be out."

Richius gave his horse an encouraging nudge. The horse obeyed, digging its hooves deeper into the soft earth. Finally the carriage creaked and broke free, rolling out of the mud. Lady Sabrina gave a happy cheer.

"You did it!" she cried, rushing over to Richius.

"Good work," said Richius over his shoulder. "Patwin, would you untie us, please?"

Patwin gave Richius a playful wink. Sabrina was looking up at Richius with plain adoration.

"Thank you, my lord. You have truly saved us."

"It was a simple thing, my lady," said Richius. "But you really must take better care. Why do you travel alone? You should have an escort."

The girl dismissed the idea with a wave. "Until today we've traveled without mishap. We will be fine until we reach the Black City."

"It isn't safe," said Richius, unconvinced. "We will accompany you the rest of the way."

"No," said the girl. "It wouldn't be . . ." she stopped, correcting herself. "It won't be necessary. Dason, my driver, looks after me well enough. He will see me safely to Nar."

"I would feel better if there were others with you. It's no trouble for us, really."

She smiled. "It's a generous offer," she said, reaching out to take his hand. "But do not worry about me. We will meet again. Go on your way. I will be well."

"Are you certain?" he asked. "It's no bother at all."

"There's no need for it," she assured him. "I am cared for, and we are close enough to Nar now not to be concerned."

"Very well," Richius conceded. "But your horses need rest badly. Will you at least see that they get it?"

She nodded. "I will make sure of it. Thank you, Richius of Aramoor. And remember my promise. We will meet again."

Richius bowed his head. "I look forward to it."

The girl curtsied, gave a small, secretive giggle, then turned and walked back to her carriage. She opened the carriage door and quickly disappeared into its dark recesses. The carriage driver waved at them, more in obligation than in friendship.

"Thanks for your aid," he said brusquely before he turned his back on them. He gave the reins another snap and was soon on the move, bearing away the Lady Sabrina of Gorkney.

Progress came slowly the rest of that day, but a bright sunrise the next morning dried up the last of the floods and had them moving quickly again. The promise of Nar's opulent hospitality drove them onward. Finally, at dusk of the second day out of Karva, they came to the hills of Locwala.

Night was wrapping its shadowy fingers around the earth, and the sun burned a hazy salmon in the western sky. The hills of Locwala were silent, but the air carried the unmistakable scent of the city. It wasn't the pungent smell of horse farms or the brackish odor of seaports. Rather it was the smell of a mystery and a fabled place. Smoky and metallic, it hung in the evening like the odor of a blacksmith's shop. And as he rode Richius thought about the city just beyond the hills. How enormous must it be, he wondered, that he should smell it here in the pristine stillness of a forest?

Tomorrow was the thirtieth day of winter.

He rode silently ahead of his men, leading them quickly along the narrow roadway. Something akin to a yearning blazed within him, for he knew that every hill might finally unveil the city he had traveled so long to reach. When at last he came to a tor with a strange glow behind it, he was suddenly sure that Nar was now only as far as an outstretched arm. Deliberately he slowed his horse. Patwin stopped beside him. They stared at the glow for a long, ponderous moment.

"We're here," Richius whispered.

Patwin sighed contentedly. "You go ahead," he said. "You should be the first."

Without a word Richius trotted his horse up the hill, and as he climbed the slope all the tales he had heard of Nar came alive in his memory. He would finally see which of them were true, and the thought made his hands tremble. Even his father had never been to Nar. He would be the first Vantran ever to look upon the works of Arkus. Slowly he crested the hill and Nar the Magnificent came into view, making the breath catch in his throat. A pale whisper passed his lips.

"Holy God . . ."

He had reached the Black City at last.

SEVENTEEN

A machine.

That's what Nar was, Richius decided. A vast, staggering machine. He toyed distractedly with the knot of his sash as he rolled the notion over in his mind. Jibben, the house slave Biagio had assigned him, had given him the vermilion sash to wear at the ceremony. It looked striking against his pitch-colored uniform, but it was made of silk and the slippery fabric caused the knot to untie itself whenever he moved too abruptly. If there was a trick to tying a sash, he had never learned it.

He had heard that Nar was big, but never had he imagined anything quite so gigantic. Nor had the tales of Naren architecture accurately described the countless looming spires that dotted the city like stars on a winter night. The towers of Aramoor Castle were dwarves beside these giants. Hands reaching from a graveyard, that's what Barret had called them. Not even the Iron Mountains seemed so high.

And then there were the fires. Nothing could have prepared Richius for these. They were everywhere, blooming out of Nar's chimneys in crimson balls, noxious balloons popping high above the dark streets. From their place atop the hill Nar had looked like a huge, misshapen flame cannon, all metal and tubes, spitting steam and fire into the night sky. The air had turned acrid even in the verdant hills, already alive with the rumbling of the city's incinerators.

They had ridden through the city under a pall of disbelief, through filthy outskirts polluted with trash and urine, past the foundries of the war labs that belched black venom into the air, hard at work with the business of bringing Liss to its knees. And they had hardly uttered a word, for what could one say in the face of it all? This was Nar the Magnificent. It wasn't at all what they had expected, but in its lavish garishness it impressed them nonetheless. They found folk of every ilk and color in its streets, and saw things as varied as potions and slaves for sale by overfed merchants. Here Richius and his companions were nameless, as niggling as the towers of Aramoor were to the monstrous bridges and cathedrals of Nar, and no one halted their begging or bartering long enough to notice them. Nor did they need to stop and ask directions to the palace, for it was visible to all, the city's onyx jewel twinkling darkly at its center.

"Damn," swore Richius, still fumbling with the sash. There seemed to be no right way to wear the thing, and he suddenly realized why his father had always conveniently "forgotten" his. But it was expected of a king of Nar to always wear his scarlet sash at state occasions, so he tried again to make the looping knot, managing only a tight, ugly cinch. He cursed just as Patwin wandered into the room, a shining scabbard of black leather and jewels in his hands. Out of the scabbard poked Jessicane's bedraggled hilt.

"What's the problem?" asked Patwin anxiously. He looked splendid in his uniform, one of the few items each of them had packed before leaving Aramoor.

"I can't tie the blasted sash. It's made of silk and the knot won't stick." Richius pointed his chin at the scabbard. "Is that it?"

Patwin handed the scabbard and sword over to Richius. "Yes. It's a good bit nicer than yours, don't you think?"

"Indeed," said Richius, inspecting the scabbard. He had wanted to wear Jessicane at his coronation, and was glad that Biagio hadn't protested. The count said only that he should have a scabbard that suited the occasion, and not wear the old ragged one he had been using. Upon seeing the size of Jessicane, however, the house slave Jibben had not been certain he could find a scabbard large enough. Apparently there were limits to even Nar's weaponry.

"It's beautiful," said Richius. "Where did Jibben find it? Did he say?"

Patwin's face twitched. "I didn't get it from Jibben."

"Oh? Where did you get it?"

"It's a gift from Biagio. He told me that Jibben couldn't find a proper sheath, and that you absolutely had to have a better scabbard if you were going to wear your sword to the coronation. I suppose he purchased it for you himself; he didn't say."

"A gift?" exclaimed Richius, examining the scabbard more closely now. It was an extraordinary piece, finely fabricated from oiled leather and studded with gems along its spine. Jessicane looked all the older in it. "Where would he find such a thing? It must have cost a fortune."

"No doubt Biagio has the fortune to spare. He probably bought it from one of those smiths we passed on the way here."

"Oh, no, Patwin. Something like this takes time to make. It's probably one of his own."

"Are you going to wear it over the sash? You'll have to make sure the sash shows, you know."

"I'd like to wear it *instead* of the sash," Richius grumbled.

"Well, you can't. Here, let me. . . ."

Patwin dropped to one knee and began fiddling with the sash, undoing the sloppy knot Richius had made. Richius watched his friend in the mirror.

"Are the others ready?" he asked.

"Yes. They're in the other room, waiting for you."

Richius nodded. The rooms Jibben had readied for him were enormous, so it didn't surprise him at all that others in the next chamber could go unnoticed. Like all the rooms he had seen in the sprawling palace, this one was astoundingly extravagant, its walls hung with tapestries and its floors laid with rich carpets. There were peasants in Aramoor whose entire homes were not as big as this one chamber.

"There!" announced Patwin proudly, getting to his feet. Richius glanced down at the sash and saw a perfectly tied tassel hanging from his side. Astonished, he looked at Patwin.

"Three younger sisters," explained Patwin with a grin.

"It's a bit girlish, isn't it? No wonder my father never wore his."

"Your father never came to Nar," said Patwin. "Besides, you have to wear it. It's your mark of kingship now."

"No, Patwin," Richius corrected. "My ring was my mark of kingship. I'm an Aramoorian first." He regarded the scabbard. It was a gift from a villain, no matter how beautiful it was. "I don't want to forget who I am."

"Don't worry, Richius, you won't. Jojustin would never let you."

Richius laughed. "Oh, Jojustin. I wish he were here to see this. I wish a lot of people were here to see this. Like Dinadin."

"Forget Dinadin," scolded Patwin, taking the scabbard and beginning to fasten it across Richius' back. "You asked him and he said no. Fine, it's his loss. If he wants to go on holding grudges, let him. Maybe when you get back he'll have learned the proper respect."

"It's not about respect, Patwin. I don't want any of you to just respect me."

Patwin stepped back, inspecting his handiwork in the mirror. "As I said, Dinadin will have a long time to think about it. Turn around."

Richius complied, turning from the mirror to face his friend. Patwin's eyes lit up.

"Wonderful. Just like a king!"

Richius smiled weakly. "Thanks."

"Nervous?"

"A little. I'm more anxious about meeting Arkus. I thought for sure he'd want to speak with me before the coronation."

"All you have to do is kiss his ring, isn't that right?"

Richius shrugged. "That's what Biagio said. Kiss his ring and pledge my allegiance to him and Nar." He grimaced at the unpleasant thought. "I hope I'm doing the right thing."

"You are. You'll be a fine king, Richius. We all know it. And we'll all be right there with you."

Before Richius could answer, Ennadon poked his head into the chamber. The embarrassed expression on his face made Richius feel like a bride dressing for a wedding.

"Richius?"

"It's all right, Ennadon," said Richius, waving the man forward. Like Patwin, Ennadon was resplendent in his Aramoorian uniform, his hair oiled and slicked back. The faint scent of perfume preceded him into the room.

"I'm sorry to bother you, but there's someone here to see you."

"Biagio?"

Ennadon nodded.

"Well then," said Richius, turning stiffly to Patwin. "I guess this is it."

"Ready?"

"I think so," said Richius, tugging nervously at his jacket and straightening his waist belt. He checked himself one last time in the mirror, then turned and walked out of the room into the connecting chamber. Barret and Gilliam were waiting there for him. So was Biagio. Though the chamber was brightly lit with glowing sconces, Biagio's smile was no less dazzling.

"Ah, you are beautiful, Prince Richius! Truly majestic. The emperor will be so pleased to see you wearing the sash."

"Thank you, Count. And thank you for the beautiful scabbard. I'm honored."

"A trifle. I just thought you should have a fitting sheath for your noble blade." The count's eyes darted to the scabbard. "It does look striking, though, doesn't it?"

"It's beautiful," said Richius. "You're too generous."

"Believe me, Prince Richius, you won't think it so extravagant when you see the feast the emperor has prepared for you. Everything is ready and waiting."

"Will the emperor be there?" Richius asked. "I had thought I would be meeting with him before the coronation. You told me in Aramoor that he has things to discuss with me."

"I'm afraid the emperor will not be at the feast, Prince Richius. He has many matters to attend to. But he will speak to you when the time is right."

"But he will be at the coronation, yes?"

"Of course," said Biagio. "The bishop will conduct a small ceremony, and then you will pledge your life and allegiance to Nar before all the gathered lords of the Empire."

Richius curled his lips into the best lying smile he had ever managed. "It sounds wonderful, Count."

"Excellent. Then we should be going."

Biagio led Richius and his comrades out of the luxurious chamber into an equally well-appointed hallway. They were high up in one of the castle's many spires. A draft made the tapestries shiver on the walls. Scurrying servants burdened with slabs of bacon and baskets of fruit made apologetic bows to them as they hurried on their way, and everywhere came the soft music of beautiful voices. The air was cool with the aromas of meats and gravies and sweet things, and the scent of flowers drifted through the hall.

"Have many people come?" asked Richius casually. He wasn't at all comfortable with having an audience, though he expected there would be a large one. Biagio did not look at him, but merely gave his polite, patronizing laugh.

"More than you might be at ease with," said the count. "Almost all the kings of Nar are here, and their wives and families, of course. Even King Panos came from Goss to be here. I'll introduce you to the important ones. Just stay close to me."

"I'll try," said Richius. To him, the idea of "staying close" to Biagio was something like the thought of sharing his bed with a war wolf, but he knew the count would be far better than he at placing the faces of the court, and so he steeled himself for a long day of handshaking.

They followed Biagio down a twisting staircase, descending each step carefully to avoid the clutter of people pushing past them. Only when the servants noticed whom they were shoving did they stop and give Biagio the obeisance his rank demanded, and a few cold glares from the count had several of them groveling apologies. Behind him, Richius' entourage was commenting about the heavenly smells, and the music rose as they finally neared the bottom of the spire and entered the palace's great hall. According to Biagio, it connected every tower of the castle—no small achievement considering the number of the looming monoliths.

There were, by Richius' estimation, at least a dozen towers, each of them containing a staircase that spiraled down to the hall. The hall's vaulted ceiling climbed high above them, its frescoed surface drawing the eye upward, its walls gilded with marble friezes depicting glorious moments in Nar's violent history. Statues of heroes with bronze helmets and broad shoulders lined the polished floor. They were men with tongue-twisting Naren names, men whose exploits were the bedtime stories of every good Naren child. Festoons of bright flowers draped the hall, garlands of honeysuckle and primrose sweetening the heady air. Here in the south of the Empire flowers grew year-round, and it was said that the emperor was particularly fond of them. Richius puzzled over this. Flowers seemed an odd affectation for a man so famous for his savagery.

When they had pressed their way another hundred feet or so, Richius saw the palace's throne room, opening off the end of the hall. The great iron doors were open wide, letting loose a wave of music. Richius bit his lip as heads began to turn. The idle chat of well-liquored onlookers hushed as they sighted him. He slowed his gait and squared his shoulders.

"We're with you, Richius," said Patwin, and Richius turned to see his four comrades flashing encouraging smiles.

"I hope you're hungry," he quipped.

Biagio leaned in closer. "I'll announce you when we enter," he whispered. "Do not worry. You won't have to say anything."

The tide of people ebbed a little as they reached the throne room, and they stepped through the metal doors. All at once a thousand heads turned to greet them. Richius looked out over the sea of richly dressed people, and watched the women curtsy and the men raise their goblets. There wasn't a familiar face among them, yet they smiled at him as if he were their brother or son. Those seated at the tables got to their feet when he entered, stopping their gorging long enough to join the cheer that rose when Biagio said boldly:

"Lords and friends of Nar, I give you Richius Vantran, the new king of Aramoor!"

There was thundering applause and the clinking of glasses. Somewhere a chorus raised their voices higher. A servant who had been waiting by the doors rushed a goblet into Richius' hand. Without thinking, Richius raised the goblet to the assemblage in thanks. Behind him, Patwin was leading his companions in a cheer, their good-natured shoulder-slapping sloshing wine out of the goblet. Yet even Biagio didn't seem to mind their boyish enthusiasm. The count laughed and called for servants to bring wine for them all, clapping his hands theatrically to the rising rhythm of the chorus.

Richius laughed, too, his mind overwhelmed by the scene, the inundation of sounds and smells and colors that made his senses reel. The throne room was decorated much the same as the great hall, with blooming flowers and sconces forged from precious metals. There were no statues cluttering the floor, but huge, mahogany tables had been brought in to accommodate the plethora of food. Casks of wine and beer stored in every corner, and everywhere collared slaves pressed through the crowd, trays of opulent little morsels balanced expertly in their palms. It was all just as Biagio had promised.

As Richius spied the congregation, it seemed to him that every nation in the Empire was represented. He let Biagio guide him slowly through the throne room, stopping intermittently to greet some of the guests. The count cocked his little finger genteelly as he pointed out those he thought Richius should remember, never being quite so rude as to look at them directly. There was King Panos of Goss and his wife Miranda, who had made her husband famous by bedding half his knights. There were Enli and Eneas, the brother dukes of Dragon's Beak, whose long-running feud for their single throne was known throughout the Empire. Queen Katiryn of Criisia had come all the way from her northern home, and Count Jahann of the Eastern Highlands had arrived with an entourage of silk-clad handmaidens. Richius greeted them all with the naive congeniality of youth. He was dazzled by the diversity; the bosomy, lavender gowns of the women of Dahaar and the modest, muted garb of the ladies from Vosk. Amber-skinned Crotan noblemen passed unnoticed by Dorians, whose own skin had been deadened to white by the nearly year-round darkness in their wintry land. And most amazingly, Richius could find only good humor in the room, without an inkling of the rivalrous bickering he had expected to see among the many folk of Nar. He smiled to himself. Arkus had staged a convincing show.

When they had crossed no more than half the room, the choir came into view. At least two dozen bright-eyed youths stood atop a short stage erected in the corner of the chamber, their mouths opened wide in song. It wasn't a song Richius knew, for it was sung in High Naren, but its forceful, angelic melody made him pause. Never in his life had he heard such perfect music. Every note was as crystalline as a raindrop. He lowered his goblet as he watched the small mouths moving to the aria, almost brought to tears by the excellence of the sound. Biagio sipped at his wine as he too listened to the music. When the song finally ended the count closed his eyes and sighed.

"Is that not beautiful?"

"Yes," said Richius truthfully. "I think that was the most beautiful music I've ever heard. What was that song? I don't think I know it."

"It's called 'Boruso Decoyo,' " said Biagio. "The song of the martyrs. It is a dirge for those killed in the service of the Empire."

Well, there are enough of those to sing about, thought Richius bitterly. But he smiled and said, "Those children must train severely to be able to sing like that. Their voices are so perfect."

"There is much discipline," agreed Biagio. "Of course, discipline alone would do little good without the procedure."

"Procedure?" asked Richius absently. Somehow he had lost Patwin and the others in the crowd, and he surveyed the expanse of bodies to find his comrades. He only half noticed Biagio's surprise at his question.

"Such music is not made easily, Prince Richius. Surely you don't think all they do is practice to sound like that?"

Richius glanced over at the chorus. Already they were clearing their throats for their next performance. But except for the extraordinary music they made, they looked wholly unremarkable in their white-and-scarlet gowns.

"What else is there?" asked Richius.

"The procedure, Prince Richius, is used to make that lovely music you heard. Each of those children has had it. Listen to them when they sing. You will not hear a single note that does not belong. Do you know why?"

"No," Richius admitted. "Why?"

"Because they are incapable of making any other sounds. When it is determined what note a child can sing most perfectly, the other cords in his throat are severed. From then on only that one note can be sung. Then, when the children sing together . . . Well, the music tells the story better than I can."

Sickened, Richius turned away. They were so much like the children he was always shooing out of the stables back home, those children whose only knowledge of music were the war croons they heard their fathers sing. The only difference was that these cherub-voiced prodigies had the misfortune of being born in Nar. Deliberately he drained his goblet, welcoming the cool sting of the wine.

"What do their parents say about it?" he asked finally. "Are they proud of what's been done to their children?"

Biagio seemed not to hear Richius' sarcasm. His smile sharpened as he said, "Why shouldn't they be proud? Not every child can be of such service to the emperor. Only the very best are chosen. It's a very high honor, and their families are well taken care of."

An attendant refilled Richius' goblet. "The *procedure* must be painful."

"Not very," said Biagio. "The children are given things to calm them."

"Really? What kind of things?"

Biagio's strange eyes flashed at Richius but he did not answer for a long moment. At last he said, almost inaudibly, "We have things here in Nar to ease pain, Prince Richius. The children do not suffer. No one who serves the emperor suffers."

Richius started to speak, but a stunning, richly tanned woman interrupted him, slipping between him and Biagio with a twist of her shapely hip. Sure that Biagio would have something surly to say about the breach of etiquette, Richius stepped back. But the count's face only brightened at the intrusion.

"Ah, you look enticing, my darling," he said, taking the woman's hand. He waved Richius closer. "Prince Richius, allow me to introduce my wife, Elliann."

Richius took the woman's offered hand. He bent to kiss it, smelling the strong odor of liquor beneath the painted nails.

"My pleasure, madam," he said, and when he looked into her dark eyes he saw the same odd transiency he had always noticed in Biagio. She gazed back at him, and yet seemed to be gazing past him, too. But he didn't stare, not at her eyes nor at her alluring figure. The Countess Elliann pulled her hand back slowly, letting Richius' fingers caress her own.

"No, Prince Richius. Mine is the pleasure." Her voice was syrupy slow, like her husband's. It had a kind of sultriness that Richius found at once attractive, and he had to force himself not to look at her eyes. With her arrogant manners and catlike gait, she was every bit Biagio's mate.

"My wife was eager to meet you, Prince Richius," said Biagio. "I have told her about you and your adventures in Lucel-Lor. Perhaps later you might entertain her with a story or two?"

Richius frowned. "Perhaps."

"That would be wonderful," said the countess. "I do like a good war story, and I've heard that Lucel-Lor was dreadfully bloody. You're not shy talking about it, are you, Prince Richius?"

"No," lied Richius. "Not really."

"I'm so glad. I have so many questions, but none of the others will talk to me about it. Not even Baron Gayle." She leaned closer, saying in a whisper, "He was there when Tharn took Tatterak, you know."

Richius nearly dropped his goblet. He turned to Biagio and asked sharply, "Is Blackwood Gayle *here*?"

"Of course," said Biagio. "Is that a problem? I did tell you all the rulers of Nar would be present."

Richius quickly scanned the giant room for Blackwood Gayle. He saw several men in the green and gold of Talistan, but none of them was the baron, and he muttered under his breath just loud enough for Biagio to hear. This was an insult beyond imagining, and he had no intention of letting it go unchallenged. To hell with etiquette. There were some things even Arkus had no right to do. He watched the people parade by, hoping to spot Gayle, to catch a glimmer of the silver mask he was said to wear now. But he saw nothing. Relieved, he settled himself with another sip of wine just as a group of revelers parted before him. There, across the crowded throne room, he glimpsed a girl. She was young, barely sixteen, with hair the color of honey. A name popped into his brain.

Sabrina.

The Lady Sabrina of Gorkney hadn't seen him yet, preoccupied as she was with wiping a wine stain off the shirt of her driver, Dason. The big carriage man looked pitifully out of place in his worn boots and bulky

woolen jacket. His hair was tousled and his beard was badly in need of a
trim, a stark contrast to the impeccably groomed noblemen milling
around him. Sabrina, however, was stunning. Her lithe frame was draped
in a gown of sapphire-blue silk that made the gold of her hair sparkle like
sunlight on an ocean. Perfectly painted lips drew back in an embarrassed
smile as her fingers worked a handkerchief into the rose-colored stain on
Dason's shirt. Though he had only just met her the day before, Richius
was comforted by her familiar face. He stepped forward without thinking, calling out to her and waving.

"Lady Sabrina!"

Sabrina ceased her rubbing and looked around the room uncertainly.
Again Richius called to her, and this time caught her eye. She glanced
over at him, confused. Then, as if with sudden recollection, she turned
from him, hiding her face with a quick twist of her head. A second later
she disappeared into the crowd, leaving her dazed driver alone with his
drink and his soiled shirt.

Richius started after her, then abruptly stopped himself. Surely she
must have recognized him. What sort of greeting was that? He frowned, a
boyish feeling of rejection creeping over him, and wondered just what
gaffe he had committed to make her act so strangely.

"Do you know Lady Sabrina, Prince Richius?" asked Biagio. There
was an overfamiliarity about the question that made Richius uneasy.

"Not really. I helped her and her driver get their carriage out of a bog
yesterday." He glanced back at the crowd into which Sabrina had vanished. "I thought for certain she'd have recognized me."

"Did you speak to her?"

Richius turned again to the count. Even his wife seemed to be hanging
on his answer.

"Briefly. Why?"

"She's an attractive girl."

"I suppose."

"There are many attractive women here, don't you think, Prince
Richius?" asked Countess Elliann. She took hold of Richius' arm and
squeezed. "A man like yourself has to be careful, or some young thing
will have her claws into you."

"Stop it, my dear," said Biagio easily. "You are making our poor guest
nervous." He removed his wife's grip on Richius. "Forgive my wife,
Prince Richius. She has an eye for fine-looking men."

"I'm flattered that your wife thinks me so, Count," said Richius. He
bowed to the countess. "Excuse me, my lady, but there are many guests
for me to greet, and I seem to have lost track of my own men." He took
her hand and forced himself to kiss it again. "It was a pleasure to meet
you. Your husband is a fortunate man."

She pretended to blush. "Maybe we can talk later?"

"I'll look forward to it. Count, you have some others for me to meet, yes?"

"Indeed," said Biagio. "Come."

Richius followed the count through the maze of perfumed bodies, past rows of tables teeming with fresh breads and colorful fruits arranged like rainbows. When they came to a suitably quiet corner of the chamber, Biagio stopped and took Richius' goblet from him, placing it and his own on a nearby table. The count glanced around furtively, his expression growing suddenly serious. He clamped an icy hand onto Richius' shoulder and drew him close.

"You have many talents, Prince Richius," he said softly. "You're a far better diplomat than your father ever was. My wife has so many of these fools sniffing around her like dogs. But not you."

"Believe me, Count, I meant no insult. I merely—"

"Do not apologize. The way you handled her was exquisite. Not many men have the courage to say no to Elliann. But you did better than that, didn't you? You had her absolutely charmed. You will do well here, I think."

"Forgive me, Count, but you must explain yourself. Your meaning is lost on me."

Biagio pulled Richius closer, taking him around the shoulder the way a father does a son. Richius glanced around the room, hoping no one was watching. But they seemed to be wholly alone, for the rest of the guests were all involved in their own conversations. Biagio pointed his finger toward the chamber's other side.

"Look, across the room. Do you see it?"

And Richius did see it. The Iron Throne of Arkus.

It was not as grand as he had imagined. In fact, he was struck by its remarkable plainness. There were no jewels inlaid in it, no ornate carvings or runes drawn in its metal. There were no cushions upon its seat, nor did its back tower pretentiously to the ceiling. There was only the rough utilitarian-ness of iron, cold and unapproachable. The throne sat stark and empty upon its tiny dais, strangely out of place in the opulent chamber, yet in all the vastness of the Empire, nothing bespoke power more than this shabby, roughly forged chair.

"Beautiful, isn't it?"

Richius had to agree. It was so much like his father's own throne that it made him wonder about the emperor that sat upon it. How simple was Arkus of Nar, conqueror of the continent, that he should be satisfied with such plainness? What kind of man had summoned him to Nar?

"It's remarkable," said Richius at last. He had many questions about the throne, all of which he decided not to ask Biagio. There was something more the count intended of this conversation. "What do you want to tell me, Count?" he asked.

"There are things we must discuss, Prince Richius. Things you should know before you meet the others."

"Others?"

"Others like myself. Men who are as close to the emperor as his own thoughts."

"I think I know these men, Count. In Aramoor we call them the Iron Circle."

"We are called that here in Nar, too," said Biagio. "It is not what we prefer to call ourselves, though."

"You speak as if I have something to fear from these men," said Richius. "Do I?"

Biagio chuckled. "Oh, Prince Richius, you have no idea!"

"Tell me."

"We are the emperor's eyes and ears. When we advise, he listens."

"So?"

"So it would be wise for you to handle the others just as you did my wife. They will be watching you, waiting for you to show the same taint of treason as your father. A stupid man might give them what they want. But you're not stupid, are you?"

Richius could hardly speak. He had never expected Biagio to be so bold about his father's treason, and he had no idea how to answer.

"Why are you telling me this, Count?" he asked. "What is it you want from me?"

"I assure you, Prince Richius, I want nothing more than to see you succeed as king."

Again, Richius made no attempt to hide his skepticism.

"You don't believe me?" asked Biagio. "You should. You already know how important peace within the Empire is to us. But the others are unsure of you. You will have to prove yourself."

"And if I don't?"

Biagio raised his eyebrows. "That would be very bad. For you see, not everyone in Nar is as forgiving as I am. And my influence with the emperor is limited. But if you can convince the others that you are not so much your father's son, they will have nothing to report to the emperor. Then you can return home to Aramoor secure in your kingship, and I can do my job without interference."

"Oh?" asked Richius. "And just what is your job?"

Biagio smiled dispassionately. "Watching you."

There was a pause between the two men that lasted only a moment, but it was long enough for a simple phrase to form in Richius' mind. It was a phrase everyone in the Empire knew, one that Richius had learned at his father's knee. It still made him shudder when he thought of it.

The Roshann is everywhere.

"Very well," said Richius finally. "It seems I have no choice but to appease these men."

"It's for the good of Aramoor, Prince Richius," said Biagio, returning Richius' drink.

"I'm sure. Where are they, then? Show me."

"One is directly behind you. Do not turn around quickly."

Slowly, deliberately, Richius turned his head back toward the throne, casually sipping at his wine. He surveyed the room lazily, wondering who he was looking for, when his eyes fixed on a conspicuously small man ahead of him. Like Biagio, the man was richly dressed. He was well under five feet tall, and he seemed not to notice them as he gazed up at the long-legged beauty towering over him, her glass poised at the level of his nose. A pair of eyes like those on a cockroach repeatedly shifted from the woman's face to her bosom.

"Who is that?"

Biagio turned away. "Don't stare," he said sharply. "His name is Bovadin. Nar's minister of arms."

"Oh, yes," said Richius. *The man who keeps the war labs busy.*

Even in Aramoor he had heard of this diminutive genius. The creator of the flame cannon and the war wagon and the acid launcher, Bovadin had the dubious honor of bringing science to Nar. He was old now but he didn't seem so, another curiosity that Richius noted, and over the decades his machines had torn down the walls and pride of a hundred cities. It was this kind of man who had made Aramoor bend its knee to Arkus without a fight. It was Bovadin who had made swords and spears as ineffectual as sticks and stones.

"Do you want me to introduce myself?"

"No. He doesn't like to talk to other men. You'll be in Nar long enough to meet him, though. He will find you when he's ready."

"But I thought you wanted me to speak to them, convince them of my loyalty."

"I want you to remember the faces, that's all. Before this day is done you will meet most of them. When you do, you will know not to say anything stupid."

Richius nodded wearily. "Who else?"

Biagio cocked his pinky toward the doors. A man in a robe of brilliant white was entering the chamber, his arms spread wide as well-wishers rushed up to greet him.

"The bishop," said Biagio.

Bishop Herrith walked with practiced grace through the crowd, patting cheeks and giving absolution out like sweets. He was a fat man but his movements were elegant. A train of cowled acolytes trailed behind him, their heads bent in silent reverence. The sight made Richius wince. Like most Aramoorians, he was not overly religious, and cared little for the rituals of the Naren priests. It was no coincidence that most of the churches they had built in Aramoor stood empty on the sabbath day. Though men like Herrith claimed that the Gods of Nar and Aramoor were one, the Vantrans had always done their best to dispel this myth.

"I don't want to meet with him," said Richius coldly. "We have priests enough in Aramoor."

"When it comes to the bishop, it doesn't matter what you want," said Biagio sourly. His eyes lingered a little too long on the holy man, making Richius suspicious.

"You don't like him, do you?" Richius said. "I can see it, the way you look at him."

Biagio shrugged. "He is close with Arkus. As am I."

"But you don't like him, do you? Why not?"

"Really, Prince, you have a boy's nastiness. You pester me over nothing. Herrith and I are . . ." Biagio paused and his face soured some more. "Allies."

"I still don't want to talk to him," said Richius.

"But you will," insisted Biagio. "You will have to meet with him after the ceremony. He will have questions for you. He'll want to know what your plans are for the church in Aramoor. Tell him what he wants to hear."

"What? That I intend to build more churches for him? I do not. I should think you would understand that, Count, being from Crote. Crotans have their own beliefs, don't they?"

"Nevertheless," said Biagio sternly. "You must have good news for the bishop if you want him to speak well of you to the emperor. Arkus is very fond of Herrith."

"I won't lie to him, not about Aramoor. We have our own ways back home. He can't . . ."

"Lower your voice," ordered Biagio, glancing around. "Prince Richius, it would be wise for you to listen to my advice. Let me protect you. Otherwise you may not have a kingdom to rule."

"Don't threaten me, Count. I already know what Arkus can do if I don't obey him. But I'm the one who must govern Aramoor. I know what my people will tolerate, so maybe you should listen to *my* advice. Am I to be nothing but a puppet?"

"We do the will of Arkus," said Biagio simply.

Richius knew the phrase. It was a line from a poem written decades ago, before Nar had the power to shake the knees of nations. Richius chuckled mirthlessly and finished the poem for the count.

"We are guided by his mighty hand."

"Excellent, Prince Richius. Remember that and you'll do well. Come, there is someone I do want you to meet."

They ventured back into the crowd, and Richius did his best to keep the phony smile on his face. The women smiled at him coyly, and those without men let their gazes linger long. When at last they reached a table full of uniformed men, Biagio stopped.

"Danar?"

A giant of a man seated at the table's head looked up at them, his face splitting in a wide grin as he sighted Biagio. He got to his feet and thrust out his hand.

"Renato!" he bellowed. "Where have you been? I haven't seen you in weeks."

"Business has kept me away, Danar," said Biagio, putting his own cold hand into the offered fist. The man was grandly attired in the indigo garb of the Naren navy. A gaggle of ribbons swam on his chest.

"I've missed you," said the man. He pulled Biagio close and added, "I have things to tell you."

"Fair news, I hope. But first let me introduce you to someone, Danar. Do you know who this is?"

The man's friendly expression evaporated as Biagio stepped aside to reveal Richius. His eyes were like all the rest of them, peculiar and cold. They flicked over Richius contemptuously.

"I know you. You're Vantran, right?"

"I am," said Richius.

"You'll have to call him King Vantran soon, Danar," said Biagio playfully. "Prince Richius, this is Admiral Danar Nicabar, commander of the Black Fleet."

Richius gave a curt bow. "I'm honored."

Nicabar said nothing.

"I have heard your name in Aramoor, Admiral," continued Richius. "When ships come from Karva they often have news of your battles with Liss."

"Liss," said Nicabar sharply, "is not a subject you know anything about, I'm sure."

"The admiral has some grand designs for Liss, don't you, Danar? Why don't you tell young Prince Richius what you have planned?"

"Happily," said Nicabar. "We have thirty new dreadnoughts being built. They're bigger than the old ones, more heavily armored and more heavily weaponed. And Bovadin has designed a new keel to make them faster. They'll be able to outrun even the schooners of Liss."

Biagio turned to Richius. "Danar is planning a final attack on Liss in the spring, once the dreadnoughts are ready. He tells me that this should be the last gasp for those pirates."

"I'd stake my life on it," added Nicabar. "There's not a chance for the bastards now."

"Tell that story I like," urged Biagio. "About what you're going to do to their sailors when you take Liss."

The admiral's grin widened. "I'm going to drown them all. They all think they're such great sailors, let's see how well they do *under* water."

The comment made Biagio giggle like a schoolboy. "And the channels, Danar. Tell him about the channels."

"You don't know it because you've never been there, Vantran, but there are these channels around the coasts of the islands, shallows they call them, like some kind of maze. I've lost dozens of ships in them. Do you know what I'm going to do with those channels?"

Richius shook his head dumbly.

"I'm going to turn them red. The men will be hauled out to sea for shark food, but the women and the babes will be bled until every channel in Liss runs scarlet."

Biagio howled with laughter and slapped Nicabar on the shoulder. So amused was he by the admiral's plans that little tears began to trickle down his cheeks. He pulled a brightly colored handkerchief from his vest and daintily blotted his eyes with it.

"Oh, I love to hear you tell that story, Danar," said Biagio. "Isn't that a delicious vengeance, Prince Richius?"

Richius said nothing. It was plain to him now why Biagio had wanted him to meet Nicabar, and he felt like a fool for being led into it. He shifted uncomfortably under the admiral's stare, cringing inwardly as Biagio put a long cold arm about his shoulder.

"The prince looks overwhelmed," said the count. "Perhaps I should take him to his seat now, let him get some food. Enjoy yourself, Danar. We will speak later."

The admiral inclined his head, letting Biagio lead Richius away from the table. There was a brief silence in their wake and then a round of poorly hidden chortles that made Richius' jaw tighten. When they were safely out of earshot, Biagio put his lips to Richius' ear and asked softly, "Well, Prince Richius, what do you say now?"

"That wasn't necessary," snapped Richius. "I told you that I know what Nar is capable of. I didn't need him to explain it to me."

"Forgive my bluntness, but I thought you should hear it from someone else. Danar has quite an imagination, and he wasn't at all pleased when he learned about your father losing the war in Lucel-Lor. He went on for days about what he would do to Aramoor, given the chance." Then, suddenly serious, Biagio added, "So let's not give him the chance, agreed?"

Richius only nodded. There were many things he would be able to do as king, but defying Nar and its Iron Circle would not be one of them. He walked soberly beside the count, and wondered how his father would have reacted to it all. Darius Vantran was a stallion, fiery and stubborn and unbreakable even under the whip of Nar. Richius had always imagined that he too would be a stallion when the time of his reign came, but now Biagio had pulled out a gelding knife. Miserably, he lifted his goblet and tilted the rest of the wine down his throat. Today, he knew, happiness would come only from a bottle.

Across the room, not far from the Iron Throne, a long table ran along the wall. Though it was large enough to accommodate a score of hungry celebrants, only four men were seated at it, their heads partially obscured behind heaps of sliced meat and fruit baskets. Richius let out a long-held breath as he recognized Patwin waving at him. Little drips of gravy fell from the mutton joint in Patwin's fist. Beside him, Barret reclined lazily in his chair while a pair of giggling maidens tossed grapes into his mouth. Next to Barret, Ennadon was hard at work constructing the largest plate of food Richius had ever seen. So high was the pile of treats that Ennadon had to balance it expertly in both hands to keep it from toppling while he spied the table for additional delicacies. Gilliam too was making good use of Nar's hospitality. He sang along with the chorus, though he clearly did not know the song. Empty beer mugs were strewn out before him like captured game pieces. It was a scene reminiscent of Aramoor, when they used to come home from a good day's hunting and gorge themselves on venison steaks, and Richius was pleased to see his men enjoying them- selves. This, at least, he had accomplished.

"I will leave you to your men for a while, Prince Richius," said Biagio. "The ceremony won't begin for some time yet, so enjoy yourself. Be care- ful with the drink, though, and remember what we spoke about."

"All right," grunted Richius, walking away from the count. Barret shooed away the girls, and he and Patwin got to their feet as Richius approached.

"Where've you been, Richius?" asked Barret. "We've been waiting for you. You'd better hurry to the beer before Gilliam drinks it all."

"Sadly, I've been told to go easy on the drink," said Richius.

"Who said that?" asked Patwin. "Biagio?"

"Yes. It seems everyone here has got their eyes on us. Biagio told me to be careful, not to say anything to offend anyone."

"Well, then," said Ennadon. "Just take a seat and don't talk." He put the plate down and held out a chair for Richius. "Here, sit."

"With pleasure," groaned Richius, practically falling into the chair. At once the steward assigned to their table placed another goblet before him. Richius sighed and stared down into the wine. A wavy reflection stared back at him, and it seemed to him that he didn't know the oxblood face in the glass. But he lifted the goblet anyway and took a deep pull of the wine, hoping Biagio was watching.

To hell with you, Biagio.

He lowered the glass to the table with a determined thud, turning sud- denly to Patwin.

"Do you know who's here?"

"Who?"

"Gayle. They actually invited that scoundrel to my coronation!"

Every head at the table turned. Ennadon's jaw dropped open in disbelief, displaying a mouthful of half-chewed food.

"What?" erupted Patwin. "Did you see him?"

Richius shook his head. "No, but Biagio told me he's here."

"But why?" asked Patwin, pushing away his plate as if the news had robbed him of his appetite. "I can't believe he'd even want to come here, not for this occasion."

"I know," said Richius. "It's unthinkable, isn't it? How dare that bastard ruin this day for us?"

"Oh, my Lord," interrupted Gilliam's pale voice. He pointed his fork toward the crowd. "There he is."

Worse, he was coming toward them, sauntering through the crowd like some green and gold golem, the buttons on his uniform straining to contain the fabric stretched across his chest. A sword hung loosely from his leather belt, slapping against his tree-trunk thigh as he walked, and his oily jet hair was pulled back in a tail and knotted with a fashionable braid of gold. Despite the warmth of the room he wore a cape of emerald wool trimmed with wolf fur. But most remarkable of all was the mask. It was just as Richius had heard, a silver façade covering the left half of Gayle's face. The eye behind it blinked, bloodshot red.

"Look at that," whispered Patwin softly. None of them had seen Blackwood Gayle since Lucel-Lor, but they had all heard the story of his maiming. A low, expectant murmur passed among them as they watched him approach the table. His blistered lips twisted into what barely passed for a grin. The beard was gone now, and his clean-shaven face showed the damage of fire. Even the skin not covered by the mask was pocked with poorly healed scabs, and the flesh on his forehead seemed to be rupturing and peeling backward along his scalp. He looked more monstrous than he had before, like a well-dressed corpse that had somehow escaped its own burial.

"Vantran," called the baron in his booming voice. "I have come to welcome you."

Richius hardly stirred. "Welcome me? How so?"

"I have come to welcome you into the family of Naren Lords," answered Gayle. "The emperor has asked me to extend my good graces."

"I see. And was it also the emperor's idea to have you come all this way to give me that message? You could have just as easily sent me a letter."

There was some chuckling at the insult. Gayle squared his shoulders and stepped closer to the table.

"You flatter yourself, Vantran," he said sharply. "Do not think you are so important to me. I have other business that brings me to the Black City."

"Oh? And what would that be?"

Gayle's broken face made a hideous smile. "Do you know how old my father is, Vantran?"

"Truly, I have no idea."

"Almost seventy. Even older than your own father was when he died, God have mercy on him." Gayle did an obscenely insincere heart-crossing. "And he's not in the best of health. When he dies Talistan will need a new king, and I am next in the royal line."

"So?"

"If I am to be king I will need an heir to follow me. And I must have a wife if I am to have an heir."

Good luck, thought Richius dryly. The only thing that had so far stopped this particular Gayle from breeding was that no woman had yet been dumb or desperate enough to accept him. Of course it was just a matter of time, Richius knew, but he thought poorly of Gayle's chances here. Better that he should look for a wife in a stable than in this roomful of ladies.

"So you've come all this way to find yourself a wife? Well, take your pick. I'm sure one of these ladies is willing to go back to Talistan with you. Perhaps you should take off your mask first, though, let them see what they're getting into."

"I have already found my woman," retorted Gayle coolly. "And she's a fine-looking wench, too. Perhaps you know her. She's here now."

"Perhaps," said Richius. "Who is she? Show her to me."

Gayle looked over his shoulder, scanning the room with his one remaining eye. He quickly pointed a gloved hand toward the doors.

"There, the one in blue."

"I don't see anyone," said Richius, straining to see past Gayle's bulk but refusing to rise from his chair. "Blue, you say? All I see is—"

Richius gasped, and Gayle burst into laughter.

"I told you she was a beauty. Her name's Sabrina. She's Duke Wallach's girl, from Gorkney." The baron's eye lit up lecherously. "And she's just of age. What do you say to that?"

"She's agreed to marry *you*?"

"Not yet, but it doesn't matter. Her father's put her on the market now that she's sixteen, and I hear he's eager to be rid of her. I have but to ask the emperor for her and she'll be mine." Gayle smacked his blistered lips, turning back to look at Sabrina. "Take a good look at her hips, Vantran. I'd wager she gives me a dozen sons."

The thought made Richius cringe. Not only did more Gayles mean trouble for Aramoor, but to think of such monsters springing from such an innocent womb made him want to retch. Yet what Gayle said was probably true; Sabrina would have almost nothing to say about whom her father and the emperor married her to, and that made it all seem even more criminal. If it happened, Richius knew, her life would be little better than hell. He glanced over at Patwin and saw that his comrade's face was white with dread.

"Maybe you should reconsider your choice, Baron," said Patwin. "You're a bit big for her, don't you think? A girl like that might easily die giving birth to your sons. Perhaps you should look for someone more sizable."

"Ridiculous," rumbled Gayle. "She'll take care of herself, I'll see to that. And if any of you whelps have your eyes on her, forget it. She's mine."

There was a finality about the word *mine* that made Richius' patience snap. He glared at the baron, saying, "Is that all you've come for? Really, Gayle, you're gloating over nothing. I certainly wouldn't choose a wench as frail as that. And she's a throwaway, you say? My lord, if her own father doesn't want her, why should you?"

"Enough," said Gayle. "I have come at Arkus' behest to give you my good wishes. Take them or do not."

"I do not," said Richius. "And I don't appreciate having you here. You may tell the emperor for me that I have no wish at all to get along with you, Blackwood Gayle. Nor do I share his hope, if that is what it is, that Aramoor and Talistan should be allies."

"You may tell him yourself," came a curvaceous voice from behind Gayle. Biagio stepped out from behind Gayle's cape, a secretive smile on his face. "Are you ready, Prince Richius?"

"Ready?" Richius asked. "For what?"

"Why, to meet the emperor, of course." The count took the goblet from Richius' hand. "I hope you haven't been drinking too much."

EIGHTEEN

Arkus of Nar was known by a thousand different names.

When he was young, so long ago now he could scarcely recall, Arkus had relished the names the vanquished gave him. They were good names, strong and full of fear. And each land that fell to his machines gave him another to tie on his armor like a ribbon, so that all the others could see him coming, brightly dressed and ready to conquer. Upon the siege of Goss he was called the Lion, and at the fall of Doria the women of that ruined city anointed him Child-Slayer. In the tongue-twisting speech of the Eastern Highlands he was the Bear; and the Crotans, who went to their knees almost without a struggle, called him the Bull. In the tall, cold hills of Gorkney he was the Ram, and in the deserts of Dahaar he was the Adder. He was the Conqueror in Casarhoon, the Plague in Criisia, and the Beast in Vosk. The twin dukes of Dragon's Beak called him Lord Protector, and the Gayles of Talistan called him father.

In Liss he was the Devil.

But of all these fanciful names, Arkus himself preferred only one— Emperor. He was old now, and he thought he had earned the simple dignity of the title. Long since tired of his ferocious nicknames, there was a part of him that acknowledged the quiet desire for recognition. He had forged the Empire out of a hundred warring cities, had led the continent into the greatest age of enlightenment it had ever known, yet no one called him Arkus the Great the way they had his grandfather, and he supposed that only rarely did anyone thank his war labs for the medicines they discovered. A century ago there had been no oil to keep the lamps alive at night, no simples to cure the blood cough, and no roads to reach the northern lands. There had not even been the day-to-day order of things that so many took for granted. All these things existed now because he had willed them into being. He was, in his mind at least, a visionary.

But they never see that, he thought bitterly. He leaned back in his chair and watched the liquid swim into his veins. It was bluer than usual, like indigo or ink. Twice the dose of a normal treatment, that's what Bovadin had said. Arkus felt a small shudder go through him. Even he, as emperor, had been hard pressed to obtain such a dangerous dosage of the drug. Biagio was always watching, making sure no harm came to him, and the count was very vocal. No one really knew what such a strong blend could do, not even Bovadin. But in the end the scientist's macabre curiosity had won out over Biagio's motherly concern, and the count had peevishly relented. Arkus was the emperor and his word was law, no matter how self-destructive some of his edicts might be.

The overturned vial that held the concoction was nearly empty, so Arkus forced himself to settle down and endure the last of it. His treatments were always so much worse when his moods were bad, and he had a throne room full of guests not to vomit on today. But he was in a melancholy mood, and restfulness would not come easily. It was the thirtieth day of winter. The chill outside his high tower was wretchedly bitter. Of late his body had become a rebellion, requiring ever more of the potion to keep it together and make it obey him. That every king in Nar might see him like this enraged him. But if this potion worked the way Bovadin supposed . . .

He closed his eyes, suddenly feverish with hope. Just enough to look strong, that was all he wanted. For the past two decades he had endured an ordeal like this almost daily, puncturing his wrist with a needle to feed himself the life-sustaining potions. He was addicted to it now. They all were. But he was so much older than the others of the Circle. Bovadin certainly looked younger than he should, and Biagio would likely have his golden beauty forever. Only he, the one who made it all possible, the one whose vision had given birth to the labs, was forced to live in the body of a mummy. It was almost the body he had had when Bovadin first discovered the potions. But only almost. Absently he ground his teeth together. Old teeth, no longer good for chewing the meats he set out for others.

"Time," he muttered. "How I hate you."

Quickly he stopped himself. He needed to relax. The young prince would be coming soon, and it would be best to have his wits about him. A little smile cracked his face. At least his mind was still sound. That, Bovadin had assured him, would probably never deteriorate. There was something about the way the potion worked on the brain. It kept the tissues vital, even when the rest of the body continued to creep toward death. And that was the problem, the damnable mystery of it all.

Across the dim chamber Lady Pennelope played lovingly on her harp. Arkus settled into the leather grip of his chair, letting her music tranquilize him. It wasn't at all like the piercing arias of the chorus. He loved those, too, but this was different. This was intoxicating. Lady Pennelope had a gift like none he had ever heard, and it was always she who soothed him and saw him through his treatments. He had no use for physicians when she was around. The chamber was cold, but she didn't seem to mind it. Like him, she was lost in her music, and she stroked the strings of her silver instrument as if she were alone in the room, the firelight of the hearth dancing on her face.

Nearly every afternoon was the same, and they played out the horrible ritual like two venerable actors. He would sink down in his heavy chair and fix the shiny needle to his wrist. The vial of whatever powerful concoction Bovadin had prescribed would start dripping into his veins, sometimes forcing him to cry out before it took him in its narcotic embrace. The lamps would be dimmed, the little pitcher of water would be iced, and they would be alone while she played for him and tried to make the treatment endurable. She would have seen him like no other ever had, twisted and in pain, greedily claiming more life that wasn't his, life he had no right to anymore. She would have seen the translucent light of his eyes start to twinkle again as the potion snatched him from whatever grave he should have fallen into. But Lady Pennelope could see none of this, for a blessedly tragic thing was amiss with her.

She was blind.

Never to tell of the things she saw in Arkus' chamber, she was his quiet, trustworthy slave, and he adored her for it. She alone had the power to make the gruesome act of resurrecting himself bearable. Her music carried him off to a place where the nausea of the drugs didn't exist, a place where he was young again. And she had a marvelous gift for playing to his moods. Today it was one of his favorites, a dark, somber melody whose name he could not recall in his maudlin state of mind. Arkus of Nar listened to the beautiful music and wept.

It was the potion, he knew, yet he couldn't stop himself. Memories flooded into his brain, as if a great wind were blowing the dust off all the portraits of his life. His boyhood in Nar City, the great, violent campaigns of his youth, comrades dead and missing—it was all a red, unstoppable torrent. Flashes of rainbows danced on his eyelids, a cabaret of dizzying colors with faces both familiar and terrifying. He saw a father in the fractured mirror of his mind: Dragonheart, the first king of Nar to call himself emperor. He saw a mother whom he'd hated with a brother whom he'd killed, and countless, begging cousins who would have slaughtered cities to ingratiate themselves to him. Trophies taken in brutal battles screamed at him, heads on pikes and the wailing of the crucified beyond the city gates.

And there were women. He had known so many of them in his time, had seduced some and simply taken others to his bed. Pretty things with breakable bodies. Princesses and harlots, gifts given by ambitious fathers, and slaves whose names he never knew. So many painted faces. They were his one great vice.

Silently he cursed his dysfunctional body. These were pleasures no longer possible. Though Bovadin and his tinkerers had tried desperately to cure his impotency, they had consistently failed. They had ground the horns of fire lizards and drizzled rose petals into tiger's milk to make him a man again, but none of their secret sciences had made him youthful enough to take a woman, and after a while he had become content to simply look and admire without touching. He knew how ghastly his appearance was, how abhorrent he must be to women now. Despite the drugs he took to sustain himself, despite the brilliant Bovadin's efforts to keep him vital, he was rotting. The drugs did a miraculous job of slowing time, but even they couldn't stop its march entirely. His old bones ached with every breeze that blew through the stones of his tower, and a stubborn roundness was taking over his back. In his youth his hair had been like a lion's, but the decades and the drugs had bleached it white and killed it so that now it hung from his forehead like blades of dead grass. Hands once capable of breaking a neck now threatened to break themselves, his brittle fingers so feeble they could hardly squeeze the juice from a fruit, and his legs were so weak they could scarcely bear his weight.

Only his eyes seemed unaffected by his age. They were as bright as they had ever been, an oceanic, iridescent blue. Like all who shared the potions of the labs, Arkus' eyes were mesmerizing. It was a side effect of the drugs even Bovadin couldn't explain, and it marked them all as the ageless, time-cheating addicts they were.

He sighed weakly. The music grew around him. Pennelope's graceful hands ran through the strings a little quicker now—the song was nearly over. When her concert was done she would leave him as she always did, abandoning her harp until tomorrow's performance. A nagging feeling of agitation crept over him. Today he ached for her to stay, for the music to continue. In his alien state, he was feeling something he had felt only rarely in his life—unspeakable fear. Two hundred feet below him, a gaggle of young and beautiful noblemen were drinking his wines and admiring his women. Fat capons and rare, bloody steaks were being consumed with abandon, and the chorus was charming the assemblage with their flawless, artificial voices. It had been six years since the last coronation of a Naren king, but in that time he had changed. Remarkably, he had actually *aged*. Except for the Iron Circle, no one had seen him since that long-ago day, and the thought of being pitied by so many smooth-skinned youths maddened him.

No. It terrified him. Worse, he had dirty business to attend to today. Somehow he had to convince Prince Richius that Nar had value, that it would be worth his while to listen to what an old, desiccated emperor had to say. It wouldn't be at all easy. Darius Vantran had been one of the hardest kings in the Empire to deal with. If his son had half the talent for skepticism . . .

But no, that was unlikely. The prince was too young to be so cynical. And he wouldn't object to what Nar had planned for him, either, not with Aramoor's sovereignty at stake. There would be some raised eyebrows, certainly, but in the end the prince would consent.

Arkus' old heart thrummed a little faster. He wondered if Biagio had done as he was told. He hoped so. It would make his own task so much easier. He hated to threaten, especially those he respected. And this one was worthy of respect. Biagio had been very thorough in his study of the prince, returning to the city with some impressive reports. According to the count, Prince Richius had served with quiet distinction in Lucel-Lor, doing the will of the Empire even against impossible odds. He had been wounded on two occasions, had held the Dring Valley against the over-whelming forces of its warlord; he had even sent several letters to his father, begging him to send more troops to the valley. Though Biagio be-lieved that the prince had had knowledge of his father's treachery, there seemed to be no indication that the prince himself approved of it, and that was what made the difference. It convinced Arkus that his plan just might succeed.

When the last of the potion had dripped into his veins, Arkus reached over and, without opening his eyes, popped the metal needle from his wrist. The action sent the customary pinch of pain through his arm, but he didn't flinch. The music went on, unabated, building to its soft, beauti-ful climax, while in his blood the potion did its unfathomable work. He could feel it, like scalding water soaking him, burning his eyes and tearing at the fabric of his skin. Tiny, invisible knives sharpened themselves on his bones, and his brain flared with the familiar agony of rebirth. When it subsided he felt alive again. He opened his eyes and watched Lady Pennel-ope lovingly caressing the music from her instrument.

"Beautiful," he said to her. She did not look up, but the unmistakable trace of a smile told him she had heard him.

A sudden knock on the chamber door shattered the moment. Arkus lifted his head expectantly, but the harpist went on plucking. The door slid soundlessly open, and Count Renato Biagio stepped inside. He closed the door gently behind himself.

"Last movement," said Arkus. "Wait, please."

Biagio waited. It took four more minutes for the piece to end, and through it all the count was motionless, his breathing as still as a lagoon. At last Lady Pennelope took her hands from the harp, stood up, and bowed her head toward Arkus.

"Thank you, my lady," said Arkus. He could already hear the glow coming back into his voice. He really was stronger, praise Bovadin. "That was marvelous."

Again Lady Pennelope said nothing, but a faint, pink blush painted her cheeks. She turned from Arkus and started slowly, carefully, to the door. Biagio quickly opened the door to accommodate her, but did not go to her side. Lady Pennelope went straight for the door, ignoring Biagio completely, and left the room. Miraculously, not a single one of the room's many articles was scuffed by her shoes or touched by the hem of her dress as she moved past them. Biagio watched her leave. When she was out of his sight he closed the door. Even by the frail light of the fire, Arkus could see the concern on the count's face.

"Well?" asked Biagio. "Did it work?"

Arkus flexed his fingers. They felt stronger. "The light. Turn it up for me."

Biagio complied, going to the nearest wall sconce and turning the little key that fed the oil to the wick of the lamp. His tall, lean shadow climbed up the wall with the growing light. Then he stepped closer, inspecting Arkus.

"You do look better," he admitted. "How do you feel?"

"Strong enough. Did you bring him?"

"It's dreadfully cold in here," said Biagio, wringing his hands together. For a normal man it would have been warm. The count went over to the giant hearth and gave a disappointing sigh. "Really, Arkus," he said fretfully. "And you wonder why you're always cold."

There was a pile of logs beside the hearth. Biagio lifted several and threw them into the fire, sending a warming shower of sparks into the air. "There," he pronounced proudly. "That's much better, isn't it?"

It was hugely better, Arkus admitted. The susceptibility to cold was just one more of the strange effects of the potions. They were all like naked little flowers in the winter, ready to shrivel in the first stiff breeze. Arkus put his own hands together and rubbed.

"Did you bring him?" he asked again, a bit sterner than before.

"He's waiting outside, but I want to talk to you first. I should warn you, he may not be what you expect."

"You already have warned me, a dozen times," said Arkus, struggling to lift himself out of the chair. Biagio offered out a hand, which the emperor gratefully accepted. At first Arkus wavered, but as the enhanced blood pumped through his limbs he quickly grew stronger, and in a moment he was standing without the count's support. Biagio hurriedly set about clearing away the clutter from the treatment, gathering up the empty vial and the tube and the ghastly silver needle, locking it all away in a giant oak wardrobe.

"Listen to me, please," implored Biagio. "I'm not so sure your plan is sound. He's different, more independent than I thought. I don't think he will do it."

"He'll do it," said Arkus. "He won't have a choice."

"But we do. You should reconsider the Gayles. They have more troops than Aramoor, and have always been more loyal."

"And more ambitious," said Arkus sharply. "Ambitious men are dangerous, my friend. We can't trust them with this."

"Respectfully, I disagree. The Gayles would never dare use the Drol weapon against us. Believe me, Arkus, I am sure of this. They speak of you in Talistan as if you were their god. They revere you, and they're certainly more eager than Aramoor to avenge themselves on the Drol. I tell you, you are making a mistake in trusting this one."

"What? You told me he would be manageable."

"I was wrong. He is different than he was when I met him in Aramoor, more sure of himself. Why, I even introduced him to Nicabar as you suggested."

"And?"

"He hardly flinched. He even had the gall to tell me that he wouldn't meet with the bishop! I only left him for a moment and when I came back I found him arguing with Blackwood Gayle. Really, Arkus, reconsider your choice. Let the Gayles prepare the way back to Lucel-Lor. The Vantran boy won't serve you. He has his father's stubbornness."

"Better that than a Gayle's guile," said Arkus. "We need Aramoor, Renato. It's the only part of the Empire that borders the Triin land, remember."

"Then we should take over Aramoor. Send the legions in, or give it back to the House of Gayle to govern."

Arkus shook his head, exasperated. "No. I don't want to fight a civil war while Liss is still a threat. You underestimate these Aramoorians. They're loyal to the Vantran blood. They would never let the Gayles govern them, not without a struggle."

"So? What are they to us? They're just a bunch of horse breeders."

"There isn't time!" thundered Arkus. "Look at me, Renato. I could be dead before we find the secrets of Lucel-Lor!" Then he softened, seeing Biagio's bruised expression, and touched the count's shoulder. "It's more than just this Drol weapon. I need to find out what other magics these Drol have. Maybe they have something I can use. But we don't have the time to drive the House of Vantran from Aramoor. We must strike as soon as possible, as soon as we finish Liss."

"You risk offending a good ally. The Baron Gayle has come a long way to meet with you. He will not take the news of Lady Sabrina well."

"Let him be offended, then," said Arkus. "We won't need the House of

Gayle this time. Prince Richius would never agree to another alliance with them anyway."

"And what do you intend to tell him?" asked Biagio, a bit sarcastically. "The truth?"

Arkus looked over at his adviser, and in a voice full of resignation, said, "Yes. If he's as smart as you say he would never believe a lie." Then he chuckled mirthlessly and added, "Besides, he'll only have to take one look at me to figure out the truth."

Biagio shrugged. "As you wish. If that is your decision I will support you, of course. Shall I bring him in?"

"Yes," said Arkus. "I am ready."

Biagio turned and went quietly from the chamber. Alone at last, Arkus went to the only window in his chamber and drew back the heavy curtains, exposing the hazy, winter sunlight. The incinerators of the war labs glowed in the distance, their smokestacks coughing ragged plumes of fire. Across the river Kiel he could see the Cathedral of the Martyrs with its towering metal steeple, and in the far-below streets children played with filthy dogs, and beggars hunted rats for their supper.

He sighed. Somewhere over the eastern horizon, too far to glimpse from his black tower, Lucel-Lor beckoned. All that magic. If only he had taken it the first time.

NINETEEN

The narrow hallway outside the emperor's chamber was still, dimly lit by a row of oil-burning sconces. Richius stood alone in the corridor, waiting for Biagio to return. He was higher up in the palace than he had been before, and the elevation made the wind beat fiercely against the walls. There were no windows in the hall, only endless gray stone. A thin scarlet carpet blanketed the floor, and a gallery of furious portraits hung on the walls, staring at him. They were renderings of long-dead kings and unrecognizable heroes, of men with gleaming bronze helmets and sharp, cherished swords. Good men of Nar, all of them.

Richius studied the paintings absently, his mind wandering in a thousand directions. He was grateful to be waiting for Biagio. The delay gave him time to think, to wonder why Arkus had summoned him. His brief stay in the palace had been pleasant, and Biagio had been better than a mother at seeing to his needs. He had been well fed, well housed, and well liquored, and all that meant only one thing—the emperor wanted something.

Anxiously he rubbed his hands together. The warming glow of the wine was dissipating, making him feel the chill more keenly. He shivered a little. Biagio had said the tower of the emperor was over three hundred feet high, apparently no exaggeration by the way his fingers tingled. But he was accustomed to the cold, and his fussings were more habit than irritation. He wanted to know what was happening down the hall. It had been several minutes since Biagio had left him, politely asking him to remain behind, and as the time ticked away he knew the count and the emperor were discussing *him*.

Despite the wailing of the wind outside the tower, the hall was remarkably quiet. Richius could hear nothing of the merrymaking going on in the throne room far below, and none of the sweet aromas of the kitchens climbed this high. In fact the hall had no odor at all, just the clean, crisp smell of winter. He was alone, and had been almost entirely so since Biagio had left him. A woman had glided by a few moments ago, her small steps taking her slowly past him. She had seemed not to notice him, and only when he startled her with a greeting had he realized she was blind. Yet even then she had not uttered a word. Nor had she accepted his offered help. She simply moved on down the corridor and disappeared, an elegant wraith haunting the dismal hall.

More of Nar's madness, thought Richius, recalling the strange, silent woman. To move about such a place without guidance was lunacy. There were a hundred staircases to trip her, unseen torches to set her dress ablaze, and any number of twists to steer her straight into a wall. Yet how confidently she had pulled her hand away when he'd offered help. She must know this place as well as Arkus himself.

He was beginning to feel quite at odds when Biagio finally reappeared. The count rounded the corner quickly, his ubiquitous grin splitting his face.

"Prince Richius?" he called. "Are you ready?"

Richius drew a steadying breath. "Yes."

"There's nothing to be afraid of," said the count. "I've known the emperor for years, and every time someone meets him they feel as you do now. But then, after they have spoken to him, they see how unnecessary their fear was. The emperor just wants to get to know you better. He never knew your father very well."

The mention of his father made Richius' heart stop. They weren't going to talk about *that*?

"I hope the emperor knows I won't speak ill of my father," said Richius cautiously. "I would like to put the bad blood behind us, but . . ."

Biagio stopped, his expression suddenly serious. "Don't believe everything you've heard about the emperor, Prince Richius. He is misunderstood. He would never ask you to dishonor your father by speaking against him."

"There's no need to hide the truth, Count. I know how the emperor felt about my father. You told me yourself how much he disliked him."

"I said no such thing," said Biagio stiffly. "It's true that Arkus felt betrayed by your father, but these rumors of hate are exaggerated. If I may say so, Prince Richius, your father was unable to think as grandly as the emperor. He could never grasp the bigger plan Arkus has for Nar. That is the only reason they were at odds."

"You know I disagree with that."

Biagio's smile waned a little. "The emperor hopes he can convince you otherwise. Come, he is waiting."

Richius followed Biagio to the end of the hall, to a door made of oak with a knocker of bronze. The fitting was fashioned into the likeness of a dragon, the striker held like a bit in its chiseled teeth. Biagio gave the knocker a light rap, then pushed the door slowly open without waiting for an answer. A warm orange light sprang from the doorway, and the comforting smell of burning wood filled the hall. Biagio entered first, holding the door open for Richius and bidding him forward. Cautiously Richius stepped inside.

The chamber was wholly unlike any other in the palace. It was also enormously warm, fed by a blazing hearth. Curiously, the room was smaller than most, certainly not as sprawling as Richius' own, and its walls were paneled with dark wood that gave off a pleasant sheen. In the corner of the room stood a giant silver harp with an empty stool beside it, and the floor and walls were cluttered with what Richius could only think of as *things*. Meaningless, endless things. Small, valueless statues sat idly upon shelves and stacks of dusty books. Unspectacular paintings hung on the walls: dreary, uninspired landscapes and portraits of nameless people. An urn of tarnished coins stood neglected by a mirror, along with a pair of chipped crystal goblets and a bowl of red, lusterless gems. A collection of dull iron weapons leaned against a wardrobe, and over the fireplace was the biggest skull Richius had ever seen. It was the bleached remains of some fierce feline. There was only one window in the chamber, a tiny portal of clouded glass with the light of the city twinkling beyond it. A thin, grey spectre stood beside the window.

"Great One," said Biagio. "This is Prince Richius Vantran of Aramoor."

Slowly the figure turned, fixing them with azure eyes. A slight smile drew itself on the wrinkled face. Arkus was dressed in a modest robe of gray silk that hung limply from his body. A golden belt cinched the robe about his waist. He was neither tall nor short, and his long hair fell haphazardly about his shoulders. The hair was the color of unclean snow, as dead and as white as the skull on the wall. Two unkempt strands of the stuff fell down across his weathered face, down between those eyes that watched with unnatural vitality. His hands were large, his fingers long and slender. He seemed to stand with visible effort, his back slightly curved despite his efforts to straighten, and all at once Richius knew he was in the presence of something ancient.

Arkus of Nar had been emperor longer than most men had been alive. He was Arkus the Venerable, Arkus the Old. He was the only emperor Richius had ever known.

Richius cleared his throat and stepped past Biagio. He fell to one knee,

bowing his head the way he had rehearsed, hoping it was the proper way
to greet an emperor.

"Lord Emperor," he said, looking at the floor.

"Rise, King of Aramoor," said Arkus. His voice was strong, incredibly
so for such a frail-looking man. There was a honey-sweetness to it, like
Biagio's voice, and an almost androgynous lilt. Slowly Richius lifted himself to his feet. Arkus was smiling at him.

"Welcome to Nar," Arkus continued. "I'm very pleased to be meeting
you at last."

"Thank you, Your Grace."

"Are you settling in well?" asked Arkus, walking over to a little cabinet Richius hadn't noticed. Inside the cabinet was a collection of dusty
wine decanters and goblets. The emperor withdrew two of the goblets
and offered one to Richius.

"Yes, very well," answered Richius, taking the goblet. "The count has
seen to all my needs."

"And your men? They are comfortable?"

"Yes, Your Grace, very comfortable."

"Good," said Arkus. "Then they can enjoy the coronation." Next he removed a particularly small bottle from the cabinet and handed it to Biagio.
He held out his goblet as the count poured. "I've spared no expense for
you, King Richius. I want this coronation to be memorable. Brandy?"

"Thank you," said Richius politely. Biagio poured. The brandy was a
warm amber tone and smelled of proper aging.

"Shall I stay, Great One?" asked Biagio, replacing the decanter in the
cabinet. "Or would you like to be alone with the prince?"

"Leave us, Renato," said Arkus. "I think we should talk alone for a
while."

Biagio smiled agreeably, leaving the chamber and closing the door quietly behind him. A rush of trepidation raced through Richius. He was
alone with the emperor, something his father had never accomplished nor
even sought to achieve. Instantly he thought of Jojustin, of how proud
the old steward would be of him now. He was, after all, doing this for
Aramoor.

Arkus raised his goblet. "To us, King Richius," he toasted. "And to a
friendship as well as an alliance."

Richius touched his goblet to the emperor's. "To us, Your Grace," he
said, then lifted the glass to his lips and sipped. They watched each other
as they drank.

"It's excellent," Richius said. "I've never tasted anything so fine."

"It's from Goss. They make the finest brandy in the Empire. I have an
agreement with King Panos there. He sends me some from time to time. If
you like, I can have him send you some in Aramoor."

"Thank you, Your Grace," said Richius, remembering Jojustin's fondness for brandy. There had been very little good wine in the castle lately. "I'm sure my people back home would appreciate that."

"I'll have it arranged. But you're not planning on leaving Nar quickly, are you? You should stay awhile. A month at least."

"We'd planned to stay a few weeks. The count said it would be all right, and I admit I'm not eager to make the long journey home again soon."

"Good," said Arkus. "I want you and your men to remain as long as you wish. The palace and anything you see within it is yours. We have fine horses for riding, and I'm sure Renato can find you a guide. The hills around the city are marvelous. I used to ride there myself when I was younger."

"Yes, I've seen them. We rode through Locwala on our way here. It was lovely."

Arkus grinned. "You'll find many lovely things in Nar, King Richius. And as I said, they are yours. Don't worry about gold. If you see something in the streets you like, simply tell the merchant who you are. No one will question you. I've made it known that you are to be welcomed by everyone in the city."

"Oh, no, Your Grace," said Richius. "I couldn't do that. I have enough gold with me. If I want something, I can purchase it myself."

"Absolutely not," said Arkus. "You're not to spend a penny while here, understand? I'll take it as an insult if you do."

He put down his goblet and walked toward a giant leather chair. As he sat down he waved Richius closer, steering him into a smaller chair beside his own. Richius sat, close enough to the enormous fire to feel its scalding heat. He took another sip from his own goblet before resting it on a stack of books. Arkus leaned back in his chair and sighed.

"You are so young," said the emperor. "Don't waste these days with righteous nonsense. Take what I can give you. Enjoy your youth and your kingship. Because, believe me, it all goes by too quickly."

A flash of pain momentarily crossed the old man's face. He smiled apologetically at Richius, shifted in his chair, then continued. "You must learn what it means to be a king of Nar, young Richius. What it means to be privileged."

"But I am privileged," said Richius. "I have a land that I love with people that care about me. What else could a king ask for?"

"Wealth, for one thing. Aramoor's not nearly as rich as it could be. And what about power? I don't merely mean the power to control people, you already have that. But do you have the power to create things? Can you change things with your power?"

"I don't know," answered Richius honestly. He thought of his father, and how so many men had willingly died for his causes. And he thought of his own men in the Dring Valley, of Dinadin and Lucyler and how they had followed him and would have died for him. Wasn't that power enough? Or was this simply why Arkus was emperor, because nothing was ever enough for him?

"I've always thought I've had power," said Richius at last. "I like to think I've done some good with it."

"I'm sure you have. You and your father have both accomplished things. But that's the past, and I'm speaking of the future."

Richius nodded. "Count Biagio has already told me you want a better relationship with Aramoor."

"I want more than that," said Arkus. "I want us to accomplish things together." The light in his eyes grew brighter as he spoke. "Look around this room," he said, making a little sweeping gesture. "What do all these things look like to you?"

Richius inspected the chamber, unsure how to answer. Despite the unkempt appearance of the place, each of its items seemed somehow loved. True, the paintings were dusty and the weapons hadn't seen a sharpening stone for decades, but there was a quality to the articles that spoke of quiet value. Richius sat back in his chair and gave Arkus the answer he knew the old man wanted.

"They look like they are precious to you," he said.

Arkus smiled appreciatively. "Yes," he agreed. "Precious is a good way to describe them. I've been told by some that these things look like nothing more than trash, but that's because they don't know the stories behind them. Every piece here has a special meaning. They're my achievements, my triumphs. My life is in this room." He sighed, surveying his odd collection. "These things aren't valuable enough to be displayed in the palace, but to me they have a worth beyond gold."

"I think I understand that," said Richius. He gave each strange item in the chamber another glance, trying to see the jewel hidden beneath the dust. When he was a child, his father used to present bronze rings to soldiers who had distinguished themselves. They hadn't been very valuable, but the trinkets were cherished by the men who received them.

"I've lived a long time," said Arkus darkly. He was still brooding over the objects in the room. "I've accomplished much on my own. But now I need your help, King Richius."

"My help? How?"

Arkus' eyes shifted to the skull mounted over the hearth. "I saw you looking at that when you came in," he said. "Do you know what it is?"

"Not really," Richius admitted. He got to his feet and reached out for the skull, running his fingers over its bleached forehead and fanged jaw. There were cougars in the hills of Aramoor with such skulls, though not as incredibly large. "It looks like some sort of cat. But I don't know of any cats this big."

"It is the skull of a Triin war lion."

"Really?" said Richius, inspecting the skull more closely. "I heard of them when I was in Lucel-Lor, but I never saw one."

"Only the Triin of Chandakkar ride the lions," said Arkus. "It's said that no other Triin can manage the beasts, that only the nomads of Chandakkar have the means to control them."

"Chandakkar wasn't part of the war," said Richius. "It was too far away. I'm not even sure if the people there have even heard of Tharn. Still . . ." He patted the thick skull ruefully. "I wish those nomads had been on our side."

"I'm sure everyone in Lucel-Lor has heard of Tharn by now," said Arkus.

Richius nodded. "Probably. But where did you get such a thing? If these lions are only found in Chandakkar, how did it get here?"

Arkus smiled. "Sit down. I want to tell you something."

Richius complied, settling back into his chair by the fire. The smoky light played eerily on Arkus' blanched face, and his eyes shone an otherworldly blue. Richius reached again for his goblet of brandy. Remarkably, he was growing comfortable. Arkus stretched out his thin hand for his own glass, took a sip from it, then said, "Did you know that I've been to Lucel-Lor, Richius? I may call you Richius, yes?"

"Yes, of course."

"Well, this isn't a very well known story, but when I was a young man I sailed to Lucel-Lor. I don't think I was much older than sixteen, and my father, who was emperor then, wanted to make a man of me. He sent me there to bring back the head of one of these lions. For you see, no one really knew if they existed, and my father was eager to find out."

"He sent you there alone?" asked Richius.

"No," said Arkus. "Not quite. I sailed to Lucel-Lor's southern coast aboard one of my father's vessels. But I did go ashore alone, yes. I was quite an accomplished hunter, even at that age, and as I said my father wanted to test me. I was to have no help from the others aboard the ship, and if I didn't return, well . . ." Arkus' voice trailed away thoughtfully.

"But you did return," said Richius. "And with the lion head."

"Yes, I did. The ship had orders to wait for me for as long as it took, since none of us knew how long it would take me to find one of the beasts. But I did find them, a whole valley of them."

Richius listened, stupefied, as Arkus went on to tell how he had finally tracked one of the lions to a giant valley, how he had seen a hundred of the beasts there, and how he had finally tracked one out of the valley again, trapping it and killing it with a spear. The young Arkus had nearly died in the venture. But in the end he had taken out his knife and methodically cut the lion's head from its torso, dragging the bloody trophy back across the wastes and finally to the shore. Upon his return he presented it to his father as a birthday gift, and never again did his father question the mettle of the heir to his throne.

"So you see, Richius," said Arkus. "My father also sent me into Lucel-Lor to fight alone."

"Yes," said Richius softly, entranced by the tale. "And you resented him for it?"

"Not at all. I loved him for it. It made me learn. Seeing Lucel-Lor gave me the fire in my belly to be the greatest leader Nar had ever known. It made me want to be emperor. Now you must do the same. You must put away the past and be the king of Aramoor your father never could be, because he never had the will to join my vision."

Arkus' eyes were glowing now with mad desire. Richius knew Arkus was leading him somewhere. Without flinching he asked the inevitable question.

"Tell me, Your Grace. Why am I here? I know you want something, but I can't guess what it is."

Arkus leaned back in his chair, rolling his goblet between his palms. "I already have told you," he said softly. "When I was in Lucel-Lor I saw things I couldn't believe. Not just the lions, but the people, too. I saw them do magic, like light fires with their minds and appear to each other in dreams. I lived among them for a time, tried to learn from them. But I couldn't. And when I returned to Nar I told my father what I'd seen, and he didn't believe me. I vowed then that one day I would conquer Lucel-Lor, something my father could never hope to accomplish, and I would gain all of their riches and abilities for the Empire. *My* Empire."

"But it never happened," said Richius. "Why not?"

"Because I made my vows when I was young and stupid. I didn't know how vast Lucel-Lor was, and there were lands on this continent to conquer first. But I waited, and when the Daegog of Lucel-Lor opened the border, I sent as many Narens in as were willing to go. They built Ackle-Nye, and they kept an eye on the Triin for me."

Richius chanced another question. "Your Grace, I must ask you this. You wanted something from the Triin, didn't you? I mean, you didn't just want to conquer them. There was something else. Tell me, please. Why did you send us there?"

Arkus chuckled, reaching out for Richius and grazing his cheek with a fingernail. "You are a sweet boy, but impatient. Let an old man tell a story, will you? Yes, it's true I wanted more than to conquer Lucel-Lor. It would have been a jewel to add to Nar's crown, surely, but there was more."

Arkus seemed to be relishing the tale, drawing it out. It occurred to Richius how lonely this man must be.

THE JACKAL OF NAR

"By this time I was already old," Arkus continued. "I had learned some patience, and was content to wait for the Daegog to slowly open up relations. As I said, Lucel-Lor is vast, and to take it by force alone would have been ruinously expensive. So I waited. I waited too damn long. Do you know why?"

"Yes," said Richius gravely. "The Drol."

"Bright boy," remarked Arkus. "The Drol indeed. I had heard of them and their leader Tharn, but I was as shocked as anyone when their damn civil war broke out. I thought it would ruin everything for me, all my chances for gaining ground in Lucel-Lor and getting what I wanted from the Triin. Those hideous Drol rose to power at the worst of times."

Richius listened, amazed at Arkus' candor and wondering still what it meant for him.

"Is that why you ordered Aramoor into Lucel-Lor?"

Arkus nodded. "I never thought the Drol would be a real threat to the Daegog. But by then Aramoor and Talistan were all that were left for us. All our ships were struggling with Liss' navy, and the loyalists in the Eastern Highlands were rebelling, too. Yet I couldn't refuse the Daegog. It was the chance I'd waited for all my life. I knew that if the Drol revolution succeeded, I might never have another opportunity to conquer Lucel-Lor."

"I'm still confused," said Richius. "I don't understand why you wanted to go into Lucel-Lor in the first place. You said you knew how vast it was, how dangerous it could be. Why take the risk?"

"Why?" asked Arkus incredulously. "Because of their power! I told you what I saw when I was there. Can't you imagine how strong that magic could make me? Could make us? If I had the magic of Lucel-Lor, there would be no more Liss, no rebellions in the Eastern Highlands. I would be the emperor of the world." He looked at Richius sharply. "And you would be one of my kings."

Richius very deliberately lowered his goblet onto the stack of books.

"But we lost," he said. He watched the emperor's face for some hint of recognition. Arkus' expression remained still as stone.

"Yes, you did," said Arkus calmly. "Because you were poorly equipped and because the Drol had a weapon none of us could have imagined." He leaned forward suddenly, and said in a twisted whisper, *"Magic!"*

Richius was stricken. Magic. That was what this was all about. He had tried to believe better of this man, but now the chorus of his father's curses rang in his ears so that all he could feel was shame and the self-loathing that comes from having trusted a thief. He remembered his strange talk with Biagio in Aramoor, how the count had interrogated him about what he had seen in Ackle-Nye, and he recalled with growing dread the countless, idle chats he had had with his men around campfires in the Dring Valley, wondering what single thing Arkus wanted from the Triin.

"What are you saying?" asked Richius.

Arkus watched him implacably. "I can see you are judging me, young Richius. Wait. I haven't finished my story yet. For you see, not only did I want something from the Daegog, but he wanted something from us as well. He wanted weapons. He wanted to be like a Daegog of old. Powerful. Strong enough to put down not only the Drol, but all the other warlords, too."

Richius shrugged, hardly surprised at the news. From what Lucyler had told him of the Daegog, he was little better than Arkus himself. "So you made a deal with him?"

"A very poor deal," replied Arkus. "The Daegog knew by now that I wanted magic from his people. He told Count Biagio he could teach it to me, but only if I crushed the Drol for him, and then helped him ruin the other warlords."

"I beg your pardon, Your Grace, but you agreed to this? Didn't you know what a snake the Daegog was?"

Arkus looked at Richius harshly. "I should be insulted by that question, but I'm not. You deserve an honest answer. Yes, I agreed. And yes, I knew he was a snake and not to be trusted. But I had already seen Triin magic. No one else believed me, not even Biagio, but I knew it existed. The Daegog told me he possessed it, and I believed him. Maybe because I wished to, I don't really know."

"But why would you believe him? If he had magic, wouldn't he have used it against the Drol?"

"No, he wouldn't have. I knew something about Triin folkways, and I knew how they felt about using magic to kill. The Drol call it the touch of heaven. But all Triin agree that any gift of the gods is for good, not harm. This is what the Daegog explained to the count. I had no choice but to trust him. For you see, the Drol would never have dealt with me if the Daegog fell."

"But the Daegog has fallen," Richius reminded the emperor. "I'm sorry, Your Grace, but you were fooled."

"Was I?" asked Arkus. "By the Daegog, perhaps, but I was correct about the magic. And now that I know that, I won't be stopped again. I want Lucel-Lor, young Richius. And I intend to have it."

"No," said Richius. What he was hearing was ludicrous, and he meant to say so. "You can't mean it."

"I do. And I need your help to get it."

"No!" repeated Richius, rising abruptly from the chair. "I won't. Lord Emperor, you must listen to me. What you're suggesting is madness. There's no way to win against the Drol. You said so yourself."

"Biagio told me you saw this weapon, Richius. You claimed it was a storm, but you know better, don't you? The truth now, tell me. You saw magic there. You saw this weapon at work."

Richius nodded dumbly, unsure what he was agreeing to. Whether the storm he saw devour Edgard was indeed a weapon, a conjuring of Tharn's ungodly magic, or whether it was some violent, freakish trick of nature he simply couldn't say. But he had seen it, whatever it was, and he knew that nothing in Arkus' vast arsenal could stand against it.

"I saw it," he said. "I don't know what it was. Maybe it was magic. Maybe not. But whatever I saw, I know it can't be beaten with horses and swords. This thing can burn us all alive. We can't win."

"We must take them," Arkus mumbled, still not looking at Richius. "We must."

"But why?" Richius implored. He fell to his knees beside the old man. "I don't understand. What do you want from them?"

Arkus broke from his trance and smiled at Richius. Slowly he raised a hand and brushed his brittle fingers across Richius' face. The touch was cold, almost dead.

"You're so young," said Arkus. "So beautiful."

"Please, Your Grace, listen to me. . . ."

"I have heard you," said Arkus. "Now you must listen to me. I know you are a man of honor. Because of that I will tell you the truth." He reached out again and took Richius' hand, clasping it firmly so that his icy fingers rested in the warmth of Richius' palm. "Do you feel that?" he asked.

"What?"

"Don't be polite. Tell me what you feel."

Richius cradled the decrepit fingers. They were frigid, like two fleshy icicles. He had held the hands of dead men with more warmth than this. Even Biagio's hands, cold as they were, had been more lifelike.

"Cold," answered Richius finally. Very gently he placed the hand on Arkus' lap.

"Yes. That's the cold of age, Richius. Age and death."

"No," said Richius. "That's not right. I've known old men before. I've never felt hands as cold as yours. And the count, what about him? Why are his hands also so cold? And why do his eyes shine like yours?" He leaned forward, confronting Arkus squarely. "What are you doing to yourselves?"

Arkus gave a little, mirthless laugh. "Trying to survive."

"How?" Richius demanded. "Some sort of magic of your own?"

"Not magic. Science. The war labs give us potions to keep us all alive. But don't look at me and judge this all. I'm not what I want to be. Look at Biagio and the others. You've seen how alike we are, haven't you?"

"Yes, but I still don't understand. What is this potion?"

"Bovadin discovered it years ago. I don't really know what it is. I don't even think Bovadin knows. But whatever it is, it has the power to keep us all alive, to keep us from aging. Only it doesn't actually do that. It only slows the process."

"Slows it? How?"

"I don't know," said Arkus again. He was growing agitated. "I only know that it's kept me alive when I should have been dead years ago. Look at me, Richius. I am over a hundred years old! Have you ever known a man to live so long?"

"Never," Richius admitted. "But what has all this to do with Lucel-Lor? This drug, does it come from there?"

"No," said Arkus. "It comes from the war labs. But you're not understanding me. I'm saying the potions aren't working for me anymore. It was discovered too late. I was too old when I started taking it, and now . . ." He paused, examining his hands, then held them out for Richius to inspect. "I am dying, Richius."

Slowly Richius rose from his knees and sat back in his chair. It was all becoming clear.

"And you think the Triin have magic to stop it? Lord Emperor, you are wrong. If I may say so, this is folly. I spent three years in Lucel-Lor. I slept almost nightly beside a Triin who was my friend, and I can tell you truthfully that I never saw magic until that last day." He sighed, almost pitying the broken old man before him. "I'm sorry for you, really. But there's no cure waiting for you in Lucel-Lor. And to be honest, there may not be any magic at all."

"Of course there is," said Arkus. "What else could have caused that storm to destroy so many men? You haven't an answer for that, have you? But I do. It was magic. I know it was. It was the sign I've waited for all my life. It proved to me I was right about the Triin, that they really do have magic. We must go back, Richius. We *will* go back."

"And how will we beat them? If you're right, if this is some sort of magical Drol weapon, how can we defeat it? We barely escaped with our lives the last time. Even the survivors from Talistan will tell you that."

"Ah, but this time you will have all of Nar behind you! No more waiting for your father to send troops that never come. No more fighting without enough fuel to keep the cannons alive. I promise you, Richius, you will have all the forces you need to conquer these Drol. My own legions will be under your command. And you won't have the Gayles of Talistan meddling with you. They won't be part of this at all."

Richius shook his head, exasperated. Clearly he wasn't convincing Arkus of the senselessness of his plan. Even if they went in with a thousand of Nar's best troops, how much good could they really do against the Drol? All of Lucel-Lor was certainly under their control by now, and that meant a brutal, bloody campaign just to gain a foothold. He remembered Edgard, and how the old war duke had warned him of Tharn's magic. Yet Richius hadn't believed him. Even now he was unsure of it. No man could control the skies. It was impossible.

"I'm sorry," he said at last. "I wasn't prepared for this. It's all such a shock."

"It's the way it must be," said Arkus. "But I don't ask this for myself alone. Think of what this could mean to you. You're one of us now. I've told you things today I've never shared with anyone, because I want you to join me. Together we can make Nar invincible. Aramoor can be the power your father always wanted it to be, stronger than Talistan or any other nation of the Empire. And you will be its king. Think of it!"

Richius did. For less than a moment he considered Arkus' proposition and knew it was insanity. Join him? He hated him. In that instant he hated Arkus more than Blackwood Gayle or Voris or even Tharn himself. Yet something kept him from flatly refusing the emperor, something more than the sheer absurdity of saying no to this man. Very clearly, very suddenly, he remembered Dyana, and that he had never actually seen her die. He knew it was irrational, that it was a hope born of pure desperation, but he couldn't stop the idea from taking shape. She might yet be alive, in the clutches of the very Drol bastard Arkus wanted so desperately to destroy. He might yet be able to save her.

Thoughtfully he bit his lower lip, rolling the preposterous idea over in his mind. There were a hundred problems to consider, any number of ways for the plan to fail. There were supply lines that needed to be opened, horses and men to train. Worst of all, there was the matter of Arkus' current war.

"What about Liss?" asked Richius pointedly. "Won't they interfere? They've kept you from Lucel-Lor before. What about now?"

"Liss won't be a problem very much longer," said Arkus coolly. "By the time we attack Lucel-Lor, Liss will be finished. Then we can use our dreadnoughts against the Drol."

"And when do you intend for us to strike? I'll need time if I'm to arrange this, Your Grace. Aramoor is poorly conditioned. We lost most of our soldiers in the last war, and have almost no horses left."

"You'll have the time you need, Richius. For you see, I need time, too. First we must defeat Liss, and that is still months away. I want you to remain in Nar for a while and rest. Then you will return to Aramoor and begin preparing your troops. By then Liss will be crumbling and the dreadnoughts will be ready to sail for the coasts of Lucel-Lor."

"All right," said Richius. A knot of nausea tied itself in his stomach. This nightmare was really happening, and he was powerless to stop it. Listlessly he drained the remaining brandy from his goblet. Arkus was watching him sharply, his face twisting into a look of sour disapproval.

"You don't really understand what I'm saying, do you?" asked the emperor. "This means as much for you as it does for me. I'm offering you the chance to share our potion, Richius, to be a part of my Circle."

"I understand what you're offering, Your Grace. But why me? There are others who would be more eager to help you. Why not ask the Gayles to do this thing for you?"

"Because they are fools and I don't trust them."

"And because Aramoor borders Lucel-Lor and Talistan doesn't."

"Of course," said Arkus. "I won't lie to you, Richius. You've already figured out why I've chosen you to do this. I need you. If this is to be done quickly, it must be done by someone with experience fighting the Drol, someone who knows his way around Lucel-Lor. But I also want you to be one of us. The House of Gayle could never be trusted with the Drol magic. But you . . ."

Are young and stupid, thought Richius bitterly. But Arkus said no such thing. The old emperor sat back and gave Richius a long, languid smile.

"You can be trusted. I know how loyally you served me in Lucel-Lor, Richius. You alone did not betray me. You won't do it now."

Richius said nothing. He had been proud of his service in Lucel-Lor, proud that he hadn't dishonored himself by running from the fight. But he had done it for the sake of Aramoor, not to please this greedy old devil. Arkus' approval sickened him.

"I won't betray you," he said softly.

"I know you won't. And don't worry. You'll be well rewarded for your loyalty. You'll be able to live forever in that beautiful body."

"No," said Richius firmly. "I'll fight your war because I must to save Aramoor. But I have no wish to live forever."

Arkus stared at him crossly, the thin, white brows knitting above his eyes. "That would be a foolish decision. Don't refuse this. I won't offer it to you again."

"You've been too kind with your gifts already, Lord Emperor. This one I must refuse."

"But this potion really works! And for someone as young and strong as you, there's no telling how long you might live. You must think before you make this choice."

"There's no need. I know what I'm saying. I don't want to live any longer than my fate has decided. Being king will be difficult enough for me."

Arkus gave an exasperated sigh. "Very well," he said. "I won't force it on you. But I am disappointed. I had hoped we might have a better relationship than your father and I endured."

"It still could happen, Your Grace," said Richius. "If you keep your promise to support me in Lucel-Lor. I have no love for these Drol. They killed my father and my friends. Nothing would satisfy me more than to have my vengeance on them. But we have no chance at all if you're not fully committed to this."

"My word will be kept," said Arkus. "When this finally happens, you'll have all the might of Nar at your disposal."

"Believe me, Your Grace, we'll need it. I'm sure the Drol have secured Lucel-Lor by now. We'll have to strike hard and quickly just to gain a foothold."

"Yes, quickly. Time is precious to me now, Richius. This must be done as soon as possible."

"I'll do my best." Richius rose from his seat and smiled bleakly at Arkus. "I'm probably being missed downstairs, and you look tired. Shall I leave you now?"

"Not yet," said Arkus, also getting to his feet. "I have one more thing to give you."

"Oh, no, Your Grace," Richius protested. "Please . . ."

Arkus interrupted with a wave of his bony hand. "This is something very special, something I'm sure you will like." He placed his frigid hands on Richius' shoulders, his eyes shining with delight. "I have found a woman for you."

Richius was thunderstruck. He blinked twice, wondering what he had heard.

"A woman, Your Grace?" he asked. "What sort of woman?"

"A wife, Richius," said Arkus. "A beautiful, young wife."

Again Richius was silent for a long moment. He stared blankly at Arkus, watching the old man's face twitch with glee. Clearly he thought his news would be welcome, yet Richius could hardly stammer a response.

"You've chosen a wife for me? But I have no wish to be married." He paused, choosing his words carefully. "I'm sorry, but this gift is impossible."

Arkus dropped his hands away and stared hard at Richius. "Why?" he asked sharply. "Have you already chosen a woman for yourself?"

"No, but—"

"Good. Because Lady Sabrina has come a long way to marry you, and I had to make her father certain promises I wish to honor."

"Sabrina? Of Gorkney? You've chosen her for *me*?"

"Don't be so alarmed. She's a beautiful girl and I'm told she's quite charming. You should consider yourself fortunate. There are others in Nar who have designs on her."

"I know, Your Grace, but I don't want to get married. Perhaps some-day, but not now."

"You must have a wife, Richius," said Arkus. "You're a king now, and the last Vantran alive. You must marry and have sons."

Richius was speechless. It was all coming too fast, the plans for war, the possibility of rescuing Dyana, and now this. Marriage was unthinkable. If by some miracle he did find Dyana alive . . .

He shook his head, unable to reason anymore. Arkus was walking away from him, replacing the crystal goblets in the dusty cabinet.

"Please," Richius implored, sounding like a pauper begging coins. "I don't want this. Find some other husband for her. Perhaps one of my own men would accept her."

"Your men? She's the daughter of a duke. She must marry into royal blood. I chose her for you because I was told she's the most beautiful girl in the Empire. I want you to have someone special. If you have your eye on some kitchen wench, forget her. You will marry Lady Sabrina."

"Your Grace—"

"Not another word," snapped Arkus. "You've already refused the potion. I won't let you refuse this gift as well."

There was a terrible, echoing silence as Arkus turned away. Slowly Richius moved toward the door. Yet before he could reach it, Arkus called back to him.

"Richius," said the emperor. "Come here."

Arkus was standing by the cloudy window, looking out over the metal metropolis of Nar. Richius moved to stand beside the emperor. A light snow was falling, dropping lazily into the filthy streets and the smokestacks of the laboratories.

"I can give her to Blackwood Gayle," said Arkus quietly, his eyes never moving from the window. "But only if that's what you truly wish. He would probably beat her, of course, and she would have you to thank for it."

"But why not somebody else? Surely there's another you can give her to. Must it be Gayle or me?"

Arkus nodded. "That's the choice. Either you agree to marry her and save me from looking like a fool with Duke Wallach, or I will give her to Blackwood Gayle. Make your decision now. I must know what to tell the baron."

Silently Richius considered his options. Sabrina was indeed beautiful, one of the loveliest creatures he had ever seen. It was true what Arkus had said. Any man would be fortunate to share his bed with her. Yet could he love her? Could he truly be a husband to her? And what of Dyana? Dead or alive, she still haunted his nights. Yet how could he condemn Sabrina to a life of degradation in Talistan? She would be little more than a slave there, another harlot between Gayle's filthy sheets. He would breed her like a horse, owning her womb until it expired or split open and killed her. And if she were barren or he were not man enough to seed her, he would beat her.

Richius stared mutely out the window. He could see the giant Cathedral of the Martyrs scratching the gray sky, and wondered if God truly had abandoned him. It seemed so.

"You won't reconsider this?" asked Richius.

Arkus shook his head. "No. I brought her here for you. If you don't want her, I shall give her to Gayle. Perhaps it will help mend his wounded pride. He won't be pleased when he learns that I've asked you to return to Lucel-Lor without him."

"Very well, then," said Richius. "If there's no other choice but that murderous rogue, I will take her."

Arkus turned back to Richius, his blue eyes once more sparkling with excitement. "Excellent. You've made me very happy, Richius. And you'll see. You're frightened now, but you'll thank me for this someday. She will make you a fine wife."

"Yes," said Richius dully. "I'm sure you're right."

"And we shall do great things together, Richius. Great things!"

Richius tried to smile. "Yes," he managed. "Great things."

TWENTY

Richius approached the garden like a stalking cat, careful not to let the Lady Sabrina notice him. As had been arranged she was waiting there for him, amusing herself with a bold little bird that had alighted on her finger. Quietly he stopped behind a statue and watched her. He hadn't seen her for three days, not since the coronation, and he wanted to be sure about her, to look at her undisturbed and reassure himself that she was indeed as lovely as he'd remembered. Sabrina did not disappoint him. She was as striking as ever amid the blooms of winter lilies, her cheeks lightly flushed, her long sapphire dress swaying gently in the evening breeze. Her painted lips were pursed in a merry whistle that made the canary on her finger cock its head inquisitively.

Dusk was wrapping its dark mantle about the city. Behind her, a thousand candled windows blinked against the encroaching shadows, and the garden's braziers bathed the balcony in orange light.

Like everything in Nar, the garden of Arkus was immense. It hung out over the palace like a giant, multicolored wing, a veritable forest against a backdrop of unyielding granite. Richius was awed by it. It was so very different from the garden back home where his father had proudly grown roses. That was a simple garden where nothing exotic grew. Not so with this place. Arkus' garden was a masterpiece of flowers, a meticulous canvas where artists worked with living colors. It was just as Biagio had promised: the perfect romantic venue for their meeting.

Richius smoothed down the wave in his hair and squared his shoulders. The bouquet of scarlet dahlias in his fist looked meager amid the bounty. It had been a long time since he'd romanced a girl, and he wondered if the token would be appreciated. She was, after all, a princess, and doubtless accustomed to suitors. He fought to still his nervousness. If only Dinadin could see him now.

Finally, his courage cresting, he stepped out from behind the statue. At once the tiny bird in Sabrina's hand took flight. She turned abruptly to face him.

"I'm sorry," said Richius softly. "I didn't mean to startle you, or your friend."

"You didn't startle me, my lord," she answered. "I was waiting for you."

Richius moved forward, her smile encouraging him closer. He offered the small bouquet for her inspection.

"Count Biagio told me you were fond of flowers," he said. "I thought you might like some of your own."

She cooed appreciatively and took the bouquet, dropping her nose into the blossoms. "Ooohh, thank you, my lord. They're beautiful."

"I'm glad you like them. I was worried you might have a room full of them by now. You made quite a stir at my coronation, you know. I think more people were looking at you than me!"

"Oh, no, my lord, I'm sure you're wrong. Most people know by now that I'm to be yours."

She stopped, catching herself, and an awkward silence rose up between them. Dutifully she looked away, casting her eyes back to the flowers. Richius was relieved she had said it first. Perhaps she was already comfortable with the idea, and he would be spared the horrible ordeal of explaining it to her. In the matter of their marriage, neither of them had a choice.

"You look cold," he said gently. "We can go inside if you like."

She shook her head. "I enjoy the winter, my lord."

Richius moved in a little closer, so that only a hairbreadth separated them, and waited for Sabrina to pull away. She did not.

"This weather reminds me of Aramoor," he said. "I miss it. Do you miss Gorkney?"

Sabrina wrinkled her forehead pensively, then shrugged. "A bit," she said. "But it's also good to be away. There are some things about Gorkney I shall not miss at all. And I've heard that Aramoor is much like my home." She paused, looking back down at the bouquet. Her smile vanished as she said, "I want to apologize for my rudeness at your coronation, my lord. I behaved badly, and I'm ashamed."

"Ashamed?" asked Richius. "Of what?"

"Please. There's no need to spare my feelings. I don't deserve it. The way I slighted you was deplorable, and I'm afraid I don't have a very good explanation for you. But we weren't supposed to meet until after you had heard about our marriage, and I was startled. I didn't know what to do, so I ignored you. I'm very sorry."

"I understand. I was able to guess why you acted that way. You knew when we met in the forest that you were coming here to marry me, didn't you?"

Sabrina nodded. "I've known about it for months," she said. "Since my sixteenth birthday. An emissary came to Gorkney with the news. He told my father that the emperor had chosen me to be your wife, and that I was to be in Nar for your coronation."

"And I thought my trip here was only for my king-making," said Richius. "I'm sorry this has happened to you, my lady. It must have been quite a surprise for you and your father."

"My father?" said Sabrina bitterly. "You needn't worry about his feelings, my lord. A daughter's not much use to a man with acres of land to tend. He'd been waiting years for that messenger."

Richius said nothing. She turned away from him again, the long stems of the flowers slackening in her grip. Awkwardly he took her hand.

"I'm not sure what type of husband I'll make," he said. "Living with me might be no better than living with your father."

"Forgive me, my lord. I seem to be doing nothing but offending you, don't I? Truly I mean no insult. I talk too much. Perhaps that's why my father wanted to be rid of me."

"Is that why he sent you here without a proper escort? Because he cares so little for you? Maybe I shouldn't say so, my lady, but your father sounds like a scoundrel. I can't imagine any man not being pleased with so beautiful and gracious a daughter."

Sabrina brightened a little at the compliment. "You're kind to say so, my lord. But I was escorted here safely."

"By one driver," said Richius, recalling the brooding giant he had met in the forest. "It was foolish of your father to send you all this way without enough men to guard you. You could have been robbed, even killed."

Sabrina shrugged. "But I wasn't, so you can stop worrying about me now, my lord. You'll soon find that I'm quite good at looking after myself."

"Indeed? Well then, I'm surprised you let your father send anyone at all with you."

"You don't understand. Dason's more than just a driver. He's my friend. We look after one another."

"He does seem to need you," Richius agreed. "I saw how you cared for him at the coronation."

"We've needed each other," Sabrina corrected. "Dason's been my only friend since I can remember. He can be difficult at times, I know, but he's a good man with a good heart. I'll miss him."

"Do you want to have him with you?" asked Richius. "You may bring him along to Aramoor, my lady. I'm sure we could find work for him there. If he's so special to you, I don't see why you should leave him."

Sabrina grimaced. "You're very kind, aren't you?" she said. "Believe me, I would have asked that favor if it were possible. But Dason is a slave, and my father owns his collar, not I."

"Then we shall buy him back for you, give him his freedom. We have no slaves in Aramoor, but I can't imagine him costing us more than a few strong horses."

"Whatever you offer won't be enough," said Sabrina. "My father won't release him, not even for a score of horses."

"Why not?"

She looked at him squarely and said, "Because my father is a heartless dragon, my lord. He has never released a slave, and has vowed he never will. And he certainly wouldn't release one simply because I wished it."

"Oh, but that's absurd," said Richius. "Why would he be so cruel as to deny you this? He may call it a wedding gift if he pleases."

Sabrina's laughter rang through the garden. "I'm sorry, my lord," she managed. "You really don't know anything about my father, do you? He doesn't give gifts and he grants no favors. Especially to women."

Richius frowned. "Your father sounds like a fool. It's hard to believe he managed to raise so fine a daughter."

"I'm more like my mother," Sabrina agreed. "But thank you for your offer. It was very generous."

"I've spent the last few days trying to think of ways to make this easier for you, my lady. I want you to be happy in Aramoor."

"Well, I do, too," said Sabrina easily. "But what about you, my lord? Are you happy? You haven't had much time to adjust to the idea. How do you feel about this marriage?"

"Honestly, I don't know yet. I hadn't intended to marry for a long time, if ever. But you are truly beautiful, and I can't imagine any man not being pleased with you."

Sabrina smiled, seemingly content with his answer. "We're both afraid," she said, "but maybe that's a good thing. When I first heard about you I thought you might be horrible, someone who would think little better of me than my father does. But I see now you're not like that at all. I knew when I first met you that you were kind and that I wouldn't need to fear you."

"Fear me?" said Richius. "God, no. I want this to be pleasant for you, if it can be. And you won't be alone in Aramoor. There are many others your age in the castle. . . ."

Richius stopped himself, suddenly embarrassed. He was talking to Sabrina as if she were a little girl worried about finding playmates. Yet in many ways she was that child. She was alone and frightened and about to lose the only friend she had in the world. And she was trusting him to take care of her. He thought about Blackwood Gayle, and how he could never satisfy this young woman's needs. And he thought of Dyana. He had promised her much the same things he was now promising Sabrina: a home, security, a place to be welcomed. That promise he had broken. He was suddenly determined not to forsake another.

Sabrina took his hand again. "Come," she said, leading him through the garden. "Let's walk together."

Quietly they moved through the flowers, avoiding each other's eyes. Soon they reached the edge of the balcony and stared out over the sprawling metropolis. Already Nar's eastern edges were dark with night. A smoky pall curtained the horizon, obscuring the newborn moon, and a murky silence floated in the air. Only the thrumming of the city's incinerators reached them on their lofty perch. The breath caught in Richius' throat, the way it always did when he looked on Nar.

"Amazing," he said softly. "I always heard about Nar when I was a boy, but I never knew it would be like this."

Sabrina seemed to shudder. "It frightens me," she said. "I think it's ugly."

"Yes, it's as ugly as death. But it is amazing, too, don't you think?"

"It's nothing like Gorkney."

"No," said Richius. "Nor like Aramoor. I'll certainly have some tales to tell them back home. This place is so vast!"

Sabrina turned up her nose in disgust. "I don't care for such big cities. I was in Goss when I was small. Even that frightened me. I can still remember all the noise and the strange people, my father arguing with the vendors in the street. It was too overwhelming for me."

"Then Aramoor should suit you well. We'll miss the winter, but the spring there is beautiful. Everybody goes riding in the springtime."

"Everybody?" asked Sabrina thinly.

Richius grinned. "Indeed, my lady. Even little children take to horses in Aramoor. I know you can't ride yet, but I'll teach you. You'll really have to learn if you want to fit in. And there's the ocean, too. It's not a big shore really, but it's rocky and pretty, like Gorkney probably. We've even a few boats if you like that sort of thing, and the Iron Mountains. Really, my lady, you'll love it."

"Yes," she said dreamily. "It sounds wonderful."

"It is," said Richius. "It's the best place I know. Mind you, I haven't really been many places, but I've never seen anything to rival Aramoor."

A crushing melancholy came over him suddenly. He had almost forgotten the dark business that awaited him back home. He let his hand slip out of Sabrina's.

"My lord?" asked Sabrina. "What's wrong?"

"I'm sorry," said Richius. "I shouldn't be talking like this to you. Aramoor might not turn out to be as grand as I say."

"I'm sure it's lovely."

"You misunderstand. There's something you don't know yet, something I have to tell you."

Sabrina's faced blanched. "What is it?"

"I'm talking of Aramoor as if it's some place you'd want to be, but it could just as easily be another prison for you, my lady. There is to be war with the Triin again, and I'm supposed to lead it."

"Oh, no," said Sabrina, her hands going to her face. "Why?"

"It is Arkus' will. I'm to prepare us for war in the spring, as soon as we return home."

"But why?" Sabrina asked again. "Why now, when we're to be married?"

"Believe me, my lady, I don't wish it. But I'm powerless. We're the only nation bordering Lucel-Lor, the only ones who can do it."

"That's preposterous. Forgive me for saying so, my lord, but everyone knows Aramoor couldn't possibly defeat the Triin. The emperor must be mad."

"Oh, indeed he is," said Richius. "But there's something in Lucel-Lor he wants, and I'm to be his message boy." He stopped, struck by Sabrina's expression. There was real worry etched on her face.

"I'm afraid for you," she said. "I've heard about these Triin. They're sorcerers. You could be killed."

"Here now," said Richius. "Don't think so blackly. I survived Lucel-Lor once and I intend to do it again. And we won't be alone. Arkus has promised me command of his legions. This time it will be different."

"Do you really think so?" asked Sabrina. There was a spark of hope in her tone that Richius couldn't bear to extinguish.

"Of course," he lied. "Tharn himself couldn't possibly stand against such might. Perhaps I shouldn't have even told you about it yet. The war probably won't last more than a few weeks anyway."

"Now you're sparing my feelings," said Sabrina. "There's no way another war with the Drol could end so quickly, and you know it. Please don't comfort me with lies, my lord. You're afraid, too. I can see it."

Richius gave a wan smile. "You see very clearly," he said. He sighed and rested his hands on the balcony's stone railing. "I am afraid. I swore I'd never go back to that place. I lost so many friends there, so many good young men. How am I supposed to do it all again?"

"Refuse him," said Sabrina. "What the emperor is asking is insane. You must make him see that."

"I cannot. I've tried, but he won't listen. Damn him to hell, Sabrina. I am trapped!"

He ended his rant just as a sentry stepped into the garden. The soldier wore the familiar black of Nar, almost invisible in the shadows of the broad-leafed vines.

"There's no trouble here," said Richius. "Leave us."

The soldier hesitated for a moment, watching them. A malevolent grin flashed across his face. Then he moved away, just as quietly as he had come, and disappeared. Enraged, Richius moved after him.

"Yes," he cried. "Go and tell your masters what I've said. Tell them—"

Sabrina's hand shot up and silenced him. "My lord, don't! I've seen these sentries everywhere. They'll hear you." She took him by the arm, leading him back toward the railing. "It won't do you any good."

"You're right," said Richius. "I should be silent. I've already agreed to it, and what's done is done. I only hope I can keep you from the danger of it, my lady. If the Drol attack us through the mountains . . ."

"I'm not worried about myself," said Sabrina. "And I don't want you troubling yourself over me, either. Look after your men and whatever else you need to when we get to Aramoor. I'll stay out of your way."

Richius shook his head. "I won't bring you home to be a kitchen wench, my lady. There will be time enough for war, but only one homecoming for you. I want it to be special. I've already sent word to my steward that I will be returning in the spring with a wife. He'll make everything ready for your arrival."

"Then we are to be married before going to Aramoor?"

Richius' eyebrows went up. "How much do you know, my lady?"

"Almost nothing. I've only spoken to Count Biagio about it, and he told me that plans were being made."

"Well then," said Richius wryly. "You'd better start arranging things. We're to be married in two weeks."

Sabrina went ashen. "Two weeks?" she shrieked, suddenly full of youthful ire. "And no one told me about it? But I haven't had any time to prepare! I have no gown, no attendants. . . ."

"Easy," said Richius. "I've asked Biagio for it to be a small wedding, very quiet. You and I and only a few of my closest companions will be there. Of course, anyone you want to invite is welcome. Perhaps your driver?"

"Yes," Sabrina agreed. "Dason should be there. I won't have much time to see him after that. But what about everything else? What will I wear? I don't know anyone here in Nar. Who will help me prepare?"

"Biagio probably has that all arranged. But I will ask him if you wish, just to be sure."

"Please," said Sabrina. "I suppose we're to be married by Naren priests, then?"

Richius nodded. "In the Cathedral of the Martyrs." He pointed out over the darkening cityscape to an elaborate, looming steeple of coppery metal. "Look there, can you see it?"

The cathedral was on the other side of the city, across the wide, winding river Kiel. It was a remarkable structure, almost as tall as the palace itself, and easily visible even at such a distance. Sabrina bristled at the sight of it.

"Might we not be married elsewhere?" she asked. "I saw the Bishop Herrith at your coronation, my lord. He seemed such an unpleasant man. Maybe we could ask that someone else perform the rite."

"I don't think we should, my lady. Biagio has already told me that Arkus cares greatly for his bishop. A request like that would certainly be considered an insult."

"All right," conceded Sabrina. "I certainly wouldn't want to risk offending the emperor. You'll need his goodwill if you expect his help."

Richius grinned at her. "You talk like you know a thing or two about politics, my lady. Do you?"

"Oh, yes," said Sabrina playfully. "I'm the daughter of a king, and you can't live in a castle without hearing about such matters. But if you would rather I was silent about it . . ."

"Not at all," said Richius. "It's just that I'm impressed. I've never known a woman to have real knowledge of politics. Most of the women in our castle are, well, ignorant about the subject. But I welcome your advice, my lady. Lord knows I'll need it."

"That might not be proper," said Sabrina. "You're a new king. Your people will be expecting you to look strong. How would they feel if they thought I was whispering orders in your ear?"

"Not orders," corrected Richius. "Advice. And I say again I welcome it. Women are treated with respect where I come from. My mother, God rest her, was loved by her people, and my father listened to her advice. I want it to be the same way with us."

"Very well, my lord. If that's what you want, I will help you in any way I can."

"Good," said Richius. He cupped Sabrina's shoulders in his hands. "Then you can start by calling me Richius."

"Richius," said Sabrina, as if trying out the word. "Yes, I like that. But what shall I call you around others? Surely I shouldn't speak to you so familiarly in front of your men."

"You needn't worry about that. Everyone in the castle calls me Richius. I'm afraid we're not very formal in Aramoor. And if I may, I would like to call you Sabrina."

Sabrina smiled. "Please do . . . Richius."

They stood there for a moment, regarding each other like two frightened strangers, and Richius didn't move or take his hands from her shoulders. There was a breeze that stirred through the garden, pulling at the hem of her dress. Her lips trembled, almost opening, begging him to come closer. And suddenly he knew it: she was in love with him.

He stopped, releasing her and backing away.

"No," he stammered. "Not yet."

Sabrina flushed. "I'm sorry, my lord," she said in a small voice. Then she composed herself, drawing a shaky breath and turning around to face him again. "I must go now. We shouldn't be seen spending so much time together."

"Sabrina, I didn't mean to—"

"No," she pleaded. "Don't say anything more." She turned and made her way from the garden.

Richius reached out for her, but when he saw the determination in her stride he let his hand fall away. He wanted to call out to her, to beg her to stop and let him explain, yet he said nothing. There were no words for what he was feeling. In the next instant she was gone, swallowed up by the vines and blooms.

He was alone.

A rigid silence cloaked the balcony. And a name floated to him on the wind. It was a name that had come to him often in the last few days. He closed his eyes and dared to think it.

Dyana.

PHANTOMS

From the Journal of Richius Vantran:

Today is the eighth day of spring, and as I write this I am blessedly alone, without the blaring horns of docking ships or the rumble of incinerators to bother me. The air is sweet again, the woods around me quiet. I have missed it all so much. It is easy to forget the taste of good bread when there is only caviar to eat, and so it is with these woods, too. Like boyhood friends these trees are familiar to me. From here I can see the castle, looking small now against my memories of Nar, and to the north all the nothingness of Aramoor is beautiful. It is perfect, and if Arkus were with me now he wouldn't need his potions to keep him alive.

After seeing home again I have decided that it is Nar itself which has driven them all mad. They are addicted to their drugs because their city is unlivable. There is too much there for the mind to grasp. Everyone who lives in Nar is like a frightened rodent, terrified of the hawks that dwell in the palace. If there is a place on earth to rival Dring for evil, it is the Black City. I don't care to ever see its like again, and to be truthful it has shaken me. I am part of this Empire now, more than I ever was before. I have work to do for Arkus. But at least I am home, and even he cannot take the spring away or stop the trees from greening.

Last night I dreamt of Lucyler again. Another damnable nightmare. I have not had a sound night's rest since returning home, and I am starting to wonder what has gone wrong with me. It is as if some of Nar's drugs have made their way into my brain. They are vivid dreams, too, so much like my own thoughts that it is hard to separate one from the other. I had assumed I was over my guilt for Lucyler, but almost nightly I am reminded of the loss. He speaks to me in the dreams, but I cannot hear him. Or it may be that I simply cannot remember his words upon my waking. Whatever it is, I wish he would say it clearly and be done. The dead should stay buried and let the living get their sleep.

Being married has been stranger than I expected. It is odd to always share my bed with someone. But Sabrina has been wonderful. Though we have been home less than three weeks, she already knows the castle as if she has lived there for years. And Jojustin and the others adore her. They keep her company at night when I am away, as I have been often lately. Only Jenna has yet to warm to her. Apparently my marriage was more of a surprise for Jenna than I had imagined. We have hardly spoken at all since I returned home, and when we do it's only to pass pleasantries. Still, I'm sure she will come around in time. Sabrina is my wife, and Jenna has to accept it. I only hope she does so quickly. I will not be around for Sabrina much longer, and she will need friends to help her through the dark days ahead.

Thankfully, Sabrina seems comfortable here. Except for Jenna, we have all tried to make the change easier for her, to show her the land and the way we do things, and to include her when we can. At first she was quiet, but now she talks more at mealtimes, and she has a talent for keeping conversations interesting. Arkus was right about her. Most men would envy such a fine young wife. She gives me my time and lets me worry when I must. I have been doing a great deal of worrying these days. Though the Drol seem satisfied with Lucel-Lor for the moment, we still have war plans to make, and I know Sabrina can sense my fear. Jenna has told her how Father was murdered in the garden, and now she is worse than Jojustin at trying to keep me indoors. It is like having both a mother and a father again. Yet I know her concern for me is genuine. I have not been as open as I should be with her, and only rarely do we share any time together. It has been hard even to steal an hour to write this journal. Still, I think she understands. These are difficult days for us all.

I have done what I can to keep this bold scheme of Arkus' a secret. So far only we in the castle seem to know of it. I had expected Jojustin to be shocked by the news, but of all of us he seems the most enamored of the plan. The idea of us all going back to war has not soured his spirits at all. Perhaps he is too old to clearly remember his own war days. Like the old father, he grieves for the possibility of our deaths, but the soldier in him rejoices. His eyes twinkle when he speaks of it. Newborn warhorses, Arkus' legions, shipments from Nar; he tells me of these things like a greedy clerk eager to put his wares to use. To him this is all a second chance, a glorious moment for showing up the Gayles and proving to the world what Aramoor can do. When I told him of Talistan's exclusion from the war he was as giddy as a schoolboy. His hatred of that breed has truly blinded him.

I myself feel no such joy. For me, a kingdom without interference from Nar would be far more welcome. Jojustin has become fond of telling me how like my father I am. He says we all must accept the rule of Arkus now. But I would rather have my father's heart within me. Let the Gayles remain the emperor's pets. Arkus' favor means nothing to me. I have tried to convince Jojustin that Nar's love for us is only momentary, yet it seems that I alone can grasp what is really happening. Lately I am surrounded by peacocks. Everyone seems to share Jojustin's stupid pride. Even Patwin is consumed with it. Perhaps that is what Arkus knew would happen. It has not been easy for any of us to live with the humiliation of our loss, but to believe we can now win against the Drol seems foolish. I have agreed to this folly because I must, but the others are senselessly willing. They frighten me. If I do this insane thing it will not be simply for the empty pocket of revenge. At least I'll know my reasons.

And it may be that all this is for nothing, and none of us will ever really have our requital. Precious little news reaches us from Nar, but the talk among the merchants in Innswick is that Liss is still holding on. God bless those hearty bastards. I'm sure Arkus and that butcher Nicabar had expected them to be on their knees by now. Perhaps those new dreadnoughts are not as wonderful as they supposed. Either way, it buys us needed time. If we are lucky and Liss manages against this onslaught, then maybe we will not need to ready ourselves for war at all. I have sent word to Biagio asking him how the war with Liss is progressing. It will be weeks before I get a reply. So much the better.

Yet this too troubles me. There is a part of me that wants this war. I know it's insane to think it, but Dyana might still be alive. Somewhere in Lucel-Lor, hiding in a cave or cowering in the bed of that devil Tharn, she is waiting for me. It is like a dream or the sense one gets of danger: no more easily seen than the air. But I know it is so. And if Liss somehow holds on, if heaven grants them a miracle and spares them from Nar, I may never have the chance to save her. It is all I have thought about these past months. I have not even whispered her name to Sabrina, but I know she suspects something. I've seen her watching me when I write, and I know she is wondering. And when I do not touch her at night, what does she think? She has been more than any man could want, yet I am unable to love her. I have tried to be skillful in avoiding her, to stay away at night until she is asleep, but I'm sure she questions me. She does not deserve such coldness in a husband.

Nor do I deserve her. I can never tell her of the terrible choice Arkus gave me, but I wonder these days if she is any better with me than she would have been with Gayle. It is only a different kind of torture I offer her, a more insidious isolation. I cannot conjure up a love for her that is any more than a man might have for a sister.

Tomorrow I will ride with Patwin to the House of Lotts. It is time to start telling the other families about Arkus' grand designs. I'm sure Dinadin will be as foolishly anxious to fight again as Jojustin. He is too young to see how the emperor manipulates us. As for Terril and the others, they will make do as always. They are old enough not to argue about war.

I have already done my arguing. No one is listening.

TWENTY-ONE

Sabrina awoke with a start.

It was barely morning. A light rain tapped against the leaded window of the bedchamber. Beside her, Richius pitched in the throes of sleep, the heavy sheets wrapped awkwardly around his legs and chest. An incoherent babble streamed from his lips. His face was white and terrible, and the little frantic movements beneath his eyelids told her he was panicked—again.

She slid away from him, gingerly pulling off the sheets. Waking him was a mistake she didn't want to repeat. He would come out of it soon, he always did. And perhaps when it passed he could sleep some more. Soundlessly she rolled off the bed, her naked feet recoiling at the chilly touch of the floor. The breeze outside the window stirred the air, making her shiver, and she quickly retrieved her robe from the bedpost. Even in early spring Aramoor was a cold corner of the Empire. She went to the window and glanced out at the day, noting the pall of clouds obscuring the sky. They had taken over the castle's master bedroom, and from here she could see almost all of the Vantran property. Every inch of it was muddied.

A bad day for traveling, she thought with a smile. *Good.*

It was a considerable distance to the House of Lotts, and Sabrina hoped that Richius would postpone the trip. Then perhaps they would finally spend some time together.

A violent shout from Richius yanked her from her daydream. She turned back to him, hurrying to the bedside. A sheen of sweat drenched his forehead and chest. He was mumbling something, saying it over and over in a bizarre, trapped voice. She cocked her head to listen, to try and piece together the fractured syntax. What was he saying? A name? Yes, she concluded quickly, a name.

At last the spell subsided and Richius was silent. Slowly his breathing fell back into a peaceful cadence. Relieved, Sabrina leaned over the bed to look at him. He was still colorless, but the perspiration seemed to be drying as she looked at him and his face was almost relaxed. She placed a kiss on his cheek, hardly forceful enough to stir a bird, and touched his damp hair. She had never really known a mother, not in any genuine sense, but she thought quickly that this is what a mother would be like, fretting over the illness of a child. Richius had been having dreams for weeks now, since returning home. It was as if some devilish fever seized him when he slept. Worse, he never talked about his dreams, but instead only offered vague apologies for waking her. Whatever these nightmares were, he considered them his alone, and his unwillingness to share them disturbed her. She was always alone in this big bed.

She went again to the window, trying vainly to locate the sun. The land was coming into flower, beautiful in the gentle touch of new morning light. Aramoor was indeed like Gorkney, and a pang she had not expected clutched at her. She missed Gorkney. She missed Dason and his odd friendship. And for some strange reason she even missed her brutish father. Today she wanted something familiar.

"Attention," she grumbled, and as she spoke the glass misted with her breath. After almost three weeks in the castle only Jojustin had really noticed her. He had even offered to teach her to ride, a promise Richius himself had made and apparently forgotten. But she wasn't in love with the old man. He was sweet and well intentioned, but it was Richius whose company she craved, that distant, beautiful man in her bed. Somehow, she had to crack the armor that kept him untouchable.

Again she looked at the sky. The rain was meager but steady. Bits of branches and blown sticks covered the courtyard, and muddy pockets of water collected in sunken corners. Soon there would be activity in the courtyard and castle halls. Her jaw tightened at the thought. They would all be making demands on Richius. Hardly a moment went by when someone wasn't looking for him. And when she would corner him at the end of the day, he would simply smile at her and say, "These are busy times."

Too busy, she thought miserably. *But not today.*

Today she and the clouds would conspire to keep him inside. Surely his trip could wait another day, though he had spoken quite anxiously about this fellow Dinadin. Maybe Patwin could see to it. She decided she would ask him.

Carefully she inched her way across the floor, avoiding the creaking of loose boards. Richius was still asleep, restful again. She was halfway past the bed when a hard edge caught her toe, nearly tripping her.

"God!" she hissed between her teeth, stifling the cry at the last moment. She was on her knees suddenly, her head bobbing at the level of the mattress. Richius gave a little moan but did not awaken. Quickly she scanned the floor. At the bedside was a small book with a leather cover. Richius' journal. She reached over and retrieved it. Usually she was glad when he left it in plain sight. It was the one small gesture of trust he managed, knowingly or otherwise, and she appreciated it. But as she held the journal in her trembling hands the image of flinging it out the window popped into her mind. Even this little book was getting more attention than she was lately, and for a brief, mindless moment she hated it.

And then another, more sinister idea occurred to her. Whatever was troubling her silent husband was probably somewhere in these soiled pages. All she had to do was open the book.

No, she thought suddenly, ashamed of the idea. *I can't. I won't. He trusts me. He does, and I can't ruin that.*

But the journal remained in her hands. She stared at it for a long moment, contemplating its secrets. There were names in here, names like codes to decipher his cryptic dreams. She could understand if she read the journal. It would be good for them both. And then he wouldn't have to talk about the war and all the ugly things that happened to him; she would know. She could help him.

"No," she whispered firmly. She placed the journal back beside the bed, tucking it slightly under the frame. A feeling of disgust writhed within her. That journal held Richius' private thoughts, and he was entitled to keep them away from everyone, even her. She rose to her feet. The skin on her knees tingled and she brushed at them, fighting back tears that seemed to come from nowhere. Richius rolled over, turning his back to her.

Attached to the bedroom was a tiny dressing chamber she used for her own privacy. It was full of clothing and jewelry, and had an elegant mirror that one could admire one's entire body in with a single glance. Sabrina stepped into the dark chamber. There was no light in the room but she closed the door anyway, shutting out the twinkling dawn. Blindly she moved across the room to where the mirror stood. Beside the mirror was a chest of drawers. Though there were a hundred things in the room to wear, stacked in piles or hung on racks in hidden closets, she didn't reach for any of them. Most of the dresses weren't hers anyway. They had belonged to Richius' mother, and Queen Jessicane had obviously been a tall woman. All her dresses needed severe altering if they were ever to fit Sabrina. But there were a few items in the room that she liked, mostly things she had brought with herself from Gorkney, and these she kept in the chest.

She opened the top drawer and felt inside. The emerald-green dress she had worn the day she had met Richius was placed exactly where she had left it. There was something in his eyes that day, something she meant to recapture. The dress, she hoped, would make the difference. Soundlessly, she dropped her robe to the floor and stepped into the dress, fussing with the ties in the back. Even in full daylight she had a problem tying the loose gold braids that cinched the dress around her waist, but in a few minutes it was done. With equal dexterity she hunted down her shoes, slipped her feet into them, and did up their laces. At last she found her hairbrush. She ran it through her hair until she guessed she looked presentable, then slipped on her favorite bracelet and went back to the door.

She peered back into the bedroom. Richius was still asleep. He was not a sound sleeper, and it surprised her that she hadn't been overheard. But his back remained to her, making it easy for her to leave. As she tiptoed past him she gave him one last look. He was beautiful, she thought sadly. Even when asleep.

Outside the bedroom the hallway was empty and cold. There were no other chambers here save for Jojustin's, and he was always one to rise early. Most likely he was already downstairs, sitting at the breakfast table with his habitual glass of hot wine. Sabrina scowled. Jenna would probably be there, too, seeing to the workings of the kitchen. It wasn't a big house, not like the one she had left in Gorkney, but it did require many of them to arise early and see to all its needs. She would have to be canny if she wanted to avoid questions. The dress would certainly provoke them.

The steps of the stone stairway echoed as she moved down them. Already tiny candles burned in the iron sconces, lighting her way and telling her that Jojustin was indeed up and at work. She found him in the little room off the kitchen where they usually took their meals. His pipe was tucked neatly between his bearded lips. Wisps of sweet-smelling smoke rose up from it, making a little blue cloud around his head. He looked up at her as she entered the room.

"Hello, Daughter," he said cheerfully. He rose from his chair to greet her. Sabrina put out her cheek for his kiss.

"Good morning, Uncle," she replied. He liked to be called Uncle, she could tell. His smile always broadened when she addressed him so. Jojustin pulled out a chair for her. She sat down with a dainty crossing of her legs.

"You're up early," he said. "Did Richius wake you?"

She shrugged. "Not really. I was restless. Perhaps it was the rain."

"Ah, I sleep like a baby in the rain," said Jojustin. "I could have slept all morning if I didn't have such a busy day planned. Where is Richius, anyway? Did he wake with you?"

"He's upstairs, still asleep."

Jojustin's eyebrows went up. "Asleep? Well, somebody had better wake him then." He sat back down and reached for the ubiquitous decanter of spiced wine. "We have a lot to do today. We're supposed to get an early start. Wine?"

Sabrina put her hand over the mug beside her. "No, thank you. But why must I wake him? I'd rather he got some sleep."

"He's riding with Patwin to the Lotts' place this morning. Didn't he tell you?"

"Is it that far? It's hardly past dawn."

"It's a fair distance, Daughter. Especially in this weather. And there are also others Richius needs to see, like Terril. He'll be gone most of the day as it is."

"But I'd hoped he would be staying around the castle today. It's so foul outside. Couldn't this trip wait? At least until tomorrow?"

"He has to get on with things, Sabrina. These plans of the emperor's are too big to keep secret. We wouldn't want the other families finding out about it the wrong way. They have to hear it from the king."

Sabrina frowned. *The king.* She still found it difficult to pin that title on Richius. He was so young. It was like those war plans or that precious sword of his: too much for him to handle.

"Why can't Patwin take the news to this Dinadin fellow himself?" asked Sabrina. "You've said yourself how dangerous it could be for Richius to travel far from the castle. What about these Drol assassins?"

Jojustin laughed. "That was months ago, Daughter. We would know if there were any more Triin in Aramoor, believe me. No, Richius must tell his people of this war himself. It wouldn't do to send a messenger. Richius needs to be seen as a leader. Besides, he has personal business with Dinadin."

"I suppose," said Sabrina. She looked about, craning her neck to see the hall outside. It was dark and empty. From the kitchen she could hear the rattling of dishes and knew that Jenna was in there, hurriedly preparing Jojustin's breakfast. And where Jenna was, one was likely to find Patwin.

"Is Patwin up yet, Uncle?" she asked casually.

Jojustin looked at her over his steaming mug. "He's outside getting the horses ready. Why?"

"I'd like to speak with him," said Sabrina. "That's all."

"It won't do you any good, Daughter. Richius has his mind set to go."

"Oh, you're so suspicious. I just want to—"

Jenna's sudden entrance made Sabrina pause. In her hands was a large plate piled high with bread and eggs. As usual she wore a plain dress of dull fabric, and she gaped at her queen's emerald gown. Sabrina pretended not to notice as she reached for the decanter.

"Good morning, my lady," said Jenna icily, putting the plate down before Jojustin. The old man seemed not to notice the animosity between them. At once he tore off a great hunk of the bread, dipped it into his wine, then stuffed it into his mouth with a sigh.

"Good morning, Jenna," replied Sabrina.

"Will you be wanting breakfast, my lady? I could bring you a plate."

Sabrina shook her head. "No, thank you."

Jenna turned to go, but not before giving Sabrina's gown another look. The coldness in her expression made Sabrina cringe. She didn't hate Jenna anymore, not since Jojustin explained things to her, but she did hate being around the serving girl. There were always little things passed between them, jealous, sideways glances at just the wrong moment. And she hated the way Jenna called her *my lady*. Anyone with half an ear could hear the venom in the title. In this informal castle, where even Richius was called by his first name, titles were more than a show of deference. They were an insult.

"Oh, Jenna," said Jojustin, reaching out to stop the girl. "Could you please run upstairs and give a knock on Richius' door? He's not awake yet and he really needs to start getting ready. Don't worry, he knows he has to get up early."

"Upstairs?" asked Jenna, almost blushing at the notion. She glanced at Sabrina.

"It's all right," said Sabrina, trying to smile.

Jenna shrugged, then went out of the kitchen toward the stairs. Sabrina sighed, placing the decanter back on the table without pouring for herself.

"I'm sorry," said Jojustin quickly. "Sometimes I say things without thinking."

"Don't," said Sabrina, waving off the apology. "It's fine."

Jojustin leaned toward her and whispered softly, "You have to give her time, Daughter. She's hurting right now, but she'll get over it. She'll find another lad to moon over soon and then you'll both be fine friends. I know it."

"I'm not so sure," said Sabrina. "Richius won't talk to her about it, and she's not willing to listen to me. I don't know what I can do to make this easier for us."

"Time," repeated Jojustin. "That's all." He propped the pipe back between his lips and leaned back in his chair, staring at her. An impish glint flashed in his eyes.

"What?" asked Sabrina coyly.

"You're looking very nice today," said Jojustin.

Sabrina cleared her throat. "Thank you."

"Is there some occasion today I don't know about?"

"No. It's just such a dreary day I thought it could use a little color. What's wrong with that?"

"Nothing," declared Jojustin. "You look nice, that's all." He smiled, and there was no malice in the expression, just the thoughtful affection of an uncle. "Listen to me, Daughter. You don't need to dress so fine to get Richius to notice you. I'm sure he sees how beautiful you are. But you're wasting your time primping today. He's got to go to Lotts'."

Sabrina rose suddenly from her chair. She could feel her face warming with embarrassment. "Patwin's outside, you say?"

"Oh, now, don't go off angry," said Jojustin. "Sit and have some breakfast with me."

"Is he in the stables?"

"Sabrina, it's raining. He'll be in soon. You can talk to him then."

But Sabrina was already gone. She moved quickly through the hall, ignoring Jojustin's echoing apology, and soon found herself in the foyer of the castle. From within the little covered chamber she could see the courtyard and the stables in the distance, hazy through the rain. There was a flickering light in the stable window, and a shadow moving against the glass. Sabrina glanced down at her fine shoes, then looked to the walls of the foyer for a coat. There was none. She could turn around and get her own coat, but that might mean seeing Jojustin again. Or Jenna.

The stable wasn't so very far, she reasoned.

She took a breath and held it, then dashed out into the rainy morning. At once her feet sank into the muddy earth, filling her shoes with water. Drops of icy rain pelted her hair and face, and as she ran she put up her arms to shield herself. Thankfully, the hem of her dress was high enough not to be muddied, and by the time she reached the stable she realized that she was mostly dry. She paused at the stable gate, releasing her breath with a weary sigh. But when she breathed in again the smell of manure and damp straw struck her like a hammer.

She had yet to visit the stables, and the pungent odor gave her a start. She glanced around. There were several horses in stalls, and some of them turned to regard her with their huge brown eyes. Implements of leather and iron hung on the wooden walls, some so strange in appearance that she could hardly guess at their use. A lamp had been lit away from the straw and the stalls. Its meager light threw her shadow against the wall as if she were a giant. And across the stable, almost invisible behind a chestnut horse he was grooming, was Patwin. He didn't seem to notice her as he worked, a cheerful whistle on his lips. Sabrina smiled. She liked Patwin. Of all Richius' comrades he was the one she felt most comfortable around.

"Patwin?" she called softly, stepping toward him. He looked up from his grooming, startled. She could see his eyes narrowing with puzzlement in the darkness.

"Sabrina?" he called back.

She moved a little closer. He stepped out to greet her.

"What are you doing here?" he asked. "What's wrong?"

"I need to talk to you," she answered. "May I?"

He smiled with encouragement. "Sabrina, a queen doesn't ask her subject if she can talk to them. *Tell* me what you want."

"I need to ask you something. A favor."

"All right," he said, surveying her dress and shoes. "But you shouldn't be out here dressed like that. You'll catch a fever."

He removed his own coat and draped it about her shoulders.

"Now," he began. "What can I do for you, my queen?"

"First, you can stop calling me that. It doesn't suit me and you know it."

"All right. What else?"

She shifted uneasily, running her muddy shoes along the earthen floor. What she wanted to ask seemed suddenly foolish.

"Go on," he prodded gently. "I'll help you if I can. Is it about Richius?"

She looked up at him. "How did you know?"

"What else would trouble a new bride besides her husband? Believe me, Sabrina, we all understand how hard this must be for you. Even Richius. But if I can do a favor for you I will. What is it?"

"Would you go to the House of Lotts without him today? I need some time with Richius alone. I need to talk to him."

Patwin's face fell. "I'm sorry, Sabrina. I can't do that."

"Patwin, please." Sabrina implored. "It would mean a great deal to me. I know Richius has business to attend to, but it's important. If I could just spend a little time with him, get him away from all this war talk for a while."

Patwin shook his head ruefully. "I can't. It's not just these war plans, either. Richius has to meet with Dinadin himself. There are things they need to talk about."

"What things?" asked Sabrina, a bit too sharply. "What's so important about this fellow anyway?"

"Dinadin's a friend," explained Patwin. "One of Richius' dearest. But they haven't spoken in months, not since returning from Lucel-Lor."

"I don't understand," said Sabrina. She was on the verge of tears now. She could hear it in the fragile way her voice cracked. "What happened between them? Is that why Richius is so distant?"

Patwin hung his head. "Sabrina, a lot happened between them. Too much to explain. And I'm not really sure it's your business."

"I think it is," said Sabrina. "Richius is my husband. I want to know what's wrong with him. If this Dinadin is part of his problem . . ."

"Only a small part," said Patwin. "Now, please, don't ask me any more." He turned back to the horse and returned to his grooming. "I've said too much already."

Sabrina snatched the brush from his hand. "You're telling me R
will talk to Dinadin but he won't talk to me, and I'm supposed to agre
that? Well, I won't. I want you to tell me what's wrong with my husband
You know, I know you do. Tell me."

Patwin's jaw clenched with anger. "There are things about what happened to us in Lucel-Lor you have no right to know."

"I'm his wife," said Sabrina miserably. The tears were coming now in
long hot streaks.

"It doesn't matter," said Patwin. He was almost pleading with her.
"Richius is my king and my friend. I won't betray him by telling you
things he won't tell you himself."

Sabrina pulled his coat from her shoulders and dropped it into the dirt,
then turned from him and went silently back into the rainy morning.
Patwin called back to her: another unwanted apology she hardly heard.

The rain was coming down harder now, drenching her dress and hair.
Mud licked at her shoes, filling them with filthy water. Yet she was only
half aware of these things. A stinging sense of loneliness overcame her as
she walked, blinded by raindrops and tears, moving without purpose
toward the hateful castle. What had started this morning as a vague hope
for companionship had become something worse than she ever expected.
She had gotten from Patwin one horrible concession: that Richius was indeed harboring secrets.

In the little foyer she took off her shoes and left them there to dry. Unmindful of the cold floor she continued on to the kitchen. Jenna was there
alone, sitting down at last for her own breakfast. When she saw Sabrina
enter she stood up. The dress she had so admired earlier was now dark
with rain. Sabrina ignored the girl's shocked expression.

"Where's Jojustin?" she asked.

Jenna swallowed hard. "With Richius," she said. "Are you all right?"

Sabrina didn't answer. She pulled out a chair and sat down. Every bit of
her tingled from the rain, and her toes were already beginning to wrinkle.
Jojustin's half-empty mug of wine caught her eye and she snatched it up,
draining the rest of it with a single quick gulp. She lowered the mug to the
table with a thud.

"Do you want your breakfast now, my lady?" asked Jenna cautiously.
There was none of the usual venom in the question.

"No," said Sabrina icily. "Sit."

"What?"

"Sit down," repeated Sabrina. "I want to talk to you."

Jenna obeyed, looking at Sabrina the way a child looks at an irate
mother. "Yes?" she asked in a tiny voice.

"I'm sixteen," said Sabrina. "Do you think that's too young?"

Jenna was silent for a long moment. Her forehead wrinkled with effort.
"My lady?"

ou think I'm too young for Richius," said Sabrina. "Is
do you resent me because I'm from a noble family and

vered with a stunned silence.
," insisted Sabrina. "I want to know what you really

sorry, my lady," stammered Jenna. "I meant no offense."

"Oh, of course you did. I know about your feelings for Richius, Jenna.
Everyone in this castle knows. Just like they all know all about my problems with him. Right?"

Jenna nodded slowly, and for a moment their eyes met, not as queen to
kitchen girl but as one woman to another. A lump sprang into Sabrina's
throat.

"Damn it," she moaned, burying her face in the wet folds of her
sleeves. "Why have I been brought here? I want to go home."

Amazingly, she felt Jenna touch her arm.

"You are home," Jenna comforted. Her voice took on the soft lilt of an
older sister. "It's just time you need now . . . Sabrina."

Sabrina grasped hold of Jenna's hand, clutching it, ignoring the sudden
madness of what she was saying. "Be my friend," she begged. "I'm so
alone here, Jenna. I'm so frightened. My God, I've already lost my husband. I need help."

"Easy," Jenna crooned, cradling Sabrina's head in the crook of her
arm. "You're not alone. We're all here for you, really. Forgive me for being so wretched to you. I was wrong. I didn't know."

"No," agreed Sabrina between sobs. "I know."

"I loved him myself," Jenna whispered. "I was hurt."

"I know. I know."

They stayed like this for a long moment, neither one speaking nor pushing the other away, and Sabrina felt at once ashamed and exhilarated.
There had been almost no true contact between her and Richius since
that night in the garden of the emperor, and now even Jenna's touch was
welcome. She felt suddenly like a child in the arms of her mother, enjoying the delightful release of tears.

"I love him," said Sabrina finally. "I don't know why but I do. But I
don't know how to reach him. He's so cold to me. . . ."

"He's preoccupied," said Jenna. "This war—"

"No, it's more than that." Sabrina pulled away and sat up, willing
Jenna to understand. "He's hiding something from me. I know he is because Patwin admitted as much. And I don't think it's these war plans or
his fears of going back to Lucel-Lor. There's something more, Jenna.
Something only he and Patwin and this Dinadin know about."

"They're men," said Jenna easily. "And good friends. They fought together. Of course they're going to have some secrets. You have to accept that."

"Good friends?" asked Sabrina, wiping her cheek with her sleeve. "Then why hasn't Dinadin spoken to Richius in months? Why is it so important that Richius go to see him today? No. I'm telling you there's something more here. And I'm losing him because of it."

"Don't say that," Jenna chided. "You're exaggerating because he hasn't given you the attention you want. You have to listen to me, Sabrina. I know Richius better than you do. Forget whatever you're thinking about him."

"He hasn't touched me since we've come here," said Sabrina sharply. "Not once. How can I not suspect something?"

Jenna simply shook her head. "Fear has a way of killing a man's hungers. It's all this talk of war, nothing more."

"You're wrong," said Sabrina. "Ask Patwin and you'll see. He'll evade you the way he did me. Ask him."

"I won't," said Jenna harshly. "And neither should you. If there is something Richius is hiding from you, perhaps it's better you know nothing of it. War does strange things to men, Sabrina. He's not the man who left here three years ago and neither is Patwin. You don't want to know everything that happened to them. A woman shouldn't hear such things."

Sabrina sat back, astounded. "Then you won't help me, either? You're just going to ignore what I've told you?"

Jenna got to her feet. Slowly, deliberately, she picked up her plate and the two mugs and began making her way back to the kitchen. But halfway to the door she turned to Sabrina.

"Please, Sabrina," she begged. "Leave it alone."

"Jenna—"

"Leave it," repeated Jenna firmly. She gave Sabrina a wan smile, then retreated back into the kitchen.

Sabrina watched her go. It was as if everyone had gone mad this morning, and she alone was sane enough to see the illness around her. Despite her status in the castle, despite her new and uneasy alliance with Jenna, she felt more isolated than she ever had before. Absently she wrung water from her sleeves, heedless of the puddles it left on the table and floor. A chill danced on her skin.

"I am truly alone," she whispered bitterly, and that unexpected longing for Gorkney returned. She wanted to be home, to be once again in her solitary rooms or to sneak into the wine cellars and gossip with Dason. But Dason wasn't here, and the only rooms she had she shared with Richius. *If only he had taught her to ride,* she thought bleakly. She would ride away from here.

Slowly she rose to her feet and stumbled out of the tiny chamber. A draft passed through the narrow corridor, icing her wet garments and pricking her skin. Upstairs there were dry clothes for her, and the solitude of her bedchamber. Surely Richius was gone by now. She made her way up the stairs as quietly as she could, spying for him at every corner. She knew he would be appalled to see her like this, and then she would have the dreadful job of explaining it all. But she reached their chamber safely, and when she stepped inside she found only rumpled linens on the bed. She peeled off her ruined dress and dropped it to the floor. It fell at the bedside in a soiled heap. It fell beside the journal she had tucked beneath the bed. And like a wicked little demon whispering in her ear, something told her to open it.

She rushed to the bedroom door and peered out into the hallway. She was half naked but she didn't care. No one. The door closed soundlessly behind her. She fell to her knees at the bedside, her hands trembling with fear and self-loathing as she picked up the tattered book. Jenna's warnings flooded her mind in a torrent. Did she really want to do this? The answer came to her with equal force.

Yes!

The book opened like a dry, yellow flower. Pages and pages of runny ink leapt out at her, undecipherable scribblings and unpronounceable names. She read in a whisper, appalled and amazed at the violence and emotions portrayed. It was as if she were looking into Richius' very soul. She skipped ahead, passing up the end of a brutal battle, and fingered her way toward the last pages.

"Dinadin," she thought aloud, scanning the scratchy penmanship for the name. If she could find him in the journal . . .

She stopped. Another name appeared. Not Dinadin. A woman's name. Sabrina's blood thundered in her temples. She fought to still her hands, to make the fingers turn the page. A feverish sense of dread nagged at her, warned her to stop, but she continued. This was something she had hardly imagined in her worst fantasies. She read on, every word stinging her like a thousand fiery needles. She read until the excerpt ended, and when she was done she dropped the open journal onto her lap, dumbfounded.

Outside the rain deepened. She looked toward the window and the black day beyond. Unable to rise, she remained on her knees, her body atremble. For she had learned what Jenna warned her not to, the one dark secret that explained all of Richius' moods and nightmares.

She had wished for a name and gotten it.

TWENTY-TWO

"What was the Dring Valley like?" asked Sabrina innocently. The question shattered the day like a pane of glass. Richius drew back on Lightning's reins, bringing his horse to a halt.

"What?" he asked incredulously.

Sabrina stopped her own horse, a chestnut mare only slightly larger than a pony, and casually tossed her hair over her shoulders. She was already growing easy in the saddle, looking more like Jenna by the moment in her borrowed breeches and riding boots. A beading of perspiration glistened on her cheeks and forehead. She threw him a smile.

"Why did you stop?" she asked. "I was doing well."

Richius stared at her, waiting for her to repeat the remarkable question.

She reined the mare around to face him, pulling only the left rein the way he had taught her. He would have been proud of her had he not been so angry. The day had been going so well.

"What is it?" she asked. "Tell me."

"I thought I'd made it clear to you, Sabrina. I don't enjoy talking about Lucel-Lor. Why did you ask me about it just then?"

Sabrina shrugged. "I don't know. The question just came to me. I've been thinking a lot about it lately."

"About what?"

"The Dring Valley, Lucel-Lor, everything. I'm worried about you. Is that so bad?"

Richius shook his head. Jojustin was right; he had been neglecting her.

"I'm tired," he said. "We should stop here and rest awhile. Hungry?"

"A bit," answered Sabrina. She surveyed the surrounding woods. Along the narrow path were a number of grassy patches for them to settle down and enjoy the lunch Jenna had packed. Cautiously she guided her horse over to the largest clearing and called back to Richius. "How about here?"

"Fine with me," said Richius. He dismounted and tethered Lightning to a nearby tree branch. "Let me help you down."

"I can do it."

"No, let me give you a hand." He had spent almost an hour this morning showing her the finer points of mounting a horse, and was determined not to have his lesson spoiled by a broken ankle. Sabrina sighed but said nothing, waiting for him patiently as he dismounted and came over to her.

"Now remember what I told you. Hold both reins in your left hand and take your foot off the right stirrup."

"I remember."

"Easy," said Richius, taking her waist in his hands. "Now swing your foot over her back. I've got you."

"I'm fine."

Sabrina slipped off the horse's back into Richius' waiting arms. He lowered her gently to the ground.

"Wonderful!" he declared proudly. "See? I knew you could do it."

He gave her cheek a peck, then took the mare's bridle, tying the horse to the same tree he had chosen for Lightning. Rummaging through his saddlebags he quickly found the bulging package of bread and cheese and cold pheasant they had brought to dine on. A bottle of brandy followed the food out of the bag. The liquor was a gift from Arkus, or more accurately from King Panos of Goss. True to his word the emperor had seen that the fine brandy was always available in the halls of Aramoor Castle. A case of it arrived almost weekly. Lastly he went back to the mare and from its saddlebags extracted a tightly rolled woolen blanket. This he handed to Sabrina, who spread it carefully on the ground by the roadside. It was a perfect spring evening, a welcome respite from the prior rains, and Richius was glad for once to be with his wife. She looked cool and beautiful and alive with youthful vigor, and he silently thanked Jojustin for the idea of taking her out. It was long overdue.

"Isn't this nice?" he said cheerfully, lowering himself cross-legged onto the blanket. He held out his hand for Sabrina and helped her down beside him. She gave him a curt little nod and started to unpack the food. He watched her as he dug a knife blade into the cork of the brandy bottle.

She had been uncharacteristically quiet since he had returned from the House of Lotts last night. Hopefully this picnic would loosen her tongue.

She handed him a sturdy-looking glass from the package and he began to pour, first her glass then his own. Laying the bottle on the blanket, he raised his goblet.

"To you," he said. "And to your excellent riding. I'm very impressed."

Sabrina touched her glass to his. "Thank you," she said stiffly. "You're a very patient teacher."

"It's easy to be patient with such a good student. You did remarkably well. I didn't expect it."

"I was eager to learn," said Sabrina. "I'd like to be able to get out of the castle more often."

There was an unmistakable iciness to the words that made Richius lower his drink. "I'm sorry, Sabrina," he said quickly. "I've been ignoring you, I know it. But I've been busy, you have to understand."

"You don't have to explain yourself to me, Richius," she said. She tore off a great hunk of the bread and handed it to him. "I know you have a great deal to do right now."

"Jenna and Jojustin said you're upset with me. Are you?"

"How could I be?"

"You *have* been very quiet today."

"Have I? I hadn't noticed. I guess I was preoccupied with the ride."

"Then you're all right?"

"I'm adjusting," said Sabrina. "It's not easy for me when you're away, but I've been managing to keep myself occupied. I had a nice talk with Jenna yesterday. Did she tell you?"

Richius nodded. He was sure Jenna hadn't told him everything.

"You were right about her," Sabrina continued. "She's wonderful. And she really thinks the world of you. She told me not to fret so much, that it's just going to take me some time to get used to life here. I think she's right." She passed an ungainly portion of the pheasant to him. "Could you cut this for me?"

Richius took the bird and began slicing it into manageable portions, first the legs, then the wings and breast. And as he cut he studied her with furtive glances.

"I had to go yesterday, Sabrina. There were people I needed to see. It really couldn't wait. You do understand, don't you?"

"Yes, I understand," she said sharply. "I told you in Nar; I don't expect you to share everything with me. As long as it went well for you, I'm happy." She paused long enough to take a bite of bread. "Did it go well yesterday?"

Richius sipped at his brandy. Yesterday had been a fiasco. "Yes," he said finally. "Well enough."

"Did you see this Dinadin fellow?"

"No," said Richius. "He wasn't there." He shifted uneasily on the blanket, desperate to change the subject.

"Really? He went out on such a dreary day, too? How terribly extraordinary. Your trip was a waste, then?"

"Not entirely. I was able to speak to his father, tell him what the emperor has planned for us. That's all I really wanted to do anyway."

"Oh, then I must have misunderstood Patwin. He told me you were eager to see your friend. He said you had something to discuss with him."

Richius felt his cheeks redden. What in the world was she asking him? And what in God's name had Patwin told her? He had never told Sabrina about Dinadin. Dinadin was a link to Dyana, and that secret he had vowed never to disclose. Anxiously he swirled his glass of brandy, faking interest in its body.

"Nothing important," he said. "He's just a friend I haven't seen for some time. I wanted to chat with him a bit, catch up on things."

"And he wasn't there to greet you?" pressed Sabrina. "Wasn't he expecting you?"

"I didn't tell them I was coming. Perhaps I should have, but I didn't."

And I didn't expect him to run like a rabbit at the sight of me, thought Richius resentfully. *Pigheaded fool.*

"It seems a shame for you to have missed him. Why don't you send word to him, have him come by the castle soon? I'd like to meet him."

Richius' patience snapped like a brittle branch. "What is this, Sabrina? Why this sudden interest in Dinadin? I told you, he's nobody. Just a friend, that's all."

Sabrina drew back, visibly wounded. "I'm sorry. I didn't mean to upset you. I was just trying to help." She glanced down at her half-eaten cheese. "You're right. I shouldn't meddle in your business."

"Don't do this to me, Sabrina," Richius said. "Forgive my snapping. It sounded like you were prying, that's all. Really, what do you want to know?"

She shrugged. "Nothing particular. Whatever you want to tell me is fine. I just want to hear you talk. We don't spend much time together and I like to know what's happening with you."

"You've got me concerned," said Richius. "All day long you hardly uttered a word and now all these questions. Have I been neglecting you as long as that?"

She looked up at him. The sadness in her eyes spoke the answer. Richius sighed.

"It'll be different now, I promise," he began. "Things are starting to come along and I won't be as needed as I have been. You'll see. From now until I leave for Lucel-Lor I'll spend some time with you every day."

Sabrina nodded. "I'd like that."

"Good. And we'll start right now. Ask me anything you like. I promise, I won't evade you."

"No, that's not it. I don't want to pry."

"But you're curious, aren't you? About the war, I mean?"

Again the innocent nod.

"Go on, then," Richius coaxed. "Anything."

Sabrina squared her shoulders and stared at him with utter seriousness. All at once, Richius regretted his bravado.

"Anything?" she whispered.

"Anything."

"All right," she said. "I want you to tell me about the Dring Valley."

"The valley? But why—"

"You said anything."

"I know, but there's really nothing to tell. It was a horrible place I'm glad to be rid of. That's pretty much the whole of it."

"No, you're not being honest. I want to know the truth about what happened there. I want to hear it from you."

"The truth is ugly, Sabrina. It's nothing for a lady to listen to."

"Then you won't tell me?"

"I will if you insist," said Richius. His voice was already starting to lower, the way it always did when Dring came to mind. "But it's not something I savor. If you're expecting some glorious story, you're going to be disappointed."

"Were there really wolves there?"

Richius nodded.

"Patwin called them war wolves," she went on. "He told me they were trained to kill."

"Patwin's being kind. They were trained to rip out our throats and leave us to bleed to death while they went after the next man. And they were trained to go after our cannoneers, so that we would be defenseless when the Drol warriors attacked. Did Patwin tell you any of that?"

Sabrina swallowed hard and shook her head.

"I didn't think so. Let me tell you something about the Dring Valley, Sabrina. We weren't men when we were there. We were food for Voris' beasts. It was the first time in my life that I realized my body was made of meat."

Sabrina looked away, pale and horrified.

"More?" he asked bitterly. "I have a hundred stories if you're interested."

"No," said Sabrina breathlessly. "I'm sorry."

But now it was Richius who was merciless. He leaned closer to her, whispering, "I could tell you about every man I lost there. I can name them all. Do you want to know how Lonal died? Or Kally? Jimsin had his neck chewed off by a wolf. Laren was decapitated—"

"Stop!" cried Sabrina desperately, putting her hands to her ears. "I don't want to hear any more!"

Richius sat back. A horrid satisfaction washed over him. It was like telling the old veterans of the Talistan war how sick he was of their tales. No one could know what he had gone through in Dring. At last he reached over to Sabrina and gave her leg a playful rub. She remained unmoving, her eyes fixed on the blanket beneath them.

"Do you see now why I never want to talk of it?" he asked. "It isn't you, Sabrina. My stories aren't fit for anyone's ears."

"Was there nothing good that came of it?" she asked. "Was all of it so bad?"

Richius considered the question, uncertain how to answer. "War brings out the best and the worst in men. I saw great courage in the valley, if that's what you mean."

"You had friends there, didn't you? Friends other than Patwin and Dinadin?"

"Of course. There were many who became my friends."

"Triin friends?"

"Sabrina, I don't understand this," said Richius. "What is it you really want to know? You're leading me somewhere, but I don't know how to follow. Tell me what's bothering you."

Sabrina straightened and flashed him a careful smile. "I'm just being silly, I suppose. I just thought if I could share these things with you, I could understand you better. I want us to be closer."

"What a favor Arkus did for me," said Richius with a sigh. "You're more than I deserve. I'll keep my promise to you, Sabrina. Now that the other families know about the war I can have others take care of business for me. We'll have more time together. You'll see."

Sabrina only nodded, her face going blank. The western sky was just beginning to flare with the ruddy haze of twilight.

"We're far from home," she said. "Shouldn't we be heading back soon?"

"Not yet," said Richius, reclining back on an elbow. "I've ridden these paths dozens of times. I could find my way back to the castle in a snowstorm from here. Let's relax awhile, enjoy ourselves. I've—"

A glimmer of white in the distance beyond snatched his attention. Something in the woods. Man-sized. He froze, fixing his gaze on the trees past Sabrina's head. It was yards away, hanging in the thickets like a pale, thin mist.

"Richius?" asked Sabrina. "What's wrong?"

Richius put his finger to his lips.

"Quiet," he cautioned. "There's someone behind you."

Sabrina stopped breathing. Her eyes widened with fear as she turned to follow Richius' stare. For a long moment they remained motionless, like two guilty children hiding in a wardrobe. Richius licked his lips. Whatever or whoever it was, it looked frighteningly like a Triin.

"Where is he?" whispered Sabrina. "I don't see anyone."

Richius cocked his chin forward. "There, by the bend. See the white?"

Sabrina's eyes narrowed. "Where?"

Richius could still see the flimsy figure in the trees, almost floating above the mossy earth. A mane of milky hair blew unnaturally in the breezeless air. The figure swayed and shimmered in the ebbing light, watching them without menace, its gray eyes full of discovery. Richius watched in horror as the thing stretched out an arm toward him.

"My God!" he said, rising unsteadily to his feet. He felt Sabrina's hand reach up for him.

"What is it?" she demanded.

"Don't you see him?" asked Richius. "Look, Sabrina. Look!"

Sabrina looked. She got to her feet beside him and stared directly at the road ahead.

"I see nothing," she cried. "Tell me what it is!"

The figure in the forest stepped out from behind the trees.

"He's smiling at me," said Richius. "My God, he's smiling!"

It ambled closer. Richius could see it more clearly now. He could see the good-natured eyes and the fibrous wisps of hair. He could see the sharp nose and the contemplating crease of the brow as the figure regarded him, not like a stranger but as one would an old comrade. And most remarkably he could see *past* the man. Not merely around him like a thing of flesh and bone, but through him and behind him to the road and trees beyond. A transparent wraith, grinning with the face of a friend.

"Heaven defend us," Richius moaned, clutching Sabrina's hand. "That's Lucyler."

"I don't see a thing," whispered Sabrina.

"But he's there, right there! What's wrong with you?"

Sabrina yanked her hand away. "You're seeing phantoms, Richius! There's nothing there."

"There is," replied Richius. A sudden understanding dawned within him. "It is Lucyler. Only you can't see him."

He took a cautious step forward. The luminous face of the Triin lit with that old, sarcastic grin. He knew it was impossible, yet Richius was overjoyed at the sight. He raised his hands in greeting.

"Lucyler," he cried. "Is it you?"

The apparition nodded. Behind him, Richius could hear Sabrina mumbling, fretting over the sickness she was sure had overcome him. He reached back a hand to silence her and moved slowly toward the translucent figure. Lucyler shook his head, as if to stop him.

"Lucyler?" asked Richius, perplexed. He started again to move forward and this time the figure's extraordinary face dimmed with a frown. It turned away, stepping back into the veil of trees.

"Wait!" yelled Richius, scrambling toward the forest. "Lucyler, come back!" He clenched his fists and drove them into the air, cursing. "Don't leave me, damn you!"

He stared into the forest, hoping to glimpse the fleeing ghost, but saw only an unending labyrinth of leaves and branches. Lucyler was gone, or hidden somewhere unseen within the tangle of trees. And he wanted Richius to follow him. There was something telling in the way he looked, something he had been screaming in dreams for Richius to hear.

"I have to go after him," said Richius. He glanced over to where Sabrina stood, her arms wrapped about her like a blanket. "I have to talk to him."

"You're mad," she said simply. "There was nobody there, Richius. Nobody."

"You couldn't see him because he didn't want you to. He has to talk to me. Alone."

"Who has to talk to you? Who's Lucyler?"

"I can't explain, not now. You didn't see him because he's a Triin. Probably it's some kind of magic, I don't know. But I have to go after him."

"You can't leave, Richius. It's going to be dark soon. What if—"

"I'll be back before sunfall, I promise. Just wait here for me. Don't move from this spot. I'll find you."

"Richius, please . . ." Sabrina implored, but Richius was already on his way into the forest. He heard her voice calling after him, yet he didn't stop or call back to her. He was on a hunt, and his quarry was already far ahead. Around him the forest thickened, the old branches of the ancient oaks reaching out for his cloak and face, and he guarded his eyes with outstretched hands as he moved with finesse through the brush. He spied every tree and hollow log, heard every bird and every croaking bullfrog. His senses were alive, more vital than they had been since leaving Lucel-Lor. He had a mission to confirm a miracle, and the zeal put fire into his steps.

"Lucyler!" he called, his voice booming through the trees. He had already come a thousand paces and had seen nothing of his friend. Again and again he cried out the name, hoping for the apparition to reappear. "I'm here, Lucyler. Talk to me!"

Nothing. He stopped. Panting, he squatted and surveyed his surroundings. Sweat fell from his brow, stinging his eyes, and he rubbed at them to clear his vision. A rabbit scampered by, startling him. His knees buckled and he sank to the ground.

"Damn it, I saw you," he said. "I know I did. Come back to me, please. Come back."

Misery seized him, just as it had when he learned of Lucyler's death. Death at the hands of Voris. A death meant for him.

Is that why you're haunting me, my friend?

Slowly he rose to his feet. Nausea coursed through him. His legs quivered uncontrollably, rubbery from the run and the nagging thought that he had truly lost his mind. There were no ghosts, his father had told him once. Only madmen. He looked up into the graying sky and thought of Sabrina. It would be impossible to explain this to her. In the morning she would be penning a letter to Arkus, begging for an annulment. And Patwin and Jojustin would hear about it, too, and look away when he passed, and who could blame them? They had a lunatic for a king.

Despondently he began the long walk back, his eyes downcast. Grime covered his boots and knees, and leaves and bits of branches clung to his hair. Viscous ribbons of sap ran down from the canopy of pines above him. Only the thought of Sabrina kept him moving forward. She was alone and defenseless with night closing in on her. If she were a man he would have left her there, but she was his wife. She needed him.

Ten paces later Lucyler stepped out from behind a tree. Richius froze.

"You have come," said the spectre in a voice not wholly human. The sound of it rang unnaturally, but it was Lucyler's voice, hard and clear and unmistakably Triin. Richius regarded the figure in wonder. It wavered in the breeze, shimmering the way sunlight does on water. It was whiter than a dove, more silent than death, and thinner than the little white vest that clings to the inside of an eggshell. Impossibly beautiful. Astonishing. Richius cranked up his courage and moved toward it.

"My wife thinks I'm mad, ghost," he whispered. "Tell me that I'm not. Tell me you exist in more than just my mind."

Lucyler, or the thing that looked like him, laughed. "I can hear you," he said gleefully. "Lorris and Pris, I can hear you!"

"What are you?" asked Richius. "Are you Lucyler?"

The figure glanced down at its hands and flexed its bony fingers. "It works!" it declared. "Richius, I am really here!"

"Are you? Are you Lucyler?"

"It is me, Richius," said the figure. "It is Lucyler."

Richius stepped back dubiously. "How can it be? You're dead!"

"Do not be afraid of me," begged Lucyler. "I am not dead. And you are not seeing a spirit. It is I, and I live."

"It does look like you," said Richius, inching closer. He reached out to touch the gauzy fabric and watched his hand pass through it.

"This is not a body," Lucyler explained. "It cannot be felt. But it is me, my friend."

"But how?" stammered Richius. "Lucyler, what *are* you?"

Lucyler held up a cautioning hand. "I cannot describe this to you, Richius. Not now. This form is difficult to hold. So listen carefully to me, I have to be quick."

"Not good enough," said Richius. "Tell me what's happened to you. This form, what is it? Are you somewhere else?"

"I am safe," replied Lucyler. "That is all I can say for now. You must listen—"

"Where are you?" Richius demanded. "You're alive and yet you are a ghost. Explain it to me. *Now.*"

"No questions!" boomed Lucyler. "There is no time. I have something to tell you and you must listen."

Richius laughed. It was all impossible, yet this hotheaded apparition was truly Lucyler.

"I'm listening," he said.

Lucyler seemed to sigh. "This form you see is a projection. I was told I would appear dead to you, but I assure you I am not. I have tried for days to reach you, to touch your mind, but I was unable to, until today."

"The dreams," said Richius knowingly.

Lucyler nodded. "You resisted me. So I took a form you could not ignore."

"But my wife couldn't see you. Why not?"

"I am appearing for you, my friend. I cannot appear to someone I do not know. Do not ask me why, it is a mystery to me, too. Oh, but I waste time. Do you remember the place you told me about in the mountains? The plateau?"

"I remember," said Richius, recalling the flat hilltop in the Saccenne Run, the rugged passage cutting through the Iron Mountains and linking Aramoor to Lucel-Lor. Richius himself had scouted it out. They had planned to retreat to that plateau if Tharn and his minions ever succeeded in ousting them from Lucel-Lor. "What of it?" he asked.

"You must go there," said Lucyler. His image was starting to waver. Frowning with concentration, he continued, "It is a safe place for us to talk. Bring provisions for a long ride. I will meet you there in three days' time."

"What? I can't leave Aramoor. And you don't even know where the plateau is. You'll never find it."

"I will find it," insisted Lucyler. "You must meet me there."

"But why? Why not come to the castle? Why all this secrecy?"

"Please, Richius," Lucyler begged. "There is no time to argue. Will you come to me or not?"

"I won't," said Richius angrily. "Not until you tell me why. If you have a secret, spit it out. Tell me what's so damn important."

Lucyler's expression dimmed. "Richius, trust me," he said. "Please. Meet me in the mountains. . . ."

"Tell me the truth, Lucyler," Richius demanded. "What do you want me for? Why this bloody magic?"

"You want proof, is that it?" asked Lucyler angrily. "Very well. I will tell you one thing only." He leaned in close and spoke a single, remarkable name. "*Dyana.*"

Richius stumbled backward. "My God," he said. "What are you telling me?"

"The woman is alive," said Lucyler. "I know where she is."

"How do you know? How do you even know who she is?"

Again the transparent hands came up. "No more questions. Do as I ask and I will answer everything. But ask me nothing more now. I cannot stay, Richius. I am losing control. . . ."

"No, God damn you, no! Don't you leave me now. Not until you've told me about her."

"Will you come to meet me?"

"Where is she?" Richius thundered.

"She is safe, Richius. I swear it." Lucyler floated a bit closer. "Will you meet me?"

Richius laughed bitterly. "Is there a choice? I will be there as you ask. But I warn you, my friend. Trifle with me in three days and I will kill you. Do you hear me?"

"I hear you," said Lucyler. "You will forgive me this, Richius. I know you will." The image began to fade. "In three days, then."

"Three days," Richius agreed. "And if you're not there I will hunt you down, Lucyler. And no magic under heaven will save you from me."

The phantom gave a sorry smile, wavered a moment, then popped like a bubble, leaving Richius alone in the gathering darkness. Painfully he pulled brambles from his hair, cursing and wondering what had really transpired. It was Lucyler, certainly, but how? And why? What ungodly news did the Triin have for him? A cold anguish gripped him. If the apparition was to be believed, Dyana *was* still alive, maybe waiting for him the way he had dreamed. He shut his eyes against the onslaught of questions. He would have to go to Lucyler, find out where Dyana was and then . . .

What? Lucyler had told him to pack for a journey. Would he guide him to her? Would he even be able to rescue her? Lucel-Lor was Tharn's now. How would he ever make his way to her unseen?

Slowly he began making his way back through the brush. Dusk was coming in ever-quickening steps, throwing twisted shadows against the mossy earth. Above him he heard the whooing of an owl as it prepared for its nightly jaunt across the sky. This was the time when the rodents cowered, when sane men went indoors. The thought quickened Richius' stride. In all her life Sabrina had probably been in the forest only this one day, and was no doubt chafing at the notion of nightfall. She would be irate, and he would have to explain it all to her. Even as he raced past the trees he considered what lies to use.

In less than ten minutes he emerged out of the forest, back to the path and the place he was sure he had left Sabrina. He quickly sighted their little picnic area with its blanket and half-eaten loaf of bread. Lightning was still tied up against the tree. The gelding turned its big eyes toward Richius in relief. But the beast was alone. The small mare Sabrina had ridden was gone—and so was Sabrina.

Richius returned home well after sunfall and entered the keep with nary a nod to the sentry at the gate. He hadn't raced back to the castle as he knew he should have, but instead took a more scenic and circuitous route. Certainly Sabrina was here by now, and if she wasn't, well . . . it would be a temporary reprieve. There was a cauldron of hostility waiting for him, and before he was boiled alive in it he wanted to sort out the thousand questions plaguing him. His hands still shook and his stomach tingled with the fearful ache of nerves. A chronic buzzing had taken over his mind, every thought tainted with dour resentment. Absently he dismounted and led Lightning to the stables. The courtyard was silent. Candles burned in the windows of the castle. They were waiting for him inside, he knew it. Even now Jojustin was pacing like an inquisitor. Richius groaned. He didn't have any answers.

When he reached the stables he was surprised to find the structure's doors flung open. A single lantern tossed its light onto a grim visage staring at him from the dimness. Patwin's face was tight with rage. Behind him, the small silhouette of Sabrina's mare stood silently chomping on alfalfa. It lifted its head for a moment as Richius entered, then turned back indifferently to its food. The horse seemed calm and well rested. Clearly Patwin had been waiting some time.

"She made it back safely," observed Richius, gesturing to the mare. "Good."

"Good?" said Patwin. "Is that all you have to say?"

Richius led Lightning past him without a glance. "Yes."

Patwin seized him by the shoulder and spun him around, his periwinkle eyes flaring. "Don't," he warned. "You'll have to explain yourself to someone tonight. It might as well be me."

"Patwin, stop." Richius scarcely recognized the desperation in his voice. "I can't argue with you, I haven't got the strength. Leave me alone, please."

"In hell," snapped Patwin, snatching the reins from Richius' hands. "I want to know what happened to you today. Sabrina came home in tears and started raving that you'd lost your mind. She said you saw a ghost! The whole castle's wondering what's gone wrong with you. How could you leave her like that? What were you thinking?"

Richius stumbled backward and sat down on a bale of hay, almost collapsing into the prickly mass. Wearily he ran his hands through his hair, uncertain where to begin. His tale was unbelievable, his actions inexcusable. But Patwin was looking down at him pitilessly, waiting for a convincing story, or at least some elaborate lie. Richius wasn't sure he had either.

"I didn't leave her," he began shakily. "Not really. Only for a few minutes. When I came back she had gone. Is she all right?"

"No thanks to you," said Patwin. "What happened?"

Richius started to speak then abruptly fell silent, unable to find sufficient words. "I can't explain it," he stammered. "God, Patwin, you won't believe me if I tell you."

"You'd better try," said Patwin. "Jojustin's been waiting for you since Sabrina got home and he's crosser than I've ever seen him. King or not, you're going to have to come up with some answers to calm him."

"The hell with him," spat Richius. "He's the least of my worries. What did Sabrina say to you?"

"That you've gone mad," said Patwin. "That you started raving about seeing some Triin that wasn't there and that you went running off into the forest to chase him. What about it, Richius? Is that what happened? Because if that's all you've got you're going to have a lot of trouble explaining it."

Richius looked up at Patwin. "Did she tell you anything else? Did she tell you who I saw?"

"She couldn't remember," said Patwin. "She just said it was some Triin you knew in the Dring Valley." Patwin's eyes narrowed. "But I think I can guess."

"It *was* Lucyler," Richius insisted. "And let me tell you truthfully—I haven't lost my mind, Patwin. I saw him like I'm seeing you now. He was there."

Patwin's expression became mournful. "Oh, Richius. Let's go inside. You need to rest."

"God damn it!" flared Richius, springing to his feet. "I don't need rest! I *did* see Lucyler. Sabrina didn't see him because she couldn't, because that's the way he wanted it. I don't know how or why, but that's what happened and if you don't believe me then I really will lose my mind! I need someone to listen!"

"All right," soothed Patwin. "I'm listening. Sit down."

Richius sighed and fell again against the hay. His head was pounding miserably and he put his hand against his forehead. In the morning he would have a headache worse than any hangover. But he smiled when Patwin sat down beside him, grateful to see the old concern back in his comrade's eyes. There was one thing he loved about Patwin; he never stayed angry for long.

"I don't know where to begin," said Richius finally. "We were eating at the roadside, just talking, and then . . ." He shrugged. "I saw him."

"What were you talking about?" asked Patwin.

"Dring," snapped Richius. "As if Sabrina didn't tell you. That's not enough to make me see ghosts, Patwin."

"But the strain of everything . . ."

"Listen to me. I'm not mad. I'm not surprised Sabrina thinks I am, but I'm not. And he didn't just walk up to me and say hello. He appeared to me. I can't really describe it, but it was like a form of him. He called it a projection."

"He spoke to you?"

"Yes. When I left Sabrina I followed him into the forest. He had disappeared but I knew he had something he wanted to tell me, so I went after him."

"It seems you found him."

Richius nodded. "He appeared to me again, and it wasn't easy for him, I could tell. He was like a ghost, all clear, white light. He told me he couldn't hold the form very long. God, he seemed as amazed by it all as I was."

"What did he say to you?"

"Very little." Richius turned to Patwin and grabbed at his sleeve. "Patwin, I need to ask you something. Will you be honest with me and tell me the truth?"

"Of course," answered Patwin. "What is it?"

"What did you tell Sabrina about Dinadin? She was questioning me. She seems to know a lot more than she should."

Patwin blanched. "I'm sorry, Richius. I guess I told her more than I intended to. She came to me yesterday morning and asked me about Dinadin. She wanted you to stay home with her and I told her that you couldn't because you had to talk to him. She asked me why, and I didn't have an explanation for her. She got suspicious when I wouldn't tell her more."

"But she doesn't know about Dyana?"

"God, no! Not from me anyhow. Why?"

Richius sat back, frowning. "She was asking me about the Dring Valley and about Dinadin. When I told her there was nothing to talk about she didn't seem to believe me. I think she suspects, Patwin. I don't know how. I never told her about Dinadin because I didn't want her to find out anything about Dyana. But now she seems to know anyway."

"It wasn't me," said Patwin gravely. "I swear it."

"Don't worry, I believe you. The question is, do you believe me?"

"I want to," answered Patwin grimly. "But Lucyler's dead, Richius, captured by Voris. How could you have seen him? It doesn't make sense."

"He's not dead. I saw him, or at least some sort of image of him. Like I told you, he couldn't hold the form very well, so he didn't have time to explain it to me. But it was him. I'm certain of it."

"But what did he say to you? If he's not dead, then where is he? Is he all right?"

"I think so," said Richius thoughtfully. "He said he was. He wouldn't tell me very much, only that he needs to speak to me. I'm supposed to meet him at our plateau in the mountains in three days."

"What?" erupted Patwin, losing all composure. "Are you serious? He asked you to meet him *there*?"

Richius only nodded.

"And just like that you're going? You really have lost your mind if you're truly considering this, Richius! Why would you agree to go into the mountains?"

"I have to," said Richius simply, still unsure if he should explain why.

"It isn't safe," said Patwin, lowering his voice. "There could be Drol scattered throughout those peaks, for all we know. I hate to say it, but did you ever consider that this could be some sort of trap? Even if it was Lucyler you saw, who knows what's happened to him since the valley? He could have turned Drol!"

"Stop!" said Richius. "Don't ever say that. I trust Lucyler with my life, Patwin. You did, too, once. He's no traitor and you know it. If he says he has to speak to me then there's a damned good reason for it."

"Really?" asked Patwin. "What is it then? If he's so keen on speaking to you, why doesn't he just come to the castle like anyone else? Why all this magic and rubbish?"

"I don't know," admitted Richius. "He wasn't able to tell me why."

"How convenient. But you're going anyway. God, Richius. What can I say to convince you? This is utter madness. Please listen and let me talk you out of it."

"Patwin, you don't know everything yet," said Richius desperately. "I wouldn't go if I didn't have to, but I must." He leaned closer to his comrade, speaking in a whisper. "He knows where Dyana is."

Patwin went ashen. "Oh, my God," he croaked. "He told you that?"

"He did."

"Where is she?"

"He wouldn't tell me. He wants me to go to the plateau. Then he'll tell me where to find her. At least that's what he promised me."

"And that doesn't sound like a trap to you? Richius, think for a minute. He could be using Dyana as bait to lure you into the mountains. I bet he doesn't even know where she is, but he knows you'll come after her."

Richius shook his head. "I don't think so. Lucyler shouldn't even know who Dyana is. I never saw him again after I left for Ackle-Nye. By the time I met Dyana, he was probably already Voris' prisoner. Besides, I trust him. Lucyler would never try to hurt me."

Patwin sighed heavily and stared down at the stable floor, kicking at the bits of hay with the toe of his boots. "Well then, I can't let you do this damn fool thing alone. If we leave in the morning we can make it to the plateau in three days. But we'll have to come up with something good to tell Jojustin. And Sabrina."

Richius reached out and grasped his friend's shoulder. At any other time he would have welcomed the company, but he knew he was going off on a fool's errand, and that there was no way he could accept Patwin's offer. Patwin was right: there probably were Drol in the Iron Mountains, just waiting for a pink-skinned human to flay. This time he would have to face the dangers of Dring alone.

"I might be gone a long time," he said. "And I don't know where Lucyler plans to take me. If Dyana is back in the Dring Valley I'm going to have to go in after her. I might not be coming back."

"If you're trying to talk me out of going with you, forget it. You need me."

"Yes," admitted Richius. "I probably do. But I can't let you risk your life for Dyana. I'm the only one who has to do this. I want you to stay behind and look after Sabrina for me. She's going to need you, too, maybe even more than I will. Especially if I don't make it back."

"Richius . . ." Patwin began, but Richius put up his hands to silence him.

"Don't argue with me about this, Patwin. I've already given it a lot of thought. This is the way it has to be. I'm leaving in the morning for the plateau—alone."

"No," said Patwin vigorously. "You're the king. It's my duty to protect you."

Richius tightened his grasp on Patwin's shoulder, trying to calm him. "It's also your duty to follow my orders. I don't give them very often, my friend. Will you follow this one for me?"

"How can I?" asked Patwin sadly. "You don't know what you'll find in the mountains or where Lucyler plans to take you. You could be riding off into your doom."

"All the more reason for you to stay behind. No offense, but if the Drol are after me, having you with me won't help much. They'll just kill you, too."

"Then I'll die defending my king," declared Patwin. "Like a Guardsman of Aramoor should."

Richius couldn't help but smile. He would miss his fair-haired friend, maybe more than anyone else in the castle. But it helped his resolve to think of Patwin swinging from a Drol gallows, and he rose decidedly to his feet.

"I wish I could say yes to you, Patwin. But I'd be a poor friend to ask you to risk your life for a woman you don't even know. Stay behind. Look after Sabrina for me. I'll be back as soon as I can."

Patwin looked up at him gloomily. "What will you tell Sabrina?"

"What I told you, mostly. Hell, she already thinks I've gone insane. I doubt she'll be too surprised that I'm going off to see Lucyler."

"Are you going to tell her about Dyana?"

Richius bit his lip. "Maybe. If she knows about Dyana already, I'll explain it to her. If not . . ." He let his voice trail off, leaving a little verbal shrug.

"Jojustin's madder than a wolf in a bear trap," warned Patwin. "He's going to want to hear your story, too. Do you want me to come with you?"

"No," said Richius, starting toward the doors. "There's no sense in you being more involved than you are already. I'll handle Jojustin. You get some sleep. I'll see you in the morning."

Richius left the stables, making his way through the dreary courtyard. As he sighted the glowing candles in the castle windows his stomach twisted. Sabrina was behind one of those frosted panes, waiting for him to return. She was probably worried about him, too, and Richius cursed himself for taking so long. Why did he always make her worry? He crossed the courtyard quickly, eager to be out of the chilly night, and stepped as silently as he could into the foyer, hoping to reach Sabrina before Jojustin sighted him. But the old man was as keen as a hawk. He stepped out of the shadows just as Richius took off his cape.

"Where have you been?" asked Jojustin icily. His thin face was twisted with fury.

"Out," Richius said evasively, dropping his cape onto a wall peg. "Where's Sabrina?"

"Don't ignore me," warned Jojustin. "I'm very angry, and I want to know where you were tonight!"

"Jojustin, it's late. I'm tired and I want to talk to Sabrina. Where is she?"

"She's in the kitchen with Jenna. She's been in a state since coming home. Explain yourself, Richius."

"Not now," said Richius, walking past his steward into the hall. "I'll talk to you in the morning." He heard Jojustin's offended grunt but kept going, ignoring the old man's ire. There was only one person he *had* to explain himself to, one person who truly deserved an explanation for what he'd done. Jojustin might stay angry with him for days, but that wasn't important. His responsibility was to his wife, and he knew he had shirked it. As he walked through the dim halls he hummed to himself, piecing together the fragments of his story and trying to arrange them in just the right way to spare Sabrina's feelings. A single question nagged at him—did Sabrina know about Dyana? It certainly seemed so to him, yet he couldn't reason how. Only Patwin and Dinadin knew about her, and neither of them had divulged the secret to Sabrina. Then it occurred to him in an ugly flash that there was only one real way she could have known. Everything that ever happened in Dring was in his journal. If she had dared even a peek at it . . .

He moved with urgency into the dining room. Beyond, he could hear Sabrina's breaking voice, and Jenna's calm, sisterly replies. He froze, trying but failing to decipher the muffled sentences. Bracing himself, he stepped into the kitchen. Sabrina was seated on a work stool, a handkerchief dangling limply in her hand. Jenna stood beside her. A fire smoldered in the cooking hearth, filling the kitchen with the greasy smell of burned fat. They both stared up at him. Frustrated tears streaked Sabrina's reddened cheeks. She wiped at them quickly with the handkerchief.

"Jenna," said Richius easily. "Would you leave us alone, please?"

Jenna looked down at Sabrina, who nodded her assent. The older woman bent to kiss the younger's forehead. "I'll be upstairs if you need me," said Jenna, then stalked past Richius without a glance.

Suddenly alone, Sabrina rose from the stool and went to the washbasin filled with dirty pots and gray, sudsy water. Her back was turned to him as she lifted a pot from the basin and began scrubbing. She seemed not to notice the water dripping onto her feet.

"I'm glad you're home," she said thinly. "I was getting concerned."

"I'm sorry," answered Richius. It was all he could manage. "I didn't mean to worry you. I was . . . thinking."

The back of her blond head bobbed as she nodded.

"Sabrina," continued Richius. "Please look at me."

Sabrina lowered her hands into the basin full of dishes. Her head slumped. "I cannot." Her sagging shoulders began to shake. He went to her and put his hands on her arms, turning her to face him.

"Please," he implored. "Let me explain. . . ."

"Explain what?" she flared, jerking from his embrace. "I really don't want to hear any more of your lies, Richius. Spare me tonight, I beg you."

Richius held firm. "I want you to listen to me. You should know the truth."

"Should I?" said Sabrina with a laugh. "Good. Then go ahead and tell me. Tell me about how you saw a Triin that wasn't there and how you left me to find my own way home in the dark. Tell me more lies about your friend Dinadin and why you never mentioned him." She stepped closer and glowered at him, her face the semblance of a demon. "And why don't you tell me about your precious Triin whore!"

Richius gritted his teeth. He took the time to calm himself before speaking again. "Patwin didn't tell you about her, did he?"

"No," admitted Sabrina fearlessly. "I read about her in your damn diary. Now I know why you never told me about Dinadin. You were afraid I'd find out about *her*." She laughed bitterly. "Don't leave your things lying around, Richius, not if you're going to be as moody as you've been."

"You had no right to read my journal," said Richius. He was less angry than disappointed, but he could almost understand her actions. "There was no reason for you to know any of it."

"I disagree. I wanted to know what was wrong with my husband, and you certainly weren't telling me. No one was."

"And you think you can know what I've been through by reading my journal? Sabrina, I tried to spare you all that misery." He looked away, shaking his head. "You can never understand."

"I think I can," said Sabrina. "You love this woman. That's why you're so unhappy. You're stuck with me when you want someone else. What's so difficult about that? I love you but I can't have you. It's the same thing."

"But you do have me," argued Richius. "I'm your husband."

Sabrina gave another short laugh. "I don't want the ring, Richius. I want the man. But I can't have him, can I?"

Richius didn't answer. He walked over to the tiny stool she had vacated and sat down, gazing blindly at the kitchen floor. He was almost relieved she knew about Dyana. It would make the rest of his news easier.

"I have to tell you something," he said weakly. "About Lucyler."

"Ah, Lucyler," said Sabrina. "That's the name. Did you find him?"

"Yes, I did. I spoke to him."

"Oh? And what did he tell you? Is he coming for dinner soon?"

Richius looked at Sabrina mournfully, unable to raise even the smallest smile. The malice on her face melted under his gaze, until she appeared as placid and beautiful as the day he had met her, stranded on the muddy road to Nar. That was months ago now, and he realized abruptly that he hardly even knew her.

"What is it?" Sabrina asked.

"I'm going away for a while, I'm not sure how long." He watched as her eyes grew wide. "I've made plans to meet Lucyler in the Iron Mountains three days from now. He has something important to tell me, something he couldn't tell me today."

Sabrina seemed stricken.

"I hope I won't be gone very long," Richius went on, "but it's hard to say. There's some danger, too. There may be Drol waiting for me when I get to the mountains. I trust Lucyler, but I don't know—"

"Oh, God," groaned Sabrina, rushing to him and falling to her knees before the stool. She took his hand, putting it to her cheek. "Don't tell me any more," she begged. "Don't go. Don't leave me."

Unable to pull back his hand, Richius let her have it, sitting in agony as she smothered it with imploring kisses. He had expected her to rage, perhaps even to strike him, but this affection was shattering. He put his head back and groaned, hating himself. At last Sabrina looked up at him. In that moment she was like a dutiful puppy, eager to please the master who had beaten her. He pulled on her hand and lifted her to her feet again, drawing her tightly to him. Her body yielded to his grasp.

"I'm leaving in the morning," he told her gently. "This is something I must do. I want you to try very hard to understand why. Will you listen to me?"

She nodded, obviously unable to speak, and dropped her head in anticipation of his story. Richius screwed up his courage. His hands trembled as they drew her onto his lap.

"You see," he began warily. "This fellow Lucyler was like a brother to me in Dring. He wasn't just another soldier. He was like Patwin and Dinadin. A friend. We trusted each other with our lives, and I still would trust any one of them to the end. Now I really can't say how he appeared to me. The Triin have magic to do some strange things, and maybe he was using some to contact me. But it was him, I know it was, and he needs me to go to him."

"But why?" asked Sabrina. "What does he want of you? Why can't he just come to the castle to speak with you?"

"He wouldn't tell me. Perhaps he can't. There's certainly more to this than he's telling me." Richius swallowed hard. "And there's more to it than I'm telling you."

"Tell me," Sabrina insisted.

"I wouldn't go if I didn't have to," Richius continued. "Even Lucyler's friendship isn't enough to lure me back into Lucel-Lor. But he told me something, something he knew I couldn't ignore."

"Something about her?"

Richius nodded. "He knows where she is, Sabrina. She's alive. He wouldn't tell me where she is, not unless I came to meet him in the mountains. After that he promised he would tell me everything."

Sabrina fell into a contemplative silence.

"Don't you see, Sabrina?" Richius asked hopefully. "I can keep my promise to her now. I can save her."

"I know about your promise. You don't need to explain it to me. It's all in your journal, after all."

Richius shut his eyes. "I want to explain it to you. I want you to know why I'm going back for her."

"I know why," said Sabrina. "Because you love her."

Richius felt like a child. He nodded dumbly. "Yes," he choked. "I do. I don't want to love her, but I do. I have since I first saw her."

The pain on Sabrina's face was wrenching. "Yes," she whispered. "That's what it's like."

"I'm under a spell, Sabrina," Richius went on. "She's done something to me. Maybe it won't make sense to you, but I was so alone in the valley. Every day I thought I would die. And every day it seemed more of my friends did die. I was losing everything fast. But then suddenly she appeared. She let me take her and I've never been the same." He looked down at the floor. "Now I want no one else. You're so beautiful, Sabrina. So beautiful. But . . ."

His voice trailed off with a sputter. Sabrina sighed then climbed gingerly off his lap. On her face was the most disquieting smile.

"This woman must be something very special. I've been trying to get you to talk about Lucel-Lor for months, but I never realized what a horror it had been for you. If you would go back there for her . . ." She shrugged resignedly. "I can't compete."

Richius stared at her, stupefied. "What are you saying?"

"Go to her," she said simply. "I can't stop you. I won't even try. You obviously love her very much." A forlorn smile played across her lips. "Maybe even more than I love you."

Richius hung his head. "God, I'm sorry," he said. There was no peace within him at her words, just a hollow, filthy feeling. Remarkably, he had gotten her consent for his wild, adulterous scheme. But he wanted more. He wanted absolution. "Forgive me," he begged. "This is something I *must* do. If I can save her, maybe I can be whole again."

"There's nothing to forgive," replied Sabrina coolly. There were no tears now. "I think you're right, Richius. I think you'll die if you don't do this. Your guilt is destroying you. It's so plain when I look at you. And I love you. Maybe someday you'll love me, too, but if that day never comes I'll continue loving you anyway, and you'll never have to say you didn't try to save her." She went to him and, lifting his chin with a finger, placed a light kiss on his lips. "I want you to return safely. Promise me you'll try."

"I promise," said Richius, almost choking on the words. "Will you be here waiting for me?"

Sabrina turned slowly and headed for the door. "I'm your wife," she said. "I'll be here."

"Don't go," Richius cried, jumping to his feet. "I don't want to say good-bye like this. There's so much more I want to tell you."

"No," Sabrina cautioned. "There's nothing more to say. I've already read it in your journal. I understand better than you think. And don't say good-bye to me. Leave in the morning without looking back. I'll wait for your return."

"Will you come to bed with me tonight?"

Sabrina shook her head. "I've made arrangements to share Jenna's chambers. I don't want to see you until you return."

"All right," agreed Richius reluctantly. "And I will return, Sabrina. Whether I save her or not. I'll be the husband you're worthy of, I swear it."

Sabrina said nothing, only smiled at him again. Moments ago it was she who had been like a child, wailing for him to love her. Now he was performing for her approval. He tried vainly to return her smile, flashing her only a tired grimace instead, and watched her leave the gloomy kitchen, dropping her tear-stained handkerchief behind her.

That night, a monstrous guilt infected Richius' sleep. It was after midnight when he finally retired, falling into a restless slumber poisoned with nightmares of Lucel-Lor. Lucyler haunted his dreams, and Dyana made appearances, too, slipping repeatedly into Tharn's infinite fog. Occasionally he would awaken, shaken out of sleep by some nameless vision, and reach over to where Sabrina should have been, only to feel the cold emptiness of vacant sheets. When at last the dawn beckoned him, he was ready for it.

He went to his closets and chose his outfit carefully, selecting a particularly militant ensemble of brown leather armor. Light enough to ride in, it was nevertheless tough enough to withstand any rigors the Drol might have planned for him. Upon the left breast was emblazoned a winged blue dragon, the crest of the Aramoor Guardsmen, its tail coiling menacingly down the left sleeve. The last time Richius saw Edgard, the old war duke had been wearing the same uniform. Richius examined his reflection in the mirror, telling himself that Edgard would have understood. He sat on the bed and laced up his knee-length boots, the ones that were unworn and polished ebony black. Lastly came Jessicane. He strapped the sword across his back, turning to admire the dazzling scabbard. A gift from Biagio, he remembered painfully. A bribe to go back and murder more Triin. Thankfully Liss was delaying that order. Now he was getting a chance to go back for Dyana without Arkus' aid.

For a very long time he stared at himself in the mirror, absently contemplating the man looking back at him. He was the king of Aramoor and the Jackal of Dring, but most of all he was a man in love. Perhaps it was a valueless love, perhaps Dyana had even forgotten about him. Yet somehow he knew she was waiting for him, that fate or a god or the force of Triin magic had delivered the news of her existence to him for a reason. He *would* find her, he promised, and if possible he would save her. If he could only get her back to Aramoor, she would be safe forever. Whatever else might happen he simply couldn't say. He was married, and would never break his vows or his latest promise to Sabrina. Dyana would be a constant temptation but at least she would be alive, protected within the borders of Aramoor.

Satisfied with himself, he tossed his traveling pack onto the bed and began rummaging through its contents. He never had unpacked from his long journey back from Nar, and found that most of the things he would need were still within the musty sack. There were bandages and salves, a small collection of tools, utensils for cooking and eating, even some baubles he had picked up in the Black City. These he placed carefully on the mantel. They were mostly wedding gifts from congratulatory lords: a silver dagger from King Panos, a ruby-eyed serpent carved out of jade from Dragon's Beak, an amulet from Dahaar. All interesting, expensive junk, the kind of things Arkus would have relished. Only Blackwood Gayle had had the sense not to present him with such a useless gift. Gayle had in fact given him nothing at all, a blessing for which he was endlessly grateful. The thought of penning a thank-you to the baron was sickening. Finally he retrieved his journal from the bedside and tucked it safely inside the pack, nestling it between a pack of playing cards and a sheathed knife. Then he cinched up the pack, slung it over his shoulder, and started out of the chamber. He was stopped by an insistent rapping on the door.

"Oh, Lord," he cursed, tossing the pack back onto the bed. There was one person he had neglected to speak to last night, the only one bold enough to knock on his door at dawn. Jojustin's irritated voice pierced the morning.

"Richius, open up," the old man demanded. "I want to talk to you before you go."

Go? thought Richius. Sabrina or Patwin must have told him. Good. It would make his good-bye all the easier. He twisted the knob and pulled the door open. Jojustin didn't wait to be invited, but strode into the chamber as if it were his own, closing the door behind him. When he saw the pack on the bed he rolled his eyes.

"Are you ready to talk now?" he asked, folding his arms across his chest. Richius assumed the same hostile posture.

"You obviously know what I've got planned," said Richius. "Who told you?"

"Sabrina. When she left you last night I went into Jenna's room to see how she was. She told me everything. Imagine my surprise. I thought we had a king here, but now I see we have only a lovesick boy."

"You're pushing it," said Richius, hoping to avoid a confrontation. "Do you want to hear my explanation or not?"

"I don't give a damn about your explanation, Richius. I'm here to help you find what's left of your mind. It's really very simple, lad. You can't go."

Richius brushed past Jojustin and retrieved his pack from the bed. "I'm going," he declared. "I have to."

"No." Jojustin positioned himself in front of the door. "I won't let you. You don't understand what you're doing."

"You're the one who doesn't understand, Jojustin. Are you so old you've forgotten what it's like to love a woman?"

Jojustin's face hardened. "I've been with more women than you've had dreams about, boy. But I never let one of them persuade me from my responsibilities. I've never turned my back on my kingdom for one. You're riding off into a Triin trap for this whore. And even if you don't get killed it won't really matter. What do you think is going to happen when Biagio gets wind of what you've done? Arkus will have our heads!"

"Arkus won't know anything about it," said Richius. "He's not about to launch his attack on Lucel-Lor, not while Liss is still standing. With luck I'll be back long before word comes from Nar."

"What if you're not? What are we supposed to tell Biagio if he comes looking for you? He's watching us, Richius. After what your father did—"

"I don't care what you tell him. Tell him I've gone hunting or something."

"Hunting?" raged Jojustin. "You think that will suffice? You've forgotten yourself, Richius. You are the king of Aramoor! You can't just leave on your featherheaded mission. This land is your responsibility. If Arkus finds out that you've gone off to talk to a Triin . . ." He waved his arms in disbelief. "It will be the end of us!"

"It won't," insisted Richius, praying he was right. "Do your part and keep this quiet, and I'll be back before anyone comes looking for me."

"And if you're killed?" pressed Jojustin. "What then? You're the last Vantran. There's no one to follow you." He shook his head. "I can't believe you would do this, Richius, not for the sake of a woman. And a Triin at that. You've lost your senses, lad, truly you have."

"Please," said Richius. "Try to understand. This is something I have to do."

"Nonsense. That's the same foolish thing your father said about abandoning you in Lucel-Lor. Look at you standing there with your fancy uniform and sword. You're the picture of him, brave and stupid and determined to ruin everything. God, I wonder sometimes what is wrong with your blood. What is it that makes Vantran kings so reckless? Arkus can crush us with a wave of his hand, but neither of you ever seem to realize that. Lord knows how we've made it this far without him coming down on us, and now you want to push him further. Why?"

"Because we aren't free!" hissed Richius. "Do you want us to be puppets like the Gayles? I'm proud of what my father did, Jojustin. I understand it now. He was trying to save lives." He paused, then added softly, "That's all I'm trying to do. Save a woman's life."

"You're betraying your country," said Jojustin. "By going to Lucel-Lor without Arkus' permission you're courting the wrath of Nar. We could lose everything."

"If I die, then we've lost nothing more than we've lost already. Aramoor will be under the boot of Arkus whether I am king or not."

"But maybe it won't be Aramoor anymore," countered Jojustin. "Maybe it will just be part of Talistan again. Have you thought of that?"

Richius wouldn't answer. The possibility of the Gayles ruling Aramoor again hadn't even occurred to him, and now that it did it made him all the more anxious to leave. He walked toward the door, nudging Jojustin aside gently with his hand. But before he left he turned one last time to his steward. He knew he owed him an explanation of some sort, something more than just lovesickness.

"Jojustin, I haven't been whole since coming home," he said softly. "Call it guilt, maybe, I don't know. But it's killing me. I'm not just going to get this girl. I'm going to find the rest of myself."

Jojustin's face turned purple. "Your life is here, Richius!" he snapped. "You don't need to run off on some fool's errand. You just need to stop being a martyr! Have some courage, man. Pull yourself together."

"I can't," said Richius meekly. "I'm sorry, Jojustin. I've tried, but I'm broken and I just can't seem to fix myself." He flashed the old man a feeble smile and headed toward the hall. "I'll be back as soon as possible. Look after Sabrina while I'm gone."

"Oh, I will," said Jojustin ruthlessly. "I'll look after all of Aramoor. I'll do your job for you, Richius."

Ignoring the gibe, Richius made his way through the quiet hall, leaving Jojustin behind. Jenna's chamber was on the other side of the castle, so he didn't much fear running into Sabrina, and he had no intention of going to her. He would do as she had asked: leave without saying good-bye. It was an odd request he meant to honor, but there was one other he hoped to see before going. He made his way down the dim stairway and through the main floor to the small dining room. There he found Patwin, half-asleep in a chair, dutifully guarding a burlap sack. The young man's bleary eyes sprang open as Richius entered the chamber.

"Richius," he said. "Is it time?"

"It's dawn," Richius answered, inspecting the sack. It was filled with dried meats and bread, the kind of foods that would last on the road. Richius gave his friend a grateful smile. "Have you been awake long?"

Patwin nodded. "Most of the night. It was hard to sleep, and I didn't want to miss you." He got slowly to his feet and dragged the sack across the table. "I packed you some food. You didn't think about that, did you?"

"Not until this morning," admitted Richius. "Thanks."

There was an awkward silence as the two regarded each other. Without words to describe his sorrow, Richius merely extended a hand. Patwin took it warmly.

"Lightning's waiting for you outside," he said. "He's shod and rested. You'll find your crossbow on him too. You haven't changed your mind, have you?"

"No," said Richius. "It's something I can't explain, Patwin. I don't know why, but I can't let it lie. I have to go back for her. I have to at least try."

"I can still go with you," Patwin offered. "Just say the word."

Richius shook his head. "I need you here to watch over Sabrina. Keep Jojustin out of trouble, too, will you?"

Patwin laughed. "That's asking a lot," he quipped. Then he added seriously, "I'll do my best."

"I know you will," said Richius. "Thank you for everything."

Patwin pulled Richius closer and embraced him. "Be careful," he whispered into his ear. "Come back safe."

Again Richius found he was speechless. He let Patwin kiss him lightly on the cheek before turning away and forcing out a farewell. Then he strode out of the room and made his way into the courtyard, where Lightning was patiently waiting.

TWENTY-THREE

orning broke like a gentle wave over the mountains. When Richius had readied himself and breakfasted on supplies, he mounted his horse and plunged forward into the Saccenne Run. The pass was just as he remembered it. The glacial, sheer faces of the mountains rose up on both sides of him, darkening the ground with their gargantuan shadows. Broken wheel struts and discarded food sacks littered the way, reminders of the days when Talistanians and Aramoorians alike poured through this narrow vein to do the unknown bidding of the emperor. There were older artifacts, too, remnants of the first Narens to go to Lucel-Lor—the merchants and the priests and all the others who tried to woo the Triin into Arkus' clutches. This was the stubborn trash that age can't waste away quickly, but must rust slowly out of existence over decades. To Richius the rubbish was like the text of a history book: intriguing, uncertain, and incomplete. It silently told the sad, violent history of Lucel-Lor to anyone keen enough to hear it.

He continued on through the passage for hours, occasionally swigging from his waterskin or stopping to give Lightning a well-earned rest. At the end of this day's journey there would be a stream where he and the horse could replenish themselves, and he knew that they had to keep moving to make the oasis by nightfall. As he rode, Richius kept a vigilant eye on the terrain, careful to notice every falling rock and intrusive sound. He held his crossbow on his lap, the bolt ready in the barrel slot. Lightning too seemed disturbed by their surroundings. The big horse moved with purpose through the Run, as eager as his master to be out of the strange, claustrophobic place. But they had many hours still ahead of them. The plateau they were seeking was far closer to Lucel-Lor than it was to Aramoor, and they would need every minute of the three days to make their rendezvous on schedule. So they continued, wary and suspicious, and by the end of the first day through the Run they found the stream. They collapsed at its banks, exhausted.

Almost four years ago Richius had done the self-same thing, a green recruit under the tutelage of Colonel Okyle. He had been terrified then, certain that he would never return home from the brutal quest Arkus had thrust upon them. Now Okyle was dead, and Richius himself had become a leader. Since then over a thousand men had died in Lucel-Lor, and if Arkus had his way, more of their brothers would be joining them. Richius cursed as he refilled his waterskins. He had called Gayle a puppet, but they were all playthings of the emperor, even he. They were dancing on a string while Arkus whistled bloody tunes.

By afternoon of his first day in the Run, Richius was more at ease. He knew it was the dangerous, lulling silence of the mountains that had produced the calm, but he welcomed the change of mood regardless. It was good not to be looking over his shoulder at every sound. The stray calls of hunting hawks no longer made him jump, nor did the sudden flight of birds assure him that Drol warriors were just around the bend. Only thoughts of Lucyler blackened his mood. His Triin friend had not appeared to him again, and the absence set him to wondering. He was risking everything on this crusade: his wife, his kingdom, perhaps his very life. There would be no friendly chatter when he met Lucyler, he decided suddenly. He wanted only to know where Dyana was.

Lightning had taken to the mountain passage like a donkey, his sure hooves guiding him steadily along the ill-constructed road. They were making good time, and found along the way more small streams from which to drink and refresh themselves. Despite the thawing ice caps whitening the clouded mountaintops, the air in the Run was mild and comfortable. Only at night did Richius need his heavy cape to keep the chill from under his leather garments. He passed the idle hours of night with a whetstone, sharpening Jessicane's pitted edge as he whistled, occasionally forgetting in his sleepy bliss the constant possibility of danger. The evening stretched peacefully into morning, and the day went by remarkably quickly.

Near dusk of the third day, Richius approached the plateau. He was very close to Lucel-Lor now, knew in fact that he could see it if he dared to climb one of the treacherous peaks surrounding him. He reined Lightning to a stop and surveyed his surroundings. The plateau was little more than an outcrop really, an odd malformation of geology that made it recognizable. It was the perfect place for routed men to retreat to, the kind of place a soldier could find even with one eye. Edgard had decided that the plateau would be the place the men of Aramoor should go were the Drol ever to get the better of them. Ironically, he had never made it to the safety of the plateau, and Richius had simply passed it on his way home from the war.

"Not much further," he told Lightning, recognizing the unique formation. The horse whinnied happily at the sound of his voice.

"You ready?" Richius asked the gelding, then squeezed his calves together to coax Lightning forward. Again he took up his crossbow, cradling the weapon in the crook of his arm. If there were an ambush waiting for him, it would be here, only miles from Ackle-Nye. His ears became acute, tuned like instruments to every sound, painstakingly aware of the crush of gravel beneath Lightning's hooves. He watched a flock of birds circling above the hills and waited for something to startle them. But when they alighted on the rough mountain face they remained there, unperturbed by their surroundings or his noisy approach.

Minutes later he sighted the plateau: a giant shelf of weathered limestone overhanging the narrow path three hundred feet below. He slowed Lightning to a cautious crawl. From here he could see no one atop the plateau, and the trail ahead was empty. Below him the ground was featureless, the only tracks those of Lightning. Lucyler would have come from the east, he knew, but even that seemed increasingly unlikely. Today was the third day. He realized suddenly that he had expected Lucyler to rush out and greet him, the way he would if he were expecting a friend. Hurriedly he urged his mount onward, lifting the crossbow out of his elbow and letting it dangle in his hand. Above him the plateau stretched out darkly. There was no path up, he already knew that. If Lucyler was waiting for him there, he would have to climb, and that meant leaving Lightning below. Furious, he dismounted and craned his neck skyward, fighting the foolish urge to call Lucyler's name. Not even a pebble fell from the loft.

"Damn it," he hissed. "Where the hell are you, Lucyler?"

He rubbed Lightning's neck as he considered what to do. If he could make it onto the plateau, he would have an unobstructed view of the Run and much of Lucel-Lor. There was a way up there, he remembered. He and Okyle had made the climb four years ago. But the plateau had never been meant for horses. It was merely to be a gathering place, a beacon for defeated soldiers to find their way home. Lightning was loyal enough to wait for him, but he had no idea who or what might be waiting for Lightning. The horse might very well wind up like Thunder had before him, helpless in the jaws of hungry wolves. But at last Richius decided it was a risk worth taking. If there were Drol waiting, there would be little one man and horse could do to stop them.

Richius led Lightning to the side of the path, then placed the ends of the reins beneath a stone. The stone would be heavy enough to keep the mild-mannered horse around if all was calm, yet leave him able to escape should anything attack him.

"Don't run off without me," said Richius good-naturedly, tethering his crossbow to Lightning's back. "I'll be back soon."

Three hundred feet of crumbling rock greeted Richius as he approached the mountainside. He could see the plateau towering above him, shadowed in the ebbing light of day. Behind him the sun was beginning its daily descent, lending an unhealthy pallor to the rock as he stepped up and dug his hands into it, pulling himself skyward. About thirty feet up he would find a ledge, and from there he could hike the rest of the way to the plateau. Grunting and sweating, he ascended the sheer wall, each inch gained with burning effort. When at last he reached the ledge he flung his body upward onto the hard rock and looked down at Lightning, giving the horse a triumphant wave.

With the hardest part of the climb completed, Richius set off for the plateau, traversing the winding ledge that would lead him part of the way there. When the ledge ended he climbed again, scuffing his polished boots and driving his fingertips into the tiny crevices and imperfections in the rock. At the end of an hour he finally reached the plateau. Exhausted, he stepped onto the long protrusion of stone and gazed out over the open expanse of sky and earth. To the east he could see the Saccenne Run, winding its formidable way through the mountains. To the west was Lucel-Lor, where the twisted city of Ackle-Nye was an indifferent pinprick on the horizon. Over the city the roof of the world glowed pink while threads of gold gushed from the sinking sun. He breathed a deep, regretful sigh. Somewhere in all that vastness was Dyana.

And Lucyler, he recalled with sudden anger.

Richius turned about, searching for the Triin, but he was utterly alone. Down the pipe of the Run he could see no one, nor did any riders show themselves out of Lucel-Lor. He stepped to the end of the plateau, looking down at the impressive drop, but saw only Lightning, patiently awaiting his return. Richius stifled a curse. The third day was drawing rapidly to a close. He had kept his word, and felt like a buffoon for doing so. Angrily he massaged the aching muscles in his arms and thighs. A bitter, chalky taste caked his tongue and he spat off the lofty perch.

"Damn you, Lucyler."

There was nothing left to do but wait. He'd come too far to retreat, and from here he could easily see both Lightning and any riders that might be approaching. Besides, night was arriving, and it would be impossible to climb down in the dark. Tonight he would spend the evening here, without a fire or Lightning's quiet companionship. And in the morning he would start the long trip home, where he would listen to Jojustin's triumphant laughter and plot some impossible vengeance against Lucyler.

For an hour and more he watched the horizon, hoping for the glimmer of a rider. The sun went down and disappeared with a final, holocaustic flare. Alone in the darkness, Richius made his way to a patch of bushes he had found near the edge of the plateau. It was a hearty collection of evergreen shrubs. Blindly he slid his body beneath it, guarding his face as best he could from the stinging rakes of branches. He would be safe here, hidden from any predators that might come looking for him—animal and Drol alike. When he had settled himself in he carefully drew his giant sword from its scabbard and set it beside him, then made a pillow of his forearm and closed his eyes. Sleep took him quickly.

He awoke from time to time, his back aching from the hardness of the ground and the chill that moved through the mountains this high up. Each time he awoke he shifted his body to make the best of his rough bed and dozed back into slumber . . .

. . . until a sound awoke him.

His eyes popped open. Through the canopy of branches he saw the far-off twinkling of stars and the pale light of a slivered moon. And there was movement, a faint scuffing of boots against the ground. He held his breath and gripped Jessicane. Slowly he rolled onto his side, trying to see down the length of the plateau, but he could see almost nothing past the mesh of sticks.

Triin, he told himself nervously. No one else could manage the climb in the dark. But was it Lucyler? A silhouette stepped into a moonbeam. White skin glistened. The unique shape of a jiiktar gleamed on its back. A man. About the size of Lucyler, Richius reckoned. And coming toward him. His grip tightened around Jessicane's hilt as he lay soundlessly in the cover of the bushes. He saw the head swing toward him, the faint dots of eyes spotting him. He made ready to spring.

"Richius?"

Richius closed his eyes, his breath coming out in an explosive gasp. Lucyler's voice was as clear and recognizable as his own.

"Richius, come out. It is me, Lucyler."

"I'm coming," answered Richius, pulling himself out of the bushes. He held his sword ready. Lucyler came closer, a magnificent smile on his face, his hair falling loosely around his shoulders, one blade of his jiiktar popping out from behind his back. A loose-fitting jacket of saffron yellow was tied across his waist with a golden braid, its wide, hanging sleeves fluttering in the breeze. No longer did he wear the uniform of the deposed Daegog. These were traditional Triin clothes, the kind favored by the Drol. Lucyler opened his arms in greeting.

"You made it," he exclaimed gleefully. "How are you? Are you well?"

"I'm fine," answered Richius. "Where is she, Lucyler?"

Lucyler dropped his hands, but the smile didn't wane. "I know you are angry with me, Richius. I will explain things to you, I promise."

"How did you find me?" asked Richius. Lucyler pointed a thumb over his back.

"I saw your horse down below. I knew you would come up here to try and find me. You were right about finding the plateau. It was not difficult."

Richius bit back an insult. His friend was very late.

"It is good to see you," Lucyler continued. He moved closer, until he and Richius were face to face. "I was not sure you would come."

"I'm here. And you have a lot of explaining to do. So start talking."

Lucyler nodded. "There is much to explain, but we should have a fire first."

"I don't have any kindling," said Richius impatiently. He put away his weapon. Lucyler took a round, red stone from his robe. A fire rock.

"I brought this up with me," he said, and proceeded to the bushes where Richius had slept. Soon a blaze was crackling and tossing out its needed warmth. Richius stretched his palms out over the flames as Lucyler settled down beside him.

"I'm ready," said Richius. "Talk."

Lucyler turned to him, his gray eyes serious. "First, she is safe. There is nothing for you to worry about."

"Does Tharn have her?"

"She is with him in his citadel in Falindar," said Lucyler gently. "He took her there when the war was lost." He paused, choosing his words. "They are wedded now, Richius."

Richius closed his eyes. "Oh, God. What the hell happened, Lucyler? Are you one of his men now?"

"Listen to me carefully, Richius. Nothing is as you remember it. Nothing."

"You're wearing Drol clothes," Richius pressed. "Have you gone Drol?"

Lucyler gave an exasperated sigh. "Will you listen to me? I will explain it all to you, but you have to hear. I know you have a lot of questions. Let me do my best to answer them, all right?"

Richius said nothing.

"I am sorry to have brought you here. You may not think so, but I am. Yet when you hear what I have to tell you, you will understand. You thought I was dead, did you not?"

"Yes," replied Richius. "Gilliam told me you were taken away by Voris while I was off in Ackle-Nye. We all thought they had executed you."

"That is what I thought would happen, too. Voris did take me prisoner. He took me back to Falindar, to await Tharn's return. He knew the war would be ending, and that Tharn was using his powers to crush the last of the Naren troops in Lucel-Lor. It was only a matter of days before it was over."

"I know," said Richius. "I saw what happened in Ackle-Nye. That's when he took Dyana away."

"It seems impossible, I know. I did not believe it myself until I met him." Lucyler's face darkened. "I spent a week down in the catacombs beneath Falindar, waiting for Tharn to return so they would kill me. They treated me well enough, I suppose, but I was alone. Then finally Tharn came to see me. He wanted you, Richius. Tharn told me he had gathered all his enemies in Falindar for something very special. I did not know what he meant, but he took me to the throne room. All of the warlords of Lucel-Lor were there. The loyalists like Kronin had been captured and were in chains. Voris and the Drol warlords were all there, too. I swear, I thought it was the end of me."

"What happened?"

"Tharn brought the Daegog in. He had captured him when Kronin's castle at Mount Godon fell, and had him tied up like a pig. He paraded him before us all, accused him of being a traitor to the people of Lucel-Lor. And then . . ." Lucyler's voice trailed off, and his face glazed over.

"What?" pressed Richius. "What happened?"

"Tharn killed him," replied Lucyler. "I do not know what he did, but he waved his hand over the Daegog, and then he died."

Richius' jaw dropped open. "Just like that?"

"Just like that. He was alive, and then he wasn't. I remember being frightened, and all the warlords started to mumble to themselves, because they all thought we were about to die the same way."

"But you didn't. Why?"

"When the Daegog fell dead at Tharn's feet, Tharn stepped onto the throne. He told us that his only enemy was dead, and that he no longer had a quarrel with us. He said he wanted peace, and that he was touched by heaven to unite us all." Lucyler's face glowed with enlightenment. "I tell you, Richius, he is not what you think he is. He is truly blessed by the gods. He has unified us. For the first time in our history all the warlords are following one man."

Richius sat back, astounded. "You *are* a Drol, aren't you?"

"Not a Drol," countered Lucyler patiently. "But I do follow Tharn now. That is why I am here. There is something we must speak about."

"Oh, indeed there is," said Richius. "Like what happens now. I came here to get Dyana back, Lucyler, that's all."

"Let me explain—"

"There is nothing to explain. You've already told me you're a traitor. All right, I accept that. Now how do I get Dyana away from Tharn?"

"I am no traitor," hissed Lucyler, his jaw tightening. "The Daegog was wrong to let your emperor in Lucel-Lor and you know it. He was weak and he was cruel. He only wanted Nar's weapons so he could destroy the warlords and rule all of Lucel-Lor like a Daegog of the past. I was wrong to ever obey him, and I am not ashamed of my loyalty to Tharn now."

"Well, you should be," said Richius mercilessly. "Tharn's a beast, and you know it. I always assumed the Daegog had been killed, but I didn't know for sure until now. And you stood by and watched him be murdered."

"You are wrong, Richius. I tried to help him. I begged Tharn to stop. But you have to understand what Tharn went through. The Daegog tortured him, broke his knees for the sport of it. Whipped him—"

"Yes, yes," Richius interrupted. "I know the story. That doesn't excuse anything. Maybe the Daegog deserved what he got, but that doesn't make Tharn innocent."

"Richius, please, listen. Tharn has ended all the fighting. He has brought peace to our nation. He let us all live as a gesture of his goodness. There is no more war anywhere in Lucel-Lor. For the first time in decades."

"So he spared your life," said Richius with a dismissive wave. "But those powers of his destroyed almost all our people. Don't you have a problem living with that? I do."

"So do I. But it was war and people die in war. I killed Triin. My own people. That's what *I* have to live with. So do not accuse me of crimes, because you do not understand."

Richius fell silent, contemplating the pain on his old friend's face. He suddenly wanted to end this bitter divide. "Tell me more," he said. "You told me Dyana is safe. Is she well? How does he treat her?"

"He is kind to her," answered Lucyler with a small smile. "He treats her like a princess. She wants for nothing, believe me."

"How do you know about her? I haven't seen you since meeting her in Ackle-Nye. Did she send you to me?"

"Tharn sent me to you," answered Lucyler. "But she knew I would be seeing you. She wanted me to give you something." He put his hand inside his jacket, rummaging around for a moment before pulling out a small gleaming object.

"My ring!" exclaimed Richius. He took it eagerly and slipped it onto his finger. It seemed like years since that day he had given it to Dyana, a key to ensure her safe entry into Aramoor. Miraculously, it had found its way back to him.

"She remembers you well, Richius. And she wanted me to tell you something. She said you would understand."

"What?" asked Richius eagerly.

"Thank you."

Richius looked away.

"Do you understand it?" asked Lucyler.

"Yes. She's thanking me for trying to save her. She knew Tharn was looking for her. That's why she was in Ackle-Nye. She wanted out of Lucel-Lor, and I told her I would send her home to Aramoor with Edgard. But your new master is a powerful man, Lucyler. He killed Edgard before she could go to him, and then used his damnable storms to abduct her. She never wanted to marry him and he knew it. But it doesn't seem like he cares, does it?"

"Tharn cares," said Lucyler calmly. "He is not the butcher you think. He is a man of peace, anointed by the gods to save us from ourselves. They have given him his powers. I never believed in his abilities before, but I see it now. He is not some evil sorcerer. He is a prophet."

Richius smiled darkly at Lucyler. "I think that's all rubbish, you know."

"You don't have to believe me. It's not why I came here."

"How did you do it, Lucyler? What was that image of you I saw?"

"Tharn called it a fetch," said the Triin. "A way of projecting oneself across great distances. It was difficult. That is why I could not talk long. But I knew where you were. I *felt* you. And your wife. She was in your mind. I saw her face. You were arguing with her, yes?"

Richius bristled at the question. "Was that Drol magic? Did Tharn teach you how to do it?"

"Not magic. Only Tharn has the touch of heaven. But I needed a way to contact you, and he showed me how. He told me anyone could do it, if they believed. I still do not understand how it works, but I was able to appear to you."

Richius dared the obvious question. "Why Lucyler? What does he want from me?"

"Your influence," answered Lucyler. He leaned back, resting his elbows in the dirt. "About a month ago a man arrived at the citadel in Falindar. The citadel is on the ocean, and the man came there alone in a little craft. This man was an agent from the king of Liss, and he wanted to speak to Tharn."

"Liss?" asked Richius. As far as he knew, no native of that island nation had set forth from its shores in a decade. "Nar has a blockade around Liss. I don't see how he could have come from there."

"He escaped the dreadnoughts of Nar, leaving Liss in the dark of night and slipping his little craft past them. His trip was difficult. When he finally arrived in Falindar he was near death, starved from the long journey. But he was from Liss, and he had with him a sealed letter from his king, which he presented to Tharn." Lucyler paused, staring hard at Richius. "What do you think it said?"

"Tell me."

"The letter was a request for help. Liss was asking for Lucel-Lor's aid in their war against your Empire. I suppose word reached them of how we had defeated Nar and ousted them from our land. The king of Liss wanted us to help him do the same."

"Amazing," said Richius. "But useless. Why would Tharn agree to help Liss? There's nothing to be gained by it."

"Oh, you are wrong, Richius. Because that is not everything the letter said. The king of Liss also had some interesting news for Tharn. The letter stated that Nar was planning another invasion of Lucel-Lor, that it would happen as soon as Liss fell. Sailors from Nar's navy were telling every Lissen they captured about how they were going back to Lucel-Lor once Liss was destroyed." Lucyler leaned closer. "They said Aramoor was already committed to the invasion. Is it, Richius? Is Nar planning another invasion of Lucel-Lor?"

Richius drew an unsteady breath, unsure how to answer. He looked at Lucyler, at the worry in his expression, and quickly made a decision.

"It's true. I heard about it months ago, when I was in Nar. Arkus wants to go back, and this time he's serious. He intends for me to lead the invasion out of Aramoor."

Lucyler sat back, stunned at the admission. "And you agreed?"

"I did. For one thing I don't share your cheerful opinion of Tharn. To me he is a butcher, and I would still be pleased to skin him alive. Remember, Lucyler, my friends and father are dead because of him. I even thought he'd killed you. And it also was a chance to go back and find Dyana. That's the real reason I agreed."

Lucyler paled. "What do you mean, your father?" he asked. "Has your father died?"

"Don't you know?" said Richius hotly. "He was killed, murdered by a Drol assassin before I got back home."

"Oh, no," said Lucyler. "Impossible."

"What's impossible? He's dead, Lucyler!"

"I do not doubt that your father is dead, maybe even murdered. But there's no way it was a Drol who killed him. I absolutely do not believe it."

"*I* believe it," said Richius. "I've been king of Aramoor ever since. Didn't you know that?"

"Richius, we hear almost nothing from the Empire in Lucel-Lor. This agent from Liss was the first outsider to reach Triin soil since the last of the Empire's soldiers left. But I tell you again—your father was not killed by a Drol."

"Believe that if you want," said Richius. "I don't really care. But I still don't understand what Tharn wants from me. Influence, you say? To do what?"

"To end the war. Tharn hopes you will go back to Nar and convince the emperor not to invade. And you are king now. Even better. Maybe he will listen to you."

The idea was so preposterous Richius laughed. "Are you serious? Why under heaven would I want to do anything for Tharn?"

"Because it is the right thing to do. Lucel-Lor is at peace now. We want no more war. And I do not think you do, either."

Richius stopped laughing at once. "You're right about that. But influence? Ridiculous. My father didn't have any, you know that. I probably have even less."

"But you must try," urged Lucyler. "Tell the emperor he cannot win. Tell him about what Tharn can do to his soldiers. . . ."

"I've told him all that already, Lucyler. He won't listen to me. Besides, I wouldn't do it if I could. Maybe Tharn's cast some spell over you, maybe you think he's some great man now, but there was a time when you hated him as much as I do. I wouldn't do a thing to help him or his regime."

"You would let more of your countrymen die, then? You would fight another war for your emperor?"

"Against Tharn? Yes, I would. I welcomed the challenge to destroy him, just as I welcomed the chance to get Dyana back. He knows about us, doesn't he? That's why he sent you here to talk to me. He knows I would listen if it meant saving Dyana."

"He knows," admitted Lucyler. "But he also thought you would listen to me. Why will you not believe me, Richius?"

"If he wanted my help he should have sent Dyana with you," said Richius. "That would have done a lot to convince me."

Lucyler looked down thoughtfully at the ground. "It is a long trip, and he thought I could convince you myself. Perhaps it is better this way, though." He turned back to Richius. "Will you not let yourself be convinced, my friend? If you saw Lucel-Lor now, I am sure you would believe me. If I could show you that it is not worth another war, would you speak to your emperor then?"

"Will Tharn release Dyana if I go back to Falindar with you, Lucyler? The truth now. Will she be free to return with me?"

"I cannot say," said Lucyler sullenly. "She is his wife. I don't know how fond he is of her or what his true intentions are. But I can say this— you will be convinced when you meet him that Tharn is a good man. You will see the peace he has brought to Lucel-Lor, and you will believe."

"I want Dyana, that's all. If he gives me her, I will speak to Arkus for him. But let me be honest with you now, Lucyler. Tharn is wrong to think me so influential. There's no way I can stop Arkus from launching his invasion. Even if he thinks me uncommitted, he will come, with or without me."

"But Tharn's power—"

"Tharn's power is what Arkus is after," said Richius. "He's heard all about it, and he's convinced now that all of Lucel-Lor has magic like that. That's what the war was all about. It's what he always wanted from

Lucel-Lor. He's dying, and he thinks Triin magic can save him. And he doesn't care how many other people have to die to get it. So you'd best prepare for war, Lucyler, because it's coming just as soon as Liss falls."

Lucyler grimaced. "Then we have a great problem. Tharn will not use his powers against the Empire. If your troops come, we will have to fight them without his help."

"Really?" asked Richius. "Are his powers gone?"

"No. But he will never use them again. He has vowed it."

"But why?"

Lucyler gave him a furtive look. "It is best not to speak of it now. You will understand when you meet him." The Triin rose and stretched his long, lithe body. "In the morning we will leave for Falindar. I have already told Tharn you could not help us, but he thinks he can convince you. You will see Dyana when we arrive."

"I don't want to just see her," warned Richius. "I'm taking her back with me. If he wants me to talk peace with Arkus, he'll have to release her. He understands that, doesn't he?"

Lucyler turned away, staring out into the blackness. "Tharn is very wise," he said softly. "No doubt he expects your demand."

TWENTY-FOUR

ount Renato Biagio stared serenely out the small window at the
perfect spring day lighting the courtyard of Aramoor Castle. It had
always been a passion of his to come up north when it was seasonable; these lands were such a pretty part of the Empire. There were
species of trees here that grew nowhere else in Nar, and lovely flowers
and animals, too. In the springtime, Aramoor was sublime. He would
have to come here more often, he decided, and stop spending so much
time in Talistan. But the Gayles were gracious to him, and allowed him to
keep a close eye on Aramoor, closer than he ever could across the continent in the capital. Aramoor was very important to Arkus. Biagio hoped
Jojustin's summons didn't mean a problem.

Popping another grape into his mouth, the count leaned back in his
chair and watched the nervous serving girl fiddle with a plate of neatly
arranged canapés. She was attractive. He liked the way she arranged her
auburn hair, wearing it long in a braided tail. Women in Crote did the
same, and whenever he saw a northerner's hair like that it always made
his lips twitch.

Because he was Crotan, he appreciated art and the form of a perfect
human body. Jenna was not perfect, not like the sculptures in his villa
back home, but she was neat and attractive and had the quiet qualities
the count appreciated in his lovers, whether man or woman. She trembled a little under his gaze.

"Jenna?" he asked casually, propping his booted feet on the table.

"Could you get me some more wine, please? I don't seem to be able to reach the bottle."

He watched with amusement as the girl hurriedly took the bottle from the table and poured him another glass, quaking under the glare of the pair of bodyguards behind him. The glass had nearly overflowed before he had to put up his hand.

"Oops! Take it easy now," he warned. "This is an expensive cape. You wouldn't want to weave me a new one, would you?"

"I'm sorry, my lord," stammered the girl. He loved the way her eyes shifted to the doorway, waiting for someone, anyone, to save her. Unfortunately, she had been the one unlucky enough to greet him in the courtyard, and at his request had stayed with him while Jojustin readied himself. It was an inconvenience he found particularly appealing. Waiting wasn't something he was good at, but it was bearable when he had an attractive woman attending him. And this was an unusual visit for him. He wasn't accustomed to being summoned to anyone's home, and the novelty of the invitation intrigued him. Jojustin's letter had reached him in Talistan only yesterday, but it sounded urgent enough for him to come at once. *Matters of grave importance,* the note had said. The count pushed a grape seed through his teeth and spat it into his palm. They had better be.

"Will I be seeing Richius?" he asked the girl. He hadn't seen the young Vantran since Nar, nor had he received any word from him. The boyish king was supposed to be waiting here, readying Aramoor for the coming invasion. He had thought Richius remarkably patient—until today. "I didn't see him on my way through the castle. Has he been told I am here?"

"I don't know, my lord," replied Jenna weakly.

What a terrible liar you are, thought Biagio. Still, he would get his answer from the old man. No doubt Jojustin's dire note had something to do with the king's conspicuous absence. Biagio sucked the juice from another grape. Behind him his entourage of Shadow Angels stood like black statues, dutifully watching the window and the doorway for any misguided assassin. They watched Jenna, too, with the hungry eyes of lonely men. Biagio made a mental note that it had been a long time since his bodyguards had been with women. He would have to remedy that soon. Perhaps a Talistanian brothel would be a necessary stop before making the trip home.

At last the door opened again and Jojustin stepped inside. Jenna loosed an audible sigh. Biagio noticed the old man's sickly pallor and the nervous way his temples throbbed. He was typically well dressed. His gold-button vest clung to his thin waist and his impeccably polished shoes glimmered. But still there was that look about him, that deliciously frightened aura that convicts have before the trapdoor swings open.

Biagio pushed his wineglass away and rose from his chair as Jenna scampered from the chamber. Jojustin closed the door behind her.

"Count Biagio," he began unsteadily. "Thank you for coming so quickly."

Biagio inclined his head. "Your letter sounded urgent, Sir Jojustin. I thought it best that matters be attended to." He watched Jojustin's eyes flick to the Shadow Angels.

"Please, sit," said Jojustin. "Your men, would they care for anything?"

"Not necessary," answered Biagio as he sat back down. "Your girl Jenna has already reminded me of their needs."

Jojustin seemed puzzled by the statement but said nothing, taking his own seat across from the count and pouring himself a liberal glass of the wine. He took three unbroken gulps before continuing.

"How was your trip from Talistan, Count? No problems, I trust."

Biagio smiled. "No problems. Sir Jojustin, I'm wondering where young King Richius is. I expected to see him here."

Jojustin's expression tightened. "I'm afraid Richius is . . . unavailable today, Count. I'm sorry."

"Oh, my. He's not ill, is he?"

Jojustin took a long time to answer, and when he did he looked away from Biagio, staring blankly into his glass. "To be honest with you, I'm not certain. It may be an illness that has taken control of him. I'm sorry, Count, I have something quite terrible to tell you."

"Go on," urged Biagio. The old steward shifted uncomfortably under his regard and the silent stare of the Shadow Angels.

"Richius is . . ." Jojustin groped for a word. "Gone."

"Gone? What does 'gone' mean, sir? Where is he?"

Jojustin swallowed hard. "Lucel-Lor."

"Eyes of God!" Biagio exclaimed. "What's he doing *there*?"

"It's a long story, Count," said Jojustin wearily.

"I have time, sir. Tell me!"

"Please," begged the steward. "Be calm. I will explain it to you the best I can." He sat back in his chair, pulling at his beard as if sorting through a great drawer full of thoughts. "Four days ago a friend of Richius' appeared to him, a Triin he had fought with in the war. This fellow told Richius he needed to speak to him, that he had important news to tell him. He wouldn't say what." Jojustin looked at Biagio, gauging his reaction so far.

"Continue, please," drawled Biagio. "I'm fascinated."

"Well, this Triin did have some news. Richius fell in love with a woman while he was in Lucel-Lor, a Triin named Dyana. But he lost her. She was taken away by the storm that destroyed Ackle-Nye, the one you think Tharn created. This Triin that appeared to Richius told him that he

knows where she is. From what I've pieced together from Richius' friend
Patwin and the Lady Sabrina, Tharn supposedly has this woman Dyana. I
think Richius went to rescue her."

"You mean he went to see *Tharn*?"

"He went to see his Triin friend," answered Jojustin. Then he added,
"But he might be going to talk to Tharn, yes. If this Triin tells Richius
that Tharn has the woman . . ." The old man's voice trailed off with a
shrug.

"When was this?" asked Biagio.

"He left three days ago, right after the Triin appeared to him."

"Make sense, man. You keep saying 'appeared.' What does that
mean?"

"I mean appeared," replied Jojustin coolly. "Like some sort of ghost.
At least that's what Richius claimed. Triin magic, by my guess."

Magic. The word hit Biagio like a hammer. That was what this was all
about; the invasion, Arkus, everything. And now to hear that a Triin
magically appeared to Richius Vantran . . . Stupefied, Biagio picked up his
glass again and took a small sip of wine, hardly noticing its flavor. He
would have to inform Arkus at once, but he was many weeks away from
Nar. Certainly Vantran would reach the Drol sorcerer long before then.
And there was no telling what they might say to each other. If Vantran
told the sorcerer of the invasion . . .

No, it was unthinkable. A roiling anger swelled up within him. Like
fools they had trusted this pup, had let him remain on the throne of
his treacherous father, and all in the name of internal peace. Now their
selfless gesture was threatening to ruin every chance they had of taking
Lucel-Lor. Slowly, Biagio slid his hand down along his thigh, to the place
where he kept his dagger sheathed. The strap snapped open with a prick
of his finger.

"You were right to tell me this, Sir Jojustin," said Biagio, forcing out
another smile. "I only wish it hadn't taken you so long."

"It was a difficult decision, Count," replied Jojustin. "I love that boy. I
tried to stop him, but he wouldn't hear me. I knew you'd find out about it
eventually." He paused, leaning forward for effect. "I do this for the good
of Aramoor, nothing more."

Biagio nodded. "Perfectly reasonable."

"Now understand me, Count, please. What Richius did wasn't treason-
ous, just stupid. But Aramoor has to be brought into modern times, and
that means accepting the rule of Nar."

"And you are loyal to Nar, aren't you, sir?" asked Biagio rhetorically.
He watched the old man's face relax.

"I am. I must be. For some reason, Darius Vantran never could be, and
now neither can his son. Darius could never realize the damage he was
causing his land. I don't want the same thing to happen again." Jojustin

lowered his eyes. "There are no more Vantrans. After Richius, a new leader will have to be chosen."

"So much like his father," said Biagio with a regretful sigh. "We are lucky to have you here, aren't we? After all, if it weren't for you, we'd still have Darius Vantran to deal with."

Jojustin raised his face and their eyes met with unexpected comprehension. Biagio smiled grimly.

"Yes, you understand me, don't you?"

Jojustin's eyes flicked to the waiting Shadow Angels.

"Don't worry about them," said Biagio. "They won't do anything unless I order it, and why should I do that? You rid Nar of a traitor, something we were loath to do. Why do you look so troubled, sir? Surely you know the Roshann is everywhere. And we never thought it was a Triin who did the killing. Didn't you think you've been a suspect all along?"

The old man didn't reply.

"Well, now you've proven yourself," continued Biagio. "Feel better, it's finally off your conscience."

Jojustin swiveled his ear toward the door and, confident no one was outside, said in a desperate whisper, "Do you think it was easy? I'm not a murderer. Not the way you might think."

"And no one's accusing you," replied Biagio. "Rather, you are a hero."

Jojustin scoffed. "I did what I had to, nothing more. Darius was ruining Aramoor. He was bringing the wrath of Nar down on us, and he didn't even care. I tried to make him listen, but he was full of righteous nonsense like his son. Someone had to stop him."

"No excuses, please, sir," Biagio interrupted. "As I said, you did us a favor. And you got away with it, isn't that extraordinary? I doubt anyone in the castle ever suspected you, not even Richius. The king must really love you not to have seen it."

Jojustin's face collapsed. "What happens now?"

"To you? Nothing," said Biagio sunnily.

"Not me," growled the old man. "What about Aramoor?"

"Oh, well, that is a tough one. Even if young Richius returns we can't leave him as king. No, we'll need someone else. I've given this some thought, you know. None of us in Nar were completely convinced of Richius' loyalty, after all. We need someone trustworthy, someone that understands Nar."

Biagio rose and went to the arm of Jojustin's chair, going down to one knee beside it. He put his lips to the steward's ear. "I have just the person in mind," he whispered seductively. "And Arkus has already given me the authority to do it should the need ever arise. It looks like that time has come, doesn't it?"

Jojustin shook his head. "I didn't do this to become king," he insisted. "I did it for the good of Aramoor."

"King?" hissed Biagio. He drew his dagger silently from his side. "I think you have me wrong, sir."

With one invisible movement Biagio grabbed Jojustin's silver hair and pulled back his head, drawing the blade quickly across his throat. The skin opened in a red, gushing line. Jojustin's eyes widened in astonished horror. His hands went to his throat and he rose from his chair, stumbling and trying to plug the wound with his fingers. He gurgled something, reaching for Biagio with a bloodied hand. Biagio batted it away.

"You've killed a king of Nar," said Biagio quietly. "That is always death."

Jojustin seemed not to hear. He fell to his knees, gasping through his severed windpipe. His eyes flared. Biagio watched him with wonder, so defiant even in dying. They bred them strong in Aramoor.

Then Jojustin collapsed, and the floor quickly pooled with blood. Biagio wiped his blade on the steward's vest while his bodyguards watched implacably. He did not hear the approaching footfalls until it was too late.

"Jojustin?" queried a young voice. The door opened and an apologetic face peered inside. "I'm sorry to bother you, but . . ."

Biagio stood up with his bloodied dagger in hand and smiled at the fair-haired intruder. "Uh-oh. Now you've caught me."

The young man's face went ashen. He stared at Biagio in frozen horror. Biagio shrugged like a little girl.

"I'm sorry," offered the count. "I've made a mess of your steward. Have you any towels?"

Bewildered, the young man remained unmoving in the doorway, his eyes drinking in the scene without comprehension. Biagio stepped toward him, gingerly avoiding the corpse. "You're Patwin, aren't you? Richius' friend? Be a dear and tell Lady Sabrina I'd like to talk to her, would you?"

"Oh, my God!" Patwin exclaimed. His eyes darted from Biagio to Jojustin, then back again. He began to sputter a question, then ran from the chamber yelling, "Sabrina!"

Biagio cursed and stalked after him, watching the young man disappear up a flight of stairs. He gestured for his Shadow Angels to pursue. The dark duo drew their swords and charged after Patwin. Biagio followed close behind.

"Now Patwin, don't make this more difficult than it must be," he sang out as he climbed the stairway. "I really hate the way things are going so far!"

When they reached the top of the stairs they heard a door slam down the hall. The Shadow Angels went to it and stood outside, waiting for their master's orders. Downstairs Biagio heard the servants clamoring, heard Jenna's scream as she discovered the murdered Jojustin. Exasperated, he went to the door and gave it a vigorous knock. Inside he heard a woman's astonished cry and Patwin's insistent urgings for silence.

"Lady Sabrina?" called Biagio. "Hello. Listen, would you come out here for a moment? I really need to talk to you."

There was something about the moment that struck the count as deliciously funny, and he giggled as he gave the order to kick in the door. A Shadow Angel drove a booted foot into the lock, splintering the wood. The Lady Sabrina gave an anguished shout as the assassins stormed her bedchamber. Patwin stood unarmed before her, staring down the bladed Angels with bare fists. Behind him, Sabrina of Gorkney looked horror-stricken. Biagio waited a moment before entering the room, and when he did he stretched out his arms in mock surrender.

"All right now, everyone calm down. Patwin, be a good man and let me talk to the lady, hmmm?"

"In hell!" snapped Patwin defiantly.

"What do you want?" cried Sabrina. "What did you do to Jojustin?"

Biagio furrowed his brow. "Ah, well, that does make me look bad, doesn't it? Forgive my rudeness, but I killed him. And I really would rather not do the same to both of you. My lady, I have need of you. It's about your husband, you see."

"Get out!" Sabrina flared. "Leave us alone!"

"Alas, I cannot," said Biagio with sadness. "Patwin, step aside, please."

"I won't."

Biagio rolled his eyes. "Good lord," he sighed.

With a snap of his dainty fingers the Shadow Angels moved, flicking their swords in a flash and pressing Patwin against the wall. While one seized the lady, the second Angel wrapped a gauntlet around Patwin's throat and pinned him to the wall, positioning the tip of his sword in the young man's mouth. Patwin gave a frightened moan as the blade slid past his lips and bit into his tongue. He held up his arms in surrender. Biagio strode over to him.

"Look at you now," said the count. "Stupid boy. Like your king."

"Let him go!" cried Sabrina. Her own captor had sheathed his sword and had his python arms coiled about her, pinning her arms and pressing the breath from her lungs. She tried to struggle but the Angel only squeezed harder, making her scream from the pressure in her chest.

"Easy, my friend," Biagio bid his servant. "She's a delicate flower. Let's not pull her petals off yet." The count put out his cold hand and brushed his fingertips over her cheek. Her skin was perfect and warm. Biagio envied her. "My lady, I need you. You're going to deliver a message for me to your husband."

"I won't!" Sabrina choked. "You bastard . . ."

"Oh, my ears," chuckled the count. "And from such a well-bred bitch. You know, it always amazes me how many people need convincing of my seriousness. Perhaps it's my easygoing manner. Well, watch closely, Lady. Then make up your mind."

The count turned his attention back to Patwin. "Young fellow, I'm really sorry about this. This is your unlucky day." Biagio made another small gesture to his servant. The Shadow Angel pushed against his sword and drove its length through Patwin's mouth, shattering the back of his skull.

Lady Sabrina's anguished wail was the loudest thing Biagio had ever heard.

The House of Gayle stood on a green and rolling tor overgrown with weedy wildflowers and surrounded by a sluggish moat that reminded Biagio of the famous Gayle paranoia. It was an unremarkable place, neither large nor excessively appointed, and it bespoke solitude and a certain serious foreboding. At the bottom of the tor was a well-trampled parade ground, a huge expanse of grass where the horsemen of Talistan pranced and drilled, and near the back of the castle was a giant stable to accommodate the many beasts of the Gayle militia, a rambling structure of ramshackle wood that gave off an evil stink on hot summer days. The House of Gayle had a twenty-foot drawbridge spanning the moat and leading into a dusty courtyard. Inside the courtyard, servants and slaves attended to the castle's needs, while on the many catwalks guardians in green and gold paced their watches and made the stout wood creak with their heavy boots. Even in the smallest hours of the night they could be heard, incessantly walking and waiting for an invasion that would probably never come.

Biagio liked the militant house. He had visited it many times over the years and always stayed in the same room, a chamber the king of Talistan had built just for imperial guests like him. When he had business in this part of the Empire, Biagio always looked to the Gayles for hospitality, and they always offered it graciously. Suspiciously, too, of course, but that was the nature of politics and Biagio never faulted them for it. The Gayles were loyal, mostly, and always spoke well of Naren ideals. Until very recently, they had been one of Arkus' closest allies.

The Baron Blackwood Gayle leaned back theatrically in his chair so that its two front legs lifted off the marble floor. Pensively, he stared out the window. A shaft of sunlight struck his half-mask, making it glimmer. On the table was a decanter of wine and some food his slaves had hurriedly served up upon the count's arrival. Biagio, surprisingly hungered by the morning's events, sandwiched a piece of meat into a chunk of bread and ate silently as he regarded the baron. He had expected Gayle's melodrama, and was waiting as patiently as he could for it to end. Behind him, his Shadow Angels stood silent, staring at Gayle through their own death masks.

"This is such a surprise," said Blackwood Gayle. He feigned offense terribly, but Biagio let him continue. "My father and I had thought you'd forgotten about us, frankly. And now to hear you need us again, well . . ." Gayle sighed loudly. "What can I say?"

Biagio shrugged and poured himself a goblet of wine. He drained the glass slowly, making Gayle wait, then even more slowly poured himself some more. Despite the temperature outside, it was cold in the castle, and Biagio despised the cold. Gayle knew this and had deliberately opened the window so that a summer breeze blew in.

"You must know the emperor meant no offense, Baron," said Biagio finally. "But only Aramoor borders the Saccenne Run. Aramoor was the natural choice for staging the invasion."

"Bah," Gayle scorned. "I think Arkus was enamored with the boy. I saw the coronation the emperor arranged for him. It is always like that for the Vantrans. They have charisma, but people don't see their treachery. I hope Arkus sees now."

"It is regrettable," Biagio conceded. He had explained what little he knew to Blackwood Gayle, and the baron had glowed at the news of the young Vantran's treachery. But like his ailing, ancient father, this Gayle was a viper, and wouldn't bend so easily to Nar's rule, not without something valuable in return. It was true what people said about the House of Gayle—that all the gold in its coffers was plundered.

"Regrettable?" said Gayle. He turned his chair around to face the count. "Is that all you have to say? My family has been loyal to you and Arkus for years. We were offended, Count, I don't mind telling you that. I traveled to Nar in good faith, not only to attend that miserable whelp's coronation but to ask for Lady Sabrina's hand. And Arkus gave her to him instead!"

Gayle was growing louder by the moment, his big voice booming through the chamber. Perhaps he truly was offended, Biagio thought. To court the anger of the Shadow Angels was certain death. But Biagio held his bodyguards in check merely with his silence, and flashed Gayle one of his malevolent smiles.

"Baron," he said musically. "Relax."

Gayle seemed to find himself. "Yes. Of course," he said mildly. "But understand what I'm saying, Count. We should have been your first choice. If you had bothered to ask me, I would have told you Vantran couldn't be trusted. Lord, I'm surprised Arkus didn't know that after what happened in Lucel-Lor."

"Yes, yes, that's all very interesting, Baron. But now we have a problem, you and I."

"You, perhaps. Not I."

You're getting bold, aren't you? thought Biagio. He stared coldly at the baron.

"Can we forget the past, my old friend?" he said with practiced charm. "Both of us have an important charge now. Arkus is very old. It pains me to say so, but I don't know how much longer he has left. Richius Vantran was to go to Lucel-Lor to find its magic. He was to bring back its secrets to save the emperor. Now you must do this, Blackwood Gayle."

Gayle scoffed. "You make it sound like an honor. It might have been had I been chosen first. I would have made Nar and the emperor very proud. I would have shown you what a real man could do, instead of a blasted boy."

"Now's your chance, then," said Biagio. He had known the best way to reach the brooding baron was through praise, and began to heap it on. "Truly, my friend, we all knew you would have done a splendid job. Certainly you would have been the emperor's first choice, but Aramoor borders the Run. And the Aramoorians would never have allowed your troops on their soil, not even to get to the mountain passage. It's politics, after all."

"Politics," the baron spat. "And what if the emperor dies? What political moves will you make, I wonder? You will have your own hands full, and Talistan may be without an ally in Nar."

"The emperor will not die, Baron. *You* will make certain he doesn't. I have come here with a gift, after all. Aramoor is returned to Talistan as of today. I thought that would make you happy."

"If the emperor died, Aramoor would be ours anyway," countered Gayle. "His will was the only thing keeping us from taking it back forcibly." The eye behind the silver mask gleamed with mischief. "Answer my question, Count. What if the emperor does die? What will you do to fend off Herrith and the others of the Iron Circle?"

Biagio smiled dispassionately. "I'm not used to being on this side of an inquisition. I must say, I don't care for it. Not at all."

Blackwood Gayle smiled back at him. "You would be wise to think on it. No one lives forever. Not even the emperor. I know Arkus is very dear to you, but you should consider the possibilities. Not only for my sake, but for your own. After all, Herrith is no friend of yours. If you do vie for the throne, he will challenge you."

"The bishop is not my concern, Baron. Arkus is. You will see to it that he does not die. You will go to Lucel-Lor and find a magic to save him. And if you find Richius Vantran, you will bring him back. Alive."

"And what do I get for this grand crusade, Count? I've already lost men questing for Arkus against the Triin. Why would I want to do it again?"

It was the question Biagio had been waiting for. Very slowly he baited his hook. "Aramoor isn't enough for you?"

"As I said, Aramoor will be Talistan's again eventually. And I can be a very patient man."

"Well, then, perhaps I can sweeten the bargain," said Biagio. He made a quick shooing gesture to one of his guardians, sending the Angel out of the room. Blackwood Gayle watched questioningly as the soldier departed, then looked back at the count. Biagio merely steepled his fingers under his chin and grinned.

"Where's he going?" asked Gayle.

"I have another gift waiting in my carriage for you. Show me some of your famous patience."

The insult silenced Gayle instantly. He got up and went to the chamber door, peering out into the hall beyond and waiting for the Shadow Angel to reappear. Delighting in the baron's puzzlement, Biagio laughed and urged him back into the room.

"Sit down, Baron, please. This might take a few moments."

Blackwood Gayle did as advised. He didn't query again. Instead he waited with Biagio for the soldier to return, and drummed his fingers on the tabletop as the minutes ticked by. At last the Shadow Angel returned—with a woman in his arms. Blackwood Gayle stopped breathing when he saw her. Despite the ropes binding her wrists and ankles, despite the wad of cloth stuffed into her mouth, he recognized her at once. Count Biagio could hardly contain his glee at the baron's astounded expression. Both men rose as the Shadow Angel dumped the struggling woman at Gayle's feet.

"Blackwood Gayle," said Biagio. "I present to you the Lady Sabrina of Gorkney, former queen of Aramoor."

"My God," groaned Gayle. He stared down at the frightened woman, nearly mute with lust and amazement. When she saw his face, Sabrina began to cry.

"Call it righting an old wrong," said Biagio. "Does this change your mind, my friend?"

Unable to pull his eyes from the girl, Gayle asked, "You mean she's mine?"

"For a little while. You see, the lady is going to deliver a message for me to her darling husband. But until then, yes, she's yours. If you agree to do this thing I ask."

"What do you mean, for a while? Have someone else deliver your bloody message. If she's going to be mine—"

"Now, now," interrupted Biagio. "Don't get greedy, Blackwood Gayle. The lady is the only one Richius Vantran will listen to. But I don't need to send the message today, not even tomorrow. Take her until then. She is yours. Do we have a bargain?"

The most inhuman grin cracked Gayle's face. "We do."

"Excellent." Count Biagio went over to Gayle and wrapped an icy arm around the giant's shoulder. Then, putting his lips to the baron's ear, he began to whisper. "Now you listen to me. If Arkus dies, you die. If you fail to find the magic, you die. If Richius Vantran escapes you, you die." He released the baron from his cold embrace and added sweetly, "If I am displeased with you in any way, Blackwood Gayle, you die. Do you understand me clearly?"

The big baron nodded.

"Fine," smiled Biagio. "I am the Roshann, Blackwood Gayle. Don't ever forget my power again."

TWENTY-FIVE

Near the border of Tatterak, the land stretched endlessly in great, rugged steppes. Tatterak was Lucel-Lor's ugly jewel, the bulk of the Triin nation and its most implacable territory. A man could lose himself forever in its desolate folds, and never know how close he was to the sea or another living being. Unlike the Dring Valley, Tatterak was a craggy, colorless land, where the frost of winter grew thick and the summer sun could scorch the skin of a salamander. Here were the salt wastes of Lucel-Lor's northern shore, stained white by eons of surf. It was the land of the snow leopard, those ravenous cats with a taste for human flesh, who came out of their mountain lairs to feed when other beasts had the sense to hibernate. At night Tatterak was a place of endless, starry skies and prowling, wide-eyed creatures, where soldiers rarely slept without a dagger by their bedrolls. And far away on the ocean shore was Falindar, the usurped home of Tharn, the birthplace of Lucyler, and the prison of Dyana.

Richius expelled a tired sigh as he scanned the hostile expanse before them. For more than three weeks they had ridden for this place, following the narrow tributaries of melting ice from Tatterak's warming peaks. He was weary from ceaseless riding, and when he saw the limitless nothingness of Tatterak he felt a wave of despair. He swore to himself, bringing his horse to a stop. Lucyler did the same.

"Tatterak," declared the Triin. There was a happy ring to his voice, as if the imposing sight actually heartened him.

"Tatterak," replied Richius dully.

Even the name was hideous. In the time of the war, hundreds of men had poured into this desolate land, fighting side by side with the warlord Kronin. It was here the war had been bloodiest, where Aramoorians died in droves. Now Richius watched the landscape struggle into spring, recalling what Lucyler had been saying; Lucel-Lor was at peace.

"I need to rest," said Richius. "I'm tired and my back's aching. Let's break for a while."

Lucyler frowned, then looked up into the hazy sky. The sun had yet to reach its zenith. They still had many hours of traveling left.

"Could you go on a little? It is not much further to Dandazar now that we have reached the border. We will spend the night there, and you can get as much rest as you need."

"The horses are tired, too, Lucyler."

"We have only been going a few hours. I know you can do better than that. You are troubled. Why?"

Richius smiled ruefully. "Bad memories. I've been doing a lot of thinking since we left Ackle-Nye. It feels strange to be back in Lucel-Lor. When I left for home, I swore I'd never return. I'm not eager to see any more." He paused, gripped with a sudden sadness. "This place reminds me of Edgard."

"I am sorry," said Lucyler. "But we have to go to Dandazar. We are low on everything, and it is the only real city around. If we do not stop now, we will starve before we make it to Falindar."

Richius nodded. He had long ago consumed the provisions Patwin had packed for him, and together they had done a fair job of depleting Lucyler's food. It was like old times again in Lucel-Lor—lean and miserable.

"How much longer after Dandazar?" asked Richius. "About a week, right?"

"About. But a week is too much time. We need supplies now. And you're right about the horses. They cannot go on without a proper rest."

"And I'm about to drop, myself," Richius admitted. "All right then. We go to Dandazar. But only for a day." He fumbled with the bulky cloak Lucyler had purchased for him in Ackle-Nye, drawing it closer around his face. The garb made him look like one of the city's many lepers, and did a good job of concealing his features. "I don't want to take any chances."

"Nor do I," replied Lucyler with a chuckle. Since leaving the city of beggars, Richius' wretched clothing had been a constant source of amusement to the Triin. But the costume was a necessity, for as Lucyler had explained, the Triin were highly sensitive about Narens now, and might well view Richius as an enemy. "Keep that cowl close around you from here on," added Lucyler. "We might be surprised by some other riders around here."

Richius was already wrapping the filthy scarf around his face, so that only his eyes shone through the tattered gray fabric. As a leper, or some other diseased outcast, he would surely be left alone. He would be safe if Lucyler did all the talking.

"God, but it's hot under here," he exclaimed. "Make sure you find us a room away from anyone else. I don't intend to wear these rags all night."

"I will do my best. And don't say 'God' anymore, Richius. Triin know that word. It could mark you."

"Don't worry," replied Richius peevishly. "I'll keep my mouth shut. And if I have to say anything I'll shout 'Loomis and Pris' the way you always do."

Lucyler tossed back his white head and laughed. "*Lorris* and Pris," he corrected. "And those are Drol gods, anyway."

"Drol gods, Triin gods . . . It's all the same to me. Maybe you should think of simplifying your religion. You Triin have more deities than a dog has fleas."

"True, there are many," agreed Lucyler. "But only a few important ones."

"Are Lorris and Pris important ones?" asked Richius. Lucyler had always been notoriously tight-lipped about Triin folkways, and Richius was in the mood to be pushy. He watched his friend's face crinkle.

"They are important to the Drol," said Lucyler tersely.

"Just the Drol?"

"Not many others worship them. Just Drol, mostly."

"Why not?" pressed Richius. "What's the difference?"

Lucyler looked at him crossly. "Why so many questions? You never cared about these things in the valley."

Richius shrugged. "We were pretty busy back then. And I just want to learn what I can about Tharn. You haven't been very willing to talk about him. What's it mean to be a Drol? How come they worship Lorris and Pris?"

Lucyler sighed. "I am no scholar, Richius. Ask Tharn yourself when you meet him."

"That's no good," said Richius. "I want to know these things *before* meeting him. Tell me about Lorris and Pris."

"If I tell you, will you ride?"

Richius nodded.

"Then let us go."

They snapped their reins and started off again, Lucyler telling the tale like a father soothing a restless child. Richius listened intently, at once forgetting the hot chafing of the cloth about his face.

"Thousands of years ago," began Lucyler dramatically, "Lorris and Pris were born in a city far in the south of Lucel-Lor."

"What city?"

"Chatti. It no longer exists. Anyway, they were twins, brother and sister. Lorris was the boy, and Pris was his beautiful sister. It is said that she was as lovely as a goddess. The two were orphaned at an early age, and had to fend for themselves. They looked after one another, and grew to love and cherish each other beyond all else."

"What happened to their parents?" asked Richius. Lucyler glared at him.

"Are you going to keep interrupting me? Let me tell the story my own way. Now, they lived on their own for many years, taking care of each other as they grew to be adults, and the legend says that the great god Vikryn took pity on the two and protected them, making sure no harm ever befell them."

"I've heard of Vikryn," offered Richius.

"He is the supreme god," said Lucyler, "the god that most Triin worship. He is said to be kind and loving, and that is why he pitied the orphans and protected them. Eventually he saw Lorris made king of his homeland, Chatti."

"Together Lorris and Pris ruled Chatti for three years. Lorris was king, and Pris was an adored princess. The people loved them both, for Lorris protected them and Pris nurtured and cared for them. That is why they are thought of as the gods of war and peace. The Drol believe that the spirits of both dwell in all people. Lorris gives men strength, say the Drol, while Pris teaches people how to love. And sometimes they grant their followers special abilities."

"The touch of heaven, right?"

"Right. Tharn has the touch of heaven. He was chosen by Lorris to free Lucel-Lor. But the touch is very rare. Lorris usually grants strength, and his sister grants love."

"Lorris is probably the favorite of most Drol, I'd bet," quipped Richius. "I don't remember much love coming from Voris."

"Drol warriors do favor Lorris," admitted Lucyler. "Men like Voris pray to him for strength and courage. The legends say that Lorris was a great warrior, perhaps the greatest ever, and all Drol warriors strive to be like him. Their wives are to follow the example of Pris. They are to be loving and attentive, just as Pris attended to her brother. And they are to be loyal, not only to their husbands but also to their villages and towns."

"Most Triin women are like that," said Richius. "Go on. What happened next?"

"As I said, they ruled Chatti peacefully for three years, but then another city rose to threaten them. This city was called Toor, and the people there were worshipers of Pradu, the lord of the dead. Now understand, Pradu and Vikryn have been enemies from the beginning of time. One is the creator, the other the taker of life, and it is said that Pradu hated Lorris and Pris, for they were favored by his enemy Vikryn. But each time Pradu tried to destroy the two or tear them apart, Vikryn stopped him."

"So Pradu started a war between Toor and Chatti," said Richius with disgust. It wasn't unlike something Arkus would do.

"That is what the Drol believe," Lucyler went on. "Remember, to Pradu a war meant more souls to fill his coffers. It did not matter to him if some of those who died came from a city that worshiped him. But the armies of Toor were unable to defeat Lorris' city. Neither was Lorris able to rid the world of the Toors. They fought to a bloody standstill for five years."

Lucyler suddenly stopped, frowning at Richius.

"Go on," urged Richius. "What happened then?"

"Chatti and Toor had both lost many men, and Lorris and Pris were desperate to put an end to the fighting. But there was nothing they could do to stop it. The Toors were as evil as their patron Pradu. They ignored all attempts by Chatti for peace. Then one day, while Lorris was out alone in the woods hunting, an animal appeared to him. The animal was a jackal."

Richius grimaced. "A jackal. That sounds familiar."

"Yes, but this was no ordinary jackal. It was the god Pradu, and it spoke to Lorris. It told him that it was actually Vikryn, and that it had a great gift for Lorris, one that would allow him to end the war with the Toors by destroying them all with a magical chant. Once spoken, the chant would wipe away the city of Toor forever."

"Did Lorris speak the chant?"

"Of course he did. He believed this animal was Vikryn and he trusted him." Lucyler's expression grew dark, and his voice thinned to a reedy hiss. "He spoke the words, and a great fire erupted in Toor, destroying the city and scattering its people."

"The spell worked?" asked Richius. "I don't understand. You said the jackal was Pradu, not Vikryn. What happened?"

"It was Pradu, and the lord of the dead had not lied to Lorris about the spell. The spell worked. It destroyed Toor. But Pradu knew something Lorris did not, for earlier that day his sister Pris had been captured by spies from Toor, and they brought her back to their city so they could ransom her."

Richius let out a low whistle. "So she was killed by the spell."

"She was killed. And Lorris, heartbroken over her death, took his own life upon hearing the news. The legend says that he lived in a giant tower, and that he flung himself out of it that very day. Without the leadership of Lorris and Pris, Chatti was plunged into chaos, and invaders from other cities swarmed in and burnt it to the ground. And Pradu got what he had always wanted. He had killed the beloved of his enemy Vikryn, and he had brought death to thousands."

"And that's why I am called the Jackal in the Dring Valley," added Richius grimly. "Because the Drol hate that animal. Why did you never tell me this?"

"Would it have mattered?" asked Lucyler. "It is just a legend anyway. But there is more to it. It goes on to say that upon their deaths, Lorris and Pris ascended into the sky to dwell with the gods, and that Vikryn still looks after them. Today they are worshiped by the Drol as the gods of war and peace."

Richius smiled with satisfaction. Legend or not, it was a fine story. "It's so sad, though," he mused. "They must have really loved each other." At once his thoughts turned to Dyana.

"Yes, it is sad," said Lucyler. "But they are remembered. Each year the Drol celebrate Casadah, their highest holy day. It is a time for remembering the lives and deaths of the twins. There is feasting and music, and the cunning-men tell stories about Lorris and Pris, so that the young children will grow to understand."

"The cunning-men? Who are they?"

"Drol holy men," said Lucyler. "Like priests in Nar. Tharn is a cunning-man. He is the highest cunning-man in the Drol sect. And this will be the first Casadah since he came to power. It is only a week away. We might even reach Falindar in time for it."

"You sound excited," said Richius, almost accusingly. "I thought you said you weren't a Drol."

"It is a celebration, Richius. A time for welcoming spring. Not only the Drol appreciate it."

Richius snorted disdainfully. He hadn't counted on arriving during a Drol holy day. "Well, I for one wouldn't mind missing it. Let's not forget my business in Falindar, Lucyler. I'm only going for Dyana."

Lucyler turned to Richius, his eyes flashing. "*You* asked me about the Drol, remember?"

"I remember. But I don't want this Casadah to preoccupy Tharn. I have business with him. I want him to attend to me."

"He will attend to you," assured Lucyler. "Believe me, you will not be ignored. Kronin himself will probably want to meet you. He has lived in the citadel with Tharn since the end of the war. He knew that I was leaving Falindar to speak to you."

"And what about him? Does he worship Lorris and Pris now?"

"Kronin is not a Drol," said Lucyler. "He does not have to be. He follows Tharn now, like I do, but he has his own beliefs. It is all part of the peace, Richius. Tharn makes no demands on the warlords. That is why he let Kronin keep Tatterak, instead of giving it to Voris in the Dring Valley. I tell you, he forgives like no man I have ever met. Kronin was spared, just like me and all the others who fought against Tharn. Even Voris has accepted Kronin."

Richius raised his eyebrows, suitably impressed. The warlords of the Dring Valley and Tatterak had been bitter enemies since anyone could remember. Even the Narens knew that. To think that Tharn had forged an alliance between the two was indeed remarkable. Still, it remained to be seen. Though each passing day made Richius trust his Triin companion a little more, the claims Lucyler made were still only words, and Richius was determined not to be swayed by hope or past friendships. The day he saw Voris and Kronin together would be the day he was convinced.

"I still can't believe Kronin is alive, not after what happened in Tatterak. Blackwood Gayle himself was forced to flee, and almost all his men were killed. How could Kronin possibly have survived? Those storms . . ."

He stopped, noticing the way Lucyler sealed his lips. The Triin looked away furtively, as if intrigued by the lifeless landscape. Richius groaned. It was so sickeningly obvious.

"He never used his magic against Kronin's warriors, did he?" asked Richius hotly. "He only used it against Narens!"

Lucyler's silence answered the charge.

"God in heaven, what a fool I've been! Of course Kronin is still alive. Why shouldn't he be? Tharn would never use his magic against his own people. Oh, no, that would be unthinkable. He's a Drol, right? But slaughter a bunch of barbarians from Nar, that's fine."

Lucyler raised a warning hand. "That is not it," he said carefully. "Tharn wanted only to rid Lucel-Lor of Naren influence. That was what the revolution was about, remember."

"So he goes ahead and burns everyone, except the Triin that are fighting against him. That sounds all right to you?"

"Of course not," snapped Lucyler. "But in the end it won the war for him, and showed the other warlords that he wanted peace. By sparing the warlords loyal to the Daegog . . ."

"Stop it," said Richius hotly. "I'm not going to be convinced."

Lucyler shrugged noncommittally. "We shall see."

They rode in silence for more than an hour, and while Richius fumed he watched the landscape change as they drove into the heart of Tatterak. The rocky plains were falling behind them, giving way to rocky hills. A perfect orange orb shone high overhead, painting the landscape with a peculiar glow, and along the uneven path pockets of twisted shrubbery buzzed with eager honeybees. An unexpected feeling of melancholy pricked at Richius. There was such a bloody history to this place. Four years ago, Tharn had just conquered Falindar and ousted the Daegog from his throne, and Kronin and his warriors were desperate to stem the Drol tide. And though they were ordered to do so by Arkus, many of Richius' countrymen were more than willing to help put down the revolution they saw as a threat not only to Lucel-Lor but perhaps eventually to Nar itself. How many people had died here, wondered Richius silently.

Like the violent campaign of the Dring Valley, Tatterak had been the stage for a dozen bloody showdowns, battles that tore the fabric of Triin life apart. But now there was no evidence of its sanguine past. Across the rolling hills there was only the indomitable blooming of spring. There were villages in these hills, filled with hearty people who had somehow endured the tragic hardships of civil war. Just how well they had actually fared was something Richius was suddenly eager to find out.

By the time they reached the outskirts of Dandazar, Richius and Lucyler were talking again. Lucyler pointed to the unmistakable outline of the place, its wood and clay buildings all too regular against the backdrop of the mountains. More a town than a city, Dandazar was nevertheless the only important place for miles, a battered and weathered beacon for weary travelers. Like Ackle-Nye, Dandazar had been a key location for the forces of Aramoor and Talistan, a place where the troops could purchase the food and other supplies they needed to survive in the harsh countryside. But unlike Ackle-Nye, Dandazar had none of the trappings of Naren influence. There were no twisted buildings here, no stone monoliths reminiscent of the Black City. There was only the architecture of the Triin, simple and pragmatic. Even from their great distance, Richius could glimpse the whitewashed roofs and smooth, sandy masonry, and on the breeze drifted the piquant scent of animals and cooking fires. It was as if some gypsy bazaar had come along and made this place its home, for Dandazar was widely known in Tatterak, and travelers from all about came to the bustling town to sell their wares and barter for needed goods.

The unmistakable pinpoints of white Triin heads were soon visible, and Richius drew the cowl closer about his face.

"Remember," warned Lucyler as they trotted toward the city. "Say nothing. If anyone speaks to you, ignore them. And don't move too quickly. You are supposed to be ill." He inspected Richius warily. "Sit low in your saddle," he urged, and proceeded to coach his comrade by slumping over. "Like this."

Richius drooped forward and rounded his back until he looked like a man near death. "All right?"

"Good. Now let us be quick. The first thing we need is a room for the night and bedding for the horses. Once you are safe inside, I will go out again for supplies."

"Find a good room," Richius reminded him. "Something private."

"I will if I can," said Lucyler. Again he looked discouragingly at Richius. "It might not be so easy to find a room at all. If they think you are a leper . . ."

"Fine," said Richius, putting up his hands in exasperation. "Let's just get what we came for and go. We can sleep in the hills tonight if we have to."

Lucyler raised his hand to quiet Richius. They were on the narrow road leading into the town, and already there were keen ears to hear them. Richius slumped down again on Lightning's back, averting his eyes from the people they passed. The Triin language was everywhere, clicking from the lips of bargain-hunting old women and frustrated merchants, and streaming out in lungfuls from the excited children that ran along the crowded corridors snaking between pavilions and shop fronts. There were animals both strange and familiar, goats and pigs and clamoring, caged fowl, and exotic birds with saffron plumage and striped bills. There were reptiles and dogs, downy rabbits and multilimbed primates, some boxed up in wooden cartons, others roaming free in the streets or resting on the shoulders of their masters. And everywhere there were cats, darting under tables and lounging blissfully in the sun, their lean bodies toned to feline perfection by the hunting of mice. It was all so much like any town square at fair time, except for the notable absence of Narens. Here there were only Triin, a sea of white skin and milky hair and pale eyes. As far as Richius could see through the thin opening of his cowl, he was the only Naren in the town. He heard Lucyler's steady voice at his side.

"Easy. Just follow me."

Richius did as his companion bid, trailing Lucyler's horse through the marketplace and doing what he could to avoid being noticed. Only a few of the gathered shoppers turned to look at them as they rode, and none seemed to take any interest. Richius suppressed a sudden shudder. Mistrust of Nar had been the cornerstone of Tharn's revolution. There was no telling how much hatred the Drol had bred among these people since.

They came to a place near the center of the market where a particularly anxious merchant was shouting and holding up headless chickens. Several horses were tethered beside the man's stall, and bags of grain and horse feed took up most of the area. There was not much of a crowd here, and Lucyler chanced dismounting, walking over to the man as Richius watched from the recesses of his cowl. After speaking briefly with the merchant, Lucyler moved casually back to Richius, looking up at him and motioning for him to come down off his horse. Richius hesitated, but a furtive wink from Lucyler convinced him to dismount. He dropped down slowly off Lightning's back, careful to appear infirm. He handed the reins to his waiting companion, who led both horses over to the man. Lucyler then dug into his jacket and pulled out several small coins, which the merchant greedily accepted. There was a brief exchange before the conversation ended. Lucyler returned to where Richius was waiting.

"He will look after the horses for the night," whispered Lucyler. "He has told me of a place at the end of the market that might have beds for us. Come."

The Triin took Richius' arm as if he were an old man and began leading him slowly through the crowded market. Richius followed along, limping the way the starving beggars in Nar City did, his back crooked painfully. Already he was feeling vulnerable without Lightning beneath him. Lucyler was quiet as they walked, barely taking his eyes off the ground as he led Richius gently by the arm. Occasionally the street would swell with people or livestock, and they would stop for a moment to let the quicker shoppers pass them. Triin children bolted by and cats scurried past their feet, and the sounds of the marketplace gradually engulfed them until they looked no more unusual than any grime-covered travelers. Like Lucyler, Richius kept his eyes to the ground, tilting his head only enough to see a few steps in front of him. He pulled the cowl closer about his face, closing it with his hands whenever someone came too near.

At last they came to the end of the market. Lucyler paused and looked around, then pulled Richius into a convenient corner. There were houses here, and the noise from the market had ebbed a little so that Lucyler's voice was clearer than before.

"I have to find the house of a man named Cavool," said Lucyler. "The merchant told me he would be around here, and that he might be willing to rent a room to us for the right price. I will tell him that you are sick, but that you have nothing dangerous to others. Then I will give him this."

He pulled out another coin from his robes, this one shiny and gold and many times larger than the ones he had given the merchant in the market. Enough to rent a healthy man a room for a month, thought Richius. Perhaps it was enough to buy a leper one night of privacy. Lucyler scanned the small houses, looking for some definitive features. A slight frown appeared on his face.

"I will have to ask around for this Cavool," he said finally. "Wait here for me. It will be quicker if I go myself."

Richius shook his head vigorously.

"I will not be long," said Lucyler. "I am sure his house is nearby. Do not talk to anyone."

"God damn it, Lucyler," Richius hissed, but his friend was already gone, leaving him leaning against one of the dozens of houses lining the street. Richius felt a desperate loneliness wash over him, and he shambled into the shadows, hoping no one would see him, or worse, attempt a conversation. But the other folk in the street ignored him, going on about their business as if he were one of them. He could hear the mild chatter of Triin through the open windows above him, could smell the exotic cooking of midday meals. Women called to their children, and old men laughed about unknown things as they drank and played dice games in little groups on the sidewalks. And as the moments passed, Richius began to feel a certain foolishness about his fears. Not only did these people not notice him, he realized suddenly, they seemed like no threat at all. There were no Drol warriors among them brandishing jiiktars, no hordes of Tharn's holy men calling out prayers. There was only the peace that

Lucyler had described, orderly and regular, as if war had never touched this place.

Richius stepped out of the shadows and into the street. He had never really been here, he realized. He had once come to this place, camping on the outskirts with Okyle's brigade, but he had never known life in Dandazar or even thought to fathom its inhabitants. Now, with the milling of all this life around him, he was intrigued, and the sudden realization that Lucyler hadn't lied to him struck him like a welcome wind.

Soon he was chancing a walk into the street, still averting his eyes but refusing to cower, gradually making his way past stalls and tables filled with the wares of a culture he hardly knew. He was careful not to wander far, but the pull of the market drew him forward. Occasionally he glanced over his shoulder to where Lucyler would be waiting for him, and each time he didn't see his friend he took another step deeper into the crowd, until he was surrounded by the city's population and their odd, throaty tongue. For the first time since leaving Aramoor, he was happy, and he glided along as if invisible, hardly bothering to stoop or limp or make any pretense to illness. The charade seemed suddenly foolish now. No one knew who he was, and all were too busy with their own doings to pay him any attention. But he was careful to keep his hands off the things for sale, for no matter how much they intrigued him he knew the hue of his skin would reveal him. So he merely observed, enchanted with the variety of things being bought and sold. At a table near the end of the street a merchant had set out a fabulous collection of silks and fabrics, a rainbow procession of colors and textures spun into robes and other garments. Richius strode over to the crowded table, eyeing the beautiful wares, and gasped at what he saw there.

Hanging from a board behind the Triin merchant was a dress of silver and scarlet so perfectly made as to be breathtaking. The smile on Richius' face broadened. Falindar was only a week away, and this would likely be their last stop before reaching the citadel. Until this moment it hadn't even occurred to him to have a gift for Dyana, but seeing the dress reminded him of her instantly. It would be a wonderful present for her. He glanced over at the merchant, who was just finishing up with a customer. Richius looked away, struggling to think. He would have to come back with Lucyler. Surely there was enough money for the dress . . .

An ear-splitting scream shattered Richius' musings. He turned to look behind him and all at once the street erupted into panic. The tide of people swarming in the square parted, and at their center Richius saw an unimaginable thing. He fell back, dumbfounded at the sight, almost stumbling into the merchant's table. What looked to him like a giant cougar was mauling a man in the center of the street. Twice the size of a warhorse, the creature towered above its screaming prey, its knifelike fangs barred, its short, brown mane frizzled with rage. Yellow eyes shone from its massive head, and its cropped tail whipped from side to side in fast, determined movements as it pinned the man beneath its paws. Like something out of Naren mythology, the beast bristled and hissed at the horrified crowd. The man wailed in shock and pain, fighting against the impossible mass of the creature and beating his fists against its legs, his clothes thick with bloody rents.

Richius searched frantically for a solution. The cat was surely enough to best a score of men, yet he could hardly bear the screams of the Triin pinned beneath the monster. He slipped his hands under his garments, feeling quickly for Jessicane's pommel. The giant sword felt insignificant in his grip. Only then did he notice that the creature was harnessed and saddled. He stared at the enraged beast, stupefied at the idea that some-one was capable of riding it. He recalled the giant skull that hung in Arkus' chamber, that bleached skeleton the emperor had called the re-mains of a Triin war lion. He had only heard of these creatures in tales, and here one was, about to tear a man's chest open. Desperately he glanced around, hoping to find the cat's master, but all he saw were the wide-eyed faces of onlookers like himself. There was no one else to save the man, and in less than a minute he would be dead.

It was all the convincing Richius needed.

Jessicane leapt out from under the robes in a silver flash. Richius dashed forward, the sword high above his head, a cry tearing from his throat. At once the cat sighted him. It lowered its head and fixed its angry eyes on him, emitting a violent roar. Richius stopped five feet before the snarling lion, waving Jessicane before him.

"Back, beast!" he cried. "Back!"

The lion snapped out a giant paw, swiping at Richius and missing by inches. Richius took a small step forward and swiped back, nicking the monster's tawny breast. Enraged, the lion stretched out farther with its limb and batted the sword away, but Richius stood firm, calling out every insult he could think of to drive the creature off its dying prey. A gasp went up from the astounded crowd. Richius pressed forward, his heart beating furiously. Where was the damn thing's rider? If it did attack him, he would never be able to outrun it, and fighting it was unthinkable. This was no dog-sized war wolf. The thing was a behe-moth. Yet still he jeered at it, poking with his sword, trying to drive it off the crumpled man. The man, too, tried to aid in his rescue, screaming and kicking and clawing. But still the cat remained there, unwilling to lift its massive paw. Finally Richius was desperate enough to attack the beast. He reared Jessicane backward in both fists. If he could harm it enough . . .

"Kajiea!"

Richius halted. A Triin man raced up to him, tugging at his cloak and dragging him off his feet. Richius stared up at the man, dumbstruck at the assault. He was unlike any Triin Richius had seen before. Long, weather-beaten garments hung loosely from his grimy body, and his skin was bronzed an unusual umber over his natural whiteness. He was tall, too, with a pair of fierce and dangerous eyes that shone like two burning rubies. His face was lean and hard, and he glared at Richius for a long moment before turning his attention to the lion. Richius could see the jiiktar poised on his back.

The beast calmed at the sight of the man. It lowered its head and retracted its claws, its eyes dawning with primitive recognition. The man walked fearlessly up to the cat and ran his hands through its dark mane, speaking to it in a low, comforting voice. He seemed not to notice the man trapped beneath it. The man's pleas had died to a dull murmur, and blood seeped from his clothes and stained the street under him. Richius struggled to his feet to face the lion rider, pointing at the dying man.

"Are you mad?" he bellowed. "Can't you see that man is dying? Let him go!"

The Triin reared back at the verbal barrage, fixing his hot eyes on Richius again, then glanced down at the twisting figure and spat. At last he cooed to the giant cat, and the beast raised its paw from the man's chest. Richius seized the opportunity, racing up to the man and dragging him away from the lion. The lion rider glared at Richius. The wounded man was barely breathing.

"You've done it, you know," he hissed. "He's dying."

Others were coming closer now. Triin women swarmed over the broken figure, pulling at his clothes and gasping at the deep rents in his flesh. Richius rose to face the lion master. The giant cat's expression had calmed to a blank stare, but his rider's face was still fixed with rage. He squared his shoulders as Richius approached, folding his tanned arms over his chest.

"What the hell is wrong with you?" Richius barked. "You could have saved him!" He knew the Triin could not understand him, but he hoped his anger would translate well enough. The man merely grunted.

"Doula un dieata," said the man in his meaningless tongue. He put his hand behind his back and pulled out his jiiktar, holding the dual-bladed staff in two fists and straddling his legs in challenge. Richius shook his head in disbelief.

"You *are* mad," he said disgustedly. The crowd was drawing nearer now, fascinated by the face-off. "I won't fight you."

The lion master stepped forward, his great, docile cat behind him, and struck Richius across the face. Richius tumbled backward, his lip gushing blood. Instantly he took up his sword.

"You little bitch-son!" he snarled. "You want a fight, eh? Well, you've got one!"

"No!"

Richius whirled around to see Lucyler streaking toward him. The Triin's face was panicked, and he jumped between the duelists, pushing Richius away.

"Don't fight him, Richius," warned Lucyler. He turned to face the lion rider. The big man's grin widened as he pushed at Lucyler with his jiiktar. Lucyler swiped it away angrily, and some words Richius couldn't decipher spewed from both their lips. After a moment the lion rider lowered his jiiktar. Lucyler took a careful step backward.

"What happened?" he asked Richius over his shoulder.

"Why are you asking me?" Richius snapped. He gestured quickly to the dying man in the street. "All I wanted to do was help that poor bastard. That's when this filthy tramp showed up. Why don't you ask him what happened?"

"I did," said Lucyler impatiently. He was still unwilling to take his eyes off the lion rider. "He says that you attacked his lion. Is that true?"

"It's true," answered Richius. "What else could I do? His beast was tearing that man apart!"

Lucyler talked to the other Triin, his voice remarkably courteous. Again the lion rider answered, and as the two spoke Richius listened intently, gleaning what little he could from the obscure words. The lion rider was calmer now, and Richius felt a faint relief as he watched him return his jiiktar to the sheath on his back.

"What's he saying?" asked Richius. Lucyler raised a silencing hand as the stranger continued. At last Lucyler turned again to Richius.

"We should go now," he said simply.

"Go? Just like that? Why? What did he say to you?"

Lucyler took Richius by the arm and led him away, moving quickly through the thickening crowd. When they were far enough from the lion rider not to be seen, Richius wrenched his arm away.

"Stop," he ordered angrily. "Tell me what he said."

"That was a lion rider from Chandakkar," said the Triin. "Do you know what that means?"

"Should I?"

"You were in great danger, Richius. Lorris and Pris, what were you thinking? I told you to wait for me near the houses!"

"That lion of his was killing someone, Lucyler! What was I supposed to do?"

"Those lions never attack anyone without reason, Richius. That is what he explained to me. That man may have been trying to harm the lion, or even steal it."

"Is that what he told you?" asked Richius, half laughing. "And you believed him?"

"You know nothing about the lion riders. What he told me was the truth. And just what did you expect to do against that animal?"

"I only wanted to save the man, that's all. He started the fight."

"Because you were a stranger and a threat. He thought that you and that other man were trying to harm his lion." Lucyler looked away, exasperated. "You could have been killed."

"I could have taken him," Richius snorted angrily. But Lucyler only laughed at his bravado.

"Impossible. Even if you did best him, that lion would have shredded you alive. They are protective that way. The bond between the lions and their masters is legendary."

"All right," said Richius. "I didn't know what I was doing. But even if that man was trying to steal or hurt the lion, is that how he should have been dealt with? No one even tried to help him, Lucyler. I just couldn't stand by and watch."

Lucyler's hard features softened. He put his hand to Richius' shoulder. "You are right," he said calmly. "I was wrong to be angry with you. But we are in danger now. They have discovered what you are."

"Let's go to the house, then," said Richius. "Did you find it?"

Lucyler nodded. "Yes, but we cannot stay there now. We'll have to go back into the hills for the night. Tomorrow I will return and get the supplies we need."

Richius sighed wearily. "I'm sorry, Lucyler. This is my fault. I shouldn't have walked off. But that damn lion . . ."

"It is all right," said Lucyler. "We will just have to wait until tomorrow to go on to Falindar. Come, we will get the horses."

Richius nodded, and the two walked quickly back to the merchant with whom they had left their mounts. The merchant shook his oily head at Lucyler, unwilling to refund the coins he had been given. But they were in a hurry, and Lucyler was in no mood to argue. They led their horses away from the market and mounted at the outskirts of the town, heading north toward the hills that would be their shelter for the night. Richius protested, telling his friend that he saw no threat from the Triin of Dandazar, but Lucyler was convinced they should leave the place, especially after the incident with the lion rider.

"They might look benign," said Lucyler as they rode out of the town, "but they do not trust Narens, believe me. That fellow Cavool would never sell a room to you."

"And the lion rider? What about him? I thought those people were outcasts. Do they trust him more than they do me?"

"He is a Triin. Even this far away from Chandakkar, he is more welcome than a Naren."

Richius shrugged, still awed by the thought of the giant cat. "I never thought I'd see one," he said. "And this far north! Why would he travel so far from Chandakkar?"

Lucyler looked mischievously at his comrade, a slight smile twisting his thin lips. "I told you, my friend, it is the peace. This is not the Lucel-Lor you remember."

"I'm starting to think you are right about that," said Richius. "And incidentally, since you're coming back tomorrow, there's a dress I saw in the market. . . ."

TWENTY-SIX

Dinadin Lotts squeezed his big body past the throngs of people and
stared in mute horror at the poster tacked to the market wall. He
had ridden hard and fast for Aramoor's square, for news of a
commotion had reached him, and an unbelievable tale was being told.
Now, out of breath and surrounded by shouting hundreds, he read the
artless scribblings on the posted paper. It said simply that Richius Vantran was a wanted man. Count Renato Biagio's signature rambled in
runny ink along the bottom. Dinadin stumbled backward into the crowd.
Around him rang the astounded accusations of farmers and the bitter
wails of women, and the word *traitor* was on the lips of children too
young to know its meaning.

"Traitor," whispered Dinadin. It was being said that Richius had left
Aramoor, that he had gone to Lucel-Lor to bargain with the devil Tharn.
Dinadin's brothers had heard it first on the road back from Innswick.
And though Dinadin could scarcely believe it, here he was, staring at a
poster that declared his friend and king a criminal. "My God," he
moaned. "What have you done, Richius?"

"He has betrayed us!" answered an old woman beside him. She poked
at him with her cane, angry tears streaking her face. "He bargains us
away to the Triin, that's what he does."

"No!" roared Dinadin, batting the cane away from his ribs. "This is
wrong. A trick!"

"A trick? Are you one of his foolish men, then? We are betrayed, boy! It's the truth."

Dinadin shook his head. "I don't believe it. I cannot!" He shifted his gaze through the crowd, hoping to spot a familiar face. Amazingly, he found one. Gilliam was wearing the uniform of the Aramoorian Guard, bold and black against the dreary backdrop of farm garb. Though Dinadin hadn't seen his fellow soldier since returning home, he raced toward him like an old friend, shouting his name. "Gilliam!" he cried, pushing his way through the crowded square. "Over here!"

Gilliam's face turned toward him, dawning with recognition. "Dinadin!" he called back. The two locked hands. "Thank God you're here. Have you heard?"

"Not everything," said Dinadin. "Why are you wearing your uniform? What's going on?"

Gilliam grabbed the lapel of Dinadin's jacket, tugging it with a disgusted snap. "What do you mean, why? What's this you're wearing? Why don't you have your own uniform on?"

"Why should I?" asked Dinadin angrily. "What the hell is happening?"

Gilliam stared at him for a long, silent moment. "You haven't heard, have you?"

"Heard what? God damn it, Gilliam, tell me!"

"The emperor has declared Blackwood Gayle governor of Aramoor. His troops are already at the castle."

"My God!" exclaimed Dinadin. "It's true about Richius, then?"

Gilliam nodded. "Yes, but it's not the whole of it. The Talistanians are saying he betrayed us, but if he went to Lucel-Lor he had good reason, I know it."

"We have to get to the castle," said Dinadin hurriedly. "Help Patwin and Jojustin."

"It's too late," said Gilliam darkly. "They're already dead. Patwin was killed defending the Lady Sabrina. And Jojustin . . ." The soldier's voice choked off, and he shut his eyes to compose himself. "I heard he was executed by Biagio. I don't know what happened to the lady."

"Patwin's dead?" asked Dinadin, his own resolve crumbling. It hadn't been so very long ago that he had spoken with his gentle comrade.

"He wouldn't renounce his vow to Richius," said Gilliam. "That's what Gayle and his dogs are demanding. Anyone staying loyal to the Vantran House is to be killed." He drew his sword and kissed its silver blade. "By God, they'll have a lot of killing to do today!"

"They're on their way here?" asked Dinadin.

"That's the word. And it looks like we're the only ones to stand against them."

Dinadin felt his face flush. "Don't be mad, Gilliam. We have to leave now, while we have the chance to get our men together. . . ."

"There are no other men, Dinadin. Most were killed at the castle. Everyone else is looking after their homes. It's up to us to fight for these folks here. We're still Guardsmen of Aramoor. We have a duty."

Dinadin nodded but said nothing. Duty or no, they were only two, and clearly no match for whatever troops Blackwood Gayle was rolling in. If the Talistanians were on their way, they would notice the brashly dressed Gilliam in an instant, and that meant a fight. Dinadin suppressed a moan. Everything was happening so quickly. Richius was gone, that much he accepted, but the rule of Talistan was no less astonishing. The House of Vantran had governed Aramoor since its founding, and there were many who would gladly die to defend its continuance. Like Patwin and Gilliam, men followed the Vantrans to their graves. It was an inexplicable fact of life in Aramoor, one that Dinadin had found increasingly unbelievable lately. His expression soured. There would be blood let today, buckets of it. He grabbed an apple from a cart beside him and took a bite, chewing it ponderously as he thought. The grocer seemed not to notice the pinching, or if he did he simply didn't care. Matters of greater weight preoccupied them all, and the commerce in the square had ground to a halt. Gilliam was talking to somebody, a young fellow with blondish hair who greedily clutched a loaf of bread to his breast. The teen seemed enthralled by the soldier and all his bold words. A crowd had gathered around Gilliam, all asking desperate questions—questions which Gilliam was hard put to answer. But despite the cacophony of voices the questions were uniformly similar—what will happen to us now?

What indeed? Dinadin asked himself. He would be told to renounce his loyalty to Richius, and his father and brothers would also. The House of Lotts would not be spared today. Dinadin's clan had a long and bellicose history with Talistan, and were as well known to the Gayles as the Vantrans were. It would take some fancy thinking to maneuver out of this one. Dinadin nibbled the apple to its core and tossed its remains over his shoulder. Gilliam was still at work fielding questions and trying to rally the group, but he was getting almost nowhere. There was real hostility among the crowd, the kind of bitterness that always grows from betrayal. These were mostly farmers, not soldiers, and it seemed that Gilliam's explanations were falling on deaf ears.

"He has not abandoned us," cried Gilliam. "He will be back. I swear it."

Some believed him. Others didn't. And while they argued Dinadin backed away. Without the might of Vantran leadership, Aramoor was little more than this ragged group of workingmen. Their army was all but gone, destroyed in Lucel-Lor, and what soldiers did remain would surely be questioning their loyalties by now. Like Darius Vantran before him, Richius had cut them loose, and the realization flooded Dinadin with rage.

"Why, Richius?" whispered Dinadin to himself. It was just one more of his friend's inexplicable actions. Just then, the familiar thunder of hooves entered the square. Ten or more horsemen, all in the green and gold of Talistan and sporting the masks of demons, brought their beasts to a snorting halt before the rowdy assemblage. Dinadin's hand dropped to his sword. A handful of the soldiers dismounted as their commander spoke. He was a lean man who wore no helmet but instead adorned himself with a peculiar, wide-brimmed hat that sprouted a tail-like feather.

"Folk of Aramoor," boomed the commander's slick voice. "I am Ardoz Trosk, colonel of the green brigade. By now you have heard of the treachery of your king. It is the order of Nar that your land has become forfeit. From this moment on, Aramoor is no more. You are a province of Talistan now, and are subject to the laws and decrees of your new governor, Baron Blackwood Gayle!"

There was the expected murmur of shock before the colonel continued. "Be cooperative, obey us, and you will not be harmed." A wave of his hand brought his entourage's swords rising from their scabbards. "Defy us, and you will be punished."

"I defy you!" came a hate-filled voice. Gilliam stepped out of the crowd, his own sword held ready in two meaty fists. "I'll not denounce my king, dog! And neither will many others!"

Colonel Trosk was unimpressed. A sigh very like a yawn leaked from his lips. "All must renounce their loyalty to the Vantran blood. Such is the will of Arkus, soldier. Lower your weapon. You will not be permitted to carry it any longer."

"Come and take it yourself," dared Gilliam. He stepped closer to the circle of gold-plated soldiers, taunting them with his giant blade. Dinadin felt his breath catch, and took his hand off his own weapon. No one was coming to the aid of this brave fool.

"You'll only give us a show," warned Trosk. "Put it down . . . *now*!"

"In hell!" growled Gilliam, then dashed toward the nearest Talistanian. The soldier had his guard up in an instant, but the force of Gilliam's overhead blow shattered the defense and the huge blade came crashing down, shearing off the soldier's arm. An astounded cry went up from the crowd as Gilliam spun to meet the onrushing Talistanians. His sword swept around, catching another in the guts and breaking through his golden armor with the precision of a scalpel. For one brief instant it looked as if Gilliam could win. . . .

But of course he could not. The remaining soldiers charged him at once, surrounding him in a circle of sharpened steel. Already the big man was breathing hard. He danced about, twisting his head and fencing away the swords that pricked and taunted him. They lunged at him, nipping at his back and thighs the way wolves do, until a hundred rents in his uniform ran red. Gilliam fell to his knees, cursing and urging them on, ignoring the men who wept for him and the mothers who buried their children's faces in their skirts.

"Dinadin!" screamed Gilliam, looking about in horror as the noose of soldiers tightened. "Where are you? I need you, boy. Help me!"

Dinadin stood, paralyzed with fear. Again and again Gilliam called out for him, the voice barely a sob when at last it disappeared. A clammy wetness soaked Dinadin's brow. He was shaking uncontrollably, as though a winter wind had set his teeth to chattering. The crowd around Gilliam backed away as the soldiers from Talistan sheathed their weapons. Gilliam lay in a crumpled mass at their center.

"Now then," said Trosk, scanning the crowd. "Who is Dinadin?"

Dinadin mouthed a silent prayer. There were people in this crowd who knew him, surely, and would point him out if pressed. He worked up his courage and stepped forward.

"I am Dinadin, of the House of Lotts," he said with mustered confidence. The colonel's head reared back with recognition.

"Lotts? Wonderful! Then you shall be the first, boy." Trosk pulled out his own sword and dangled it at his side. "Come closer."

Dinadin complied, inching cautiously toward the horseman. When he was face to face with the snorting warhorse he stopped. "Do it," he said harshly. "Just make it quick."

Trosk smiled sardonically. "You know the law now, Lotts. Will you obey it?"

The question hung in the air with the heaviness of an anvil, and all watched Dinadin for his reaction. The offered sword lay loosely at the horse's flank, awaiting an answer. A twitch of the hand could bring it to his throat. Dinadin was silent.

"Will you renounce your loyalty to the House of Vantran?" asked Trosk impatiently. "Swear all your allegiance to Nar?"

Hot tears were coming in streaks now. Embarrassed, Dinadin wiped them away, burying his face in his sleeve. The eyes of the masses burned into him, waiting and wondering what they would see. And as they watched him his every thought was of Richius. Richius, dear friend and betrayer. It had been far too long, he decided in that moment. Perhaps if he hadn't shunned his king, things would have turned out differently.

Slowly he reached out and touched the blade. The thought of running his wrist over its edge briefly raced through his mind. But what shame was there in this, truly? What unworthy cause had Gilliam died for? They had all been duped into loving a clan of traitors. Perhaps the price of stupidity was a nation's sovereignty.

In grief and anguish, he leaned forward and kissed the sword from Talistan.

TWENTY-SEVEN

On the eve of Casadah, the great holy day of the Drol, Richius and Lucyler arrived at the citadel of Falindar. They had made it to the north of Tatterak, where the cold sea lapped against the rocky earth and the mountains were tall and secretive. On such a mountain the citadel towered, precariously poised near a sheer cliff face bleached white by the violent surf a thousand feet below. Only one passage led to the citadel, a well-built road wide enough to accommodate the royal processions of the citadel's former master, and studded along its length with monolithic torches so that the way to the place was both lit and shadowy even in the smallest hours of the night. Like the awesome constructs of Nar, the citadel of Falindar dominated the horizon, its cleanly formed spires at once bleak and beautiful, hued an eerie pink by the crescent moon.

The wind was sighing as Lucyler brought his mount to a halt. A haunted smile cracked his tired expression.

"We have made it," he said solemnly. There were seabirds in the distance, drifting wraithlike in the moonbeams, and the torches stirred fitfully in the breeze.

"Welcome home," said Richius. He stared up at the citadel in reverence, awed by its unnatural beauty. He had heard stories of this place since the time he first came to Lucel-Lor. It was the birthplace of the revolution, and in the hearts of all who struggled here the name "Falindar" had a certain infamy. He watched Lucyler's eyes glow, and wondered if he had looked the same upon seeing Aramoor again.

"Did I not tell you it was beautiful?"

"It's more than I expected," answered Richius. "No wonder Tharn kept it for himself."

"No, Richius, please," Lucyler implored. "Let us not have that argument again. Not now."

Richius agreed, but the little tugging at his conscience wouldn't be ignored. Falindar had fallen on the first night of the revolution, victim of a Drol attempt to free their leader from the citadel's prison. The attack had forced the Daegog into exile, and had thrown Lucyler and the other men loyal to the Triin leader into chaos, scattering them to the corners of Lucel-Lor. Just how Lucyler had come to forget his plight was a mystery to Richius. But then he looked again on the magnificent citadel and he understood. The place was a diamond, shimmering darkly in the night. It was perhaps the finest man-made thing Richius had ever seen, so much more holy than the Cathedral of the Martyrs in Nar. For all its science and superstructure, the Black City had nothing to rival the beauty of Falindar.

"I'm envious of you," he said quietly. "Come, let's go quickly. The sooner I'm done here, the sooner I can return home myself."

"It is late, Richius. I doubt you will be seeing Tharn tonight."

"Late? I've traveled for three weeks to get here. I'm sure your lord can endure the inconvenience of some lost sleep."

Lucyler made to speak, but the sudden appearance of an approaching rider silenced him. The horseman blazed out of the darkness, unmistakably Triin in his militant ensemble. His hair didn't gleam white, but instead was dyed cucumber green, and half the wild face beneath the shocking mane was green, too, smeared with greasy paint. A jacket of indigo covered him to the loins, girthed by a brilliant sash of gold. Around his head was belted the narrow skin of an animal, and doe-hide boots with long, looping laces rose up the length of his shanks. He was a picture of madness as he raced through the night, his loose clothes streaming out behind him like the tail of a comet.

"One of Kronin's," Richius remarked. He had seen this ilk before, many times. "A messenger?"

"A herald," replied Lucyler. "We have been seen."

The rider drove his horse furiously down the winding road, the obligatory jiiktar glimmering on his back. When he reached the newcomers he pulled back on the reins, bringing the lathered beast to a snorting stop. A great smile stretched across his painted face as he regarded Richius. Richius stared back at him.

"Joaala akka, Loocylr," said the warrior, tipping his head in respect. Lucyler returned the greeting with the same slight bow.

"Joaala akka, Hakan."

The warrior then turned to Richius, and this time his bow was slow and deep. He did not look upon Richius as he spoke, but kept his eyes fixed to the dark earth as he extended a long, incomprehensible greeting. When the stream of words finally ended the head stayed bowed. Richius looked questioningly at Lucyler.

"This is Hakan," said Lucyler. "One of Kronin's warriors. He welcomes you to Falindar and says he is pleased to meet you . . . *great king*."

Richius warmed to the man at once. "How should I answer him?"

"You can simply say thank you. Say *shay sar*."

"Shay sar, Hakan," said Richius, wrapping his tongue the best he could around the strange words. Hakan at last lifted his head. There was a disquieting awe to his expression, as though he expected something more. Richius had to look away.

"Why is he looking at me? Did I say it right?"

"I warned you, my friend," chuckled Lucyler. "You are a curiosity here. Yes, you said it right. Hakan is merely amused to see you." Lucyler turned to the warrior and spoke a few more words, to which Hakan replied with laughs and nods.

"I have told him that you are happy to be here," said Lucyler. "And that you are impressed by his home."

"His home? I thought it was Tharn's now. Do all of Kronin's men live here?"

"The citadel is home to many, as you will see. Kronin is Tharn's protector now, and all of his warriors are, too. When the war ended and Kronin's castle at Mount Godon was destroyed, he was brought here to live and continue his reign over Tatterak."

Hakan nodded agreeably, as if he understood. "Kuaoa akei eiunb, Kalak."

Richius felt his heart stop. Kalak? He turned to Lucyler and watched the Triin's face go even paler.

"Did he call me Kalak?"

"He does not understand," said Lucyler quickly, then broke into a string of words aimed squarely at the puzzled warrior. Hakan bowed his head again, uttering some low, apologetic gibberish.

"He asks your forgiveness," translated Lucyler. "He did not understand your offense. No insult was meant."

"Obviously not," said Richius, embarrassed by the man's apology. "Hakan," he said loudly. "Stop now. Lucyler, how do I tell him to stop?"

Lucyler spoke the order for him, and Hakan at last straightened, careful to speak only to Lucyler. Then the warrior bowed again to each of them, turned, and started off back up the long, dim road.

"He will go tell the others we are coming," said Lucyler.

"Kalak," spat Richius. "Am I never to be rid of that horrible name?"

"You are well known by that name here, Richius, but it is no insult.

Remember, Kronin and his people hate Voris as much as you do; more perhaps. That is why you are talked about here. They are not Drol. When they call you the Jackal, they do it proudly. You are the enemy of their enemy."

"I thought you told me Kronin and Voris are at peace now."

"And so they are. But that does not mean they care for each other. They endure the peace for Tharn's sake, nothing more."

"Your Tharn must really be something for so many men to follow him," said Richius caustically. "Perhaps he is a better sorcerer than any of you realize."

Lucyler ignored the gibe. "You will see for yourself soon enough."

"Indeed. But I won't meet him dressed like this," Richius said, peeling off the rancid garments he had disguised himself in since leaving Ackle-Nye. One by one the buttons of his cloak opened, until at last the leather of his uniform shone in the moonlight. He undid the cowl from around his neck and head, then stripped the cloak from his arms and back like the shedding skin of a snake. Once again he was in his armor of dark leather, displaying the proud blue dragon on his left breast. *Something for Tharn to see,* he thought. Something to remind him of a slaughtered war duke.

"There," he declared, dropping the disguise to the ground. "Much better."

Lucyler took the jiiktar off his back and prodded at the clothes with the weapon, hooking them with the curved blade and snatching them up.

"What are you doing?" asked Richius. "I'm not putting it back on, Lucyler."

"It is not for you," replied the Triin coolly. "There are many who can use such clothes. They should not be wasted."

"Wasted? But they're rags."

Lucyler quietly tucked the grimy clothing into his saddlebags. As if reminded of something, Richius peered into his own bags, satisfied to see a scarlet swatch of silk peeking from beneath his own folded clothes. A childlike grin danced on his face as he fingered the fine fabric. Dyana would adore it, he was sure.

"Ready?" he asked Lucyler eagerly. The Triin gave a gruff reply and they started up the smooth road toward the citadel. The air grew colder as they climbed, filling their noses with the briny scent of the sea. They could hear it dashing against the shore far, far below, could hear too the subtle cries of gulls as they winged through the night. It took them many minutes to crest the mountaintop, and when they did Richius felt dwarfed by the magnificent structure. Two immense gates of brass dominated the façade, flanked by twin spires of silver that disappeared into the blackness above them. On every wall and every terrace was a blooming tangle of vines. There were no battlements, only gardened balconies where little silhouettes shimmered in the moonlight like lovers on a river of light. The pale glow of the torches bathed the citadel in orange and sent their shadows winging against the silver stone, and the stone itself seemed vital and new, as if polished to a jewel's luster.

"You didn't exaggerate," said Richius, his head tilted back to find the end of the endless spires. "I am speechless."

The citadel's gates were opened wide to greet them. Richius pushed Lightning forward, not bothering to wait for his friend. From within the giant, enclosed courtyard he could hear voices, all chattering in the mysterious tongue of Lucel-Lor. Somewhere within these walls was Dyana. Would she be waiting for him? He peered through the court, and one by one the faces there popped into focus. A hush dropped over them as Richius rode into their midst.

He had expected to see nobles here, or whatever Tharn was calling his lackeys. What he saw instead was every form of destitute humanity. It was as if all of Ackle-Nye had been jammed into the place.

"Lucyler," he called over his shoulder. "What is this?"

They were coming up to him now, their eyes filled with a kind of childlike wonder. Old men and women, children with grimy faces, the ragged, the lame and the broken. Was this Falindar? Richius looked over the dirty heads to the high walls and noticed at once that they were barren, stripped of every kind of ornament, leaving only dark outlines where once, he was sure, things of value had been displayed. There were no paintings, no statues, no chandeliers or candelabras or gilded curtains. There was no carpeting, no tapestries hanging from the vaulted ceiling, no gold and no silver. Astounded, Richius gazed down on the swarm closing in around him. They were smiling at him. Each face wore the same ingratiating grin the warrior had shown. And there were warriors in this dismal mix, their blue garb unmistakable amid the drab grays and browns of the peasant folk. None spoke but all watched, fascinated by the Naren nobleman.

"What is this, Lucyler?" Richius asked again. "Who are these people?"

"They are the lost of Tatterak," replied Lucyler. "The ones left destitute by the war." He dug into his saddlebags and pulled out the ratty cloak, tossing it into the crowd. A quick little man in tattered clothes snatched it up.

"Do all these people live here?"

"Not all. Many live in the hills and try to farm. But there is not much left for them. Gayle's men were not as kind as your Edgard, Richius. In the last days of the war they destroyed everything they could, burning villages and even forests so the people here couldn't build new homes. Most of them have no place else to go. That is why they are here, for shelter and food. This is a place of the people now, by Tharn's decree."

"But it's been almost a year. Surely they have rebuilt by now."

Lucyler shook his head sadly. "They are trying, but there is not much left to build with. Tatterak is mostly rock. So all are welcome in the citadel now, to live here if they wish or to simply take a meal. There is not much food, but it is rationed and everyone gets something."

"Dear God," whispered Richius. "I had no idea things were so bad here. Why didn't you tell me, Lucyler?"

"Because I did not want you to worry about the woman. And because I wanted you to see it for yourself. You did not believe me when I told you Tharn is a man of peace. But here is the proof. Everything of value has been stripped from this place and given to the needy so that they may barter for the things they require. This whole area was ruined, but Tharn is trying to restore it."

"But they were not so poor in Dandazar," Richius pointed out. "What happened here?"

"Dandazar was far from the war. All the lands between here and Mount Godon were ruined. It is like this almost everywhere there was fighting. All burned. All gone."

Richius threw up his hands. "I don't understand this at all," he said bitterly. "Tharn was the cause of the war. Have all these people forgotten that? He is to blame for their plight, yet they follow him. It doesn't make sense."

"Tharn has united them," Lucyler said bleakly. "He is touched by the gods."

"Nonsense. Look at this mess. None of this would have happened if not for him. You say he brought peace to Lucel-Lor, but all I see is the destruction of war. He freed Lucel-Lor from Nar only to ruin it." Richius paused, shaking his head. "Where is Dyana? Is she living here with these refugees?"

"Do not worry," said Lucyler. "The woman is well looked after. She lives in the upper rooms of the citadel in her own chamber. Tharn takes care of her."

I'm sure, thought Richius angrily. *Just like he takes care of the rest of them.*

"I want to see her," he demanded. "Now."

"First you should see Tharn," said Lucyler. "Dyana is his wife, after all."

"Fine. As long as it's quick."

They began to dismount when a figure appeared out of the crowd. The gathering parted a little as he neared. A warrior, Richius realized at once, and something more. He was taller than the other Triin, but no less thin, with a body as lithe as a reed. His hair was streaked with shades of lime, and his eyes shone steel gray past the green belt of paint encircling his face like a blindfold. He wore the indigo jacket of Tatterak's tribe, but his was cinched not with a sash but with the wide, spotted hide of a snow leopard. The same skins draped from his narrow shoulders in a cape that dragged along the floor as he walked. Here among the tattered he looked truly regal, and Richius guessed his identity instantly.

"Kronin."

Kronin, warlord of Tatterak and archnemesis of Voris the Wolf, glided through the crowd effortlessly, his head high and determined as he locked eyes with Richius. Two golden chains linked around his boots jingled with his stride, as did his bracelets and dangling earrings. In less than a moment he was before them. And then the warlord of Tatterak fell to one knee before Richius, bowing his head to the floor. He took Richius' hand in his own and brought it carefully to his lips, then placed the most gentle of kisses on it. Amazed, Richius glanced over at Lucyler for an explanation, but the Triin seemed as stunned as he was. This was a greeting one would expect in Nar, not from a warlord of Lucel-Lor. Richius was shocked that Kronin would even know of the custom.

"Joaala akka," said Kronin silkily. "Tew banney Totterahk jin joanay." The warlord rose to his feet without waiting for an answer. He regarded Richius dutifully.

"Kronin greets you, Richius," began Lucyler. "He says it is a high honor to meet you, and that you are welcome in Tatterak always."

Richius beamed. "Please tell him that this is a great honor for me as well. Tell him that I have heard much of him, and that he is spoken of in Aramoor as the bravest of all Lucel-Lor's warlords."

Kronin's face split with a wide smile as he listened to Lucyler's translation. Again he spoke, directly to Richius.

"He says your words glorify him," Lucyler continued. "He wishes that he had been with you in the valley, and that you had been able to slay Voris."

Richius laughed, unsure how to answer. For a man at peace, Kronin still seemed obsessed with his Drol enemy. Kronin laughed, too, a brassy guffaw that belied his lean stature. Then the warlord of Tatterak hooked his thumbs into his leopard-skin belt and sighed.

"Eedgod," he said sadly. When Richius shrugged he repeated the word, this time pointing to the dragon insignia emblazoned on Richius' breast. "Eedgod."

"Edgard!" realized Richius. "Yes. Lucyler, tell him we were of the same brigade."

Kronin nodded as Lucyler translated, then broke into a fanciful speech, raising and dropping his arms and putting his hand to his heart.

"Edgard was a great man," said Lucyler. "The warlord says he was broken by the news of his death."

Richius smiled bleakly at Kronin. "I understand. Thank you, Kronin. Shay sar."

Kronin cooed like a boy at hearing his language from Richius. "Tryn?" he asked.

Lucyler shook his head. "Eya," he answered the warlord. "Kronin wanted to know if you spoke our tongue," he explained.

Kronin pointed his finger at himself, then to Lucyler, then to Richius. He spoke very slowly, as if trying to give Richius time to understand.

"What's he saying, Lucyler?"

"He says that he will be here for you, too. If you need anything, you are to come to him. He also asks that you sit with him at the feast tomorrow."

"Feast? What feast?"

"In celebration of Casadah. Tharn has invited all of Tatterak to share in the celebration. Falindar will be open to everyone, and there will be a banquet in honor of the day. Kronin asks for your company at the banquet."

Richius gestured skeptically at the peasants filling the hall. "How can Tharn afford a banquet? These people look starved."

"Everyone has been saving their best for Casadah," said Lucyler. "And anyone who has food has been asked to bring it so that it may be shared."

Kronin nodded, feigning understanding. He was waiting for an answer.

"What shall I tell him, Richius?"

"Tell him I would be honored to feast with him tomorrow, but that I may be on my way early. I will enjoy his company as long as I can. Ask him also if he would be willing to answer a question from me."

Lucyler translated, and Kronin nodded.

"Please ask him if I may see Tharn tonight. Tell him that I have much to discuss with his master."

Lucyler hesitated, then asked the question anyway. Kronin's smile melted away. He turned to Lucyler and answered in a low, distressed voice. Lucyler exchanged more words with the warrior, then glanced at Richius.

"I am sorry, Richius," began Lucyler haltingly. "Kronin says you cannot meet with Tharn tonight."

"But why? Doesn't he know I'm here?"

"He has been told. But Kronin says that he is . . . occupied."

Richius could hardly hide his exasperation. "Occupied? What's that supposed to mean? Ask him again."

Lucyler shook his head. "I will not. He has explained it to me already. It is impossible."

"What about Dyana, then? Can I see her?"

Lucyler's face crinkled. "That is not possible, either."

Richius looked from one to the other before putting the fractured pieces of their conversation together. "He's with her, isn't he?" he asked.

"Tharn is with his wife," replied Lucyler. "I am sorry, Richius. But listen to me, it is not what you think."

Richius laughed bitterly. "Oh, no. I'm sure you're right. What do you think they're up to, eh? A card game?"

"Easy," warned Lucyler. Kronin was staring intently at Richius, obviously confused by his outburst. "You must trust me. What you are imagining is wrong."

"I'm a grown man, Lucyler. You needn't spare my feelings. Tell Kronin I accept what he has said and that I'll see him tomorrow."

"Richius, let me explain. . . ."

"Just tell him, Lucyler."

Lucyler did as Richius asked. Kronin listened courteously, bowing to both of them when the conversation was over then disappearing into the crowd. When he had gone Richius let out a gigantic sigh.

"I'm very tired, Lucyler," said Richius. "Could you find me some quarters?"

"Yes, you should rest. Come, I will take you up into the north tower."

Lucyler led Richius through the courtyard to a place where they could take their horses, conversing with the man there to look after them. Richius was careful to take all of his belongings with him, unstrapping his saddlebags and his crossbow from Lightning's back. They then went through a confusing maze of hallways, all as bleak as the great hall, and finally up an endless spiral staircase fitted with oil lamps along its curving walls. They climbed for what seemed an eternity, coming at last to another labyrinthine circuit of halls.

"This is where the better quarters are," said Lucyler. "My own rooms are up here."

Richius looked around, unimpressed. The place seemed as barren as the rest of the citadel. But he relished the quiet, thinking that soon he would be blissfully asleep behind one of the hall's many doors. And then another, more interesting thought occurred to him.

"Are Tharn's quarters here?"

"No. They are in another wing of the tower. Come, I will take you to my chamber. You can sleep there for the night. Tomorrow I will find you quarters of your own."

They came to a narrow, rounded doorway near the end of the main hall. Outside of the chamber was a sconce holding a small candle, already burned half away. The candle was unlit. Lucyler took it from the sconce and dipped its tip in a nearby oil lamp, setting its wick aflame. When he opened the door to his chamber the tiny flame painted the room with a dull orange glow.

"Come in," said Lucyler quietly, waving Richius into the chamber. Except for the small illumination of the candle flame and a struggling sliver of moonlight from the window, the room was dark. It was not much bigger than a room one might find in an inn, and hardly as well appointed. There was a single bed of wood covered with a cotton mattress, a washbasin with a water pitcher, and little else. The floor was strewn with miscellaneous items, clothes mostly, and some books with bindings like those in the Empire. A chair in the corner of the room was also buried under a stack of possessions, unrecognizable in the darkness. Richius couldn't help but wonder which of them would wind up sleeping on the chair. He added to the mess by dropping his saddlebags and crossbow by the doorway.

"There is not much room," said Lucyler apologetically. He put the candle gently into a silver holder by the bedside. It was the only thing of seeming value in the place.

"It's fine," replied Richius cheerfully. "Hell, I'd be happy to sleep on the floor after what we've been through."

"No need. Take the bed. I will not be coming back tonight."

"Oh?" asked Richius, trying to cover his pleasure. He sat down on the bed, testing its comfort with a slight bounce and finding it exquisite. "Why not?"

Lucyler hesitated for a moment before answering. "I have things to attend to. I must let people know I have returned."

Richius was already pulling off his boots. He dropped them to the carpet with a thud. "You're going to see Tharn, aren't you?"

The Triin grimaced with embarrassment. "Not just Tharn. There are others I must talk to, friends I have not seen in a long while. Are you hungry? I could fetch something."

"But you will see Tharn."

Lucyler sighed. "If I can, yes. If he is not occupied."

"Occupied," said Richius. There was that horrible euphemism again. "When you see him tell him that I wish to meet with him as early as possible tomorrow. If he is not occupied, of course."

"You are worrying yourself over nothing, my friend. Tharn is not with Dyana the way you imagine."

"You keep saying that, Lucyler, but you never explain yourself. I've been asking you about Tharn for weeks now." He lay back on the mattress. "Are you ready to tell me yet?"

He heard his friend shuffle toward the door. "Tharn will be at the feast tomorrow. I could explain it to you, but it is best you see for yourself. Trust me tonight, and do not worry about Dyana. You will sleep better if you believe me."

"I'm too tired to argue," said Richius despondently. He rolled over and blew out the candle, so that all he could see was Lucyler's pale face in the doorway.

"Rest well. I will see you in the morning," said Lucyler gently, then silently closed the door.

Richius listened to the booted feet disappear down the hall, until all he could hear was the distant cry of wind and his own rhythmic breaths. Closing his eyes, he nestled his head back against the mattress, trying to push Dyana from his thoughts. Yet his mind's eye was filled with her. Tonight he would lie awake and think of her in the arms of his enemy, and torture himself over the sweetness of their love-making.

The great feast of Casadah was to be held in the giant banquet room on the ground floor of the citadel, close to the kitchens and the great-hall-turned-orphanage. All day Richius watched the transformation of the citadel, marveling at the women scurrying through the halls balancing trays of strange dishes, and at the men who came through the gates of the place burdened by the carcasses of freshly killed animals. Children scrambled underfoot, excited by the sounds and smells of the coming celebration, and folk from everywhere in Tatterak streamed into the citadel laden with baskets of their best. Musicians played on unusual pipes and sang their foreign, haunting songs, and holy men walked through the crowds telling stories and leading fiery prayers to Lorris and Pris, the gods for whom the day was consecrated. And all prepared themselves for the same thing Richius anticipated: the coming of Tharn.

It had been a quiet morning. Lucyler showed Richius the sights of Falindar, carefully avoiding the subject of Dyana and remaining conspicuously quiet about Tharn. They had gone to the very top of the citadel, to stand upon its wondrous roof garden and try to guess just how many miles they could see. The Drol had been given a flawless day for their holiday. The sky was a cloudless blue, and the gentle spring sun painted the hills and the sea with its brilliance. From their mountain perch they could see the endless plains of Tatterak stretching outward, halted only by the ocean that crashed against the citadel's founding cliff. And they watched the processions of pilgrims come—whole families on foot and wanderers on horseback—until by noon the road was choked with them and the common areas around the castle rang with the din of happy celebrants. The exotic scents of unknown herbs and seasoned meats drifted through the castle's many halls, and outside in the yards teenaged Triin wrestled playfully with Kronin's warriors and cajoled their female peers with displays of boyish charm. All was perfect, just as Lucyler promised—except for one thing.

Dyana was nowhere to be seen.

Not that Richius had expected to see her. He had guessed by Lucyler's shiftiness that he would not be seeing her until he first spoke to Tharn, and that wouldn't happen until after the feast. Perhaps tonight, he told himself anxiously, and did his best to relax into the mood of the day. When the feast finally came near sundown, he was famished from an afternoon of sightseeing. They watched in the crowded courtyard as the sun began to vanish behind the mountain peaks, the moment, Lucyler explained, when the feast of Casadah could begin. The great gathering finally hushed as they anticipated the coming of their cunning-man.

"We can go inside now," said Lucyler. "There is only enough space in the banquet room for some of us. The others will feast out here."

"Where will Tharn be?" asked Richius. "I want to see him first."

"He will speak to the people after the feast. Come, Kronin will be waiting for us."

Richius followed Lucyler into the citadel and down the halls packed with people, who viewed him with only passing curiosity. The banquet room was on the side of the castle nearest the ocean, a fair walk even when the place was empty, and they had to push their way across the floor, carefully navigating the maze of knees and elbows. When they finally reached the banquet chamber they found that it too was swelled to capacity, its huge windows all but invisible behind a curtain of white Triin flesh. Richius felt a passing uneasiness. The place was swarming with saffron robes, the favored garb of the Drol caste. There was a sprinkling of Kronin's blue-jacketed warriors, but for the most part it was a hive of yellow. Richius paused at the doorway, suddenly losing his prior appetite. They were all men, with long white hair like Lucyler's and serious expressions on their faces, and the only females in the room were modestly dressed servingwomen who floated daintily through the group with platters of steaming food.

Were all these sober men Drol priests? Richius hadn't expected to see so many. Gradually he inched into the room, hoping to go unnoticed until he found Kronin. The tall warlord was at the other end of the chamber, talking loudly with a trio of his men. Every head in the place turned as the first of them sighted Richius. The talking thinned to a curious murmur.

"Do not be worried," said Lucyler confidently. "You are Tharn's guest tonight."

Richius tried to harden his expression and they moved through the gathering toward Kronin. There were two conspicuously empty chairs near the warlord. A grander chair was beside Kronin's own, no doubt meant for Tharn.

"Did you speak to him last night?" asked Richius.

"I did. And now you will see why I've kept secrets from you."

Richius said nothing more, satisfied that he would soon have some answers. The talking in the chamber politely resumed. When they reached Kronin, the warlord stretched out his hands and greeted them loudly.

"Gaaye hoo, awakk!" proclaimed Kronin, looking around the room defiantly. He took Richius' hand and pulled him forward, placing an unexpected kiss on his cheek.

"Kronin greets his cherished friend," explained Lucyler with a chuckle. "And he wants everyone to know it."

"Shay sar, Kronin," said Richius, carefully pulling back his hand. The warriors whom Kronin had been speaking with dismissed themselves with flowery bows. Kronin bid them to their chairs, then sat down, his jewelry jingling like chimes. Richius sat next to the lord of Tatterak, grateful to have at least one ally in this room full of Drol. He leaned over to whisper in Lucyler's ear.

"Are all the men Drol cunning-men?"

Lucyler nodded. "They have come to celebrate this day with their leader. You should feel honored, Richius."

"I suppose," replied Richius dully. In a strange way he did feel honored. Voris wasn't here, and neither were any of the other warlords who had been loyal to Tharn during the war. Other than the cunning-men, only he, Lucyler, and Kronin were present, three men who had dedicated themselves to Tharn's destruction. Now Lucyler and Kronin wore smiles in the presence of the revolutionary, and the mystery of it all was about to be revealed. Shortly he would meet the man who had stolen his love and murdered Edgard.

Bring him on, he thought coldly. *I am ready.*

The scores of cunning-men took their seats at the round tables. The voices stilled. From outside the banquet room an anxious murmur grew among the Triin gathered in the hall. Soon the murmur became an impassioned cry.

Richius knew that his nemesis was near.

He tried to still his thundering heart with a few slow breaths, but the electricity of the moment had charged him. The chorus outside the banquet chamber intensified, droning on and on as the minutes passed and Tharn moved through the crowd toward his waiting cunning-men. Endless shouting and hopeful voices, all ringing out in praise for this man who had brought them war and widows. To Richius the sound was unfathomable. Never once had he heard such devotion for a leader, even in the heady days of his father's reign.

And then the chorus suddenly ebbed, as if Tharn had stilled it with a wave of his hand. The eyes in the banquet room fixed on the hall beyond, and the cunning-men rose silently from their seats. Kronin and his warriors did the same.

"Rise," whispered Lucyler, getting to his feet. Richius got up, waiting for a giant to step into the chamber. What he saw instead made his jaw slacken.

A stooped figure appeared in the doorway, one atrophied hand clutching a cane that shook beneath his weight. He was dressed in the saffron robes of a Drol holy man, his face partially covered by a hood that did little to obscure his poisoned features. He pulled himself with evident pain across the smooth floor, his gnarled walking stick barely supporting his drooping frame and the palsy-stiffened leg that dragged behind him. His face was a diseased mask of scars and sores, and his scalp was bare in parts where the tangled hair had fallen out in clumps. Two dark eyes shone from the depths of the cowl, and the lips that curled around the malformed jaw were spotted with yellow blisters. Tharn's left arm dangled at his side, its hand tightened into a useless club. Like the lepers and wounded veterans he protected, his body was a shattered, shambling mound of crooked bones and cracked skin, and when he moved his anguish projected itself to all who watched him struggle. It was as if old age had heaped all its worst maladies upon one young man, wrecking forever the good looks nature might have intended. To be complimentary was to say he was grotesque.

Richius watched with forced effort as Tharn dragged himself slowly through the banquet hall, amazed at the sight. How had this broken thing inspired the Drol to victory? It seemed impossible. And in all the stories he had heard of Tharn, never once had such infirmity been mentioned. Surely a man so deformed would have had names other than "Storm Maker." Tharn the Hideous would have been more apt, for it looked like he could hardly summon a cup of water, much less a storm. Richius understood with sudden clarity what Lucyler had been hinting; there was no way this man could share a bed with a woman. For him, the simple act of walking was exhausting.

When Tharn had made it halfway across the room, Kronin stepped forward and helped him the rest of the way to his chair. When he was sure his master was steady, Kronin released him, going back to stand beside his own chair. The crowd bowed their heads as Tharn raised his good hand and spoke.

A prayer, Richius guessed. Lucyler bowed his head with the others. Richius did not. He listened to Tharn's emaciated voice, like the straining of some untuned harp, sickly fascinated by the broken sounds. Even speaking seemed to sap the man's energy. He was not old, yet his voice was ancient, at times vanishing completely beneath the rasping of mucus. Yet he did not cease, but continued on with his prayer, finally lowering himself gratefully into his chair when he was done. When he was safely seated he bid the others to sit as well. Kronin clapped his hands, and the servingwomen in the corner came to life again. From outside the doorway several more women entered carrying a collection of instruments of ornate Triin design. At once the conversation sprang up again, and Kronin took his seat, a huge smile stretched across his face. He slapped Richius playfully across the back, forcefully enough to send his knees banging against the table. The warlord and Lucyler both laughed.

Richius laughed, too, albeit nervously, and shifted his eyes around the room to where the women were setting up their instruments.

Typically Triin, he thought cynically. The goddess Pris had done nothing to improve the lot of her gender.

The musicians started playing and singing and Richius began to relax, finally chancing a glance in Tharn's direction. The master of the citadel was engaged in conversation with another holy man, over his shoulder. Richius leaned closer to Lucyler.

"Not what I expected," he whispered. "What happened to him?"

"Later," replied Lucyler softly. "When we are alone."

"But—"

"Shhh."

Tharn was speaking again. He raised his scarred hand and gestured toward Richius, then to all the men seated around the circular tables. Servingwomen darted through the crowd, placing their platters of food before the hungry warriors. Kronin's men began devouring the stuff as they listened.

"What's he saying?" asked Richius. "Is it about me?"

Lucyler was laughing. "Yes, my friend. He is telling the cunning-men not to let your presence upset them. See how they look?"

It was true. The faces in the chamber were uniformly somber. Tharn pointed again at Richius.

"King Vantran," he rasped awkwardly. It had obviously been a long time since he had spoken the tongue of Nar, and the words sounded foreign even to Richius. The cunning-man had none of Lucyler's eloquence with the language. Tharn cleared his throat and started again, looking at Richius apologetically. "King Vantran. Welcome."

"Answer back in Naren," said Lucyler softly.

Richius straightened to address the monarch. "I thank you for the welcome, Master Tharn, and for your kindness in having me sup with you on your holiday."

Tharn managed what looked like a smile. "These others do not want you here, King Vantran. This is what I was saying."

Richius shrugged. "Then that is their problem, Master Tharn."

A scratchy laughter roiled out of Tharn's throat, followed by a fit of coughing. "It is, King Vantran." He settled down and looked at Richius seriously. "You wish to talk, I know. Lucyler has told me you are . . ." He paused to think of the word. "Anxious, yes?"

"Very," answered Richius.

"We will speak," said Tharn. "Tonight. Now we will eat. Casadah, King Vantran."

Richius turned to accept a cup of some steaming liquid from a servingwoman. The drink was thick and foul, like peppered vinegar. He raised the cup to Tharn in mock salute.

You asked me to come, remember? he mused. It upset him that Tharn was so willing to put him off, but he brought the cup to his lips and drank anyway. The hot liquid bit ferociously into his palate, startling him.

"What is that?" he barked, dropping the drink to the table and cupping his wounded lips. He could feel the blisters already starting to rise.

"Tokka," said Lucyler, enjoying his own cup with Kronin. "A spiced berry wine. You have to drink it carefully."

Richius pushed the cup away. "Or not at all."

"It is a traditional drink among the people of Tatterak," warned Lucyler. He pushed the cup back under Richius' nose. "Kronin will be offended. Drink."

"It's terrible, Lucyler. I can't."

"Pretend then."

"Tokka," said Kronin, prodding Richius with his elbow and pantomiming taking a drink.

"All right," said Richius wearily. "Tokka." He took another sip of the impossibly peppery liquor, almost gagging at its noxiousness. The serving-woman assigned to their table was setting down more cups and platters of food, each one less appetizing to Richius than the one before. There were whole fish swimming in green gravies, boiling bowls of red soup, and sliced meats piled high in leaning stacks, so fresh and raw that blood still dripped from the platter. Despite his hunger, the procession was unendurable. He watched the Triin devour their delicacies bare-handed, for there was no silverware on the table, only circles of puffy bread for grabbing up whatever looked enticing. Lucyler and Kronin dipped continuously into the communal platter placed before Richius, and the clatter of dishes being passed around sounded through the banquet room. The musicians played and sang, the warriors ate like ravenous dogs, and Richius swayed in his seat, sickened by the noise and the unpalatable odor of the cuisine. Kronin nudged him none too gently in the ribs.

"Ish umlat halhara do?"

Lucyler leaned over to translate. "He wants to know why you do not eat."

"I'm not hungry," said Richius politely. Kronin scowled at him, as if he understood the lie.

"It does not matter if you are hungry or not, Richius. On Casadah everyone eats. These people have endured starvation just for this day."

"I can't eat, Lucyler," said Richius through gritted teeth. "It's disgusting."

Lucyler reared back, stung by the insult. He put down his wedge of bread and grabbed hold of Richius' sleeve, pulling him close. "For over a year all I had to eat was whatever slop you and Dinadin could cook up. And I never complained. Now eat."

Richius recoiled. "You're right," he said sheepishly. "Dinadin was a terrible cook."

They both laughed and Lucyler picked out something he thought Richius could tolerate, a soupy lentil mixture for dipping breads and vegetables in. It wasn't too hot, and if he ate sparingly Richius found that he could stomach it. The sweetmeats and tangles of octopus tentacles he left for Kronin, who seemed to have a love for such bizarre fare. The warlord ate without end and barely broke for conversation, and it was easy to tell his favorites from all the stains on his lapel. Lucyler was less extreme. He consumed his food daintily, the way he always had in the Dring Valley, careful to choose things he knew he would finish without waste. His manners were more like the cunning-men than the warriors. While the warriors ate as if they were about to battle giants, the Drol holy men seemed more concerned with conversation than with the plethora of food. They spoke genteelly, raising toasts to Tharn and sometimes joining in the more sedate songs, and at their master's order were wholly unconcerned now with the Naren among them.

Tharn too seemed undisturbed by Richius. He hardly looked at him at all, only occasionally flashing him one of his deformed smiles. The master of Falindar ate practically nothing, playing with his food the way a child does and drinking water instead of wine. Richius followed Tharn's example, waving over one of the women to fill his now-empty tokka cup with the blessedly tasteless drink. The water slid down his burning gullet like a spring breeze. He turned to offer some to Lucyler, who simply shrugged indifferently.

"I don't know how you can manage this food," said Richius. "It's so hot."

"You will get used to it."

"No, thanks." Richius glanced around the table and saw that the others were well liquored now, engaged in overloud conversations. A good chance to try again, he reasoned. "Tell me about Tharn," he whispered to Lucyler. "What happened to him?"

"No," said the Triin, exasperated. "The others may hear us."

"No one's going to hear us. They can't even understand us. Come on, tell me. Is it a disease?"

"Not a disease," answered Lucyler. "A judgment."

"What do you mean? Someone did that to him?"

"The gods made him this way."

"The gods? Oh, no, Lucyler. Don't say it."

"Keep your voice down," chided Lucyler. "I told you about his powers but I did not tell you why he will not use them anymore, remember?"

Richius nodded. It was one of the things about Tharn he was most curious about.

"Do you recall that day in the valley when I told you about the Drol?"

"You said they would never use magic to harm another living being, I remember. So?"

"Is it not obvious?" asked Lucyler. "Look at him."

"Lucyler, he has leprosy, or some other disease. That doesn't prove anything."

"He was not diseased until he used his powers to end the war, Richius. He used them to kill your Naren brothers, and the gods punished him for it."

Richius rolled his eyes. "You're really falling for him, aren't you? You never believed that nonsense before. It's a coincidence, nothing more."

"It is not coincidence," said Lucyler. "His power is from heaven. But the gods give their gifts for unknown reasons, and they are never to be used to kill." Again he gestured toward Tharn. "You see the consequences there. He delivered us from Nar, and now he suffers for it."

"Well, he'd better be willing to pay again," said Richius blackly. "He'll need his powers if he hopes to defeat Arkus."

"He will not do it again. He has sworn it. The gods have spoken to him through his body. He knows now that what he did was wrong."

"Oh, I think he'll change his mind," said Richius playfully. "When he sees the legions of Nar."

"He will not!" said Lucyler, slamming his fist down on the table and rattling the glasses. The others around the table glanced at him, but he continued fiercely, "Can you not see what has happened here? He is a prophet, Richius. Sent by the gods to unite Lucel-Lor. And when he broke with them he suffered. To me it is very plain."

"All right," said Richius. "Believe what you want, I don't care. I'm only here for Dyana. I will speak with him tonight. If he releases her, I'll talk to Arkus for him and be on my way in the morning. I only hope he means what he says. He will talk to me tonight, won't he?"

"He has much on his mind," replied Lucyler. "There is a reason why he did not see you last night."

"And you're not going to tell me what it is."

Lucyler sipped languidly at his drink. "Right."

"Your loyalties have certainly changed," said Richius, more disappointed than angry. "I remember a time when you didn't keep secrets from me."

Lucyler sighed. "*Times* have changed. You do not know Tharn the way I do, not yet at least. If you did you would understand."

"I don't want to understand, Lucyler. I just want to get Dyana out of here."

They ate in relative silence for a time, until a small Triin woman entered the banquet room. She was dressed in a simple white frock, unremarkable except for the blotchy crimson stains it bore. An expression of worry suffused her face. She dashed across the banquet room and up to Tharn, bending down to whisper in the monarch's ear. Tharn's hideous face blanched, his eyes widening horribly. There was an abrupt exchange between the two before Tharn struggled to his feet, calling out to Kronin to help him. The warlord sprang from his chair and was at his master's side in an instant, lifting him up and guiding him toward the doorway. The music and eating stopped, and all watched with alarm as Tharn painfully left the room, obviously pushing his body to its limits as he limped away.

"What is it, Lucyler?" asked Richius. "What's happening?"

"It is what I warned you of," answered Lucyler. "I'm sorry, Richius. You will not be seeing Tharn tonight."

TWENTY-EIGHT

When Renato Biagio was a boy, he lived in splendor on the southerly island of Crote, a tiny nation renowned for its wine, its love of art and food, and its temperamental inhabitants. For nearly two centuries the Biagio family ruled Crote, growing fat on its olives and the sweat of its peasants, and ruling their dominion from a sparkling villa of marble and gold, a palace surrounded by beaches and crystalline seas and hung with giant windows that drank in the island's hot sun and turned the skin of the royal family amber.

The young Renato enjoyed a regal existence in his ancestral home. His every need was met instantly, and his every curiosity was satisfied by his father's many servants. When he grew to manhood, there were slaves to pacify his lusts. Like most Crotans, Renato Biagio's tastes were varied, and keeping himself from boredom was always a challenge. He had books and music rooms to occupy his mind, men and women to please his body, and all the wealth of a Crotan nobleman with which to explore the world. But he was landlocked in those days, for in his youth the world beyond the seas was dangerous. The Black Renaissance was sweeping the continent, and little Crote was soon to be caught up in Arkus' grand design. Ever restless, Renato Biagio watched the Black Renaissance swallow nations, watched the ideals of Nar and its passionate emperor with youthful longing, and hoped for the day when it would reach the untouchable shores of his island prison. His father, a man of meager imagination, was quite incapable of foreseeing the military giant his foppish son would become.

Talistan wasn't Crote. It was cold and rugged, and the people here had the skin tone of cadavers. But it was quiet in the House of Gayle, and the inactivity afforded Biagio time to consider things. Since Blackwood Gayle's departure to Lucel-Lor, some weeks ago now, the castle had seemed deserted. The absence of the baron and his army had given Biagio time to plan. Only occasionally was he interrupted here, usually by servants seeing to his numerous needs, and he never once saw the ailing king of Talistan, Blackwood Gayle's decrepit father. Like his son, Tassis Gayle had always been loyal to Nar, and he had given his blessing to let the head of Arkus' Roshann use his home as a command base.

And command he did. Biagio had worked wisely these past weeks, hurrying Blackwood Gayle and his horsemen into Lucel-Lor to find a cure for the emperor. He had conscripted the fools of Aramoor, enslaving them to Talistanian masters, and he had sent the Lady Sabrina to the citadel of Falindar in search of her wayward husband. Sure that he was doing all he could to aid his beloved Arkus, Biagio was moderately satisfied. He had even summoned an old friend to the House of Gayle.

This morning Biagio awoke at the same time he always did, just past dawn. As was customary, the house slave assigned to him provided him with a light breakfast of tea and biscuits and a little jar of jam. Biagio dressed before pouring himself a cup of tea, then took his steaming drink to the giant window and opened it, stepping out onto a sizable balcony. His chambers provided a magnificent view of the cold ocean, and though he usually shunned the cool morning air, Biagio decided to rest a moment outside and let the sea remind him of his far-off Crote. He dragged a chair out onto the balcony and sat down, sipping at his hot beverage as his sluggish blood thawed. A slight tremor rippled through his hand, making his teacup shiver. The count put a palm to his forehead and felt the skin. Freezing, he decided with a frown. He would need another treatment soon. It was a small matter really, since he never traveled anywhere without his life-sustaining drug, but the treatments were uncomfortable and bothersome, especially when he had things on his mind. Tonight, perhaps. Or definitely tomorrow . . .

The count stopped fretting when an object on the horizon snared his gaze. His sharp eyes focused out across the sea. A ship was approaching. A very large ship. Count Biagio smiled.

"Hello, my friend," he said, getting to his feet. "Welcome to Talistan."

It took the *Fearless* almost an hour to reach the coast. The giant flagship of the Black Fleet crested the seas like a leviathan, parting the waves effortlessly under its enormous keel. Its triple masts and dozen dark sails swelled with the ocean air, bearing the warship toward land at a speed that seemed impossible for such an immense craft. At its center mast, flying high and proud, was a single flag of black.

Count Biagio greeted the arrival of the *Fearless* with glee. It had been far too many months since he had seen the proud vessel, and the sight of the beautiful war machine heartened him. She was the pride of the Black Fleet, the terrible messenger of Arkus. Rimmed with flame cannons and stout with fighting men, she was unequaled in all the world's navies. Just like her commander.

Admiral Danar Nicabar stepped lightly from the dinghy that brought him ashore, his polished boots sinking fast into the wet sand of Talistan. When he saw his old comrade, a devious grin cracked his rocky face. He was a tall man, and only rarely did his countenance change to express pleasure. Like his flagship, Danar Nicabar was peerless, the most excellent naval commander the Black Fleet had ever produced. Because he was a member of the Iron Circle, his eyes shone the same narcotic blue as Biagio's, a trait all who used the drugs shared. He was crass and terrible, and Biagio counted him among his closest friends.

"Danar," said Biagio with exuberance. The delicate count waited for Nicabar to step out of the mud before going to meet him. They embraced. Biagio kissed the admiral's cheek, ignoring the inquisitive stares of the sailors that had brought the officer ashore, then took Nicabar's giant hand and led him away.

"You've come quicker than I expected," said Biagio. "I'm glad."

"I am not," said Nicabar harshly. "Renato, what am I doing here?"

Biagio smiled. He had expected the admiral's poor reaction to his summons. "When did you get my message? Where were you? Near Liss?"

The admiral shook his head. "Off of Casarhoon. We were on our way back to Nar City when your message arrived. I had news I wanted to bring Arkus." Nicabar looked up at the looming House of Gayle in the distance. "Renato, what is all this? What's happened?"

"It's a very long story," sighed the count. He put his arm around Nicabar's shoulders and directed him toward the castle. "Come. There are too many ears here."

Nicabar didn't protest, but let his fellow Naren guide him along. As they walked, Biagio explained the recent happenings in Aramoor and Talistan, how Richius Vantran had betrayed them and how Blackwood Gayle had been tapped to take up the mission. Nicabar listened without interrupting, nodding severely when he heard of Arkus' dire state.

"This is why I'm going to Nar," the admiral explained. "I've heard about the emperor's state. I thought my news from Liss would hearten him."

Biagio's eyebrows went up. "They are beaten then? Finally?"

"Very nearly," declared Nicabar with pride. "They haven't been resist-
ing us or attacking. I think their schooners are finally finished."

Very diplomatically, Biagio looked away. "My friend, don't take
offense. . . ."

Nicabar stopped walking and scowled. "I'm not wrong, Renato. Not
this time. I tell you, I have them. Liss will fall within the month. That's
my promise. I only need the emperor's word to finish them. If he gives it
to me, I will take him myself to see their death."

"Is that why you're going to Nar?" laughed Biagio. "To prove yourself
to Arkus? The emperor cannot travel, Danar, you know that. Really,
what an asinine idea."

"Is it? I thought Arkus could do with the news. Maybe it would do
more to revive him than these damned drugs."

Biagio held up a finger. "Listen now," he cautioned. "I haven't called
you here to argue. I need you, Danar. Arkus needs you."

"For what?" asked Nicabar impatiently. "I have work. . . ."

"Stop. Your mission in Liss is ended, at least for now."

Danar Nicabar went ashen. "What . . . ?"

"I need your ships, Danar. It's important."

"What for?" growled Nicabar. "Liss is down, I tell you. Another
month and—"

"Another month is too long," snapped Biagio. "I need your ships *now*.
They have to begin landing troops in Lucel-Lor."

"No," roared Danar. "My dreadnoughts aren't cargo barges! They're
warships. I won't allow it."

Biagio struggled for patience. "Blackwood Gayle is riding for Lucel-
Lor with his horsemen. I've already summoned a legion from Nar City to
follow him in. But they're on foot, Danar. They'll have to take Ackle-
Nye, and then the Dring Valley. It could take them forever to subdue
Lucel-Lor that way. We need to land troops throughout the territories,
deal with the warlords one by one. I need ships to do that."

"I already have a mission, Renato," said Nicabar defiantly. "To take
Liss."

"I'm changing your mission."

"You're not admiral of the fleet! Who are you to change my mission?"

The question was absurd, and Biagio could tell Nicabar regretted it.
"You're a good friend, Danar. I will forget that question."

Danar Nicabar inclined his head in deference. He was the head of the
Black Fleet, one of the highest military men in all of the Empire, but that
title was nothing to the sway Biagio had over Arkus. Except for the Bishop
Herrith—a man whose influence over Arkus was almost magical—
Renato Biagio was clearly the emperor's favorite, and didn't need an im-
perial seal to change the direction of the navy.

"I don't ask this lightly, Danar," continued the count. "I know you think your honor is in the balance. But if you're right about Liss, they will wait for you."

Nicabar closed his eyes and gritted his teeth. "They may rebuild. Without the blockade . . ."

"They will wait. And this mission in Lucel-Lor is more important. The Triin land is too vast to take through the Saccenne Run alone. We need your navy, Danar. We need to land troops throughout their continent if we're to find the magic in time for Arkus."

"We all die, my friend," said Nicabar. "Even Arkus."

"No. Arkus cannot die. He is immortal. He will go on forever. Like his Black Renaissance." Count Biagio smiled sadly. "We will see to that, Danar. You and I, and Blackwood Gayle."

"Gayle is a coward and a clown," sneered Nicabar. "You shouldn't have trusted him with something so important."

"I had no choice. The Vantran boy betrayed us, and Blackwood Gayle was our only option."

Nicabar tapped his fingertip against Biagio's skull. "You're slipping, old man. Didn't I warn you about Vantran?"

"You did," admitted Biagio. "And I tried to warn Arkus. But it was too late."

"And now he's made a fool of you," laughed Nicabar. "My poor Renato. How will this look to Arkus, I wonder? And to Herrith? Oh, the bishop is having a good laugh at your expense, I'm sure. Don't you think?"

Biagio closed his eyes and in his keen mind summoned up a picture of Richius Vantran. "The boy may have won a battle, Danar, but not the war. I've already sent his wife to him with a message. When he gets it, he will learn what it means to trifle with Count Biagio."

TWENTY-NINE

Three days after Casadah, Richius was still waiting for Tharn.
He passed the long hours exploring the citadel and its mountain, and writing in his journal about his frustrations. On the night of the holy day he had been given his own quarters, a sparsely furnished room in the north tower not far from Lucyler's room, with a window that overlooked the ocean and let him write by moonlight. Lucyler was gone most of the time, off on errands or some other mysterious business, leaving Richius to wander through Falindar unchaperoned.

The citadel had been remarkably quiet since the holy day. There were no more pilgrims swelling the halls, just the usual homeless peasants and their flocks of children, all of whom stayed on the ground floor, never venturing high enough for Richius to hear them. What little he did hear from the warriors and servants he couldn't understand anyway, but occasionally he caught snippets of the name "Tharn" and wondered how the master of Falindar fared.

It had been blood he had seen on the woman's clothes, he was sure of it. Lucyler denied it, but it didn't matter. Something was terribly amiss in the citadel, something grave enough to keep Tharn from making his address to the people who had ventured to Falindar to hear him. Richius could only assume it was Dyana who ailed. He had begged Lucyler to tell him more, but his friend only offered him transparent lies, telling him that nothing was wrong. So Richius was left to worry, alone and terrified for Dyana and wondering just when Tharn would finally keep his promise to speak to him. It would have to be soon, Richius reasoned. War was brewing. Tharn would have to act quickly if he truly hoped to stop it.

On his fourth morning in Falindar, Richius awoke to the usual breakfast of bread and honey, a welcome treat that Lucyler always placed silently near his bedside while he slept. Each morning he devoured the food hungrily, hoping that soon he would be eating Jenna's fine cooking again and smoking a pipe at the hearthside with Jojustin. Bread was frighteningly scarce in Falindar, and what little there was was rationed. But Richius was a guest here, Lucyler had explained, and since he found everything else unpalatable he was given as much as he wanted, a privilege Richius tried not to abuse. When the night finally came he was always starving again, and his sleep was punctuated by thoughts of breakfast.

This day he wrote while he ate. Careful to make his bread last, he tore off tiny bits from the round loaves, dipping them liberally in the small crock of honey just as he dipped his quill in the inkwell. Fresh morning light poured into the dull chamber as he lay on his soft bed, his breakfast tray poised neatly on a chair beside him. Since coming to Falindar he had written more than in all the few weeks prior. Time had been sparse for writing when they were traveling through Lucel-Lor, and what little notes he had jotted in his journal had been written by moonlight just as weariness was overtaking him. Now he had all the time needed, and made use of it by describing the changes he had seen in Lucel-Lor.

Today's entry began with a bleak confession.

Lucyler was right, he penned at the top of the page. *There is peace in Lucel-Lor, a kind I would never have imagined. They follow their madman with love.*

He paused. Was Tharn a madman? Richius still wasn't sure. Tharn was a murderer, certainly, but his sanity remained in question. Perhaps when they spoke he would learn the truth. . . .

There was an unexpected knock on the door. Richius raised his head curiously, startled by the intrusion. Only Lucyler had visited him since coming here, and Lucyler never knocked. Richius lowered the quill and set his journal aside, going to the door and pulling it open carefully. On the other side was Kronin, looking wholly unfamiliar without his usual face paint. He wore no jewelry, either, and his shirt was sorely wrinkled. The warlord's eyes were dull from lack of sleep. He bowed to Richius as the door opened.

"Tharn," he stated simply. He pointed to Richius, then down the empty corridor.

"He wants me now?" asked Richius. Kronin looked at him with puzzlement. "Yes, of course." Dashing back into the chamber, he sat down on the bed and pulled on his long boots, then tore off a great chunk of bread and stuffed it in his mouth as he did up the laces. Kronin watched

him indifferently, shaking his head when Richius offered a loaf for sharing. Before they left the room Richius tucked his journal neatly in his bag,
hiding it beneath the dress he had purchased for Dyana. Then he ran his
fingers through his hair, patting down his cowlick as he followed Kronin
from the chamber.

All was quiet as they moved through the empty hall. At just past dawn,
very few of the citadel's inhabitants were awake, and Richius walked as
soundlessly as possible, careful not to disturb those still asleep. He trailed
Kronin down the endless staircase until they came to another passage
halfway down. Narrow and gloomy, the passage led them to yet another
flight of spiral stairs, which they began to ascend.

The south tower, Richius guessed. It was where Lucyler had told him
Tharn was quartered. Most likely he would find Dyana here. A schoolboy excitement rippled through him. He could almost feel her presence as
he neared her, and the faint memory of her sweet-smelling hair ignited in
his mind. *At last,* he told himself silently. *At last.*

But he would have to speak to Tharn first. He steeled himself as they
reached the top of the stairs.

Like the hall that led to his own chambers, this one was furnished in
the new style of Falindar, its bare walls decorated only by an occasional
lamp or candle. It had as many doors as its sister tower, too, all presumably leading to poorly appointed apartments. He listened intently for a
familiar voice as they strode down the hall, cocking his head slightly at
each passing door. Only an occasional snore reached him.

Up one more small flight of stairs, they came at last to a partially open
door. Dusty sunlight and the sound of labored breathing leaked from the
bottom of the portal. Kronin knocked once, then pushed the door open
and stepped aside for Richius. The room was larger than the other chambers, though no more spacious, for it was cluttered from floor to ceiling
with shelves and stacks of books and papers. Across the room, near one
of its three windows, was an ancient desk, also covered with papers. As
Richius stepped into the room the man seated at the desk looked up.

"Come," croaked Tharn listlessly. He looked tired, his skin all the
more hideous in the sunlight. Kronin walked away without dismissing
himself and Richius stepped into the room. There was an empty chair beside the desk, the only furniture not burdened by a load of manuscripts.
Tharn bid Richius to sit.

"Thank you," said Richius uneasily, taking to the chair. Tharn no
longer wore his cowl, but instead let his scalp shine in the morning light.
Scars of red and yellow boiled up from his skull where the hair had died
away, and what hair there was grew in spotty patches, long and unman-
ageable and lacking the customary Triin sheen. Richius studied him. He
had seen victims of such awful diseases before. Leprosy was common in

the Empire, and among the Naren beggars who once filled Ackle-Nye. His own troops had battled terrible, flesh-rotting foot ailments in the moist Dring Valley. But Tharn's case was shockingly severe, and Richius could only imagine the unendurable pain of it. He recalled with morbid irony his audience with Arkus, and how the emperor and his fiendish circle had all taken drugs for years to sustain themselves. How laughable that they thought this broken man owned the secret to eternal life. Tharn was in far more need of their narcotics than they were of his useless magics.

Tharn shifted awkwardly in his seat, trying to straighten his back as he faced Richius. "I have not thanked you for coming here," he said thickly. "You have done me a service."

"I have good reason for coming," answered Richius. "You know why I'm here."

Tharn nodded. "My wife."

"Dyana," Richius corrected. "Lucyler tells me she is well."

"She is well."

"May I see her?"

"Soon."

"You mean as soon as she is able, don't you?" ventured Richius. "Is she ill?"

Tharn seemed surprised by the deduction. He considered his answer for a moment before saying, "She is almost well now."

"I would like to see her," pressed Richius. "What's wrong?"

"Nothing. Not anymore. She rests now."

Richius was becoming agitated, and he knew it showed. "I've come a long way to see her."

"Why?" probed Tharn curiously.

"She's the reason I'm here," Richius said simply. "You know that."

"Perhaps I can convince you of other reasons. We have much to discuss."

"Not without seeing Dyana," said Richius. He didn't like fencing with the man. He didn't even like looking at him. "I'm afraid I must insist."

Tharn leaned back in his chair, rubbing his good hand with his bad one. "Forgive me, King Vantran. I have wasted time. But it was necessary. Can I have more of your patience? My wife is soon to recover. You can see her then."

"I mean to take her back with me," said Richius ruthlessly. "Do you understand that?"

"It is what I expected."

"Will you let me?"

Tharn was silent.

"Master Tharn," said Richius calmly. "I know what you want from me, and you know what I want from you. We can make this work if you let Dyana go."

"I have spent some time in Nar, King Vantran. It is not a beautiful place. Why are you sure she would go with you there? She is Triin. She belongs here."

"My country is a better place than most in Nar."

"And you have a life for her there? Lucyler has told me you are already married. What will Dyana do in Aramoor?"

Richius frowned, unable to think of a retort. "Let me talk to her. I am willing to let her decide."

"You know little of our ways," said Tharn. "Women do not decide such things. But you may speak to her, in time."

"I don't have time, Master Tharn. I must leave for Aramoor soon, by the morrow if possible. There is business waiting for me. And you know of what I speak."

"I do. It is why I have asked you here. Lucyler tells me you have no influence in your Empire. Is this so?"

"Not entirely," Richius lied. He knew it was the only chance he had.

"Are you willing to use it for us?"

"I've named my price. Release Dyana, and I will speak to Arkus for you. More than that I can't promise."

Tharn leaned closer, his expression earnest. "You must do your best, King Vantran. Tell him there is nothing here for him. Tell him it would be dangerous. Say what you must."

Richius nodded agreeably, all the while remembering he had told his emperor all this and more. There was nothing anyone could say to Arkus to turn his mind from invasion. One could speak to the emperor of lives, but that would be meaningless to a man who thought of death as a worthy end for his enemies.

"It will be difficult," said Richius. "Arkus thinks you have magic. And after all, you do."

Tharn looked away, hiding his face. "My gift is no use to your emperor."

"It's more than just your *gift*, if that's what you wish to call it. He thinks there is magic in Lucel-Lor to heal him, to keep him alive. He's obsessed with it, and he'll do whatever he can to take it." Richius folded his arms, studying Tharn. "I'm willing to try for Dyana's sake, but you should be making ready, Master Tharn. Arkus may simply come without me."

"No, no, he must not," croaked Tharn. "Lucel-Lor has peace now. You have seen it."

"That means nothing to the emperor. You would be wise to consider the proposition from Liss. If you can join with them, you should."

Tharn was shaking. "No. No more war! I will not fight again." He clutched at Richius with his twisted hand, grabbing at his sleeve. "You must do your best. You have a duty."

Richius snatched back his hand. "Duty? You presume a great deal. This isn't my war; I didn't start it."

"Your duty is to Aramoor," pressed Tharn. "I know you want to stop this war."

"All I want is Dyana!" roared Richius, springing to his feet. "She's the only reason I'm here. I don't care about your ideals or your country anymore, and I don't owe you a damned thing. Nor will I feel guilty if Nar crushes you, *Drol*." He spat out the word like a curse. "If I do this thing it will be for my own sake. So what's your answer? Will you let Dyana leave with me? Because if you don't, I promise you ruin. I'll do everything I can to see that Nar destroys you!"

Tharn reared back, amazed at the outburst. "Such rage," he whispered. "Why?"

"Why?" sneered Richius. "You have murdered almost everyone dear to me. I would rather see you in hell before helping you, but I want Dyana freed."

"I am no murderer," said Tharn defensively. "And I know about your father. You are wrong about this."

Richius gritted his teeth. It was the same infuriating lie Lucyler had claimed. "No one else could have done it. My father was loved in Aramoor."

"Beloved kings are assassinated more often than tyrants," said Tharn. "And I know in Nar it is not so uncommon. Why can you not believe your emperor capable of this crime?"

"No," retorted Richius. "I might have thought that, too, but my steward saw the killer. He was Triin."

Tharn shrugged, obviously unconvinced. "Sit," he requested gently. "We argue for nothing."

"Not nothing," said Richius, taking his seat again. "Everyone says you're a man of peace now, but I'm not convinced. It was you who started all the bloodshed. I might be the only one left who remembers that, but I know it's true. My friends died because of you. How do you have the courage to ask anything of me?"

"I am shameless," said Tharn. "Everything I do is for my people and my gods."

"Pretty words," said Richius. "But they don't change the past. This is your mess. You let the spirit out of the bottle. You used your magic and the whole world saw. Now Arkus wants what you have, and he's not going to stop until he gets it."

"Do not speak to me of magic," growled Tharn. "When I was in Nar, everyone thought I was a sorcerer because I was Triin! Your people are ignorant. They see magic in everything they cannot understand."

"But are they wrong? I saw Lucyler do magic. He said you taught him how."

"A simple thing," scoffed Tharn. "If your mind was open, you could learn it, too. But no one can learn the trick of my evil power." He looked away distractedly, turning his ravaged face to the floor. "It is the touch of heaven, and it is for me alone. I cannot give or teach it to your emperor."

There was honesty in his voice. Though it was all nonsense to Richius, it was clear that Tharn believed it for his own misguided reasons, and there was a certain tragedy to the tale. Tharn was a devout Drol, a leader of his people, and yet he truly thought his gods had deformed him for using their gift to deliver his land.

"I will tell Arkus what you have told me," said Richius, "if you let Dyana go."

"Would you risk a war for a woman, King Vantran?"

"Would you?"

"Aramoor could be as hurt by a war as Lucel-Lor. Are you ready for that? And what of the things you have seen here? Lucyler has told me much about you. He says you were saddened by what you and your Empire did here."

"What happened to Lucel-Lor didn't happen because of Narens alone," said Richius. "You were the one who burned the grain fields. You were the one who ordered the massacre at Falindar. This is your war as much as it is my emperor's."

"I admit that," said Tharn solemnly. "I am not a perfect man. I have made mistakes."

"Oh, indeed!" said Richius. "And you're about to make another one, aren't you? You have no intention of freeing Dyana, do you?"

"You speak as though she were a slave, King. She is not. She is my wife."

"It's the same thing to her, I'm sure."

"I will not talk of this," said Tharn defensively. "She is a woman. Her feelings in this matter are meaningless. We have peace, King Vantran. That is all you need to know. And you cannot deny it, can you? You have seen it."

"That's why you brought me here, isn't it?" asked Richius angrily. "Because you thought I would see the land at peace and be convinced to do as you ask." He rose again, the fury swelling inside him. "You never intended to let Dyana go with me...."

"She is my wife, King Vantran."

"She doesn't want to be with you! That's why I was taking her to Aramoor, to get her away from you."

"We were betrothed," said Tharn unflinchingly. He watched Richius with his emotionless eyes, as if what he was hearing was utterly meaningless. "She intended to break her father's vow."

"I know the story. She was too young to know what was happening to her."

"It is the way of things here, King Vantran."

"No," said Richius bitterly. "I was there when you stole her away, or have you forgotten? I saw what you did to her. That's not the way things are here. You may be a hero to these others, but I know what you really are. You're a coward. In Nar they call you the devil. I think they may be right."

"In Liss they call Arkus the devil."

"Then I am surrounded by devils, for you enslave Dyana like Arkus enslaves nations."

"Are you certain?" asked Tharn. "You have not spoken to her. She might be unwilling to go with you."

"Maybe," admitted Richius. "But I want her to tell me that, not you. Let me see her. Let her speak for herself."

"In time you will see her," said Tharn. "But I must have your answer, King Vantran. Will you do this thing for us? Remember, it is the peace of Aramoor we speak of also. Many lives . . ."

"You've made your case, Tharn. My answer depends on Dyana. If she wishes to remain here, I will consider it. But if she wishes to go and you don't let her, there will be no peace between us. And I warn you, if I find you have threatened her in any way . . ."

"There will be no threats," replied Tharn coldly. It seemed to Richius that he had finally said something to offend him. Tharn twisted away from Richius, taking up his pen and returning his attention to his books. "When she is ready I will send for you," he said. "Think on what we have talked about."

"And you do the same," said Richius, going to the door. "There's not much time. If the emissary from Liss is right, Arkus is finally wearing them down. When he does he'll come for Lucel-Lor."

Tharn waved him away in awkward frustration. "Good day, King Vantran."

Richius strode out of the chamber, slamming the door behind him. He paused outside the chamber. Tharn's breath wheezed from behind the door, followed by a trio of hacking coughs. Somehow the monarch had managed to keep himself together long enough to speak with Richius, and now the exertion of the conversation was plaguing him.

Good, thought Richius pettily. His brain was on fire as he began walking through the hall, tempted to kick in every door until he found Dyana. How dare that monster bring him all the way here only to rebuke him! Even Lucyler had tricked him. He cursed himself, hating his own love-blindness. It should have been obvious. Tharn had conjured a storm to take Dyana from him. Why would he give her back now when he knew Richius wanted peace as much as any of them? Angrily he thundered down the stairs of the south tower, his boots echoing like cannon fire on the stonework. Today he was a great fool, and every bone in him rattled with disgust.

Near the end of the hall linking the citadel's two towers he found the stairway that led to his chamber. His thoughts remained dark throughout the steep ascent. It would be difficult to get Dyana out of here. Kronin's warriors were everywhere, and Lucyler couldn't be counted on anymore. Both the warlord and his friend had been turned by the charismatic freak, made forgetful of their bloody pasts by talk of peace. He was alone now, and would have to depend on his own wits to spirit Dyana away.

A few early risers passed him on the stairs, mostly women starting to attend to the citadel's daily needs. They were traditionally dressed in their colorful but modest wrappings and long, dragging skirts that barely left their ankles visible. Their faces were mostly covered, too, shielded from the sight of all but their husbands by a clinging veil of silk. Whenever a man crossed their paths they always looked the other way, a custom Richius found particularly galling this morning. He had stopped bowing to them days ago when he realized they would only ignore him, and the thought of Dyana in such a groveling role heated his already-boiling blood.

His room was near the end of the hall. When he approached it he paused. The door was ajar. Had he forgotten to close it?

Carefully he moved toward the door. There was sunlight in the room, creeping out between the passage and the wall. An unsettling quiet stilled the air. Someone was inside; he sensed it. Probably Lucyler. He would want to know how the meeting went. Richius pushed open the door, dreading the coming conversation and forcing a smile onto his lips.

A wizened ghost smiled back at him. Richius stopped in the doorway, stunned by the sight of her. She sat silently on his bed, her fragile hands clasped before her. To anyone else she might have been unrecognizable, but Richius knew her in an instant. Her name slipped from his lips in a tight sob.

"Dyana."

Her smile broadened as he stepped closer, greeting him with word-less warmth. But this wasn't the Dyana he had lost in Ackle-Nye. There was less luster in her eyes, less depth to the white hair. Her dainty hands shook a little, and her skin was too pale, even for a Triin. She seemed to be struggling to hold herself erect. Yet amazingly she was no less beautiful.

Richius went to her slowly, his throat constricting with emotion, and lowered himself to her feet. She put out her hands for him and he took them, kissing them twice before placing his head in her lap.

Dyana stroked his head for long moments, caressing his hair and calm-ing him with her soothing touch. Words would not come. Too much emotion, the shock of it all, kept him bent like a frightened child, unable to straighten and face her. It occurred to him suddenly that he had feared her dead, and that he hadn't dared to voice his fears, not even to himself. Now she was here, touching him again, and the perfume of her hands and thighs was fragrant and heady and irresistible.

"Dyana," he moaned. "I'm sorry."

"Be still," she said sweetly.

And he was. Her voice was melodious, as it had always been in his dreams. Slowly he lifted his head, staring into her gray eyes. An invisible burden showed in her face and the lines about her mouth. She was pale and unhealthy looking. Hair fell in limp threads about her forehead, and an unsteady tremor rippled through her hands. He reached out and touched her cheek. It was hot. She recoiled from his touch as if it burned.

"What's happened to you?" he whispered. "What's he done to you?"

Her smile was forlorn. "He is better than that," she said vaguely.

He took her hand again, squeezing it gently so that it caused no pain. He could feel the troubling shiver in her fingers. "You're ill. I can see it. What's wrong?"

"I am just weak," she admitted softly. "There is no more trouble." Again she smiled, leaning back on the bed. "It is good to see you again."

"Yes, it is. But how did you get here? Does Tharn know you're here?"

"He does not keep such an eye on me. He thinks I am resting."

"As you should be, no doubt," said Richius. "Here, lay back." He rose and took her tiny, slippered feet in his hands, lifting them easily and coaxing them onto the bed. Dyana complied, evidently grateful for the bed as she twisted to fit her body into the mattress' contours. "Better?" he asked.

Dyana had closed her eyes. "It is better."

Richius shut the door to the little chamber, then cleared his half-eaten breakfast off the chair beside the bed and sat down. He studied her, worried by her obvious weariness. But he saw no scars or bruises, only the sleepy lines of stress. Her breathing was regular, pleasant to listen to, and her face was unveiled, though the rest of her garb was traditionally Triin.

"What will happen if he discovers you're gone?"

"He will be angry with me," said Dyana indifferently. "He worries."

"Why? What's wrong with you?"

Dyana opened her eyes to look at him. "I will tell you. But first I want to know how *you* are. Your friend Lucyler told me you were coming." She glanced down at his hand and smiled. "He gave you back your ring."

"Yes, he did," said Richius, holding it out for her to admire. "And he gave me your message. You shouldn't have thanked me, Dyana. I failed you. I promised to protect you and I let you get captured."

"I knew you would come back," she said sadly. "I knew you would think you failed me and return for me. But listen now. You did not fail. You did what you could, I know. I saw you on the bridge when I was taken away. I saw . . ."

She broke off, turning her bitter face away. Richius went to her, sitting down beside her.

"I'm here now, Dyana," he said. "And I'm going to keep that promise I made you. I'm going to take you away from him."

She shook her head. "No. No, you cannot."

"I will. I've already spoken to him about it. He knows you're the only reason I've come here. He'll listen to me, I'm sure. And if he doesn't, we'll leave anyway."

Dyana sighed miserably. "I do not know why you are here, Richius. Tharn tells me almost nothing. What is happening?"

"You don't know? Didn't Lucyler tell you?"

"No. I have only spoken to him a few times. Once was just after I told Tharn about you, and once about a month ago. That was when he told me he was going to speak to you and bring you back here. I gave him the ring so he could prove to you I was alive, but I didn't understand why he was going to see you. I asked him to explain but he would not." Her face tightened with confusion. "The last time I saw him was yesterday. He told me you were here. Richius, tell me what is happening. Why has Tharn brought you?"

"Easy," said Richius. "I'll explain it to you, if I can." He took a deep breath. If she didn't know about the coming war, it would surely be a shock. "There's going to be another war," he said. "Arkus is planning to invade Lucel-Lor, and he wants my country to help him. Tharn heard about his plans, and now he wants my help to stop the emperor. He thinks that if I speak to Arkus he will listen to me."

"Because you are king now."

"You know about that?"

"It is what Lucyler told me."

"What else did he tell you?"

"That you have a wife." Dyana watched Richius' face and added quickly, "I know all of this, Richius. It is all right."

"It's not," said Richius. "I'm sorry, Dyana. I'm so very sorry. I didn't want to marry. I couldn't forget you but—"

She leaned forward and put a finger to his lips. "Stop," she ordered. "I am not angry."

"Good, because now I intend to keep my promise. I'll get you out of here, one way or another. I've given Tharn till tomorrow to make a decision. He knows that keeping you here would mean an end to peace between us."

Dyana closed her eyes. "Oh, Richius. I wish you had never come."

"Why do you say that?" cried Richius. "Dyana, you're going to be free. I'm going to take you back to Aramoor, like I promised."

"I cannot," she said. "I cannot go with you."

"God damn it, don't be afraid of him! That's what he wants, the evil bastard. But I won't let him take you away from me this time. I have all of Nar behind me now and he knows it. He has to listen."

But the more insistent he was the more she shook her head, until finally she put up her hands to stop him. "No!" she cried. "No, it is impossible. I cannot leave."

Richius drew back, exasperated and terrified by her words. What magic had Tharn worked over her to bend her will so completely? She was hardly the Dyana he knew anymore, the girl willing to sell herself before wedding the devil of Lucel-Lor. He got up from the bed and looked down at her beautiful, mysterious face, trying to glean some insight from her eyes. But they were mute, as incomprehensible as her words.

"Explain this to me," he insisted. "Why can't you leave him? Do you love him?"

"I do not."

"What, then? Has he threatened you? Because if he has—"

"He is gentle with me, Richius. He would never do that to me."

Richius moved closer to the bed. "Then what is it? I've come a long way for you, Dyana. I won't be turned away without reason."

Dyana stiffened. "Another war," she muttered. "This must not happen."

"Why can't you leave?" asked Richius ruthlessly. All the tenderness was gone from his voice. He lifted her chin with his hand, feeling the bone beneath the taut skin. "Answer me," he demanded. "Is it your sickness? Are you afraid? What?"

"Come with me," Dyana said, getting up from the bed with visible effort.

"Where are you going?"

"Follow."

He watched her move unsteadily to the door, then sprang forward and opened it for her. "You can hardly walk," he said, putting out his arm for her. "Here, let me help you."

"No, please," she said, pulling away. "Others might see."

"Dyana . . ."

"I am fine. Come."

He followed her out of the chamber and into the hall, then down the staircase, which she negotiated with difficulty, at last accepting his help when she was sure no one was around. The citadel was quiet, and he eased her soundlessly down the stairs until they reached the place where the hall that led to the other tower began.

"Are we going to your room?"

Dyana nodded but said nothing.

"What about Tharn? Won't he see us?"

"My rooms are not near his."

Her rooms were in the south tower, a good distance from Tharn's. There were more windows in this hall, all letting in the warm spring sunlight, and a plush carpet blanketed the floor. The carpet gave thickly underfoot, letting Richius feel its obvious quality even through his boots. Several fixtures of tarnished gold were fastened to the wall, along with a handful of ivory and jade inlays. It was truly a royal residence here, like all of the citadel had once been. Scattered conversations echoed through the hall, the polite voices of women behind the nearest doors. Richius paused, fearful they would be seen.

"Who's here?" he asked softly.

"Servants. Women who attend to me."

The answer made Richius' eyebrows shoot up. It seemed that Tharn spared no expense when it came to Dyana. While the rest of the citadel lived in relative squalor, she was Tharn's pampered queen. A little pang of jealousy coursed through him.

"Here," she said, coming to an open door. Richius peered into the chamber. It was sunny and bright and remarkably clean. A woman not much older than Dyana stood in the far corner of the room, fussing over a waist-high piece of furniture. The chamber was large and she couldn't hear them until they were close behind her. She gave a startled cry when she noticed Richius, then reached out for Dyana. Dyana struggled to calm the woman, putting up her hands and talking rapidly, obviously explaining that nothing was wrong. The woman stared wide-eyed at Richius, unconvinced until Dyana practically pushed her out the door, shutting it behind her. When the argument was done Dyana nearly collapsed. She put her hand to her forehead and leaned against the closed door, breathing far too heavily. Richius went to her, catching her up in his arms. She didn't protest, but let him support her. Again Richius felt the sickly frailty of her body and knew there was something terribly amiss.

"Oh, Dyana. What's the matter with you?"

She gestured to a chair near the corner where the woman had been. "There, please. Let me sit."

The tall, trough-shaped piece of furniture was by the chair, covered with lace and ribbons of white linen. Four sturdy legs held it upright, and a canopy of fabric stretched half-open across its top. Richius guided Dyana to the chair, curious about the odd item. It looked like a blanket case. He could see swatches of downy fabric creeping out over its sides where the canopy was pulled away. When Dyana was seated he peered inside. Something pink stared back at him.

"Oh, my God," he whispered, backing away. His eyes flicked to Dyana. She didn't look at him. "That's a baby," he stammered, and the reality of the moment struck him like a bracing wind. "A baby!" he said again. "Dyana . . ."

"My daughter," said Dyana softly. She glanced up at Richius apologetically.

Richius was stupefied. He tried to collect himself, chancing another peek into the cradle. The tiniest infant he had ever seen writhed beneath a swaddling of lily-soft cloth, her eyes fixing on him with unfocused interest. Ruddy cheeks blew out minute puffs of air as she breathed, and when she saw him she whimpered unhappily.

"She's beautiful," Richius whispered sadly. Lucyler had lied to him, and he could hardly veil his bitterness. "I suppose I was wrong about Tharn. Lucyler told me he couldn't have you."

Dyana reached out and touched his hand. "Look more closely," she urged.

Confused, Richius did as she asked, gently pulling back the canopy and studying the babe. Newborn, he deduced. He had seen newborn babies back at home, and they always had the same red complexion and pinched appearance. This one was no more than a few days old. She was nearly bald, too, with only the barest threads of fawn hair curling up from her scalp. The fingers of her right hand snatched feebly at the air, balling into a walnut-sized fist. Cautiously he reached into the crib, slow enough for her to see him coming. Her eyes tried to follow his hand, and when he touched her head she blew a bubble from her mouth. Richius laughed.

"What's her name?" he asked, too fascinated to address Dyana directly.

"Shani," replied Dyana. There was a hint of pride in her tired voice. "I named her after a cousin—someone I loved."

Richius looked up at her. "Someone that died?"

"Yes," said Dyana sadly. "When she was very young. I told you about her once. Do you remember?"

Richius did, and the memory was torture. "In the valley," he whispered. "She was trampled by a horse."

"And I blamed you for killing her. I don't know if I ever apologized to you for that."

"There's no need," said Richius. He looked again at the child. "Hello, Shani," he cooed, stroking the baby's neck the way one would a puppy. "Hello." He spared a glance at Dyana. "She's beautiful," he said again. "Just like her mother."

"And her father," said Dyana. "You are not seeing her, Richius. Look."

"Why?" asked Richius, suddenly alarmed. "Is she sick? Oh, does she have Tharn's disease?" He studied her closely, looking for some telling sign of illness. Other than the normal blemishes of a difficult birth, he saw nothing extraordinary about her.

Except for her eyes. They were unusually dark and oddly shaped. Not deformed, as one might expect of Tharn's offspring, just different. More round than the usual narrow eyes of Triin. But Richius had never seen a Triin infant before. Perhaps it was normal. Perhaps they all had eyes like . . .

He jumped back from the crib, as if an adder had suddenly appeared in the baby's place. "God in heaven," he exclaimed. "Is she mine?"

The floor seemed to move beneath him. Quickly he took a breath, then another. Dyana was watching him anxiously. She reached for him, grabbing his hand and trying to pull him closer, but he snapped it back with an angry scowl.

"She's mine!" he roared, bringing his hands to his head to contain the imminent explosion. "Damn it all, she's mine!" His eyes closed and his jaws clenched and his fists shook against his ears.

"Richius," Dyana managed. "I—"

"You didn't tell me! You gave me back this damned ring and didn't tell me you were carrying my child! Lucyler, too, damn him to hell!"

"I hoped you wouldn't come," she said angrily. "I asked Lucyler not to tell you. I never wanted you to know."

"You're as mad as he is," he railed. "She's my baby. I should have been told!"

"Why? There is nothing you can do. Do you not see that?"

"Like hell," spat Richius. "I'll take you both back. Shani can live in Aramoor, too. I'll look after both of you. My wife already knows about you, Dyana. She knows. . . ."

Dyana was shaking her head. "It cannot be."

"Of course it can," Richius insisted. "I'm king of Aramoor now. I can protect you and the baby. Nothing will happen to her there."

She looked up at him, the skin beneath her eyes red and sagging. "He lured you here," she said. "He knew you would come for me. It is his way, to manipulate."

"And it worked," admitted Richius. "But I'm here now, and he knows he has no choice if he wants peace with Nar."

"He will not let me leave," said Dyana. "He loves me, Richius. He has always loved me, I told you that once before. When we were children, he was always doing things for me, bringing me flowers and gifts. And he would try to be a man for me, to impress me by riding horses or climbing trees." Dyana laughed. "He was different then, and I liked the attention. But I have never been able to understand his love. It has always been too much, too heavy."

"Does he know how you feel about him?"

"It does not matter. He is Drol. He is wedded to me and that is the end of it. He would never let another man take his wife away. It would be the highest disgrace. Now do you see why I cannot leave? He would have to kill us both before letting you take me. His honor would demand it."

"Then we'll go without his permission. We'll sneak away at night if we must."

"He would find us, like he did last time. And then we would all be in danger. I cannot take such a chance with Shani. I will not."

There was an awful logic to it. She was right and Richius knew it. Tharn would find them if he meant to, and the risk to the infant was un-questionable. Dyana had survived her abduction by Tharn because she was young and strong, but Shani would be like a mote of dust in one of Tharn's storms, blown into oblivion. A sour curse sprang from his lips and he dropped to the floor, rocking with his chin burrowed into his chest and his arms about his knees. He needed to think, but nothing was coming to him. They were trapped, without allies or escape. Tharn had beaten him.

"Damn you, Tharn," he hissed. He couldn't even return to Aramoor and plot his vengeance on the cunning-man. Dyana and Shani were here, hostages against any military retribution. "Dyana," he groaned. "Help me. I don't know what to do."

"You must go back. You must leave us here, Richius."

"How can I leave you with this madman?" he asked. "God, she's my daughter!"

"Tharn is not mad," she said mildly. "He looks after me, and he has promised to care for Shani, too. He knows that she is your child."

"Are you certain about this? Is there any chance she is his?"

"None," said Dyana. "You have seen how ill he is. He is not able to be with me, Richius. That is why my rooms are not near his." She smiled, trying to cheer him. "Please believe me. I have learned much about him. His illness has changed him. He is kind and gentle, like you. And I am not afraid of him."

"But you don't love him."

Dyana shrugged. "No. But I know he loves me. Shani's birth was hard. I was close to death, I think. But he stayed with me through it all. He did not care for himself, but watched me and slept by me."

"Casadah," said Richius. "That was when the birth started, wasn't it?"

"Yes," said Dyana with a shudder. He could tell she was still weak from the ordeal and that the memory of it was painfully fresh. "Shani was born the morning after. I do not remember much, really. There was so much blood, and Tharn was talking to my women, telling them to help me. He thought I would die. I thought so, too. But he stayed with me. He was there when she was born."

"When I was in Aramoor I used to dream about you," Richius said softly. "I didn't know if you were alive or dead, but you were all I could think about. I was so angry with myself for leaving you, for letting you down. And then when Arkus said he was sending me back to Lucel-Lor, I told myself that maybe you would still be here, and I could find you and take you back home." He laughed. It all seemed so pathetic now. "My God. What a fool I am."

"No," said Dyana. "You did more than anyone could have. Somehow I knew when I met you that you would find a way back here. But it is over now, Richius. We have separate lives. I am Triin and you are Naren, and we are both wedded."

"Yes," Richius admitted. "Wedded." He thought of his bride back in Aramoor. She would be waiting for him, worrying. He knew he didn't deserve Sabrina any more than she deserved the curse of a neglectful husband. But Arkus had cast both their fates for them, just as Dyana's father had written her future when she was a mere girl. They were all game pieces being moved whimsically across a board, unable to still the hands of their masters. He stared listlessly at the floor, searching for an answer that never came. "What shall I do?" he said softly.

"Leave us," said Dyana firmly. "We will be well here, I promise. Tharn is good. And he cares for me. You must go home to Aramoor. You must do as Tharn asks. Can you do that? Can you stop this war?"

"No," said Richius. "The emperor won't listen to me."

Dyana looked at him oddly. "I do not understand. You told Tharn you could help him."

"Tharn thinks that because I'm a Naren king, Arkus will care what I say. He's wrong. Getting Arkus to change his mind is impossible."

"But you will try, yes?"

Richius was silent. He was very quickly becoming Tharn's whore, and the thought of helping the freakish holy man made his insides clench. But now there was Dyana and his daughter to consider. Things were different, just as Tharn knew they would be.

"Richius," ventured Dyana carefully. "Tharn is very wise. He would not ask this of you if it were not important. He has brought peace to Lucel-Lor. He is—"

"Please," said Richius, cupping his hands over his ears. "Not you, too. I can't bear it. Everyone is convinced he's some great man. Forgive me, but I don't see it."

"Not a great man," Dyana corrected. "A good man. You do not know him, Richius. He has changed, I swear it. He is like he used to be, when we were young. He cares about his people. We are everything to him."

"Lucyler tells me he thinks his gods deformed him. I think he's just diseased. What do you believe?"

"I think he is touched by heaven," replied Dyana. "I think the gods have made him special. And I think he knows this, and it has humbled him."

Richius shook his head in disbelief. It was as if they all suffered from some mind-dulling dementia. Did the past mean nothing to them? Slowly he rose from the floor and peered once more into Shani's cradle. The infant fidgeted.

"My daughter," he said sadly. "How can I leave her? You ask the impossible of me, Dyana."

"It is how it must be," Dyana answered. "I wish there was another way, but . . ." Her voice trailed off with a shrug.

"I know," said Richius. He reached down and lightly felt Shani's tiny head, marveling at the sensation of her downy hair on his finger. In that moment she was more magnificent to him than the towers of Nar or the ancient forests of Aramoor or Falindar's bright citadel. He would slay an army of Tharns for her, but he had no weapons for the fight. Silently he closed the cradle's canopy.

"I want to see her again before I leave," he said over his shoulder.

Dyana walked up behind him. "You are going, then?"

He nodded.

"Will you speak to your emperor?"

"I'll leave in a few days," Richius replied dully. "I want to give Tharn time to think about what I told him."

"Will you, Richius? Will you talk to him?"

Richius turned and stalked away. But when he made it to the door he hovered there, unable to cross the threshold. Dyana was staring at him curiously.

"Richius?"

"For months I have thought about you, Dyana," said Richius softly. "I'm like Tharn, obsessed with you, and I can't find the strength to forget you."

"You must."

"I don't want to. I'm in love."

Dyana colored.

"It's a foolish thing, I know," said Richius. "But I had always hoped that maybe when I saw you again, you might tell me that you have thought of me these past months, too." He tried to smile at her. "Have you ever? Maybe just a little?"

Dyana turned away. "It is not a thing to speak of," she said icily. "I am married to Tharn."

It wasn't an answer, and the evasiveness of the statement made Richius hopeful. He took a tiny step closer to her. "Just a little, perhaps?"

Dyana did not turn, but her shoulders slumped slightly. "When I was carrying Shani, Tharn was with me always, caring for me and seeing to my needs. He was like a true husband to me. And when I was birthing, he nursed me and held my hand. But Shani has always made me think of you, Richius. Even when she was in my belly." At last she turned to look at him, and her eyes were heavy with sadness. "You are not so easy to forget, Richius Vantran."

Richius smiled hopefully. "Dyana . . ."

"That is my answer," she said curtly. "It is all I can say to you. And if you love me as you claim, you will do this thing for me and our child. Will you? Will you talk to your emperor?"

Richius left the room without replying.

THIRTY

On Falindar's bleak mountain, on the side that faced the sea, the cliff face dove down a thousand feet to the rocks and wash below. Almost nothing grew here, for the ground was rocky, and the view to the endless ocean was unobscured except for one remarkable tree. It was ancient, tall, and weather-gnarled, with coiled branches that never dropped their foliage, even in winter. Leaves of gold and summer green changed hue with the seasons, and its trunk terminated in a web of roots that burst from the earth as they struggled to crack their rocky foundation. No one knew how the tree had gotten here, or how it garnered nourishment from the soil, but it was widely thought of as a gift from the sky wraiths, those lesser Triin gods that floated above the earth and dwelt sometimes on beautiful mountains. Because of this and its peculiar fruit that ripened in the early spring, the tree was renowned among Triin, an artifact taken as proof that the gods existed and that they loved their mortal children.

Lucyler didn't know if the tree was a gift from heaven or a trick of nature. He only knew that he loved the tree; that the tree gave him solace and made him thoughtful. In the days before the fall of Falindar, when he was the Daegog's privileged man, he would come to the tree and pick off one of its citrusy fruits, savoring it while he watched the sea dash itself against the shore. Those had been carefree times, when all he had to worry about was his Daegog's security and the boring press of daily life. Tharn and his revolution had changed all that forever, but the tree was still here and it still gave fruit, and it still made Lucyler ponder mysteries.

Today he needed the tree.

He reached into its thorny branches and plucked off a ripe red fruit. The branch sprang backward, startling a thrush and sending it skyward. It was a mild morning, a good morning to enjoy the serenity of the mountain. He sat down on an outcropping, his feet dangling off the cliff wall, and gently began peeling away the fruit's skin. A spray of juice struck his face and he smiled.

The sea was tranquil. He spied it as he ate, sucking out the tangy juice from the fruit's segmented interior. Birds skimmed the ocean in their perpetual quest for food, and the sky above was azure and cloudless. The fresh scent of briny water drifted on the breeze, and the sun was gentle on his face—so warm that its touch made him sleepy. But he hadn't come here to sleep today. He had come to think, for he was troubled, and the day's excellence did little to leaven his mood. He had betrayed a friend, and the guilt of it was killing him.

Two days had passed since he had spoken to Richius. Tharn had informed them both of his decision separately, and now it was up to Richius to decide what happened next. The discovery of his daughter had made Richius cold and distant. He didn't come to meals, he didn't speak with anyone, he didn't acknowledge knocks on his door. Sequestered in his room, Richius took in the food left for him in the hall only when he heard Lucyler's footfalls leaving. They all worried about him, even Tharn, but they didn't press him, and they were ignorant about what was going on behind his chamber door.

My poor friend, thought Lucyler mournfully. *I am sorry.*

And he was sorry. Genuinely. He skipped over the last few weeks in his mind, playing over his tactics and looking for mistakes. His one great regret was that he had listened to the woman. Dyana was wrong to keep the news from Richius, Lucyler knew that now. He should have told his friend of the pregnancy the moment they met in the Saccenne Run. But Dyana had been adamant, and hopeful that Richius would not come at all. She explained that there was no sense in telling him of the baby if he decided not to return for her. It would only make him want to come more, and there was nothing for him here.

Lucyler frowned as he chewed on the fruit's soft pulp. It had seemed good reasoning at the time. But Richius had reacted badly, and Lucyler was sure he was resentful.

"Damn," he muttered. He shouldn't have done it. Now his friend was lost to him, this fine, irreplaceable friend. Making it up was impossible; deception couldn't be erased. They had had a code in the Dring Val-

THE JACKAL OF NAR

ley, and had kept each other alive by following it. He had broken that code. He would miss Richius greatly.

And then, like a faint breeze, he heard him. Lucyler turned his head to see him standing some yards away, his arms hanging purposelessly at his sides. Lucyler licked the sticky juice from his lips, then waved Richius over.

"Sit," he said as Richius' shadow fell on his back. The shadow hesitated a moment before it moved. Richius sat down on the ledge carelessly, tossing his feet over the edge and staring blankly at the horizon.

"Why didn't you tell me?" Richius asked. He didn't turn to look at Lucyler, but asked the question to the wind. Lucyler shrugged.

"I am not sure now."

"Not good enough. Dyana told me she asked you not to tell me. Is that true?"

Lucyler nodded.

"And you listened to her? Why, Lucyler? How could you keep such a thing from me?"

"I said I do not know," Lucyler replied. "She asked me and I did it. Maybe I was wrong."

"You *were* wrong."

Lucyler turned to regard his friend. Richius looked older now. Three days' beard growth obscured his face and his hair was tousled and oily. Wrinkles creased his clothes and his eyes were sad. He sat with his shoulders slumped, his hands clasped loosely against his stomach as he rocked distractedly in the breeze.

"All right," Lucyler conceded. "I was wrong. And I am sorry. I thought I was doing the right thing. Dyana hoped you would not return, and she knew if I told you about the child that you would certainly come."

"But you knew I'd come anyway," said Richius. "You and Tharn planned it that way."

"That is not so," said Lucyler, shaking his head vigorously. "I never lied to you."

Richius finally turned to look at him. "Didn't you? I asked you if Tharn would let Dyana go. You never answered me. That's just as bad as lying about it, Lucyler. Call it what you want, but you let me go on believing he would free her." His chin sank into his chest. "And that's what hurts me most of all. I thought we were friends."

Lucyler's heart fractured. "Never doubt it," he said quietly. "You are dear to me, Richius, whether you believe so or not. But I thought at the time Dyana was right. And perhaps she was. Is it really good to know you have a child here whose life you can never be part of? This did occur to me. I was not doing it to hurt you."

"And what about Tharn? Did you know he wouldn't let Dyana go with me?"

The question made Lucyler grimace. He wanted to lie, to extricate himself from guilt with a simple fabrication, but he screwed up his courage and said, "Tharn never told me he would not let her leave with you. But I suppose I knew it, yes."

Richius' head drooped a little more. Lucyler raced to explain himself.

"You have to understand. It was the only way to get you here. Would you have been willing to speak to Tharn if Dyana was not here?"

"Of course not," said Richius. "I would rather speak to the devil himself."

"Then you do understand." Lucyler lowered the fruit and stared at Richius pleadingly. "How else could I have gotten you here if not for Dyana? I told you Tharn was good, I told you there was peace here now, but you would not listen. It was only Dyana that made you come here."

"That's right," said Richius hotly. He lifted his head and glared at Lucyler. "Do you want to know the truth, Lucyler? The truth is I don't give a damn about any of you anymore. If I could I'd go back to Nar City and tell them everything I know about you, where you are and what weaknesses you have—everything. I would destroy Falindar if I could, and everyone in it, because you all bloody deserve it. But I can't do that now because of Dyana and the baby. I can't have the revenge I deserve."

Lucyler felt a hopeful spark flare up within him. "So you are going back to help us?"

"That's all you want, isn't it?" Richius asked sourly. "Haven't you been listening to me?"

"I have," snapped Lucyler. "But you have not been listening to me. Look around, Richius. The war is over. Lucel-Lor has peace. Dyana's safe, whether you want to admit it or not, and your baby will be well cared for. Things are not perfect, but Tharn is trying. He cares about his people, more than the Daegog ever did. I know because I knew them both. Life will be better here because of Tharn, because he is strong and the warlords will follow him. Whether or not this lasts is up to you."

"Up to me?" Richius flared. "You're as bad as Tharn. I don't have that kind of influence with Arkus and you know it."

"But you can try."

There was an awkward silence as Richius sighed and ran his hands through his hair. He looked crazed, like an animal chewing off its own foot to escape a trap, and for a moment Lucyler was afraid. Not for himself, for he knew that Richius would never harm him, no matter how enraged or bitter he was. He feared for Richius, and for the sanity that seemed to be slipping away from him.

"Richius," he said gently. "I was wrong to do this to you. I used you, and for that I am sorry. Do not forgive me, but do not let this stop you from making a good decision. Think of all those here who have deceived you. They will suffer if this war happens. And think of Aramoor. . . ."

"Stop," said Richius. "You and Tharn think you know me so well, don't you? You know just what to say to make me do your bidding."

"Richius, I—"

"No, Lucyler. I'm right. But the awful thing is you're right, too. I don't have a choice. I know I don't. You and Tharn have seen to that. You've learned well from him, my friend. You've learned how to manipulate people. He's quite a master at that, isn't he?"

"There was simply no other way," said Lucyler again. "Right or wrong, I had to get you here. I had to make you see what was at risk."

"I see," said Richius. "I see." He glanced down at the fruit on the rocky ground between them, picking it up and inspecting it. "Is this from that tree?"

Lucyler nodded. "It is called a heart fruit. They only ripen a few days a year. But when they do . . ." He raised an eyebrow. "Try it."

Richius sniffed at the half-eaten fruit. "Smells nice," he commented, and took a bite. His eyes lit up as he mumbled, "Good."

"I thought you would like it," said Lucyler. "I can get you some if you like."

"No," said Richius. "Save them for the others. We have fruit enough in Aramoor." He handed the heart fruit back to Lucyler. "Here, you finish it."

Lucyler took it and set it back down. "Richius," he asked carefully, "will you tell me what you have decided?"

Richius looked away distractedly. "He's not going to change his mind, is he?"

"No," answered Lucyler. "I am sorry."

"Why not, Lucyler? He knows I love her. He knows she doesn't love him. Why is he keeping her from me?"

"It is not like that exactly," Lucyler explained. "It is not that he wants to keep you apart. He wants to keep her with him. He loves her also."

"Do you know that for certain?"

"She is very beautiful, Richius. And he is . . . well, less than beautiful. It is like that for men here. A beautiful woman is important for men like Tharn. Others follow him. They strive to be like him. And yes, I think he does love her."

"Then he will take care of her? And the baby?"

"I have no doubt. You should see him with her, Richius. He glows when she is around. He is more obsessed with her than you are, I think."

"Dyana's told me," Richius admitted. "She said that he has always loved her, even before they were betrothed. I guess I was hoping she was wrong."

Lucyler shook his head. "She is not wrong. His love for her is a strange thing. It is something fierce. And his sickness makes him love her even more. She is very beautiful. I think he feels less monstrous around her. But he is good to her. And that is all you should worry about."

Richius seemed satisfied. He nodded to himself, as if in deep thought, saying, "All right then. I will leave in the morning for Aramoor."

"Will you speak to Arkus for us, Richius?"

"You know I will. I have no choice. I can't let this war happen if Dyana and Shani are here in Falindar. But don't deceive yourself, Lucyler. Just being here is treason. When Arkus learns of it, he won't be in a mood to talk. I'll be lucky if I get out of the Black City alive."

"I know. That is why I am going with you."

"What?"

"I cannot ask you to do this without taking the risk myself. And I have already told Tharn I am going. It is done."

"Then undo it. You'll have a lot less chance of surviving this than me, Lucyler. What do you think goes on in Nar? Arkus will have you locked up in one of his war labs before you know what's happening. He'd just love to get his hands on a Triin."

"I am prepared for the worst," replied Lucyler calmly. "We will face this together."

"Then you might as well say your farewells now, Lucyler. You won't be coming back."

Lucyler merely shrugged. He had expected Richius' argument, and had already reached all the same conclusions. It changed nothing. He would either die in Nar trying for peace, or he would die in Lucel-Lor fighting a war. Death came to everyone. What really mattered was how it came.

"I've told Tharn not to expect too much from us," he said. "But I doubt he was listening. He has faith in us, I fear."

"Faith," spat Richius. "Then he is a fool. He should put his faith in Liss. He should fight with them like they've asked. With their help Lucel-Lor might stand a chance. Unless of course he uses his power."

"You do not understand," said Lucyler. He was tiring of this argument, of trying to explain the subtleties of Drol life to Richius. Not everyone could grasp it, he knew, particularly non-Triin, but he had hoped Richius was smarter than that.

"You're right," said Richius. "I don't understand. I wish I could see him as you do. This would all be easier for me."

"You will see the truth of him in time, Richius. Just like I did."

Clearly, Richius disagreed. He rubbed thoughtfully at his beard, his eyes darting with the passing seabirds. They sat there together a long moment, their legs perched over the sea wall, and a gust of ocean air blew back their hair. White-capped waves shimmered in the distance, tossing up tasty trophies for the hovering gulls. The song of the sea was crisp on the mountain and they lost themselves in it, swaying slightly to its constant, iambic rhythm.

Tomorrow, thought Lucyler sadly. It was too soon. He had missed Falindar terribly during his long excursion to Aramoor. He wasn't eager to say farewell again—and this time it might be for good. He flicked the rind of the heart fruit off the cliff edge, mindful that it would likely be his last. The fruit plummeted downward and disappeared.

"Will you see him again before we go?" asked Lucyler.

Richius shrugged indifferently. "Why should I? He's made his decision and I've made mine."

"What about Dyana and the little one?"

"Tonight I'll say good-bye to them both," said Richius. "If Tharn lets me, that is."

"Of course he will," said Lucyler. "You need only ask. I'll tell him myself if you like."

"No," said Richius. "I'll do it." He closed his eyes and sighed. "Am I a fool, Lucyler?"

"What?"

"Am I a fool?" asked Richius again. "I feel like one. I should never have come back. I don't know what I expected to find here."

"I think you know," said Lucyler gently. "You expected to find Dyana willing. You imagined she would be waiting for you, did you not?"

Richius opened his eyes and stared at his friend. "God, I'm stupid, aren't I? She hardly even knows me. And I hardly know her. Yet I love her, Lucyler. I can't explain it, but I do. I've loved her since I saw her. She was enough to make me leave Aramoor. And I never thought anything could drag me back here."

"Love is a mystery, my friend," offered Lucyler. "Sometimes it takes years to grow. Other times an instant is enough."

"And sometimes it never grows at all," Richius concluded.

Lucyler started to speak but abruptly broke off, cocking his head toward the citadel. Someone was calling his name, barely audible over the rushing breeze. He stood up at once and scanned the distance. A man was coming toward them, a warrior of Kronin's, racing down the sloping hillside.

"What is it?" asked Richius, getting to his feet. He followed Lucyler's gaze until he himself sighted the running man. The warrior moved with purpose along the rocky ground, his arms and legs pumping furiously. Lucyler felt his insides ice.

"Trouble," he whispered blackly.

"Loocylr!" came the echoing cry, rolling down the mountain like an avalanche. The man was waving now, frantically waving a hand above him as he ran. Lucyler waved back, then motioned to Richius.

"Follow me," he called over his shoulder, dashing madly to meet the warrior. Richius was close on his heels.

Together they thundered up the slope to where the warrior in blue and gold had halted, his face flushed with exertion and dripping perspiration. He spoke in a flustered croak, his words disjointed. Lucyler listened, piecing together what he could as the man rambled and pointed, first to Richius and then to the towering citadel over his shoulder.

"What's he saying?" asked Richius.

Lucyler said shakily, "There is someone for you in the citadel. Tharn wants you to come at once."

"Someone for me? Who?"

"He does not know," Lucyler explained. The man was still talking. "He only knows Tharn wants to see you, in the banquet room. Something important."

They began the long, winding journey back to the citadel, leaving the bewildered warrior behind. Richius easily kept pace with Lucyler, digging into the rocky earth with his hard boots and sending shards of gravel into the air. Panic energized them, propelling them up the hill and into the relatively flat yards around the castle. The grounds were empty. They looked at one another cautiously.

"No trouble," said Richius. "What is this?"

Lucyler shrugged, then started off again into the covered court of the citadel. They didn't run now but rather walked briskly, taking notice of the people they passed and seeing nothing unusual. The banquet room, the warrior had said. Lucyler peered down the hall. All was quiet. Whatever was happening apparently wasn't common knowledge. Several people passed them on their way, hardly sparing them a glance. Lucyler tossed Richius a confused look, then started off down the great hall that led to the banquet room, with Richius on his heels. Their boots echoed ominously through the cavernous hall as they walked. Richius was breathing heavily. A nervous sweat had erupted on his forehead and he licked his lips impatiently as his eyes scanned for trouble. They paused as they neared the closed doors of the banquet room. Lucyler put his ear to the ornate portals and held his breath. Inside he could hear an occasional, unrecognizable voice, but it was too muffled to be distinguishable.

"Someone is inside," he whispered. "I do not know who."

"Open it," Richius directed.

Lucyler rapped twice on one of the doors, then pulled it slowly open. At once he saw Tharn. The cunning-man's face was dreadful. He nodded slightly as he recognized Lucyler. Other heads turned toward the door; Kronin and two of his warriors, all standing with their jiiktars held loosely at waist level. And then Lucyler saw another man as he pulled the door wider, an unknown figure in shining black leather with a gilded cape and a helmet of silver. He was tall and lean, and when he turned to the doorway his masked face displayed a horrible death's-head, the perfect likeness of a human skull rendered in metal. A long, thin sword dangled from his belt. Lucyler faltered. Richius pushed past him. His friend recoiled when he noticed the soldier.

"My God," whispered Richius. He stopped in the doorway. Lucyler came up alongside him. Both men's eyes fixed on the malevolent figure.

"Who is he, Richius? Do you know?"

"Come," ordered Tharn. His voice resonated with angry power in the hollow chamber. His expression was tight, even bitter, and his blistered lips twisted in the semblance of a snarl. He was watching the odd man closely, doing nothing to hide his contempt. Kronin and his warriors watched the soldier, too, their jiiktars poised. It was then that Lucyler noticed the box at the soldier's feet.

It was the size of a small chest, forged from battered irons and barely large enough for a modest collection of books. A stout lock dangled from a web of chains wrapped around its lid and casing. The soldier, seeing Lucyler regarding the chest, stepped aside so he and Richius could view it clearly. He inclined his gruesome head to one side, and the silver skull seemed to smile.

"Who is he?" Lucyler whispered.

Richius was too stunned to answer.

"Come in," said Tharn again. His gnarled walking stick shook in his feeble grip.

"Is this King Vantran?" asked the golden voice from behind the silver mask.

Tharn looked at the soldier contemptuously before saying, "Richius, this *thing* is here to speak with you. Do you know who he is?"

"Not precisely," answered Richius in a shrinking voice. "But I know what he is."

Lucyler was lost. It seemed that everyone knew what was happening but him. "Well?" he asked impatiently. "What is he then?"

"He is a Shadow Angel. A messenger of Arkus of Nar. And I'm certain he has business with me."

Now Lucyler stepped forward, moving between the strange soldier and his friend. "What business have you with the king?"

The Shadow Angel gestured to the chest at his feet. "I am the emperor's humble herald. I bring a gift for the king of Aramoor."

Richius moved to get closer, but Lucyler held out a hand. "What is this gift?" he asked. "How did you get here?"

"To the first question, it is a gift between the great Lord Arkus and Aramoor's king. I know not what it is. To the second, I have come by ship to deliver His Majesty's present." The Shadow Angel slipped a hand into his black vestments, moving slowly so as not to alarm the armed warriors. Kronin eyed him coldly but didn't stop him. An envelope of crisp parchment appeared in the messenger's hand. He held it out past Lucyler for Richius. "For you," he said, bowing his head slightly. Lucyler snatched the envelope away.

"Give it to me," said Richius rigidly.

"No. It is nothing good, Richius, I am sure."

Richius touched his friend's shoulder. "Please," he said softly.

Lucyler thought to argue then stopped himself, seeing the determination in his comrade's eyes. He passed the envelope over.

"You will find a key inside," offered the Shadow Angel. "It will open the lock for the chest."

They all watched as Richius slid his finger under the wax seal of the envelope. Inside was a single piece of paper and the promised key. He held the key in one hand and the letter in the other as he read.

"What is it?" asked Lucyler anxiously. Richius dropped the letter. It floated to the floor. "Richius," Lucyler pressed. He was agitated now, near panic. "Richius, tell me."

Richius walked past Lucyler to the chest. The Shadow Angel backed away. Kronin and his warriors moved to subdue him, but a terse order from Tharn stopped them.

"Leave him," spoke the cunning-man in Triin. He struggled to his feet, balancing himself precariously on his cane. "Not yet."

Richius knelt before the chest, fumbling with the key and finally fitting it into the lock. The mechanism sprang open. Richius pulled the chains away. He was shaking visibly now, his hands hardly obeying him as they worked the latches. Sweat beaded on his forehead and cheeks and his breathing came in great, labored pants.

The box creaked partially open, revealing a sliver of its dark recesses. Lucyler craned his neck over Richius' shoulder. He could see nothing.

"Dear heaven," Richius whispered. "Oh, heaven, no . . ."

He flung open the chest, the lid flying backward and crashing against the floor. Lucyler tried to see but Richius was standing. His hands went to his head and his voice rose from his throat in a tortured cry.

The cry became a scream. Richius collapsed, scrambling backward away from the box, his legs flailing, trying desperately to be away from the thing in the chest.

Commotion erupted in the chamber. Kronin raised his jiiktar. The Shadow Angel straightened for the blow. Tharn lurched toward Richius, his palsied hand outstretched. Lucyler looked into the box.

A face he barely recognized stared back at him, mottled with decay and topped with a filthy mass of blond hair. Its eyes were open in perpetual death, blue and horror-stricken. Lucyler felt a rush of nausea. He reached down and grabbed the open lid, slamming it shut and roaring out to Kronin, "Kill him!"

Kronin's jiiktar flashed. The Shadow Angel's helmeted head toppled from his shoulders. And Richius' screams went on and on.

When Richius had at last quieted and had been escorted from the banquet chamber by Lucyler, Tharn stepped over the decapitated body of the soldier from Nar and painfully stooped to retrieve the strange letter from the floor. Kronin and the warriors watched him inquisitively, as curious as their master about the contents of the correspondence. Tharn's crimson eyes squinted as he read the scratchy penmanship.

> To the Jackal of Nar,
> The girl was everything I'd hoped. Sleep lightly. We are coming for you.
> With great hate,
> Baron Blackwood Gayle, Governor of Aramoor Province.

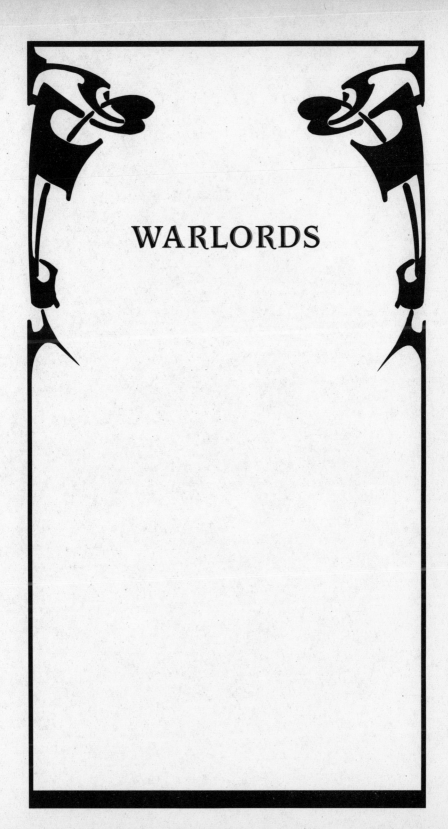

WARLORDS

From the Journal of Richius Vantran:

We were married by a church neither of us believed in, on a wintry but beautiful day. Sabrina was the loveliest bride in the Empire. Her white gown had been specially made for her by the dressmakers of Countess Elliann, and when she first appeared in the cathedral everyone fell in love with her. I was a lucky man that day. She was perfect. But I never told her so.

Count Biagio stood in for Sabrina's father. I remember how proud he was to do it. I don't know if he has children of his own, but Sabrina didn't mind and it seemed to make Biagio happy—something we all agreed was a good idea. Arkus wasn't there, and I was glad for it. Except for Biagio, his wife, and the bishop, only my friends witnessed our wedding. Patwin stood by me the whole time, and though I missed Dinadin it was good to have Patwin so near.

After the wedding, Sabrina told me she wished her father had been there to see her married. I don't know why she always cared so much for that cold bastard, but his absence affected her deeply. She was right, of course. He should have been there to see his daughter wed. Now he'll never see her again.

I have been wondering how Arkus will explain all this to Sabrina's father. He is not such an important duke, nor is Gorkney a very important place in the Empire. Perhaps Arkus will simply say nothing, or perhaps her father just won't care. He never cared for her while she lived, and I doubt her death will impress him. But does Arkus have heart enough to *realize what he's done? For some reason this question perplexes me. I am in awe of his brutality now. He is not a man to me anymore.*

But it's not Arkus who has ruined me. Would I have ever believed it possible before? It seems so obvious now, I cringe to remember my blindness. Jojustin's story never made sense, yet I suppose I loved him too much to question it. The garden gate was locked, that's what he had told me, and the assassin had climbed over the wall to reach Father. But the garden gate was never locked. Father wouldn't have it that way. To him it was everyone's garden. He would open it to the servants and the stableboys. Not even the threat of a Drol assassin would have made him lock those gates.

So I am left only with Jojustin to suspect. Only he would have dared speak of my journey here. Only he was so enamored with Aramoor as to see my love as treachery. And only he loved Aramoor enough to kill its king. I would hate him for it if I could, but I think I have no hatred left in me. We have all killed for stupid ideals, and all our murdering only makes us suffer more. If my uncle still lives, then he is already punished beyond anything I could do to him. He is living in an Aramoor he always dreaded—one ruled by Gayles.

Still, I may be wrong about him yet. Dear Jojustin. Could you have done this to me?

All my loyal friends are gone now. I have seen how Arkus builds his Empire. I know that those who would not renounce me have been killed. Most likely Patwin died first. He was always loyal to a fault, and I'm sure he did his best to save Sabrina. As for Gilliam and the others, I suspect they were executed. The servants, too, probably, unless they had the sense to forsake me. If God is good he will have given them such insight. Except Jenna. Women do not do well in Talistan, and she is better off dead than sharing Gayle's filthy bed.

And perhaps that is what frightens me the most. At least I know Sabrina is dead. Whatever monstrous things Gayle did to her are over. But I can only guess at the tortures the rest of my people must now endure. Somehow, be it through Jojustin or some other fiend, Arkus has found out about me. He knows that the same taint that ruled my father has ruined me for Nar. He will not be so merciful with Aramoor this time. By giving Aramoor over to the House of Gayle he has destroyed us, possibly forever. Aramoor has only me for a champion, and I am in no circumstance to fight. Now they must endure the cruel governing of Blackwood Gayle, the very thing Jojustin sought so desperately to avoid. And so we have both failed our kingdom, and we are damned for it.

I have not seen Dyana since that day. I cannot bring myself to see her. If I didn't love her so foolishly I would never have made this trip, and Sabrina would still be alive. Dyana has sent messages to me through Lucyler. She wants to speak with me, to comfort me I suppose. But it all seems so pointless now. I should never have come to Falindar, and now that I'm stuck here I don't know what my place is. Tharn has been gracious. He has given me leave of the citadel, and has told me I may stay as long as I wish. As of now I see little choice. There is no home for me to return to, and though I am loath to accept his hospitality, I am a man without a country now, and would be a vagabond if not for this majestic roof. I have made a mockery of my father's throne, and now our enemy sits upon it in my stead. Someday maybe I will oust Gayle from my place, but that day is far away and I no longer command armies to make it happen. Today Gayle is the victor.

But I will have my vengeance on the baron from Talistan. For Sabrina alone I will see him slain, and he will rue the day he made us part this way.

Tharn has started to rally his people for another war. It's inevitable now, and he knows it. Amazingly he has asked me for help. He thinks my knowledge of Naren tactics can be useful. How poorly he knows me. These days I can handle a sword and little else. I just don't trust my instincts anymore, and my advice would only lead his warriors to a routing. But Tharn has been adamant. It seems he's not used to being refused, and he has a way with his people. Already Kronin's men are chafing for this fight. I pity them for their ignorance. For all his education and books, Tharn doesn't realize the machinery Arkus will mass against him.

Nor does he understand the emperor's inhuman thirst for life. The Drol speak of death as a doorway, an arch one passes through to reach another world. They don't fear death the way we of Nar do, and they cannot comprehend Arkus' desperation to cheat it. I've tried to explain this to Tharn but he doesn't hear me. He talks only of beating back the Naren tide. He gives pretty speeches and everyone adores him for it, but they don't know of the weapons of science or the emperor's fanatical legions. They remember us of Aramoor and Talistan and think that we were Nar's best. If they knew better they would be afraid.

The Shadow Angel that brought me Sabrina arrived here by ship. To me that means Arkus has finally ended his siege of Liss. There will be dreadnoughts on the shores of Lucel-Lor soon. They will surround this land like a noose and they will strangle it. If Tharn is as wise as everyone believes he will make the pact the Lissens want. Perhaps their navy can protect these shores, and let the fighting take place on land, where I know these Triin are best. I see little hope for their cause, but they are strong and they are many, and if the Lissens ally themselves with Tharn this may yet be a war to challenge Arkus and his legions.

THIRTY-ONE

It was the dress that made Dyana realize Richius wouldn't talk to her. Or more precisely, it was the note pinned to its sleeve.

For seven straight days Dyana had sent Lucyler to Richius, offering her condolences and begging him to come see their child. Lucyler always returned with polite refusals, explaining that Richius had nothing to say. Then, three days ago, Lucyler had come to her with the dress, a lovely brocade of scarlet silk that looked valuable even crumpled from the saddlebag. The note on its sleeve was from Richius. In that odd way men often have of being senseless, Richius had decided that staying in Falindar would be much more tolerable if they never saw each other again, and if he could accept that she belonged to another man. The dress, the note went on to say, was an apology. Dyana accepted it reluctantly.

But she thought of him often anyway, and she thought of him now as she put her infant daughter to her breast, fearful that the babe would grow up without knowing the father who lived just a flight of stairs away. He was a peculiar man, she decided, full of all the strange Naren idiosyncrasies her own father had warned her about. It distressed her that he would not speak to her. This was his way of acting strong, she knew, and yet it seemed uncharacteristically weak. At first she had been sure he would come to her once the shock of his wife's death had passed, but as his refusals mounted she realized there was something more in his silence. For some unknown reason, he suffered from the same lovesickness as Tharn, and it was making him foolish.

She opened her shirt and let Shani latch on, smiling at the pinching discomfort. This was their quiet time together, the late-afternoon feeding when the chamber was cool and all her attendants were busy with other tasks. Now that she was accustomed to feeding her daughter she enjoyed this time, and would look out of the window toward the sea as Shani gently suckled and cozied up against her breast.

Dyana was much stronger now. No longer did she need the wetnurse who had fed Shani the first few days. But the nurse was still around, dispensing invaluable advice on how best to perform this motherly act. She had taught Dyana how to hold the baby and how to get her to drink, and how to keep her from getting too hungry so that the feedings weren't an attack. At first nursing had been a painful nuisance, but as Dyana mastered the delicate art she found a sense of wonder in it. She was never more in love with her daughter than when she put her to her breast.

"Shani," said Dyana, brushing at the fine hair atop the infant's head. "You are hungry today."

Shani squirmed a little in her blanket as Dyana sat back. Beyond the window bright sunlight played on the distant waves, and the warmth diffusing through the glass felt good on her face and neck. Effortlessly she held the baby in the cradle of her arm and watched the slow progression of the ocean.

A melancholy settled over her. Tharn had made quite a home for her here, so much different from her uncle Jaspin's home in the Dring Valley. It was like she was a little child again, spoiled by her affluent father. All her needs were met even before she voiced them, and it seemed like every morning started with a perfect sunrise. She held no title, for Tharn vehemently disdained such things, but she felt like a queen regardless—one of those regal women from Nar who painted their nails and had slaves taste their food. And though her husband wasn't fully functional, he was gentle with her and respectful, a claim few Triin women could boast. She wasn't his equal, of course, but he did speak to her, sometimes with amazing candor. Drol cunning-men seldom talked to their wives about anything more important than meals, but Tharn was unusual in this regard and she was grateful for it. He was even passionate in his own impotent way, always concerned for her health before his own, which was never less than dire.

So why was she so unhappy?

An image of Richius flashed through her mind. Lately thoughts of him were becoming irksome. He had made his decision. It didn't matter if she disagreed with it. She had a husband and a child to care for. Richius would have to care for himself.

But she missed him. Amazingly, she was fond of the strange fellow from Nar. He was gentle like Tharn, but much more vulnerable. His frenzied screams when he had discovered his dead wife had become the talk of the citadel, and there were those among her own attendants who spoke of him as less than sane. Dyana did not share their sentiments. When she had learned of his wife's execution, she had cried for them both. There was something bitingly tragic about him, something that made him always push his way back into her thoughts.

She glanced down at the suckling Shani, tracing a finger over the small contour of her ear. She had his features, his eyes and colorful hair. These things would mark her all her days in Lucel-Lor. But she also had her mother's features, the thin bones and frail face, and these things too would mark her if she ever ventured outside Triin borders. And so she was very much like Richius, an innocent youth made homeless by circumstance. She was the Jackal's daughter, and only Tharn's grace protected her from those who hated her father.

Her mood soured a bit more. War with Nar was imminent now. She could lose all of them—Richius, Shani, even Tharn. Not even the high walls of Falindar could protect them from the Empire's weapons, that's what Lucyler was saying. Instinctively she held Shani closer. They might need some sort of miracle to survive, and it was the responsibility of each of them to pray for one. Drol or non-Drol, they all had the work of the faithful to do.

Dyana herself was not very faithful. Until very recently she hadn't even believed the gods existed. Seeing Tharn's broken body changed that. Like hundreds of others, she had witnessed the cunning-man's powers and the terrible toll the lords of heaven had exacted on him. To her, Tharn was vital proof that gods indeed held sway in the world, and if he said to pray then she would pray with all her strength, and hope that her voice reached the ears of caring powers.

"I pray for you," she said to the nursing infant. She always addressed Shani in Triin. It was Tharn's one demand. "I pray for your peace and your life."

But will it be enough? she wondered. It was commonly known that Tharn would never use his arcane abilities again. This time the gods would need to devise a different means to save them. This time all the demons of the Empire were against them, and though she knew much less of Nar than did her husband, she knew enough to understand the threat they posed. Nar had the weapons. She had already seen the handiwork of a flame cannon. The Triin had only jiiktars and courage.

"And Tharn to lead us," she added thoughtfully. The realization heartened her. He was a fanatic, too, capable of inspiring his people to great deeds. He had already organized the warlords and put an end to their bitter squabbles. If he could do that, then surely he could unite them in war against Nar.

"Tharn will save us," she whispered gently. "Do not worry."

Shani obviously wasn't worried. She continued to nurse, oblivious to her mother's words. Dyana smiled lightly. Shani was such a good baby, not at all like those other terrors she had heard about when she was carrying. Even her wetnurse had commented on the child's mildness. Dyana was proud of her.

A sudden shuffling outside her door startled her. Quickly she pulled Shani away and drew her garments close. But then she recognized the sound of her husband and relaxed as she heard his rapping on the door.

"Husband?" she ventured. "Come in."

The door creaked slowly open and Tharn appeared. He looked at her apologetically.

"Dyana, can we speak?"

Dyana unclasped her hand from her shirt and let it hang open again. "Yes," she answered. "But I am nursing. Do you mind?"

Tharn glanced down at her open shirt and for one brief moment something like lust flared in his eyes. But he looked away quickly, closing the door with a clumsy effort.

"I do not mind," he said. He turned back to her but would not look at her again, choosing instead to distract himself with the view outside the window.

Poor man, thought Dyana as she brought Shani back to her. She could almost feel his struggling. He always hid it well, but sometimes, like now, it bubbled to the surface and was plain to any woman who had ever seen desire in the eyes of a man. Tragically, Tharn could do nothing to ease his appetites. He couldn't force himself on her if he wanted to, and for some odd reason she pitied him for this. Carefully she arranged her shirt closer about her bosom.

"You look thoughtful," she said.

Tharn seemed disappointed. "Do I? Forgive me. I am . . ." he shrugged, "preoccupied."

"Do you have bad news for me?"

"Not yet," replied Tharn dully. "But there are troops massing in the Saccenne Run. I think they will strike Ackle-Nye soon. When they do, then I will have bad news for you."

Dyana was silent. She knew that whatever Tharn wanted from her, he would ask her in his own time. He shuffled closer to the window, ignoring her for a while as he stared out at the day.

"I need you to do something for me," he said finally. "I would not ask you normally but you are the only one who can do this."

"I will do it if I can," answered Dyana.

"Is the baby well?" he asked.

Dyana nodded. "Yes."

"Strong?"

"She is strong."

"And you are strong, too, yes?"

He was still not looking at her and his evasiveness unnerved her.

"I am well now, husband, do not worry. What is it you want me to do?"

"It is a good day outside, not too cool. Perhaps you should take the child out for some sun and air."

"Is that your favor?"

"No," said Tharn. "Not exactly." At last he turned to look at her, and all the lust was gone from his expression. He shuffled closer, dragging himself next to her with his cane. She looked up into his serious eyes and felt a nervous flutter.

"Husband?"

Tharn stooped nearer. "What I am going to ask you is important, Dyana. But you may refuse me if you wish. I will not be angry. Do you understand?"

Dyana nodded. She didn't really understand but the pretense made him continue.

"Your man from Aramoor. He is not well. He is not thinking clearly. Do you know this?"

"I have hardly spoken to him," answered Dyana evasively, suddenly wondering how much Lucyler had told him.

"That is because he will not see anyone. My wife, I know you have tried to speak to him. You may admit it. I have not come to chastise you."

"Husband, no . . ."

"Do not lie," warned Tharn. "It is too easy to read your thoughts. You care for him, and have been trying to speak to him. I know this."

Dyana fussed with the baby, hating the way he spoke to her. But she had been indiscreet. She knew she should apologize, but the words would not come. Thankfully, Tharn seemed not to expect an apology.

"What is it you want from me?" she asked icily.

"I have been trying to get Richius to help us. He has knowledge that we need. But he will not listen to me or Lucyler. I think he might listen to you. I want you to convince him to help us."

Dyana's head sprang up. "Husband, I cannot. He will not see me. You know this already."

"If you go to him he will not turn you away, I am certain. He will not be able to because he loves you."

Dyana feigned a laugh. "He does not."

"I have no time for your games, woman," Tharn said roughly. "He loves you as I do. And I know you think much of him. To be honest, I am jealous. Now, may we continue with important matters?"

"Yes," said Dyana. "But I will not seduce him. And I will not deceive him, as you have."

Tharn's expression hardened. "Do not task me. I'm not asking you to deceive or seduce him. I only want you to convince him that he must help us."

"No, husband," Dyana insisted. "I cannot see him."

Tharn backed away a step, then said calmly, "Dyana, I have already told you I would not be angry if you refused me. But I want you to let me explain myself first. We are in trouble. If the word from Ackle-Nye is true then thousands of Naren forces are already poised to strike at us. And none of us knows as much about them as Richius. He may be our only hope."

"You are wrong. . . ."

"I am not done," he interrupted firmly. "They will be using weapons none of us have ever seen before. And their tactics will be new, too. We will be fighting the legions of Nar this time, the emperor's own troops. It will not just be men from Talistan or Aramoor. Richius can tell us what to expect. Even if he will not fight with us, he has knowledge we can use. I have learned all I can from my texts. I need him."

He leaned forward on his stick, satisfied with his speech.

"That is all of it," he said. "Now you can make a proper decision."

"And if my answer is no?"

"Then that is a proper decision for you."

Dyana laughed. "And you will be disappointed."

"I will," said Tharn. "But I will respect the decision." He moved in a bit closer. "I could order you to do this, you know. You are my wife. Most men do not grovel as I do."

"Husband, I do not think you realize what you ask of me," Dyana said boldly. "He has already told me not to try to speak to him. He wants nothing to do with me anymore, and though I do not understand why I know that he means it. And it is likely that he means what he has told you. If he does not wish to help you, I cannot change his mind."

Tharn's expression become earnest. "Dyana, if you go to him with the baby, if you show him what he is fighting for, I am sure he will listen."

"The baby? I will not manipulate him so."

"We must manipulate him," said Tharn sharply. "We must make him see everything. He has a child here! Let him tell you to your face he will abandon it. I do not think he can do it."

It was a horrible suggestion, and it appalled Dyana to hear it. Worst of all, she thought it just might work. Tharn saw things very clearly. He had already looked into Richius and found a caring soul there, one incapable of leaving his daughter to die.

"I know he cares about both of us," said Dyana. "But perhaps he doesn't think he can help us."

"He has already told me that," said Tharn. "It is nonsense. He just needs confidence, a reason to believe in himself. That is why it must be you, Dyana. I cannot get him to listen. He hates me and perhaps he should. But he loves you. He will do as you ask."

The presumption made Dyana chuckle. "Husband, you make too much of me. He has been strong enough to refuse to see me."

"So go to him without request. Do not let him refuse you. He is on the greens, Dyana, grooming his horse. He is alone."

"You want me to go now?"

Tharn nodded. "When you are done here, yes."

"No," said Dyana. "It is too soon. Perhaps when he is over his wife's death . . ."

"There is no time for him to grieve," said Tharn. "If you are going to do this, it has to be now. The Naren troops in the Run could strike at any time. Once they enter Lucel-Lor there may be no stopping them. There is also their navy to worry about." He pointed out the window toward the restless sea. "They could start landing men here soon, right outside our doors. We are in danger, my wife. We cannot waste time." His expression softened, and he bent nearer. "I'm sorry, but if you're going to refuse me I must know quickly. I have plans to make that cannot wait. The warlords have already been summoned for council. In less than a week they will be here. I have to be ready for them."

Dyana's face lit up with alarm. "The warlords? You've summoned them here? All of them?"

Tharn nodded nonchalantly. She could tell he perceived her fears. "All who can make the journey."

"And Voris? What of him?"

"I am expecting him," answered Tharn coolly.

Dyana bristled. For a wise man, Tharn could also be remarkably stupid. He already knew the danger this posed to Richius, and obviously he thought it acceptable. But Richius had to be warned. She would have to see Lucyler again, and make certain he told Richius about the Dring warlord's arrival.

"I want Richius at the war council," said Tharn. "He can tell us all what to expect. I need him on our side, Dyana. Only you and Shani can convince him to join us."

Shani made a bleating sound and a trickle of milk foamed from her mouth. Dyana lifted the babe off her lap and examined her. There were still times when she couldn't quite manage feeding the baby, like when she was distracted. She rose from her chair and passed by Tharn without regard, then placed the infant in her ornate crib, arranging the blankets comfortably.

"This is unexpected," she said finally. "I don't know if I can help."

"The choice is yours," conceded Tharn. "I will try to respect whatever you decide."

"You say Lucyler cannot convince him? He has tried?"

"More than once. I fear Richius no longer trusts him."

Dyana nodded dully. "I will answer you soon," she said. "By tomorrow morning." She could almost hear the smile crack on Tharn's face behind her. Under her breath she mouthed a tiny curse. Tharn always got what he wanted, damn him.

"I will wait for your decision," he said, then turned and shambled out of the chamber, closing the door as he left.

Dyana absently did up the buttons of her garment, ignoring Shani's cranky cries. She wanted to go to Richius, to show him his daughter again and listen to him weep about his wife. She wanted to sit down next to him and talk for hours about little things, and get to know him like she never could before. But none of these things were possible, because she was married to Tharn, and Drol love was terrible. All that she could do was tempt herself with Tharn's mission, talking to Richius of war and councils and battles and death instead of the things she wanted to talk about. That was her bleak choice; speak to him for Tharn or not at all.

It was a surprisingly easy decision.

Just as Tharn had promised, she found Richius outside on the greens, tending to a brawny brown gelding. The "greens" were really just a collection of grassy slopes on the citadel's south façade. More like an untended farm than a garden, they were overrun with colorful wildflowers and industrious honeybees. Because of their romantic trappings, they were a favorite place for men to take their lovers. Or, if they had no lover, to take their horses.

Richius didn't see her as she approached. He was busily brushing the horse's lustrous coat, taking each stroke with affectionate slowness. The steed wore a blissful expression, enjoying every moment of its master's attention. Dyana slowed and lightened her footsteps, blocking Shani's face from the sharp sunlight with her hand. Richius' tall shadow wavered on the grassy earth. She stepped into it.

"Thank you for the dress," she said nervously. "It is beautiful."

His brush hand stopped in mid-motion, hanging in the air for a moment before falling to his side. Next his head fell. She heard his plaintive sigh.

"You got my note," he said without facing her. "I'm sorry, Dyana. I meant what I said."

"I have brought the baby to see you," said Dyana quickly. At once he turned around. His serious face brightened when he saw the bundle in her arms. "You said you would come to see her. You never did, so I thought I would bring her to you."

"Dyana . . ."

"You are her father, Richius. If you are going to live here you should get to know her."

Richius looked contemplative. He dropped his grooming brush to the ground and moved closer to them, his eyes darting from one to the other and finally coming to rest on Dyana's face.

"I'm glad you've come," he said. "I've missed you."

And I have missed you, she thought. But she didn't tell him that. Instead she held out the child for him.

"Hold her," she directed. "You have not yet, and you should."

Richius hesitated.

"Here," she said encouragingly. "I will show you how."

"No, I know how," he said. "It's just . . ."

"What?"

"I'm afraid to hold her. I'm already in love with her, Dyana. If I hold her I don't think I will be able to let her go."

Dyana hurriedly put the baby into his arms, not waiting for him to refuse again. He was surprised by her actions but he took the infant up quickly, fumbling with her swaddling blanket as he tucked his arm under her buttocks and neck. The entire exchange happened without a single bleat from the baby. Dyana beamed at him.

"You have done this before," she said. "Where did you learn?"

"There were plenty of children back home," said Richius. "Someone was always pregnant." He laughed. "My father was constantly offering to watch the babies of the servants. The servants, mind you. He was king! He loved children, but every time they needed cleaning he called me to help him." Again he chuckled. "God, I hated that."

"But you learned well. Look, she is still asleep."

They both peered beneath the blanket into Shani's expressionless face. Only a rivulet of spittle distinguished her from a statue. Richius raised her gently to his lips and placed the smallest of kisses on her forehead. His eyes remained closed for a very long moment. When they opened again they were different.

"Thank you for bringing her," he said. "I was wondering if I would ever see her again."

"You had only to ask. I would never keep her from you. I tried to tell you that. Why would you not listen to me?"

As soon as she asked the question she regretted it. She knew why Richius had refused to see her. He had already explained it to her and here was the proof of it, painted all over his face. He loved her. Even being close to her was painful for him. That she did not yet share his pain so acutely only made her hate herself more. He went over to his horse, tugging on the beast's reins just once and walking back toward Dyana. The horse followed him.

"Let's sit for a while," he suggested.

Together they moved through the flowering grass to the edge of a smoothed rock, its surface well worn by thousands of prior squatters. They sat down on the outcropping, the horse stopping contentedly behind them, and Richius kept the baby in his arms, rocking her gently and singing her a barely audible lullaby. Dyana listened, impressed by the simple beauty of his voice. When he was done he glanced at her peripherally, a hint of embarrassment sparking in his eyes.

"That was pretty," she said. "What was it?"

"Just a song from Aramoor. I think my mother used to sing it to me when I was young, but I can't remember. I didn't know her very well."

And I do not know you very well, thought Dyana. There was a sudden tightness in her chest. *But I want to.*

"Did she die when you were young?"

Richius frowned. "I was about five when she died. She had a cancer. My father didn't tell me much more than that, but I remember waiting for her to come back. She never did."

"It must have been terrible for you."

"It was. But I think it was worse for my father. Friends of his told me he was never the same after she died. He wanted to have lots of children of his own, but she was too sick to have more after I was born. It's not good for a king to have only one son, you know. He always tried to protect me, but when the war came in Lucel-Lor, he had to send me." Richius' face tightened. "He was a good father," he said softly. "Not perfect, but I know now that he did his best."

"I am sorry for you, Richius," she said. "You have had such loss. I grieve for you." She hesitated, then added quickly, "And your wife."

Richius looked up from Shani and stared at her. She could hardly stand the burning emotion in his eyes, and yet she was glad she had spoken the word. *Wife.* There was so much to know about this dead woman. Curiosity seized her. She didn't even know the woman's name. Before she could stop herself she was speaking.

"What was she like, your wife?"

Richius seemed stunned by the question. He reared back, his eyes widening.

"That's an odd thing to ask," he said. "But I'm happy to answer, if only so people can remember her. Sabrina was the most wonderful girl in the world. I didn't know it, but she was. And the worst thing that ever happened to her was marrying me."

"Was she very beautiful?"

A smile stretched across Richius' face. "Beautiful beyond words. Every man who saw her loved her, and would have married her if they had the chance. She had blond hair and deep eyes, and her face was like something from a portrait. Yes, beautiful."

"Did you love her?"

"Ah, well, that's a difficult question."

"Did you?"

"She was easy to love," said Richius. "I think I loved her as if she were my sister, someone who needed my protection. Obviously I wasn't any better at protecting her than I was at protecting you. But I did care about her. Maybe not as much as she deserved, but I did."

"You are like your father then. You did your best."

"I failed her, Dyana. Just as I failed you. It's what I'm best at these days. Is there a Triin word for failure?"

"I will not tell you it," said Dyana. "I will tell you a better word. Say *neensata*."

"What?"

"*Neensata*," repeated Dyana more slowly. "*Neensata*. Say it."

Richius grimaced. "Ninshata." Dyana chuckled.

"*Neensata*," said Dyana, pointing at Shani. "That means daughter. Shani is your *neensata*." She pointed at herself, then to Richius. "*Jayato* and *dayator*."

"Mother and father?" guessed Richius.

"Yes. You are good at this, Richius. You know more Triin than you think. One more," she said, and made a circular gesture that included all three of them. "*Kafife*," she said. She was disappointed when she saw his eyebrows knit.

"I don't know," he said. "Something that means all of us?"

"Yes. All of us. Mother, father, and daughter."

He puzzled over it a moment more before his face collapsed with sadness. "Family."

Dyana nodded. "Family. We are a family, Richius."

"No," argued Richius. "We are not. You're married to Tharn."

"That changes nothing. Shani is our daughter. We are family. *Kafife*."

"Dyana—"

"You think you are alone here, Richius, but you are not. I am here for you. I will do what I can for you. Lucyler, too. He is your friend, no matter what you think of him now. He cares about you. He worries as I do. We are all *kafife*."

Richius smiled lightly. "You are kind to me, Dyana. I appreciate it. I didn't know how much I needed to talk to you until now."

"You can come to me whenever you want," said Dyana. "Tharn has not forbidden me to see you. Just do not come to my chamber unannounced. If you send word to Lucyler, he will arrange it, and I will tell Tharn you are coming."

"He's not like other men, is he?" asked Richius. "Drol, I mean. He doesn't guard you like other Drol guard their wives."

"He trusts me," replied Dyana. "Or he does not want to offend me by treating me poorly. I have told you, Richius, he is good to me."

"I see that. I'm pleased."

Dyana glanced away then. She remembered why she was here, and she was sure her face was coloring with guilt. There was still the ugly matter of Tharn's plans to discuss. She would have to broach it carefully. But she was too ashamed to continue the farce, and didn't want to complicate it with lies. She loved the honesty he had shown her and wanted desperately to reciprocate.

"Richius," she said weakly. "I must tell you something. You will be angry with me."

Richius looked at her. "What is it?"

"I have not come here just to show you the baby," she confessed. "I must have words with you about something important."

"What is it?"

"I am here for Tharn. He has asked me to speak to you for him. He wants your help, Richius, and he thinks I can get it from you."

Richius gave a short laugh. "Your husband is persistent. He's already had Lucyler try to enlist me, and he's come to me twice himself. Now you? Lord, he never quits, does he?"

"He believes what you know of Nar will be valuable to him," said Dyana. "Are you angry?"

"No," answered Richius easily. He looked down at Shani. "I'm still glad you've brought the little one to see me."

"There is something else," said Dyana. "Tharn is organizing a war council. He has summoned all the warlords to Falindar to talk of the coming battle with Nar. All of the warlords, Richius."

Her words didn't seem to register. He toyed with the baby, putting his finger under the blanket and tickling her gently. Shani, who was awake now, bubbled at the attention, her little face twisting with dimpled smiles.

"So?" asked Richius.

"You're not listening," she said anxiously. "Voris is coming here."

The mere mention of the Dring warlord erased all the pleasure from Richius' face. He slowly retracted his finger from beneath Shani's blanket.

"Voris," he whispered. She could see his apprehension. Apart from Tharn, there were few names that had engendered such fear in the loyalists of the Daegog.

"He will be here within the week," said Dyana. "Tharn told me so himself. When he comes, you might be in danger. You must be careful, Richius. If he bears you grudges Tharn may not be able to protect you."

"Voris coming here," said Richius incredulously. "It's astounding. I can't believe he'd risk entering Tatterak, not with Kronin still alive."

"Kronin will do nothing to him, and while he is here Voris will be polite to Kronin. They are at peace now because of Tharn, and will do nothing in front of him. But you are different. Voris has no reason not to quarrel with you. You are not Triin. Even if Tharn forbids it he might try to harm you."

"Then I will be very content to stay far away from him," said Richius. "Maybe he doesn't even know I'm here. Frankly I see no reason to tell him."

Dyana frowned. "But you do not understand. Tharn wants you at this war council. Voris will see you there."

"I know what Tharn wants, Dyana. I won't be there."

Disappointment surged through her. She reached out and touched his arm. "You will not go to help them?"

Richius shook his head. "I cannot."

"But I thought—"

"What did you think, Dyana? Did you think your coming here would change my mind? Well, you're wrong. I'm glad you brought the baby to me, I'm glad we spoke, but it changes nothing. I can't help Tharn, and I'm not sure I would even if I could."

"Richius, please listen to me. Tharn has told me there are already troops gathering in the Saccenne Run. Soon they will be ready to attack Ackle-Nye, and after that there may be no way to stop them. But you know things. You might be able to save them. Without your help they will certainly die."

Richius looked at her ruthlessly. "Understand something. They're all going to die with or without my help. I've already told Tharn he doesn't have a chance, but he's too stubborn to listen to me. The best he can do is gain the help of Liss and prolong the end. Lucel-Lor doesn't have the power to stop Nar this time. Arkus will come here with everything in his arsenal, and they're going to roll through here and kill everyone, including you and me and our little girl, and there's not a damn thing I or anybody can do to change that."

Dyana was horrified. "Do not talk like that, or we are doomed."

"We are doomed!" insisted Richius. "Doomed to hell. What does Tharn expect me to do? Build him a navy? Start some war labs so he can make flame cannons? The only reason we lasted so long in the Dring Valley was because we had Naren weapons to hold back Voris' warriors. Now imagine thousands of Naren troops all armed with those same weapons. What kind of chance do you think these people would have? That's what your husband is up against, Dyana. It's hopeless."

"It is not hopeless," countered Dyana desperately. "This is a big land, Richius. It has many, many people to defend it. Even your emperor cannot kill them all."

"Couldn't he?"

"There are still reasons to fight. I cannot believe you would give up so easily. You came all the way here just for me, and now you will not give Tharn or Lucyler just a little help? You are not the same person, Richius."

"That surprises you? I've lost everything I was fighting for: my country, my friends, everything. This is not my war anymore."

"There's nothing for you here to fight for?"

"Nothing."

"But Aramoor had things you cared about?"

"Of course. My father for one thing, and my uncles. They were my family."

Dyana smiled at him, and watched the color drain from his face. She reached into his arms and pulled away Shani, who gave a petulant cry at leaving her father. Then she rose and turned to go, saying but one word over her shoulder as she left.

"*Kafife.*"

THIRTY-TWO

The siege of Ackle-Nye lasted barely a day. When it was over, best estimates put the number of Triin casualties at over three thousand. Naren deaths totaled less than fifty.

Ackle-Nye, the city of beggars, fell to an overwhelming force that poured out of the Iron Mountains and did not stop the slaughter until everything alive was dead. It was a meaningless victory, for everyone in the imperial ranks expected to annihilate their foes, but the shockwave it sent rippling through Lucel-Lor galvanized the Triin. They had not thought the blow would come so soon, or that it would be delivered with such deliberate hate. They could not imagine that the walls of a city could be pulled down so quickly, or that the nozzle of a flame cannon could be aimed at a child. In the deserted territories surrounding Ackle-Nye, travelers claimed that the city's fires and choking plumes of smoke could be seen for miles, and on that night when Ackle-Nye crumbled and lit the sky like another setting sun, the city of beggars earned a different name—the burning city.

Nar had begun its war of terror. In the great tradition of Arkus and his lineage, they started by eradicating the starved and desperate, those Triin refugees that had flooded Ackle-Nye in the closing days of the war in the hope of scratching out a life. Nar had come with its armored horses and spiked machines, lumbering into the city at dawn with their flame cannons glowing. They were fueled and armed for a long fight, and they had come prepared to slaughter. The war wagons rolled in first, nightmarish vehicles of iron pulled by primeval, horned monsters and armed with a single long-range flame cannon poised perilously on their roofs. Capable of pumping a stream of burning kerosene two hundred feet or more, the war wagons were the pride of Nar's arsenal. They were the heralds of Ackle-Nye's destruction, and painted on their sides in bold Triin lettering was the genocidal message *"After today, there will be no more of you."*

And so it was as the dark message predicted. Three thousand Triin were dead by twilight, burned or hanged or mutilated, their corpses left in gigantic piles outside the smoldering city as food for rats and carrion birds. Not a single child was spared, not a single woman was taken into slavery. All were killed, for this was Arkus' warning to all Triin—that no mercy would be found. The old, wicked glory of Nar burned bright and terrible that night. And at the forefront of his legions was a man with a silver mask and half a face, a giant whose standard was a charging horse and whose voice boomed like thunder as he cried out for his nemesis the Jackal. Those who saw him thought him a resplendent demon in his armor of green and gold. Those who knew him thought even worse.

This was the story of Ackle-Nye's fall, or at least a reasonable telling of it. By the time the tale reached Falindar, no one in the citadel knew for certain how accurate it was. They only knew what Richius told them: that Nar was easily capable of such an atrocity.

Richius himself had not been shocked by the news of Ackle-Nye's fall. He had expected it to be fast and brutal. What he had not expected was to hear from Blackwood Gayle so soon. The baron of Talistan was wasting no time in finding him. He was Arkus' favorite again, with all the resources of Nar at his disposal, and he was using them to raze Lucel-Lor in search of one man. Richius had no illusions about the baron's agenda. To be sure, Gayle wanted vengeance on Tharn, but he wanted the Jackal more.

And perhaps it was this more than anything else that convinced Richius to help Tharn. He told himself it was for the sake of Dyana and the baby, but he knew a more sinister reason lurked in his heart. Blackwood Gayle was coming for him. He no longer had to plot a furtive mission into Talistan to find him. He wanted to run a blade along the baron's throat, and he didn't care if he was caught doing it. It was as if he had sworn one of those serious Triin oaths, that he would exact his revenge at any cost, even his own life—which, despite Dyana's kind words to the contrary, had become meaningless. Dyana and Shani would live or die without him, but the death of Blackwood Gayle was an irresistible temptation. He craved it.

When word of Ackle-Nye's destruction reached Falindar, Tharn disappeared into his chambers to grieve. He did not emerge again until the warlords of Lucel-Lor began arriving at the citadel. Boawa of Sheaze was first. The River Snake, as he was fondly dubbed, arrived with an entourage of leather-clad warriors and a gift of steel for the master of Falindar, a gleaming jiiktar forged by a master smith and engraved with runes that read *"Death to Nar."* Because he had arrived before any others, he was favored with one of the citadel's largest rooms, and in the manner befitting a warlord he quickly declined the ostentatious chamber so that he might stay with his men.

Soon after Boawa others began arriving. Almost every day saw another proud caravan entering the citadel. There was Delgar of Miradon and Praxtin-Tar of Reen, who traveled to Tatterak together despite their former rivalry. From the mountain keep of Kes came Lord Ishia, and out of the dreary eastlands came Shohar, dragging behind him his own tribute to Tharn, a collection of Naren skulls he had gathered in his first war against the Empire. There were over one hundred of the gruesome trophies, each one lovingly polished to an ivory sheen.

Others came with less remarkable gifts, gold and weapons and wives, all of which Tharn accepted gracefully, though he freed the women to become house servants and handed the weapons out to Kronin's warriors. He greeted each warlord with measured respect, never thanking them too profusely nor honoring them with too deep a bow. And each warlord he met returned his aloofness with profound regard, displaying their belief that he was touched by heaven and that he alone could deliver them.

The last to come was Gavros of Garl, and upon his arrival Tharn ordered the war council to begin. Preparations were made on the greens, for it was explained to Richius that the council must be held out of doors, where the gods of the sky could look down upon them and shroud them in protective moonlight. There were torches erected on the slopes and tables set with foods and wine and offerings of leopard teeth and snake venom. Braziers of incensed coal were readied so that their scented smoke could rise to heaven and awake the sleeping deities of the air, and wells were dug around the tables so that blessed water from the ocean could be brought nearer and ensure that the immortal lords of the sea would have a place to rest and hear the prayers of the faithful.

For Lorris and Pris, patrons of this Drol ritual, a very special wreath was laid on the center table. Woven from wildflowers and thorny vines, it was as large as a wagon wheel and its circular shape was meant to symbolize the unending devotion shared by the sibling gods. Golden candles were set along the ring, and were to be lit one by one by each of the gathered warlords. Richius watched the preparations in fascination, and while he watched and asked naive questions, he waited for Voris the Wolf. He waited until nightfall, when the ceremonial torches on the greens were lit and the moonlight played down on the gathered faces. But the Wolf never came.

"Will he be here, do you think?" Richius asked Lucyler. They were seated beside each other on a blanket spread out on the ground near one of the short-legged tables. The other warlords were starting to gather, waiting for Tharn to arrive. The war council would begin when the cunning-man lit the candle in the center of the wreath. Already the braziers were smoking, sending up their mystical signals. Lucyler caressed his jiiktar nervously, polishing its twin blades with a cloth so that both were unblemished. So enamored was he with his reflection in the steel that he hardly glanced at Richius.

"Tharn seems to think so," he said without moving.

Richius looked around. The odd Boawa had just arrived with his train of warriors, and was kneeling in prayer before the wreath on the center table. Shohar and Ishia were already here, as were most of the others, but Voris was conspicuously absent. So too was Kronin, a coincidence that Richius found immediately disheartening.

"He should have been here by now," said Richius anxiously. "The Dring Valley's not that far away. And where's Kronin? Shouldn't he be here?"

The mention of Tatterak's warlord caught Lucyler's attention. He finally raised his head and surveyed the assembly of armed warriors, clearly puzzled by Kronin's absence.

"Perhaps he is with Tharn," he offered.

"Maybe," mused Richius. He was growing more uncomfortable by the moment, doing his best to ignore the astounded stares of the warlords. He watched Boawa and his men kiss their jiiktars as they finished their prayers, seating themselves near the center table. The warlord's expression did a particularly comic twist when he sighted Richius. Richius looked away.

"I wish he'd hurry. These warlords make me nervous."

"Be calm," said Lucyler. "Nothing is going to happen to you."

"Do you think Tharn will want me to speak?"

"That is why you are here. Tharn wants the warlords to know what we are facing. Nobody knows better than you, Richius. Do not be afraid. Just tell me what you want to say, and I will translate. If they have any questions, answer them directly. Do not look away from them. You would appear weak."

Richius groaned. He had just done a fine job of appearing weak to Boawa. He looked again at the warlord, trying to make eye contact. The man from Sheaze ignored him.

"Are these all the warlords of Lucel-Lor?" he asked.

"Just about. Except for Voris and Kronin. And Karlaz, of course."

"Who's Karlaz?"

"From Chandakkar," said Lucyler. "The leader of the lion riders. He is not a warlord really, just a clan head. Tharn sent a messenger to him, asking him to come here. The messenger was sent away." Lucyler snorted. "Tharn should never have bothered."

"I don't know," said Richius. "Those lions could be useful against Gayle's horsemen."

"Richius, it would not matter if Tharn got down on his knees and begged them to come."

"How come?"

"Because they want to be left alone. When the Daegog asked them for help against Tharn, they ignored him. Now they are ignoring Tharn. They are a selfish lot that have no loyalties to anyone but themselves."

Richius merely nodded, remembering his violent clash with the lion rider in Dandazar. He had been such a fierce man, almost paranoid. It was easy to understand why Lucyler disliked them.

"If they're so bad why did Tharn want them here?" he asked.

"Because he wants all of Lucel-Lor united. That's why he has called this council, to ensure the loyalty of all the warlords and to organize our defense."

"He'll need their loyalty to even have a chance of stopping Arkus this time," said Richius. "I told you he would use everything he has. He's already sent in the war wagons."

Lucyler sighed. "War wagons. Even their name is terrible. What did you say those creatures are called?"

"Greegans," said Richius. "They come from the north of the Empire, near Gorkney. They're raised from birth to pull those wagons."

"Tharn says they are almost unstoppable. Is that true?"

Richius shrugged. Despite what they all thought of him, he was hardly an expert on Naren armaments. "That's what I've heard. I've only seen them once, when I was in Nar City." He glanced around at all the jiiktars, wondering how many blows it would take to crack the armored hide of a greegan. "They don't actually fight, they just pull the wagons. The flame cannon does the damage."

"Another miserable weapon," Lucyler said, examining his jiiktar. "Not a weapon for a real man."

"No? You liked them well enough in Dring."

"That was different," said Lucyler slyly. "We had them. Voris did not."

They both laughed, then fell quickly silent as a shadow passed over them. The figure of a bare-chested man was blocking out the moonlight. He walked past them toward the other warlords, a trio of similarly naked warriors trailing close behind him. On each of their pale backs was carved an identical tattoo, a ferocious bird of prey with outstretched wings. They were all bald except for a long, white ponytail sprouting from the back of their heads. Each wore leather armbands around both biceps, and the tallest one, the one who had cast the massive shadow, also wore a studded belt of well-worn buckskin. Their muscled bodies glowed in the flickering orange torchlight, making them seem more like spectres than men.

"Who is *that*?" Richius asked. He had never seen a more savage-looking Triin in his life.

"Nang," Lucyler whispered. "Warlord of the Fire Steppes."

Nang was like something from another time, a thick-skulled primate with the eyes of a cat and a serpent's sharpened teeth. He knelt down before the center wreath, bowing his head to the dirt then lifting it with a piercing cry. He sang his monstrous prayer until all the breath was gone from him, and when he was done he undid a tiny bag from his belt and tossed it onto the table.

"Another gift?" Richius asked. Lucyler shook his head.

"Not a gift. A spirit bag. Nang's people believe the soul of an enemy can be captured in such a thing. The bag holds herbs and stones meant to imprison evil. Nang is giving it to Tharn so that he may capture the soul of his enemy."

"Who would that be?" asked Richius.

Lucyler grinned at him. "Do you think your emperor has a soul to capture, my friend?"

"I don't know. But if he does, that bag's just about the right size."

There was an easiness to their banter reminiscent of other times, and Richius was glad to be with Lucyler again. Perhaps it was because he was the only friend left to him in the world, or perhaps it was because they were at war again, and war forces men together. Either way, Richius didn't care. Lucyler was himself again, open and honest. Now when he spoke, Richius believed him.

A group of robed cunning-men stepped onto the torchlit green, their heads bowed in silent contemplation. They walked past the gathered warlords, sitting cross-legged on the blanketed ground beside the center table. The table was almost full now. Only space for two more remained. Tharn was one of them, of course. The other, Richius presumed, was Voris.

Or Kronin, he thought with sudden alarm. He glanced around the assembly again, but the painted warlord was nowhere to be seen. Lucyler gestured to the cunning-men.

"Almost time," he whispered. "Tharn will be coming soon."

Richius suppressed a nervous flutter at the thought of addressing the warlords. He hoped Kronin would arrive soon. At least his would be a friendly face. Lucyler followed the lead of the other warriors, placing his jiiktar on the ground beside him. A soft breeze stirred the torches and the water of the wells. The conversations were politely muted. None of the foods or wine had been touched yet. Richius reminded himself that none of them had come here to eat.

"I will be glad when this is over," he said quietly, "and all these warlords go back home." He sighed and tried to relax, folding his arms over his chest. From the corner of his eye he glimpsed something white approaching slowly. It walked up beside him and stopped. Richius turned to look at it.

A dog? The animal stared back at him, its tongue drooping lazily from its mouth, and sat itself down on its haunches. For the smallest of moments Richius puzzled over it, until he realized that the beast was not a dog at all but a snow-white, smiling wolf.

"God!" he exclaimed, rearing back from the animal. "Lucyler, look at—"

From somewhere behind him a giant hand grabbed Richius' collar, lifting him off the ground. He sputtered, fighting the iron grip and turning to stare into an enraged white face. He knew at once who it was. Voris stared back at him, his bared teeth menacing. He released Richius' collar, taking him instead by the lapels and shaking him with wrathful exuberance.

"Kalak!"

Richius panicked. He kicked at the warlord's legs, landing one powerful blow on his shin before being tossed bodily backward. He landed hard on one of the tables, saw the decanters of wine and platters of food explode into the air. A sharp pain ricocheted through his body and the breath shot from his lungs. He tried to right himself. Lucyler's panicked shouts mingled with the sudden growling of the wolf. Richius scrambled. Wine covered his face, dripping into his eyes as he rolled over onto his stomach. Voris' pointed boot thundered into his rib cage. He bellowed in pain, reaching desperately for the only weapon he could find, a sturdy metal decanter sprawled over on the broken table. He grabbed it, sprung to his feet, and swung.

Amazingly, it caught Voris in mid-lunge, crashing against his bald pate with a peculiar, bell-like ring. Voris howled and stumbled backward. Richius staggered to his feet. All around them astonished warlords were staring, their jaws slung open in amazement. The wolf watched also, its muzzle lowered and a baneful growl rumbling from its throat. Lucyler had his jiiktar in his hand. He was dashing toward Voris and crying out a warning.

Voris removed his own jiiktar and in a single blinding movement flicked its long blade at Lucyler, catching him in the wrist. Lucyler cursed and fumbled his weapon. Blood gushed from the wound. Voris barreled past him, knocking him down with a shoulder. Richius readied himself, cocking back the decanter for another blow.

Voris stopped his charge. He held out his jiiktar then dropped it in front of him.

"Jara min, Kalak," he said through a taunting grin. Slowly he stepped over his weapon.

"You want me?" railed Richius. He threw the decanter at the warlord, who batted it away effortlessly. "Come get me!"

"Richius, stop," called Lucyler. He was crawling to his feet, nursing his bloodied hand. Voris only had to glance at him. The wolf turned from Richius to Lucyler, stopping the Triin with an angry growl.

"Eesay Voris," yelled Lucyler. "Hara akka Tharn!"

Voris laughed. "Tharn bena naka tor. Tassa Kalak!"

"Richius, he means to kill you," warned Lucyler. "Defend yourself."

It was stupid advice. Richius was already preparing himself for the tangle. He glanced past Voris to the two jiiktars laying uselessly on the ground. If he could reach one . . .

But no, they were too far. A torch then. He ran to the nearest one, yanking it free and holding it before him. Voris only seemed amused. He put out a jeering finger, gesturing for Richius to come closer.

"Jara min, Kalak."

Richius seethed. His side burned with pain from Voris' kick, and he slumped slightly as he took a step closer. The torch was heavy, too unwieldy to be of any real use. He dropped it and charged forward. Voris danced aside. The warlord's amused laughter echoed but Richius ignored it, rolling past and snatching up his discarded jiiktar. He jumped to his feet, holding up the weapon triumphantly. A cheer went up from the crowd.

"Now, you big bastard," he hissed. "I'm ready."

The jiiktar flashed, raking across Voris' chest. The warlord fell back. His robe split open in a thin, red rent, exposing his bloodied chest. He cried out and his wolf turned in alarm, just long enough for Lucyler to employ his own weapon. One blade caught a leg, shearing it off. The other finished the beast with a slash to the throat. Voris bellowed with fury. He tried to reach his slain pet, but Richius held him back with the jiiktar.

"Don't you goddamn move!"

Voris glared at him. He brought up his fist and shook it at Richius, then spit a wad of saliva into his face. Lucyler came up alongside Richius, his own jiiktar held ready.

"Go," he ordered. "Get back to the citadel. Find Tharn."

"Like hell I will," said Richius. He raised the jiiktar, determined to slice at Voris' throat.

"Stop," begged his friend, grabbing his sleeve.

Richius halted. "Damn it, Lucyler, why shouldn't I?"

"Leave," ordered Lucyler. "Now."

"No. I can't, Lucyler. I won't."

"You will," came a scratchy voice behind him. Richius turned to see Tharn standing barely five feet away. He stepped between the two combatants, his broken body trembling with barely contained anger, and put up a hand to Voris. He spoke to the warlord in a slow, measured voice. Voris shook his head briskly.

"Ahda!" he protested. He pointed at Richius, threatening him with a waving finger. "Pogoa isa Kalak."

"What's he saying?" asked Richius.

"Back away now, Richius," said Lucyler. He placed his own weapon on the ground then held out his open hands for Voris to see. Richius stood fast. "Do it," demanded Lucyler. "Quickly!"

"I won't," said Richius. "Not until you tell me what he said."

Tharn turned to regard him. "He said that you are filth," he replied blithely. "And that your presence here is a disgrace. Now move away."

"He attacked *me*, cunning-man," said Richius. "Let him back away first."

"You have already drawn blood," said Tharn. "Be content with that. He cannot yield before these others."

"It is over, Richius," Lucyler pressed. "Please . . ."

Richius stared hatefully at the bloodied warlord, seeing every bit of his ire mirrored in Voris' eyes.

"If he agrees not to attack me again, I'll lower the weapon," he said. "But I want to hear it first."

Tharn translated Richius' terms. Voris answered with a sardonic smile and some obviously insincere words.

"Not good enough," said Lucyler. "Richius, he says he will not harm you while Tharn is here. Tharn, make him say he will not harm Richius at all. Make him swear it."

Tharn and Voris exchanged more heated words. Finally the warlord nodded and took a step back.

"He did not swear it," said Lucyler.

"Nor will he," wheezed Tharn, turning on Lucyler with disgust. "You forget yourself. He is a warlord of Lucel-Lor. Remember that. Richius, give him back the jiiktar. Now, please."

There was an irresistible quality to Tharn's voice that made Richius relent. But he would not hand the weapon back to Voris. Instead he opened his hand and let the warlord's jiiktar fall contemptuously to the dirt.

"Let him get it himself," he said, then turned and walked away. Lucyler's loyal footsteps were close behind.

The table they had been sitting at was ruined now, so they found a more conspicuous place closer to the main table and sat down. The closest warlord was the feral Nang, who gave what Richius thought was an approving smile when he looked at them. Lucyler wiped the perspiration from his face, then reached for one of the decanters of wine, pouring himself a liberal glass of the stuff and drinking it down in a series of unending gulps. He set the cup down with a sigh.

"Lorris and Pris, you are not to be left alone, my friend. Wherever you go someone tries to kill you!"

"Arrogant bastard," said Richius. Several warriors were already clearing away the mess of the dead wolf. "I should have done it," he mused. "I should have finished him when I had the chance."

"You had no chance," said Lucyler easily. "Voris would have killed you."

"What? I had the weapon, Lucyler. He had nothing."

"He would have gotten it away from you, Richius, just as he did from me." Lucyler raised his bloodied hand and showed it to Richius. "He is big, but he is quick."

"Oh, Lucyler!" exclaimed Richius. "I'm sorry, I forgot."

Carefully he took his comrade's wrist and examined the wound running across the open palm. The gash bubbled each time Lucyler's fingers flexed.

"You have to take care of this," said Richius. "Get a bandage on it."

"Not now. You need me here."

"Lucyler, you're bleeding. Go back to the citadel and get a dressing. Come back when you can."

"If I leave you will not understand a thing they say," said Lucyler. "And I do not trust Voris." He offered Richius his sleeve. "Here. Use my jiiktar and cut off this sleeve. It will do well enough for now."

Richius took the scythelike weapon and began the clumsy work of removing the sleeve, careful not to slip or move too quickly. The sleeve tore easily under the sharp blade, leaving Richius with a long tube of fabric. He shredded it into strips and gingerly dressed Lucyler's hand, dabbing at the blood as he worked. When he was done Lucyler tested the bandage with a fist.

"Good. Thank you."

"It won't do for long," Richius warned. "That cut's pretty deep. You'll need to get stitched up."

"After the council," said Lucyler.

"Lucyler?" ventured Richius.

"Umm?"

"Thanks."

Lucyler nodded quickly. "It is what friends do, Richius. Now settle down. Tharn is coming."

The crippled holy man lurched across the sloping ground toward the main table. As he moved, the congregation hushed. Voris walked slowly alongside Tharn, carefully keeping pace with him. The warlord seemed unaware of his own wound, which had soaked his scarlet robes. Electric anticipation charged the air. The incensed breeze was sweet. Ocean surf sounded in the far distance. Tharn made it to the table and raised his clubbed hand to heaven. When he spoke his voice was like jagged lightning. Lucyler leaned close to Richius and translated.

"Lorris and Pris and the powers of earth and sky. Cast down your strength on us, the defenders of your faith. Grant us the might to cleanse your blessed kingdom, so that we may slay those without virtue who defile you."

Tharn reached for the center candle, pulling it free and igniting its wick with a nearby torch. Orange light danced on his skin. He said a few more words then passed the candle to Voris, who used it to light another of the wreath's candles and mouthed a solemn oath.

"Death to Nar."

One by one the candle was passed to the warlords, and each arose in turn to light another flame and speak the same dire oath. When each had taken their turn, only one candle was left unlit.

"Kronin's," explained Lucyler in a whisper.

Tharn bid Voris to sit, and lit the candle for Tatterak.

"We unite to still the hand of evil." He placed the largest candle back in the center of the wreath. "May the spirits of the world guide us, and make our council wise."

"Death to Nar," the warlords shouted in chorus.

"May the might of Lorris make the weakness of our flesh as iron. May the love of his sister Pris inspire us for the battle."

"Death to Nar."

Tharn turned his face toward the sky again and mumbled some inaudible words. His saffron garments glowed with the mystical aura of the candled wreath. Tendrils of hair fell around his shoulders like white snakes, and he raised his palsied hand into the air. He finished his prayer with a rasping cry then lowered his hand and faced the gathering.

Richius gasped. Tharn looked almost vibrant. His face still wore the same poxlike lesions, but his eyes were vital and clear, no longer shot through with webs of bloody veins. He breathed deeply and forced a smile past his crooked jaw, then sat himself down between Voris and Shohar of Jhool. It was a glimmer of Tharn's power Richius never expected. He looked inquisitively at Lucyler, but his friend hushed him with a slight shake of his head.

"Richius," said Tharn in Naren. "It is good you are here. Lucyler, you will tell him everything we say, yes?"

"Yes," replied Lucyler.

Tharn gazed out over the group. As he spoke Lucyler whispered in Richius' ear.

"Great ones of Lucel-Lor, you honor me by coming here. I thank you."

Each warlord gave a stone-faced nod.

"The dragon of the west has awakened. Did I not tell you that it would? Did you not all know in your hearts that one day the many-headed beast would come to devour all of us? But this is not a time for blame. We are united now. We are strong. Lorris and Pris watch over us. They have given us their power and wisdom. They have made the blind to see."

Tharn's eyes flicked momentarily toward Richius. Again the warlords nodded.

"Does he mean *me?*" asked Richius incredulously.

"Ackle-Nye is in the hands of our enemies," Tharn continued. "You all know this. You have heard of the rape of our poor brothers. The city of beggars is ash now, and outside its rubble Naren soldiers set up camp. Already they are starting to spread through the countryside."

He summoned Voris to speak.

"This is true," said the warlord. "Scouts from my land have seen the approaching flags of the Narens. They are coming for my valley in great numbers. Soon there will be war again in Dring."

"As there is war nearby, here on the very shores of Tatterak," added Tharn. "There has been a landing of Nar's Black Fleet, east of here near Harada. As we speak brave men are fighting and dying." He gestured to the solemn candle, the one he had lit for Tatterak. "You have noticed the missing lord of this land. Kronin is not here for this council, for at this moment he and his warriors are defending us. I know not how the battle goes for them, but they are trying to keep the Narens from reaching Falindar. Nar cannot land their ships any closer to the citadel, for the shores are too rough here. So they must fight through Tatterak to take us. We will see that they do not.

"But we must also protect ourselves from their fleet, and so I have asked the help of the hundred islands. Liss has already sent an emissary, requesting our aid in their struggle against the Empire. It is my belief now that this war has ended, that Nar has decided to use all its strength against us. But the Lissens continue to fight. I have sent back the Lissen emissary in a new ship with orders to tell his king that we are with him. Together Liss and Lucel-Lor will slay the dragon of Nar. If they can protect our shores, Nar will only be able to come at us through the Saccenne Run. And that will be our salvation."

Richius listened intently. This Tharn was brilliant.

"You must all pray mightily for the Lissen to make it home again. Even Nar fears the schooners of the hundred islands. From what the emissary has told me, their navy has not suffered greatly under the blockade of their homeland. He claimed that they have long reserved more than fifty ships for the day when they could break free and attack the shores of Nar itself. So you see, my great allies, we are more than strong. The emperor thinks we are weak but we are not. We will send him this message in blood!"

A rousing chorus broke from the warlords and they banged their jiiktars on the table, spilling wine and food. Tharn's face erupted in a triumphant smile.

"Oh, my friends," he cried. "This is our greatest task, to be men in the face of demons. Because we are united we are powerful, but this must never wane. Only doom will profit from our quarrels. Nar alone cannot defeat us, not with all their mighty sciences. Only we can defeat ourselves. This war council must be as one. And we will speak with one voice." He paused and looked at them seriously. "My voice."

No one challenged him. The beating of jiiktars grew louder and Nang let out a blood-chilling war-whoop. Voris got to his feet and held his weapon high above his head, letting his ruined robes hang open and his bloodied flesh shine in the moonlight.

"We are one with Tharn!" he bellowed proudly. "Drol and not Drol, we are brothers!" Slyly he looked over at Richius. "Even our enemies are delivered to us," he proclaimed.

Richius shifted uncomfortably, thinking to rise then dismissing it. He heard Lucyler's faint order to stay calm. Every baleful eye turned toward him. Tharn smiled at him encouragingly.

"Yes," agreed the cunning-man. He looked questioningly about the gathering. "Do you know who sits with us at this council? Do any of you but Voris recognize this great enemy?"

Richius cringed. "What's he doing?"

"Easy," whispered Lucyler. "Trust him."

Tharn struggled to his feet. "This is Kalak," he cried. "You know the name, yes? Kalak of Aramoor. If you do not know him then ask the warlord Voris. Kalak alone kept the Drol of Dring from slaughtering the weak Narens he protected. As you have seen they still hate each other." He glared at Voris and then at Richius. "This too shall end. All of you will respect Kalak. For this is a king who has lost his kingdom to aid us. And I have plans for him, just as I have for each of you."

"What?" Richius blurted. "What plans, Lucyler? What's he talking about?"

Lucyler shrugged. "I do not know."

"I'm just here to answer some questions. He'd better know that."

"I told him," said Lucyler with some annoyance.

"You have all done well by coming here," Tharn continued. He was placid again, and had his hand on Voris' shoulder. "But we are not complete yet. There is no one here from Chandakkar."

A low murmur rumbled through the crowd. Tharn silenced them with a scowl.

"Quiet now. You may hate who you wish, but this is a battle for all Triin. They should be here with us."

Voris shook his bald head. "The lion people are not to be trusted," he said firmly. It was the first time any of them had interrupted Tharn. Surprisingly, the cunning-man seemed pleased by the challenge.

"I could lecture you on brotherhood, my friend," said Tharn with deference, "but you most of all know about loyalty, so I will not question your instincts. I do not know if the nomads can be trusted. But we must be willing to find out. We need them."

"We are enough without them," argued Voris. "You may beg them to come, but they will ignore you, just as they did last time."

Another of the warlords spoke up, Shohar from Jhool. He nodded his agreement. "The lion people are notorious," he said in his brittle voice. "They know nothing of sacrifice, and they worship none of our gods. I would rather fight without them than beg their help."

"We do not beg," countered Tharn. "We ask. When they understand the threat they will listen."

Voris chuckled. "You are always too good, Tharn. Is there nothing you cannot forgive? At least these others here had the courage to fight against you. But Chandakkar turned you away, and turned away the Daegog. They are without honor."

"Words," said Tharn. "None of us knows enough about them to make such a claim. You argue with Kronin over a tract of land and you say that he too is without honor, yet he may be dying for our cause as we speak. If you and he can ally together, why not we with Chandakkar?"

Voris glanced away. "Kronin and I hate each other no less."

Tharn moved closer to him. "There was a time when you would never have breathed the air of Tatterak. Now here you are, sitting down with those you once called evil. Think on that, my friend."

"No, Voris is right," came Shohar's shrill voice again. "I myself have over one thousand warriors. Most of these others have at least that many. We do not need Chandakkar's help."

"No?" said Tharn. "How many is that, Shohar? I have looked at the numbers myself. It is a goodly amount, to be sure. But it is not enough to stop Nar. Even if Liss does keep them off our shores, they are already pouring through the Run. We need to stop them there. The lions could do that well."

Shohar thought for a moment, then asked, "Is that your plan? To stop the Narens at the Run?"

"There is no other way. If we are ever to stop them we must take control of the Run. But it cannot be done quickly. The Narens already have the region secured. And it cannot be done with jiiktars and horses. We need to surprise them in the mountains. For that we need the lions."

"They are coming for my valley," said Voris impatiently. "*My* valley. I will not depend on the nomads to defend us."

"You will defend yourself," said Tharn. He looked around the gathering. "All of you will. My only plan for the nomads is to use them against the Narens in the Run. Once we close off the passage Nar will be unable to send more troops in. Then we will deal with those left on our soil."

"First the nomads must be convinced to help," said Shohar. "That will not be easy."

"Perhaps they do not know what happened to Ackle-Nye," suggested Tharn.

"Or perhaps they do not care," said Shohar.

Tharn's face soured. "When they see that their own lives are threatened, they will join us."

"Until then we must make plans," said Voris anxiously. "We cannot wait for them."

"Nor will we," said Tharn. "As I have said, I have plans for each of you. Lucyler?"

"Rayamo, Tharn?" said Lucyler.

"In Naren," Tharn ordered. "I want Richius to understand us."

Richius straightened at the mention of his name. The sudden sound of his own language was oddly strange.

"Lucyler, you know Kronin well. You know Tatterak, too. You must help Kronin. Nar is too close. We must defend ourselves, keep them from Falindar. I want you to do this."

"Willingly," answered Lucyler. There was a glint in his eyes, the kind of foolish zealousness Richius had seen far too often.

"Gather the warriors still in the citadel. Take them and go where you are needed. Fight with Kronin or without him, I care not which."

"I understand," said Lucyler. "But what of Richius? Is he to come with me?"

"No. I need other things from him."

Richius could take no more. He cleared his throat and stood up alongside his companion. "Tharn," he began haltingly. "You know why I'm here. I've agreed to help you with information. If you have other plans for me I wish you'd tell me now."

"Wait," warned Tharn. "It would be better."

"No. Tell me now. I'll probably refuse anyway, and you will have your answer all the quicker."

"Very well," said Tharn. He turned to the gathered warlords, telling them all to eat and drink while he attended to Richius. The warlords wasted no time in reaching for the wine decanters. Only Voris refrained. Tharn asked him to rise, and the two made their way alongside the table to Richius and Lucyler. Richius bristled as the warlord of the Dring Valley approached, quietly wondering what Tharn had in mind for him.

"We will speak in Naren," Tharn said. "Lucyler, explain what I say to Voris, please."

"I will tell him," answered Lucyler warily. Tharn stared hard at Richius.

"Voris knows nothing of what I am to tell you, King Richius. Do not be surprised by anything he does now."

Voris frowned as the translation became clear. He prodded Tharn to continue.

"He doesn't looked pleased and neither am I," said Richius. The sense of impending dread was agonizing. "What is it you have planned, Tharn? If it's to work with this maniac . . ."

Tharn lifted a hand. "Lucyler . . ."

"I will not repeat that," Lucyler assured him.

Tharn smiled. "Yes. Be careful what you tell Voris."

"My God!" cried Richius. "That is what you want, isn't it? You expect me to work with Voris!"

Voris became incensed. He glared at Tharn, angrily demanding some explanation.

"Tell us everything, Tharn," implored Lucyler. "Please."

"King Richius, you heard what I said about the Empire's troops, yes? They spread through the countryside. They will strike Dring soon. If they take it, they can divide us. You know this."

Richius nodded. He knew very well the strategic value of taking the Dring Valley. He had spent nearly two years of his life trying to do the very same thing. With no luck.

"Dring is where you are needed. I meant what I said to the others. You may not think so, but your surviving Dring was like a miracle. I know because Voris has told me so. You are clever. This is needed in Dring. With you and Voris both there—"

"Voris is enough for anyone," said Richius. "Trust me. He can handle his valley without my advice."

"It will be more than advice," said Tharn. "I want you to command there."

"Kalak?" thundered Voris. His face purpled and a stream of protests rolled off his tongue. Tharn sighed heavily, letting the warlord exhaust himself before replying. Voris was wrathful and loud, Tharn as peaceful as a lake. Richius threw up his hands in disgust.

"This is ridiculous. Lucyler, tell him to forget it. Maybe he'll listen to you. He doesn't seem to hear a damn thing *I* tell him."

"Richius, calm down," said Lucyler easily.

"Stop telling me to calm down!" Richius flared. He turned back to Tharn. "Tharn, I'm going back to the citadel. Tell this madman he can stop arguing with you, because I agree with him. He doesn't want my help and I don't want to help him. Fine." Richius started away but Tharn grabbed hold of his arm.

"Stay!" hissed the cunning-man. Another angry order quieted Voris. Tharn released Richius' arm and spat at his feet. "Both of you are sickening!" he raged. His voice resonated with remarkable vigor. "See these others here? They watch you and they think you are fools. You are like children. But I care not of your pride, either of you! You must do this thing. Must!"

As Lucyler translated the Drol's tirade, Voris shrank back with shame. He bowed his head to the ground, avoiding Tharn's eyes. But Richius roiled at the insults. He pushed past Voris and stuck his finger into Tharn's face, punctuating each word with it as he snarled.

"You have used me for the last time, Tharn. I agreed to help you and this is what I get for it? You know how I feel about Voris. How could I not hate him?" He shook his head in disbelief. "Everyone thinks you're so wise, but this is one of the stupidest plans I've ever heard."

Tharn's eyes smoldered. "Come with me," he rumbled, then turned his back on the astonished trio and slowly shuffled away from the war council. All the warlords watched him depart but said nothing, and the silence made Richius at once self-conscious. He glanced at Lucyler.

"Just me?" he asked.

"I think so," answered his friend. Voris was already walking away from them, returning to his place at the council table.

Richius stiffened. "If he thinks he's going to change my mind . . ."

"Go with him and find out," urged Lucyler. "I will stay here with the others."

"But your hand . . ."

Lucyler shooed him away. "Forget about it. Go."

Reluctantly Richius agreed, going off along the dark slopes after Tharn. The cunning-man had made very little progress, and Richius overtook him easily. Tharn was breathing hard, as much from ire as exertion, and was mumbling to himself distractedly as Richius came up behind him.

"What do you want from me, Tharn?" Richius asked acidly. "I've already given you my answer. You're not going to convince me otherwise."

"Silence for once," Tharn snapped. "Follow me."

"Why? Where are we going?"

"Where we can talk without other ears. Now come."

Richius followed, letting Tharn guide him wordlessly back to the citadel and through the place's tall doors. The trip was arduously long, made more unbearable by Tharn's stony silence. Each time the cunning-man faltered, Richius reached out for him, and each time Tharn pulled angrily away, not even opening his mouth for an insult. They were alone as they entered the citadel, but Tharn kept going, past the indoor court and past the dingy rooms where crippled men talked and busy women settled children down for sleep. Finally, when they reached the main stairs, Richius stopped.

"Tell me where we're going," he said as politely as he could manage.

Tharn did not turn around but instead put his foot on the first riser of the stairs. "Up."

"You can't get up those stairs without help. Don't even try."

A second later Tharn's foot slid off the riser. He tumbled backward into Richius' arms.

"I told you, you fool," said Richius. Tharn struggled to right himself and Richius let him go. "Now, if you want to go upstairs, you'll either let me help you or we'll talk down here. It's your choice."

"Upstairs," Tharn conceded breathlessly. "Please."

"All right," said Richius, taking the man's arm and securing it around his shoulders. He put his own arm around Tharn's waist, fighting a wrench of nausea at the sensation of loose skin beneath the saffron robes. Tharn gasped with pain, and Richius quickly eased his embrace. "Better?"

Tharn nodded. "Yes."

"Good," said Richius, guiding Tharn up the stairs. "Careful now. We'll go slowly."

"Yes, slowly."

Inch by agonizing inch they made their way up the spiral staircase, bypassing any who came down the narrow passage. Some offered help, others politely ignored them, and Tharn greeted each of them with an impatient wave. Richius gritted his teeth against the sickening stench of rotting skin. He had never been so near Tharn before, and wondered how the cunning-man himself endured the odor. It struck him suddenly that Tharn was barely five years his senior, and yet he was helping him up the stairs as if he were ancient.

"Much further?" asked Richius. His back already ached from the awkward gait.

"To Dyana's chamber," Tharn replied.

"Dyana? What are we seeing her for?"

"Take me to her."

Thankfully Dyana's chamber was not as high up as the others in the citadel. When they reached the hallway leading to it Tharn spilled out of Richius' arms. He started off down the hall without a word, at once regaining his recent iciness.

"You're welcome," muttered Richius loudly. Tharn ignored him.

"Come," he ordered.

The hallway was dim and quiet. Dyana's chamber was near the end of the corridor. Tharn traversed the distance with remarkable speed and rapped insistently on the door. A long pause went by with no answer. Richius guessed that Dyana had already retired for the night. But before Tharn could knock again the door pulled cautiously open and Dyana peered out. Bewildered, she looked at Tharn and then to Richius, then finally back to Tharn.

"Husband?"

Tharn pushed the door open with his cane. Dyana stumbled backward. She was dressed in a simple gown that told Richius she was indeed readying herself for sleep. She blinked at her husband in alarm.

"What is it?" she asked. Tharn did not step inside the chamber.

"King Richius is going to the Dring Valley," he said tersely. "He will be leaving in two days. He will need an interpreter. You will go with him."

Dyana stared at him as if she hadn't heard. "Husband?"

"What?" erupted Richius.

"Teach him our language so he can learn," Tharn continued. "It is important, Dyana. Do your very best."

"I don't understand," Dyana stammered. "Why must we go to the Dring Valley?"

"Richius is needed there," said Tharn. "And you are the only one who can teach him."

"But Shani—"

"Take the infant with you. Voris will look after you both."

Dyana's look was baleful. "Husband—"

"Do not argue with me!" snapped Tharn. "Now sleep. You will need to be rested." He hooked his hand around the door handle and pulled it closed, shutting Dyana away. Richius could hear her astonished curse behind the door.

"Are you insane?" he asked. "You want her to go with me? Why?"

"You need an interpreter," said Tharn. He went to another door and knocked. This time it opened quickly. The nurse Richius had seen in Dyana's chambers days ago appeared. Tharn tossed off some quick demands and she stepped out into the hall, wrapping her arms around him just as Richius had. Slowly they made their way back to the stairway.

"Don't ignore me," said Richius, keeping pace with them. "I want to know what this is all about. Why should she go with me?"

Tharn would not look at him. "You do not speak the language and Lucyler is needed elsewhere."

"Rubbish. What's the real reason?"

"That is it."

Richius grabbed hold of the nurse's arm and yanked her away. She shrieked and shrank backward, sending Tharn to his knees. The cunning-man cursed and glared up at Richius.

"Leave me be!" he hissed, fumbling to rise. Richius did not offer a hand.

"Tell me the truth."

"I have told the truth! You are needed in Dring. We cannot lose the valley."

"Not that," Richius barked. He held back the nurse with a warning hand. "Tell me the truth about Dyana. Why must she go with me?"

"Because she isn't safe here!"

Richius faltered back a step, stunned. He watched Tharn struggle to his feet. The cunning-man's expression was terrible.

"Tharn," began Richius weakly. "I don't understand. Explain yourself."

Tharn rubbed at his forehead pensively. "She is not safe here," he repeated through gritted teeth. "I must send her to Dring with you. I have no choice."

"You're worried about her? But she'd be safer here, surely."

Tharn pulled himself up with his walking stick. "No," he said. "There are many here in Falindar who know about you and Dyana." He looked at Richius curiously. "Does that surprise you? Yes, I can see that it does. I am not so blind myself, you know. She has not been the same since you arrived. Little things distract her." Tharn's face was sour. "It seems carrying your child has affected her."

Embarrassed, Richius could only shrug. "But why isn't she safe here? You're her husband now."

"There are many who think she is tainted from being with you. The child, too. They would kill her if they could."

"They wouldn't dare."

"They would," Tharn insisted. "Not all Drol are as I am. They see how she is, like a Naren woman. And they know the child is yours."

"But no one would harm her with you around," said Richius. "You can protect her better than I can."

"I will not be here to protect her much longer. I must go to Chandakkar. I must make Karlaz listen. If I do not return Dyana and the baby will be in danger. So they must go with you to Dring. She will be safe there. Voris will protect her. He is sworn to me."

"These others are sworn to you, too," countered Richius. "Aren't they?"

"Not like Voris. He is a friend of many years. He is a brother to me. He will protect Dyana." Tharn's face darkened. "And you will, too, I know. I have seen how you glow when you look at her. I am not as blind as you think."

"Tharn . . ."

"Do not deny it. I do not fault you. And I do not blame Dyana, either. She has a monster for a husband. Of course she would find *you* compelling."

Richius couldn't answer, so stunned was he by the man's honesty. More, he was intrigued. Had Dyana really changed since he'd come here? Was she enamored with him, too? The notion made his heart race.

"Tharn, I can't go to Dring. You don't know how Voris and I feel about each other."

Tharn laughed. "Oh, yes, I do."

"Then you know you ask the impossible. Voris will never work with me."

"He will because I have ordered it," said Tharn. "He will do as I say. Believe me, he is better than you think of him. And he needs you. The Dring Valley is too important. If it is lost, then the war is lost. You must help us, Richius, you must. We all must stand together."

"Easy," urged Richius, taking the man's arm. He waved the nurse over. Hesitantly she took hold of Tharn. "Go back to the council. I'll think on what you've said."

"No. I want your answer first. Dyana thinks you are a man of strength. Will you show us some strength now? Go to Dring. Defend it. Have your revenge on your emperor that way."

"It won't work. . . ."

"It will," Tharn said. "But you must put aside your feelings, as I have. Do you think I wish to send Dyana with you? I do not. But you have need of her, and I cannot leave her here. I do not trust you, but I have no choice. So you see? Even I am tangled in my plans. But know this. I am a Drol. I will not let you disgrace me. And Voris will be watching you."

"That sounds like a threat," remarked Richius sharply. "You shouldn't threaten someone from whom you need a favor."

"You will defend Dring because it is right to do, not because I ask it. As for Dyana, I do not believe she would risk being with you. She knows I love her. Call it an obsession if you wish, but I cannot stop it. I have never been able to, and I have tried. It is like that for you, too, is it not?"

Richius nodded sadly. "Yes."

Tharn smiled at him. "I do not hate you, Richius Vantran. I think my wife is right about you. But do not rival me for Dyana. Where she is concerned, I cannot stop myself."

It was a grim warning, and Richius accepted it grudgingly. He had already seen the lengths the cunning-man would go to for possession of Dyana, and he had no wish to repeat such violence. Especially not with Shani involved.

"Go back to the others, Tharn," he said. "Let me at least have the night to think."

Tharn inclined his head slightly, then let the nurse guide him away down the winding staircase.

For a long moment Richius stood alone in the hall. His side still ached where Voris had kicked him, but it was a distant ache, hardly noticeable. He thought of going to Dyana while Tharn was occupied, but the idea seemed somehow dishonorable. Tharn loved her. That was as evident as the moonlight. Richius stared down the hall toward Dyana's closed door, knowing that she was as troubled and confused as he was. Someone should explain it all to her, he thought.

He would do it. Just not tonight.

Dyana awoke the next morning determined to speak to Tharn. Now that his war council was over, he would have time for her, she reasoned, and even if he didn't she would make him see her. It was just past dawn and she was fussing with Shani, feeding the baby and cleaning her, and waiting for her nurse so that she might leave her daughter in search of Tharn.

She was incensed. Not only for being ordered around like a dog, but for being given the impossible task of teaching Richius their language. Worse still, she dreaded the thought of returning to the austere Dring Valley. Almost a year had passed since she had fled that awful place, stealing away with Falger and the other refugees, and she had promised herself that she would never return, certainly not while the Drol held sway. Now her husband was ordering her back there, and Dyana didn't know which she hated more—her impotence at being commanded or the thought of living with Voris.

"Damn him," she muttered as she put Shani into her crib. Tharn could be such an enigma. Just when she thought him kind, he turned back into an adder. And this time he had bitten her hard. This time, she knew, she would not be able to dissuade him. There had been a wildness in his eyes last night, a frightening singleness of mind. For whatever inscrutable reasons, he had made his decision. She would have to go to Dring. But not without a protest.

When the nurse arrived, Dyana left her chambers and started down the stairs that would take her to her husband's study. Tharn always rose before the sun and spent an hour in devotion, then whiled away the rest of the morning with his books. He did not care to be interrupted while he read, and more than once had chastised servants for disturbing him. It was his ailments that made him cranky, she knew, and so usually she left him alone, never troubling him until he emerged from his offices of his own choice.

But not today. Today she had business with the master of Falindar, and had nary a care for his precious solitude. She was almost at the bottom of the stairs when the sight of Voris made her halt. The warlord was coming up. He stopped when he saw her.

"Woman," he said thickly. "I was coming to speak to you."

Dyana straightened. "That is presumptuous of you. Those are my private quarters, upstairs."

"What I have to say to you should be said in private." The warlord gestured for her to turn around. "Back to your rooms. We will talk there."

"We will not," said Dyana hotly. "What is it you want, Lord Voris? Have you a message from my husband?"

Voris' face seized. "What I have to tell you is from me alone, woman. And if you would rather hear my insults in a stairway, so be it." The warlord ascended another step, so that he was face to face with Dyana. "I am to escort you to my home. I am to protect you there. Have you been told this?"

"I have," Dyana answered, not hiding her own distaste. "So?"

"I bring you a warning. I know you have feelings for the Jackal. I know that child is his. But let me tell you something. I will not allow you to disgrace your husband with that criminal. Not while you are under my charge. Tharn is sending you with me so that I may protect you, but I will protect him as well. His virtue is in my hands now. I will not let you disgrace him."

Dyana gritted her teeth. "How dare you?" she seethed. "Do not tell me my mind, Warlord. I am a grown woman."

Voris laughed. "Yes, this is the fire I have heard of. Oh, Tharn has always been so enamored of you. I cannot see why. To me you are nothing but a wild harlot."

"Get out of my way," said Dyana, brushing past him.

Voris seized her arm and pressed her against the wall. "I am not done with you."

"You are!" spat Dyana, wrenching free. "And you will not ever touch me again."

"And you will not let that Naren pig touch you, either, wife of Tharn. I will know it if he does. In my valley I know all."

"Then you should know I have no intention of being with the Naren," said Dyana. "I know who my husband is."

"Indeed?" barked Voris. "Tharn is far too trusting of you. I have warned him about you for years, but he would never listen to me. Now he tells me that I do not know you, that you are a good woman. But I do not want to know you, harlot. I do not want to hear your poison, and I do not want you spreading it through my valley."

"There is no cause for worry," said Dyana. "I want nothing to do with your followers."

"Good. Do not prove me right about you. For if you disgrace Tharn, I swear to you I will kill the Jackal, with Tharn's blessing or without." Voris fixed his blazing eyes on her. "And I might do the same to you."

Before Dyana could respond, Voris the Wolf turned and went back down the stairs, leaving her alone. She took one more step downward, then stopped, suddenly unsure what she would tell Tharn. Sometimes she forgot that she was a prisoner, but then things like this happened and the bars became visible again. Tharn wouldn't care about her complaints. He was a good man. She hadn't lied to Richius about that. He was kind to her, and gentle. But he owned her, and there was nothing she could ever do to change that.

Slowly, Dyana made her way back up the stairs toward her spacious, gilded cage.

THIRTY-THREE

In the days prior to leaving Falindar, Richius busied himself with plans for the Dring Valley's defense. He remained in his chambers for long hours, working well into the night as he scribbled maps by candlelight and thumbed through his journal to recall past misadventures.

Tharn had given him an ambitious project, for neither he nor Voris was willing to speak to the other, and Richius was forced to rely on his memories of Dring as he drew his maps.

It was a slipshod method at best. Having spent most of his time in the trenches just outside the valley's deep core, he had never seen all of Dring. It was a thick, forbidding place, but more than that he could not say. Castle Dring was in the center of the valley, and he had never been there, and to the south were marshes and swamps, which the Naren forces would certainly avoid. The heart of the valley was absolutely overrun with vegetation, so Gayle's horsemen and the war wagons wouldn't pose much of a threat. Richius knew the dense center of Dring would be relatively easy to defend. Voris and his warriors would have the advantage there. It was on the outskirts of the valley, where the land was flat enough for both horse and greegan, that the threat would be the greatest. This was territory they would probably lose quickly.

But they would have to try, and Richius set to work planning an elaborate scheme of trenches and traps for the war wagons and cavalry. There would be long spears to deal with the horsemen, and shields to deflect the fire of the flame cannons. Archers would have to be positioned in every trench so that they could pick off the infantry, and whatever war wolves Voris possessed would have the unenviable task of tangling with the monstrous greegans. Richius set it all down on paper and gave it to Tharn to pass along to Voris. Voris passed it along grudgingly to his men. The warlord of Dring didn't question the plans, however, but sent his warriors back to his valley with orders to begin the work Richius had directed. It was an uncomfortable arrangement, and Richius resented it. So too did Voris, and on the eve of their leaving for Dring, the warlord made his feelings plain.

That morning, Richius said his good-byes to Lucyler, who at the direction of Tharn had gathered the remaining warriors in the citadel and set out for the rough outer reaches of Tatterak to find and kill those Narens that had landed on their shores. It was a melancholy farewell, and it soured Richius' mood. He whiled away that afternoon in his chamber, jotting down notes in his journal and missing home and fretting over how Dyana and Shani would manage on the long journey to the valley. She would be the only woman on the trip and would need to feed the baby. Her privacy was the issue pestering him when he heard the knock on his door.

"Who is it?" he asked, setting aside his pen. There was another knock. Richius got out of his chair with a groan and opened the door. Outside was a grim-faced cunning-man, one of Tharn's devotees. The man handed Richius a note and departed without a word. The note read very simply, *"Come see me now."* It was not signed but the nearly illegible penmanship told Richius it was from Tharn.

"Where?" wondered Richius aloud. Stuffing the note into his pocket, he stepped out of his chamber and closed the door. He guessed that Tharn would be in his study, poring over his own collection of maps and books, and he sauntered casually down the narrow hallway, confused by the message but unconcerned. Tharn would be leaving in the morning, too, and probably wanted to know what progress Richius had made in his plans. Richius was sure he had enough to satisfy the Drol.

The Drol priests in the hall outside of Tharn's study stepped aside when they saw him coming. Since the council, the citadel had been alive with activity, and it was rare to be able to walk the place's corridors without seeing at least one of the ubiquitous holy men. They encircled Tharn like a shroud now, never letting anyone interrupt him unless they had known business. Richius scooted past them without regard. The door to Tharn's study was closed. A conversation leaked out beneath it. Richius cocked his head to listen. Tharn's voice was rasping in Triin. He hesitated a moment longer, wondering who else was in the chamber and hoping it was Dyana. But the cunning-men were watching him, so he knocked lightly on the door. At once the conversation stopped.

"Tharn?" he asked politely. "It's Richius."

Some shuffling noises sounded before Tharn's voice answered, "Come."

Cautiously Richius pushed open the door. He spied Tharn seated at his desk behind a pile of parchments and sloppily stacked books. The Drol leader looked up with a frail smile. There was a shadow on his face from the person standing by the window. Richius opened the door wide enough to see Voris' face. The warlord of the Dring Valley crossed his arms over his chest and made a grimace of contempt as he noticed Richius.

"Come in," urged Tharn. "Close the door, please."

When the door closed the room fell under a tense silence. Richius waited for Tharn to speak, chancing a curious glance at Voris. The warlord stared back. Tharn sighed, and gestured Richius toward the small chair by his desk. Richius remained standing.

"Very well," said Tharn impatiently. He blew back a strand of dirty hair from his forehead and leaned back in his seat. "Richius, do you know why you are here?"

"No," replied Richius. "Tell me please. I'm already anxious to leave."

Tharn chuckled mirthlessly. "It gets colder day by day around you. Why not sit? We have business."

"I'll stand. Thank you."

"Then I will sit," said Tharn. "And you and Voris can be as uncomfortable as you wish. But do not fight, please. I am too tired for it."

A reluctant smile broke on Richius' face. Regrettably, he was liking Tharn these days. It made it difficult to stay angry.

"We are all tired, Tharn," he said easily. "If your friend doesn't attack me again, I promise not to throw him out the window."

"If you want to die for something, make it for something valuable." He gestured to the chair again. "Now please . . ."

Richius relented, pulling out the chair and sitting down. He crossed one leg over the other and leaned backward, making every effort to seem relaxed. "Now," he said, pointing his chin toward Voris. "What's he doing here?"

As if he understood the words, Voris stepped forward and broke into an angry retort, pushing his finger into Richius' face. Richius swatted it away and sprang out of the chair, bracing for another fight. He didn't see Tharn's cane flash until it crashed against his shin. Before Voris could back away the cane struck again, cracking against the warlord's leg. Both men fell back with a howl. Cursing, Richius dropped into the chair, rubbing the bone to dull the pain. He scowled at Tharn and the cunning-man grinned.

"Now we can talk," said Tharn. "You will listen, yes?"

Richius nodded.

Tharn bid Voris closer with his stiffened hand. The warlord sighed dutifully and obeyed. Only when he was satisfied that he had an attentive audience did Tharn continue.

"We all go in the morning," he said seriously. "And I want things understood. Richius, Voris has made suggestions to me."

"I'm sure."

"Hear me now. He is not pleased with your plans for Dring. He disagrees."

"Disagrees?" Richius sat upright in his chair. "He's had four days to disagree with me. Why's he telling us this now?"

"He wants changes."

"No," said Richius. "No changes. He was supposed to start ordering the things I asked for. Didn't he start yet?"

Tharn nodded. "He has already sent some of his warriors ahead. The defenses you asked for are being made."

"Good. So what's the problem?"

"There is no attack plan," replied Tharn. "He wants to see an attack plan."

"There *is* no attack plan. You asked me to help defend the Dring Valley. So all right, I'm doing it. If you want an attack plan, ask him for one."

"He has already given me one. I want your ideas on it." Tharn shifted effortfully in the chair and produced a small map from the desktop. He held it out for Richius to inspect. It was of the Dring Valley. To the west were dozens of blotchy black pen strikes representing the approaching forces of Nar. To the east were a series of vertical lines. Richius guessed these to be his defense trenches. He shrugged and tossed the map back onto the desk.

"So?"

Voris spoke up, addressing Tharn directly. Tharn nodded as he listened.

"Richius, Voris wants to attack the Narens. He says that it would surprise them and that they could be overtaken with enough men. Do you agree with this?"

Richius choked back a laugh. "Attack them? Is he serious? With what? He'd need an army to overcome their forces."

"He proposes using all his warriors and wolves for the strike. He says the surprise would even out the numbers."

"He's wrong, Tharn. They'd be slaughtered. Even if they could surprise them, Nar has too many men ready. Attacking them would be suicide."

Tharn passed on Richius' words to Voris. The warlord argued vehemently.

"Voris wants you to know that he has built up his forces since you left the Dring Valley. He says that he has over two thousand men now. Enough, he says, to have destroyed you."

Richius smiled. "History. Besides, he's not just up against Aramoor this time. Lord, haven't you explained that to him? If he fights them on the flats he'll have to deal with the war wagons and the horsemen." He glanced mischievously at Voris. "And if we'd used horses we would have beaten him."

Tharn's bloodshot eyes rolled back in his head. "Enough, please. Now tell me, will you support this or not?"

"I will not," said Richius. "It is foolhardy and dangerous. Nothing good can come of it, I promise."

"Richius," said Tharn thoughtfully, "before you decide you should consider everything. The horseman you hate will be on the flats. It may not be possible for you to get to him otherwise."

"I know," answered Richius. He had already considered his slim chances of reaching Blackwood Gayle in the thick, inhospitable valley. It changed nothing. "I stand by what I've said. Will you support me?"

Tharn smiled grimly, addressing Voris over his shoulder. The warlord's face mottled with crimson as he listened. When his master was done, Voris spoke again, crossing his arms and throwing back his head. Tharn frowned and didn't translate.

"Well?" asked Richius. "What did he say?"

"He says that you are a coward. He says that your plan is a coward's plan." Tharn rubbed his atrophied hand distractedly. "Are you afraid to die, Richius?" he asked. "Because Voris thinks that you are. You should know that he is not."

"I'm no coward," replied Richius. "But if Voris isn't afraid to die, tell him to go ahead with his stupid plan. He'll be dead within an hour. And his valley will be no safer for it."

Tharn lowered his head. "And that is what we want, is it not? Very well. You know I do not think you are a coward, Richius. But you may have to convince Voris. Understand what I have done to him. He is a warlord of Lucel-Lor. What I have asked of him is a great dishonor. Because he is loyal he obeys."

"Does he?" asked Richius. "I mean really obey you? None of your stories now, Tharn. I want the truth. Don't let me get all the way to Dring just so he can slit my throat."

"You will be safe. I would not send Dyana with you if I did not think so. I am only warning you not to anger Voris. I will not be in Dring to protect you, and if he thinks you are less than what I have told him . . ."

"I understand," said Richius. He could see that Tharn was looking for a concession, so he added, "I'll try not to anger him."

Voris listened dumbly to their banter. He nudged at Tharn's chair leg with his foot impatiently, and Tharn explained to him what had been said. The warlord seemed satisfied. He gave Richius a sly smile.

"Now tell him to forget his plans," directed Richius. "Tell him to do things my way."

This Voris found less amusing. He made a sound like a whimper. Surprisingly, though, he didn't argue the point. He merely bowed to Tharn and left the chamber, ignoring Richius as he walked by, leaving the door to the chamber open. Richius rose and closed it.

"You told him?" he asked.

Tharn nodded wearily. "You have much to prove to him, Richius. Be careful."

"I will if I can," said Richius. "But he has to listen to me. Voris is wrong about attacking the Narens. If you don't believe me yourself—"

"I believe you," said Tharn. "I only wanted to be sure of your answer. Voris is a man of strong will. He always feels he must act. You are asking him to do nothing."

"Not nothing. I'm asking him to defend his valley. And to use his head for a change. Even he must know how foolish his idea is. He just wants to look like he's still in control." Richius shrugged indifferently. "If it's that important to him, maybe he should be."

"No," said Tharn. "It must be you. Only you know what Dring will be up against."

"I'm no expert, Tharn. I grew up in Aramoor, remember? And when it comes to the Dring Valley, no one knows it better than Voris. Really, maybe you should reconsider."

"No need. You have shown me what I wanted to see."

"What was that?"

"You are strong, like Voris, but smarter. I worried you would want to attack the Narens so you could get to the Baron Gayle. You surprised me. I am pleased."

Richius lowered his gaze to the floor.

"You take good news badly," said the cunning-man. "Why?"

"Sabrina," said Richius. "She deserves to be avenged. Maybe Voris was right about me. Maybe I am afraid."

"We are all afraid, Richius. We would not be men otherwise."

"Voris isn't afraid. You told me so yourself."

"I lied. He is afraid. He fears for his valley and his family. He fears for his pride, too. You think he is mad but he is not. He is simply unknown to you."

"But at least he's willing to go after Gayle. And Gayle didn't kill his wife."

Tharn waved the remark away. "These doubts you have are nonsense. A real man protects the people he cares about. That is all Voris is trying to do, and that is what you want, too. I have asked you to protect the Dring Valley. By doing so you are protecting Dyana and the little one. You are right not to attack the horseman. He and his brigands would slaughter you."

"All right," agreed Richius. "Point taken."

"Good." Tharn grinned. "And do not worry. The time may come when you can get to the horseman. When it comes, you will know it."

Maybe, thought Richius. *I just hope I'm ready for it.*

Tharn was pushing papers across his desk again, using his good hand to rummage under the stacks of books. "I want to show you something," he said. "Very interesting." At last he found a tattered parchment and his eyes lit up as he handed it to Richius, who inspected it with halfhearted interest. It was no bigger than a page torn from his own journal, and the Triin writing jotted across it was faded and runny. The parchment had that peculiar, warped texture paper always gets when it has been wet.

"What is it?" asked Richius, studying the foreign words. There were not many of them, but the sparsity made the paper no easier to read.

"See the signature?" Tharn asked.

"I don't read any Triin, Tharn. I'm sorry. What does it say?"

Tharn stretched forward and ran his yellow fingernail along the signature. He said very slowly, "Cha Yulan."

"Cha Yulan?" asked Richius. "What's that mean?"

But suddenly he knew what it meant. The old battle cry of the Dring Drol. Cha Yulan. The Wolf.

"This is from Voris, isn't it?" he asked. Tharn didn't answer. Richius dropped the parchment onto the desk. "Why are you showing me this?"

"That letter came to me two years ago," said Tharn. "When the war was not yet over. You were in the Dring Valley then."

Richius picked up the letter again, wondering which word was *Kalak*. "What's it say?"

"It says: 'My son is dead. I will kill the man from Nar.' "

Richius shut his eyes. The letter trembled slightly in his hand. "My son?" he asked. "Whose son? Voris'?"

"His name was Tal," said Tharn. "He was fourteen when he died. A warrior, just made. It was in the valley."

"Oh, no," Richius groaned. "Please don't tell me that. His son was killed? I didn't even know he had a son."

"One son. Three daughters. They are all still alive. Tal is dead."

"Damn!" Richius hissed, balling his fist around the note and slamming it down on the desk. "Is that why he hates me so much? Because he blames me for killing his son? God's death, how was I supposed to know? I killed a lot of people, Tharn. Too many."

"Think not of it. Anyone could have killed him. I doubt it was you."

"That's not what I'm saying. Doesn't anyone know how hard I worked to protect the people in the valley? I could have massacred them like

Gayle would have, but I didn't. And now to hear this . . . It's a nightmare!"

"What did you think?" asked Tharn. "That only old people die in wars? Tal was a warrior. He died a hero."

"That's not how Voris sees it."

"That letter was written long ago. He was in grief. And I did not show it to you to upset you. Nor to help you understand Voris, either. You miss something."

Richius threw the letter onto the desk. "What?"

"Can you not see? Voris is like you. He hates you, but he works with you. He knows it is best."

"He's nothing like me, Tharn," argued Richius. "He's a beast."

"But he *is* like you," Tharn insisted. "He hates you for killing his son. You hate me for killing your Edgard."

There was a childlike innocence to the words that made Richius falter. He realized suddenly that his hatred of Tharn had all but evaporated. Tharn smiled, his crooked grin full of warmth.

"You understand," he said knowingly. "Now we work together. You and Voris, too. We learn."

"That's a lot to learn, Tharn. Voris lost a son. He has a reason to hate."

"Hate and hate. No more hate!"

"I'll do my best," said Richius.

"Your very best, or Voris will not trust you. And you must learn our language, too. Listen to Dyana and study. It is important you understand us."

"I'll try," said Richius. "But there may not be time for much study. Things are going to get pretty busy, you know."

"Dyana will teach you and you will make time. I have told her this is her duty. She understands." A melancholy veil drifted over Tharn's face then and he looked away. "Yes," he mumbled to himself. "She understands."

The pensiveness in the Drol's voice nudged Richius' curiosity. "Tharn? What is it? What are you thinking about?"

"About Dyana," Tharn confessed. "She seems troubled. She has been . . ." His face wrinkled as he searched for a word. "Distant, I think. She will not speak to me now."

"She's probably just worried about you, that's all. She's afraid you won't make it back from Chandakkar. That's the way women are."

"Worried?" asked Tharn. "About me?"

"Of course," said Richius. "That surprises you, doesn't it?"

Tharn looked away. "I am not much of a husband."

"Neither was I," said Richius. "It doesn't make them care about us any less."

Tharn lifted his clubbed hand and stared at it, turning it slowly as he studied the pits and scars bubbling his skin and racing up his forearm. A questioning horror dawned on his face.

"I'll tell Dyana not to fret so much when I see her," Richius hurried to say. "I'll tell her the warriors will protect you. She'll believe that."

"No," said Tharn. "No warriors."

Richius stared at him for a long moment. "No warriors? You mean you're going to Chandakkar alone?"

"Not alone. Cunning-men are coming with me. Three of them."

"You're going to Chandakkar with these priests? Oh, no, Tharn. You need warriors with you. It's too dangerous not to take them."

"All warriors are needed here in Tatterak," said Tharn. "I will be fine without them."

"But Chandakkar could be overrun with Narens by now. You can't go there unprepared. You could be killed!"

Tharn put up his hand. "Stop," he ordered. "It is decided. Falindar cannot be left unguarded. Now speak no more of it, please. I am going to Chandakkar with my cunning-men. We will convince Karlaz of the lions to help us."

Richius chanced an honest question. "What if you can't, Tharn? What if the lion people won't listen to you? Do you have another plan?"

The light in Tharn's eyes dimmed a little. "They must listen. We need them. There is no other way to take the Saccenne Run. Only the lions can do that."

"There is another way," said Richius cautiously.

"What?"

"You," Richius said. "You can stop them at the Run or anywhere else. You know you can. All you have to do is try."

Tharn stumbled to his feet. "How can you say this? Do you not see me? Look!"

Richius struggled to keep his voice level. "I've seen you, Tharn. You are ill, that's all."

"Ill? I am cursed! Look at me, man. I am grotesque!"

"A skin disease," said Richius. "Leprosy, maybe. I don't know what it is but it's not a curse. You've not been damned to live like this, not by your gods."

Tharn's face went blank. "You do not understand," he said. "I have used my touch to kill." He made a sweeping motion over his body. "This is the consequence."

"No, not a consequence," said Richius. "A coincidence. Your power isn't a curse. You saved Lucel-Lor with it once. You can do it again."

"No," said Tharn wildly, collapsing into his chair. "Never say so! I am punished. It is true." He buried his chin in his chest and his voice became a broken whisper. "I am a freak. Unlovable to any woman."

Richius went over to the cunning-man, kneeling down beside him.

"Tharn, there are medicines that can help you. It doesn't have to be this way. You don't have to be in pain all the time."

"It is what the gods want," said Tharn. "Have you no belief? What more proof do you need than my wretched body?"

"But these medicines—"

"These medicines are Naren. There is no way to get them. And I would rather suffer than beg aid from the likes of the Empire. This I deserve. To deny the gods their vengeance on me would just be another crime."

Richius stood up. "You are wrong," he said. "You could save Lucel-Lor with your powers."

"No," replied Tharn. "*You* are wrong. You have much to learn about being Triin. The gods do exist, and they give men burdens. Listen well to Dyana, Richius. She never believed, but she does now. She will teach you these things."

Richius nodded slowly. "If you say so. But I'll need more than your word and your disease to make me believe it. Be well on your journey, Tharn. And good luck."

Tharn's eyes welled with sadness. "Richius," he said softly. "Remember what I have told you. Prove yourself to Voris. Be careful around him. He is a good man. Try to believe that."

THIRTY-FOUR

Past the midnight hour, when the moon was at its apex and the lingering moans of far-off surf drifted through the air, Tharn wandered alone through the splendid halls of Falindar, his face awash with candlelight. The stone floors tapped out his shuffling progress as he moved, slowly and with effort. The candle dish trembled in his hand, spilling burning wax onto his thumb, yet in all his pain it was but one more tiny torment, and the master of the citadel hardly noticed it. His mind was feverish. A rush of thirst and fascination pushed him on, making him drag his palsied leg ever closer to Dyana's chambers.

She would be asleep. She might even be angry with him. But Richius' words had kept him awake all night, and he could not leave his wife on the morrow without one last audience. He was afraid, fearful of the death he might find in Chandakkar, and terrified that he might never again look upon the woman who held his heart. He was a monster and he knew he was, and the thought that someone so lovely feared for him had humbled him to tears. Sleep was impossible. Tonight he craved the warmth of human flesh.

Dyana's flesh. The flesh that had always been denied him since his boyhood. When they met, so many years ago now he could barely recall, he had not been of an age to understand his yearnings. But they were deep and relentless even then, and they haunted him at night or when he was alone. It had been his greatest joy to hear their parents had betrothed them, and he had waited for her to come of age, enduring the hungers of his manhood without lying with another so that on that day when he tasted her at last he would be unspoiled. Unpolluted.

He thought of her often in those days while he waited for her to flower. He took her memory with him to Nar and thought of her as he watched the imperial ladies rouge themselves until their faces were red and drug themselves incoherent. And upon his return he thought of her still, and told his Drol tutors of the lovely wife awaiting him. He had bragged on her, and when she broke her father's vow she had given him only one choice. So he hunted her.

Tonight, he hunted her again. She was his wife now, and that meant he owned her. If his body would allow he could have forced himself on her anytime he wished it. But he no longer wished it. Perhaps this was love.

She shared the hall with her nurse and handmaidens, he reminded himself, and so moved as quietly as possible to her door. Carefully, he tucked his cane under his armpit and reached for the latch. She never locked her door, for he did not require her to do so as many husbands would. It was a small token of trust, and he supposed she appreciated it. His useless hand turned the knob slowly, losing its weak grip before finally twisting it open. A telltale creak whined from the hinges as the door swung open and the light of his candle swept inside.

Nervously Tharn entered the room, closing the door behind him with the weight of his shoulder. The latch shut with a quiet click. He surveyed the bedchamber. Moonlight streamed in through the windows, lighting Shani's crib. The baby was sleeping soundlessly under her swathe of blankets. Dyana's bed was against a far wall. He could see her dozing, unaware of his intrusion, her arms bare, her hair falling around her. An aching thundered in his breast, setting his skin aflame. The candlelight flickered on her white flesh, exposing her perfection.

He lingered in the moonlight. He felt ashamed and juvenile, like a curious boy kept forever from manhood. Yet he could not leave her, and he thought again of Richius Vantran, and how he too suffered under the same bewitchment. But Dyana knew she was his wife, and that gave him title over her and dominion. Even with his broken body, she was his forever. He wondered darkly if she were his reward for delivering his land, or just another of his patron deities' cruel jests.

Quietly, he stalked to the bedside. Dyana stirred, her eyelids flickering against the candlelight. Quickly he shielded the flame, blocking it from her sight. He had thought she had settled back to sleep when her eyes popped open. Tharn took a hurried step away from the bed. Dyana started with a shallow cry and drew back against the headboard.

"No," Tharn whispered. "Do not be afraid, Dyana. It is me."

Dyana's eyes narrowed. "Husband?" she ventured. "Is that you?"

"It is," admitted Tharn, embarrassed. "I am sorry I frightened you."

"What is it?" asked Dyana, sitting up. "Is something wrong?"

"Nothing is wrong," answered Tharn. He could see she was confused and stepped back to the bedside. She squinted at him, dazed and maybe a bit frightened, and he wondered just how ghastly he appeared in such murkiness. Dyana pulled the sheets closer around her body as she stared at him.

"Husband? What is it?"

Tharn could hardly answer. All the courage that had taken him this far vanished in a flash, abandoning him to the same puerile anxieties he always felt around his wife. He started to stammer a response, but abruptly stopped himself.

"It is nothing," he said finally. "I just wanted to see you before I left. Be well, Dyana."

As he started back toward the door Dyana called after him.

"Husband, wait," she pleaded. "Tell me what is wrong."

Tharn hovered near the door, watching his wife's impossibly deep eyes. He put the candle down on a dresser and inched closer to her bed. Dyana had dropped her fearful look and now seemed only concerned.

Concerned, thought Tharn. Like Richius had said.

"I am leaving in the morning," he said. "For Chandakkar."

Dyana nodded uncertainly. "I know."

"I am your husband," said Tharn. His lip began to tremble. "Have I been a fair one, Dyana?"

"Yes," said Dyana quickly. She waved him closer and took his hand. Her touch burned. "More than fair. You have been a gentle husband."

Tharn frowned. Gentle was not what he hoped for tonight.

"And you are happy here?" he asked. "And is the baby happy?"

"I am happy," said Dyana. There was enough sadness in her tone to tell she was lying. "Shani is healthy and growing. Yes, husband, we are both well."

"In the morning I will be leaving," he said again desperately. "Maybe for a long while. It is a bad road to Chandakkar. . . ."

Dyana stared at him, clearly puzzled by his words. "You must take care of yourself. Be wary. Listen to your cunning-men, and do not ride too hard. Rest often."

"I will miss you," he managed to say. "I will miss looking at you. You are beautiful, Dyana. Have I ever told you that?"

Dyana looked away. "No," she said awkwardly. "I am glad I please you."

"Oh, yes," said Tharn sadly. "Very much."

And then she looked up at him, and a sudden understanding dawned on her face. Terrified, he thought to leave, but she was staring at him in silent amazement, comprehending the thing he was hinting. Yet there was no revulsion in her eyes, only the endless mercy of womanhood.

"I am your husband, Dyana," he stammered. "I . . . I care for you. I . . ."

Dyana did not let him finish. She rose from the bed and drifted closer, putting her finger to his lips. Tharn hushed. Anticipation roiled through him, quickening his heart and drumming in his temples. He watched as her lips curved into the most serene smile.

"And I am your wife," she whispered. There was no dread in her eyes, only a kind of easy acceptance.

"Dyana," he breathed. "I am afraid."

"Do not be," she crooned, taking his hand. "Nothing will hurt you. No more pain, my husband."

He sat down on the bed and watched her, wide-eyed in the candlelight. She took a light step back and smiled at him, then pulled the straps of her gown over her shoulders. Tharn felt a dizzying rush at the sight of the smooth flesh. His mouth dried up, and in the moonbeams she was something holy, the light of heaven visiting earth. Her gown dropped to the floor and she stood before him in exquisite nakedness, beautiful and electrifying and perfectly crushing to his fragile self-image.

"We will be together tonight," she whispered. "And I will thank you for taking such care of me."

But when she came to him and began removing his robe, Tharn panicked.

"No," he pleaded, clutching for her hands and pulling them away. "Dyana, I . . . I am afraid."

"Be still," she said gently. "I will not hurt you."

"No, no," he repeated desperately. "You have not seen me. I am a horror to look at, a monster. . . ."

"You are no monster," said Dyana. Again she put her hands to his shoulders and gingerly started working down the robe. Tharn closed his eyes and felt the fabric being pulled down around his chest and arms. In a moment he was exposed to her, all his boils and ravaged flesh, and he dared not open his eyes for the stricken look he was sure he would discover. But Dyana did not gasp, nor did he hear her turn away. Instead he felt her warm palm press his naked chest. When he opened his eyes she was still with him, her expression as soft as the candlelight.

"Husband," she said through a smile. "You have been very good to me. You were with me when Shani was born, and I have not forgotten that kindness. Let me do this thing for you."

Tharn smiled back at her. "There is not much for you to do, Dyana. I am hardly a man at all."

"Then lie with me," she said. "Share my bed and let me hold you. You are so alone, my husband. I can see it in you."

Tharn barely stifled a sob. "Oh, yes," he groaned. "I hurt, Dyana. My body . . ."

"Shhh," she directed, wrapping her arms around him. With the lightest touch, she placed his head on her shoulders. Tharn began to weep, sickened by what he was. He felt her hand brush his back and heard her gasp.

"They tortured me," he explained. "They broke my knees. . . ."

"Easy," Dyana crooned. "Easy."

"And now look at me," Tharn went on. "I am in such pain, Dyana. Why has this been done to me?"

"I do not know," Dyana answered. "But tonight you are a man, my husband. A whole man."

"I am not," said Tharn. "I can never be again. I have done unspeakable things. I have so much blood on me, and I am damned."

"You are a savior, husband," said Dyana, stroking his oily hair. "You are touched by heaven. Lorris knows your mission. Have faith in him."

Tharn wanted to scream. He had loved his patron once, so much that he had used his gifts for death. And yet the touch in him was a curse, a dark, purposeless ability he knew he could never use again. Richius was right. He could end the war with a thought. But how much more pain could heaven punish him with? How much could he endure before madness conquered his sanity? He could rule the world with his gifts if he wanted to, he could think of stopping Arkus' black heart just as he had the Daegog's. But he had done that once, and the price had been this tortuous body. If he did it again, he was certain the price would be his soul.

"Dyana," he said sadly. "I love you."

The silence he had expected followed. But he was not angry with her. He knew that tonight she was loving him in the only way she could.

THIRTY-FIVE

On a grim, gray morning, Richius and Dyana followed Voris out of Falindar. They had Shani with them, and less than a dozen of the warlord's warriors to protect them. No one of consequence bid them farewell, not even Tharn, for the cunning-man had already left to begin his own arduous journey.

It was not a fine day for traveling. The perfect weather that had so blessed them had receded, leaving in its stead a gray drizzle that had them each soaked by the time they reached the bottom of Falindar's wondrous mountain. Only Dyana and Shani were spared the misery of the climate. They traveled together in a small carriage that had once been the conveyance of the Daegog's wife. Despite the carriage's diminutive size, it had ample room inside its cab for Dyana and the baby, and it offered the privacy a woman with an infant needed. It kept them both warm and dry, even as their driver endured the inclemency outside.

The fog was murky on the hillsides that morning, and Richius watched it roll across the terrain with a genuine sadness. He was leaving behind the vastness of Tatterak for the claustrophobic forests of Dring, and his guide was a man who had once sworn to kill him. Less than a year had passed since he had left that place, swearing never to return, and there were still times when the nightmares were fresh and as vivid as yesterday's memories. Enduring it again would be an effort. He would have to remember that there was a stake involved.

All that first day Dyana did not open the sliding door to her litter. She remained inside, even when the rain slackened enough for her to enjoy some air, choosing the solitude of her own thoughts instead of the subdued chatter of her fellow travelers. It was as Tharn had said: she had become distant. Only when the caravan finally stopped for the evening did she emerge, relieving herself quickly in the woods and accepting some food from Voris. She thanked the warlord briefly, then returned quietly to the wagon. She didn't even spare a glance to Richius, who ate alone that night with only his horse for companionship, and who slept apart from Voris and his warriors beneath a muddied blanket and a steady, melancholy drizzle.

That night, amid the buzz of crickets and the patter of rain, Richius could hear his daughter's faint cries behind the thin walls of the wagon. He rested his head on the filthy earth and watched from afar as Dyana's lithe silhouette lifted Shani to her breast. In the dark he was contented by her shadow, and his loneliness ebbed a little.

On the second and third days the rain deepened, and by the fourth day it seemed that the narrow road would become a swamp. They were near the border of the Dring Valley, in a region known as Agar Forest. The forest, Richius knew, was the infamous tract of land Kronin and Voris had clashed over for years, and he wasn't surprised at all to see the warlord's face clench as they rode through it. For Richius, it was the only source of amusement there had been since leaving Falindar. He had endured Voris' gruff orders for him to keep up, and he was weary from lack of sleep. Lightning, who had twice the breeding of any of the other horses, kept pace with the caravan easily, never missing a step even as Voris' own horse struggled with the dubious roadway.

Each night the same, tedious ritual took place. They would camp and light a cooking fire, and the warriors would prepare a simple meal. Dyana would stay alone in her coach, sometimes cracking the door enough for some fresh air but never speaking to anyone but Voris. Richius would gather up a plate of whatever unappetizing fare was offered, then sit alone with Lightning as the warlord and his men caroused and laughed and generally ignored him. And all the while Richius chanced glances toward the wagon, hoping for a signal from Dyana and never getting one. It was an irritation he found unsettling, and by the fifth day he had had enough.

That day the sun finally made an appearance. Agar Forest was behind them, and the general attitude of the caravan was good. Dyana had at last opened the small door to her coach, letting in the sunlight. They were in the Dring Valley now, and Tatterak's jagged, open spaces had become a fond memory. Another two days and they would reach Castle Dring. Richius decided to make his move.

Voris and the other warriors were ahead of Dyana's carriage. The warlord was talking and gesturing to the surrounding terrain. His audience was enamored by whatever tall tale he was telling, and even the coach driver seemed to be listening. A good time to slip in close, reasoned Richius, and coaxed Lightning to the side of the coach. He stared straight ahead and cleared his throat. Dyana was reclining with Shani in her arms, but when she saw Richius she leaned slightly out the open door.

"Richius," she whispered. "What are you doing?"

"Me?" he asked coyly, not taking his eyes from the road. "I could ask the same of you."

The driver heard him and turned to look. Richius smiled at him. The man turned back around.

"You shouldn't be talking to me," warned Dyana. "Voris may see you."

"So let him. You're supposed to be teaching me to speak Triin, aren't you? He knows that."

Dyana was contemplative. "Not now," she said after a moment. "Maybe when we reach Dring. When we can be alone."

"Why are you ignoring me?" asked Richius flatly. He liked the cold preciseness of the question, the way it made Dyana flush. She toyed with the baby, feigning surprise.

"I am not," she said.

"Yes, you are. I haven't seen you for days. How come?" Now Voris heard them. The warlord tossed a warning scowl over his shoulder, which Richius blithely ignored. "Are you angry with me?"

"No," said Dyana quickly. "Not angry. Please, I cannot explain."

"Is it about Tharn? Are you angry with him?"

No answer. Richius grinned.

"That's it, isn't it? You're worried about him. He told me you wouldn't speak to him."

Dyana scowled at him. Her voice was ice as she said, "You men are all so smart." Then she reached for the door and slid it closed.

Dumbfounded, Richius let the carriage pass.

But he was determined to get an answer, and that night, when the moon rose and a fog settled down and all the others were asleep, he twisted silently out of his bedroll and stalked toward Dyana's coach, avoiding the dying light of the fire. The warrior who had driven the coach was asleep against a tree, his jaw slung open in exhaustion. Richius moved past him silently, then past the sleeping Voris, masking his footfalls beneath the warlord's copious snores. He reached the coach and sneaked around to the side, well hidden from any restless eyes, and pressed his ear to the wall. What sounded like a baby's breath reached him through the cloth. But there was no movement. He peeked around the front of the coach, satisfied that Voris and his men were asleep, then moved back to the door and put his mouth to it.

"Dyana," he whispered. "Dyana, wake up."

He held his breath and listened. Nothing.

"Dyana, it's me, Richius. If you can hear me, open up."

Now Shani started to stir, awakened by his voice. She let out a disgruntled whimper. Richius smiled. *Good girl. Wake up Mother.* He scratched at the door with his fingers, hoping Dyana would see the fabric bulge. Shani's whimper grew to an irritated cry. Richius could hear Dyana starting to wake.

"Dyana."

There was a short, panicked gasp, followed by a stretch of confused silence. The shadow of Dyana's head bobbed as she strained to see past the cloth door. Richius tapped on the white fabric.

"Dyana, it's me," he said. "It's Richius."

"Richius?" she answered unsteadily. "What do you want?"

"Let me in, I have to talk to you."

The door slid open quickly and Dyana peeked outside. She looked at him, then past him. "What is wrong?" she asked. "Are you all right?"

Richius put up his palms to quiet her. "I'm fine. Nothing's wrong. I just need to speak to you."

She blinked. "Now?"

"Yes," said Richius. He squeezed his head and shoulders into the cab, looking about for some empty space. There was precious little, but he flashed Dyana an ingratiating smile and asked, "Can I come in?"

Dyana pulled her blanket closer. "Richius, what do you want? It is very late."

"I want to talk to you. Please. No one will see us."

"We will be at Castle Dring soon," said Dyana, shooing him away. "We can talk then."

Insistently Richius pushed himself farther into the cramped cabin, his foot missing the cranky Shani by inches. Dyana snatched up the baby and stared at Richius in disbelief.

"I don't want to wait until we get to the castle," said Richius sternly, pulling the door closed behind him. "We must talk."

"Why?"

"Dyana, I don't understand this. What's the matter with you? You haven't spoken to me since we left Falindar. Why are you avoiding me?"

Dyana turned away from him. She began fussing with the baby, adjusting her swaddling and rocking her to silence. Richius reached out for her, lightly tracing the skin of her hand. She flinched at his touch.

"Dyana, what is it? Tell me, please. You're frightening me."

"How can you not know?" asked Dyana. "It should be plain to you. We are together now, Richius. Without Tharn."

Richius shrugged. "We'll be all right without him."

"No. Do you not see? Look what he has done to us. He has left you alone with me. You are free from him now."

"Is that why you're afraid?" asked Richius, instantly offended. "Lord, Dyana, how could you think such a thing? Don't you know I would never harm you?"

Dyana looked at him pleadingly. "You misunderstand me."

And then suddenly he did understand. He could hardly speak or even breathe. He reached out for her again, and this time she did not shrink away.

"I am thinking of the baby," she said. "Voris will kill you if he thinks you have dishonored me."

Richius chuckled. "He will not, Dyana. He's Tharn's friend, and Tharn told him to work with me."

"No, you do not understand. Voris came to me, Richius. On the night of the council. He warned me not to disgrace Tharn. He said he would kill you if I let you touch me."

"When were you going to tell me this, Dyana? I should have known sooner."

"I was trying to avoid you," she said with annoyance. "But you are so stubborn. He must not suspect anything from us. He will kill you. And maybe me. He thinks I am bad for Tharn. He will take the baby from me. . . ."

"No harm will come to Shani," said Richius. "Or to us."

"Tharn loves me so much, Richius. He is sick for me. Voris knows that. And . . ." Dyana's eyes filled with confession. "I spent the night with Tharn."

"You did?" Richius said, not hiding his astonishment. "How?"

"He came to me, the night before he left. He was so sad, and he wanted me, wanted to be cared for. He shared my bed. And I felt nothing for him but pity."

"Tharn is miles away, Dyana. He cannot harm us."

Dyana shook her head. "No. Voris will tell him. He must never see us together, Richius. Never. Please . . ."

"Easy," crooned Richius. "Don't be afraid. I will not come to you again on the ride. But when we reach the castle—"

"No, not even there. Nowhere, Richius."

Richius sighed. "Tharn told you to teach me," he said. "So teach me. That way we can be together without making Voris suspicious."

"Can we?"

"I can be strong. We can still talk and see each other. You can teach me your language. Let Voris be suspicious. He won't have any proof. We won't give him any."

Dyana bit her lip. "The baby . . ."

"Shani will be safe. We won't betray Tharn. I promise you that. But I cannot be away from you."

"Nor I you."

Richius beamed. He kissed his finger, then put it to her lips. "Until the castle, then," he said, and didn't wait for her reply before silently opening the coach's door and springing out. He waved at her and she nodded, then closed the door.

Richius skirted around the coach and surveyed the campsite. The first thing he noticed was the silence. Voris' incessant snoring had stopped. He peered through the darkness to where the warlord slept, but he could not see the man's face clearly, only the steady rise and fall of his chest. Richius eased past him, never once taking his eyes from the man. When he was barely ten feet away he noticed the flashing of eye whites. Voris was staring at him. Richius froze.

Unsure what to do, Richius did nothing. The warlord's face contorted into a disapproving grimace. And then, remarkably, Voris shut his eyes and rolled over.

THIRTY-SIX

The Black City, as Nar had long been called, earned its name from the constant clouds of ash and smoke that drifted eternally above the city. It was an apt name, and particularly suited the place on warm spring days, when the wind was impotent against the heavy pollution choked up by the incinerators. On such days the sunlight struggled to reach the earth, and the shadows of the labyrinthine skyscrapers were rich and dark. There was a mood to the city on these days, a colorless depression shared by all in the ancient capital. It struck both the beggars in the streets and the royal fops in their posh apartments, for it was an ailment of the mind and crushing to the human spirit. Those with means escaped the city on these days, taking horse or carriage or boat to a place where the air was more natural. There were many places in the Empire a man could go to find clean skies. Count Renato Biagio had seen almost all of them. But he always considered himself lucky when he came home again, back to the bizarre city he adored. Nar was his truest love, more so even than Crote, and every time he saw its jagged silhouette he swooned.

Yet today, as he raced through the corridors of the black palace, he hardly noticed the splendor of his home. He had been called back to Nar unexpectedly, and the shock of it had jarred him. Biagio was afraid. For the first time he could remember, something valuable to him was at mortal risk, something more dear to him than Nar itself.

"I came as quickly as I could," he told Bovadin as they darted up the stairway. The little scientist had greeted his coach at the palace gates.

Biagio hadn't waited for an explanation. They talked while they ran, Bovadin trailing in Biagio's wake as he attempted to answer the count's endless questions. *When did it happen? Is he strong enough to speak? How long has he been asking for me?* Biagio only half heard the answers. His thoughts were on fire, as they had been for all the three long weeks since he received Bovadin's urgent plea to return. He had still been in Talistan when the letter came. From there, he had arranged transport aboard one of Nicabar's warships. The ship was called the *Swift,* but the journey had still seemed agonizingly slow.

"He will be glad to see you," said Bovadin, already winded from the climb. "It will cheer him."

"What is it?" asked Biagio over his shoulder. "The drug?"

"Just age," replied the scientist. It was the answer Biagio dreaded.

They stopped when they came to the corridor outside the emperor's bedchamber. It was unbearably warm. There was a blazing fire in the hearth at the hall's far end, spitting flames up the chimney. Biagio's perpetually cold flesh drank in the warmth like a flower.

"We've been keeping him as warm as possible," explained Bovadin. "It doesn't seem to be doing much good. His skin is like ice."

Biagio tossed off his cape and handed it to Bovadin as he hurried to the door. The scientist grabbed his arm. "Wait," he urged. "I want to prepare you."

"Is it that bad?"

"He can't walk, and he can't see. He can talk reasonably well, but hearing is difficult for him. You'll have to speak loudly."

Suddenly Biagio couldn't move. It was all too much, and his voice constricted in his throat. "My God," he whispered. "Can't you do anything for him?"

Bovadin crinkled his insectlike nose. "I'm not a wizard. The drug can only do so much."

"Well, make it stronger," said Biagio. "Double it: anything."

"I've tried all that. Nothing works. I'm sorry, but he's grown immune to it. It'll probably happen to us all eventually."

"I don't care about eventually," snapped Biagio. "You have to do something *now*. Find a different drug. Make up some new potion. Kill a hundred virgins, I don't care. Just do something!"

Bovadin stiffened. "I'm trying. But it's not that simple. And he's not expecting *me* to save him, my friend. It's *your* turn."

Biagio didn't reply. All his life he had known this moment would come, and now that he faced it he was like a child, fearful of the monsters in the closet. He hesitated outside the bedchamber, hovering just out of range of the knob. Arkus was more like a father to him than any man had ever been. The thought of life without the cruel genius was unbearable.

"Does he know I'm here?"

Bovadin made the most serene face. "No. He knows I sent for you, that's all. Nicabar is in with him now."

"Danar? What's he doing here?"

"Arranging troop transports to Lucel-Lor," sniffed the scientist. "Your orders, I believe."

Biagio nodded. "Good. While he's here we can discuss things."

"Not too much," warned Bovadin. "Don't get Arkus excited. I've already heard how things are going in Lucel-Lor. You haven't found anything yet. The emperor doesn't know that. He's been asking Nicabar about the war, but so far we've been able to keep things from him. He's going to ask you, so be careful what you say."

"I will," said Biagio. There was really little choice. Bad news could ruin Arkus now. He would have to be optimistic.

He reached for the ornate doorknob and twisted, pulling the door silently open. Immediately the scent of burning wood assailed him. In the corner of the lavish chamber was another hearth, rumbling with the same monstrous fire as in the hall. Biagio could hear its insistent crackling over the muted conversation. Against the wall was a massive iron bed, thick with lavender pillows and silky, cream-colored sheets. A golden harp stood unused by the bedside, a little stool resting vacant beside it. And reclining on the bed—so lightly that he hardly made an impression in the mattress—was the reedy, emaciated body of Arkus. His bony hand rested in the meaty grip of Admiral Danar Nicabar. The admiral did not see Biagio standing in the doorway.

"Danar?" called Biagio softly. He forced himself to step into the chamber.

Nicabar turned to glare at him, then his hard features softened with recognition. He waved Biagio forward.

"Who is it?" asked Arkus, lifting his head to stare blindly at the door. Gone was the golden voice, replaced by a hoarse croaking. "Danar, is someone here?"

Danar patted the emperor's hand as Biagio approached. "Yes, my lord," he said cheerfully. "Guess who?"

"Do not play with me, Danar. Is it he?"

"It is I, Great One," declared Biagio. He looked down at the man in the bed, almost weeping at the sight of him. "I have come as you've asked."

"Oh, Renato," breathed Arkus unsteadily. His voice quivered. "Renato. I knew you would come; I knew it."

"Of course I came," said Biagio. "I came as soon as I could."

He motioned for Nicabar to remove himself from the bed and quickly took his place, picking up the emperor's brittle hand. Biagio studied his sickly features, gazing into his dim eyes. The shimmering, preternatural blue was gone, replaced by a murky glaze of cataracts. A network of veins striped his face, and he seemed not to notice the viscous stream of spittle dripping down the desiccated skin of his jaw. Biagio swallowed and mustered up his strength.

"My lord, how are you feeling?"

"I am in hell itself," replied Arkus. "But I am better now that you are here, Renato. Oh, so much better."

"Bovadin told me you fell ill. I was in Talistan when I heard the news. Forgive me, my lord. I made the journey as quickly as I could."

Arkus attempted a smile. "You are here. That is what matters. You can stay with me now."

"Yes, Great One. Whatever you wish. You know I will do it."

Arkus tried to clasp his hand more firmly, but the muscles of his fingers only quivered. He let out an irate groan. Biagio stroked his hair to quiet him.

"Do not try to move," he said. "You are very weak. Bovadin says you must rest. Lie still. I am with you."

"Danar?" called Arkus weakly. "Are you still here?"

"I am, my lord," said Nicabar, coming to the bed.

"Danar, tell Renato what we've been talking about. It will interest him. Listen, Renato."

Biagio looked up at Nicabar and the admiral shook his head. He understood at once.

"Great One, this is not the time for such talk. You must rest. Danar and I will speak later."

"I am not an infant," said Arkus roughly. "And I am still emperor. Do not treat me as if I were already dead. Danar, tell him."

The admiral cleared his throat and said, "It may be nothing, really. You already know we've broken off our siege of Liss."

"Yes," said Biagio. "So?"

"Well, I think we're not through with them yet. I've had some interesting reports while you were traveling, Renato. It seems the schooners of Liss are on the move."

"What?" Biagio sputtered. "That's impossible! You told me the schooners were destroyed."

"Not all of them, apparently. My dreadnoughts have sighted them. They were heading for Lucel-Lor."

Biagio felt a desperate tightness in his chest. He glanced at Arkus, who was nodding dumbly. Nicabar shrugged, unable to explain the odd phenomenon.

"You hear, Renato?" asked Arkus. "Even as I die those Lissen pirates torment me!"

"But Lucel-Lor?" said Biagio, looking to Nicabar. "Why? It doesn't make sense."

"Obviously the Triin have found allies," said Arkus. "Common cause against us, you might say. What matters now is not why, Renato, but what we shall do about it. Danar claims there are at least a dozen of the schooners."

"Probably more," added Nicabar. "A dozen is all we've seen so far."

"And they're faster than our dreadnoughts," Arkus continued. "They could keep us from landing more troops on the Triin shores."

"They mustn't," said Biagio. "Danar, you have to stop them."

"We will try," said Nicabar. "But it won't be easy. Our lord is right. They are much faster than our own ships. Catching them will be difficult."

Biagio wanted to argue, but he held his tongue for his emperor's sake. If Liss was allowed to aid the Triin, the conquest of Lucel-Lor could become a slow, protracted stalemate. And that meant no cure for Arkus.

"Danar, you must do your best," directed the count calmly. Then he laughed and said, "These Lissens are a distraction we don't need!"

"You spare me," said Arkus darkly. "They are more than a distraction. They could ruin us. You must not let them, either of you. Do everything you have to, but stop them, do you hear?"

"We won't fail you, my lord," came Nicabar's reply. He seemed eager to leave, licking his dry lips as he spoke. "If there are only a dozen of them, they should pose little threat."

"A dozen ships," said Biagio, tossing off the notion as if it were nothing. "And how many dreadnoughts do you have, Danar? At least that many, yes? And the old war barges, too? These Lissens will be nothing to you. Really, Great One, you worry needlessly. We are already on the ground in Lucel-Lor. Let the Triin look to Liss for help. They will be but a petty annoyance."

Arkus smiled, appreciating his count's elaborate lie. "Renato, I will hold you to that," he said. "And you, too, Admiral."

Nicabar blanched. "I should leave you now, my lord," he said, backing away. "You and the count should talk. I will come to you again this evening. If you need anything—"

"I will send for you," said Arkus. "Thank you."

Nicabar bowed to the blind emperor, shot Biagio an insulted look, then turned and left the chamber. Arkus waited until the admiral closed the door before he moved again. He took hold of Biagio's hand with a grip as weak as water and closed his blind eyes.

"Oh, Renato," he sighed, breathing the name like a prayer. "I am so happy you are with me. I get nothing but lies from the others. The truth now, my friend. What news from Lucel-Lor?"

It was the question Biagio had been dreading. He forced up a sunny voice and lied. "Good news, Great One. We have the Triin on the run."

Arkus waited a moment for the count to continue, frowning with impatience. "And?"

"Well, Gayle has been doing a fine job," answered Biagio evasively. "I'm sure you've heard about Ackle-Nye. It was a complete success, and Gayle's men are on their way to the valley." He patted the emperor's hand. "Your legions are with him, and Nicabar's navy has started to land men on the coasts. By summer—"

"Renato!" demanded the emperor. "What news?"

Biagio faltered. "I'm sorry, Great One," he stammered. "We've found nothing yet."

Arkus' hand stilled, then the lips curled around the awful word, and it came out of his throat in a small, terrified whisper. "Nothing." His hand started to tremble, and he looked toward Biagio. "Nothing?"

"No, Great One. Not yet. But we've only just begun our search. Surely in the Dring Valley, or in Chandakkar—"

"It's there, Renato. Look for it!"

"We *are* looking, Great One. We're doing everything we can. Gayle is tearing Lucel-Lor apart for you. If there is a cure, he'll find it."

"He must hurry. There is no time to waste." Arkus shut his eyes and a tiny tear squeezed out from under a lid. "Lord in heaven, save me. I cannot walk, Renato. I am blind. My heart is next, I know it."

"No, Great One," soothed Biagio. "You will walk again. It is probably nothing more than some rheumatism. Your eyes, too. Bovadin will have another potion for you. Soon we will be walking in the garden together."

"I love your optimism," said Arkus. "But I am dying. And I swear to God I cannot stand the terror of it." The tears were dripping onto the perfumed pillows. "Help me, Renato. I am afraid."

"Do not be," said Biagio firmly. "I won't let you die, Great One, I swear it. If there is a magic in Lucel-Lor to save you, I'll find it. I will rip it out of Tharn myself."

"Yes, find it," begged the emperor. "Quickly now. God, that bastard boy has ruined me. Don't let him get away with it, Renato."

Biagio's eyes narrowed. "No. That I promise you, no matter what happens. I will bring you back his skull."

"Why, Renato? Why did he betray me like this? I gave him everything, a wife, a kingdom, his whole damn inheritance. I could have taken his worthless life, but I didn't. Why has he done this to me?"

"It is in his blood, my lord. Some sort of gross disease. Don't blame yourself. He duped us both. It is true what the Triin say of him. He is a jackal."

"I want him," said Arkus. "Before I die I want him brought to me."

"We will have a greegan suck out his eyeballs for the blindness he has caused you, Great One. But do not talk of death. You are Arkus of Nar. You cannot die."

"But I am dying, I am. . . ."

"I will save you, my lord," said Biagio. He stroked the old man's hand and stared down at him, amazed and devastated by the ancient husk. "Do you believe in me?"

"Always," replied Arkus. "You have always been my trusted friend, Renato. I know you will save me."

"Good. Now rest. Sleep if you can. I will see you again tonight." Biagio bent and kissed the man's fragile face. "Dream of good things, Great One. You will be whole again."

Colonel Ardoz Trosk was almost a full head shorter than Dinadin, even with his snakeskin boots on, but Dinadin had never met a man who terrified him more. He was the kind of man who pulled the wings off butterflies when he was bored, and he never let an Aramoorian conscript pass without an insult. As colonel of the green brigade, Trosk was Blackwood Gayle's senior military adviser, a duty he relished and expected those beneath him to respect, even those Aramoorians unfortunate enough to serve with him. There were not a lot of them, just Dinadin and perhaps a dozen others, but they were a constant source of amusement for the sardonic colonel, who made sure they were always assigned the most menial details. Dinadin's specialty was picking up after their horses. And he performed his task with the constant hope of placating Trosk enough for the colonel to ignore him.

You'll be fine, Dinadin told himself as he followed Trosk through the narrow streets of the village. *Just do what he says and you'll be fine.*

They were fifteen miles from the Dring Valley, and about to ravage another nameless town. Like so many others they had come across, this town had expected them, and had even chosen a member of their community to speak with them. The poor bastard had only gotten one of Gayle's signatory throat-cuttings for his trouble. Surrender, Gayle had explained weeks ago, was unacceptable. Every time they came across another village Dinadin cringed, for he knew that once it was searched and Gayle was thoroughly satisfied, it would be burned to the ground just like all the others.

The last few weeks had been the worst of Dinadin's life. He had done things even a priest could never forgive, and he prayed for death every time his eyes closed. He followed orders with blind obedience, numbing himself in the hope that a Triin jiiktar would find him. But the legions of Nar were cutting the Triin down like weeds.

As always, Dinadin straggled behind Colonel Trosk. Already the familiar cries of panicked villagers filled the air. The legionnaires, those black-garbed imperial heralds, were kicking in the doors of the small houses and dragging out the people inside. Dogs barked incessantly and children wailed. Somewhere ahead of them Blackwood Gayle was at work directing the carnage. Trosk rode ahead of his group, a smile of contentment on his face.

"Magic," he snarled. "That's what we're looking for, boys."

The men nodded. There were five of them including Dinadin, each wearing the same boldly colored uniform of a Talistanian horseman, and all handpicked by Trosk to follow him into the village. Dinadin was the only Aramoorian among them. The dubious honor made him ride a good distance behind. In the weeks since joining Trosk and his brigade, Dinadin had been deft in avoiding the colonel. It seemed that Trosk was satisfied simply to have him shovel dung.

Until today. Each time they reached a village, Trosk picked another of the Aramoorians to accompany him personally. It was, Dinadin surmised, the colonel's way of initiating them. Today was his turn.

"Lotts!" Trosk growled over his shoulder. "Keep up, goddamn it!"

The legionnaires and horsemen were gathering the men in the center of the village; the women and children were kept apart. It was the same ghastly ritual as always. First the men would be questioned, then the women, each under the threat that the other would be killed if they resisted. Dinadin tried to look away. He would have cupped his hands over his ears if he could. Triin women were wrestling with soldiers, trying to yank back their stolen children. The men stood stone-faced and mute in the streets.

Why don't you run? he urged them silently. *Don't you know what's going to happen?*

But of course they knew. They knew their fate as well as their murderers did. It was simply unavoidable. Ackle-Nye had tried to fight, and the result had been no less bloody. There was a pathetic kind of hope in the eyes of the Triin they saw after that, a foolish idea that if they cooperated, perhaps they would be spared. It might have been that way if Richius were running the war, but this was Gayle's campaign now. And like everything Talistan did, it was vicious.

They slowed as they reached the center of the village. There, beside a well and a wooden bench, a group of legionnaires had assembled a throng of Triin children. Another Triin was talking to them, one who had surrendered in a previous raid and whose passable knowledge of the Empire's language made him worth sparing. There were several of these interpreters now, men who thought it better to live as slaves than to die with their brothers. Whenever the rolling army came to another town or village, the interpreters went to work, trying to coerce the newly conquered people into surrendering whatever magical items or knowledge they might have. So far the effort had proven an utter failure. For Dinadin, that was the one bright note in their whole dismal operation. He watched with sick fascination as the Triin interpreters smiled at the children, trying to calm them. By now Dinadin knew the lines by heart.

Your parents are safe. Don't worry. Just tell us where the magic is.

But there wasn't any magic. It was all like Lucyler had told him so many months ago. They could burn down a hundred villages, they could open up a million Triin chests, but all they would discover was blood. Magic wasn't hidden under a child's bed. If it existed at all it was in the air and the soil and, perhaps, the mind. But Gayle and the others were unconvinced and were consumed with their mission to find and bring back anything that could help the emperor.

"It's here," Blackwood Gayle had told them. "We just have to find it."

But they never would. Dinadin knew that now. He stopped his mount some ten paces from Trosk's horse and watched as the colonel's freakish smile broadened. Sometimes his love for war was disgustingly obvious. Here he could let his sadism soar, and never be accused of doing anything but his duty. He was the perfect soldier, hard and lean and unspeakably cruel. Dinadin hated him. He hated the way he cocked the brim of his feathered hat and the way he laughed when others suffered and the way he called grown men *boys*. Given the chance, Dinadin would have killed him.

"Pin 'em down good, gog," Trosk ordered the Triin interpreter. "Don't let 'em hold nothing back."

The interpreter spoke in a rush. He was begging the children to listen to him, to quiet down and answer his questions. Dinadin begged silently along with him, waiting for Trosk to explode. The colonel's face went from interest to boredom in less than a minute. He kicked the interpreter in the back with his pointed boot.

"Well? What's the story?"

The interpreter swallowed hard. "They know nothing, I think. It is hard to tell."

Trosk rolled his eyes. "Stupid gogs." He signaled for his horsemen to follow and snapped the reins of his mount impatiently. "All right, let's move it out, boys. We got a lot of doors to kick in."

Dinadin followed soundlessly, his mouth as dry as the stones beneath him. It would be impossible to avoid the carnage this time. He tried to still his thundering heart, forcing down the wave of nausea. A tiny prayer sprang silently from his lips. He was no murderer, but today the butcher was watching.

They moved quickly through the streets, avoiding the other swarms of soldiers and the handful of homes already set alight. A woman was screaming, her garments and hair engulfed in fire. Dinadin could hear the insistent flailing of her arms as she tried to bat out the flames. By the time her wailing stopped, they were well past her.

Trosk's horse stopped abruptly as the colonel jerked back on the reins. One by one the horsemen halted behind him. Trosk sat as still as a pole, his gaze locked onto something in the distance. Dinadin traced the colonel's gaze to a collection of tiny wood and paper houses. There, in the narrow avenue between two of the homes, was a small girl of perhaps thirteen, with a shiny metal object in her hand. The colonel's face lit up with a lecherous longing.

"Mmmm, hello," he rumbled.

Their eyes met for a brief moment. The girl clutched the object to her breast. Trosk's tongue darted out to wet his lips. The girl gasped, then dashed off into one of the houses, slamming the door behind her. Trosk let out a perverse groan.

"Oh, my. What a little beauty you are." Then he turned to smile at his troops, his face a perfect mask of mischief. "What do you say, boys? Ready for some fun?"

Dinadin shut his eyes. It was unthinkable. He tried to speak but couldn't, and the others were already grunting their approval. Trosk laughed and hurried his horse into a gallop. The others rushed to follow him.

I can't let this happen, Dinadin told himself. *Please, God, help me.*

God didn't answer. Dinadin was alone and he knew it. He raced off after Trosk, hoping an idea would occur to him. He would have to reason with the colonel, make him see the horror of his plan. If that didn't work . . .

Trosk was at the house. He threw himself off his horse and started toward the door. Dinadin leapt off his horse and scrambled up behind him. The colonel flashed him one of his arrogant grins.

"Time to make a man of you, Lotts," he said, then smoothed out the rim of his hat and smashed in the door with his boot heel. A sharp scream broke from inside the house. Trosk stuck his head through the doorway.

"Hello, sweetling," he called. "Ready for Ardoz?"

Dinadin strained to see past the colonel. He noticed the girl cowering in the corner of the room. The metal object was still wedged in her fist, but what it was Dinadin couldn't say. Beside her was another figure, a very old man with a stooped back and razor-sharp wrinkles. Outstretched before him was a dull-looking jiiktar. The girl clung defiantly to his side. Trosk frowned.

"Forget about her," Dinadin urged. "It's not worth it. Let's go."

Trosk glared at him. "Go? What do they bed in Aramoor, Lotts? Sheep? I'll not forget about her because of some old gog."

The colonel stepped over the threshold, his hands raised plaintively before him.

"Easy now," he crooned. "No one wants trouble."

The old man raised the jiiktar higher. Trosk hesitated, then gestured to the others behind him.

"There's a whole lot of us and only one of you, friend. Put the blade down and no one gets hurt. Simple, right?"

The old Triin hesitated, clearly seeing the hopelessness of his plight. Trosk took another step forward.

"Leave it alone, Colonel," begged Dinadin. "He could hurt you."

"Quiet, you ass," growled Trosk from the corner of his mouth. "He's listening to me, can't you see that?"

Dinadin saw perfectly. He held his breath as Trosk took another step. The girl whimpered, the metal thing in her grip shaking. It was a statue, Dinadin realized then, a gold and silver rendering of a human figure. Trosk had spied it also.

"What's that you have?" he asked the girl gently. "Something good? Ooohh, yes, it's very pretty. You're pretty, too. What's your name, darling?"

He was talking and inching forward, until he was less than two feet from the old man. He was looking right at the girl when his arm shot forward. A spray of blood erupted from the old man's nose and he crumpled, dropping the jiiktar to the floor. Trosk watched him struggle to rise, then put his booted foot down hard on his hand. The old man cried in pain. Trosk ground his heel into flesh.

"There now," he said happily. "That's much better. I am a colonel of Talistan, in your filthy country to try and save my emperor. Don't you ever threaten me, gog. Ever."

He punctuated the last *ever* with a final drive of his foot. The Triin's ancient bones popped under the pressure.

Now the girl was in a panic. Her eyes darted around the room, but everywhere the men of Nar were closing around her. She kept the statue close to her, and in a moment of mad insight raced for the small space between Trosk and Dinadin. Dinadin started to step aside as the girl came toward him, but Trosk snatched at her skirt and dragged her backward.

"Where the hell are you going?" he asked viciously. "I've been through a lot for you, you little bitch."

The girl scratched at him as she struggled to free herself. Trosk caught her hand and yanked her closer, then grabbed a tuft of her hair and pulled her head back. She let out an ear-splitting scream when he licked her face. On the floor the old man was begging Trosk to stop, his nose and jaw covered in blood. Trosk tore open the girl's bodice and dug his teeth into the exposed flesh of her neck. He had her against the wall now, her shoulders flat against the exposed brick. At his feet the old Triin was grabbing for his legs.

"Damn it!" Trosk spat, kicking the man backward. "Lotts, you idiot. Don't just stand there, get rid of this trash!"

Dinadin didn't move.

Trosk stopped molesting the girl at once. The little statuette she'd been guarding fell to her feet. He wrapped his meaty fist around her throat and pinned her to the wall as he turned to scowl at Dinadin.

"Are you deaf, boy? Kill him!"

Dinadin slowly shook his head. Trosk's dark eyes flared with rage, then suddenly the colonel laughed.

"No?" he asked. "Are you refusing my orders, you Aramoorian troll?"

"I won't kill him," declared Dinadin. He heard the brittleness in his voice. "My God, he didn't do anything. He's just trying to protect her."

Trosk smiled, ignoring the struggles of the girl as she tried to loosen his grip on her throat. Her breath was coming in desperate rasps. The other infantrymen watched, too frightened or surprised by Dinadin's boldness to move. The colonel's grin was unearthly.

"You won't kill him?" he asked. "All right. Then let's see what type of men they make in Aramoor, Lotts." He pulled the girl forward by her torn bodice and tossed her to Dinadin's feet, where she collapsed into a sobbing mound. "You don't have to kill the gog, Lotts. All you have to do is take the girl. Now, right here in front of us."

The girl was on her knees between Trosk and Dinadin, looking from one to the other in a confused panic. Dinadin stared down at her. Trosk pulled his ruby-studded dagger from his boot.

"I won't," said Dinadin unsteadily. "You can't make me do this."

"Why not?" asked Trosk. "Don't you like ladies, Lotts? Or have you just been waiting for us to find a fine-looking boy? Is that what you want? A boy?"

The colonel kicked at the girl, coaxing her toward Dinadin. She yelped and crawled closer, pulling at his pants leg and moaning for mercy. Dinadin moaned, too, trying to brush her away, to be rid of her haunting eyes and pleas. He wanted to run, to leave them all behind in the dingy little house and hide himself where Trosk would never find him. But the girl kept dragging him back.

"Do it," demanded Trosk. "Take her if you're man enough."

"No," said Dinadin. "I won't. Do you hear me? I won't!"

Trosk showed Dinadin his dagger. "You'd better," he warned, stooping to lift the old man's head and putting the blade to his throat. "Or else."

"Don't," begged Dinadin. "Please don't do this."

"What's the problem?" asked Trosk angrily. "You're a man, aren't you? She's a girl. Take her."

"Colonel . . ."

"Take her, you weasel, or I swear to God this gog dies!"

The old man wasn't moving. He was staring up at Dinadin through a slick of blood, Trosk's hand propping up his bruised head. The girl was still at Dinadin's feet, crying and pleading. Dinadin put out his hand to calm her.

"Stop," he begged her. "Oh God, please stop. I'm not going to hurt you. I'm not."

"Do it, Lotts," urged Trosk. "Now."

"No!"

Trosk sighed. "Good Lord, you're a stubborn one," he said. "All right then, have it your way."

He drew his blade across the wrinkled flesh of the old man's throat. The man's eyes widened in shock. Trosk released his head and he fell to the floor, clutching at the air and reaching for the girl, who was screeching now. Dinadin's nausea spiked. He saw Trosk looking at him with disgust. The colonel was going for the girl. For one brief second Dinadin thought to stop him, but again that old fear cemented his feet to the floor. Trosk took hold of the girl's hair again and pulled her to her feet, tossing her against the wall.

"Better now?" asked the colonel bitterly.

Dinadin couldn't answer. He was choking up bile and trying to wipe away the worst of it with his sleeve.

"You haven't saved her, you idiot," said Trosk. "In fact, I think maybe we'll all take a turn at her. Except you, of course. You can go find yourself that little boy you want so badly."

The colonel turned away and went toward the wall. Next to the girl was the object she had tried so hard to protect, the little statue of gold and silver. Trosk picked it up and examined it for a moment, then returned to Dinadin and handed it to him.

"Here. This might be something useful. Take it outside and give it to the legionnaires. Do you think you can do that?"

Dinadin could only nod as he accepted the object. He took one last look at the cowering girl, sick with guilt over her coming fate, then down at the Triin with the open throat. The old man had finally stopped thrashing. A river of blood ran along the uneven floor. Dinadin found enough of his voice to speak.

"Colonel—"

"Get out of my sight," said Trosk, turning away.

Dinadin hesitated, then moved slowly backward. His head was pounding as he reached the doorway and stepped into the smoky daylight. Already the girl's pleas had begun anew. Dinadin rushed away from the house, forgetting his horse, his hand clasped over his mouth. He ran to the center of the village, toward the legionnaires with the gathered children and the sobbing mothers and the stricken men. He ran so quickly he did not see the looming figure of the green and gold horseman until they nearly collided. Dinadin glanced up into the rider's face.

"Baron Gayle," Dinadin stammered. "I'm sorry, my lord. I didn't see you."

Gayle stared down at him contemptuously. "Lotts, isn't it?"

"Yes, sir," answered Dinadin. "Of the green brigade."

The baron motioned to the object in Dinadin's hand. "What is that?"

Dinadin hesitated. He didn't know what it was. He hadn't even glanced at it. Quickly he inspected it, discovering it was in fact a statue of a man and a woman. Deities, probably.

"Give it here," Gayle ordered impatiently.

Regretfully Dinadin handed the statue to the baron. Gayle looked at it for a moment, scratched at its surface with his fingernail, then hissed with annoyance. "More Triin garbage," he said. "Do you know what we're doing here, Lotts? We're trying to save our emperor. This . . ." he dropped the statue into the dirt, ". . . is worthless."

And then he was gone, trotting past Dinadin without regard. Dinadin waited until the baron was out of sight before retrieving the statue. He lifted it up carefully to the sun and brushed the dirt away. The statue sparkled in the light, the two figures dazzling and graceful, one of gold, the other of perfect silver. It was an heirloom the girl had risked her life for, a lump of precious metal near priceless in the Empire. But it had a different value to Dinadin. He would keep it, he decided, and if he could he would avenge her.

"I'll remember you, girl," he choked, then walked slowly back toward his horse.

THIRTY-SEVEN

Ten days out of Falindar, Richius and Dyana reached the valley. On the afternoon of the eleventh day, they crested a hillside and saw Castle Dring.

It wasn't actually the castle itself they saw first, but rather its soaring watchtower, erupting from a green blanket of trees around its base, reaching into heaven like a giant's rocky arm. It was a welcome sight for both of them, and they would have marveled at it had they not been so exhausted. The long trip from the citadel had winded them all, and when the prominent watchtower at last came into view, the weary travelers let out a collective sigh.

"Finally," crowed Richius. He happily patted the neck of his horse. "There she is, boy. We made it."

Around him the faces of the warriors broke into triumphant smiles. Dyana was hanging out of her carriage, craning for a better view. The cylindrical structure gleamed in the distance, its multifaceted façade glowing like a jewel. Richius trotted his horse over to her.

"Pretty impressive," he remarked. "That's going to be our home for a while."

"Not too long, I hope. It is dreary."

"Oh, I don't know," said Richius. For him, the haphazard stonework had a definite warmth. "It reminds me of my own home back in Aramoor. I think I like it."

Voris began barking orders to his men. One of them broke rank and started down the hill in a gallop. Dyana caught the puzzlement on Richius' face.

"He is going to tell the others we are here," she said. "Be ready, Richius. They will be waiting for us."

"Waiting for us? What do you mean?"

"I do not know. Voris simply told him to make ready." She smiled mischievously. "Maybe they want to meet you."

Richius scoffed. "Right. And maybe I should have stayed in Falindar."

They both laughed, but a little shudder went through Richius anyway. He was in the Dring Valley now, about to step over Voris' threshold.

"I'll have to check the front," he said blackly. "See if Voris' men have been doing as I asked."

"Tomorrow," replied Dyana. "There will be time enough for all of that. Tonight we rest. And in real beds, too."

"Umm, that does sound nice. Tomorrow then, unless Voris has other plans for me."

Dyana looked at him sternly. "It is not the warlord's plans that matter, Richius. What do *you* want? Remember, this is your battle now."

"But it's still his valley, Dyana. I don't want to cross him. Tharn warned me not to."

"Tharn also wants you to take command here. Do not let Voris intimidate you, Richius. He will if he can."

Richius chuckled. "Oh? And how do you know so much about him?"

"He is a man," said Dyana. "That is all I need to know."

Richius was readying an answer when Voris rode between them. He pointed at the watchtower, speaking directly to Dyana.

"Eeasay. Nobata Kalak hoorensay."

Dyana nodded and Voris rode off, starting down the slope toward his home. When he was out of earshot, Richius asked, "What was that about?"

"He says you are to follow him."

Richius stiffened. "Follow him? Why?"

"I am sorry, Richius. He did not say."

"He's very secretive, isn't he? Very well. If that's what he wants." He started off after the warlord.

Voris was trotting impassively along the narrow path in front of him. Richius looked into the net of tree limbs above his head, peeking through them to the dapples of blue heaven. The watchtower was almost invisible behind the leafy canopy. Beneath him the road had thinned to a rocky path, strewn with smooth stones and bordered by scarlet wildflowers and dense patches of weedy grass. He heard a brook bubbling in the distance and the throaty honking of waterfowl, and it struck him again how much like Aramoor this was. This wasn't the monstrous, forbidding Dring he remembered, with its tangles of secretive trees and ever-looming shadows. It was as if he were home again, in a part of Aramoor he had simply never discovered. The air was thick but wonderfully breathable, replete with the mossy scents of nature's slow processes. A dragon-fly winged by his nose, and in the trees squirrels chased each other from branch to branch, frolicking without regard to the strangers invading their primeval home. Cheerful robins sang above him, warbling their melodies, and where the broken trunk of a tree had fallen a hive of industrious wasps busied themselves with the construction of a paper house.

All this Richius imbibed like the sweetest liquor, absently stroking Lightning's neck. He thought of Dyana in her slow-moving carriage, and wondered what her reaction would be to all this beauty. Dreary, she called it. Richius laughed to himself, sure that she would be regretting her hasty assessment. He wished suddenly that she was here with him, so they could discover the loveliness of the path together.

Then he heard the first wolf cry.

It tore through him relentlessly, stopping him in mid-breath and leaching the color from his face. Off in the distance he heard another and then another still, ghostly howling that pierced the heart of the forest. Richius cocked his head to listen. He had to fight Lightning, who whinnied at the sounds. There were dozens of them, all baying the same melancholy tune. Worse, it was coming from the path before him. He glanced ahead to find Voris and saw the warlord's crimson tunic swaying nonchalantly as he continued forward, heedless of the doleful wolf-music.

Richius hesitated. Those were war wolves, and they were just ahead of him, waiting on their haunches for a coming meal. A clammy perspiration rose on his brow, and his mouth dried till his gums were like sand. Voris was disappearing behind the veil of trees as he neared the castle. The warlord stopped suddenly and looked over his shoulder.

"Kalak," cried Voris, waving Richius on. "Eeasay!"

Richius seethed. "Don't task me, you bastard."

Voris was still staring at him.

"All right," conceded Richius softly, "but I'll get you for this," and started off again down the path. This time Voris waited for him. The exuberant song of the war wolves grew in volume as Richius approached. Voris' grin widened. And then the forest parted like a curtain behind him, revealing Castle Dring.

It was like the ruins of some ancient Naren stronghold, a fortified amalgamation of mismatched stone and jagged mountain rock, so poorly thrown together that the place seemed about to crumble under its own gargantuan weight. Its glass panes were frosted with a timeless film of grunge, and its granite foundation listed noticeably eastward, lending the place a decidedly crooked appearance so that the windows and balconies formed the face of a cretin child. The base of the giant watchtower sprang up out of the castle's side in a leaning spike of crumbling stones, and on every pillar and bowed gable were the artistic imprints of a better time, architectural nuances that had once made the castle a fitting home. Discolored gargoyles with weather-broken claws sat atop rounded turrets, and the headless remains of a leaky water-statue stood in the clearing near the base of the watchtower, her naked feet and calves mired in clinging yellow lichens. There were missing shutters and vine-covered fences, collapsing catwalks and a stairway that seemed to lead nowhere.

Richius would have laughed but for the serious face of his host. Voris was still staring at him as he approached, his furtive smile growing wilder by the moment. And then Richius saw past Voris to the castle grounds. The warlord made a great sweeping gesture toward his home and the minions there to greet them.

"Bonata, Kalak."

An army of red-robed warriors stood off to the side farthest from the tower, their shocking manes of white hair oiled and gleaming like the polished jiiktars they held poised beside them. Stone-faced and immaculate, they stared straight ahead, their eyes and jaws set with ceremony. And there too were the war wolves, those howling beasts with the red eyes and yellow fangs, their necks encircled with stout collars and leashed together with chains. There were at least two hundred warriors and a dozen of the wolves, all brought out to greet the return of the lord of this dilapidated keep. A handful of other men stood out before the others, men of rank denoted by golden crests threaded through their robes. They too held jiiktars, bejeweled and leafed with precious metals.

Home again indeed, thought Richius. They were all like spectres to him these Drol of Dring, creatures of a netherworld he'd hoped long buried. With their long, white faces and gray eyes, they were things both less and more than human. He set his jaw and stared back at them.

"For me?" he asked the warlord sarcastically. "Really, I wish you hadn't gone to the trouble."

Voris ignored him and started toward the castle grounds. Richius forced Lightning after him, making the steed obey. The men with the golden crests bowed to the warlord as he approached, then straightened and held up their jiiktars in salute. A crashing cheer broke from the ranks of the gathered warriors.

"Cha Yulan!" they sang each time the jiiktars rose. "Cha Yulan! Cha Yulan!"

Voris dismounted and held up his hands. There was a great, pacific smile on his face. The cheering stopped at once. The warlord dropped slowly to his knees and placed his open palms on the loamy earth and kissed the ground of his homeland. The warriors cheered again, whistling and shouting and stamping their feet. Voris rose and held up a triumphant fist.

"Jahani!" he shouted madly. "Jahani Dring!"

Dyana's carriage was finally winding into the clearing with the rest of the caravan. When she saw Richius she ordered her driver to stop, then jumped out of the vehicle, Shani held in a little bundle against her breast. Richius raised his eyebrows.

"This I didn't expect," he called to her. "What's going on?"

Dyana strode over to him, spying the baying wolves and trying to hide the babe in the folds of her dress. "They are greeting their returning lord," she explained. "It is a custom among the warlords. These are his warriors, his loyal men."

"And this is all for my benefit, I suppose. God, he really puts on a show. Look there. What's he doing?"

Voris was climbing onto the massive stump of a long-fallen tree. The warriors hushed as he inspected them, casting an approving eye on each in turn. He took a deep breath and let it out with a satisfied sigh.

"Matusa ben Dring!" he called to the gathering.

There was no cheering this time, just the reverent silence of a captivated army. Even the war wolves had ceased their welcoming cries. They sat back on their haunches like trained house pets, their tails still and their pointed snouts held high for their master. Richius climbed down from Lightning's back and stood beside Dyana, fascinated by the incredible sight. He had to hold the horse to keep it from bolting.

"What's he saying?" he asked Dyana.

Dyana started to translate.

"Great men of Dring!" began Voris. "You honor me. I know when I see you that I am home again. When I look at you, I see our power!"

Now, as if they had been waiting for a sign, the men of the Dring Valley let forth a chorus of *Cha Yulan*.

Voris struck his fist into the air. "I am the Wolf!" he declared. "And this is my valley!" He lowered his voice and growled, "No one will take it from me."

This electrified the army. They stamped their feet and beat their jiiktars together, hooting their approval. Richius felt the charge, too. He listened to every translated word of the warlord's speech, transfixed by the figure prancing on the tree trunk. Voris bared his pointed canines.

"Nar is at our heels, my warriors. Their cowards are coming for us with their terrible machines. But am I afraid? I am not. Because this dragon that stalks us walks on feet of straw! It is a beast without a soul. It knows nothing of land or loyalty or the power of our living gods."

A cool breeze stirred through the grasses and Voris licked his lips to taste it. "Our valley is free, my warriors. Now and always it will be so. We are together again, made strong by the will of Lorris, and we will defend our land. We will defy the dragon of Nar!" He lifted his booming voice to the sky and cried, "Do you hear me, Black Ones? We defy you!"

"We defy you!" returned the crowd. "We are with the Wolf!"

"Be still now, and listen," Voris continued. "We are set a great task. Men of Dring, the time has come to again offer battle in defense of our country. Invaders poise to despoil us. The dragon comes to devour our lives and our honor. And it is strong. They come to us in great numbers, these things from the Black Empire, but I would fight them if they were a million. They have weapons of science to burn us, but I would fight them with my fingernails alone. For this great valley, my home and yours, and for the honor of our wives and sisters, I would fight them to my dying breath."

An unexpected fervor seized Richius. He had never known this Voris, the orator, and now he was set afire by the warlord's words. The crowd was still as Voris moved on his wooden stage like a practiced dancer, gesturing to the trees and the sky above, riding the intangible wave of emotion. He stopped speaking and smiled at the crowd, then jerked his thumb in Richius' direction. Richius stiffened.

"And we are not alone, my friends," said the warlord. "Heaven is with us. Lorris and Pris guide our hands. They have delivered to us our great enemy—the Jackal."

Every head in the crowd turned at once toward Richius, who felt a surge of hot color in his face. Their cool gray eyes bored into him, shredding his courage and causing a lump to spring into his throat. Dyana's hand leapt invisibly to his arm and squeezed.

"Do not worry," she whispered.

He cleared the dry blockage from his throat and looked back at the men of Dring. Voris was continuing.

"He has been chosen, my friends, picked by the hand of Lorris himself. No, you say? Is he not a heretic? True, a heretic he may always be, but what more proof do you need of heaven's hand than the humbling of this once-hateful creature? I say Lorris has brought him to us, and so says Tharn himself!"

At the mere mention of Tharn's name, the heads of the warriors began nodding in agreement. Voris seized the opportunity.

"I follow the Lord Tharn," he declared proudly. "And I am not too great to refuse his bidding. In his wisdom he has set the Jackal above me, but do I question him? I do not."

"Ooohh," remarked Richius, "you are good." He looked over to Dyana, and watched her face contort.

"He lies," said Dyana.

Richius shook his head. "No. Don't you see? He's making it possible for me to do my job."

"What do you mean?"

"The men will listen to me now. If they think I'm some delivered villain chosen by Tharn, they will follow me."

"Tharn has charged the Jackal to save us. We must all help him. You are expected to show yourselves worthy, men of Dring. Be worthy of the women you love. Be worthy of your children's respect. Be worthy of my faith in you. I follow the word of Tharn, and you shall follow my word. Together we can win back our valley. Strength and valor is what I ask of you. Do not betray me."

There was a sober silence. Voris let his army bow to him, then stepped down from the tree trunk. No one spoke or even lifted their heads. The warlord strode over to where Richius and Dyana stood, an expression of disgust on his face.

"Utumbo toobay isa, Kalak," he said to Richius. "Do toobay bis." Then he turned and walked back toward the castle. Richius looked inquisitively at Dyana.

"Voris says that he has done his part," Dyana explained. "You must now do yours."

The congregation started to disperse, and a small man stepped up to Richius and Dyana. From his dress and serious features Richius knew he was one of Voris' lieutenants. Older than Voris by far, he reminded Richius at once of Jojustin. He bowed to Richius courteously, and then to Dyana, careful not to stare at either of them. When he spoke his voice was rough but polite.

"His name is Jarra," said Dyana. "He is Voris' *Dumaka*."

"Dumaka?" asked Richius. "What's that?"

Dyana puzzled over the question for a moment. "I do not think there is a word for it in your language, Richius. He is like a teacher. He schools the other warriors. You might call him a war master."

"A war master, huh?" said Richius, openly impressed. "I'll have to remember that. So what's he want with us?"

"He says he has been ordered to take care of us."

Richius laughed. "Just like Jojustin. Very well then. Please tell the war master I'm very tired. I would like a bed."

Dyana made the request and the Dumaka nodded, walking away and beckoning them to follow. But when he noticed Richius leading Lightning, he stopped and pointed at the animal.

"He wants you to leave the horse, Richius," said Dyana.

"Leave him? Where?"

Jarra explained some more.

"The Dumaka says your horse will be looked after with the others. Please, Richius, leave him."

Richius frowned.

"This is about trust, Richius," said Dyana. "If you cannot trust them with your horse, how can they trust you with their valley?"

The war master stared at Richius inquisitively, waiting for his reply. At last Richius shrugged.

"Tell him to be careful. Lightning has breeding. He's not like these other bone-bags."

"I will tell him," said Dyana. She explained it all to the war master, who made a disgruntled face but seemed to comply, calling over one of the warriors and giving him a list of explicit instructions. Dyana smiled at Richius. "All right?"

"I suppose," replied Richius. "Now let's find those beds."

They followed Jarra across the grounds, careful to stay as far as possible from the war wolves still leashed in the yard. Shani gurgled as they neared the looming castle. Dyana rocked her gently to quiet her. There was a huge gate of wrought iron to greet them. They passed through it silently and entered the keep. Inside they found the same careless architecture that marked the castle's exterior. The walls bulged with uneven brickwork and a few broken chandeliers hung crookedly from the ceiling on chains of tarnished gold. What sparse furnishings there were consisted mostly of wooden chairs and tables, all plain and utilitarian, strewn haphazardly throughout the hall. The floor was irregular and tiled with cracked blue stones, and dirtied sunlight poured into the room from an odd collection of octagonal windows cut into the walls in lopsided trios.

Yet despite all the antiquity of the place, it was not dreary. Activity sounded in the halls, and above them the warped ceiling thumped with movement on the upper floor. A coursing excitement permeated the keep and the air was fresh through the open windows. Smiling warriors pushed by them, and eager children clung to the hems of their mothers' dresses. Dogs barked and wolves howled, and it was all like a carnival to Richius, who had never guessed his nemesis capable of fostering such emotion in his people.

Jarra led them up a small flight of stairs leading to a sunny wing of the castle decorated with tall, multipaned windows and a reasonable view of an overgrown garden. A warped wooden door stood at the end of the hall leading to a sunlit chamber. This, Jarra explained, was where Richius would be staying. It was a small room but well appointed, with a desk and some chairs and, most importantly, a thick-mattressed bed. On the desk was a tablet of writing paper and several maps, and beside these someone had placed a decanter of water and a basket of bread and fruit. Richius chose a perfectly ripe apple from the basket and handed it to Dyana, who accepted it gratefully.

"This is fine," he said cheerfully. "Just fine. But what about you, Dyana? Where will you be?"

"The Dumaka says that I am to stay with Voris' wife," said Dyana angrily. "I do not think the warlord trusts me."

"Oh, he trusts you," said Richius. "It's *me* he wants to keep an eye on. Don't worry. You can come down here to instruct me."

Dyana shook her head. "I cannot. Richius, we spoke of this already. We must not make others suspicious." She cocked her head slightly toward the listening Jarra. "We will find a more open place for your instructions."

Richius smiled at her. "Of course. I'll see you later then?"

"At the evening meal. The Dumaka says we are both to attend. It is Voris' wish. It will be at sundown."

"I'll probably be asleep by then," said Richius. "Will you come down to get me?"

"No. I will meet you in the hall where we came in." With her face hidden from Jarra, she flashed Richius a smile. "Sleep well. I will see you tonight."

Richius watched them disappear down the hall, then shut the door to his chamber behind them. He went back to the basket of fruit and selected a piece for himself, a fist-sized citrus with dimpled skin and the scent of a powerfully ripe melon. A spray of juice erupted as he peeled back its pithy skin. There had been precious little good food on the long journey to the castle, and far less privacy. Now he was enjoying both with equal vigor. He sat down on the bed and leaned back against the wall, watching the trees sway outside his window as he ate.

In less than a minute he was asleep.

When he awoke, many hours later, the sunlight had stopped pouring in from the garden window. Richius lifted himself groggily from the mattress, surprised by the heaviness of his head. He rubbed his eyes and strained to see in the dim chamber, remembering suddenly that there was a dinner waiting for him downstairs. Hungrily he patted his stomach, eager to fill it. He was growing curiously accustomed to the odd cuisine of Lucel-Lor, and the thought of it no longer sent his insides pitching. There was a mirror on the wall farthest from the bed. He went to it, running his hands through his hair and inspecting the red creases the mattress had made on his face. It was then that he noticed the clothing.

While he slept, someone had deposited a new outfit in his chamber. It consisted of a plain white shirt and a pair of doeskin trousers, simple Triin clothes like those worn by farmers. He picked up the shirt and admired it. It was wonderfully clean, and his own shirt was soiled beyond recognition. The trousers were well-made, too, comfortable looking, with a drawstring front that made a belt unnecessary. Eagerly he stripped off his filthy clothes and pulled on the trousers, sucking in his breath while he did up the drawstrings. It was a reasonable fit, and the soft fabric felt marvelous against his skin. Then he grabbed the shirt and put it on, too, fastening each button slowly as he watched himself in the little mirror, laughing gleefully at his reflection. In the strange outfit he looked neither like a Naren or a Triin. Rather he seemed an odd mix of both. He decided the look suited him.

Downstairs, the main hall of the castle was almost deserted. He skirted along its perimeter looking for Dyana and hoping Voris would not find him first. Outside he could see the sky darkening through the octagonal windows. Dyana should be waiting for him. He turned a corner and started down another corridor, empty except for a man and a woman he didn't know, just beginning a passionate kiss. They both started at his appearance, and the man straightened in embarrassment as he recognized Richius. Richius smiled at him awkwardly.

"I'm sorry," he offered. "I'm looking for someone."

The warrior sort of shrugged. "Ja coca vin?"

"Hmm, maybe. I don't understand a word you're saying. And you don't understand me, either, do you? Never mind. I'll find her myself."

He left the corridor quickly, going back the way he had come, trying to find the little staircase he had descended and deciding to wait there for Dyana. But when he slipped by a small door he stopped. Behind it he heard a tiny voice talking to itself. Curiously he cracked open the door and stuck his head into the chamber. A small girl sat cross-legged on the floor, reading a book by candlelight. Reading, to Richius' great astonishment, in Naren. When she saw him she stopped and looked up, and he knew instantly that she wasn't frightened.

"Who are you?" he asked directly. The girl seemed amused by the question. She was barely ten years old, but the face she made was decidedly adult.

"I live here," she answered. Then she looked him up and down and said, "You do not. You are an Empire man."

Richius grinned. Hearing his own language come from the lips of this waif was utterly fantastic.

"Yes," he said, inching into the room. "I'm an Empire man. My name is Richius."

"You are Kalak," she said. "Father told me you were here."

Richius shook his head, trying to be gentle. "My name is Richius," he repeated. "Not Kalak. Who's your father?"

"Father is warlord," replied the girl.

"Well, you can call me Richius, anyway," said Richius, unsure if he should even continue the conversation. But the girl had entranced him. "What's your name?"

The girl pointed to herself proudly. "I am Pris."

"Pris? Like the goddess?"

"Yes. Father says I am beautiful like her. Strong like her, too. She is my patroness."

Richius squatted down beside her and pointed to the book in her hands. "You're a very good reader," he said. "What is this book?"

"Bhapo's book," said Pris. "He gave it to me. I learn from it."

Bhapo, Richius knew, was a Triin term of affection. It usually meant an uncle or some male cousin. He peered into the open book lying in her lap, trying to read its upside-down print.

"Who's Bhapo?"

"Bhapo Tharn," replied Pris. She looked at Richius excitedly. "You know Bhapo?"

"Oh, yes," said Richius. "He's not my bhapo, but I know him. Did he give you this book?"

Pris nodded. "To teach me."

"It's a very nice book. Can I hold it?"

Without hesitation Pris gave the book to Richius. "You read Empire words, too, yes?"

"Yes," said Richius, thumbing through the pages. It was a book of Naren poems, very old and probably very valuable. It was plain to see why the girl cherished it.

"You read for me?" asked Pris. "You read good?"

"Oh, I don't think I could read these poems as well as you, Pris," said Richius with a smile. "You have such a pretty voice. How did you learn to speak Naren? Did Tharn teach you?"

"Bhapo teach me before big war," said Pris. "He gave me book before going away. He say I best student, learn fast."

Apparently, thought Richius. He skimmed the text of some of the poems, amazed that a child so young could comprehend such complex sentences. Even Naren children her age couldn't read at her level. Obviously Tharn had seen some genius in her and had chosen to encourage it. And clearly Voris had been indulgent.

"Your father doesn't mind your reading about Nar?"

"Father wanted me to learn, to be smart and strong like my patroness." Then the little girl's face darkened. "But he made me stop for Tal."

Richius froze. "Tal, your brother," he whispered.

Pris' gray eyes lost their twinkle. "Father says you killed Tal. Blamed Empire men for Tal dying. Made me stop reading then. But I kept book. I still read and learn."

"Is that why you're hiding in here?" asked Richius. "So your father doesn't see you?"

"Father would be unhappy," said Pris. "I get no more books from Bhapo." She flashed a furtive smile. "But I learn anyway. You can help me. Read for me, yes?"

Richius got up and closed the door, suddenly worried they would be discovered. "I'm sorry, Pris," he said to her gently. "I don't think I should. Your father would be very angry with both of us if he knew."

"Just one," she implored. "You read one for me. Here, I show you."

She grabbed the book and rifled though the pages. When she found the poem she was looking for she handed the book back to him with a grin. Richius accepted the book regretfully and glanced at the poem. Predictably, it was a love poem, the type of old-fashioned verse that had become all too rare in militaristic Nar. Pris leaned back attentively, waiting for him to begin.

"Pris, I can't read this for you. I don't want to get your father mad."

"I am not afraid of Father," replied Pris. "Are you?"

"It has nothing to do with that. I'm just trying to respect his wishes, that's all."

Pris clearly didn't believe him. "Read for me," she said sweetly. "Please."

He was about to relent when he heard his name being called. Dyana's voice held a distinct note of concern. Pris wrinkled her nose in disappointment. Richius went to the door and opened it. He saw Dyana down the hallway, searching for him, and he called her over with a wave.

"Dyana, over here."

Dyana's expression went from relief to puzzlement. "Richius, why are you hiding in there? I have been looking for you. It is time to see Voris."

"I'm not hiding," said Richius. "Come in. I want you to meet someone."

Dyana stepped inside and saw Pris sitting on the floor. The little girl smiled at her precociously. "Hello."

"Hello," replied Dyana. She turned quickly to Richius. "Who is this?"

"This is Voris' daughter," said Richius. "Her name is Pris. Say something to her in Naren."

"What?"

"Go on," Richius urged. "Anything."

Dyana looked at Pris suspiciously, then said very softly, "Hello, Pris. My name is Dyana. How old are you?"

"I am almost ten," replied Pris. "You are a pretty lady."

Richius laughed. "Isn't that amazing? She speaks better than some Talistanians I know!"

Dyana knelt down next to Pris and examined her, as if unsure she were truly Triin. "Remarkable," she whispered. The compliment made Pris sit up straight.

"Are you Kalak's woman?" asked the girl.

"No," said Dyana. There was a touch of sadness in her tone that Richius approved of. "I am not."

"She is your bhapo's wife," explained Richius. "She's here to help us. Dyana, isn't she something? She learned Naren from Tharn, and from reading this book he gave her. It's just a bunch of poems, but she picked it up."

"Here," said Pris to Dyana, patting the floor beside her. "You sit. Kalak is going to read for us."

"Oh?" said Dyana. "How wonderful."

Richius flushed. "It's just a poem she likes, Dyana. She wants me to read it for her." He looked at Pris. "And I never said I would."

"Please," begged Pris.

"Yes," chimed Dyana. "Please, Richius. Read it for us."

Richius glanced down at the book. For some odd reason he wanted to read it for Pris, and now that Dyana was here he wanted to read it even more. They both watched him, and they were too compelling to refuse.

"This poem doesn't seem to have a title," he began haltingly, "so I'll just start." He cleared his throat and waited for Pris and Dyana to settle down. "Ready?"

"Yes," said Pris happily.

But Richius had no sooner opened his mouth when a frantic cry erupted. A woman bolted into the chamber, startling them all. Pris jumped to her feet. The woman was screaming in pure panic. She rushed over to Pris and grabbed her, pulling her close and cradling her head against her legs. Her face lit with anger as she cowered in the corner of the room with the girl, speaking so quickly that her words ran together in a babbling, incoherent stream. Richius drew back.

"Dyana, what the hell is this? Who is she?"

"Shhh," ordered Dyana. "This is Najjir, Richius. Voris' wife."

Pris was protesting through her mother's skirt, but her mother didn't hear. She continued berating Richius. Dyana stepped between them, trying to calm the woman. Richius still had the book in his hand. He stood there mute, unsure if he should stay or go, wanting to help and not knowing how.

"Kalak!" cursed the woman, spitting at Richius. "Kalak!"

"I didn't do anything," said Richius, backing toward the door. "Tell her, Dyana."

"I think you should leave," said Dyana carefully. "Now."

"Dyana, I didn't do anything wrong. Make her understand."

"Just go, Richius," said Dyana sharply. "I will explain it to her when she calms down."

"God damn it." Richius turned to leave and saw a shadow in the doorway. Voris was staring at him. His bald head was red with rage.

"Nogiya asa?" asked Voris hotly, looking at his hysterical wife. The woman pointed to Richius and said the hateful word.

"Kalak!"

Voris' eyes bulged from their sockets. He stepped aside and gestured to the door. Obediently his wife departed, dragging Pris, who gave Richius an apologetic look before disappearing into the hall. Dyana hurried to defend Richius, firing off a flurry of explanations to the warlord. But Voris would hear none of it.

"Kalak!" he thundered, barely controlling himself. Richius guessed easily what was the matter.

"Tell him I didn't hurt her," he told Dyana calmly. "Tell him I only came in to talk to her."

Dyana tried to speak, her voice all but inaudible against the warlord's bellows.

Richius held up his hands, finally shouting, "Enough!"

Voris stopped yelling. He scowled at Richius.

"Enough," said Richius again. "Voris, listen to me. I didn't do anything to your daughter. I never would." He held up Pris' little book. "Here, this is all we were doing. Just reading some poems."

Voris snatched the book away from him, listening to Dyana's translation of his explanation. The warlord waited until she was done, nodded, then looked directly at Richius and spoke.

"He says that Pris is not to read this language," said Dyana. "He wants to know if she told you this."

"She told me," confessed Richius. "Tell him I'm sorry. I shouldn't have gone against his wishes."

Voris took the apology badly.

"That is not good enough," said Dyana, translating Voris' furious words. "You are in my house now. You will follow my ways."

Richius nodded. "Yes. You're right. I'm sorry."

Voris went on, his voice still shaking with ire. He paused and waited for Dyana to translate. Dyana did not.

"What is it?" asked Richius. "What did he say?"

"I am sorry, Richius, I do not understand him. He says you are to stay away from his children. If he sees you near them again he will kill you. He says that you will not take another of his children away." Dyana looked at Richius questioningly. "Do you know what that means?"

Richius nodded gravely. "I do. Tell Voris he has nothing to worry about. I will stay away from his family. Tell him also that I'm sorry about Tal."

"Tal? Who is Tal?"

"Just tell him."

Dyana did as he requested, passing on the cryptic message to Voris. The warlord scowled at Richius, the pain of his loss was clearly evident. When Voris spoke again there was a slight unevenness in his tone.

"Voris says that he hates you, Richius," said Dyana, clearly confused by the exchange. "He does not know if he can do what Tharn asks of him."

"Tell him I understand. We must both do our best. I'll do my best to prove myself to him. And I won't go near his children again. Promise him that for me, Dyana."

Dyana made the promise. Voris simply nodded.

"One more thing," said Richius. "And be careful how you tell him this. I don't know if I had anything to do with Tal's death, but if I could bring him back I would. Tell him that, Dyana."

"Richius, I do not understand any of this," said Dyana. "Who is Tal?"

"Voris' son. I'll explain it to you later. Just tell him, Dyana. Please."

Reluctantly, Dyana agreed. They both watched Voris for a reaction, but his face never changed. Instead he glanced down at the book of poems in his hand, shaking his head ruefully.

"Did you tell him?" Richius whispered.

Dyana nodded. "Everything."

But Voris seemed disinterested. He sighed wearily and stuck the little book in his sash. He did not look at Richius again, but spoke directly to Dyana only briefly before leaving the room. Dyana raised her eyebrows in surprise.

"He still expects us for the meal," she said. "He wants us to hurry."

Richius didn't answer. Dyana gently touched his arm.

"Richius," she asked carefully. "Did you kill Voris' son?"

Richius shrugged. "I honestly don't know."

"Is that what this was all about?"

"He wants me to stay away from his children, and I don't blame him. Go to dinner without me, will you? I'm really not very hungry anymore. I will see you in the morning. Maybe we can start my studies then."

Dyana's voice was soft in the half-light. "I will have a servant bring some food to your chamber. Sleep well. We will be busy tomorrow."

"Good night, Dyana," he said, and left the chamber. Nearby, Voris' voice echoed down the cavernous halls, and Richius quickly decided to go in the opposite direction, toward the main gate. He stepped out into the cool spring evening, savoring the earthy fragrance of the air. To the west the sky was a peculiar purple, to the east a violent vermilion. The infant night was ripe with stars. Moonlight rested on the broken statues in the abandoned garden. In the trees, nocturnal hunters readied to take wing, rustling and preening for the night's work. An illusory peace had settled on the valley like a blanket.

Richius spied the watchtower, gazing up to its twisted peak so far above him. That was where the real peace was, he decided. The structure was connected to the rest of the castle, but it had its own entrance, a narrow slit cut into stone. There was a guard stationed there, a young man in the typical garb of a Dring warrior. He bowed to Richius as he approached.

"I'm going up," said Richius. He pointed his index finger toward heaven. "Up. All right?"

The guard nodded. "Doa trenum."

"Fine," said Richius, squeezing past him. "Whatever."

Inside, the watchtower seemed much smaller. Darkness soaked every corner, held at bay only by a single torch hanging defiantly against a wall. Except for the torch and the formidable staircase spiraling ever upward, the tower was empty. Richius grabbed the torch from the wall and began ascending. The stone risers were gritty beneath his feet, and his boots crunched on untold layers of filth as he mounted the steps, keeping his arm outstretched before him. The world had dropped away, and all he could hear was the scrape of his feet and his own labored breathing. Stale air filled his lungs, making him cough. Ahead of him, the stairs unfolded endlessly out of the blackness. He thought to turn around, go back down and forget the peace he might find at the pinnacle, but he was sure he was closer to the top now than he was to the bottom so he continued his climb, hoping each step would be the last. Finally he saw the end of the staircase, bathed in the unmistakable glow of moonlight.

"Thank God," he said, and the sound of his voice startled him.

He heard other voices in the dark, then stepped up into the pinnacle of the tower, into a chamber surrounded by glass and awash in the pale light of heaven. Two more red-robed warriors were inside, staring out through the glass in boredom and talking between themselves. They started when they noticed Richius.

"I'm sorry," Richius offered, embarrassed. "I didn't know you'd be up here. I'll go."

He made to turn around but the warriors called his name.

"Kalak?"

"Yes," said Richius. "All right, yes, I'm Kalak."

The two warriors sized him up, nodding and cocking their eyebrows. They spoke and chuckled to each other. Then one came forward and directed Richius toward the windows.

"Dring," said the man. He smiled. "Dring."

Curious, Richius went to the window. All around him was the Dring Valley, rolling and verdant and dark. This wasn't the Dring of so many nightmares. This was a primeval Aramoor, wild and lush, a force of nature. He put his nose to the glass, trying to forget the graves he had dug here.

"Yes," he said. "Dring."

And then a strange light came alive in the distance. Richius watched it glow, unsure of the cause. The warriors watched it, too. It flared like an orange star, burning in a single bright puff before dimming, then glowing a steady crimson. Another sparked to life, then another, and soon the horizon was ringed with them, tiny pinpoints of flame set against the western sky.

Richius clenched his teeth. A memory came to him like a hammer blow, a recollection of fire and kerosene and igniters glowing red against the night. He moved back from the window.

"So it begins," he whispered. "God save us."

THIRTY-EIGHT

High in the watchtower of Castle Dring, in a dark, hidden belfry of its vaulted pinnacle, was a giant, antiquated bell. In the better days of the castle's youth, the bell was rung by the lord of the keep on occasions of celebration and, sometimes, of peril. It sang for the people of Dring for nearly two centuries, alerting them of prayer time and warning them of the occasional, episodic crusades of invaders. Its voice was clear and perfect, woven as tightly into the fabric of the valley as the howling of wolves.

But like so much of Castle Dring, the bell was more fragile than it looked. On the day that Voris the Wolf wrested the valley from its previous warlord and personally rang the bell to proclaim his victory, the bell cracked, killing forever its angelic voice and bringing forth only a jangling, ear-crunching din. The bell was never rung again.

For twenty-three years the bell hung silent in its belfry, collecting rust and spiders, and being neglected by the new lord of the valley, who raised children that never heard the bell's song and who warred occasionally with another warlord from the north. Nevertheless, it was a time of good things in Dring. Even without the bell, the devout of the valley knew when to kneel for prayer, and the holidays still came without the bell to ring them in. People still farmed and grew up happy, the birds still migrated with the seasons, and flowers always bloomed in the spring, just as the gods of the earth had sworn.

Yet the bell was never wholly forgotten. There were many who remembered the great bell of Castle Dring, including Voris himself, who had once proclaimed to Jarra the Dumaka that he would ring the bell again if the valley he cherished was in mortal danger.

So, when Richius and the warriors burst into his dining chamber with news of the Naren invasion, the shrieking bell sliced open the night. Riders had come from the front, confirming the dreadful news that Nar was on the march. It was a call to arms everyone in the valley expected. Shortly after dusk the ringing began. To Richius' ears, it was like something out of hell itself, and as he thundered toward the front, following Voris and Dumaka Jarra by torchlight, he was grateful to hear the sound dying out behind him. It was nearly midnight, and every creature in the valley was alert, awakened by the pounding bell and the hammering of a thousand hooves. The forest pulsed with eerie orange light as the defenders of the valley rode forth from Castle Dring, jiiktars and torches in hand, headlong against the mechanized invaders.

And as they rode, two hundred strong to bolster their brothers at the front, the warriors of the Dring Valley sang their terrible war songs and cried to heaven for strength and victory. They sang as Voris directed them, their voices bold and heavy, so that the shrill music of the bell fell away behind their chorus like the soft bleating of a lamb.

Richius held fast to the reins of his gelding Lightning, following Voris' lead down the thin, meandering corridor cut through the forest. A fearful excitement bubbled up within him. Those were flame cannons he had seen, he was sure of it. They were being warmed for imminent battle, probably a dawn attack. He glanced up at the high moon. Midnight. Six more hours.

"How far are we from the front?" asked Richius over his shoulder. He felt Dyana's arms tighten around his waist.

"Not far," she called into his ear. "Voris says less than an hour."

Richius grimaced. The last time they were on horseback together, they were running from Tharn's storm. Now they were running down the gullet of peril again. He let the sweetness of her breath warm the back of his neck, loving the closeness of it and hating himself for agreeing to let her come. Neither he nor Voris had wanted Dyana to accompany them to the front, but her argument had been sound. Without her, she had claimed, he and Voris would be unable to speak to each other. So they had left Shani in the care of Voris' wife, Najjir, with the insecure hope that they wouldn't be orphaning her, and rode off with Voris and his Dring defenders.

"Remember your promise," Richius counseled. "You leave as soon as I say so. I don't know how long the defenses will last."

"And you leave with me," she replied. "It is what Tharn would want."

Richius nodded. He hadn't actually agreed to leave with her when the defenses inevitably crumbled, but his silence seemed enough to appease her. Tharn wouldn't want either of them at the front, but it was a necessity the cunning-man had obviously overlooked. Richius needed to direct the battle himself. And for that he needed Dyana.

Ahead of him he saw Voris' bald head gleaming orange in the torchlight. The warlord's horse was kicking up a wake of earth. He was the only one who rode alone. Even Jarra the Dumaka shared his mount with another man, just like the hundreds of others behind him did. They were a great, fast-moving caravan snaking through the night and bringing men to battle, and the valley's shortage of horses wasn't going to stop them.

Stay to the trail, Voris had warned them. Only the trail was safe. There were traps in the forest now, ingenious things of Triin design. There were thousands of sharpened sticks in the ground, their tips dipped in snake venom, the tireless toil of hundreds of Dring women. The trees were strung with bladed weapons so that a misplaced step could sever a limb, and nets filled with rocks hung in the branches, waiting for unwitting heads to crush. It was all meant to keep the invaders to this narrow path, the only way in or out of the valley's deep forest. This was Richius' grand design, part of a plan he had worked on until his brain was numb, and he soon would see if it was enough.

They darted through the forest until the bell behind them had fallen silent and the voices of the warriors grew hushed with introspection. Richius knew the grasslands where the Narens were positioned were close now. An almost tangible smell of kerosene filled the air. Nar would have dozens of flame cannons and war wagons ready. Night had hidden them from his sight in the watchtower but he knew they were there, cloaked in darkness and waiting for the dawn.

Come the dawn then, thought Richius, gritting his teeth. *We'll be ready, too.*

For nearly another full hour they rode, until at last a glimpse of the defenses could be seen. Here was where the forest thinned and gave way to a huge, sunken plain of grass and poppies, and between the forest of towering oaks and the flats was constructed the elaborate perimeter Richius had devised. A smile stretched across his face as he saw it, bathed in the light of defiant torches and manned by legions of crimson-draped warriors. They were on catwalks between trees, and on platforms built into the sides of gigantic trunks, and hanging from rope bridges and wooden scaffolds a hundred feet off the ground. Richius saw their white faces all around and above him, peering down at him from everywhere like a million nocturnal birds. A wild excitement rippled through the forest.

"Cha Yulan!" came the familiar song. "Cha Yulan ta!"

Cha Yulan ta. The Wolf lives.

Voris struck his fist into the air and spurred his horse into a gallop. Almost standing in his stirrups, he answered the call of his warriors with a frenzied battle cry, shattering the night with his voice. Jiiktars rattled in the trees, and on the ground dozens of warriors raced up to them, cheering and welcoming the warlord with outstretched arms. Jarra followed Voris, and Richius followed Jarra, and one by one they brought their horses to a halt.

"Look, Dyana," said Richius, surveying the trees and the trench he could now see beyond them, with its giant shields and its deadly barricades. "It's all perfect, just like I asked."

And it was more than perfect, more than Richius had imagined in all those long hours locked in his room in Falindar. The perimeter was something Nar itself would have designed, an intricate creation of wood and ropes and earth. In the trees were the catwalks where the bowmen waited, and beyond the trees, bordering and protecting the forest, was a long straight trench manned by another thousand warriors. The trench itself was guarded, too, rimmed with a barrier of sharp spears stuck into the earth at an angle meant to impale a charging infantry. Tall shields of wet logs, lashed together and covered with animal hides, were erected behind the spears, meant to protect the men in the trench from the scorching blasts of flame cannons, while in front of the spears, leashed with heavy chains, were packs of hungry war wolves, waiting to be loosed. The plain itself was crisscrossed with ropes and razors and pitted with deep traps dug to swallow slow-moving greegans.

Richius dropped from Lightning's back and helped Dyana down. Around them the hero's welcome continued as the men of Castle Dring took up positions beside their brethren, and Jarra shouted orders, straining to be heard over the triumphant voices of the warriors. Richius took Dyana's hand and squeezed it.

"They've done a fine job," he said. "It's everything I asked for and more. This war isn't over yet."

"But will it be enough? Can we win?"

It was the same impossible question everyone was asking. "I really don't know," said Richius. "I don't know what they've sent against us yet. We'll see in the morning, when it's light."

He looked up toward the nearest trees and saw the observation platform he had ordered, hanging high above the ground between two large oaks. There were several men on the deck, all staring out across the battlefield. A flimsy rope ladder dangled from it, barely reaching the ground.

"There," said Richius, pointing toward the platform. "We'll be able to see more from the deck."

Dyana nodded and explained this to Voris, who followed them toward the rope ladder with Jarra. Richius pulled on the ladder to test its strength, then coaxed Dyana onto it.

"I'll be right behind you," he said. "Go slowly so it doesn't shake too much."

Dyana scurried up the first few rungs like a squirrel. She smiled down at Richius playfully. "All right."

Richius followed her up the ladder. Next came Voris and then Jarra, and the combined weight made the ladder groan. But it held, and when Dyana reached the top a warrior was waiting with an outstretched hand. Richius stepped onto the deck after her and went to the edge of the platform, leaning out over its railing and surveying the dark battlefield. He could see the pinpoints of flame cannons and cooking fires far off in the distance. He guessed from the distance between lights that there were at least several hundred men camped just outside the valley. Dyana came up alongside him just as he let out a worried sigh.

"What is it?" she asked nervously. He pointed toward the lights.

"I can't really tell from here, but there's a lot more activity than I saw from the watchtower. Those flames are spaced far apart, too, which means at least a whole division."

"How many is a division?"

Richius turned to look at her, suddenly sorry he had allowed her to come. "A lot," he answered honestly.

Dyana's expression was resolute. "We are a lot, too."

She was right. Down in the trench were at least a thousand men and boys ready to defend the valley, some armed with jiiktars, others with no more than a sharpened shovel. Peasants and warriors stood side by side, a wall of white flesh against the coming onslaught. And of course there were the wolves, over a hundred of them, slobbering and howling in their eagerness for blood. It was all as Richius had ordered, precise in every detail, and he was oddly pleased. He remembered what his father had once told him, that there are moments in a soldier's life when he knows he's doing right, even in the face of doom.

"My father would be proud of me now, I think," he said quietly.

Dyana smiled at him. "I am proud of you, Richius. And if Sabrina were here, she would be proud of you, too."

"Sabrina," he whispered. "I would do anything to change her fate. But the most I can do now is avenge her." He looked at Dyana seriously. "He's out there, Dyana. I feel him. Gayle is out there, waiting for me."

"Do not," she warned. "You need your wits about you. If he is out there, he will not be able to get to you."

But will I be able to get to him? wondered Richius. The thought was overwhelming. He turned back toward the black expanse of battlefield and considered his chances of stopping Gayle and the legions of Nar.

How many of them were there, hidden behind the cloak of night? It all depended on the numbers. If there were only a few brigades, they might win the day. More, and their chances were slim. A whole division would overrun them—not quickly, but certainly. The notion made Richius shudder. There were people in this valley, people he knew. One of them was his daughter.

Voris strode up alongside him, gesturing broadly to the perimeter and directing Dyana to translate.

"He wants to know what you think," Dyana said.

"His men did a very fine job," Richius admitted. "I'm impressed. You can tell him that for me. He should know."

Dyana explained this to Voris and the warlord's face lit with pride. He started pointing out the details of the perimeter, as affected as Richius by the sight of it. They were at least a hundred feet off the ground, with the whole of the field before them.

"We'll direct the battle from up here," explained Richius. "Dyana, make sure he knows not to give any orders without me. I want to be careful how we use what we've got."

Voris grunted unhappily as Dyana explained this to him, but otherwise the warlord did not protest. He passed the order along to Jarra, who called it down to the men on the ground. Richius saw their expressions darken. They would be taking orders from the Jackal now. He would have to be wary, he decided, and make sure Voris wasn't embarrassed.

They spent the next hour pacing the deck and staring up at the moon, waiting for dawn to come. The defenders in the trench had fallen silent, some asleep, most lost in melancholy thought. Spring breezes carried aloft the scents of fear and perspiration, and a mile away the twinkle of flame cannons flickered. The night was warm and oppressive, and as Richius watched the moon make its long journey across the sky he felt his eyelids drooping with fatigue. He whiled away the idle minutes toying with Jessicane and fighting back the surreal spell of the Dring Valley.

Eventually, he sat back against one of the huge tree trunks holding up the deck. Dyana was asleep beside him, her breathing soft and peaceful. Across the deck sat Voris, his meaty hands clasped around his knees. The warlord stared at him impassively. Richius chanced an encouraging smile. Voris responded with a little nod and closed his eyes.

Progress, thought Richius wryly. He closed his eyes, too, not really wanting to sleep but unable to stay awake.

When he awoke, some hours later, Dyana was standing over him.

"Richius," she said nervously. "I was just going to wake you."

He blinked hard and struggled to his feet. "Why? What is it?"

"Dawn," she said, pointing eastward. Over her shoulder the horizon was brightening.

Richius peered over the rail. Darkness still dominated the west, but he

could just make out the faint outlines of things moving. Far below in the
trench the warriors and peasants stood in rows, their faces locked and determined. Voris and Jarra were at the railing, too, speaking anxiously.
They quieted when they noticed Richius.

"Can you see anything?" asked Dyana.

Richius shook his head. "Not too much," he said. "Not yet."

They waited as the sun rose sluggishly in the east and sprinkled the
earth with its rays. Gradually the western horizon brightened, revealing
the forces positioned there. Richius leaned out over the railing. Sunlight
glinted on black and silver metals. Thin wisps of smoke climbed into the
sky. Things moved. Big things. Richius held his breath. Voris prodded
him. Richius held up a hand.

"Wait."

It was all in the numbers, he reminded himself. What had Arkus sent
against them? A division? More? The deck fell silent as they all awaited
the verdict. As the pall thinned, the first of the greegans lumbered out of
the fog.

"There," said Dyana, pointing toward the monster. "You see?"

"I see," replied Richius gravely.

Soon there was another and another still, until there were fifty or more
of the horned beasts in sight, each pulling a tracked and armored war
wagon. On top of each wagon was a long, needle-nosed pipe, most
sprouting twisted hoses, others with an odd-looking bellows. These were
the acid launchers, the air-powered guns that could fire a canister of
caustic liquid nearly a thousand feet. Behind the wagons were rows of
legionnaires—infantrymen with sabers and spiked maces, advancing out
of the mist in staggered waves. The ranks of infantry seemed to fill the
horizon, while behind them, still only barely visible, was the heavy cavalry of Talistan, prancing under the banner of the House of Gayle.
Richius heard a disturbed murmur ripple through the trench below.

"Almighty God," whispered Richius. He glanced over at Voris. "We're
in trouble."

"How many are there?" asked Dyana incredulously.

"Too many," said Richius. "We're going to need help."

"Help? From where?"

"Anywhere. Anyone who can pick up a weapon. God, Dyana, look out
there. This perimeter can't hold against that many men. Not for more
than a day at best. We're going to need reinforcements. Fast."

Dyana stared at him. "Richius, this is everyone. There are no more
men in Dring."

"Then they'll have to come from somewhere else. Tatterak maybe, or
the Sheaze. Hell, anywhere. But we have to send for help now, before
we're completely overrun."

Voris, who had been listening intently, stepped between them. He glanced at Richius questioningly.

"Tell him, Dyana," urged Richius. "We don't have enough men to stop them. He can probably see that for himself. Tell him we need help."

Dyana explained it to Voris and Dumaka Jarra carefully, then waited for the warlord's response. Voris looked thoughtful and ran a hand over his bald scalp. He conversed with Jarra for a moment, sighed, then shook his head.

"Voris says that it is impossible," said Dyana. "He says the only warriors near enough to help are in Tatterak, and that they are also under attack."

"Dyana, listen to me. That's a host of Nar's ground forces. And if they're here, then they can't be in Tatterak, too. I don't know what kind of numbers Arkus is landing on the shores, but I'm sure it's nothing like what's here in Dring right now."

"He will not do it, Richius. He will not ask Kronin for help."

"But we need it. Damn it, Dyana, there isn't time for this nonsense. Now you tell him we need Kronin's help fast, or those troops are going to overrun this valley in a week. Tell him, Dyana. Every word."

Dyana did as Richius directed, and when she was done the warlord folded his arms over his chest and shook his head again. Dyana listened to his response then started to translate, but Richius interrupted her.

"Stop. I don't want to hear any more of his excuses." He scowled at Voris, stepping right up to him and saying fiercely, "Warlord, I'm ordering you in the name of Tharn to send a messenger to Tatterak at once. We need help, and I don't give a damn where it comes from. I'm supposed to protect your valley. I don't want to, but that's the way it is. So if you don't give me what I want, understand that you're disobeying your Lord Tharn, and that whatever happens here is your own bloody fault!"

Voris seemed stunned. He demanded an explanation from Dyana, and when it came his face purpled. But Jarra was at his side, calming him with his smooth, authoritative voice. They argued for a moment, until finally Voris grunted and went to the edge of the deck.

"Ki easay," he said begrudgingly.

Dyana let out a relieved breath. "He will do it. The Dumaka agrees with you, Richius."

"Thank God," said Richius. "And thank you, Jarra," he said to the Dumaka.

Jarra bowed, but seemed to take no pleasure in the victory. He summoned one of the warriors on the deck and gave the order to ride to Tatterak immediately. The warrior accepted the charge without challenge and disappeared down the rope ladder. Jarra then went to the railing to stand beside Voris.

"I don't understand him at all," remarked Richius. "We need help. Can't he see that?"

"He sees," said Dyana easily. "But what you have asked of him is a great dishonor. Now come. You must see to things."

They went to stand beside the warlord and looked out over the field. The greegans were closer now, too far to see well but close enough to gauge their numbers. At least fifty, Richius concluded. And just over a hundred war wolves to stop them. It would be a difficult feat. He had counted on having at least three wolves to bring down each greegan— a creature a Naren poet had once compared to a mountain. With their plated flesh, greegans were practically immune to arrows. Only the powerful jaws of the wolves stood a chance of puncturing their hides.

Down near the trench, the wolves picked up the musty scent of their prey and a wild baying issued from their throats as they strained against their bonds. They would be able to run under the ropes and blades strung along the field, and the greegans, far too late to outmaneuver the traps, would have to deal with both. So too would the infantrymen, who Richius was sure had never faced such a bedeviling adversary as the war wolves of Dring. A wicked sense of satisfaction raced through him. It would be good to be on this side of their teeth for a change.

"When the war wagons enter the perimeter," he said to Voris, "that's when we'll let the wolves go. Have your archers in the trees make ready. We'll fire off a few volleys when they get in range."

Dyana translated and Voris agreed, calling out the order to the hundreds of bowmen along the network of catwalks and in the trench below. The warlord himself picked up a bow from the deck and handed it to Richius, who accepted it with a smile. They each chose an arrow from the quivers strung haphazardly about the platform and notched them in their bows. Richius pulled back on the string to test its tension.

"When I give the word, we let 'em fly," said Richius.

Amazingly, Voris grinned at him. "Kirh ata Narr," he said.

Richius looked to Dyana. "What did he say?"

"Do you not know those words by now?" asked Dyana. "He said 'Death to Nar.' "

Richius nodded soberly. "Kirh ata Narr, indeed."

For long moments they watched as the greegans pulled the war wagons closer, and soon the weapons poised on their roofs were clearly visible. Most had flame cannons. Others, perhaps ten in all, were outfitted with acid launchers. These would be the real danger. But the men in the trenches had all been given shields, and when the peculiar whistle of an acid cannister was heard overhead, they were instructed to hide beneath their shields or any other object large enough to cover them. Richius remembered Edgard telling him that there was always a dull thump when an acid launcher fired. He hoped that sound and the whistling of the projectile would be enough to warn them.

"Get ready," warned Richius. The greegans were almost in range. The flame cannons and acid launchers began tracking upward. And in the trench and trees, the Triin of Dring braced themselves against the bizarre death machines rolling forward, as defiant and hard as Richius had ever seen them. In the far-off haze, the banner of Blackwood Gayle snaked in the breeze, and the long sabers of his proud horsemen shimmered in the new morning. The black-armored infantrymen drew up their maces and swords and marched in flawless order behind the greegans.

When they reached the perimeter Richius tilted his bow into the air. "Ready?" he called to Voris. "Hold for my word. . . ."

The warlord passed the order down the line, and the trees sang with the squeaking strain of tightening bowstrings. Plumes of smoke roiled up from the flame cannons. The greegans lowered their horned snouts to charge. Richius closed an eye and with the other drew a bead on the closest war wagon. Inside it, he knew, a sweating operator was deciding when to charge. It was like deciding when to die.

"Ready . . ."

On the roof of the wagon was a flame cannon. It tracked its long nose toward the trench. Richius held his breath. First the blast, then the charge, that's what he would do. The wolves would have to be loosed now.

"Yulans!" he cried.

Outside the trench, the wolf keepers loosed the bolts on the collars of their pets and sent them streaming forward like a hundred-fingered hand.

"Fire!"

Every man with a bow sent an arrow screaming into the air, over and ahead of the charging wolves, straight for the hearts of the infantry. The legionnaires stopped and each fell to one knee, bringing up their shields against the coming rain of shafts. The wolves rushed forward, slipping effortlessly under the wires strewn across the perimeter, racing in howling trios toward the invading greegans. Inside the first iron wagon, the cannoneer squeezed his trigger. There was a flare and a rumble as the liquid fire shot across the battlefield. The men in the trench ducked behind ten-foot walls of wood and skins. Arrows rained down on the infantry. The river of fire poured across the field, blasting the wooden barricade. Orange heat exploded and tore at the animal hides, scorching them and sending up a bright chain of acrid smoke.

The shield held.

Behind it, the men joined in Richius' cheer, readying themselves for the next blast.

The infantrymen were up again—fewer now, but not by many. Richius ordered the Triin to lower their bows. It was time to see what the wolves could do. The beasts were all over the field now, throwing themselves onto the giant greegans. An awful braying rose as the horned monsters tried to charge but were stopped by the lines of rope and the relentless teeth of the wolves. Snapping jaws wrapped around thick legs, tearing open the gray, wrinkled skin where it was thinnest. The greegans kicked at the wolves and swiped at them with their horns, impaling some but missing most. From somewhere back near the cavalry a trumpet sounded, and the infantry rushed forward.

There was a sharp cracking, and the air turned red. Richius called out for the men to cover themselves. He brought up his own shield as a shaft of flame cut through the trees, shearing off a clump of nearby branches. Richius grabbed Dyana, dragging her down onto the deck and covering her body with his as another stream of fire blasted overhead. But the aim of the cannons was made random by the war wolves, who were now climbing onto the backs of the wailing greegans and sinking their dagger-like teeth into their stout necks. One greegan fell and then another, and Richius could see the infantrymen racing to the rescue of the war wagons, which had almost come to a standstill in the labyrinthine rope maze of the perimeter. A handful of wolves collapsed under the heavy maces of the soldiers before they realized what was happening. But they were wise, these beasts, and quick, and in a flash they had analyzed these new ene- mies and set upon them with vigor. They jumped on the infantrymen, pushing them onto their backs and pulling off their helmets with their teeth.

Richius rose and pulled Dyana to her feet. Voris and Jarra were hang- ing over the rail, ignoring the shower of sparks coming down like rain as they shouted orders down to the trench. Around them the trees rustled as men busied themselves notching arrows to bows. Richius raised his own bow and ordered another volley. The arrows screamed skyward over the greegans and wolves and into the far columns of infantrymen, who were now charging the perimeter. Inside the battlefield the ropes and traps were tangling greegans and soldiers alike. The air filled with the hiss of wooden shafts and smoke and terrible, inhuman shouts.

And then another sound reached the deck. Richius cocked his head to listen. The acid launchers were in range, their huge, baglike bellows ex- panding and collapsing with a sucking thump. In the sky a metal cannis- ter was twisting toward them, whistling as it sprayed out a thin, yellow rain. Richius raised his shield over his head and shouted into the trees.

"Shields!"

"Basa!" echoed Voris, understanding Richius' mime. "Basa!"

Less than a second later the men on the catwalks disappeared behind their hand shields. Overhead the cannister shivered and burst, and from the sky came a burning shower, hissing and steaming.

"Hold your breath," Richius ordered Dyana. "Don't breathe until I tell you!"

But others did breathe. An agonized moaning rocked the catwalks as several of the defenders dropped to their knees and put their hands to their throats, coughing up mucus and blood. Richius felt a sizzling on his leg and bit back a holler. He glanced backward and saw a drop of yellow liquid burning through his boot and boring into his calf. Around him the deck cooked, sending up faint wisps of pale smoke, while beneath him Dyana was perfectly still, too terrified to move or breathe. Men were falling off the catwalks, tumbling to the hard earth below as they screamed and scratched at their blistering throats.

Finally the yellow rain ended. Richius hurried to his feet and looked at Dyana. "Are you all right?" he asked breathlessly.

"I am," she answered, but she was clearly shaken. Across the deck Voris and his Dumaka were rising also. The warlord raced over to Dyana, who gestured quickly that she was fine. Then Voris turned to Richius with the same concern in his eyes. Richius shook his head.

"It's nothing," he said. "It just caught my leg."

It wasn't nothing, but there was no time to tend to it. The acid had already stopped working its way under his skin and now there was only pain. Richius ignored it and went back to the rail. On the perimeter, the wolves were still worrying the greegans. Several of the mammoth beasts had fallen into the ditches pocking the field, the wagons they were pulling half-buried. All about the field soldiers hacked at the ropes, desperate to reach the barricade before a wolf or quarrel caught them. The unluckiest were caught in the fire of the flame cannons, which were detonating constantly now, strafing the barricades and slicing through the trees. Fireballs cascaded off the shields and bounced backward onto the field, catching men and animals alike, and all the while the Triin of Dring loosed arrows into the air with inhuman speed.

But the perimeter wasn't holding. The ropes were coming down and the wolves were thinning. Richius strained to see past the smoke clogging the field. Maybe twenty wolves were left, and the Naren numbers were swelling. A handful of wagons still lumbered forward. Another bolt of fire crashed into a trench shield, and the thump-thump of acid launchers popped in the distance. Skyward came a trio of fizzing cannisters, spraying down their watery poison on the trench and disappearing into the trees. The rain of arrows ceased as the Triin sought cover, ducking under shields and holding their breath till their faces blued. There was more choking as the searing acid seeped into lungs, and on the field men were vomiting blood. Above him, Richius could hear leaves steaming. His eyes stung, and he covered his face with his hands. Rivers of tears gushed down his cheeks. He heard Voris roar in agony and struggled to open his eyes. The warlord was still firing into the field, holding his breath as he plied his bow like a madman.

"Voris, get down!" Richius shouted, chancing a breath. He tasted the bitter fumes on his lips. Another cannister was sailing through the air, heading directly for the deck.

Richius sprang to his feet and raced toward Voris, barreling into him and pushing him down. Together they sprawled across the platform just as the acid cannister crashed against the deck. There was a popping hiss and the cannister burst. Dyana screamed for Richius. Richius covered Voris. And then, as if a surgeon were peeling away his skin, he felt the back of his shirt melt away and a thousand burning needles puncture his flesh.

Richius screamed, scrambling toward the end of the deck. The pain was agonizing. Someone was pulling off his shirt. He opened his eyes and saw Voris' giant body smothering him, rolling him over and ripping off his garment. On the other side of the deck, Dyana was fighting to reach him. Jarra was pulling her backward. And in the middle of the deck the acid was eating through the planking, spitting and smoking as it chewed like termites through the wood.

"Richius!" screamed Dyana, struggling against Jarra's insistent grasp. Voris turned and growled at her, then lifted Richius off the deck and hoisted him over his shoulder. Richius felt the world spinning. Out on the field a flame cannon was leveling its nose toward them. Voris dashed for the deck's other side. The wooden platform groaned. Jarra was pulling Dyana toward the rope ladder. The flame cannon fired. A bolt of fire ripped overhead. Voris jumped.

He landed heavily on the far side of the deck, his weight splintering the platform. Voris' foot went through the weakened wood and he stumbled. Richius sprawled headlong across the deck. Quickly he turned, his scorched back throbbing as he stretched out a hand for Voris and pulled him out of the hole. Behind him he heard Jarra begging Dyana to leave.

"Go," Richius ordered her. "Go! We'll follow."

Dyana obeyed, hurrying down the ladder. Jarra waited a second longer, then descended himself. Next came Richius. He could hardly control his muscles, but he managed with Voris' help to slip onto the swinging ladder. Beneath him Jarra was close behind, waiting and guiding his every step. When he was halfway down the ladder Voris followed, and one by one they dropped gratefully to the ground. Above them, the deck collapsed.

Amidst the falling rubble, Richius fell breathlessly to his knees, doubling over in agony. Dyana rushed up behind him and inspected his back.

"How is it?" he asked, almost unable to speak. Dyana was silent for a very long moment. Richius could see her worry reflected in Voris' face.

"Richius, we have to get you back to the keep," she said carefully. "Your back is . . . bad."

"I can't leave, Dyana. Not yet. But I want you to go. Have one of the warriors take you back before the shields fall."

"I am not going without you," she said. "And there is nothing left for you to do here. Your back needs tending."

"No, I'm needed here!" Richius glanced up at the ruined platform, then searched the trees for another reasonable vantage point. "I have to see what's happening."

Voris said something harsh, making shooing gestures at Richius.

"He says you should leave, Richius," said Dyana. "You are hurt. You have to go now."

"No. We have to stop those acid launchers. The line won't hold if we don't. I have to get to the trench."

He was on his way to the line when Dyana grabbed his arm. "Richius, listen to me, please. It's over. The trench is lost. There's nothing more to do. We have to go, call retreat and fight from the forest like you planned."

But Voris was already heading toward the trench, with Dumaka Jarra on his heels. Richius had to follow.

"Dyana, go back to the castle," he said. "I'll join you as soon as I can."

"Richius, you promised. There is nothing you can do. You will only be slaughtered like the rest of them."

"I can't leave now, Dyana. I *can't*. They're depending on me. They need me. Please. Go back to the castle and wait for me there. Have one of the warriors ride with you. I have to think of a way to stop the launchers."

"And what if you cannot?"

"Then the perimeter falls and I'll join you back at the castle. Now go, Dyana. Hurry."

It seemed forever before she relented, her lips brushing his lightly in an unexpected kiss. "Be safe," she said.

He let her hands slip away. "I will."

She left him, and as he watched her go Richius heard a commotion behind him. In the trench men were shouting, taunting their Naren adversaries to advance. Very deliberately, Richius undid the clasp of his scabbard. He drew Jessicane slowly as he turned toward the trench. Flame cannons erupted ahead of him. He saw smoke and fire, smelled the cooked flesh.

Voris helped him into the ditch. In front of them a wooden shield trembled with the impact of cannon fire. The warlord ignored it.

"Nobata acana toss, Kalak," he said proudly.

"I don't know what you're saying," said Richius, "but if you'll have me I'm here to fight with you."

Voris laughed. "Kalak es Cha Yulan," he declared, pointing between the two of them. There was more incredulous laughing. "Kalak es Cha Yulan!"

Richius beamed. "The Jackal and the Wolf!" he said. "Yes, I understand."

And for the first time Richius could recall, the Wolf of the Dring Valley smiled at him. Not a sinister smile, but a warm, genuine one. Together they climbed onto the narrow planks lining the inside of the trench and looked out over the battlefield. Every muscle in his back raged but Richius put the pain out of his mind, holding Jessicane out before him as he watched the flames sizzle and explode against the shields. Across the field he saw the infantry charging toward them, free at last of the wolves. Only a few greegans still pulled war wagons, and these were mostly far away, while behind them all, waiting for their chance to run the defenders underfoot, were the horsemen of Talistan, their grotesque demon masks shining in the sun.

Voris was shouting at his warriors, ordering them to continue shooting. The infantry was so close now that the Triin arrows had little trouble penetrating their leather gorgets. Wave after wave of soldiers rushed forward, swinging their weapons and screaming wildly. Two acid launchers popped in the distance, sending cannisters into the trees beyond the trench, while Triin bowmen stood recklessly on the catwalks, daring the acid to reach them as they picked off the attackers.

Yet despite their efforts, Richius knew it would all be over soon. Without the wolves there was no way to stop the war wagons, and the shields that had withstood so much punishment were starting to shudder under the cannon fire. Soon they would collapse, leaving them defenseless. From the trench they might be able to withstand the infantry indefinitely, but the cannons and launchers would ruin them. He searched for an idea, a way of slowing the handful of greegans still slogging toward them. Arrows certainly couldn't do it. Most of the monsters already looked like pincushions. They needed another option, and they didn't have one.

"Damn," he spat bitterly. "It's over."

Voris seemed to understand him. He called over to Jarra, who immediately passed the order to retreat. Warriors began pouring out of the trench, while in the trees their comrades covered their escape, focusing their fire on the nearest infantrymen, who were now only yards from the barricade of sharpened spears. Jarra herded the men out of the ditch, funneling them into the narrow path leading to the woods. And as they moved they dropped their bows to the ground and held out jiiktars. It was time to take the fight to the forest.

"Come on, Voris," urged Richius. "We have to get out of here."

Voris shook his head, gesturing toward his men. Clearly he was determined to leave last. The shields were buckling as the force on them increased. Already a seam was opening in the log wall nearest them, letting through lashing tongues of flame. Close by, another shield was engulfed in flame, sending up a torrent of gray smoke. The periodic thump of acid

THE JACKAL OF NAR

launchers grew ever louder. Richius peered out across the field, blocking his eyes from the glow of burning kerosene. The soldiers were fighting their way through the barricade, slowly squeezing past the spears and spikes as the barrage of arrows pressed down on them. Bodies littered the battlefield, corpses with throats torn open and heads blasted away, and wounded greegans moaned in distress as they pulled themselves aimlessly through the tangle of ropes, their legs gnawed to tatters by the wolves, who now lay in mangled heaps about the perimeter. It was a nightmare of carnage. Richius started to look away, but saw instead a green and gold standard waving through the haze.

Baron Blackwood Gayle sat imperiously atop his black charger, flanked by his standard bearer and a man with a peculiar, feathered hat. He was unmistakable in his silver mask and long, braided ponytail. Behind him waited his cavalry and infantry. Patiently the baron surveyed the field, waiting for the barricade to come down before ordering his own men to charge. Even from such a distance Richius could discern the arrogant smile splashed across his disfigured face.

"Gayle," Richius whispered, climbing back onto the narrow deck. He moved as if possessed. He barely flinched as flames shot by, and all the agony of his burnt skin was gone, submerged by a consuming hate. Voris was yelling at him, beckoning him down, but he ignored the warlord's order. Like a bare-chested savage he hoisted Jessicane over his head and howled across the battlefield.

"Gayle, you whoreson, I'm here!"

Soldiers tumbled through the barricade. Acid cannisters whizzed overhead, drizzling poison. Richius twisted to avoid the deadly spray. Behind him, he heard Voris calling.

"It's me!" he cried. "Kalak!"

Off in the distance, Blackwood Gayle's head tilted. The bright mask turned curiously to the trench. Richius lifted Jessicane higher.

"Kalak!" he shouted again. "Look here, you bastard! It's me!"

Gayle's body seemed to twitch. He sat up in his saddle, then suddenly put his fist in the air and shook it.

"Yes," cried Richius madly. "You see me." He waved his sword like a flag, yelling his Triin nickname over and over. Gayle flicked his reins and started charging. Richius let out a triumphant howl.

Without thinking he crawled out of the trench, into the space between the ditch and the barricade. Gayle was covering the distance with incredible speed. Richius staggered to his feet. Ten yards away he could see the snarling, shocked faces of the legionnaires, hacking their way through the barricade as they struggled to reach him. A flame cannon leveled a shot, destroying a section of a wall behind him. Incensed, he held out Jessicane and cursed.

"Come to me, you clumsy murderer!"

"Kalak!" came an insistent voice from behind. Richius turned to see Voris slogging toward him. The warlord stretched out both of his hands and took hold of Richius' arm.

"No!" Richius barked, twisting out of Voris' grasp. "Leave me be. It's Gayle!"

Voris roared something and wrested Richius' sword away. Enraged, Richius tried to reclaim it, but Voris struck him hard across the face. The world blurred. Voris wrapped an arm around Richius' waist and started dragging him backward. The pain of the embrace was unspeakable.

"No," he moaned. "You don't understand. It's Gayle, it's Gayle."

Through the gauzy smoke he caught sight of Gayle still charging the barricade. The soldiers broke through. Shouts rose in his ears. Then he was in the trench again, still being dragged by Voris. The warlord was calling for help. Richius could hear the man's labored breathing. Seconds later, dozens of white hands were on him, pulling him away.

"No," he said again. "You don't know what you're doing. . . ."

Then the skin of his back ruptured with a pain as hot as fire, and the world blackened. And as he faded out he heard Voris' angry voice, cursing him.

THIRTY-NINE

When the harsh mountains of Tatterak had faded away and the terrain had flattened into yellow savanna, Tharn knew they were approaching Chandakkar.

It had been a sickening journey, one that had depleted him, and he was glad their trek was nearly over. He could smell it. Like a hunter, he could taste the change in the air. Chandakkar wasn't rugged like Tatterak or lush like Dring. And it wasn't hot like the Fire Steppes, or cold like Ishia's mountain. It was simply Chandakkar, the separate and defiant land of Karlaz. Here, among the grasses, there was nothing familiar to give them comfort. For two days now the land had been sloping gradually downward. They were in a valley now, a vast plain overrun with tall, amber plants that bent like wheat in the wind. Without really knowing why, they had all slipped into a contemplative silence.

Tharn took a small sip from a waterskin and leaned back in the carriage. Unable to steer the horses himself, he always rode in the back while his cunning-men took turns driving. It was a warm day, sticky and close, and his boils itched madly. So far, water hadn't been a concern, but they conserved it anyway. They had no maps to follow, no idea of what lay ahead. A desert, perhaps, and that meant water would very quickly become precious. So Tharn capped his skin after the tiniest sip, burying it under his seat to keep it cool. Their conveyance had a canvas top that could be pulled overhead and shield them from the sun, but Tharn didn't like the feeling of confinement. He wanted to see Chandakkar, to experience it like he had Nar.

Besides, watching their surroundings was all any of them could do. Tharn had brought three young men with them, all full of youthful vigor, and all cunning-men devoted to his Drol ideals. But they were equally devoted to Tharn himself, and knew that their master appreciated silence. So they spoke only rarely, and let their leader linger in the back of the carriage.

Tharn appreciated every moment of the silence. For now at least, he was no one again, without the pressures of Falindar or war. With the easy slipping of day into night, it seemed that none of his torments existed, and that Nar was only a nightmare. Surprisingly, he thought little of his mission. Karlaz would help them, or he would not. The logic of it put Tharn at ease. He felt powerless, an innocent at the mercy of fate, and the simplicity of it was wonderful. He was enjoying something he had not known since his boyhood—peace.

Only the memory of Dyana made him restless. He ached for her, more now than he ever had before. Part of him regretted the night he had spent with her. It had been so sublime, like heaven but better, he was sure. She had treated him as a man, had seen past his monstrousness, and had set his skin on fire with her touch. It had crushed him to leave her.

And of course, he thought of Richius.

She was starry-eyed for him; he had always known it. When she carried Shani she had cried for him, for the absent father of the thing growing inside her. He had thought it would pass, that it was only the natural yearning a woman has for any man who has impregnated her. In time, he had hoped, she would forget Richius and see him as the child's father. But now Richius was in Lucel-Lor. There could be no stopping the fire between them. Tharn sank down a little in the carriage. It had been pity that had made her lie with him, he knew that. He looked at himself, studying his malformed body in the sunlight and hating it. Richius was nothing like him. The Naren was perfect—except for being Naren, but Dyana had never minded that. She was still the heretic she had always been, enamored with the Empire and its astute barbarians. And Richius was a young man, with all the normal hungers. He could satisfy her. The thought tightened Tharn's jaw. He didn't hate Richius, or at least he didn't want to. He had used him horribly, though, and he wondered now as he watched the clouds overhead if there hadn't been some vengeance in his design.

I am not evil, Tharn decided. *But I have done evil things. Lorris, help me. Help me with my rage.*

As he had been for months, Tharn's divine patron was silent. The Drol kept his eyes closed, considering the question himself. Voris would kill

Richius if he moved against Dyana. He had not ordered it, but he had not had to. It was the way of things between Tharn and the warlord, part of their alliance. Was that evil? Was the murder of Edgard evil? It was all blood for a cause, but sometimes that answer didn't satisfy Tharn. Lorris was a mystery to him now. Once he had been sure of his god's desires, so sure he had slaughtered hundreds with his gift. And the act had earned him his wretched body. Sometimes, when he was alone and most in pain, he blamed Lorris, not only for his agony but also for his loneliness. If he were a man and whole like Richius, he might have Dyana for himself.

But it was impossible. She could never love him, and that knowledge broke his heart. He took a deep breath of the clean air and expelled it in a loud sigh. Nagrah, one of the priests he was traveling with, rolled over from his nap and looked at him.

"Master?" said the younger man. "Are you all right?"

Nagrah was barely twenty, a devotee from a good Drol family. Tharn liked him. Usually, he appreciated the young man's concern. But not now.

"Fine," he snapped, sure he sounded unconvincing.

Nagrah frowned. Tharn was never short with any of them. "Your pardon, Master, but you are not fine. You have been silent all day. What is it? Are you ill?"

"Look at me," said Tharn. "Of course I am ill." But then he softened, saying, "I am really fine. I am just . . ." He shrugged. "Thinking."

"Of Chandakkar?" asked Nagrah excitedly. Like the others, Nagrah had eagerly accepted Tharn's request to go to Karlaz. He was a priest, barely, but he had a boy's adventurous spirit. Tharn smiled at him.

"No, not Chandakkar. Something far less important. Do not concern yourself."

Nagrah gestured to the openness around them. "We have all day, Master. Maybe many days. Why not talk?"

"Because I am not in the mood. Now be quiet; let me rest."

Nagrah looked hurt, but didn't press his master. He simply averted his eyes, letting them linger on the beautiful grassland and pretending he was unaffected by the rebuff. Tharn regretted his harshness. They were all good young men. And strong. He had picked them because of their vigor. But they were curious, and curiosity, he had learned early on, shouldn't be snuffed out. His own father had made that mistake.

"All right," he said, straightening painfully. "Let us talk." With his cane he banged on the bench seat in front of him. Raig and Vorn, Nagrah's Drol brothers, both turned around. Raig had the reins in his hands. "You two, listen to me," started Tharn. "Young Nagrah wants to talk. And I have things on my mind. Let us exercise our brains a little."

"Master?" asked Vorn incredulously. Tharn never addressed them so casually. Vorn seemed both pleased and shocked.

"Talk," said Tharn. "You know what that is, do you not? Our lives need not be all prayers, you know."

"I know, Master," replied Vorn. "I pray *and* I talk."

"Good. Then talk to me. I have a question. Nagrah, listen closely."

Tharn sat back against the shallow boards and made himself as comfortable as he could. Nagrah and Vorn leaned in closer, keen to hear their master's question. Raig had turned his eyes back to the road ahead, but he cocked his head to listen.

"I have been wondering something," Tharn went on. "About cruelty. I am wondering where it comes from."

The young men puzzled over the question, not really understanding it. Tharn watched with amusement as Nagrah tried to hurry an answer. The aloof Raig beat him to it.

"Evil," Raig pronounced confidently. "Cruelty comes from evil."

"Evil," Tharn echoed, considering it. "Hmm, maybe. Like the Narens, Raig?"

"Yes. The Narens are evil. It makes them cruel. Only evil men could do what was done at Ackle-Nye."

"Is this a game, Master?" inquired Vorn. He had a suspicious bent that reminded Tharn of himself.

"No, not a game," said Tharn. "Oh, you three think I have all the answers, but I do not. I wonder things, too. Sometimes it helps me to philosophize." He poked Nagrah with his cane. "Well? What do you say?"

"I think Raig is right," said Nagrah. "Evil makes men cruel. Why are you wondering this, Master?"

"I ask the questions. What about the warlords? Are they cruel?"

"No," replied Raig over his shoulder. "They are warriors."

Tharn's smile was precocious. "When Delgar fought Praxtin-Tar at Reen, he buried fifty captured warriors up to their necks on the shore and waited for the tide to come in. Before they drowned the crabs and gulls ate out their eyes. Does that qualify as cruelty to you, Raig?"

It took a long time for Raig to answer, and Tharn watched as his pupil bristled. "Yes, I suppose," agreed Raig finally. "Maybe Delgar is evil."

"Delgar is helping us now. He's fighting with us against the Narens. Does that make us evil?"

"Master, what is this about?" asked Nagrah. "I do not understand. We are not evil."

"Hush, boy. I never said we were. Raig, tell me. Is Delgar evil, or are you wrong about the cause of cruelty?"

Raig shrugged. "I do not know."

"I think Raig is wrong," said Vorn. "Delgar is cruel. Shohar, too. But they are not evil."

"No," said Tharn. "I agree with you. They are honorable men, both of them. Brutal, perhaps, but honorable. As are we all." He looked straight at Nagrah. The young man looked back, clearly troubled. "Right, Nagrah?"

Nagrah could only shrug, and for a moment their minds met. Nagrah knew Tharn was troubled. That was why he had forced him to talk when Tharn was content with silence. The Drol master thought about his question, and how he had been cruel to Richius and Edgard, and how he had kicked the Daegog's teeth across the throne room. Even Dyana had suffered his cruelty. But Tharn never once considered himself evil. Something else had moved him to such madness. With their eyes still locked, Tharn addressed Nagrah softly.

"Nagrah? Why are men cruel?"

Nagrah's expression was heartbreaking. "Men are cruel when they are weak, Master. Men are cruel when they have desires and are frustrated."

And then Nagrah spoke no more. The young man turned from his master and looked again out over the plains, and there was no more reason for any of them to speak.

Later that day, when the sun was high and full with noon, Tharn awakened from a restless nap. He looked over the side of the rocking carriage and found they were in a swamp of dry grass, higher even than a man's waist and dotted with ancient, thick-limbed trees with wide, spreading canopies of leaves. He made a quick assessment of the sun's position and decided it was time to stop. A rap of his cane got Raig's attention.

"Stop the carriage," he ordered. "Rest time. And prayer time."

Raig obeyed at once, drawing the pair of horses to a stop and setting down the reins. He and Vorn both climbed into the back of the carriage for some water and food. Nagrah began digging into the supplies. Tharn, whose back felt broken with fatigue, decided to stretch himself with a walk.

"Eat," he directed as he got unsteadily to his feet. "Rest. I will be back soon."

Nagrah looked up. "Where are you going?"

"To pray," said Tharn. He pointed with his cane into the high grass. "Out there."

"No, Master. It is too dangerous." Nagrah got to his feet and took Tharn's wobbly arm.

"Relax, boy," said Tharn. "Help me down."

"The grass is too tall," Nagrah protested, complying. "We will not be able to see you."

Tharn sighed. "I have not needed a wetnurse for a long while, Nagrah. Now eat and rest yourself. I will be quick."

He heard Nagrah's protests over his shoulder but ignored them, hobbling off into the tall grass, beating down the worst of it with his cane. It was dry here, and the grass beneath his feet hissed as he flattened it. Before long he was almost out of sight of the carriage, thoroughly invisible when he knelt. His knees gave an awful groan as he eased to the ground, setting aside his cane. He drew in a breath of sweet air to cleanse his mind. Above, the sky was cloudless. In the distance he could hear the youthful, argumentative voices of his cunning-men. This he blocked out, too, shutting his eyes and listening to the wind.

And Tharn prayed. . . .

He spoke to Lorris and to Pris, he asked for guidance and for strength, and for all the usual prayerful things, but he also asked for forgiveness for his cruelty, and he thanked his gods for opening his eyes to what he had become. With help, he would change, he told them. He had almost finished his lament when a sound behind him broke his thoughts.

Tharn muttered a little curse. "Nagrah, please . . ."

Tharn opened his eyes and turned around, and his breath stopped with a gasp. Six feet before him was the biggest animal he had ever seen, its feline head lowered to the ground, its yellow eyes bright with interest. Tharn froze. The big cat's ears drew back and for a moment it was invisible in the tawny grass. Tharn reached very slowly for his cane. The huge eyes tracked him, unblinking.

He wanted to flee, but there was nowhere to run. And running wasn't what Tharn was best at anyway. Carefully, painfully, he brought up one knee, then the other, until he was standing.

"Easy," he whispered. "Easy . . ."

The beast's eyes narrowed and a low growl rumbled from its throat. Tharn put up his hands.

"No, no. Easy. I am nothing. No trouble."

He took one step backward. The cat didn't pursue.

"Good," he crooned. "Good . . ."

"Master!"

The lion turned in a blur. Nagrah was coming, his face rigid with alarm. Behind him were Vorn and Raig. The lion roared and gathered itself to spring.

"No!" Tharn screamed, swatting at the beast with his cane. Again the lion turned. It opened up its mouth, bared its pointed fangs, and raised a flashing paw.

And the world just disappeared.

FORTY

Arkus of Nar was on a ship, sailing.

His hair was black and his limbs were strong, and he was a young man again. Barely twenty, he supposed. From the prow of the warship he could see the great expanse of ocean, and the sky was a deep, impossible blue, the kind of color that only appears in dreams. It was a giant ship, this sister of the fleet, yet he was alone on its deck and his solitude did not frighten him. Because he was young he had only one name—Arkus. It was not time yet for his Black Renaissance: not time to be dubbed the doom of the world.

Far out to sea the coast of Lucel-Lor beckoned, a shimmering break on the horizon. He had traveled far and hard, and had endured the jealous looks of the sailors who had borne him here. Arkus was not a ruler today, and wouldn't be for years. Today he was only a hunter, sent to behead a mythical beast of Lucel-Lor. He would present the lion's skull to his father, he decided, and prove his worth. His father would be pleased, and he would see that he had raised a fine and fearless heir.

Curiously, as happens in dreams, the sky began to darken. Arkus looked over the side of his ship. Beneath the keel the sea began to foam and boil, and from its depth arose a reptilian head, and then another, and then two more, all on the smooth torsos of snakes. They towered above the ship and its single passenger, staring down at him angrily. Abruptly the ship ceased its movement. Arkus of Nar gazed up at the serpent and commanded it out of his way.

"I have need of Lucel-Lor, monster," he shouted. "Do not fight me."

All the beaked heads scowled. "Who are you?" they asked. "And what is your need?" The heads seemed to speak at once in a hissing chorus.

"I am Arkus of Nar," he answered defiantly. "Someday master of a continent. Are you the guardian of Lucel-Lor?"

"We have many names," said the heads together. One smiled a dragon's smile. "I am Tharn," it said. Then its brothers joined in.

"I am Liss."

"I am the Magic of Lucel-Lor."

"And you?" asked Arkus of the head that was silent. "What are you called?"

The head that hadn't spoken now loomed higher than the rest. "I am Richius Vantran," it boomed. "I am the Jackal. The betrayer."

"We are all who fight you," said the heads, laughing, and the sea began to pitch so that Arkus could hardly stand. "We are keeping you from living."

"No," bellowed Arkus. He went to the railing of the ship and shook his fist at the hellish thing. "I am immortal. I do not fear you."

"In your youth you were immortal," said the head that called itself Magic. "And you feared nothing then."

"But you are old now," added the head called Vantran. "Old and weak. You are dying."

"I am not!" Arkus cried. "I fear no one. I am here at my father's beckoning, to capture and kill a lion and to bring back its head."

The head called Liss began to howl. "You have killed us! And now we will kill you!"

"No," Arkus protested. "I must go to Lucel-Lor. You must let me pass. Peace, Liss. I promised you peace. . . ."

Now all the heads were wailing, and Arkus felt their accusations tearing him, dragging him back to his awful reality. Cold gripped him, and the unspeakable pull of age. He gripped the rail harder to steady himself.

"Stop it!" he cried. "Stop, I demand it!"

And the head that called itself Richius Vantran lowered itself on its prehensile neck and regarded Arkus with all the venom of the world. "You demand nothing from us, old man," it hissed. "We defy you, for you are weak. You can't even see us! You are blind."

Arkus put his hands to his eyes. He knew the dragon spoke true, and the rightness of it shattered him, startling him awake. The sound of his hearth-fire roared in his ears, but he could not see its flames. All was black, as it had been for weeks now, and Arkus of Nar cursed his blindness and screamed an unholy scream.

·   ·   ·

It had taken nearly an hour for Biagio to calm the emperor. Since returning to Nar City, Biagio had foregone his usual apartments for a small chamber near Arkus', so that he could handle any emergencies. He had heard Arkus' wails even before the monarch's servants, and had rushed into the chamber to find him delirious with fear, clutching and tearing at his eyes. And though he was far stronger than his emaciated ruler, Biagio had needed nearly all his strength to subdue Arkus, so powerful was his delirium.

Arkus slept now, aided by a powerful elixir Bovadin had concocted for just such an outburst. Biagio watched Arkus from a chair by the bedside. He was exhausted. It was well past midnight. The tall tower groaned. A fire roared in the hearth. Biagio fought to keep his eyes open. He had promised Arkus he would stay with him.

It was a bitter thing, the count decided, to watch someone beloved rot away. Even he admitted that Arkus hadn't much time. Bovadin couldn't say how long the drugs would sustain him, but Arkus was weaker by the day. His bowels loosed every bit of food he forced down and, except for his occasional rages, he was as weak as a kitten. Even if there were some great magic in Lucel-Lor, Biagio doubted Gayle could bring it back in time.

And that was the terrible agony of it. For those of the Iron Circle, time had always been an ally, a force they could stop when other mortals went on aging and dying. Biagio himself was well past fifty, but he had the appearance and virility of a twenty-year-old. His skin was bronze and he was beautiful even by Crotan standards. He was a vain man with an affinity for mirrors, and seeing Arkus so misshapen horrified him. It was not fitting that a great man should die so.

Biagio closed his drooping eyelids. Arkus had regaled to him his terrible dream, and now the count could see the white dragon, its four heads taunting Arkus, taunting them all. *Liss,* thought Biagio hatefully. They were the cause of this all, them and that bastard Vantran. Liss had single-mindedly destroyed Arkus, had prevented Nicabar's troop landings at almost every turn. They had come to rely solely on Blackwood Gayle's ground offensive, and although the baron had done a remarkable job of slaughtering Triin, Lucel-Lor was simply too vast. Though they held the Saccenne Run securely, it might be months before Gayle broke through completely, months Arkus didn't have.

"Oh, God, I need more time," Biagio whispered. "More time, that's all . . ."

He could do it if Gayle hurried. If Gayle could reach Tharn, perhaps the holy man himself could save Arkus. Biagio's mind turned on this for a moment. He would torture Tharn himself if necessary. And when Arkus was safe and alive, he would pull out Tharn's eyeballs.

"I would love that, holy man. To see you die . . ."

Arkus stirred. Biagio got up from his chair and went to the bedside.

"Renato . . . ?" gasped the emperor. Biagio had to strain to hear the soft voice.

"I'm here, Great One," he replied. "I'm right here. Are you all right?"

The wizened head nodded. "Is it morning?"

"Not yet. Not for several hours." Biagio looked toward the window. Past the thick curtains, all was dark. Only the occasional blast from a smokestack lit the night. "Can't you sleep? You should try. Bovadin says you need rest."

"Bovadin is my mother hen," rasped Arkus. "Like you."

Biagio smiled sadly and took his master's hand. The appendage seemed smaller by the day. "We are worried for you, that's all. We want to see you healthy again."

"Yes, yes," agreed Arkus. "I must recover. Work to be done."

"Much work, my lord. The world still needs you. I need you."

Arkus' frail fingers curled around Biagio's hand. A trace of a grin appeared on the cracked lips. "Thank you for being with me, Renato. You are my truest servant."

"Always, Great One."

"Yes, always. It was always you."

Humbled, Biagio went to his knees at the bedside. He put his chin down on the mattress and stared long and hard at Arkus, aching for more praise. He *was* Arkus' truest servant. He had always been. It wasn't the bishop or Nicabar or Bovadin, nor any other of the Iron Circle. Only he was so loyal and steadfast. Only he adored Arkus as a father.

But all fathers died, he supposed. And the sons were left to go on alone, uncherished. Biagio had a wife and a gaggle of cousins, but they were no more his family than the blood father he had slain. He had heard the call of Arkus and it had pulled him like a religion. It had given his life dimension. Now, as he watched the Great One fade, his existence seemed flat again.

"Great One?" he asked softly.

"Yes?"

"I am doing my best for you. You know that, don't you?"

There was a long, painful silence. At last the emperor gave a sullen nod. "You are trying," he said weakly. "I know that."

"The Lissens are devils, my lord. If not for them, I would have taken Lucel-Lor by now. And you would not be in such pain. But it will end, Great One. I swear it. We will take Lucel-Lor, and you will be whole again."

Even as he said it, Biagio knew it was a lie. But it was a lie he needed as much as Arkus. It comforted them both.

"I have been thinking, my friend," said Arkus. The words came with effort and he swallowed hard to continue. "What shall I do first when I recover? Who should be first to taste my vengeance? The Lissens?"

"Nicabar would like that," said Biagio. "He is anxious to go after their homeland again."

"We will do that. Yes, we will. When I am well and Lucel-Lor is mine, I will sail to Liss myself and slay their king. You will come with me, Renato. It will be glorious."

"Glorious, my lord."

Arkus gave a satisfied sigh, and in his blind eyes Biagio could see the memories skipping backward. Where is Arkus now, he wondered?

"And the Vantran boy," Arkus continued. "I want him brought to me. Right away. I want to see him swing, Renato. We will have a public execution."

"Gladly."

"You will see to it then? Have him brought to me?"

Biagio hesitated. "We are trying, Great One. As I said . . ."

"Now, Renato! Can't you do this for me? Do I ask so much of you? He's but one man."

"All right, yes. If that is your wish, my lord, we will make every effort to bring him here."

Arkus reached out and brushed his count's face with a finger. "Renato, I die."

"No, Great One. You can never die."

"Perhaps. But it may be that nothing can stop this. So I want one last thing from you. Find me Richius Vantran, and bring him back to me. I must see this before I'm gone. Now promise me."

"Yes," choked Biagio. "I promise. On my own eyes, I will bring Vantran here for you."

Arkus slackened. "Good," he said. "Good."

"Great One?" Biagio probed gently. "May I ask you something?"

"Anything, my friend."

Biagio licked his lips, fighting down his nervousness. "If you die—and I say *if*—what will become of us?"

Arkus' face hardened. "What are you asking?"

"It is nothing," said Biagio, waving it away.

"Do you think I'm dying, Renato?" asked Arkus sharply.

"Great One, you said yourself . . ."

"I do not expect you to agree. You're supposed to be saving me!" Arkus trembled. "God in heaven, how can you speak to me like this? I suffer and you think only of your ambition!"

"No, my lord! I'm thinking of Nar, of your Black Renaissance! If you die Herrith will fight me for the throne. Unless . . ."

"What?"

"Unless you choose your own successor."

There. He'd said it. The emperor drew a deep, pensive breath.

"You are my truest servant, Renato," said Arkus softly. "Is that not enough for you?"

"Oh, yes, my lord, it is. I want nothing more than to serve you."

"Then why do you speak to me of death?"

"For Nar, Great One. That is all. . . ."

"I will not die!" Arkus thundered. "I will not. Not now or ever!"

Biagio watched, horrified, as the emperor dissolved into tears. Arkus shut his blind eyes and turned away, cursing and shaking. Biagio took Arkus' hand and waited for the tantrum to pass, and suddenly he knew he would never have his answer. Arkus feared death too keenly to ever pass along his throne.

"I'll sleep now," sniffed Arkus. "Stay with me, Renato. I'm afraid of my dreams. Wake me if I scream."

"I'm here, Great One," said Biagio. He kissed the emperor's desiccated forehead. "Rest."

A few moments passed before Arkus dropped into a fitful slumber. When he was certain his emperor was asleep, Count Biagio arose from the bedside and went to the door. He spared one last look at his master, then, confident that Arkus would not soon awaken, left the room and summoned his Shadow Angels.

FORTY-ONE

"Here, Dyana," said Najjir. "These are the leaves you want."
Dyana looked over Najjir's shoulder. The leaves were small but thick, textured with a downy fuzz. Najjir picked one of them from the bush and held it up, then snapped it in two. As she pulled the sections apart, sticky threads of sap ran from the leaf.

"You see? Just like I told you. This will help him."

Dyana poked at the strings of sap, breaking them like spiderwebs. They felt cool on her finger, just as Najjir had said they would. Her mood brightened, buoyed by the thought of helping Richius at last. For four days he had lain in agony, nearly paralyzed with pain from the awful wound. Now it looked like he would finally have some relief.

Since returning from the front, Richius had been in too much pain to allow even the lightest of touches on his flayed skin. But he had rested since, and could probably bear the application of the poultice. He was waiting for her to return with the stuff, as eager as she to know if it would work.

"How many do we need?" she asked, reaching into the bush and starting to pick off the leaves.

"Slowly," Najjir cautioned. "Do not bruise them or the sap will run out. And do not pick the plant bare. The medicine does not last long, and we will be needing it for others."

Of course, Dyana cautioned herself. *The others.* There were dozens of them now, many with burns as bad as Richius'. But Najjir had told her there were other plants. Fine. Then this one should be for Richius. She picked off the leaves as Najjir watched, placing them quickly into her collecting basket. Thankfully they were not far from the castle. Surely they wouldn't spoil before she could use them. Najjir joined in the picking, her hands moving deliberately as she dropped the leaves into Dyana's basket. Dyana smiled.

"Thank you so much, Najjir. You will not be sorry."

Najjir gave an embarrassed nod. "I only do what my husband would want me to do," she answered. "He told me to help you look after Kalak. That is what I am doing."

Dyana bit back an insult. In less than a week Voris' wife had gone from being a complete stranger to something like a friend. They shared a room together, and between women that meant sharing secrets. For though Dyana had been silent about her past, she knew Najjir could read her thoughts anyway. She was uncanny that way. Dyana didn't know if she liked Najjir or not, but as she picked the lifesaving leaves, she knew one thing for certain—she was grateful for the woman's aid, no matter how grudgingly given.

"When Voris comes back I will thank him for your assistance, Najjir. He should know what a help you have been."

Najjir puffed a little at the compliment. Like all Drol women she was devoted to her husband, almost to the point of slavery. Voris was the center of her world, and Dyana knew she would do anything to please him. Devoutly religious, Najjir rose every morning at dawn for an hour of prayer with the other women of the keep, readying themselves for a day of servitude. It was an austere life, but Najjir embraced it, because she loved Voris and his love defined her. Three daughters and a son had sprung from her womb, and still she was eager to give her master more children. She was a good mother, and she was always willing to help Dyana care for Shani, but they were the antithesis of each other and they both knew it. Najjir was the perfect Drol woman, and Dyana was, by Drol sensibilities, a harlot.

"My husband will be home soon," said Najjir. "He may wish to see Kalak when he returns. You may tell him about my help then, if you wish."

"If he returns tonight, I will tell him gladly," said Dyana, careful not to shatter the woman's hope. Voris had been gone for three long days, ever since he had brought back the wounded Richius, and each day the siege of the valley continued, Najjir fretted over her missing husband.

"Tonight he will come," said Najjir confidently. "I feel it, Dyana. He wants to be near me again."

"I am sure he does," replied Dyana. "And I am sure he will return as soon as he can, tomorrow if not tonight."

Najjir made a sour face. "It has to be tonight. I cannot bear his absence. Pris pity me, I miss him. And I worry."

Dyana stopped picking and eyed Najjir sympathetically. "Do not worry. He will return."

"Oh, Dyana, you must think me such a fool. It is not even a week he is gone, and I cry for him like a girl. And you have been without your husband so much longer than that. How do you stand it?"

It was a trap Dyana had been waiting for. She sidestepped it with a shrug. "I do not worry like you do, Najjir. Tharn is very wise. I know he will come back for me."

"But it has been so long, and he is alone in Chandakkar. Pris pray I am wrong, Dyana, but he may already be dead. Does that not frighten you?"

Dyana had to think before responding. She knew Najjir was baiting her. "Of course I fear for him. But he is stronger than you know. He can look after himself."

"You are so strong," remarked Najjir. "It is easy to see why he chose you. A strong wife is important for a man."

"He did not choose me," said Dyana sharply. "Our parents arranged our marriage when we were both too young to know better."

"Still, he is lucky to have you," said Najjir. She sat back on her heels, kneeling in the soil and watching Dyana intently. "You are very beautiful. I am sure you could have had any man you wished."

"Perhaps."

"And you are lucky to have him, too," Najjir continued. "Have you considered that?"

"He is very kind to me, if that is what you mean. My parents could have done worse."

"Dyana!" shrieked Najjir. "How could you speak so poorly of your husband? He is the leader of all Drol. The deliverer, touched by heaven. You speak of him as if he were some farmer!"

"He is a fair man. He is gentle with me. There is little else I would ask from a husband. As for being Drol, he knows that I am not and he respects it. For that I am grateful. Are these such terrible things for me to say, Najjir?"

"Certainly not," said Najjir. "But do you not know he loves you, Dyana? He has spoken about you for years, every time he came to the valley. There are many women who never get the love of their husband. Can you not see how fortunate you are?"

The conversation was wearying. Dyana took the time to stretch her aching back before answering. "I know I am more fortunate than most women, even though I had no choice in husbands. But I would not have married Tharn if I could have avoided it. And you already know that."

The older woman smiled. "We are women, Dyana. It is not our place to make such decisions for ourselves. When I was very young I thought my husband the most terrible of men. I had heard he had conquered the valley and that he was cruel. And when we learned he was looking for a wife, all the girls in my village were afraid. We were told he would be riding through our village to find a wife, and our parents made us dress for him and stand there while he inspected us. All of us prayed we would not be his choice. But do you know what happened?"

"Should I guess?"

Najjir laughed. "I was younger than you are when we married, and I was so afraid. Yet as I grew older I realized he knew what was best for me, and that he had chosen me for a reason. Just like Tharn has chosen you, whether you believe so or not."

"Najjir," said Dyana gently. "I am not like you. I am glad you are happy with Voris, but I think women should be free to make these choices for themselves. Why should I honor a decision made by my father when I was a girl?"

"Shhh, Dyana. Do not speak such lies. You've been around that Naren man too long, I think. He has poisoned your mind."

"No," said Dyana. "I have always been different. Do not blame Richius for what you dislike about me."

Najjir seemed hurt. She rested a hand on Dyana's shoulder and asked, "Am I so harsh? If so forgive me. I never meant to offend you. And I do not dislike you, Dyana. To be true it has been wonderful having you share my chamber. I feel like a girl again, talking to a sister."

Dyana lowered the basket and sighed. "Then why so many questions, Najjir? Why do you talk to me as if I were some fool?"

"Because I worry about you, and decisions you make. Choices can be dangerous for a woman, Dyana."

"What do you mean?"

Najjir leaned forward. "The child is not Tharn's," she whispered.

Dyana started. "Did Voris tell you that?" she asked.

"I do not need my husband to tell me something so obvious. Shani has her father's eyes. She has Kalak's eyes."

It was an accusation Dyana hadn't expected. Najjir had never been so bold before. Dyana picked up her basket distractedly, then held it out for Najjir.

"Is this enough?" she asked stiffly.

Najjir nodded. "It should be."

"And how do I use it? Just rub it on his back?"

"Gently, yes. But Dyana, please listen to me." Najjir reached out a hand and snared her wrist.

"No, Najjir," said Dyana, wrenching away. "Please. I have heard it all before. From Tharn, from my women back at Falindar, from everyone. I do not want to talk about it anymore."

She started back for the castle.

"Dyana, stop." Najjir seized the basket, and a handful of leaves toppled out. Dyana dropped to her knees, snatching up the leaves that had fallen. Najjir hovered over her, waiting for her to rise.

"Give me the basket," Dyana ordered. "I have to get to him quickly."

"There is time," said Najjir. "I want to talk to you first."

"Later." Dyana reached for the basket but Najjir pulled it away.

"Even before you came here, everyone knew the stories of how Tharn's wife had birthed a child that was not his. We all thought you had been raped, but that is not so, is it? It was Kalak."

Dyana put her hands to her ears. "Stop. . . ."

"I can see it when you look at him. Even Voris knows. You are in love with him."

"I have to go. Please . . ."

Still Najjir held the basket away. "He is a Naren, Dyana. A murderer. Kalak killed my son!"

"That is a lie!" Dyana cried. "Richius would never have murdered your son. Not knowingly."

Najjir's face crumbled. Slowly she handed the basket back to Dyana. "Then it is true," she said. "You defend him. You do love Kalak."

Dyana didn't know how to respond. She took the basket and dropped the few leaves that had spilled back into it. Najjir made no attempt to snatch it away.

"Have you been with him?" Najjir asked.

"No."

"Good. It must stay that way. If Voris knew—"

"Voris knows all he needs to," said Dyana coldly. "And nothing will happen. You must trust me, Najjir."

"I do. But this love of yours is doomed. Kalak is Naren, and you are already married to a Drol cunning-man. You could be killed for what you are feeling."

Dyana laughed bitterly. "Killed for what I am feeling? This is the life you would have for your daughters? Najjir, I was not made to serve a man, even a great man like Tharn."

"But you can be happy, Dyana. As I am."

Dyana slid down onto the grass, wrapping her arms about her knees and looking up at Najjir. "Happy? I have never been happy. Not since I was a girl. Not since I knew what it meant to become a woman."

Najjir dropped to her knees beside Dyana. "And what is so horrible about being a woman? I am not unhappy. I accept what I am."

"And that is why we are different. You can be happy being a slave. Not me. Not even to a husband who is fair. And Richius . . ." She broke off with a smile. "You do not know him, Najjir. No one here does. He is special. I knew that when I first met him. When I am with him, I feel like an equal. I feel like I belong."

"A dream," chided Najjir. "You are young and heartsick. I am sure you mean no more to him than any other."

"You are wrong," said Dyana sharply. "He has given up everything for me. There were enough women in Nar for him to bed, but he returned here for *me.*"

"Then he is heartsick, too. He is not so much older than you, still young enough to be fooled by infatuation. Do not destroy everything you have for him, Dyana. He will not be there forever. And think of the child. What sort of life can she have with a Naren for a father? She will never—"

"Najjir, I have never planned on deceiving Tharn. He wants only my loyalty, and I will not break that. I know I can never be with Richius."

Najjir dropped her gaze. "I hate him," she said. "But I do not hate you. I am sorry for you."

"Do not be." Dyana rose. "And you are wrong about him, Najjir. I wish you could see that. I wish your husband could see that. He is a good man. He deserves more than your hate."

"My hate is all I have had since Tal died," said Najjir simply. "Do not take it away from me."

There was nothing Dyana could say to that, so she thanked Najjir with a nod, then turned and went back toward the castle, leaving her friend to search out more of the forest's remedies. Dyana navigated the narrow path back to the castle carefully, emerging from the woods within minutes. Castle Dring loomed large in front of her, shadowing the yard. She entered the keep. The women of the castle looked at her oddly as she passed and made whispered comments to each other. Dyana ignored them. Of all the women she had met in the castle, only Najjir had made an effort to welcome her. While the others tended the warriors of the valley, she tended Richius alone, and she knew the attention she lavished on the Naren was raising more than a few eyebrows. Still, she had made an attempt to join them. When the first of the wounded had returned from the front, she had offered her help and had been uniformly rebuffed. Now, four days later, she wasn't about to explain herself to the gaggle of gossipers who would rather their men die than receive aid from the hands of a harlot.

Fortunately, she found the hall leading to Richius' chamber empty. A tiny tremor of excitement ran through her. He would be so pleased she had found the leaves. Now that his back was firm enough to touch, the ointment would be a relief. She knocked on the door.

"Richius?" she asked lightly.

A hoarse, sleep-deprived voice answered her. "Come in."

She opened the door. Richius was lying on his stomach with his raw back exposed. He was propped up on his elbows with a pen in his hand, fussing over a small book. His hair was oily, and the smell of perspiration assailed her, but his tired eyes brightened when he recognized her.

"Dyana," he rasped. "Did you find them?"

She showed him the basket.

"Oh, thank God," he sighed. "Thank God."

"Najjir showed me," said Dyana, going to the bedside. "She is sure it will help. I hope she is right."

"Me, too, but go easy on it, all right? My skin still feels like it's on fire."

"I will be careful," she said. She sat down on the bed and examined his back. It still horrified her to see his wounds. They were worse than any burns she had ever seen. Even Tharn's lash marks seemed minor in comparison. There was no bleeding anymore, but the skin remained the color of an apple, a luminescent red with flaking scales of dried pus. Meandering furrows ran from his shoulders to his waist, carved into his flesh by the insatiable acid.

"I am going to touch you," she warned. "Be ready."

Gingerly she reached out a finger and probed the flesh. At once he stiffened. He had cried like a baby when he had first awoken in the castle. Najjir had tried to keep him asleep by burning a herbal incense, but the pain had been too great. Even bandages had been too much for him to endure, so they had left the wounds exposed to the air, hoping they would dry without too much scarring. But just like the agonizing pain, the scarring had been unavoidable, and now his back looked like pulverized meat, so that even breathing was a labor. That he had fought on after being burned earned the respect of Voris and the other warriors, but like so many of Nar's weapons the acid was insidious, and had waited until hours later to do the worst of its work. That night Dyana had not slept at all.

"How does that feel?" she asked, pressing her finger lightly into his skin. He winced.

"Hurts."

Dyana forced a sunny tone. "Do not worry. Najjir promised me this would work." She picked one of the leaves from the basket and snapped it in two, drizzling the sap onto his back. There was precious little of the stuff. Resolutely she picked out another leaf and did the same.

"It's cold," commented Richius. "Feels good."

"It should feel better when I rub it in." As Dyana worked, she gestured with her chin to his book. It was open to a page filled with poorly penned lines and scratchy notes. What looked like a map dominated one side of the page. "What are you doing?" she asked.

"This is my journal," he said. "I've been working on something. I'm glad you're here. I want to talk to you about it."

Carefully she squeezed more of the sap onto his back. "Is that a map?"

"Of Dring. Listen, Dyana, I've been thinking. I have some ideas about beating back the Narens."

She cracked open the last leaf and spread the sticky sap on her hands. "Ready?"

Richius braced himself. "Yes." He laid the journal on the floor and lowered his head.

"I will be careful," she promised him again. He managed a broken smile.

She steeled herself, and with all the delicacy she could manage placed her sap-covered palms on his back. As she did, his entire body seized. Instinctively, her hands jerked back.

"I am sorry," she said. "Richius, I do not want to hurt you. . . ."

He shook his head. "Go on. Do it."

She replaced her hands. This time, the sticky stuff was colder. She could feel its coldness seeping beneath her fingernails. Gradually she moved her palms down his back, working in the rest of the sap, running her fingers over the scars and cavities cratering his flesh. Amazingly, Richius sighed.

"It's working," he said. "Sweet God, it's working."

He closed his eyes, letting her massage his tattered skin and smooth the soothing ointment into every tortured crevice. She worked gently, talking to him as if he were a child. The sticky lotion felt good on her hands, cool as autumn. She loved the way it felt between her fingers, and the way her fingers moved over his body. She loved his body. Battle had ravaged it, but it was still beautiful.

Her hands stilled.

Richius opened his eyes. "Why did you stop?" he asked.

"Because I am done," she lied. "Better?"

Richius stretched. "Yes," he said. "Much better. Dyana, thank you. That was unendurable. . . ."

She almost touched his cheek but checked herself.

"What is it, Dyana? Is something wrong?"

Dyana shook her head. "No, nothing. I will tell Najjir the leaves have helped you. She will be pleased."

"I doubt that," said Richius. "But thank her for me anyway."

"Can you turn now?"

He maneuvered himself onto his side, leaning against his elbow. She saw how thin he had become. Except for his back, all the skin on his face and chest was the sickly shade of milk, and the bones in his shoulders popped out unnaturally. He had refused food since coming back from the front. It was time to get him healthy again.

"You must eat," she said, going to the little table by the bed. There she found a cloth beside his washbasin and wiped the worst of the sap from her hands. "Let me get you something."

"Wait," he urged. "I want to talk to you first."

He stretched out over the bedside and tried to retrieve the little book from the floor. She hurried over to him and picked it up.

"Don't move too much, Richius," she chided. "You might feel better but your skin still needs to heal. It will take time."

"I haven't got time, Dyana," he said, accepting the journal and flipping quickly through its pages. "That's why I've been working on a plan. Here, let me show you."

Dyana knelt down beside the bed, close enough to feel the heat of his breath. "You were supposed to be resting," she said. "Now that I see you are strong enough to write, we can begin your lessons."

"Tomorrow," said Richius. "Or later tonight, if you want. But first I want to show you this."

He stopped turning pages and poked at one, directing Dyana's eyes downward. It was a map of the Dring Valley, badly drawn but legible. Little black marks showed the Narens surrounding the valley. In the center of the valley was rendered a watchtower, Castle Dring, while at the bottom of the page ran a collection of squiggles, drawn so roughly they resembled nothing Dyana could imagine. She gestured to them with her chin.

"What is that?"

"That's what I want to talk to you about. There are marshes in the south of the valley, right?"

"Those are marshes?"

Richius looked at her scornfully. "I've been sick. Anyway, I'm right about the marshes, aren't I? I've heard the whole area between the bottom of the valley and the start of the Sheaze is covered with them."

"Najjir would know better. But yes, I think so. Why?"

"I've been trying to figure out a way to beat back the legionnaires now that they've made it into the forest." He looked at her, as if suddenly remembering his usual question. "There's nothing new to tell me, is there?"

"No," she assured him. Even at his sickest he had asked how things were going, always trying to get involved. "Voris has not come home yet. Neither has Dumaka Jarra. But the wounded keep saying they are holding on. You were right about the forest traps. They have slowed down the soldiers. The warriors are saying they have lost only a little ground."

"What about Kronin? Has anyone heard from Tatterak yet?"

"Richius, it has not even been a week."

He nodded bleakly. "Voris and his men won't be able to hold out forever. Gayle's going to let the legionnaires clear the traps for him. Once he finds a way of getting his cavalry into the forest, there won't be a way to stop them from reaching the castle. I know his tactics, Dyana. He'll secure the areas around the forest path, then he'll come charging in. We have to think of a way to defeat them before that happens."

"Is that what you have been working on?" she asked. "A plan to defeat them?"

"Yes, and it all has to do with these marshes. Think about it. We can't fight the horsemen because they're in the open grasslands. What we need to do is push them into the forest before they're ready. Or . . ." He pointed to the squiggles at the bottom of the page. "Get them into the marshes. We could ambush them there. The horses would be stuck, and even the legionnaires wouldn't be able to move. We could beat them there, fighting on our own terms."

He smiled at her, and his expression told her he was waiting for a reply. But an obvious question nagged at her, dampening her exuberance.

"Yes, it is very good," she said reservedly. "But how can we get them into the marshes?"

"*We're* not going to," said Richius slyly. "Kronin will."

"Kronin? Oh, Richius, you should think more on this. It may not be a good idea."

"But I have thought about it," said Richius. He pushed himself up to sit on the edge of the bed beside her. "I have it all worked out. I know it can succeed. Gayle won't be expecting any more warriors to come at him. With that kind of surprise we can have him heading south before he knows what's happening. And when he gets into the swamp, the rest of us will be waiting for him, in the trees and everywhere, just like now. Only they'll be stuck. They won't be able to retreat. We'll have them, Dyana."

"Easy," said Dyana. "All I am saying is that you should not be sure Kronin will come. He may feel the same as Voris does. And if he thinks—"

She caught herself then, snagged on her thought.

"If he thinks what?" pressed Richius.

"No, nothing," said Dyana quickly. "I am sorry. It is unimportant."

"I can always tell when you're lying," he said with a grin. "Tell me. What were you going to say?"

She hesitated. "Kronin might not come, because he might think there is no need to come."

"No need? Why would he think that? If the messenger Voris sent tells him how many Naren soldiers are here, he'll know we need his help."

"That is not what I am saying," corrected Dyana. She looked down at the ground as she spoke. "Kronin and Voris only stopped their war because Tharn told them to. But no one has heard from Tharn for many weeks." She closed her eyes. "Kronin might not help us if he thinks Tharn is dead."

There, she'd said it. She braced herself, waiting for the room to erupt with Tharn's lightning. Najjir would have said she was wishing for it. A dark feeling of shame writhed in her. Maybe she was. Beside her she heard Richius' sweet, reassuring voice.

"Dyana, look at me."

She opened her eyes. He was smiling at her, the way he always did when she needed him.

"Don't grieve for a man who's not dead," said Richius gently. "Tharn is alive, Dyana. I'm sure of it."

"Are you?" she asked. Sometimes he was right about the worst things.

"Yes. I can feel it. He's too strong and stubborn to die while Nar is in Lucel-Lor, believe me."

"Oh, I believe you," she said. "I believe you." She swallowed the lump of emotion in her throat. "Yes, you are right. Of course you are. Forgive me. I am a fool."

"You are just concerned about him, that's all. To be honest, so am I. But we'll hear from him soon, as soon as he is able. Don't worry."

She tried to smile. "I will not. But I am still not wrong, Richius. Najjir has told me others are starting to wonder about Tharn. If Kronin thinks Tharn is dead, he may not come."

"He'll come," said Richius. "If he can. He's a man of honor. And I think he'll feel he owes it to me. But it all depends on the coasts. If the Naren fleet is still landing troops, he may not be able to help us. We're blind here, Dyana. We don't know what's happening. For all we know Tharn could have already sent word to Falindar, or the Lissens could be beating back the Black Fleet. . . ."

"Stop," said Dyana firmly. "You have to rest. You might feel well but you're not. The pain will be back."

"But there's more medicine, right? I can just put more on."

"Yes, but it will not help you heal. For that you need rest, at least another day in bed. Tonight I will come back to see you. If the pain has returned we'll use the medicine again. But you must not try to do too much. And put that book away. Try to sleep."

"Yes, sleep," he said dreamily. It had been days since he had slept for more than an hour. The word worked its charm on him and his eyelids started to droop.

Then in the doorway she saw the shadow of Voris. She gasped, startling Richius, who sat up at once.

"Voris," sputtered Richius.

Dyana felt a wave of color rush into her cheeks. She lowered her head and greeted the warlord.

"Welcome home, Lord Voris."

Voris nodded at her wearily. In his hands was his jiiktar, covered with mud and splattered along its braided hilt with red blotches. His eyes were dim and haunted, and his soiled clothes hung from his big body like limp rags. A filthy bandage wrapped one forearm, while along the other ran scars like those tracing Richius' back. The warlord moved into the room with heavy steps, so exhausted he seemed about to drop. But he mustered up just enough strength to cast Richius a crooked smile.

"How is he?" asked Voris.

"He has been resting. Your wife has been helping me with him."

Voris stepped up to the bed and examined Richius' wounds. "Where is my wife?"

Richius straightened. "Dyana, what's he saying?"

"In the woods around the keep, gathering more leaves for the burned," said Dyana to Voris. "She is very eager to see you again."

"And I her." Voris was still looking at Richius. "Now that he is awake, tell this boy what a fool he is. Tell him I should have killed him for trying to save me."

There was nothing but good humor in the warlord's tone. Dyana smiled at Richius. "The warlord thanks you, Richius," she said. It wasn't entirely true but she was sure neither of them would care. "He says what you did was brave."

"That's not all he said, I can see it in his eyes. But you may tell him he is welcome. He did, if I recall right, do the same for me."

"His color looks bad," remarked Voris. "And why so thin?"

"He has been unable to eat from the pain. Do not worry. I will see he eats a full meal tonight."

"Yes, take care of him," said Voris, gazing down at Richius with tired, laughing eyes. "We will need him again as soon as he is able. Not too soon, mind you. Just when he is able."

"Ask him what's happening, Dyana," said Richius eagerly. "What's going on? Why's he back here?"

Dyana smiled. "He has many questions, my lord."

"He will have his answers later," replied Voris. "I have only just returned. I am tired and hungry and I wish to see my wife." He headed for the door. "See that he eats soon. He needs strength."

"What did he say, Dyana?"

"Later, Richius," said Dyana. "Rest now."

"But I want to tell him about my plan."

"He has only just returned, Richius. And he needs rest, too."

As if understanding Richius' anxiety, Voris took a step again toward the bed. "Things are going well enough, Kalak. And you are not the only one I have come home to see. Family, Kalak. Kafife."

"Kafife, Richius. Remember? He wants to see his family."

Richius nodded.

"Kalak should rest now," said Voris to Dyana. His face made a peculiar expression and he directed her with his eyes toward the doorway. "Come outside with me. I want to talk."

Dyana froze. *Najjir,* she thought blackly. *You have betrayed me already.*

But no. Voris hadn't seen her yet. What could he want? She nodded and headed toward the door, tossing off a reassuring smile to Richius. "I will come back tonight with food," she told him. "Sleep."

Richius watched them go, then she closed the door to his chamber. Once in the hall, she had the courage to look at Voris again. He was staring at her. Wearily he gestured for her to proceed him down the hall. She did as he bade, taking small steps to prolong the trip as she tried to determine what the warlord might want of her. She had reached the end of the hall when he stopped her.

"You have been taking good care of Kalak, I see."

"I have done my best."

"Good. Tharn would want that. It is our duty to see that no harm comes to him, both yours and mine. You know this, yes?"

Dyana stiffened. "Of course."

The warlord's eyes became two shrewd slivers. "You are a bold one, aren't you? Fine. Then tell me the truth about something. I have seen you and Kalak together. I have seen the way you look at each other. Do you think your husband dead, woman?"

Horror. Dyana fought to keep the shock from her expression. "Dead, my lord? Why would you ask me that?"

"I am very tired, woman, and in no mood to play with you. Do you think Tharn is dead? The truth now. I will know if you lie."

"My lord, what are you accusing me of?"

"Do not lie to save Kalak," declared Voris simply. "This is not the threat you think it is. I want to know if you are craving for the Naren. I have accused you of this before. I must know if it is so."

Dyana looked away, feigning disgust. "Really, my lord. You should be careful what you say to me. If Tharn were here would you speak so to me?"

Voris gave her a terrible look. "I have known Tharn almost as long as you have, woman. Do not think to threaten me with his name."

Dyana didn't back down. "Then why do you ask me such criminal things? If you know so much about us, why not let us be?"

Voris didn't answer, but there was an inscrutable twinkle in his eyes, almost like a laugh. He simply stared at her for a long moment, blinked, then turned and left her, going off toward the castle entrance where the woods were and where, presumably, he would find his wife.

A sick feeling coiled around Dyana's mind, and she cursed herself for her indiscretion. She leaned back against the cold stone and stared dumbly at the cracked ceiling. What, she wondered, would Voris do now?

FORTY-TWO

Tharn awakened to the sound of his own unpleasant wheezing. He was in a room, or what looked like a room, in a home of primitive canvas. His head swam. An amazing knife of pain sliced across his face as he opened his eyes. The room spun for a moment as his eyes adjusted to the blurriness.

No, Tharn realized. *Not eyes. Eye.* He brought a shaking hand to his face and felt the bandage covering its left side, blotting out half his vision. As he touched the flesh the pain roared anew.

He was alone in the dim chamber. A soft mattress of woven grass cradled his aching body. Over him was a soft blanket, while on the ground next to him sat a bowl of water and a cloth, both bloodied. An uneasy feeling gripped him, as though he had been gone for a very long time.

"What . . . ?"

He tried to speak but his voice was a croak. When he tried again it hurt. He hurt. Quickly he took stock of his pains. It wasn't just his head that burned. So did his arm and chest. It wasn't just the usual pains that plagued him, either. These were new agonies, clawing into his flesh like a thousand wasp stings. Where was he? Where were the others? He had been in the carriage, and then he was here.

The memory of the lion awakened. The lion had attacked him?

"Oh, Lorris," he choked. "Help me. . . ."

Again he tried to move, but all he could do was roll helplessly onto his side. His atrophied arm had been bandaged, too. As he moved the blan-

ket slid off him, and he realized he was naked. Except for the fresh strips
of cloth over his chest and arm, he was exposed to the world, and the
sight was horrifying. His eyes darted around the room, at once spotting
his clothes. Someone had washed them and laid them neatly over a chair.
Near the chair were his boots, the special ones that fit his malformed feet.
These too were tidied up, all the mud scraped from them so that the
brown leather shone. Frustrated, Tharn tried to crawl toward them,
dragging himself across the stone floor. He made it barely a foot before
exhaustion overtook him.

"Damn it," he cursed. Already he was breathing hard. The small effort
set his head to pounding. His body collapsed to the floor, and again he
could feel the darkness of unconsciousness approaching.

"Help me!" he cried. "Raig, Nagrah, help!"

As if he had summoned a servant, Nagrah hurried into the room. The
young man gasped when he saw Tharn sprawled across the floor.

"Master!" cried Nagrah, rushing to Tharn's aid. "Stop! What are you
doing?"

Tharn could scarcely answer. "Nagrah . . . where . . . ?"

"Do not talk," ordered the priest. He slid his arms under Tharn and
gently pulled him back onto the mattress, doing his best to arrange
Tharn's mangled limbs. Weary beyond words, Tharn closed his eyes
against the pain of the manipulation. Finally Nagrah put a hand to his
forehead and felt the diseased skin. Tharn sighed at the touch.

"Still feverish," Nagrah commented, more to himself than to Tharn.
He knelt down and looked intently into Tharn's single eye. "Master? Can
you hear me?"

"Yes," answered Tharn weakly. "What is this place?"

"Shhh," soothed Nagrah. He brushed a hand gently across Tharn's
cheek the way a mother would. "Master, please. You are very ill." Then a
smile crossed Nagrah's face. "But you will be all right now."

"What is wrong with me?" Tharn gasped. He had so many questions,
and they were all spilling out of him. "What happened?"

"Later," replied Nagrah.

"Now," snapped Tharn. "Nagrah, tell me. Where are we?"

The young man gave Tharn a dissatisfied look. "Master, please, rest.
We can talk later."

It was agony, not only the pain but being treated like a child. Tharn
gritted his teeth and grabbed hold of Nagrah's cloak, hissing, "Tell me!"

"All right," Nagrah conceded. Gently he uncoiled the fingers from his
sleeve. "We are in Chandakkar."

"All of us? The others are safe?"

"We are all safe, Master. Thanks to Karlaz. This is his village."

"The lion," Tharn sputtered. "What happened?"

Nagrah's expression soured. "I am sorry, Master. It was my fault. I startled the creature. You struck it, and it went for you. Do you remember any of it?"

Tharn reached into his memory, pulling up the hazy recollection. He remembered praying, and seeing the lion. After that, nothing. He shook his head.

"No," he said. "Not really. Am I bad, Nagrah?"

"You were. But you will be fine now."

"Karlaz. He is here?"

"We are in his village," Nagrah repeated, slowly this time so Tharn would hear it. "That lion was his, I think. He was with it in the valley. When it attacked you, he stopped it, called it off you."

"Not soon enough," Tharn growled. "What happened to me? My face?"

"It struck you, Master. It reached out for you when you hit it. You were bleeding badly from the chest. But your face is not too bad."

"No," said Tharn bitterly. "It could not get much worse, could it? But where is Karlaz now? Where are the others? Get them, Nagrah. Bring them here. We have to talk."

"*You* have to rest, Master. Much has happened you don't know about. I will explain it all to you, but not now. When you are stronger . . ."

"There is no time," Tharn argued. "Karlaz is here. We must hurry. The Run . . ."

"I have already told him about the Run, Master. He knows why we are here. He has been waiting for you to awaken to talk with you about it."

"Will he help us?"

"Master, he will not talk to me. Only you."

"Then bring him here," Tharn demanded. Again he tried to prop himself up. "Damn it, boy, stop wasting time. How long have I been here, anyway?"

Nagrah grimaced. "Three days."

Tharn's one eye blinked in disbelief. "I have been sleeping for three days?"

"Mostly sleeping. Some dreams. Are you hungry?"

Tharn realized he was famished. "Yes. And thirsty."

"I will bring you food," said Nagrah, getting up to leave.

"Bring me Karlaz!"

"I will tell the others you are awake, Master. If Karlaz can come, he will."

Nagrah left the room, exiting through a small door that led out into the daylight. But it was not he who returned with food and drink. A woman entered the chamber minutes later, bearing two steaming bowls. She was older than Tharn, small and hearty looking, with fast, evasive eyes that avoided the cunning-man's gaze. Her dress was meager, utilitarian, mostly stitched calfskin, and tight-fitting. Tharn thought her appropriate for this plain home. She came to him and set down the bowls, one filled with steaming broth, the other with a thick grain porridge. When she showed him the food he smiled at her.

"Thank you," he said. "But I need help."

She had already foreseen his need and offered him a spoonful of broth. He sipped it down hungrily, enjoying the heat of it in his throat. She fed him without speaking, and when the bowl was emptied he nodded his thanks and put up his hand.

"You are kind," he said. "Who are you? What is your name?"

The woman ignored him. Tharn frowned.

"Do you speak my tongue?" he asked. "I am Tharn." He pointed to himself. "Tharn."

She nodded but still looked away. Tharn could tell she understood him. Next she reached for the porridge and offered him some. It too was a delight, and he swallowed it down greedily. But halfway through he refused the next mouthful.

"Talk to me," he pleaded. "Who are you?"

"I am no one," she answered. "More?"

Tharn shook his head. "No, not now. Are you one of Karlaz' people?"

She didn't answer him. When he refused another spoonful of food, she rose from the floor and left the room, leaving him to puzzle over her silence. Tharn fell back against the mattress, his belly full but his feelings wounded. Clearly she spoke his tongue. There was a dialect difference, but that was all. He sighed, frustrated. Where was Nagrah?

Half an hour later, a figure appeared in the doorway. Tharn had almost fallen asleep again, but the sight of the man startled him awake. He was a giant, barrel-chested and as broad as a bridge, with a mane of hair that was both Triin white and sunlight gold. Around his shoulders and muscled breast he wore a bandolier of woven silk, green and red and studded with lions' teeth. A collection of silver rings graced his thick fingers and long ornaments of gemstones dangled down from his ears. Tharn knew at once that this was Karlaz, warlord of Chandakkar. The cunning-man sat up, trying hard to look presentable even in his nakedness. The master of the lions strode into the room, towering over Tharn and looking down with knife-sharp eyes.

"You are Tharn," he boomed. "I am Karlaz."

Tharn nodded eagerly. "Yes, Karlaz. I am Tharn. I . . . uh, thank you for coming. And for saving me. My man Nagrah told me what you did for me." He blushed a little at his uncovered body, drawing the small blanket over himself. "I am grateful."

Karlaz was humorless. "Nagrah tells me you are well now. Well enough to talk?"

"I am all right now. I can talk. And we must, Karlaz. I must speak with you, ask your help. . . ."

Karlaz silenced him. "I know what you are asking. Your men have explained it to me."

"Then you will help me?" Tharn asked hopefully. "Great Karlaz, I have need of you and your people. All of Lucel-Lor needs you. If . . ."

Karlaz turned and walked to the door. It was open and the sunlight struck his face. For a long moment he stared outside, then back to Tharn, and then again outside. Curious, Tharn craned his neck to see past the giant, but all he could see was Karlaz.

"What do you know?" asked the lion master.

"What? I am sorry, I do not understand. I do not remember much, if that is what you mean."

The giant's face was unreadable. He stood staring at the mystery outside the walls, his silence making Tharn ever more anxious.

"Where are my cunning-men?" asked Tharn. "I expected to see them here."

"They are well," replied Karlaz. "Do not worry over them."

But Tharn was worried. Something about the warlord's manner disturbed him. He seemed distant, as if his mind were preoccupied with a thousand other things. Tharn cleared his throat to get Karlaz' attention.

"I would like to see them," he said politely.

"No. They are not here because I do not want them here. We will talk alone."

"All right," agreed Tharn. "But please, come closer." He brought a hand to his face. "My eyes . . ."

Karlaz looked at him sharply, then walked over. Tharn felt drowned within his shadow.

"You are Tharn," he stated again. "Even here in Chandakkar we have heard of the Storm Maker. But I wonder something. Why would anyone with heaven's touch come to me for help?"

"Great Karlaz, I am not what you think of me. I am just a man."

Karlaz gave a skeptical laugh. "Not just a man. A cunning-man. You call the clouds. I know these things, Drol. I know what you can do. So why do you not do it?"

"It is not the way of heaven, Karlaz. Not my way. Not anymore. I have the touch, that is true. But I cannot use it to kill. Not even Narens. I did that once." Tharn slid the blanket off of him, revealing his entire horrid body. "You see the result."

A trace of revulsion flashed in the giant's eyes. "You believe this?"

"I know it," declared Tharn. "The gods have given me this burden. I would destroy the Narens if I could, but I cannot. Not alone. I need you and your people." Tharn reached up to the warlord, earnestly offering out his hand. "Please, Karlaz. I have traveled a long way. Do not send me back without your help."

Karlaz did not accept the offered hand. "Until a week ago, you would not have been welcome here, Storm Maker. We are not Drol, and we have no wish to join you. I wonder what you know of us, to have the boldness to make your request."

"Karlaz," said Tharn sternly. "I am not asking a favor. It is not just *my* life that is in peril, but yours as well. All Triin are in danger from Nar, even here in Chandakkar. If we do not take the Saccenne Run, if we do not stop Nar's men, all that we have will perish. And if you do not believe this, then you are a fool."

Karlaz' eyes lit with fury. "Can you walk?" he demanded.

"No," said Tharn.

Karlaz went to where the holy man's clothes were waiting. He picked up the cloak and held it out for Tharn. "Dress," he ordered.

Tharn grimaced. "I cannot. Not without help."

"Give me your hand," said Karlaz. He bent down and stretched out his huge fingers for Tharn, who put out his hand warily. Karlaz took it and yanked Tharn to his feet effortlessly. The cunning-man gave an anguished wail from the wrenching, but Karlaz ignored it. Naked, he stood there propped in the giant's arms, held up like a doll. Karlaz arranged the cloak over his shoulders like a shawl.

"What are you doing?" asked Tharn breathlessly. "Karlaz, stop. . . ."

But Karlaz wouldn't listen. He ignored Tharn's pleas, lifting him in his arms and going to the door. When they were just outside the threshold, Karlaz lowered Tharn to the ground, keeping one arm wrapped beneath his armpits to steady him.

"Look!" the warlord demanded. "Look and do not lecture me!"

Now out in the sunlight, Tharn could see the village. He brought up a hand to shield his eye from the light, and through his fingers saw the devastation. Most of the homes were burned and there was litter everywhere, broken sticks and weapons and the ruins of collapsed houses, their roofs caved in with fire damage. Amongst the rubble were others like Karlaz, bronze-skinned Triin with gold-white hair and long, somber faces. Tharn's eyes widened in horror. At his feet was a mangled flame lance.

"By Lorris," he gasped. "What happened?"

"You see, Drol?" raged Karlaz. "I know Nar, too."

Tharn was stunned. At once he forgot his ailments and aches. "Karlaz, what happened here? Tell me."

"They came," said the warlord. "In their black ships, with their fire weapons. They found us here, unexpecting. They . . ." His voice choked off. "They slaughtered us. We knew nothing, they just came, too quick for us." He closed his eyes and groaned. "And I could not stop them. I had no time to call the lions."

"When was this?" Tharn demanded. "Where are they now?"

"They came five days ago. From the sea, at night. When we were sleeping!"

"What happened?" Tharn pressed. "Tell me everything."

"Tell you what, Drol? You still have an eye. Look!" He swept his free arm over their surroundings. "They did all of this. We fought them but they were too many, and we were unprepared. They were in a rage, like a gale storm sweeping over. They were looking for something. I do not know what."

"But you beat them back," said Tharn. "How?"

"We fled to the valley of lions," said Karlaz. "Where I found you. I called the lions, but when we returned the Narens had gone."

"Gone? You mean they left? Then they will be back, Karlaz. You must—"

"They will not be back," said Karlaz. "Their ships are gone from our waters."

Tharn shook his head. It was aching again. "Karlaz, none of this makes sense to me. Why did the Narens leave? What happened to them?"

"Inside," said Karlaz. "I will tell you."

The warlord took Tharn back into the home, one of the few houses unscathed by fire, and roughly set him back down on the mattress. Tharn took a few breaths to steady himself. He was nauseous, probably near fainting, but he fought it back.

"Now," he said. "What happened to the Narens? What happened to their ships?"

Karlaz smiled. "There was a man here in the village when we came back with the lions. Strange looking. Thin. Not like you or I. Not like any man I have seen. He spoke the tongue of Nar, I think. There were others with him. Men of the sea. We could not talk to each other, but I understood his meaning."

Tharn listened, amazed at the tale. "A man? Who?"

"Prakna," said Karlaz. "He called himself Prakna. He took me to the water, where his ships were. He pointed to where he had attacked the black ships. But his ships were different." The warlord's smile became serene. "They were like dragons of gold. Water demons but beautiful. And big. They were Prakna's ships."

"Prakna," said Tharn, a little bell ringing in his mind. He *had* heard the name, from the Lissen emissary. Fleet commander of the Hundred Isles of Liss. "Gods, they were Lissens! Lissens, Karlaz. Did they say so?"

"I did not understand their words," said Karlaz. "But they came from the water. They attacked the Naren ships and drove them off. Prakna went after them."

"How do you know?"

"Because Prakna did this," said Karlaz, then used a flattened hand to mimic a ship on the ocean. When the fingers nose-dived, Tharn understood. "He will sink them as he promised," Karlaz continued. "He had many ships with him. The Narens were afraid and fled."

Tharn was overjoyed. In his most hopeful dreams, he had never dared think the Lissens would come to their aid so quickly. He wanted to find this Prakna, to kiss him and fall to his knees in gratitude. They had an ally now, one who might just stem the tide of the invasion.

"Karlaz, listen to me closely. With the Lissens patrolling our shores, the Narens will not be able to land any more troops by sea. They will have to come through the Saccenne Run. That means they will be sending all the troops they can through it. They already own the mountain pass, and Ackle-Nye. We cannot take it alone, not without your help." Tharn's lone eye was imploring. "Karlaz, we need your lions."

Karlaz' face was emotionless. "A week ago, I would have sent you away, Storm Maker. We had a good life here, free of you and your revolution. But that has changed. My heart is full of vengeance now."

"Then you will help me?" asked Tharn.

"We will call the lions, and the warriors from the other villages," said Karlaz. "But we must have a bargain, Drol. When this is done, you will leave Chandakkar. There will be no Drol here, ever."

Tharn nodded grimly. "Agreed."

"You will rest now. It will be days before you can make the journey from here. And days still before the other warriors arrive. Rest, and I will make ready."

"Then call your lions, Warlord," said Tharn. "You will have your vengeance."

FORTY-THREE

A thick rain fell steadily through the night. Voris the Wolf crouched in the mud, hiding his white skin and wild eyes behind the curtaining branches. Behind him, Dumaka Jarra and a trio of warriors waited, enveloped in darkness. Voris moved silently, parting the low tree limbs the tiniest fraction. In the road before him was the war wagon, one wheel broken and hanging from its axle, its other wheels mired in soggy earth. Five legionnaires paced impatiently around the wagon, trying to calm the spooked greegan still tethered to it. The men watched the forest for their invisible enemies. One held a flame cannon ready in his grip, sweeping the dark trees with its nozzle. Voris could see their nervous eyes behind their helmets. They were afraid. The warlord smiled. He held up a finger and beckoned Jarra forward. The old man slithered through the mud to kneel down beside his master.

"Five," he counted in a whisper. "Maybe some in the wagon."

Voris shook his head. "No. See? It's open." He pointed to a soldier dressed differently from the rest, the one with the flame cannon. "He works the machine. It is empty."

Jarra gave a slight nod, straining to see. The hatch at the top of the wagon was indeed open. "Five of them, five of us," he remarked. "What now?"

"Now we make them suffer."

He dropped his hand and let the branches spring back, closing over his face. Five and five. The odds were good. It was dark and he was Triin and that was good, too. He knew his prey would be blind. He leaned back on his haunches, considering things. First the man with the flame cannon, then the others. As for the beast, they would kill it, too, if they could. Voris wiped mud and water from his forehead. He was exhausted. The fighting had been ferocious, and every day they lost a little more of his precious valley to the horde. He and his warriors had the skill, but they were woefully outnumbered. Even the traps they had laid for their enemies did little to slow their advance. In time, Voris knew, the Narens would clear the traps, allowing the horsemen to come. Then they would fight their last battle at Castle Dring—and they would die.

But not before the Wolf made his mark. In Dring the animals were vicious, and Voris had a message to send. Quietly, he moved to where his warriors waited. They were three young and eager men, the kind who didn't mind bloodletting. Voris gathered them into a huddle and spoke.

"You are ready?" he asked. Each man replied with a silent nod. Voris smiled. "I will take out the one with the cannon first. He will not fire it. He will not see me. When he is down, rush in. We will be too fast for them. Jarra, watch for the acid launcher. There may yet be someone inside."

"I will watch," replied the old man.

"Be quick. Cut the bellows before anyone can see you. If we are killed, I do not want the launcher used again."

"I will be quick."

Voris set his jaw and turned back to the road. He would have to get close. The underbrush cracked and squished beneath his boots, the noise masked by the insistent rain. He held his breath, attuned to every sound. The Narens hadn't seen him. Jarra and the warriors were gone now, swallowed up in the darkness. Tonight there was no moon, no light at all. Yet Voris could see, and he delighted in his Triin blood.

When he was sure he had traveled far enough, Voris turned slightly and headed back to the road. Instantly he heard the Narens. His vision focused in the blackness, peering through the trees. The filthy barbarians talked amongst themselves, watching their dark surroundings. A thrill went through Voris as he bent into a hunting stance. He heard the blood rush through his ears, felt the quickening of his heart. Out came his jiiktar, sharp before him, broken into two scythelike swords. He inched his way through the vines and branches. Yards away, the Narens milled around the war wagon, cursing the greegan and their own misfortune. The one with the cannon moved its glowing nozzle nervously. Voris the Wolf licked his lips.

He was on them in a moment, bursting from the bushes. Screaming, flying, he charged the one with the cannon, flashing his blades. The cannon turned, the trigger squeezed, and a stream of burning kerosene shot across the roadway, lighting Voris for the briefest time as it blew past him. The Wolf howled and brought down his blades, severing an arm and then the neck. The head toppled into the mud. Soldiers screamed in shock and fright. Out of the trees came Dumaka Jarra and the warriors, screaming, their weapons glowing invisibly in the darkness. The Narens scrambled backward. The greegan kicked up its big horn and howled. . . .

The legionnaires of Nar were blind in the melee. Voris fell upon one, driving his blades against his armor before the soldier even saw him. The Naren sword went up uselessly. The jiiktar met it and slid down its shaft, cleaning off the fingers holding it. The soldier screamed in agony. Voris grabbed his head. He pulled off the helmet, rolled the man into the mud, then sunk his teeth into his nose, tearing off a chunk of flesh. Horrified and blinded with blood, the soldier cried out, begging for mercy. Voris swallowed the man's fear whole, loving it. He balled up a fist and drove it repeatedly into the soldier's skull until it cracked.

"CHA YULAN!" he howled. "CHA YULAN TA!"

The Wolf lives.

Jarra had made it onto the war wagon. The frenzied greegan bucked. Two warriors went to it and worked their blades on its windpipe, hacking as if at a tree trunk. The monster fell with a crash, wailing like the storm. Four more soldiers remained, all blind, all fearful of the white wraiths around them. Voris heard the hiss of steel swinging for his head. He ducked and let the blade whistle past, rolling and then springing up to meet his attacker. Two more times his jiiktar slashed, two more arcs of blood. Leather and chain mail buckled open under the quick blades, slicing into vital veins. The Naren stumbled, horrified at his own open throat. He put up his hands and fell to his knees, gasping as a waterfall of blood cascaded down his chest. Voris drove a boot into his metal face, denting the helmet and forcing him backward.

On the war wagon, old Jarra roared as he tore open the bellows with his weapon. The acid launcher groaned. The bellows swelled with a rush of air. Alarmed, Jarra jumped from the wagon just as the bellows exploded. The fabric bag popped like thunder and a cloud of yellow acid spewed up into the sky. The warriors instinctively protected themselves, diving into the mud. Voris looked up into the sky. He tried to run and found he couldn't. The Naren soldier had a hand wrapped around his ankle. Down came the acid in the rain. Voris kicked at the man and broke free. But the acid was on him. It chewed into his shoulder, cutting through his clothing even as the rain began washing it away. Voris bit back the pain and grabbed hold of the Naren who had seized him, lifting him in a rage and tossing him bodily into the upturned horn of the dead greegan.

"Kill!" shouted the warlord.

His warriors charged the Narens at their master's order. Dumaka Jarra joined the fray, leaping on one from behind and wrestling him into the swampy earth. Voris went to his aid, stomping the man's face with his heavy boot until the body stopped moving and the helmet oozed brains. They were all screaming now, drunk on blood. Voris heard the wails of the two remaining Narens. His warriors were already on them, cutting them down. The Wolf fell back against the wagon, his shoulder on fire with pain. He tore off his shirt and howled so that every Naren on earth would hear him.

"I am the Wolf!" he roared. "Dring is mine!"

When the rain finally slackened, the clouds parted to reveal a brooding moon. The insects had come out again to sing. The camp buzzed with their music. Up high in the birches nocturnal animals hunted, shaking the leaves with their movements. Voris sat back against a tree trunk, staring at the moon through the white limbs. Exhaustion had settled over the camp. It was very late now and only lookouts were awake. Voris ran a soiled cloth over his soiled jiiktar, polishing away the gore. Tired beyond words, he still found sleep impossible. Like the moon, he brooded.

Black thoughts soaked his brain. This part of the forest was peaceful, but not far away the legions gathered, soon to force another battle. Voris groaned at the idea of morning. They had clashed with the Narens in a dozen melees and he had lost scores of men. He had killed scores, too, but their numbers seemed unending. In time, Nar would deplete them. Despite its vastness, the Dring Valley had limited bodies to throw against the Empire, and every day that number dwindled bit by bit. The legionnaires clearing the forest of traps continually advanced. Too soon, they would be at the doors of Castle Dring. Voris made a monumental push to stifle his emotions. Najjir was home, waiting for him. Home.

"You do not sleep?" came a voice. Dumaka Jarra dropped down beside Voris, ignoring the wet ground. "Why?"

Voris shrugged. He wasn't in the mood for company. "Restless. Things on my mind."

Jarra leaned back against the tree trunk with his friend. Together they stared at the moon, exchanging sighs. The war master had a subtle way about him. Voris knew he would have to wait for his advice. Wraiths of clouds skirted across the sky, gray things with wings of vapor that looked to Voris like doves. Jarra smiled at the sight of them. It was always this way in Dring. The gods had been good here.

"I think you should sleep," said Jarra at last. He did not look at Voris but kept his old eyes fixed on the moon. "We need you strong. Tomorrow they will come again."

"Tomorrow and tomorrow and the tomorrow after that," said Voris. "They will never stop. They are like the moon, without end."

"We have won battles. It is not so hopeless."

Voris scoffed. "How many battles have we won? We lose ground every day."

"The acid shooters, they are not so many anymore."

"And that is why the Narens are keeping the rest of them out of the trees," reminded Voris. "They are waiting for the armored ones to sweep the traps. After that, they will charge in here with the horses. They will force us back to the castle."

"We are still many."

"Not so many."

"We are strong," argued Jarra. "We have the heart. The Narens do not."

"I would trade my heart for another hundred men," said Voris. "I would give anything to save this valley. This is my land. To lose it to these barbarians . . ." It was a thought so sickening Voris couldn't speak it. He put down the weapon he was polishing and brought his knees to his chest, wrapping his arms around them. "I would rather lose Dring to Kronin."

Jarra laughed. "Ah, now that is a big boast!"

"It is true. I cannot bear this loss, my friend. I cannot allow it. There are too many depending on me." Again he thought of Najjir. She had been a fine wife. The Narens would violate her, he was sure. Just as they had Kalak's wife. Even Tharn's wife would suffer, a thought that made Voris curiously sad. He had never cared for the heretic, but time and battle had softened him to her. And he was supposed to protect her. Tharn was expecting that, at least.

Tharn.

Another giant loss. Dead, probably, and this Voris couldn't bear, either. The weight of the world pressed down on his shoulders, threatening to snap him.

"I am so tired," he said softly. "So tired . . ."

"Sleep now," urged Jarra. "I have set up watchers on the borders and in the trees along the road. They will warn us of any trouble."

Voris didn't reply. He didn't want to sleep, not if it meant waking up to all of this. In his boyhood he had dreamed of war. They were good dreams, full of victories. No one important ever died in them. Wives weren't raped and murdered. Or daughters. If the Narens had any humanity at all, they might spare his youngest. Pris and her precocious smile popped into his mind, making him smile.

"When they see what I have left them, they will fear me," said Voris.

When Voris and his men had killed their opponents, they had skinned them and hung their remains from the trees with their sword belts. Voris hoped the Narens would see what he had done.

"They will call you a savage and a madman," replied Jarra. "That is all. The Narens do such things themselves. They will not be so dissuaded by it."

"Then I will do it to their generals," hissed Voris. "To that big one, Blackwood Gayle. I would like that, to peel off his skin. I would give it to Kalak as a reward."

"Kalak would rather do the skinning himself, I am sure," laughed Jarra. The old man looked at Voris curiously. "You are thinking of Vantran a lot these days. Why?"

"Am I?"

"I can tell you are thinking of him. You change when I mention him."

"Kalak has done me a service," said Voris. "I am grateful for it, and that is all. You imagine things, old man."

"Kalak has done well for you. You were wrong about him. You see that, and it bothers you."

"*You* bother me, Jarra," said Voris. "I was fine until you sat down. Leave me now. I am thinking."

The old man looked back up at the moon. Voris relaxed. He hadn't expected Jarra to go. And Jarra wouldn't go, not until he had his answer.

"You want to be right?" asked Voris. "You are. Kalak is better than I thought. And yes, I have been considering him. And yes, it does bother me. Should it not?"

"I suppose. You still grieve for Tal. But Tal died defending Dring. Now Kalak might do the same. So maybe they were not so different."

Voris shrugged. "Maybe." He didn't want Kalak dying for Dring. For some reason, the young king seemed to have lost too much already. He was without a home, nearly friendless. He didn't even have a woman, a luxury all Triin men took for granted. If Kalak died, Voris knew he would grieve for him.

"We cannot keep them back forever," said Voris. "A week more. Maybe less. We will have to make plans for the defense of the keep. Kalak can help with that. It would be good to put his brain to use."

"He knows these Narens well," Jarra admitted. "Tharn was right about him."

"Yes. He was right."

"And Tharn's woman? What of her?"

"She will die, like the rest of us," said Voris. He closed his eyes. "Tharn, forgive me."

"Do not talk so among the others," scolded the war master. "Most think Tharn is still alive. If you do not, they will not, either. Then they will not fight as well."

"Jarra, you are pestering me," snapped Voris. "Leave me alone now."

It always took such sharpness to shoo Jarra away. The war master left, his feelings uninjured. Voris watched him go. He loved Jarra. The old man was like a father to him. He had been war master in Dring since Voris had taken the valley. The Wolf simply couldn't imagine life without him. To Voris, Jarra was the Dring Valley, old and forever. He had thought Tharn would be like that, too, but then the gods became fickle and crippled him. Now, just like Dring without Jarra, Voris couldn't comprehend Lucel-Lor without Tharn.

He thought of Dyana, and how he had always warned Tharn against her. But she had been too beautiful for his friend to resist. Voris crinkled his forehead. She was lovely, in a sort of undomesticated way. He supposed he could understand the attraction. And Dyana had made Tharn happy in his last days. For that, the warlord was grateful. He had never thought the girl capable of such kindness.

It was just one more thing he had been wrong about.

FORTY-FOUR

Richius healed quickly over the subsequent days, anxious for word from Voris and receiving none. He whiled away the hours sitting up in bed, waiting for Dyana to make her appointed visits with food and more of the cooling medicine that had made the skin of his back supple once again. After a few days of the ointment he could tolerate a shirt and short walks outside to get some air. He ate well, devouring everything Dyana brought to him, scribbled furiously in his journal about the Naren siege, and entertained himself with violent fantasies of revenge against Blackwood Gayle. Maps had become a hobby, and he regularly drew pictures of the Dring Valley and the marshlands to its south, planning for the time when Kronin and his warriors would come to their aid and help push the Narens into the wetlands for a sodden demise.

But he was frustrated, too. It wasn't so much the war he missed, but he hated the horror of the unknown. Like everyone in Castle Dring, he had no idea how close the Narens were to the keep, or how many of the valley's defenders remained. Voris and his warriors might be turning the tide, or they might be pressed against a wall with blades at their throats. And here he was, stuck in a prison, ignorant and comfortable while others fought to defend Dyana and their child.

Only the time he spent with Dyana made him forget their predicament. She had a way of making hours speed away. She came to him daily with his meals and little bits of gossip about what was being said, how the wounded were telling stories of their small victories, and how the Narens had never seen such fierce fighters—all the usual bravado of dying men. She talked in hushed tones about Najjir and the other women of the keep, and occasionally even mentioned Tharn. And she always left the door to his chamber open when she came to him.

She had taken her mission to teach him her language seriously, and set about the task with alarming vigor. For an hour each day she kept up a cool exterior while she taught him the most rudimentary of Triin sayings and extolled the virtues of the Triin alphabet. He soon found that he was only a fair student. Triin was unlike the languages of the Empire, which to his thinking were far more fluid. Everything he uttered in Triin sounded like little more than baby dribble. But Dyana was patient with him, gently coaxing each word off his tongue with determination, and by the end of a week he was sounding more like a Triin and less like a troubled infant.

Best of all, Shani was often nearby to encourage him. For some reason, Dyana had become less wary about bringing their child to see him. She would shrug off the oddness by saying that Najjir was too busy to tend the infant, but Richius could tell by the way she encouraged him to hold their daughter that there was something more to it.

Weeks had passed since any of them had heard from Tharn. Once, in the thickness of his pain, he thought he had glimpsed Tharn speaking to him in a dream, but when he awoke the apparition had gone, and he remembered how long it had been since the cunning-man had left for Chandakkar. He had grieved for Tharn that night, sure his old adversary had died. In the morning his fears had abated, but like everyone else he still wondered where the lord of Lucel-Lor had vanished to. Chandakkar was remote and dangerous, and Tharn might already be a stomach-souring lump in the belly of a lion.

But Richius never voiced any of these fears to Dyana. She and Tharn were not lovers, but they were man and wife, and Richius guessed that most of Dyana's sadness grew from her worries over her husband. So they avoided the subject and enjoyed what time they had together, while outside the castle walls, the war for their lives raged on, and more men died telling foolish stories of foolish bravery.

And then at last Voris returned to Castle Dring. It was on a night when the rain was falling hard, the thunderous release of a hot day's humidity. Richius was in his chamber when the knock came. It was Dumaka Jarra, the war master. Richius had been clearing the debris of his evening meal, chewing on a bone as he opened the door. Jarra made a disapproving face.

"Jarra," said Richius. He put the bone down, embarrassed to be eating in the presence of the gaunt war master. "What is it? Has Voris returned?" He pointed out into the hall. "Voris?"

"Voris," answered the old man with a nod. He turned and gestured for Richius to follow him. "Gomin easa ar, Kalak."

"He's waiting for me? Just wait a moment," said Richius. He hurried over to where his boots were lying and slid one onto his foot, then hopped toward the door as he slid on the other. The haggard war master bid him to follow, leading him out of the chamber and into the hall. There he saw a congregation of people, wide-eyed and eager for news of their lord. The Dumaka put up a hand to part them, growling at them to step aside.

Richius trailed the Dumaka through the hall toward the back of the keep. It was quieter here, darker, with few windows and only a handful of torches to light the way. Richius had never been in this area of the castle before. He suspected it was where Voris had his own chambers and those of his family, and he never wanted to chance running into the precocious little Pris again. Several wooden doors hung crookedly on the western wall, and the ceiling was high and sooty from years of burning torches. An elaborate spider's web clung to an out-of-reach corner. Jarra came to one of the doors, rapped on it twice, then pushed it open. Richius peered over the old man's shoulder. Inside the chamber was a low circular table with green pillows strewn around it. Soft fabrics decorated the walls. A candelabra burned serenely in the center of the table, casting its glow on two silent figures. Voris sat cross-legged and long-faced at the far side of the table. Beside him knelt Dyana, her head dutifully bowed. She hardly stirred as Richius entered.

"Voris?" he ventured.

The warlord forced a smile. Dumaka Jarra stepped into the chamber and sat down on the floor beside Voris. Both men eyed Richius mournfully. Unsure if he should sit or remain standing, Richius waited for Voris to speak. At last he did, and his voice was thin and brittle.

"The warlord asks you to sit," explained Dyana, keeping her head bowed as she spoke. Richius felt a queer uneasiness inch up his spine.

"What is it?" he asked. "Is something wrong?"

"I do not know," answered Dyana. "Sit, please."

Richius did as Dyana asked, lowering himself to the floor between her and Voris. He tried to make her look at him, but she wouldn't. Voris' expression was vacant. Beside him, his Dumaka wore a stony mask.

"I'm listening, Voris," said Richius. "Tell me what's wrong."

Dyana translated, and Voris gave a bitter laugh. He pulled up a sleeve and stretched out his forearm for Richius to see. The scars crisscrossing his skin were a violent shade of purple.

"Acid launcher," remarked Richius. "Yes, I understand. Have you stopped them yet?"

The warlord's reply was short. Richius struggled to piece together the snippets he understood. What he heard didn't make sense.

"He has not," said Dyana. "He wishes to know how you are, Richius."

"Me? Who cares how I am? Come on, Dyana, ask him what's happening."

"The warlord wishes you well, Richius," chided Dyana mildly.

"I'm much better," he said. Then, "Easa, Voris. Fine. Thank you. Shay sar."

Voris seemed pleased by the answer. Then his eyes grew melancholy, and he pulled down his billowy sleeve to cover his wounds. He sighed so loudly his breath stirred the candle flames. When he spoke, he did so directly to Richius.

"Voris wants you to know that our time is short," said Dyana. "He says the Narens are very near now. Soon the horsemen will be coming, and he will not be able to stop them." Her voice caught for a moment before she could right it. "He says we have only days left."

Richius was stunned. He had seen the numbers massed against them, had witnessed the carnage Gayle and his henchmen could occasion, yet he had never really considered that Voris would utter such words. His throat constricted. If he was lucky he would die anonymously with the others. If he were not, he would be dragged to Nar City in chains. He thought of Dyana and Shani, and the horrors they might be forced to endure.

"Days," he whispered breathlessly. He would never let Gayle take his family. He would have them all drink poison first.

"Richius?" said Dyana. "Are you all right?"

"Fine," said Richius distantly. "Fine . . ."

"The warlord wants you to know that you have honored him. He asks your forgiveness that he has failed you."

"No," said Richius. "I won't hear it. We aren't beaten yet. There's still time for Kronin to reach us. Go on, Dyana, tell him about my plan."

Dyana raised her head. "Richius . . ."

"Tell him."

Reluctantly Dyana explained Richius' plan to Voris, who listened attentively before smiling at Richius and shaking his head. Dumaka Jarra chuckled.

"Voris says Kronin will not come," said Dyana. "He says Kronin is probably enjoying this as much as your horsemen."

"No," said Richius sternly. "I don't believe that. Voris, listen to me. Kronin will come, he will." Frustrated, Richius tried to make the warlord understand with a flurry of hand signs and a string of fractured Triin phrases. At last he gave up and fell back into Naren. "I know Kronin better than you do. He's not the man you think he is. He has honor, like you. Honor. Yaaso, Voris. Kronin yaaso. He will come to help us. When he does we can push the Narens into the swamps. We just have to hold on until he gets here."

Voris put up his hands, not waiting for Dyana's translation. Dyana listened then translated for Richius.

"Voris wants you to stop being so foolish," she said. "He says you are too young to believe this, but there is a time when every warrior dies. You must accept it."

"Maybe," said Richius. "But I won't accept it until I know for certain. If we give up now, we'll never know how long we could have held out. Maybe long enough for Kronin to come or Tharn to return. *Maybe.*"

Voris seemed exasperated. He looked to his companion for guidance, but Jarra merely tossed off one of his cavalier shrugs. "Kalak oahnal benagray," said the Dumaka.

"The Dumaka thinks you are brave but stupid, Richius," said Dyana. Then she stole a glance at him and added, "But I am with you."

"Then convince them, Dyana. Please. I don't have the words. How can I make them see that it's only a matter of time? Kronin will come, I know he will. He'll come because he's dedicated to Tharn—just like Voris and the rest of them."

"Richius," said Dyana cautiously. "Tharn may be dead."

"So what if he is? Does that mean Kronin will just let Voris and his men be slaughtered? I don't think so. He's devoted to Tharn's ideals, not just the man. He's just like Voris. Loyal."

Voris interrupted, telling Dyana to explain it all to him. Dyana complied, and the warlord's face once again dimmed with doubt. This time when he spoke, he was very firm.

"You do not know him as well as you think you do," said Dyana for Voris. "He is a serpent. If he thinks Tharn is dead he will happily let us be murdered."

Richius got to his feet and stood before Voris. "No. I no more believe that than I believe you would let Tatterak fall under Nar's heel. You're so blinded by hate that you can't see that. But I put it to you, Voris. Would you let Kronin and his men fall? Would you not help them?"

Voris waited a very long moment before replying. His answer was more like a grunt than a sentence.

"The warlord says he would not let them die," says Dyana. "He would save them for Tharn's sake, and the sake of all Triin."

"Of course," said Richius. "That's the only real answer a warrior of Lucel-Lor could give. Why would you think Kronin would give any other? Believe me, Voris, I beg you. Fight on. Don't just let Arkus and his bastards take your valley. It isn't over yet. I swear it."

Voris listened to Richius' appeal with interest, a wan smile brightening his face. Dyana translated it all.

"The warlord wants you to know that he will never lay down his weapons. He promises you he will fight on as long as he can, and that he prays you are right about the serpent Kronin."

Richius nodded. "I am right. You'll see, Voris. We just have to hold on."

Voris got to his feet. "Coala con, Kalak," he said quietly.

"We are done," said Dyana. She rose and faced Richius. "The warlord wishes to rest now, Richius. And it is late. We should all go to our chambers."

"Will he be staying?" Richius asked. "Voris, will I see you in the morning?"

Dyana asked the question, and Voris nodded, shooing them toward the door as he spoke.

"Yes," said Dyana. "He will be staying. The Narens are getting close to the castle now. He says we will use the castle as our fortress."

"I understand," said Richius. He wanted to return to his chamber, to be alone and think on what had been discussed.

The halls of the keep were almost empty now, but he could hear the nervous voices of men and women behind the closed doors lining his way. They were talking about the siege, he knew, and how desperate their predicament had become. Voices seemed so much louder when they were desperate.

When he reached his tiny chamber he found the door closed tight. Had he closed it? He couldn't remember. Gingerly he pushed it open, wondering if he would catch someone in the chamber. But there was no one. The candle he'd been reading by had burned down to a waxy nub, and the remnants of his meal still lingered on his bed. But beside the plate, placed in plain view, was a book. It lay open and spine up, as if someone had been reading it and didn't want to lose their place. And it was vaguely familiar to Richius. He went over to the bed and picked it up, careful to wedge a thumb beneath it to hold the page. It was the book he had seen Pris reading, the collection of Naren poems. Curiously, it was open to the same poem she had wanted him to read. He smiled as he remembered and silently read the poem.

> Bright lovers with an ocean between them,
> search the horizons forever.
> Doves bear love notes across the sea,
> against the raging winds of heaven.
> Eternity laughs,
> and builds for them prisons.
> Black dawns, where angels beg the night for mercy.

Astonished, he closed the book. This was more than a mere coincidence. This was a message. Someone had left this book for him, and if it was Pris she had done so under another's direction. And there was only one person who would have made her do it.

Richius moved purposefully from the room, passing through the castle like a ghost. Voris would be expecting him. He steeled his nerves as he went back through the dingy hall to the little, windowless room, pausing just outside its threshold before stepping through. Dumaka Jarra was no longer with Voris. Instead he saw Pris sitting in her father's lap, giggling while he brushed long braids from her eyes. Voris looked up at Richius expectantly. Richius tossed the book onto the table.

"What's this?" he asked sharply.

Pris seemed surprised by his action, even hurt. The gleeful grin melted off her face. But Voris barely flinched. He reached out his long arm and retrieved the book from the table, handing it to his daughter.

"What is this, Voris?" repeated Richius firmly. "If you have something to tell me, get it over with."

Pris jumped to her father's rescue. "Kalak is angry with Father?" she asked. "Why?"

"Pris, will you tell your father something for me?" asked Richius.

"I am here for that," said Pris.

"What?"

"I am here to talk for you and Father. Talk. Father has been waiting."

Richius softened his voice. "Did you leave that book in my room?"

Pris nodded. "For Father. My poem, Kalak. Remember? I showed it to Father when he was angry with me for being with you. Liked it, he did. He asked me to give it to you." Her eyes narrowed. "Was it wrong?"

"Why did he want me to see it, Pris?" asked Richius. "Do you know?"

Pris frowned, then came up with the most plausible answer her young mind could. "He liked it?"

"Would you ask him for me? Ask him why?"

Pris started to ask but Voris put a finger to her lips and spoke first. His voice was clear and sweet, and he looked deep into her eyes as he spoke, never letting his tone slip above a loving whisper. Pris absorbed it all with puzzlement, clearly missing most of its meaning. She was a genius with language, but the tangle of adult emotions still eluded her. When her father was done, she turned to Richius.

"Kalak knows the pretty woman?" she asked.

"Dyana," guessed Richius easily. "What about her?"

"You love her."

Richius didn't know what to say. His eyes flicked to the warlord then back to the girl. "Yes."

Pris grinned. "She loves you."

Oh, Lord, thought Richius. He fought to quell his growing panic, determined not to back down. But Voris simply stared at him.

"Father says you want each other," said the girl. She pointed to the book in her hands. "Like in the poem. Love. Good like him and Mother."

Voris stopped her and carefully explained himself again. Pris nodded impatiently. Then her face darkened, and Voris put a hand on her head and stroked her hair.

"What's wrong, Pris?" asked Richius anxiously. "What's your father saying?"

"Bhapo," replied Pris. "Father worries."

"You mean Tharn?"

Voris nudged her, and Pris made an effort to stifle her tears. "Yes. Kalak, do you see?"

"I'm sorry, Pris, I don't see," said Richius. He went to them and knelt down on the soft carpet. "Help me, please. I don't know what you're saying. What's your father trying to tell me?"

"He wants you with the pretty woman," explained Pris feebly. "Before you die. No more time. Bhapo gone. . . ."

"Easy," crooned Richius. "It's all right. I think I know what your father means." He leaned back, amazed, and stared at Voris. "He's telling us to be together."

"Yes, yes," sniffled Pris. "Together."

Voris' big thumb swept a tear from her cheek. The warlord looked at Richius, trying to express himself with his face alone, silently convincing Richius of his meaning. Richius shook his head in disbelief. He leaned forward to comfort the girl, who was crying now for her beloved Tharn and for her father and mother and everyone else she thought would soon be dead. Richius placed a soothing hand on her knee and Pris collapsed into sobs. Voris made no attempt to pull his daughter away.

"Do you know what you're saying?" Richius asked the warlord. "Have a care. I love her dearly, it's true. But she is Tharn's now, and he might yet be alive. There is still a chance, you know."

"Tharn kyata fa," said Voris sadly. He drew a circular gesture in the air, signifying time passing or something very far away. "Tharn kiv Lorris."

"You think Tharn's with Lorris," said Richius, understanding the warlord's words. He shrugged. "I don't know. Maybe. You might not believe this, but I hope he's alive. He's my friend, like he's yours. I'm not willing to give up on him yet." He rose and smiled bleakly at Voris and his weeping daughter. "Thank you," he said. "Thank you for letting us love each other. I will tell Dyana what you have said. We will decide together."

The warlord nodded, then bent his neck to kiss the top of Pris' head. "Sala sar, Kalak," he said quietly.

Richius bid good-night to Voris in the warlord's own language. "Sala sar, Voris."

The next morning, Richius awoke early and went in search of Pris. He found her where he had expected, stealing away time in the small room where he had first discovered her, jealously devouring one of the household's other books, an old Triin manuscript with faded pages. As he had hoped, though, she still had her book of Naren poems with her, and when he asked her to borrow it she handed it to him willingly. He thanked her, promising her she would have it back within the day, and tucked it into his belt beneath his shirt so that no one would see it. He left the tiny room and set out toward the chamber of Voris' wife, Najjir, where he thought to find Dyana. Dyana was nursing Shani when he knocked on the door. Thankfully, Najjir was nowhere to be found.

Dyana was surprised to see him so early. Her breakfast of rice porridge was still waiting for her. She tucked Shani into her crib, buttoned up her shirt, and made a sour face at Richius.

"You should not have come," she said. "Someone might have seen you."

He wanted to tell her he didn't care, but he contained it with a mischievous grin.

"Can you come with me?" he asked.

"Voris is with Najjir," whispered Dyana. "You will have to wait to speak to him."

"I don't want to talk to Voris. I want to talk to you. Can you leave Shani for a while?"

She glanced at her uneaten breakfast. "Will you wait for me? I have not eaten."

"This is better than porridge, Dyana. Find somebody to look after Shani. I'll meet you out in the yard."

"The yard? Why there?"

"Just meet me outside as soon as you can. Around the back by the statues. Don't let anyone know where you're going."

"All right," she agreed.

He closed the door and looked about before slipping out of the hall. The yard was deserted except for a pair of tight-lipped guards. He bounded past the warriors and went around toward the rear of the castle where the grass was overgrown and he could hide behind the pitted marble of a ruined statue. There he waited for Dyana.

Minutes ticked away, but eventually she appeared, wearing a pair of thigh-high doeskin boots, perfect for the wasp-infested grasses of the yard.

Good girl, thought Richius happily.

She came up to him, hazarded a glance over her shoulder, then asked, "What is it, Richius? What is wrong?"

"Nothing's wrong," he assured her. "Come with me."

"Where are we going?"

"Someplace nice."

He took her hand and led her back toward the rear of the keep, where the grass was even higher. Two days before, he had discovered a small path that meandered through the woods. The path had taken him to a tiny, crystalline brook full of smooth rocks and shiny fish with gemstone eyes. He had spent more than an hour there, perusing his maps and his journal, and wishing he could bring Dyana there with him. Now Voris had given him leave to do so, and a childlike excitement surged through him so that he could hardly keep from breaking into a run as he guided Dyana toward the path. But Dyana hesitated as she saw the trail, stopping at its threshold.

"Oh, no," she protested. "No, Richius, we cannot."

"Yes, we can," he said gently. "I found a place I want you to see. Come on, it isn't far."

"But someone might find us, see us together. No, Richius. We must go back."

"Dyana, trust me. I have something to tell you. When I do you'll understand. Come with me, please."

Hesitantly she agreed, letting Richius take her hand and lead her onto the path, which was so narrow only one of them could proceed down it at a time. Over their heads, tree branches weaved into a net spotted with dancing birds, and ahead of them little furry things darted out of their way. Richius cocked his head to listen.

"Hear that?" he asked cheerfully.

Dyana paused. "Water?"

"A brook. I found it the other day when I was exploring the keep. It's beautiful. I wanted you to see it."

Annoyance made Dyana's eyes narrow. "Is that why you brought me out here? Richius, we could be seen. . . ."

"It's not just a brook, Dyana. It's not much further. I'll explain it to you there."

Less than ten yards later the path opened up to reveal the brook. A ribbon of sunlight bounced off the water and Dyana gasped. Richius smiled. It was prettier than he remembered it. They skirted the muddy bank, using the flat stones along its side as a bridge and coming to rest in a sunny clearing. The sounds of the bubbling brook filled their ears. Near the water was a large rock, perfect for resting on. Long ago someone had carved a word into it; a name, Richius supposed. He showed it to Dyana, who laughed when she read it.

"What does it say?" asked Richius.

"It says Najjir," Dyana giggled. She traced a finger over it. "It must be very old."

"It must be," agreed Richius. "I can't imagine her carving her name into a rock now. She's so . . ." He tried to think of something inoffensive. "Strict."

"You do not know her, Richius. She is not as you believe. She is only different. You are used to Naren woman. Najjir is Drol. And she helped me care for you, remember."

"I remember," said Richius. "And I'm grateful." He dusted off the rock with his palm and bid Dyana to sit. "Now I've something else to show you."

Dyana dropped down onto the stone and looked up at him. "What?"

"This," he said, and reached under his shirt to retrieve the book. He held it out for Dyana. "Do you recognize it? It belongs to Pris."

"Her book of poems," said Dyana. "Yes, I remember. How did you get it?"

Richius rifled through the pages until he found the poem he wanted, then handed her the book. "Here," he said. "Read that."

Dyana took the book and read the poem aloud. When she was done her eyes lingered on the page for a long moment.

"How did you get this?"

"Pris left it for me last night when I went down to talk to Voris. It was in my chamber when I returned. Voris wanted me to see it."

"Gods," Dyana swore. "Then he does know. . . ."

"Dyana, don't worry." Richius took her hand and held it. "I spoke to him about it. It's all right. You won't believe what he said to me!"

"Do I want to hear?"

"This you do. Voris knows all about us. He knows how we feel." He looked deep into her eyes, now filled with such enormous apprehension, and said, "He wants us to be together."

Dyana blinked, then reared back. "What?"

"Isn't that amazing?" The thrill of the news made him bubble like the brook. "It's true, Dyana, I swear. He told me so himself, last night. He wants us to be together!"

"But why?" asked Dyana, still shocked. "Why would he say such a thing? I am married!"

"To Tharn," explained Richius. "But Voris thinks Tharn's dead, and that we only have a short time left. He knows we love each other, and that we want to be together. Call it a gift, a way of thanking me for helping him, I don't know. But he wants us to be happy for these last few days." He knelt before her, ignoring the mud soaking his knee. "We can be together, Dyana."

Dyana shook her head. "No. We cannot."

"Why, Dyana? No one's heard from Tharn in months. How will he ever know what happens between us now? Even if he is alive, Voris won't tell him."

"Have you forgotten everything, Richius? It does matter. You once told me that Tharn warned you not to pursue me. Voris' blessing is not enough. If Tharn is alive, then he will find out what we have done. He will, because he is Drol and he loves me. I am glad we no longer need to hide our love from the warlord, but it changes nothing. I am sorry, we cannot be together, not the way you wish."

Richius looked at her carefully. "Dyana, this is hard for me to say, but I think Voris is right. Tharn could be dead." He fell back and sighed. "We don't have much time ourselves. I want to love you, at least for a little while before I die. And I know you want the same thing, too."

"You made a promise to me. You told me you would never risk Shani. Do you remember?"

"Dyana . . ."

"Do you?"

She touched his cheek and he nodded. He did remember the abominable promise. Dyana smiled at him sadly.

"It does not matter who knows of our love, Richius. Let the whole world know. Even Tharn already knows our feelings. He sent me with you so you would protect me. He trusted you. And me. But he must never think we have been lovers. It is our actions that could doom us, not our hearts."

"Dyana, Tharn's probably dead. . . ."

"Probably?" asked Dyana. "Probably is not enough for me, Richius. You do not know Tharn. He is a survivor. I must know he is gone before I can be with you. There is too much to risk."

"I can't bear this, Dyana. Am I supposed to find proof of his death first? Will we never be together?"

"Not while Tharn lives. Not if our little one is to be safe. We—"

She stopped suddenly and held her breath. Her eyes froze on something over his shoulder. Richius turned at once, following her gaze toward the forest across the brook.

"Dyana?" he asked. "What is it?"

"In those trees," she whispered. "I saw them move."

Instinctively Richius dropped his hand to his side, but Jessicane wasn't there. He focused sharply on the woods, trying to catch a glimpse of what Dyana had seen. But he saw nothing.

"Are you sure?" he asked. "I don't see anything."

"Someone is there," said Dyana. Her eyes were locked on the trees. "A man. He is looking at me."

Then Richius saw it, a hint of white skin and a small rustle of leaves. It was a man. A Triin. Richius could just make out the spark of two gray eyes.

"You there!" he called, getting to his feet. "Who are you? Come out and show yourself."

The branches were still.

"Come out," Richius demanded. "Or shall I come in there?"

He had no intention of going into the trees, but the tone of his voice made the hidden man step forward. Very gradually his face emerged from the thickets, a thin white face, painted half green. His hair was green, too, dyed the color of new grass, and around his chest was draped a long blue jacket, belted with a golden sash. A jiiktar was strapped to his back but he held up both hands as he came forward, carefully showing his peaceful intent.

"Vantran," said the man. "Min voco Vantran."

"Richius!" blurted Dyana. "He says he is looking for you."

It was the same man Richius had seen when first approaching Falindar, the one Lucyler had called Kronin's herald. Richius tried to recall his name. Was it Hakan?

"Hakan?" he called to the warrior. "Is it you?"

The warrior's face glowed. "Vantran!" he said, and splashed across the brook toward them, babbling excitedly. When he reached them he bowed deeply to Richius, greeting him with more gibberish Richius couldn't recognize.

"Dyana?" Richius asked.

"His name *is* Hakan," said Dyana. "Do you know him, Richius?"

"Not really. He greeted me when I came to Falindar. He's one of Kronin's men. What's he saying, Dyana? Is Kronin here?"

"Yes," Dyana cried. "He *is* here, Richius. Kronin has come. And Richius . . . Lucyler is with him."

FORTY-FIVE

To call the lions is to speak with the gods.

So Karlaz had said. It was a gift, much the same as Tharn's own, and the warlord had been unable to explain it further. Or unwilling.

In the days during his recuperation, Tharn had much to ponder. Isolated in the shabby house, his cunning-men gone, he was denied the company of the trees and wildlife. He was, in a sense, a prisoner of his own inadequate and damaged body, and because he was so weak he recovered slowly. It was a painful, boring process, and after a week he had begun to feel the weight of his own loneliness. To Karlaz' stoic people he was still Storm Maker, a Drol, and even the woman who attended to him seemed unwilling to warm to him. He had learned her name was Kreena. And that was all he learned. Kreena fed him, washed him when he needed it, and was never more than a shout away. She had nursed him back to a semblance of health, all the while leaving him to his own brooding solitude.

And Karlaz had come to him infrequently. The master of the lion folk was preoccupied with matters of great weight, and only seldom came to speak with the Drol. Karlaz ordered Tharn to rest, and Kreena kept that mandate, making sure that Tharn never wandered far from his mattress. Together they planned, Karlaz and Tharn, and what passed for a grudging friendship developed between them. Tharn liked Karlaz. To him the warlord was honorable, like Voris and Kronin. But as the days and nights progressed, Tharn grew ever more restless. He wanted to know what was happening outside his four walls. He begged the quiet Karlaz for information, for a scrap of news, but Karlaz was like Kreena. Neither one of them gave Tharn any more than he needed.

Until today. Today Tharn turned his face skyward, loving the sun and its heat. He was on a ledge overlooking the valley of the lions. All the world seemed at his feet. Up here, high with the bracing wind, he thought of what Karlaz had told him. Here a man really could speak to the gods.

Tharn looked down into the valley. It was a dry land, overrun with tall, spidery brush that turned the earth to amber. Trees of dull green with huge, ballooning canopies dotted the plain, their branches ripe with fruit and birds, and lions lounged in the shade, exhausted from the heat and hunting. The grasses shuddered with their stalkings, their spiked tails jutting up like shark fins, frightening the flocks of egrets and the meaty, lesser beasts that were their prey. Near the south side of the valley was a sluggish river, thick and dark from the lack of rain, where thirsty lions and crocodiles drank. A wind brushed its breath across the water, making it stir in the sun. A wayward leaf fell from a tree. Tharn watched it all with awe, enraptured by its beauty. Perhaps it was his mood or the thrill of being in the light again, but it made his throat constrict. He felt whole again, a man like any other. He felt powerful.

Karlaz and the warriors gathered around the ledge. The warlord had summoned them from the villages and they had come, jiiktars sharpened and long hair braided for war. On their faces were the implacable masks of vengeance, that same austere countenance Karlaz wore and never dropped. They had gathered at their master's bidding eager for blood, to avenge the deaths of their brothers, and to show the might of Chandakkar to the barbarians from Nar. Tharn thrilled at the sight of them. They reminded him of Dring's wolves—lean and hungry, and a little wild around the eyes. Men could be beautiful, he decided, like the valley. He was not beautiful but he was one of them nonetheless, and the notion made him proud. Soon they would fight for the Saccenne Run. Soon Naren skulls would be crushed in the powerful jaws of lions, and the emperor would tremble at the might of Lucel-Lor.

Tharn took satisfaction in the thought. Like Karlaz, he himself had been busy, even in his recuperation. He had sent his cunning-men away, each bearing a message to a different warlord. Karlaz had sent messengers, too. Kronin, Shohar, Praxtin-Tar; they would all be told of Liss' involvement, if they hadn't known already. The messages bid them to meet at the outskirts of Ackle-Nye, where they were to await the arrival of the lions. Kronin himself would lead the attack. It would be a crushing blow, a tide so powerful even the Narens and their machines wouldn't be able to stand against it. Tharn had only one regret about his plan—he wouldn't be there.

Too weary and ill to make the long trip to Ackle-Nye, Tharn planned on bringing Karlaz to Dring first. There Tharn would wait until the war was over. He would rest and make himself well again. And he would be with Dyana. A smile stretched across his face. She would be proud of him. He knew she would.

"What now?" Tharn called to Karlaz. The warlord was with two of the warriors, a burly pair from his own village. When he heard Tharn's question he frowned.

"Be silent," said Karlaz. His warriors fell back as he took a step closer to the ledge. On his back was his jiiktar, held by a stout leather belt across his naked chest. The wind rose. Tharn remained dutifully quiet. He watched as Karlaz inched thoughtfully to the edge of the rocky ledge, spilling a tiny avalanche of stones down the slope. One by one the hundred gathered lion riders took their jiiktars from their backs and held them out before them, arms locked straight, weapons parallel to the ground. There was a tangible hush over the rush of wind. Down in the valley, the lions went about their usual business, oblivious to the ceremony above. Tharn's eyes darted down to watch them. They drank and slept and sired, and seemed to care nothing of their masters on the ledge.

Karlaz drew his own jiiktar from his back. Its twin blades sparkled with a blinding glimmer. He grasped its shaft in both fists and raised it above his head, stretching it out toward heaven and pointing his face to the sky. Eyes closed, he stood like this for long moments, silent, maybe praying, leaving Tharn to puzzle over his actions.

Then Karlaz screamed.

Deafening, shattering, he raised his voice to the gods and shook the valley with his thunder as the cry trilled from his throat. Like the blast from a cannon his voice fired into the sky, tearing open the peace of the wind and the valley's nature, flattening the silence until all that existed was Karlaz. The warlord cried without end, without breathing, pushing his lungs beyond anything Tharn thought possible. Tharn gazed down into the valley. The grasses had stopped moving. The lions fell still. Each in turn raised its giant head to the hillside, staring up at the wailing master of Chandakkar. Karlaz' voice went on, impossibly, his flesh reddening with effort, his forehead flushed and sweating.

Now the warriors joined in, mixing their voices with the warlord's. Like Karlaz they raised up their weapons, screaming their inhuman song, breaking down the walls of heaven with an insistent pounding of sound. Astonished, Tharn could only watch the spectacle, watch as the lions of the valley rose to their feet and gazed up at Karlaz, their yellow eyes dawning with a primitive intelligence. A male of the pack stepped out from the grasses, craned its muscled neck, then roared.

And then they were all roaring, a chorus of monsters singing with the men, reviving an ancient song of battle. They roared and it was beautiful. Slowly, carefully, Tharn picked his way to the ledge to stand beside Karlaz.

Then Tharn raised his cane into the air and screamed along with the waiting warriors.

FORTY-SIX

Lucyler of Falindar peeked his face through the brambles and smiled. He had been too long from the hunt, and the distance to Dring had been too far. On the grassy plain below milled his quarry, unmistakable in their golden armor. But today they weren't proud horsemen of Talistan. Today they were victims.

"There they are," he whispered. "Like pigs in a pen."

He stepped aside for Kronin to see, cautioning the warlord to silence. Though they were far away on a hillside, their faces painted green, there was always the chance that a sharp-eyed scout would spot them. Kronin slid in next to Lucyler and gingerly pushed away a handful of branches. He peered down the slope and grunted with satisfaction. The horsemen were sitting around in dumb boredom, idle except for the industrious few who groomed their mounts or polished their blades, awaiting the order that would send them at last against Castle Dring.

And there were the acid launchers. Three of them. There had once been a dozen, or so Richius had claimed. Hakan had returned to them full of Richius' stories. Just thinking of his friend made Lucyler grin. He had wanted to see Richius himself, but there hadn't been time. There was just time enough for the plan.

"The launchers," said Lucyler. "See? The wagons with the big sacks on them."

Kronin nodded impatiently. "Where is Gayle? I cannot see him. And who is that one? The one with the feathered hat?"

Lucyler looked out over the camp, trying to locate the big baron from a clouded memory. He had seen Gayle only once, and that was over a year ago. All he could recall about the Talistanian was his size and his imperious voice. Silently he scanned the camp, hoping to catch a trace of him. Gayle was the prize they were after. Even Kronin salivated over slaying his old ally. None of them had forgotten the baron's awful gift to Richius. But if Gayle was below, he was lost in the sea of green and gold uniforms or hidden inside one of the small pavilions. At last Lucyler shrugged.

"Maybe he is there, maybe not. In one of the tents probably. No matter. There are the war wagons."

He stepped back to let Hakan have a look. Hakan moved in eagerly and made a small whistling sound as he sighted the wagons. He had never seen one before, and had only terrible tales to measure them against. He weighed the sight of them and decided their prowess hadn't been exaggerated.

"Big," he said.

"But unmanned," added Lucyler quickly. "At least as far as I can see. If we move quickly we can douse them and be off before anyone can stop us."

"Yes, quickly," agreed Kronin. He too stepped out of the bushes. "The launchers have to be taken or they'll be able to stop our charge. There are not so many of us for surprise to be enough." He turned to Hakan. "Are your men prepared?"

Hakan nodded. "The skins are all filled. We await your word, Warlord."

"Do not be heroic," scolded Lucyler. "Just get the oil on the wagons and get out of there."

"I will give the signal for the archers to loose when all of us are clear," Kronin put in. "Lucyler, you will ride with me. We will take the wagon in the center, the one by the man with the hat. If he is important, he might lead us to Gayle."

There was so much iron in the warlord's voice that Lucyler couldn't keep his chest from swelling. They had all ridden hard for the valley once word of Voris' predicament had reached them, and none of them knew what they would find here. A ruined castle? Richius and Voris swinging from trees? There had been a massacre of sorts, but it had included Triin and Narens alike, and Richius and Voris had both told Hakan that the odds would be even. A final, decisive moment had arrived in Dring's history, and it seemed odd to Lucyler that he and Kronin should be part of it. But they were all part of a greater brotherhood now, without the rancor that had once dominated their thinking. Tharn would expect no less of them.

And they owed it to Liss, those brave, magnificent mariners whose hatred of Nar had eclipsed everything else in their lives, including reason.

The schooners of Liss had kept the dreadnoughts of the Black Fleet off the shores of Tatterak, so that only those Narens that had already landed were a threat. And there were so few of them now that only a fraction of Kronin's men could contain them. So they had ridden for the valley with their own land secure, and the peace of mind that if they returned at all, it would be to a land at relative peace. Tatterak was safe for the time being. Dring was another matter entirely.

"Go back, Hakan," ordered Kronin. "Tell the others to make ready. Come get us again in one hour. We will attack then."

"And you, Warlord?" asked Hakan. "Will you wait here?"

"With Lucyler, yes," said Kronin. "I mean to keep an eye open for the criminal Gayle."

Hakan bowed reluctantly and left them, silently stalking farther up the hill and disappearing. When he was gone and all they could hear was the slow rush of wind and the rustling of leaves, Kronin turned to Lucyler.

"There are still many of them," he said frankly. "Vantran's plan is good but risky. This might not work at all. You know that, yes?"

"I know," answered Lucyler. "But I know Richius, too. He is clever. He has worked this all out, I am sure."

Kronin settled down on his haunches. He smiled at Lucyler. "You do this for him? Nothing more?"

"I do it for Lucel-Lor," replied Lucyler. Then he thought for a moment and added, "And for my friend, yes. I owe him for some old wrongs. And what about you, Kronin? To be honest you surprise me. You hate Voris even more than you hate Gayle. Is your faith in Tharn so strong?"

Kronin laughed softly. "Stronger than I would have guessed," he confessed. "And I too owe the man from Aramoor a debt." The laughing vanished and a mournful look settled upon the warlord's face. "Debts are sometimes hard to repay."

Richius and Voris left Castle Dring under the cover of darkness. Two hundred men followed them. They were without horses or provisions, slogging their way south through the valley's thickest parts, heading toward the marshlands. It was barely a half-day's journey, and with only their jiiktars and Richius' giant broadsword to slow them they moved like an army of ants through the brush and tangled trees.

Richius held his scabbarded sword at his side as he trotted over fallen trees and under spear-shaped branches. He was near exhaustion, but the ground was starting to soften. They were close now.

But he was so tired. His muscles moved by force of will alone. Sweat poured from his forehead, stinging his eyes, and giant black mosquitoes swarmed around his face, puncturing his flesh with their knifelike stingers. It was a hot day in Dring, the hottest he could recall. Sunlight chewed through the net of trees, bearing down on them mercilessly. Ahead of him, Richius could see the back of Voris' robe soaked with perspiration. The warlord's neck was pocked with insect bites. A constrictor moved in the trees, regarding them with its reptilian eyes, and a rotting stump spewed up a foam of white termites. The air took on a tangy stink, the smell of wet decay. Somewhere ahead of them something large splashed through a pond. It might have been a monkey or some giant fish, but Richius ignored it, closing off his mind to the sound. There were enough visible monstrosities to occupy his fears. He didn't need imagination here. Once again he was in the Dring of his nightmares, the evil, suffocating underbelly of the valley.

But soon it'll be over, he assured himself. Lucyler and Kronin were coming. With luck they would reach the swamps by nightfall. The thought put an extra spring in Richius' step. Soon the valley would be free of Narens, and he could return to the keep and tell Dyana how he had watched Gayle sink to his knees in the bog and beg for mercy, and how he had killed him anyway. Dyana and their daughter would be rid of Gayle's threat forever. And he would have avenged Sabrina. Finally.

They continued on this way for long minutes, never sharing a word, rationing their energies as they fought their way deeper into the darkening marshlands. And then, at last, Voris stopped. The warlord held up a hand to halt his company. Dumaka Jarra shouted back an order, and man by man the column of exhausted warriors stopped moving. Richius stood next to Voris. Before them was an oozing expanse of muddy earth, so sodden and unstable that only frogs and insects could light upon its surface without breaking it. Overhead the trees were high, thick with leaves that blocked out the worst of the sun's cutting rays. The air was perceptibly ranker. Voris tested the ground with the toe of his boot and his foot disappeared. When he pulled it out, it was covered with a slick of green, noxious muck. He grunted, then glanced up into the trees, gesturing toward the high, concealing branches.

"Do o dae," he said. "Ta, Kalak?"

Richius looked up into the trees and a smile split his face. "Perfect."

"Lotts! Stop hiding and get over here. We're talking about you again."

There was a chorus of laughter as Dinadin stepped out from behind his horse, his grooming brush still in hand. He flicked his colonel a disinterested look, trying to quell the little flutter of terror that always came when Trosk called him. "Colonel?"

"Take a seat, waterhead," ordered Trosk. "You're missing some good stories about your king." Trosk pointed to the empty space on the ground beside him. "Here."

Dinadin went to where Trosk and the others were huddled around a burned-out campfire. They all gave him the same skeptical look as he sat down beside the colonel. Trosk removed his feathered hat and ran the back of his hand over his forehead, wiping away a pool of perspiration.

"Damn. It's hotter than a whore's bedroom out here." He fluffed up the long yellow feather before replacing his hat and cocking it down over his right eye. "You hot, Lotts?"

Dinadin nodded.

"Still not talking to me, huh, you little bastard? Hell, that's all right. I got other friends."

The others in the circle flashed menacing smiles. Dinadin grimaced. Even before they had raped the village girl, he could barely stand the sight of them. Now when he looked at them he was sickened. That girl still gave him nightmares. How did these devils dare to look at him so accusingly?

"You're taking good care of your horse, Lotts," said Trosk. "That's just fine. You go on cleaning yourself up. I want you to look real pretty when we ride into the woods to take apart your king and that dumpy little castle he's cowering in. I want him to see us all coming." Trosk looked off into the distance, toward the giant watchtower whose peak could barely be seen bobbing up above the tree line. "You think he sees us now, Lotts?"

Dinadin wouldn't reply.

"No? Let's try anyway. Come on, Lotts. Wave to your old friend." The colonel started waving toward the far-off tower, then quickly turned his gesture into an obscenity. There was more malicious laughter from the soldiers. "Hello, Jackal!" cried Trosk. "We're coming for you!"

Dinadin felt his mood crumble. They *would* be coming for Richius soon. The word from the infantry was that Voris' resistance was collapsing. Today or tomorrow, Gayle would give the order to ride for the castle. Amazingly, Dinadin felt a pang at the notion. It wasn't the reunion with Richius he would have liked. There was a part of him that wanted to sneak off and warn his old friend, to fight by his side once again against these evil men. But he was thinking of another lifetime, a man he was no longer. His eyes lingered a moment on the distant watchtower.

Are you up there, Richius? Would you turn me away?

Trosk turned his attention to one of the small pavilions dotting the camp. There were only two of them. Trosk and ten men shared one. Gayle alone inhabited the other. Trosk stared at Gayle's tent contemptuously, and his voice dipped to a whisper.

"The baron is going mad, I think. Since seeing Vantran on the barricade he talks about nothing else." He turned to Dinadin and chuckled. "You might want to send your old king a warning, Lotts. Tell him Blackwood Gayle's coming for him with a gelding knife!"

"We have to catch him first," offered one of the men in the circle, a filthy-haired lieutenant. "That castle might not look like much, but it's no doubt well manned. Vantran's probably got the whole thing rimmed with traps by now."

"Gayle thinks the castle will come down in less than a day," said Trosk. His eyes glinted wildly, the same way they did when he had first glimpsed the peasant girl. "If we're lucky he'll let us have some trophies. But not Vantran. He's to be taken alive. Maybe you'll come in helpful for that, Lotts. Maybe he'll trust you."

"What?" asked Dinadin incredulously.

"Do you think you can do it? Talk him into surrendering? It'll look good for us all if you do."

They were all watching him. "I don't know," Dinadin mumbled. "Maybe."

"It's how such things are done, Lotts," snapped Trosk. "You'd know that if you were any sort of man." Then he laughed again. "But I forget myself. You're not a man, are you?"

Dinadin got to his feet indignantly. "I'll go back to my grooming now," he said. "If we're done, sir."

"Ooohh, I think I've finally said something to make the boy bristle. Is that right, Lotts? You mad at me? 'Cause if you are it'd break my heart."

More insane laughter. The heat of the day and the insult mingled to make Dinadin's face boil. For one fleeting second, the thought of kicking Trosk in his arrogant face shone gloriously in his mind. It would almost be worth it. But only almost.

"Whatever you say, sir," said Dinadin. There was the barest trace of sarcasm in his tone. "You're always right."

"Yes," agreed Trosk seriously. "Remember that."

Dinadin almost turned to go, but something off on the hillside made him pause. He stared out into the distance, shading his eyes with his hand. Something was moving, something colorful.

Trosk looked up, and every head around the circle followed. Somewhere behind them another soldier was shouting. A confused excitement galvanized the camp. All around, men were springing to their feet. Trosk stood beside Dinadin, snapping up the brim of his hat with a fingernail.

Warriors. Scores of them, thundering down the hillside in a blazing mass, their jiiktars held as high as the screech of their inhuman voices. They poured out of the trees, yelping and kicking up clods of brown earth as they hurried their horses onto the plain, their faces green and horrible, their hair billowing emerald.

"Colonel . . . ?" said the filthy lieutenant. He seemed lost. "What . . . What's happening?"

Trosk was speechless. His jaw had dropped open. Around them, the other horsemen had begun to move, scrambling onto their horses or searching frantically for misplaced weapons. Dinadin reached into his mind, trying to find a solid place to anchor himself. His horse. He had to get his horse. But Trosk wasn't moving. . . .

"Colonel?" he ventured. "What should we do?"

Before he could answer Blackwood Gayle burst out of his tent. He was more than ten yards away but Dinadin heard his booming voice as if the baron was standing next to him.

"Fires of heaven," exclaimed Gayle. "That's Kronin!"

Hurriedly the baron began shouting, ordering his men to find their mounts. He himself dashed for his own black charger, tossing himself onto its back. He scanned the camp, and when he saw the dumbstruck Trosk he swore.

"Trosk!" he bellowed madly. "On your horse, man! Protect the launchers!"

The order snapped Trosk out of his stupor. "The launchers," he muttered. He turned to Dinadin with all his old menace. "Ready to be a hero, Lotts?"

The furious sound of bloodthirsty men pounded in Lucyler's ears as his horse hurtled headlong down the hillside. A white heat welled up inside him. The Talistanians in the camp had seen them. Orders were being shouted. Men were clambering onto horseback. It was all wonderfully sloppy, and Lucyler bared his teeth as he joined in the chorus of his companions, screaming like an animal as he charged into battle. Beside him, Kronin was an avenging angel, a long-haired nightmare that sang and moved with a serpent's speed and a hurricane's implacable might.

Lucyler lowered his head and held his jiiktar close. The beast beneath him snorted as it stampeded down the hill, toward the little collection of war wagons and the still-dozing monsters tethered to them. The acid launchers atop the iron vehicles were flaccid. The great bellows didn't stir. Lucyler felt a rush of triumph. If the launchers weren't manned . . .

But someone had read their minds—the peculiar man with the hat. He was shouting and pointing at all the wagons. Lucyler cursed.

"Kronin!" he shouted over the din of hammering hooves. With the blade of his weapon he gestured toward the trio of wagons. Kronin glimpsed the man and frowned.

"Faster!" ordered the warlord. "Faster now!"

And they went faster, Lucyler and Kronin, speeding toward the center wagon as Hakan and the others broke rank and dashed toward the flanking vehicles. Behind them, still hidden in the trees, a score of archers awaited the outcome of their mission. Lucyler let his hand drop to the deerskin sack bouncing against his horse's side. Hakan and his men were similarly burdened. Even Kronin's horse was slowed by a bulging bag. And if they should split . . .

No, Lucyler corrected himself. The skins were strong enough. Their plan would work if they were quick.

They were on the plain now, the war wagons clearly in sight. Talistanian steel scraped out of scabbards. And then, as if a great, dark sun had risen in the center of the camp, Lucyler saw the maniacal figure of Blackwood Gayle atop his ebony horse, one gauntleted fist throttling the hilt of his sword. A long tail of braided hair trestled off his head, and a shining mask of silver glinted on his face, so that only one scarlet eye blinked with life. He was surrounded by mounted horsemen, defiantly calling out to the men of Tatterak even as they washed toward him.

The horsemen were organizing. It would be a battle then. But Lucyler was sure they would win. The Talistanians were outnumbered, and their protective fence of legionnaires was a mile away, still fighting in the forest with the rest of Voris' zealots. Without the infantry of Nar to bolster them, the horsemen were too few to stand against the indigo wave crashing toward them. They would *have* to retreat.

The wagon was only yards away now. The man with the hat seemed perplexed. He drew his saber and started off toward the wagons, calling after another man behind him. Lucyler grinned. They would never make it.

"Come!" urged the warlord as he prepared to leap from his saddle. Hakan and the other teams were close behind, while behind them hurried the wild fighting men of Tatterak. A greegan sleeping near its wagon opened a bleary eye at the commotion. Suddenly another of the beasts awoke, the one chained to the center wagon. It saw the oncoming army and howled in alarm, lumbering clumsily to its feet.

But Kronin was too close now. The warlord brought his horse to a skidding halt beside the monster and swung the blade of his jiiktar against the greegan's throat. The blow glanced off. Kronin screamed in rage, then stabbed at the beast with all his might, forcing the point of his blade through the thick skin. Amazingly, the blade snapped. There was a gush of dark blood and the creature bellowed, thrusting up its horn. Its front legs buckled and its huge head thrashed, and Kronin climbed off his mount, narrowly escaping the sweeping horn as he snatched the sack of oil from his horse. The horse whinnied and drew back, and as it reared the greegan's horn plunged into its belly.

Kronin staggered back, horrified. A fountain of blood splashed against his face. Lucyler reached him and brought his own horse to a halt. The warlord's mount gave an anguished cry as the greegan withdrew its horn, pulling with it a knotted mass of entrails. The horse fell twitching to the ground. The greegan whirled, blinded by the blood. Lucyler heard men shouting. He grabbed hold of Kronin's arm and pulled, directing him onto the roof of the war wagon, which pitched as the beast that pulled it thrashed.

"Go!" Lucyler called. Kronin lost his footing, slipped, then quickly righted himself, still balancing the skin full of flammable liquid. When he reached the roof he tore open the drawstring with his teeth and inverted the sack, pouring out the viscous contents and soaking the wagon.

"Now yours!" cried the warlord, reaching out for Lucyler's oil skin. He did the same as before, dousing the vehicle with its contents, careful to make sure the wooden parts of the wagon were well coated. The pitching of the greegan only helped slosh the oil about, and when he had nearly emptied the second sack he took the last of its contents and tossed them onto the animal itself. As the warlord worked, Lucyler hazarded a look behind them. There in the hills he could see the archers, peeking out from their verdant hiding spots with their bows held ready. A glowing brazier of coals sent up a reed of thin smoke.

"No more," Lucyler shouted. "The soldiers are coming. We have to go."

Kronin jumped from the top of the wagon as Lucyler hurried to his horse and tossed himself onto the beast's back. The man with the hat was coming toward them, waving his saber and cursing. The other man with him seemed in a daze. He had clamped a helmet over his face and followed the hatted man haphazardly, a good ten paces behind. Lucyler smiled to himself. They would never reach the wagon in time. He extended out a hand and helped the warlord climb onto the horse. Kronin had dropped his broken jiiktar and was staring in disgust as the wounded greegan trampled it into the bloodied dirt, splintering it.

"The others are done," said Lucyler, watching Hakan and his fellows race away from the camp. Lucyler jerked the reins and spun his horse toward the hill. All they needed now was a signal.

As they began their escape, Kronin cupped his hands around his mouth and let out an ear-splitting shriek. Up in the hills the archers dipped their arrow tips into the burning brazier. Lucyler let out a giddy laugh. They would get Kronin another mount, then they would join the others on the battlefield. They would find Blackwood Gayle and they would gut him. He laughed louder, and saw the archers tip their flaming arrows skyward.

And then he saw something else, another bright object twinkling in the corner of his eye. He turned his head. It was a young man, hardly more than a boy, garbed in the uniform of a Talistanian horseman. But he wasn't on a horse. He had fallen to one knee and was staring at them, a huge, metallic nozzle balanced precariously on his shoulder. The nozzle smoked and sparked, as if ready to explode. Beside the man was a cannister with a spiderweb of lines running to the metal nozzle.

Lucyler cursed. Up in the hills the archers drew back on their bowstrings. The man with the flame cannon trembled as he heard the thunder of approaching warriors. He pulled the trigger.

There was a roaring blast. The world turned orange.

Trosk watched the arrows climbing skyward. The buzz in his brain had settled to a low hum, but he still didn't know what the hell was happening. Gayle was behind him, shouting incomprehensibly, and the idiot Lotts was bumbling after him, talking to himself. The colonel followed the arrows through the sky, unsure what to do. He was near the war wagon and knew the giant vehicles were the targets of the incoming arrows. The Triin scum had covered the wagons with something, no doubt explosive.

"Lotts!" he cried over his shoulder. "Hurry up, you fool. We have to get the wagons to safety."

The big Aramoorian clamored forward, stopping yards away from the wounded greegan. Trosk held up his hands to the animal.

"Easy, you big idiot. I just want you to move."

If the creature heard him it did not obey. It merely wailed in pain, pulverizing the dead body of the horse as it thrashed about. Trosk stole a glance toward the sky. Mere moments remained.

"Move, damn you!" he shouted, then backed quickly away from the targeted animal. Dinadin arrived next to him just as the shower of flaming arrows came down. The wagon erupted in flame, its huge bellows expanding in an instant. The licking flames caught the rump of the greegan and ignited the oil smeared across its back. The greegan wailed and lunged forward. Trosk yelled and stumbled. Blackness filled his vision as the greegan rumbled forward, then collapsed, its two front legs crumbling beneath its gargantuan weight. Trosk twisted, trying to jump clear of the falling beast. His face and chest hit the ground and he clawed madly at the dirt, cursing. He saw a shadow dropping over him, saw Lotts' horrified face, then more blackness and a pain so indescribable he thought his lungs would burst.

The greegan had fallen. It lay across his crushed legs, slobbering blood and dragging itself over him, grinding him into the ground and shattering his bones.

"Lotts!" he screamed. Blood filled his mouth, gushing up from his insides. "Lotts, help me!"

The Aramoorian didn't move. He merely stood there, his face hidden behind the grotesque demon mask, and watched as Trosk reached out for him. Trosk felt an icy panic seize him. He couldn't move.

"Lotts, you idiot, help me! My legs are caught. Help me, goddamn it!"

And still Lotts didn't stir. Trosk twisted his neck and saw the wagon immersed in smoky fire. The greegan had stopped moving. But now the bellows of the acid launcher were moving, blowing up like an enormous balloon.

"Lotts, please!" Trosk cried. Hysterical tears were running down his face. The bellows made a weird, unhealthy screech. "Please!" he screamed again. "Lotts, I'll give you anything! Anything!"

The Aramoorian took a small step forward. Trosk's heart leapt with hope.

"Do you remember the girl?" came the inhuman voice beneath the helmet. "There's only one thing I want, Colonel. And I'm getting it right now."

Then, without another word, Lotts turned and walked away. Trosk twisted again and saw the groaning bellows through the flames, stretched to an impossible size. A trickle of yellow steam rose from a pinprick in its surface. The hole widened with a shudder, vomiting up a cloud of corrosive vapor.

It was the last thing Trosk saw before his eyeballs burst.

The first thing Lucyler saw when he opened his eyes was the sky. There was an insistent pounding in his temples, and the sky was bright, burning his skin with its heat. His face hurt. His arms hurt, too. Men were calling after him. He heard his name as if from a great distance. And he heard Kronin's name.

Kronin. Where was he?

Lucyler struggled onto his side. There was a figure in the grass next to him, its limbs unnaturally twisted. Lucyler put his hand to his face, remembering the concussive blast that had knocked him from his horse. His face ached. The sleeve of his blue jacket hung from his left side in tatters, and the white skin beneath had been singed a ruddy red. The pain was unspeakable. Lucyler crawled to where the figure lay, dragging himself with his good arm. He pushed away the tall grass and saw Kronin sprawled facedown in the dirt. The warlord's hair was almost gone, burned away from his scalp. There was a giant tear along his back, a rent that had ripped through his clothing and devoured his flesh so that the bony facets of his spine protruded. Kronin wasn't moving, not even to draw the slightest breath.

"Oh, no, no," Lucyler moaned, slumped over the warlord's corpse. Hakan and another warrior rode up. There was a long, grief-stricken silence before the herald spoke.

"Kronin is killed!" he said incredulously. "He is killed. . . ."

Around them horses thundered past as the men of Tatterak rode toward their enemies, but Lucyler didn't lift his head. He stayed draped over the dead warlord, feeling the warmness of Kronin's bloodied back on his chest and letting the steaming fluid drench his clothes. He was sobbing, and he didn't know why. Was Kronin so great a friend? Barely able to straighten, Lucyler lifted himself off the inert body. Hakan was staring at him sorrowfully.

"We will avenge him," seethed Lucyler. "We will fight these men and we will push them into the swamps. And we will drown them there."

"Come off me, you little bastard," spat Richius as he worked the tip of his dagger under the mouth of the leech. It was the last one, or so he hoped. Somehow he had missed it. The swamps, Voris had neglected to tell him, were full of the slimy parasites, and he had spent the last few hours impatiently working them off his flesh with his blade. Except for this one. This one had eluded him, climbing up his pants leg and onto his back. He hadn't felt it until a moment ago.

They had crossed the thickest parts of the swamps, waist deep in muck until they each found a perch to support their weight. And when they had climbed up into their hideouts the sickening work of removing the parasites had begun. It was a filthy, exacting surgery, one that Richius hurried through as best he could, and the numerous cuts on his legs betrayed his sloppiness. But he had gotten almost all of them.

He bit his lip as he twisted his body, balancing carefully on the branch with one arm as he put the other behind his back and worked with one hand to dislodge the parasite. He felt the length of its slimy body for its mouth, maneuvered the blade under it, and flicked it, digging out a piece of his own flesh in the process.

"Son of a . . ."

But the leech was off. He pinched it between his fingers and squeezed until it popped, then dropped it into the water below. Beside him he heard Voris laugh. The warlord, who was roosted in a nearby tree, had been watching his antics with amusement. Richius sheathed his dagger and smiled ruefully at Voris.

"Thanks for telling me about the leeches," he mumbled as he buttoned up his shirt. Jessicane hung from another branch an arm's length away, dangling safely within reach in its soiled scabbard. It was almost dusk. A weird calm had settled over the moors. Richius could scarcely hear the faint conversations of the Triin hidden in the treetops around him. The heat of the day had broken, but the rotten smell of the swamps was a constant plague. Yellow fumes floated over the waters, croaking up from bubbling pools, and the throaty songs of frogs droned endlessly through the trees. In the distance the distressed cry of a waterbird rang out as something pulled it beneath the waters. The air was thick, rank with humidity, and Richius' drenched clothing hung from him like rags. His scalp and face itched from a thousand mosquito bites. He wanted to go home.

Wherever that was.

To Dyana. To Shani. Wherever they were, he wanted to be. Anywhere he could be a man again, instead of a tree-climbing predator. He wasn't a jackal anymore. He had become a jaguar, waiting for its meal to pass beneath him so he could spring and break its neck. Were jaguars maneaters, he wondered?

A sound echoed through the moors. A warrior splashed toward them. He was shouting, pointing behind him. Richius froze. There was no doubt what the signal meant. He glanced over toward Voris.

"Are they coming?"

Voris gave a disquieting nod, then drifted backward into the branches and silently disappeared.

Dinadin urged his horse through the muck, forcing the steed deeper into the swamps. His armor had become an oven. Ahead of him, barely visible through a slick of perspiration, Gayle led the procession of horsemen into the darkness. The baron was cursing, screaming at them to hurry. Behind them they could hear Kronin's warriors closing in. They had battled the raging Triin until they could stand no more. That's when Gayle had called retreat. But the baron had led them into something far worse.

"Go on, damn you!" Dinadin shouted at his horse. The beast snorted and plowed on, already knee deep in green ooze and sinking fast. Black leeches swarmed over its legs and underbelly. Dinadin kicked his heels into the horse's side. He didn't want to die here. . . .

Behind him he heard branches snapping. The warriors were closer now. They were on foot. It had all been a trap and they had followed Gayle into it. Dinadin cursed himself, cursed Gayle and Trosk, too. He pulled out his sword again and craned his neck to see behind him. The water was moving, the trees starting to waver. They were coming.

"All right, you gogs," Dinadin snarled. "No more running!"

He had no sooner drawn his sword than he heard a scream in front of him. He whirled around and saw a giant red creature drop from the trees onto the horseman he'd been following. Soon another fell and then another, toppling the Talistanians off their mounts into the stinking waters. Dinadin panicked. He looked up into the trees just as one of the redrobed men fell on him. There was a blackness and a wind-knocking jolt. Dinadin felt the reins slip from his grip. He tried to shout but something thick and warm ran into his mouth, choking him.

He was under water.

In a raging panic he twisted, knocking the man off him and bursting out from beneath the swamp. His sword was gone. The red man was charging toward him.

"No!" he cried, pulling off his helmet and swinging it wildly. The helmet collided with the Drol's head and sent him careening backward. Dinadin tried to run but was waist deep in viscous filth. It sucked at him, drawing him down even as he fought to move forward. Breath was coming now only in gasps. Panic seized him. Weaponless, he pushed himself through the melee. Drol warriors still dropped from the trees. The horsemen were screaming, swinging blindly at the red phantoms. And there was Gayle, off his horse and on his belly in the water, skulking through the carnage and darkness so that only his silver mask could be seen.

"Gayle!" Dinadin cried. "I see you, you bastard. I see you!"

He hurried toward the escaping baron, forgetting the Drol falling all around him and the warriors of Tatterak on his heels. He would die here, he was sure of it, but there was one more score to settle before that happened.

"Coward!" he shouted. "Come back!"

But Gayle had a healthy lead. Dinadin lunged after him, lumbering from side to side, brushing away watery scum with his hands. He could catch him, catch him and kill him. . . .

Another red shape fell from the skies, clipping Dinadin's shoulder. He spun, slipping and dropping to his knees. Foul water flowed into his mouth. He tried to right himself, get back onto his feet, but this Drol was huge. He caught hold of Dinadin's neck and dragged him backward into the water. Beneath the foam everything was a blurry green. Dinadin twisted his eyes skyward to see the struggling ribbons of sunlight and the bubbles of his own breath breaking the surface.

The fighting lasted barely an hour.

When it was over, Richius collapsed against the trunk of a tree and sank to his knees. Bloodied water ran around his shoulders. He was covered with leeches again. So were the bodies that floated facedown about him. Across the swamp he saw Voris cradling a warrior in his arms, carrying him to a muddy bank. He saw the exhausted men of Tatterak falling into the supporting arms of the Drol. Dusk had fallen, bringing with it a peculiar heat, and the stink of decay and rotting flesh. Next to Richius a water snake was feeding on the open wound of a Talistanian corpse. A giant insect crawled into the frozen mouth of a severed Triin head. Men splashed by, made mute by the carnage and their own unspeakable exhaustion, and the cheerless victors set about the grim task of pulling out their dead.

Richius could hardly move. The acid wounds on his back were screaming. A Talistanian sword had nicked his forehead, and a trickle of blood ran down his face. The insatiable mouths of a hundred leeches sucked greedily at his flesh. He swayed, almost falling face-first into the mire, then righted himself and emptied his stomach into the water next to him. He would have collapsed again if not for the sound of a familiar voice.

"Richius!" came the call from across the swamp. Richius managed to raise his head just enough to see Lucyler coming toward him. The Triin's face was scarred with soot, and his garments hung from him in tatters. A scarlet bloom of broken blood vessels ran the length of his arm and shoulder, and he moved with the uncertainty of a drunkard, panting as he trudged through the ooze.

"Lucyler," Richius gasped, going to meet his comrade. They met on a swale, knee deep in filth, and Richius fell into Lucyler's arms, all the strength drained away from him.

"We did it," said Lucyler. "Richius, we did it! They are beaten."

"Beaten," echoed Richius. He could hardly speak, but the power of the words bolstered him. "God, I can't believe it."

"Believe it, my friend," said Lucyler. "But you are wounded. We have to get you out of here."

"No," said Richius, pulling away from his friend's embrace. "I must see Kronin, him and Voris together. Where is he, Lucyler?"

Lucyler's expression paled. Richius closed his eyes.

"Oh, no," he moaned. "Dead?"

"Back on the plain. Flame cannon."

Richius reached out for Lucyler's damaged arm, almost touching the wound but stopping short. "Is that what happened to you?"

"We were both on my horse. I did not see the cannon until too late. I am sorry, Richius. But you should know he did this for you. He told me so."

"Voris is the one who should know," said Richius. "I want him to know Kronin died saving him, too."

Lucyler smiled grimly. "Time enough for that later. Now we have to get you out of this swamp."

"I can't leave yet, Lucyler. I need to find Gayle. Is he dead? Have you seen him?"

Lucyler looked around at the ghastly collection of bodies. "I do not know," he said. "I do not remember seeing him at all, not after coming to the moors."

Richius clenched his fist. "Don't tell me that, Lucyler. He has to be here. He has to. . . ."

"If he is, we will find him," Lucyler assured him. "He could not have escaped us. But the leeches . . ."

"Forget the leeches," Richius snapped. "I want to find Gayle!"

He started off through the maze of bodies, prodding at every Talistanian corpse with the tip of his sword. The bodies rolled over effortlessly, regarding him with their dead eyes. Those that still wore helmets had them unceremoniously removed, as one by one Richius tossed the demon helms angrily over his shoulder.

"Richius, calm down," chided Lucyler. "He wore no helmet. Just his mask."

"He's not here, Lucyler," Richius growled. "Damn it all, he's not here!"

But there were more cadavers to inspect, scores of them. Richius left Lucyler behind, trudging back out to the deeper water. There was a large body there, large enough to be Gayle, half-hidden under a web of mossy reeds. Richius splashed toward it, ignoring Lucyler. He was consumed with the idea of Gayle's escape. When he reached the body in the reeds he grabbed hold of its booted ankles and pulled, dragging it toward him.

"Gayle, you whoreson," he roared. "Tell me it's you!"

But it wasn't Blackwood Gayle. Rather it was a younger man—a boy really—with hair turned brown by the swamp's filth and skin stippled with insect bites. A great crack had been dealt to the armor around his belly, exposing his swollen innards to the wet poisons of the swamps. The man groaned as Richius yanked at him, opening his eyes to stare at Richius with a delirious gaze. There was only the barest hint of life left in that stare, and a weird, speechless recognition. Richius let go of the ankles.

"Sweet almighty," he whispered. He staggered back, clutching his own belly in sympathy and horror. "Lucyler!" he called. "Lucyler, come quick. It's Dinadin!"

Dinadin blinked, and a peculiar smile appeared on his face.

"Richius?"

It was nightmarish. Dinadin was barely alive, his skin like ashes, his belly torn open and spilling blood. Richius hurried over to his comrade, dropping Jessicane down next to him. He forced his hand onto the wound, pushing back the distended innards. He put his arm under Dinadin's head and cradled it, forcing himself to look again into the insane gaze.

"It's me, Dinadin," Richius stammered. "It's me. I'm here." He turned and called again, "Lucyler, get the hell over here!"

Lucyler was hurrying toward them. Dinadin's smiled widened.

"Lucyler's here, too?" he asked weakly. "Lucyler's dead. . . ."

"No, Dinadin. He's alive. We're all alive. The three of us together."

"Like old times . . ."

"Hang on, Dinadin. Please. Just hang on. I'm going to get you out of here."

"We're in Dring. . . ."

"Yes," said Richius, pushing gently on Dinadin's stomach. His friend was babbling, talking nonsense, and all he could think to do was agree and try to calm him. Lucyler hurried up to them, panting, and looked at Dinadin, his gray eyes widening in shock.

"Gods," Lucyler gasped. "What happened?"

Dinadin flashed his crooked grin. "You're alive," he croaked. "Lucyler . . ."

"He's delirious," explained Richius hastily. "We have to get him out of here. Fast. Help me with him."

Lucyler looked at Dinadin's wound and blanched. "Richius," he said gently. "There is no way—"

"Help me with him, goddamn it! He'll die in this hole if we don't get him out of here."

"Richius, he is dead already. Lord, just look at him!"

"Oh God, Lucyler," Richius moaned. "Just help me with him. Please." He tried to lift up the swaying head but Dinadin hardly budged.

"I'll get Voris," said Lucyler. "He's strong enough to lift him."

While Lucyler darted off into the swamps, Richius stayed with Dinadin, cradling his head and trying to keep his insides from gushing out. Dinadin's expression broke as he glimpsed Lucyler leaving.

"Where. . . ?" he gasped. "Lucyler?"

"He's going for a horse to get you out of here," said Richius easily. "Don't worry, Dinadin. Just hang on, all right? We're going to get you someplace safe."

"Am I sick?"

The question was so ludicrous that Richius didn't know how to answer. "You're going to be all right," he said desperately. He tried to keep the tremor out of his voice, but Dinadin seemed oblivious to it anyway. There was a distant glaze to his eyes, as if he were lost in a dark room and couldn't find his way out. And each time his heart pumped his insides quivered, reminding Richius just how tenuous a grasp Dinadin had on life. He had to get Dinadin out. Now.

"Voris!" he called over his shoulder. He saw the warlord's head twist toward him. "Voris, help!"

The warlord crashed through the water, hurrying to Richius. Dinadin stiffened.

"Voris?" he hissed.

"Easy," crooned Richius. "We're gonna get you out of here. Someplace safe."

Voris arrived, gasping for breath. He looked down at Richius and the wounded Dinadin and shot them a confused look.

"Kalak?"

"Not me," said Richius quickly. He pointed his chin toward Dinadin. "Him. We have to get him out of here. I need your help. He's heavy. Too big for me. Too big."

The warlord seemed to understand. He bent closer and looked at Dinadin's wounds, then glanced back at Richius and somberly shook his head.

"It's bad, I know," Richius said. "But we have to try. You'll help me, yes? Help me?"

Voris grunted and started to reach out for Dinadin, but Richius stopped him.

"No," he said, putting up his hands. "We need a horse. A horse. Lucyler's getting one. We'll wait. Wait for Lucyler."

Richius was talking so quickly he was sure Voris couldn't understand a word. But the warlord backed away, dutifully waiting while Richius kept the pressure on Dinadin's wound, crooning to his friend in a gentle whisper. Dinadin's breathing quickened. He stared at Voris, shivering and perplexed.

"Voris," he mumbled darkly. "Voris . . ."

"Quiet, Dinadin. Don't try to talk. Just take it easy. You'll be out of here real soon. And we're going to take you somewhere safe. Safe, all right? Just hang on."

Richius heard a commotion behind him and turned to see Lucyler leading a leech-laden horse through the waters, pulling it forward with his good arm. The horse brayed wildly but Lucyler held the reins tight, dragging the animal closer. It was one of Talistan's huge beasts, the type that followed orders only when given with a crop in hand. The horse reared and flailed its hooves, making Lucyler put up both arms to defend himself.

"Richius," called the Triin. "Help me with this monster!"

The horse broke free and Richius cursed. He gently lowered Dinadin's head into the reeds and splashed toward Lucyler, who was already chasing the thrashing animal. The Triin leapt for the reins and caught them, yanking on the bridle. When Richius finally reached him, the horse had settled into an obstinate stance.

"The damn thing will not move!" swore Lucyler. He was hunched over, wincing and favoring his wounded arm.

"He's afraid," said Richius. "Stop yelling and give me the reins."

Lucyler passed him the reins, then stopped in mid-motion, his eyes wide. Richius whirled to see Voris standing in the water, watching them as they struggled with the horse. Behind him was Dinadin—on his feet. Dinadin was stumbling toward the warlord, the grimy broadsword Jessicane raised above his head. The shadow of the weapon fell across Voris' shoulder. It was moving before Richius could scream.

"NO!"

The blade came down. Voris' expression lit with shock. A fountain of blood spurted from his shoulder, a huge gash opening at the base of his

JOHN MARCO

neck. Dinadin fell forward, toppling himself and Voris into the water. Richius and Lucyler leapt toward them, forgetting the horse as they half-ran, half-swam after the submerged men.

"Voris!" Richius cried. He had taken hold of Dinadin and was pulling him off the buried warlord. Lucyler reached into the water and pulled Voris free. The warlord was jetting water from his mouth and blood from the rip in his neck. Voris choked and struggled to breathe, putting his hands to his neck as he shook uncontrollably in Lucyler's grasp. Dinadin hardly moved. Richius laid him aside and went to Voris.

"Voris," he said desperately. "Can you hear me? It's me, Kalak."

Voris opened his eyes and looked at Richius. "Kalak?"

"I'm here," said Richius. Lucyler had Voris' head in his lap and was holding the flaps of skin closed with his hand. But the blood was pumping through the Triin's fingers. Each heartbeat sent a new plume of it spraying forth. Voris' expression was dimming fast.

"Kafife, Kalak," he said breathlessly. "Kafife. Kafife . . ."

"What?" said Richius. "I don't understand. What are you saying?"

And then Voris was gone. His eyes simply closed and he fell limp in Lucyler's grasp. Richius began to shake.

"Oh, God, Dinadin," he moaned. "What have you done?"

Behind him he heard Dinadin's hysterical laughter. "I did it, Richius," he said. He retched up a ball of blood. "I killed the Wolf. We're safe now. We can go home. . . ."

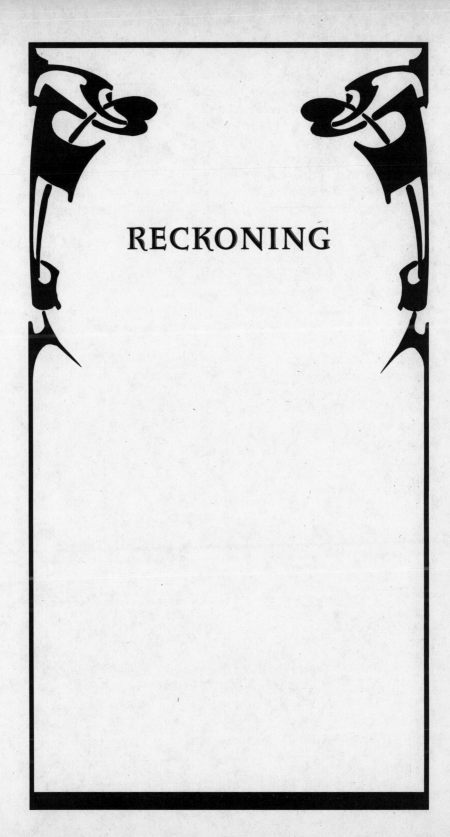

RECKONING

From the Journal of Richius Vantran:

We found Dinadin's horse with the other Talistanian beasts. There was a note in his saddlebag to his father. I couldn't bear to read it, so Lucyler read it for me. If only I had known the misery my poor friend was in, I would have done something, somehow. But he is gone now and all I can do is cherish his note and hope that one day I can return it to his father, and explain my terrible treachery. I know the note could never have been delivered any other way. Even Dinadin knew that. It speaks of Gayle in the worst of terms. Dinadin begged his father to help him, then tucked the note in his saddlebag, never to be seen.

But I've seen it, my friend. I will not forget you. At least you saw Lucyler before you died.

The statue we found with the note is a sad thing, the last remnant of the girl Dinadin tried to save. It was so like him to hold on to baubles. And what a horror it must have been for him, not to be able to rescue her. His note screams with grief. I'm keeping the statue in my chamber now, and that's where it will stay until I leave here. I have nothing else to remember Dinadin by. The horses we will keep for our own. There are just a few of us now, but even fewer horses. We will need them if Nar should come again.

I have not told Najjir how Voris died. She would never have let me bury Dinadin so close if she knew. Even Dyana doesn't know the truth of things, and I have no plans to tell her. She barely remembered Dinadin, even after I explained how she had met him so long ago in Ackle-Nye. How unjust her lack of memory seems to me. Now he is a mystery to

Dyana and Najjir both, just a lump of freshly turned earth out in the gar-den. Soon the lichens will grow over him and only his grave will remain, hidden. They will forget about him here in Lucel-Lor, but somewhere back in old Aramoor his father will wonder why he hasn't returned. He will petition the Gayles for an answer, and they will shrug like black-hearted idiots and say that Dinadin was only one of many who died here.

Like Voris. And Kronin. And maybe Tharn. But not me, and not Gayle. We still live, though God won't tell me why. If I am charmed then it is a damnable magic, for I know I should be dead like the others, and if justice exists at all Gayle would be lying dead beside me with my fingers around his throat. He is a sorcerer, that one. Each time death comes for him he talks his way free. I don't know how he managed to slip us, but we tore that swamp apart looking for him, and he's too big for a snake to swallow. He cheats death as well as I do.

For me, others take the arrows. It will be hard to live here without Voris. I see the bitterness and blame in Najjir's eyes. If it wasn't for you, her eyes say, my husband would still be alive. My children would not be fatherless. I wish you had never come. And what can I say to her? Voris told me to look after them. That's what he meant when he died. Kafife. Family. Lucyler had to explain it to me. Maybe it's because Jarra wasn't around, or maybe he simply trusted me in those final moments, but he has left me with a great burden. I know almost nothing of this valley, yet I am its protector now. If it is the honor Lucyler claims I will do my best, but I will make no promises. Najjir still hates me, and there are only a handful of warriors left. This is not the kingdom I was born to rule.

And Lucyler won't be here to help me. He has left on fool's errand to find Tharn. Kronin's men have left, too, to deliver the awful news of Kronin's death. If they are lucky they will find Tatterak at peace. We have all taken a great toll, and if there is any more fighting to be done the other warlords will have to do it. Dring has been almost emptied of fighting men, and without Kronin to lead them the warriors of Tatterak may soon lose heart.

We need Tharn. Our good fortune is temporary at best. Dring is safe, but for how long I do not know. The time to strike the Run is now, but we haven't the warriors or leaders to accomplish it. Soon fresh troops will be pouring through the mountains, marching out of Ackle-Nye again. I thought we might have victory, but without Tharn all our fighting has been for nothing. This nation bleeds for him. It is a body without a soul, inadequate to the task. He has left on his foolish errand and been killed, leaving us all like orphaned children. I would never tell Dyana how I feel, but I think she already knows my mind. If Tharn still lived he would have told us so by now. He would have sent an apparition to warn us, or some other weird demon. We are alone, as fractured without him as in the days of the revolution.

So I have only the bleak companionship of my thoughts and this bottle of sour wine that Jarra has found. There are privileges in being the lord of this castle, I suppose, but I would willingly trade the warmth of this drink for Dyana's touch. If only I could share her faith. I want to believe, as she does, but Tharn was so frail when he left. Even if he did make it to Chandakkar, the lion riders or the trip back certainly killed him. I mourn for him. More, I mourn for the mystery of his death. I need proof of his end to convince Dyana. Without that we may forever be apart, and I will rot in this castle till I die or more Narens come to kill me.

May I admit something terrible? I am not the man I was. This war has devoured me. I burn for Dyana. She taunts me with words of love, shows me my child, makes me adore them both then keeps me away from them. And I am starting to hate her for it. I hate her strength, for I do not have any of my own left. I hate her fidelity to Tharn. Like a loyal dog she waits at the door for a dead master. And I'm still jealous of that twisted holy man, who even in death keeps Dyana away from me. Heaven burn me, I am so alone.

FORTY-SEVEN

The knock came as Richius penned the last word in his journal. It was late, past the hour of cordial visitors, and the sudden rapping startled him, making him nearly tip the bottle of wine on his desk. He pushed the bottle aside and groaned. He was drunk, too drunk to hold a proper conversation. The knocking came again, more insistent. Richius drew an unsteady breath.

"It's late," he mumbled. "Who is it?"

"Richius? It is me, Dyana."

Richius straightened. He rose quickly and started for the door, then saw his grizzled reflection in the mirror, with his overgrown beard and disheveled hair. And of course there was his breath. Anxiously he smoothed down his tousled hair and went to the door.

"Dyana?"

She greeted him with a thin smile. She was not dressed for sleep as would have been customary, but instead wore a dress still stained from laboring in the kitchen. Najjir was with her, her eyes cast solemnly down. Unlike Dyana, she wore a soft shift of jade silk, belted lightly around her waist with a sash embroidered with flowers.

"What's this?" asked Richius.

"May we come in?" asked Dyana. "I will explain it to you."

Richius stepped aside and gestured them into the room. Najjir kept her eyes focused on her slippers. Dyana's expression was despairing. She looked at the bottle on the desk beside the open journal, then back to Richius.

"You are busy?" she asked.

"I'm getting ready for sleep," said Richius. "It's very late, Dyana. Is something wrong?"

Dyana grimaced. He could tell she was getting ready to lie.

"No," she answered. "I only wanted to bring Najjir to you."

"Why?"

Dyana shifted uneasily. "I was hoping Lucyler had explained this to you," she said. "Did he?"

"Did he what?"

"Tell you about your lordship?"

Richius felt his patience boiling away. "Dyana, what the hell is going on here? Why have you brought Najjir to me?"

"Because she is yours now," said Dyana stiffly. Her words seemed to be coming with great effort. "You are lord of this castle at Voris' bequest. He asked you to take care of his family."

"So?"

"So his family is yours now, to do with what you wish. Are you understanding me, Richius?"

Richius was mortified as the idea slowly came clear. "What are you saying? That Najjir is my wife now?"

"Not your wife," Dyana corrected. "Your property. As is this castle and everyone who serves it. The warriors, the daughters of Voris, everyone. They have been passed to you. You know this already." Dyana was near tears, but she held her head high as she continued. "Did Lucyler tell you none of this?"

"He told me that I was to look after Voris' family."

"And what did you think that meant?"

"I don't know," said Richius. "I'm not a Triin, remember?"

Dyana remained calm. "It means you are lord here. Master of the valley."

"No," said Richius. "I've not accepted the charge. It was an accident of Voris' death, Dyana, that's all."

"Richius, you do not understand. He passed his family on to you. That makes you warlord."

"But I don't want to be warlord!" cried Richius. "Don't you understand? I'll look after them if I can, for as long as I can, but I'm no Triin." He looked at Najjir, who still did not look up but kept her head dutifully bowed. "I can't have her, Dyana. Lord, it's immoral."

"It is the way of things here," said Dyana. "It cannot be changed."

"Oh, like hell. Najjir hates me. I know it and so do you. How could you bring her here like this?"

Dyana's face was carefully blank. "I do this only for her sake. She is Drol. You must understand what that means."

Richius took her hand and squeezed. "But I don't understand. Why should she do this to herself? I don't desire her. I desire you."

"Drol, Richius. They have customs. She is without a husband now, without a lord to serve. You must be that lord. Najjir cannot live without a master. She would be as nothing without one, like dust."

"Dyana . . ."

"Hear me," said Dyana gently. "Take her or do not take her. But do not discard her. It would be her death. She has nothing else, Richius."

"No." Richius took Dyana by the shoulders. "I have a family already. You and Shani, you're my family."

"I know," said Dyana. "But I am still Tharn's wife. . . ."

"He's dead, Dyana. He's not a threat to anyone anymore, not even our enemies."

"Richius, you have been drinking," said Dyana, her voice shaking. She tried to smile at him. "Let go of me. Please."

And he did. Richius went to his desk and collapsed in his chair, burying his head in his hands. After a moment he felt Dyana's touch on his shoulder.

"Will you do this for me? It is not like you think. This is not a gift. Najjir needs you. If other men in the valley hear that you have discarded her they will come and claim her for their own. She will be forced to leave the castle. It must be you, Richius."

He could not answer. Dyana pressed a hand to his shoulder, her touch burning as keenly as the acid of the war labs.

"Richius?" she ventured. "Please do not send her away. Ignore her if you wish, but do not put her aside. You must see what it is like to be a Drol woman. She needs you."

"Yes, yes," Richius roared. "She needs me. Tharn needs me. Voris needs me. All right then, I'm here. Your bloody gods have made a slave of me. So go, leave me to this new duty. I'll let you know tomorrow how well I perform."

"Richius . . ."

"Go!"

A long moment passed. Deliberately he peeled his hands from his face. Dyana was gone, and Najjir, who had taken on the color of an icicle, was waiting for him. He leaned back in his chair and regarded her. She was surprisingly lovely. A decade older than him at least, but with features not unlike Dyana. Even in her prosaic fear she was artistic, like one of those broken statues in the yard, a neglected masterpiece. He could imagine her as a queen, or a portrait hanging in Arkus' gallery. Vulnerable. Dutiful. Beautiful.

"I'm drunk," he said sluggishly.

Najjir merely nodded as if his words were meaningful.

"You don't understand a thing I said, do you?" he asked. "You don't even know why you're here. Maybe because one of your nasty gods took away your husband and gave you this filthy barbarian instead." He laughed, and the sound of it startled him. "Can I tell you something? You're right. I am a barbarian. A beast. That's what happens to a man when everything is taken from him."

He rose slowly and stared at her. "Are you afraid of me?" he asked. "You needn't be." He inched closer. "I wasn't always a beast, Najjir. I used to be a king. Can you believe that? I was civilized once."

His voice had taken on volume. Najjir closed her eyes. He closed the gap between them. "I came from a country where men didn't take women as slaves. I had a wife that I respected but I let her die."

Then Najjir simply crumbled. She could not look at him, or bear to have him look at her. She sank down on the floor and began to sob, rocking as she mumbled and crossed her hands over her shoulders.

"Voris," she moaned. "Voris . . ."

Richius staggered away from the broken woman, backing into his desk. The wine bottle tipped and rolled onto the floor. Najjir's cries jangled in his ears. He looked at her, unable to console her, and simply let her grieve.

In a corner of Ackle-Nye, in a ramshackle tavern with its roof partially collapsed, Baron Blackwood Gayle of Talistan sat staring at his atrocious reflection in a goblet of wine. He was on his sixth glass, and thoroughly enjoying the dull intoxication. It was a hot night. The humidity pricked the tender skin beneath his silver mask, causing an ungodly itch, and because he was alone he slid a slender fingernail under the precious metal to scratch.

Alone. There was a time when he relished solitude, but recently there had been too much of it. All his horsemen were dead, killed by that Aramoorian devil, and the only company he had now were the accusing stares of the legionnaires. He heard what they were calling him, the whispered slurs exchanged when he passed. Gayle the coward. Gayle the fool, who couldn't capture Vantran even with an army. He had ridden back to Ackle-Nye without his vaunted horsemen, and the Naren garrison in the city were understandably suspicious—too suspicious to believe his tale. He should have died with his men. That's what a real commander would do. Even Cassis, the puppet commanding the garrison, had dared to look cross-eyed at him.

"Piss on you, Cassis," he mumbled. A pair of legionnaires seated across the room turned to stare at him, then abruptly looked away. Gayle thought to rise, then stopped himself. There was nothing he could do but

endure their mirth. He was a baron of Talistan, but that title was meaningless now. When word of his failure reached Nar, they would oil the
gallows for him.

And that was the hell of it. He really had *tried*. He had slipped the
noose around Vantran's neck, yet somehow the Jackal had outwitted
him. And everybody knew it. There were even some who were calling
Vantran a genius, a military mastermind. He had routed the legionnaires
in Tatterak, destroyed the horsemen in the Dring Valley, even managed to
work some charm on the seafaring devils of Liss. He had become a sorcerer like his new master Tharn. Some said he was unbeatable.

But Blackwood Gayle knew better. Every man could be defeated, especially a pup like Vantran. The Jackal had been lucky, but luck invariably
ran short. And when it did, Gayle planned to be there waiting. Furiously
he scribbled down notes on his map of the Dring Valley. All he needed
was a chance, and enough men to follow him. If Vantran was still holed
up in that dismal castle, then he was vulnerable. The Drol of the valley
might have beaten back his horsemen, but they had paid a terrible price.
They were too few to protect Vantran against another assault. All he had
to do was sneak back in.

Somehow.

"Do you think you've seen the last of me?" he rumbled. Again the soldiers glanced at him. Gayle raised his head. "What the hell are you staring at?" He got to his feet and put his hand on his sword pommel. "I'm
not so drunk I can't grind both of you into pulp. And if you think I'm jok-
ing, why not find out? Because I would love it!"

The legionnaires put down their drinks, got up very slowly, then turned
and left the tavern. Gayle gave a hoarse laugh.

"Yes, yes," he called after them. "Who's the coward now, eh? You're
too good to sit with me but not good enough to fight me? Get out of here,
you craven bastards! Go back and lick Cassis' boots!"

He dropped back into his chair and laughed, pouring himself another
glass of wine. It was good to know he could still intimidate. At least he
had that. In the morning he would write to his father, asking him to send
more troops. He hated to grovel but there wasn't a choice. He had already failed Nar, and would probably hang for it. But before he did there
was a vendetta to settle. For that he needed troops.

Since returning to Ackle-Nye his command over the legionnaires had
evaporated. General Cassis had begun questioning his every order. Now
every member of the garrison was waiting for word from Nar, like dogs
waiting for their owner's whistle.

The door to the tavern hung open on its creaking hinge. Blackwood
Gayle felt the lazy hand of sleepiness graze him. He was very tired, but
sleep had eluded him lately, so he decided to remain in the tavern, at least
until he finished his current bottle. Without realizing it, he lowered his

head to the table, setting it down on the wet ink of the map. Within a few moments his eyes closed, dragging him off to sleep.

But soon he awoke out of an unpleasant dream. Someone was standing over him, prodding his shoulder with a gloved finger. Alarmed, Gayle bolted upright.

"What . . . ?" he sputtered, staring into a helmeted face. A shining metal skull looked back at him. Gayle's insides seized.

"Baron Blackwood Gayle of Talistan?" came the voice behind the helm.

"I am he."

The Shadow Angel reached into a pouch at his gilded belt and pulled out a small piece of paper. Handing it to Gayle he said, "I am a messenger from Count Renato Biagio."

Gayle fought to steady his hands. Though his eyes were blurry from sleep, he could see Biagio's wax seal on the letter, the crest of his island home of Crote. He broke the seal, hesitated, then opened the letter and read.

> My Dear Baron,
> Our emperor is near death, and I assume from your silence that you have failed to find a magic that can save him. If this is not a foregone conclusion, have your men continue their search. You, Baron, are given another charge.
> This messenger is one of my private guardians. He is part of a contingent that will be arriving in Ackle-Nye. You are to take these men and capture Richius Vantran, delivering him to Nar City before our great emperor expires. It is his dying wish that the Jackal of Nar be brought here for trial, and I have promised him this final victory. The emperor's time is being counted in days. Do not fail.
> Cordially,
> Count Renato Biagio

Gayle stared at the page for a moment, trying to keep the giddiness at bay. "When was this letter sent?"

"I rode from Nar City four weeks ago," replied the Shadow Angel.

"Four weeks?" Gayle scratched at his mask thoughtfully. "And what news have you heard since coming here?"

"I do not listen to gossip as a woman. I am under orders from my count. I was to seek you out and deliver this message. Now I have done that." The soldier inclined his head. "I await your bidding."

"My bidding? Explain."

"Baron," began the soldier impatiently. "In three days' time my brothers will arrive in this city. You are to take us to find Richius Vantran. We

will capture him alive and bring him back to Nar. To do this we are to follow your orders."

"Just how many of you are there?"

"One hundred," replied the soldier. "Enough."

Oh, yes, thought Gayle. *Enough indeed.*

"These men," Gayle continued, "do they know of their mission?"

"They know only that they are to meet you here and follow your orders. I will be here to explain the rest to them."

An inward smile broke beneath Gayle's silver mask. "What's your
name, Shadow Angel? The rank on your cape says captain."

"I am Odamo, a captain of the count's guardians."

"Your accent sounds Crotan. Are you?"

"Proudly so, Baron."

Gayle leaned back and got comfortable, putting his feet up on the rickety table. "Well then, Captain. I have a service for you. I want you to set
out for Nar in the morning. There's a message I want delivered to your
count."

The Shadow Angel watched as Gayle sipped at his drink, then took up
his pen again and began writing, jotting quickly in the margins of Biagio's
letter, concealing his scribblings with a cocked shoulder.

He began.

> Dear Count,
>   Thank you for the contingent of soldiers. By the time you read
> this letter you will know how badly I need them. You may tell
> the emperor that I look forward to my hanging. If he is not dead
> by then, perhaps he can do the honors himself. Please tell him
> also that his dying wish will not be fulfilled. Vantran is mine.

He signed it politely, *Your devoted servant, Blackwood Gayle.*

"There," he said cheerfully, folding the letter and handing it to the soldier. "Now make all haste with it. And don't read it, or I'll know. That
letter is for the count only. You may stay the night to rest but I want you
to leave by dawn. This note must be delivered by your hand alone. Take a
ship or a horse, I don't care how you get there. Just see that he gets it. Do
you understand?"

The skull helm was still for a long moment. Finally a voice issued forth.
"Baron, the men that are coming are under my command."

"They are under my command now," corrected Gayle. "Did the count
not tell you to follow my orders?"

"He did."

"And are you not sworn to die if the count bids you?"

"I am. But . . ."

"Captain," snarled Gayle. "You are a Shadow Angel. You will do exactly as I tell you. These matters are not for a brain your size. Trust your master. Trust me. Do you hear?"

"Yes, Baron. I will obey."

"Good. Now go. And don't worry about your men. I will be here when they arrive. Everything will be explained to them."

When the dawn finally broke, Dyana was still awake. Najjir had not returned.

She would not have expected it from Richius. Still, she had only herself to blame. She had rejected him, then handed him another woman. How could she condemn him for being a man?

"So he is lost to me," she said softly, spying Najjir's empty bed. She wondered what it had been like for her, lying with him, enduring his kisses. He had been tender with her, of course. He was always tender. Soon he would desire her nightly. She would go to his bed willingly the next time, and they would have a child and he would forget about Shani. . . .

Abruptly she stopped herself. Such thoughts would only drive her mad. But she would not be here when Najjir returned. That she simply couldn't face.

The floor was cold on her bare feet, speeding her along as she dressed and pulled on a pair of soft leather boots, the ones that reached to her thighs and were good for walking through tall grass. She had a destination in mind, someplace Richius had thought very special. She wanted to see it again before he shared it with Najjir.

Outside the chamber she found the hall empty and silent. Shani was asleep in a nearby room, carefully tended to by the nurse that looked after all the warlord's children. Not even a whimper issued from beneath the door. Dyana shut the door to her own chamber and tiptoed through the hall. The sun was just rising, burning off the chill of night. Blessedly, the yard was empty.

She hurried down the stairs, through the dingy hall, and out of the iron gates without seeing another soul. Since the siege of the valley there were only a handful of warriors left, and these were mostly wounded men, tended by the widows of the castle. The dearth of men made maneuvering the castle grounds oddly convenient. When she reached the yard she headed for the rear of the castle, passing the huddle of neglected sculptures. The sky was still gray, and she had to work to locate the path in the dimness, but she soon found it hidden in the shade of an elm. Then, satisfied no one was watching, she disappeared into the woods.

The darkness made navigating the narrow path difficult. Dyana kept her eyes on the ground and one hand stretched out before her. Above her, the thick cradle of tree limbs blotted out most of the sun's rays, but she reminded herself that it wasn't far and soon she heard the burble of running water. Before long she saw the break in the trees and the little alcove where the stream bubbled merrily in the light. She moved toward the clearing eagerly, but stopped as she noticed a figure nestled against the backdrop of trees. It was Najjir, sitting with her head bowed on the smooth rock, tracing her fingernail over her name. Dyana halted behind a tree and watched Najjir, watched the little river of tears dripping onto the cold rock and the way the breeze rippled her tired strands of hair. She was still dressed in the silk shift she had worn to Richius' chamber. It clung defiantly to her body against the morning chill. There was a vacant expression on her face as one by one she spelled out the letters with her fingers, finished, then repeated the process. Dyana stepped out from behind the tree.

"Najjir?" she asked anxiously. As she approached the older woman's head tilted slowly up. Dyana hurried up to her side and put a gentle hand on her shoulder. The silk and skin beneath it were like ice.

"What are you doing out here?"

"See my name?" asked Najjir blankly, gesturing to the letters carved into the rock. "Voris wrote it for me."

"Najjir, you are freezing. Let me take you inside."

"It is pretty here. Voris used to take me here when we were young. I am comfortable here."

Dyana reached down and took Najjir's hand. "You are not dressed to be out here, Najjir. Come with me. We will go inside and get you changed."

Najjir jerked her hand away. "I want to stay."

"Najjir, what is wrong with you? Have you been out here all night?"

"All night, yes. I wanted to be alone. I wanted to get away from Kalak. And you."

Dyana sank down beside the woman and put her arms around her shoulders. "What happened?" she asked carefully. "Did he . . . ?"

The question trailed off. Najjir followed her meaning. "No," she answered. "He did not. He might have, but I screamed and frightened him. Then I left him. I think he wanted me to go." She turned to Dyana and her eyes widened. "He is mad, Dyana. Kalak is mad."

Dyana stiffened. "He is . . . troubled."

"You were not there. I know. I saw his eyes."

"But he did not hurt you?"

Najjir looked away. "No. He merely watched me. I do not think he could have hurt me, he is so . . ."

"Kind?" Dyana suggested.

"Alone," corrected Najjir. Her head slumped and she began to weep, great sobs rising up from her belly. Dyana tightened her embrace and held the woman, rocking her and coaxing out the tears until they ebbed enough for speech. "I cannot go on like this," said Najjir. "I cannot. Kalak is not my lord. He never could be. I . . ." She choked on another sob. "I want my husband back."

Dyana let Najjir weep, but in her heart she rejoiced, redeemed by Richius' refusal of her friend. Najjir might think him mad, but she was wrong. It was not insanity that drove him. She had seen brutes who would have forced themselves on a protesting woman. But not Richius. He was the truest man she had ever known.

"Will you let me take you inside?" asked Dyana.

Najjir didn't respond.

"Najjir, you will be sick if you do not warm yourself. Please, come inside. Let me put you to bed. You look exhausted."

"I do not want to see him," said Najjir. "I cannot be with him, Dyana. I cannot."

"Be still, Najjir. You have nothing to fear from Richius, you know that. Remember, we were the ones that made him see you last night."

"I was wrong," said Najjir. "I would rather have no master than him. Please, Dyana. Tell him this for me."

"Oh? And what will happen to you? And your family? No, Najjir. You need Richius. He is the lord of this valley now."

Najjir's face darkened. "It should have been Jarra," she said bitterly.

"But it is Richius. And if you do not want him to touch you, he will not. I promise you that. But you know what will happen to you if you are without a lord. You will be prey for any man who comes to claim you. And Richius won't be able to stop them, because you will have renounced your loyalty to him."

"I do not know what to do, Dyana," she moaned. "I am afraid of him."

"You were the one that made me take you to him, Najjir. I have done that for you. He will not harm you, but you do not want to believe that. What you must understand is that he wants no part of this lordship, but he has no choice."

"He could leave," said Najjir sharply.

"He could," Dyana agreed. "And forget Voris' request of him and forgo you and your family, leaving you to be snatched up by some cruel farmer, and the valley to be torn apart by fighting. But he will not do that, because he is a man of honor." Dyana rose and stared down acidly at Najjir. "Maybe someday you will see that."

Dyana turned to go, then heard Najjir's desperate plea.

"Dyana, wait, please. . . ."

"No, Najjir," Dyana snapped. "What did you think I did for you last night? I love Richius. You know that. But you made me bring you to

him so that he would protect you. Now you want him to forget about
you, after I have explained to him what will happen if he does? No. I will
not do it."

"Dyana, I cannot be his woman. I cannot bear the thought of it."

"Then tell him yourself," said Dyana coldly. "I want no part of it."

She turned and strode away, but had taken no more than three paces
before a fiery pain tore through her temples. Her knees buckled and she
shrieked, putting her hands to her head and shutting her eyes. Behind her
she heard Najjir's cry, felt the woman's worried hand grasp her shoulder,
but still she sank into the muddy bank, blind and in agony as a disem-
bodied voice thundered in her head. The blurry image of Tharn's face
flashed through her mind, a phantom at once flesh and ethereal. The
mouth was moving, the broken teeth chattering words, garbled sounds
punctuated by an animal's roar and the throaty click of an unknown
dialect. Dyana tried to stand, moaning as the images flooded her mind.
Najjir's hands were there, bearing her up.

"Dyana!" came Najjir's terrified voice. "What is it?"

"Tharn," choked Dyana. She opened her eyes and still saw the phan-
tasm face of her husband. "It is Tharn. He is here."

FORTY-EIGHT

Jarra awakened Richius with a single word. Dyana.

It was all Richius needed to break the hold of sleep. He followed the Dumaka through the halls as he hastily buttoned up his shirt, the dirt of the yard scraping his bare feet. Out near the gate he saw Dyana lying with her head in Najjir's lap. A small crowd of women had gathered around them, eyeing Najjir in her nightclothes. Dyana had her eyes shut while Najjir brushed a gentle hand across her forehead.

"My God, what's happened?" asked Richius as he rushed through the throng. He knelt down beside Dyana. "Dyana, what is it? Are you ill?"

Dyana shivered. Finally she opened her eyes. "Tharn," she whispered. "He is coming."

Richius looked at Najjir but the old woman shrugged. The crowd began murmuring among themselves. Richius turned to glower at them.

"Get away, all of you." He gestured to the Dumaka. "Jarra, get them out of here."

Jarra began shooing away the curious crowd. Richius bent over Dyana. Her skin was hot, misted with perspiration. A wild panic fevered her eyes.

"Dyana," he said gently. "I'm here. I want you to tell me what's wrong. What about Tharn? Is he talking to you?"

"Yes," she said. "And no. I see him, but I do not understand. He is in my head, Richius. It hurts, it hurts. . . ."

"What hurts?"

"He is coming," said Dyana. "Very near. Others are with him. Beasts. He is talking to me, shouting. . . ."

"Easy," crooned Richius. "Don't speak. We'll get you inside." He tucked his hands beneath her legs and shoulders and lifted her gently from the ground. Listlessly she wrapped her hands around his neck.

"He cannot talk," she moaned. "He tries, but he cannot. He is ill, I feel it."

"I'll take you inside. You'll feel better. Quiet now, quiet . . ."

"Very near," she said again. "I must wait for him."

"Wait for him in bed," said Richius, and carried her out of the yard through the castle gates. Jarra and the confused Najjir followed, shadowing him through the hall until they reached the bedchamber Dyana shared with Voris' wife. The Dumaka waited at the threshold while the others stepped inside, and Richius placed Dyana lightly on her bed. He pulled off her long boots, drew the covers over her, and watched her shut her eyes.

"Tharn looks for me," she gasped. "But he cannot find me."

"If he's coming he will be here soon enough," said Richius. "Try to rest. It will pass. I'll wait here with you. Nothing will happen, I promise."

"My mind, he is inside it. He does not know. . . ."

"Dyana, please. Try to be still." He took her hand and patted it. "Close your mind to it. I'm not going to leave you."

He glanced over at Najjir, who was watching their exchange with a sorrowful expression. She looked away as their eyes met. Carefully Richius slipped his hand out of Dyana's.

"I'm right here," he assured her, but slid off the bed and went over to Najjir. He had hardly noticed her garb, the same shift she had worn to his room the previous evening. Now she looked lost, more like a girl than a woman. Deep lines of fatigue and worry scratched her face. Richius stood before her and opened his arms.

"I am sorry about your husband," he said.

Najjir took a flustered breath and said something he did not understand.

"She asks that you forgive her," Dyana explained.

Richius shook his head. "No. There is nothing to forgive."

Najjir's expression softened. She bent her head in a bow, then went over to Dyana's bedside. The two women spoke for a moment, and Najjir leaned forward and lightly kissed Dyana's forehead. Dyana gave a little laugh as Najjir rose and left the room. Richius watched her disappear through the door before going back to Dyana's bedside.

"What did she say?" asked Richius.

"She told me I was right about you," she answered. Her gray eyes opened again and she regarded him. "I know you did not touch her, Richius. I know what happened last night."

Richius brushed a strand of hair from Dyana's face. "And you? How are you now?"

"Better, I think. Tharn is gone. I cannot see him. But he was calling to me, Richius, looking for me. Something is wrong. He is ill; he is weak. His mind would not focus on me. I could feel his pain, his fear. Oh, Richius, what is it?"

"I don't know, Dyana," said Richius. "But if he is near we will find out soon. Now close your eyes and try to sleep."

She closed her eyes and tilted her head into the pillow. Before long she had slipped into a shallow sleep. Richius remained at the bedside, watching quietly. Tharn was near. He had used the same magic he had taught Lucyler to enter Dyana's mind, but somehow the jolt had been unfocused, overwhelming. Perhaps it was as Dyana guessed. Perhaps he was ill and crying for help. And what were the beasts chasing him? Lions? Or had they already raked their claws over the cunning-man's body, and his last scream was echoing in Dyana's brain?

The minutes ticked by and soon became an hour. Dyana barely stirred. Strands of silver hair dangled around her face, and her breathing was deep and serene. Richius stayed with her, moving off the bed to an uncomfortable wooden chair in the corner of the room, waiting for her to awaken but wanting her to sleep. It had no doubt been an exhausting night for her. It had been for him, too, and evidently Najjir as well. Two hours into Dyana's slumber Najjir poked her head into the room, checking on her friend's condition. She smiled lightly when she saw Dyana asleep, gave Richius a courteous bow, then left. She was the only visitor until Dumaka Jarra came.

The old war master knocked once on the door, but didn't wait for Richius to call him in before entering. He went over to Richius, saw that Dyana was still asleep, and whispered into his new master's ear.

"Tharn."

Dyana stirred a bit at the sound of the name. Richius stared at Jarra in disbelief. "Tharn? He is coming?"

Jarra nodded and pointed upward. "Uasit toa."

"The watchtower?" asked Richius.

"Yes," said Dyana groggily. She opened her eyes. "They can see him from the watchtower. He is coming."

Jarra went on talking, half to Richius and half to Dyana, motioning excitedly with his hands as he spoke. Dyana sat up in bed, astonished by the tale. It was all too fast for Richius to follow.

"What's he saying?" he asked impatiently.

"He comes with lions," replied Dyana. "Dozens of them. They are in the forest now and will be here soon."

"How does he know it's Tharn? Dyana, can you feel anything?"

"No. He has stopped trying to speak to me. But they show the banner of Falindar, Richius. It is Tharn."

Richius got to his feet. "Then I must go to meet him. I must tell him what's happened to Voris. Jarra, you should come with me. Dyana, tell him I want him with me."

"I will go, too," said Dyana. She tossed off the covers and flung her feet over the bedside. "He will be expecting to see me."

"No, Dyana. You need rest, and we don't know what kind of condition he's in. If he wants to see you I'll bring him here."

"I will go," said Dyana adamantly. "I am his wife and I must greet him."

She left the bed and retrieved her boots from the corner of the chamber, pulling them on and talking to Jarra. The Dumaka nodded his understanding and eagerly straightened out his garments, wetting his lips as he prepared to meet the supreme Drol. Richius took hold of Dyana's hand and led her from the chamber, and the three of them stepped out into the sunny yard. Another crowd had gathered there, including Najjir and her three daughters. The castle's few remaining warriors had arranged themselves in a neat line, their jiiktars slung over their backs, their chests puffed out in homage to the approaching master of Falindar. But there was someone very special missing, Richius knew, and he dreaded telling Tharn of it.

As long moments drifted by, the crowd became anxious. Richius looked at Jarra. "How near are they?" he asked. He formed the question in Triin. The Dumaka shrugged and gave an incomprehensible answer.

"The watchman in the tower said they approach," Dyana explained. "The Dumaka was told they are close, that is all."

They all had their eyes fixed on the path leading from the forest to the yard. The warriors were as silent as stones, while the modestly garbed women of the keep bantered lightly among themselves. Dyana shifted distractedly beside Richius, her thin face twitching nervously. Richius leaned closer.

"Don't worry," he whispered. "Nothing is going to happen. He doesn't know anything."

A rumble carried through the forest and the tops of the trees began to quiver. The sound and movement seized the crowd. The archway of branches stood empty and dark. A bizarre chorus issued from the woods. And then a head appeared, a monstrous thing with yellow eyes and a cavelike mouth rimmed with oversized teeth. Attached to the head was a giant body of tawny fur and a whipping tail barbed with ribboned spikes, and around the body were bands of leather riding tack supporting a stout saddle. In the saddle was a bronze-skinned man with hair the color of faded gold, and behind that man was Tharn.

Tharn, unmistakable in his red rags and soiled bandages, who crooked one arm around the lion rider's waist and let the other dangle uselessly at his side. His diseased skin shone like curdled milk. The giant beast carried the two men into the yard and a parade of lions followed, each bearing another long-haired, leathered rider. Falindar's banner hung from the muscled flank of Tharn's cat, and the cunning-man lifted his malformed head as he saw the gathering in the yard. His eyes flicked from face to face, then came to rest on Dyana.

Yet there was something wrong in the way the eyes moved and the way the head tilted and the body swayed, almost uncontrollably, in the saddle. Tharn's shoulders slumped with weariness, and there were scars on his face that Richius had never seen before. The bronzed rider drew the cat to a halt.

"Tharn!" cried Richius. Tharn's gaze shifted from Dyana to Richius and a weak smile bubbled onto his face.

"Richius," said the Drol weakly. "Come and help me, please."

Richius and Jarra hurried up to Tharn, holding out their arms and easing him off the lion's back. As usual, the cunning-man was feather-light. He collapsed into Richius' arms.

"Tharn, what happened?" asked Richius. "What's wrong with you?"

Tharn was breathing so heavily he could hardly respond. "You were right," he said. "The journey was too much for me." He gestured to the silent man atop the lion. "This," he said reverently, "is Karlaz."

Karlaz of the lions took his place on the floor by the round table and, without waiting for the others, began devouring the food and drink Najjir had brought for them. He was, as Richius quickly discovered, a man who did not trifle with words, but instead preferred to grunt and nod and to use every other part of his body rather than tire his tongue. That he saved for eating.

"Are you feeling better now?" asked Richius.

The cunning-man nodded. It had taken him more than an hour to catch his breath, and in that time Richius had arranged for them all to meet. Now he, Tharn, Jarra, and Karlaz sat around the table in Voris' former meeting chamber, sipping at strong spirits and watching Karlaz tear into joints of fowl with his teeth. Only Dyana sat apart from them, kneeling behind Tharn in the customary manner of a Drol wife. The look on her face betrayed her disgust. Tharn had requested that she attend the meeting, and like the good wife she was forced again to be, she reluctantly complied. Richius did his best to keep his eyes off her.

"Can you tell us now what's happened?" he asked.

"As I said," Tharn began, "Lucyler told me of Voris' death. We met up with him not far from the valley. He gave us the banner to hang on the lion."

"No," said Richius. "What happened to *you*? You weren't this bad when you left for Chandakkar."

"I was ill enough," said Tharn. "But I had an encounter that worsened me." He pointed to his face, and the fresh scars lining his left side. "This is from one of the lions. I was attacked in Chandakkar. That was when Karlaz and his people found me. But I was asleep for days, unconscious. My cunning-men explained to him why I was there, but he would not speak to them, only to me. They cared for me and I rested." He glanced over at Karlaz who, at the mention of his name, was grinning through a mouthful of food. "He saved me. He was in the same valley I was attacked in. His people had fled there." Tharn looked sad and serious. "The Narens attacked them, Richius."

"What happened?"

"They attacked before we arrived. As I said, Karlaz and his people fled into the lion valley, but there was much destruction. Many died. It was a Naren fleet. They slaughtered dozens before Karlaz could return with the lions to fight them."

Tharn turned and smiled at Karlaz. "This is a great man, Richius. He would have refused my request, but he saw what the Narens did. They convinced him of their own evil."

"But what happened to the Narens?" asked Richius.

Tharn smiled. "Did Lucyler tell you about Liss?"

"He told me they were helping to keep the Black Fleet off the coast."

"And so they have been. Karlaz returned to the village to fight them, but they were already gone. Liss had attacked their ships and beaten them back. The captain of the Lissen fleet spoke to Karlaz. The lion master claimed it was Prakna."

"Prakna? Who the hell is that?"

"Fleet Commander Prakna is the supreme commander of the Lissen navy. He was there in the village. He told Karlaz he would sink the Naren ships." Tharn beamed. "We have an ally, Richius."

"But what happened to you? Why were you gone so long?"

"The lion. I am not so hearty, you know. It did me damage. When I was able to travel again, we set out for Dring. I was still weary. I did not know then that Voris had been killed, and I wanted to know what was happening here. On the way we met Lucyler. He explained the rest to me." Tharn's face grew grim. "Did he die well, Richius?"

Richius frowned. Just what had Lucyler told him?

"He died with honor, defending his valley."

Tharn nodded. "Good. He deserved that, at least." He glanced about secretively then whispered, "I know of your lordship here. We will speak of it later."

"Can you get me out of this, Tharn?"

"Later. Now we must talk of more important things. I will finish my tale. You know already that I was ill. It took me a long while to recover, but when I did we left Chandakkar. I was not wholly well, and I am still not as you can see. Most of my strength had gone." He turned and regarded Dyana. "That is why I harmed you, my wife. Forgive me, it was not meant. I wanted only to speak to you, to see if you were here and well. But my strength, it failed me. I thought I was close enough but my mind would not reach you. The fetch can be dangerous if not done well. Perhaps it was foolish of me to try."

Dyana tossed off the apology. "I am well again, husband. Do not be concerned."

Tharn smiled. "I am glad you are well. It was only my eagerness to see you that made me try and speak to you. I have missed you."

Dyana did not reply.

Richius felt suddenly awkward. "You say you met up with Lucyler. When was this?"

"Five days ago," replied Tharn.

"He told you about Kronin?"

"Yes," said Tharn sadly. "Another giant loss. I grieve for him. We had become almost as brothers." He sighed. "But I waste time, and I have news for you, Richius. These lion riders have come to attack the Saccenne Run. They will ride for the Run in a day or so, after they have rested. All is in place now. The war is almost over."

"What do you mean, all is in place? There are still hundreds of Naren troops in Ackle-Nye, and more will be coming. I agree the lions are a help, but—"

"Before I left Chandakkar," said Tharn, "I sent messengers to all the warlords of Lucel-Lor. Some were the cunning-men that went with me to Chandakkar, others were sent by Karlaz. But they all bore a letter telling them to ride for Ackle-Nye with all the warriors they could. I did not know then what had happened here in Dring, but Liss was already ending the battles on the coasts and I knew Kronin's men would be able to deal with the Narens that had already landed in Tatterak. That was almost three weeks ago, Richius."

Richius was stunned. "So they're all riding for Ackle-Nye as we speak?"

"If they can, yes. There will be thousands of warriors at the outskirts of the city by the time Karlaz and his lions reach the mountains. They will attack the Run and ruin the Naren escape. The other warriors will take Ackle-Nye." Tharn's eyes flashed. "It is over for them, Richius. They have no chance."

Richius leaned back on his heels. *Tharn the avenger,* he thought suddenly. He had heard the Drol called that once, a very long lifetime ago.

He was the dark angel of Lucel-Lor again, the sorcerer who counted Naren lives as cheaply as grains of sand. Again he had outwitted the masterminds of Nar, again he was arranging a holocaust. And Richius had joined him in the black crusade, and the thought of murdering so many men barely ruffled his scruples. A little part of his soul grieved for his dead conscience.

"When do we leave?" he asked. "There aren't many of Voris' warriors left, but we can be in Ackle-Nye in two days."

Tharn shook his head. "You will not be going, Richius. Nor will I. I am too sick to make the journey, and I know from speaking with Dyana that you yourself have been badly wounded. You will stay here with us. So will Jarra and the others."

"Stay here? But why? I'm fit enough to fight. And Jarra—"

"Jarra is old and deserves the chance for some peace. So do the other warriors who fought here. So do you. You say you are fit, but you are not. I knew when I saw you. You look barely able to stand."

"Tharn . . ."

"No more. I have made my decision."

"It's not your decision to make. I don't need your permission to ride for Ackle-Nye."

Tharn shrugged. "You could do that. But I think you would probably collapse on the way. And even if you did not, no one would listen to you. When I sent my letters to the warlords, I told them Kronin would be in command. I also told them that if you were there, they were not to let you fight. They would capture you, Richius, and bring you back here. With Kronin dead, Lucyler will be in command. I have already told him so, and have sent him back to Tatterak. I also told him not to let you fight."

"Why are you doing this to me?" Richius asked. "I've been nothing but loyal. I've given all I can to—"

"Enough," ordered Tharn. "Karlaz will leave with his men the day after tomorrow. They will ride for the Run and they will take it, and the other warlords will take Ackle-Nye. You and I will have no part in this, Richius."

Tharn turned to Jarra and began gibbering in Triin, obviously explaining it all to the old war master. Jarra took the news poorly, but did not question. When Tharn was finished, Jarra turned to Richius and spoke.

"He wants to know if he may leave now," explained Tharn. "I have told him everything and said we are done here. He awaits your dismissal."

"Yes," said Richius in Triin, waving at the Dumaka. "You can go now, Jarra."

Jarra stood, bowed deeply to Richius and Tharn, and left the room. Then Tharn turned to Karlaz and, very cordially, dismissed him, too. The lion man seemed unperturbed by the request, taking his food with him before going. Lastly Tharn spoke to Dyana.

"Will you leave us, too, my wife? I wish to speak to Richius alone."

Dyana chanced a sideways glance at Richius, sighed, then vacated the chamber. Richius leaned back and scowled at Tharn.

"I want an explanation," he said. "Why are you keeping me out of this? I have just as much right to fight as anyone. More even."

"And you deserve to know my reasons," said Tharn. "I am not going because I am sick. You are not going because you are not sick."

"Oh, Lord. Is it back to your riddles already? Please, Tharn, a straight answer for once. Why won't you let me go?"

"Because you are not Triin, and because you still have your life ahead of you. Richius, understand me. I asked you to defend the Dring Valley. You have done that for me. Your task is finished here. There is no reason for you to fight for us anymore, and I will not let you die needlessly. I can save you now, and I will. You will stay here, and you will live."

The way the cunning-man was trying to save him infuriated Richius. But then he realized how similar it sounded. Once, he himself had tried to save Dyana.

"Tharn, don't try to save me. I want to defend Lucel-Lor. Is that so different from what Lucyler and the others are doing?"

"They are Triin and you are not. They must die if the gods call them to defend this land. But the gods do not call you, Richius. Perhaps they have used you, brought you to us for your help, but they are done with you now, and you are still alive. I will make sure you remain so."

"But I have nothing! Why should I live?"

Tharn gave a sympathetic smile. "I have met Narens like you before. Always they speak of having nothing. But your heart still beats, yes? You still have breath? You have life, Richius. If you were infirm and cursed like me, I would grant your request. But you are healthy and young. I cannot let you risk that anymore. I needed you once, but no longer."

"Then I am needed nowhere," said Richius bitterly. "Aramoor is gone, and Dring doesn't need me. My lordship here is a farce."

"It is not a farce," said Tharn sternly. "It is the way things have always been done. Voris passed his family on to you. *They* have need of you." Then his expression softened and he added, "But if you do not wish to remain here as lord, you do not have to. I have the authority to change it. You may pass the lordship to Jarra if that is what you want."

"That's exactly what I want," said Richius. "As quickly as possible."

Tharn nodded. "It shall be done. But you should think on it first, Richius. This castle could be a new home for you, a new life. If you leave here, you will be a stranger wherever you go. You can, of course, come back to Falindar with us. You may live there as long as you wish, and will not be held to our laws. I ask only that you do not question the way we live our lives as Drol."

Richius bit his lip. His life was slipping away from him, and there was nothing he could do to stop it. Tharn was alive. He had lost Dyana forever.

"You are right," he said. "I will have to think about it. Don't mention anything to Jarra or Najjir until I give you my decision. I'll need some time to think."

"Take time," said Tharn. "Consider everything, and know that to us in Tatterak you are a hero."

Richius uncrossed his legs and rose. "Wonderful," he said bleakly. "But if you ask the people in Aramoor I'm sure they'll tell you differently."

"Richius," said Tharn. "There is something else." The cunning-man's gaze hit the floor evasively. "This is difficult for me. But you and Dyana . . ." Tharn sighed. "She has been true to her vow to me. I can tell. I should thank you."

"Tharn, don't," implored Richius. "I can't speak of it. You're back now. I've lost her. I know that."

Tharn smiled. "I did not trust you when I left for Chandakkar. I am glad you are better than my fears."

FORTY-NINE

On a balcony overlooking Nar City, on a morning brisk with a northern breeze, Count Renato Biagio sat alone among the flowers, his eyes swollen red from a night of tears and prayers. The sun was new and yellow, and he could see it burning defiantly past the nebulous smoke of the war labs. Beside him was a holy book, an heirloom from his father, its pages dog-eared from generations of devotion. He had spent the entire night out here, fasting and praying with the book to his forehead, staining it with frustrated tears as his emperor lay dying.

Biagio had never been a religious man. Though Arkus had bid all of the Iron Circle to submit to the one God—the God of Bishop Herrith—Biagio had never really had the faith. He was a defiant man, like the sun he was watching, determined to burn away the darkness with the power of his own intellect. But when he was desperate, when he felt small, he sometimes turned to heaven. This night he had prayed mightily, and somehow he knew his pleas had failed. Bovadin hadn't come out to tell him of any miracles, and Biagio knew in his tortured heart that his most beloved was perishing.

Arkus wouldn't survive the day, that's what Bovadin had said. The old man's mind was gone now, unable to even distinguish a friendly voice. Like Biagio's. The count closed his eyes. At last the tears had stopped. He wasn't mournful anymore, he realized, just angry. He even felt abandoned, and this new emotion puzzled him. He resented the old man for leaving him. What was he without Arkus, after all? He was the head of the Roshann, he had allies, but he had consigned his life to the ideals of Nar, and now those ideals were breathing their last and coughing up blood. Within hours, the world would be a very different place.

And Arkus was himself to blame for this, at least in part. Stubborn to the last, the emperor still refused to believe the inevitability of his own demise. Already the Iron Circle began to hover around like buzzards. Herrith was with Arkus even now, chanting his nonsense about heaven. There would be a struggle for the throne, maybe a bloody one, and for such an insightful man Arkus had foolishly allowed it to happen. Biagio shuddered, sick with the thought of Bishop Herrith's prayers. Praying to a God that didn't exist.

"Damn you!" Biagio raged. He rose from his chair and picked up his book, flinging it off the side of the balcony. The book plummeted from sight. When it was gone Biagio reached for his chair, smashing it against a statue of a woman. The chair shattered against the marble. Biagio fell to his knees, shaking and sobbing. He raised his face to the sky and spat, imagining the missile striking the face of God.

"I hate you!" he screamed. "You deaf monster, I hate you!"

God had failed him, just as he had failed Arkus. There was no magic in Lucel-Lor. There was only death and solitude and revenge. He had promised Arkus life and delivered only ruin. He had not even captured Vantran. Vantran. Biagio smoldered. That boy would suffer someday.

"Do you hear me, God?" Biagio cried. "You can take Arkus, but you'll never save Vantran! I will burn every church, I will kill every priest to get him. You're protecting him, I know. But you'll never save him!"

"Renato!"

Biagio looked up to see Bovadin standing at the entrance of the balcony. The little scientist wore an expression of shock.

"What are you doing?" asked Bovadin. He hurried over to the count and offered a hand. Biagio growled and batted it away, rising to his feet without aid.

"Leave me," he roared. "I told you, I don't want company!"

"Listen, you fool. Arkus is asking for you. You should come inside now, be with him."

"He's calling for phantoms, Bovadin. He doesn't even recognize me."

"He's dying," snapped Bovadin. He grabbed Biagio's cape and pulled him around. "Are you listening to me? He's dying!"

"I know!" cried Biagio. Again he was on the verge of sobs. "So let him die! Let him leave us to war." Bitterly, Biagio turned away and went to the edge of the balcony. "If there's a hell, I swear he'll be in it, and all of us after him. All but Herrith."

"Renato," called Bovadin. The midget padded over to the count and slid a tiny, consoling hand onto his back. "You'll regret this. Please, come with me. Before it's too late . . ."

"It is too late. He's already dead."

"But Herrith is with him. Maybe Arkus will speak and Herrith will hear. . . ."

Biagio laughed mirthlessly. "Arkus won't say it. Even now he can't admit his dying. He'll never pass the throne to me."

"Then you must make him," urged Bovadin. "If you demand it, he may listen. Please, Renato. For all our sakes. Won't you try?"

"It's impossible. You know him as well as I. He'll never give up the throne. It will be up to us to fight for it." The count fell to one knee and put both hands on Bovadin's small shoulders, staring into the insectlike face. "I'll need you with me," he whispered. "I've already spoken to Nicabar and some others. They've already agreed to join me. What about you?"

"Don't make me choose. Not yet. Not while there's still a chance."

"With me or against me, Bovadin. Which is it?"

Bovadin locked blue eyes with the count. "With you. If you try to talk to Arkus."

"Bovadin, it's no use. . . ."

"Try," insisted the scientist. "Or I'll stand with Herrith."

Biagio stood and towered hatefully over the midget. "Stand with Herrith and I'll have you killed. You know I can do it."

"Talk to Arkus, or no more drugs," countered Bovadin.

An expert interrogator, Biagio quickly scanned Bovadin's face and concluded he wasn't lying. And without the drugs to keep them vital, they would all soon wither.

"Very well," agreed Biagio. "I'll try."

He let Bovadin lead him back into the palace. Grim-faced slaves, all attired in black, lined the hallways to Arkus' bedchamber. Candles and incense burned on the walls, more of Herrith's holy nonsense, and a handful of the bishop's acolytes knelt in the halls and prayed loudly for the emperor's soul. Biagio passed them disdainfully, carelessly stepping on their flowing robes as he moved through the palace. A pair of Shadow Angels stood at the open door of the emperor's rooms. Quickly they stepped aside as Biagio and Bovadin approached. Biagio paused at the threshold and steadied himself. He was sure his request would send the emperor into a rage. Very slowly he stepped into the room. Bishop Herrith was poised over Arkus' bed, cradling the emperor's hand in his own. Arkus lay unmoving in the sheets. When he saw Biagio, Herrith flashed a spiteful smile.

"I'm sorry," said the bishop. "You're too late, Count. The emperor is gone."

All the world fell upon Biagio in a sudden avalanche. Beneath him his knees buckled. He reached out for Bovadin and the midget fought to prop him up. Herrith raced over and seized an arm before Biagio could faint. Insistently the bishop conveyed him toward the bed. There on the mattress was Arkus, static and breathless. Renato Biagio closed his eyes, anguished by the sight.

Arkus of Nar was dead.

FIFTY

The host of Lucel-Lor gathered on a hill overlooking the fortified city of Ackle-Nye. The morning was bright, and the glare from the sun set the city of beggars alight so that it glowed with Naren ugliness. Two thousand strong, the warriors waited impatiently for their leaders to hand down the word. Each had traveled from a different corner of the vast Triin land, eager to taste imperial blood. Horses snorted unhappily and dug at the dirt with their hooves, ready to charge down the hillside, while unmounted warriors talked uneasily amongst themselves and fiddled with their arrows. A pall had settled over the city, a lack of movement that bespoke apprehension. Ackle-Nye was closed up tight. The warriors had been seen and they knew it, and not a man of them feared the lack of surprise. The warlords had told them of the gun emplacements in the towers and the well-armed garrison stationed in the city. Drunk on bloodlust, nothing would deter them.

Near the top of the hill three men waited apart from the rest, their eyes fixed intently on the city at their feet. Mounted on heavy horses, their white hair blowing, they watched as the growing sun filled the world with light and made the shadows of the mountains smaller. Lucyler of Falindar shifted uneasily in his saddle. Unlike the others, he had no love for what was coming nor for the burden Tharn had handed him. Of the two thousand men gathered, nearly seven hundred were his own to command: the blue-jacketed warriors of Tatterak, who had been left masterless by the death of Kronin. Tharn had promised Lucyler that they would follow him and they had done so without question, yet Lucyler still felt uncertain. He wasn't a warlord. Neither was he a general.

But he had done his best, and this morning's martial meeting was the result. Praxtin-Tar and Shohar had followed him loyally, as had Karlaz and Nang. Lucyler's eyes moved past the city to the mountain passage winding in the distance. At his orders, Karlaz and his hundred lion riders were waiting there, invisible amongst the rocks. Behind them, near the end of the Saccenne Run, was Nang. The savage from the Fire Steppes had also come to Ackle-Nye for the appointed rendezvous, as eager as the rest to fall upon the city. He had brought two hundred men, the most he could gather from his tiny territory, and had forcibly marched them over the mountains to take up position in the Run. Whatever the lions didn't devour, Nang would.

Lucyler waited atop his horse. Dreadfully sure the Narens would say no to his terms, the little note he held seemed ridiculous. But he had to try. He supposed there were nearly a thousand soldiers in Ackle-Nye, and though he had them outnumbered, Lucyler hoped to avoid a bloody conflict. He wanted them to retreat, to leave their weapons and go home. Then he could close up the Run forever, and they could all return to their families. Lucyler glanced down at the parchment. On it were Naren words he had written himself.

> Garrison Commander—
> Surrender. Leave your weapons and retreat. If not, you will die.

He hadn't signed it, because he knew the commander of the garrison had never heard of him, and the fool need only to look out his window to see what he was facing. It was probably a hopeless gesture, but Lucyler had to try. Nearby on the hillside, the warriors of Kronin watched him curiously, hoping his plan would fail. They followed him without question, because it was the will of Tharn, but they grieved for their fallen master and hungered for revenge. Nang did, too, and Praxtin-Tar. Shohar, always eager to fight, had simply shrugged at Lucyler's plan. Clearly, he thought Lucyler's chances slim. He had traveled farther than any of the warlords, and his thin face looked paler than usual. In Lucel-Lor, they called Shohar the "Skull-Taker." It was said his throne was built of them. As for Praxtin-Tar of Reen, Tharn had said he was a trustworthy but vicious man. Good in a fight. Not so good at peace.

Of all the warlords who had come to Ackle-Nye, only Karlaz seemed reasonable to Lucyler. The master of Chandakkar had suffered under Nar, too, but he seemed less eager than the others, more humane somehow. He had told Lucyler that he only wanted to do this thing and then go home. Lucyler liked Karlaz.

"The light has grown enough," said Lucyler. "They should see us all by now."

"Surprise would have been better," argued Praxtin-Tar. "You have ruined that."

The warlord from Reen was a tall, intimidating man, and when he sat on his horse he looked like a centaur. He had powerful eyes that bore down hard, and long, spidery fingers that twitched when he spoke. His banner was a raven, and all of his men had one tattooed on their cheek. Praxtin-Tar's was black and oddly animate.

"It is what Tharn wanted," Lucyler explained. "For all of us. If they leave peacefully, the outcome is the same."

"The outcome perhaps," said Praxtin-Tar. "But not the glory. My men traveled here for battle, as did Shohar's." He looked to Shohar for support. The smaller warlord merely shrugged.

"We will do it my way," said Lucyler firmly. "Your way if I fail. That garrison is heavily armed. Why take the chance?"

Praxtin-Tar leaned closer. "Because it is what they deserve." He scoffed with disgust. "If you were Kronin—"

"I am not Kronin," said Lucyler sharply. "And you are not my superior, Praxtin-Tar. This is *my* army today. You joined it. You will do as I say."

Lucyler's venom quieted the warlord. Praxtin-Tar grunted unhappily and said no more. Lucyler steeled himself.

"I will take the letter myself," he said. "I will have my men follow me in. You both stay on the hill and watch. If anything happens, come down. Not before. Understood?"

Praxtin-Tar nodded. "Understood."

"I do not agree," said Shohar. He had a shrill voice that reminded Lucyler of a bell. "Lucyler, you should remain here. You are the leader. If you are attacked, you might be killed. Let me take your letter. It will do no good, anyway."

Lucyler thought for a moment, considering the option. It was true he could see far more from up here. Wasn't that what generals did? He thought of Richius, and wondered what his friend would have done. The answer came to him in an instant.

"No. I will take it down myself. One leader to another. It might impress them."

Praxtin-Tar laughed. "If all of us on this hill do not impress them, do you really think you will? Do not be a fool. Shohar is right. Let him take the letter. You are needed more than he is." He smiled evilly at Shohar. "No offense."

Shohar smiled back. He wore golden silk robes and might have been handsome if not for the insanity in his eyes. "Agreeing with you makes my stomach turn, Praxtin-Tar. Stand back a little. I might get sick on you." Shohar went to Lucyler and stuck out his hand. "Give me your message. I will take it down for you. An army is useless without a leader."

Reluctantly, Lucyler handed over the paper. "All right," he conceded. "But just give them the letter. Do not say or do anything else."

"Of course not," said Shohar dryly. "I am not as dumb as some, you know." He took the letter and stuffed it into his robes. "Praxtin-Tar, if you see us in trouble, try not to take your time."

"I will ride as fast as I can," joked Praxtin-Tar, "in the other direction."

Shohar laughed shrilly and drove his horse away, down the slope a little toward his men. He began gathering them for the ride toward the city. Lucyler watched him go, fearful of the response he would get.

General Cassis, commander of the garrison of Ackle-Nye, stood at the end of his balcony, craning his neck to see. The building he used for his office stood obliquely to the hillside, but he could make out enough to know he was in trouble. His expert eyes counted fifteen hundred Triin, maybe more, some on horseback, most on foot. They were arranged in colored regiments the way Triin do, each group no doubt belonging to a separate warlord. Behind them in the eastern sky the sun was rising, throwing their shadows ominously down the hillside. Scouts had sighted them days ago but had put their numbers at far less. Now gathered, they looked like an entire legion.

Cassis put his hands on the balcony's railing and gripped it hard, keeping himself steady as he leaned forward. The narrow streets had fallen silent. The highest buildings in the city had long-range flame cannons in position, and a platoon of handhelds had been dispatched at the city's mouth, a first line of defense Cassis knew would buy him some time. At last count he had 653 men under his command—not including Blackwood Gayle, who had abandoned them some days earlier. Cassis had been over the math several times. Even with their weapons and the security of the walls, their chances were terrible.

"Goddamn gogs," he muttered. "Should have wiped them out the first time."

The first time, Cassis had been in Nar. He was a career soldier, a move he was regretting more by the minute, and had spent his life guarding godforsaken hellholes like Ackle-Nye. When he was younger his father had told him that soldiering was the only real profession for a man. He hated his father now, and he hated the advice even more. He hated being garrison commander. It was a rotten position that granted title without advantage. While Naren lords lounged around plush apartments, he slept in filth and made what home he could out of abandoned buildings. They were all fops, the Naren lords. Cassis spit over the side of the balcony, imagining a royal head beneath him. Now he was surrounded by Triin savages ready to pull his fingernails out, and it was all thanks to Arkus. Cassis gritted his teeth. He wouldn't die for that bastard. Not here.

Cassis turned to his aide, who had been standing some paces back on the balcony. Colonel Marlyle's face was the color of milk. Curdled. "Colonel, I want you to tell the cannoneers in the towers not to open fire until we've drawn them in. Each burst has to count. You've got good men on them?"

Marlyle nodded. "Yes, sir."

"Enough fuel?"

"Yes, sir. I think so."

"Don't think so, Marlyle. Make goddamn sure. All three of them. I don't want any of them running short."

Marlyle grimaced. "Two, sir."

"What?"

"There's only two long-range guns, General. They can't get the third one working. Broken fuel line, I think. No spares."

Cassis put his hand to his forehead. "Colonel, get that bloody thing working. I don't care how, and I don't want excuses. Do it, or I'll throw you to that horde myself."

"I'll try, sir," said Marlyle, blanching. It was an impossible order and Cassis knew it. Despite the commitment the Black City had promised, the Saccenne Run was a long route. Spare parts, like food and medicines, ran out quickly. And no one had foreseen their current situation. Cassis had already sped messengers to Talistan, but he knew reinforcements would never arrive in time. When they got here, they would all be hanging from trees.

"Colonel, I want you nearby. Things are going to get ugly fast unless we keep communications open. Don't run off on me. And don't engage the enemy yourself. Have a guard of horsemen around us. Get them ready in the city center. I'll be down soon."

Marlyle nodded again, his gaze shifting to something over Cassis' shoulder.

"They're coming," said Marlyle. He pointed to the hillside. "Look."

"I see," said Cassis calmly. A large group had broken off from the rest and were riding toward the city. All in gold, they looked to Cassis like a sunrise. They didn't ride hard but kept a casual gait. A single horseman rode before the others, his head held high.

"Terms?" suggested Marlyle hopefully.

Cassis frowned. He had never heard of a warlord offering terms. And even if they did, he could never accept them. More Naren nonsense. The general tried hard to look confident.

"Colonel, carry out my orders. Get that cannon operational. And arrange the horsemen in the city center. Meet me there."

"How many, sir? A dozen?"

"Fifty," said Cassis.

"Fifty? Sir, if I recall that many men to—"

"Do it!" flared Cassis. "Go. And get my own horse ready."

Marlyle obliged, leaving Cassis alone on the balcony. The general looked back over the approaching warriors. The one in front seemed to be smiling. Even at such a distance, Cassis made out the flash of teeth. The message would be for him, he knew, so he straightened his uniform, mouthed a little prayer, then followed Marlyle out of the chamber.

Shohar the Skull-Taker rode purposefully toward the city of beggars. Behind him, his four-hundred-strong force of warriors kept pace, their faces frozen. The warlord was a small man and tried very hard to sit tall in his saddle. His immaculate golden robes of silk fell daintily around his chest and thighs, and his long hair flowed neatly around his shoulders, kept in place with azure ribbons. Neither strong nor muscular, he had a reputation for skill and cleverness that made him proud. Being so slight of build, some said he looked like a woman. These were dead men, mostly.

Shohar thought very carefully, reining up his horse so that it ambled at a snail's pace. Ackle-Nye loomed large in front of him. He could see soldiers milling in the streets, so many black dots. He caught a glare out of one of the towers and knew the reflection was a cannon. Long-range, the kind that could pick him off from here. If he listened very closely he could hear voices echoing through the streets, the anxious sound of shouted orders.

Shohar had always liked Lucyler of Falindar. And he had always honored Tharn. But neither of them were warlords. They simply couldn't understand. It was different for him and Praxtin-Tar. They were men of war, born and bred. To ask them to change was like asking a river to shift directions.

The Skull-Taker brought his warhorse to a halt, turning it so that it faced his troops. They stopped with their master. On the hillside Shohar could see Lucyler looking down on him. Praxtin-Tar was there, too, and all the warriors who were waiting to see the outcome of his mission. A delicious tremor went through him. Shohar reached into his robes and took out the note Lucyler had given him. He couldn't read Naren but he knew what it said, and the words nauseated him. Smiling like a madman, he held it up and showed it to his warriors. Then, making sure Lucyler saw clearly, he closed his fist and crumpled the letter, letting it fall to the ground.

"Take skulls!" he shrieked. "Today we are avenged!"

Lucyler watched the goings-on at the bottom of the hill, in a moment of frozen incredulity. Shohar was saying something; Lucyler didn't have to read his lips. The warlord had dropped the note to the ground. Even now it tumbled away in the breeze. His warriors were shouting, cheering, making ready to charge. Lucyler groaned. Next to him, Praxtin-Tar was chortling. Lucyler shook a fist at him.

"You!" he flared. "You planned this!"

"I did not," laughed Praxtin-Tar. "By Tharn, I swear it!"

"What is he doing, Praxtin-Tar? Tell me!"

"I do not know," answered the warlord. "Again, I swear."

Lucyler didn't know what to believe. Already a ripple of uncertainty was passing through the men on the hill. They looked to him for guidance. Even Praxtin-Tar stared at him questioningly. Down below, Shohar was screaming and charging toward the city, his oversized jiiktar slicing the air. A clarion sounded inside of Ackle-Nye. Two towers glowed menacingly. Shohar's troops had broken formation and now followed their leader, horses thundering, footmen running their hearts out.

"Damn you, Shohar," hissed Lucyler. "Damn you!"

"Your orders," demanded Praxtin-Tar. "We join them?"

A beam of fire tore from a tower, exploding among the charging warriors and setting the earth aflame. Seconds later another cannon detonated. Three horsemen behind Shohar fell, the ground ripped away beneath them. Shohar continued as if nothing in the world would stop him.

"Lucyler?" shouted Praxtin-Tar. "We must join them. Now!"

Lucyler shut his eyes, trying to subdue the worst of his ire. "I hear you, Praxtin-Tar. I hear you." He wanted to let them die, he wanted to let Shohar's own skull be taken, but there was still an objective to be won, and so he gave the order.

Karlaz of the lions waited atop his giant battle-cat, his bronze skin and the beast's tawny fur camouflaging him among the rocks. He was high up in the Iron Mountains with the meandering Saccenne Run far below, and the sun was hot against his flesh. With him were fifty other lion riders, all atop their own mounts, all belted and ready for war. Across the divide of the passage ·were fifty more such warriors, but they were as well concealed as Karlaz, and the warlord had trouble spotting them among the rocks. To his east, farther down in the Run, waited the warlord Nang, a creature who reminded Karlaz more of a monster than a man. Like himself, Nang had been given the job of taking and holding the Run—a mission that seemed particularly well suited to the hearty, naked men of the Fire Steppes. Karlaz and his lions had borne Nang's warriors over the worst parts of the mountains, but no doubt they had made the rest of the way themselves, barefooted.

From his rocky perch Karlaz watched the city. It was an ugly place, gutted with fire and unbalanced by strange architecture. Karlaz had never seen structures so tall. He had heard of Falindar but he had never seen it, and he wondered if the palace of the Daegog looked as atrocious as this thing from Nar. Anaka, his lion, let out a low growl. The beast could sense the coming battle and the anticipation of blood made it restless. Karlaz leaned forward and pushed his fingers roughly through Anaka's mane, calming him. Anaka was a male, more powerful than most riding lions, but despite his size, the beast responded better to an easy touch. The lion ceased his rumbling and settled down, lowering his head a bit. He too watched the city.

Then his ears perked up as he heard a sound. Along the mountainside, every lion and rider raised their heads in turn. Karlaz listened closely. Voices. Shouts. He set his jaw, sorry to see that Lucyler's plan had failed. An orange bolt sliced across the horizon, followed by another and a far-off concussion. The lions roared, grateful for the noise. Karlaz stiffened, holding Anaka firmer. It was the signal he had dreaded. He ordered Anaka out from behind the rocks so that all his comrades could see him, then reluctantly shouted the order to attack.

General Cassis found his horse in the center of the city. As ordered, his aide Marlyle had assembled fifty horsemen to protect him. From here he could watch and conduct the battle safely, at least for a time, and he would be in plain view of the men he asked to die for him. Up in the towers the long-range cannons had opened fire, but there were only two of them. Cassis looked around for Marlyle. He spotted the colonel on a street near the front of the city, desperately shouting orders to a platoon of infantry guarding the road. They had only two handheld cannons and Marlyle was apparently telling them how to use the weapons. Cassis could almost read his mind. Short blasts, he would be telling them. Conserve fuel and set up a diagonal crossfire. He saw the two cannoneers take their positions on opposite sides of the streets. Cassis trotted his horse toward the colonel.

"Marlyle! I told you to stay close. Get over here now!"

His aide hurried over, pushing through the crowds of legionnaires hurrying toward the city entrance. His face was flushed and his eyes jumped fearfully.

"Report," Cassis ordered.

"The first wave is at the city entrance," gasped Marlyle. "I've sent a platoon of cavalry out after them. The—"

A rushing blast tore from the nearest cannon tower, making Marlyle duck. Cassis looked at him impatiently.

"And?"

"The cannons have already taken out some of the first wave."

"What about the third cannon?"

"It's still down. I've got some engineers working on it, trying to cannibalize a fuel line from some of the broken handhelds. It might take time."

"We don't have time!" roared Cassis. "Get some archers in the tower instead. Do it now. And place a battery of archers near the western street. Make sure they block it off. I want it barricaded so the gogs don't overrun it. If they do it'll be bloody hand-to-hand. Go!"

Marlyle grunted and rode off. Cassis steered his horse over to the group Marlyle had been working with. He looked down the street and could see the armies clashing as the gogs pushed their way into Ackle-Nye. Behind the first wave the rest of the warriors were pouring down the mountainside. Another blast from the flame cannons detonated in their ranks. The charging horses split into two directions as they came for the city. Archers along the western barricades pumped arrows into the battlefield. Triin bowmen returned fire, their whistling shafts raining down into the city. Soon the streets would glow with fire as the hand cannoneers opened up. Cassis trotted toward the relative safety of the city center, into the protective folds of his guardians.

Lucyler hurried his horse into the melee. He was chasing Shohar, but the wild warlord was already into the city streets, hacking off armored heads even as flames erupted around him. In the mere minutes since attacking, Shohar's zealots had made stunning progress, pushing back the first line of defenders and crushing the small cavalry brigade sent out to stop them. The warriors of Tatterak and Reen had joined the battle and fought side by side with Shohar's own, an irresistible horde sweeping over the city outskirts. Lucyler had ordered a line of bowmen to concentrate fire on the barricades, to try and soften them and make the advance easier, but the guns in the towers had trained fire on the bowmen and were decimating their ranks. This wouldn't be a battlefield war, Lucyler realized. This would be like fighting in a stone jungle.

Hakan and the other warriors of Tatterak had taken positions near the western barricades and were fighting their way into the city. Lucyler had broken away to chase down Shohar. He spotted the warlord galloping down a narrow street. Two handheld cannons were spitting flames toward him. Shohar ignored the fire as if it were rain. He had twenty horsemen with him, their bloody jiiktars ready to chop down the defenders.

"Skulls!" the warlord screamed. "Skulls for Lucel-Lor!"

Blinded with rage, Lucyler hurried after him. The street erupted with an orange glow. Shohar's big horse jumped to the side, avoiding the blast even as it took down three of his own men. The soldiers at the other end of the street braced themselves. They raised their swords and pulled their triggers. Again they missed Shohar, who galloped into the middle of the street, raised his jiiktar high, and watched in glee as his men engaged the legionnaires. The cannoneers fell in an instant, hacked to pieces by the blades of the warriors. Kerosene leaked from severed hoses as the weapons dropped to the stone roadway. Shohar laughed as if someone were tickling him.

"Shohar!" Lucyler cried. "Damn you!"

He brought his horse up to the warlord and grabbed hold of his golden robes, tearing him from his saddle. Shohar fell to the ground, stunned, and looked up at Lucyler with his maniac's eyes.

"How dare you!" Lucyler spat down at him.

Shohar casually retrieved his jiiktar, seemingly oblivious to the battle around him. He bowed deeply.

"It is the way it is, Lucyler of Falindar," he said. "The way it must be."

"I did not want this!" Lucyler roared. "Neither did Tharn! How dare you disobey me?"

Shohar smiled. "You may have my head when this day is over. But not before I take these skulls." The warlord got back on his horse. "You will thank me for this someday, you and Tharn both."

And then he was gone, driving his horse deeper into the city, leaving Lucyler alone in the carnage. Lucyler watched him go. Overhead the air thundered with the hot might of cannons. An arrow flew by him, followed by a hundred more. Lucyler ignored it all. Today they would avenge Ackle-Nye, and he was powerless to stop the slaughter. Soon Karlaz and his lions would join the battle, and there would be no stopping the unleashed beasts of Chandakkar. They would feast until their bellies were full. And if any Narens tried to escape, to flee into the Run, they would face the animal warlord Nang.

Lucyler felt oddly alone. Slowly, he turned his horse around and rode back toward his men.

"They've taken the western barricades!" Marlyle was out of breath and panicked. "The gogs are overwhelming the perimeters, and streets four and five. One and two are holding, but they won't for long. We have to fall back, sir!"

General Cassis quelled his terror. He had already fallen back as far as he could. Much farther and they would be in the Run. Barely half a mile in front of them, the defenders of the city were fighting the Triin who had flooded into the city. It was bedlam now. Fire had taken over the outskirts and huge pyres of rubble sent oily plumes of smoke into the sky. The cavalry Cassis had sent against the gogs had been nearly wiped out, and riderless horses galloped wildly through the streets, frenzied by the flames and butchery. Marlyle put their numbers at well under three hundred now. In less than an hour they had lost half their men.

"We have to take cover in the buildings," said Marlyle. "We can't be out in the open."

Cassis shook his head. "Take half my guard and seal off this street.

We'll make our stand here. If we must, we can still escape into the Run from here. Call the cannoneers back here, too. We'll need them to defend our position."

"Sir, if we recall the cannons the gogs will just gain ground. The hand-helds are the only thing stopping them."

Cassis wasn't listening. "Order the towers to concentrate fire in front of streets one and two. They won't be able to reach us if they can't make it down those roads." Cassis spun his horse around and ordered twenty of his guard into the front. The horsemen obeyed without question, galloping out of sight around a corner. Marlyle didn't move.

"Colonel, don't go deaf on me. Carry out my orders."

"Sir, we'll die if we don't take cover. Haven't you heard what I said? The gogs are heading this way. What good are . . ."

Marlyle's words trailed off. His eyes widened and fixed on something in the distance. Cassis turned to see what had silenced his aide, and was no less horrified for it. There, climbing over the rubble of the city's western wall, was an army of the strangest monsters Cassis had ever seen. As big as greegans but a hundred times faster, they looked like prehistoric mountain lions, their ears pressed back against their heads, their mouths hissing as they sighted the soldiers.

"Oh, my God . . ." whispered Cassis. "What are those?"

"Chandakkar," gasped Marlyle. "The lions . . ."

Now Cassis panicked. In front of him were a thousand screaming Triin, ready to pull his heart from his chest. He had thought he could retreat to the Run, but now that option had vanished. He was surrounded, and the thought made him tremble.

"Marlyle," he said. "Engage them."

"What?"

"Engage them!" barked Cassis. He drew his sword and pointed toward the coming cats. "Attack. Now!"

"General, no," sputtered Marlyle. "How? We can't fight them!"

General Cassis moved in closer to his aide. His eyes burned with all the hatred he had ever felt, all his lifelong regrets. "Soldier, I'm not ordering you to fight," he said. "I'm ordering you to die."

Lucyler had retreated to the hill, alone, to sit and brood over the battle of Ackle-Nye. He sat on the grass as a spectator might, watching the city burn for a second time and listening to the hoarse shouts of dying men. Some of them were Kronin's men, he supposed, but the supposition didn't bother him. Like Shohar and Praxtin-Tar, Kronin's men had wanted this. They were warriors of a different ilk than himself. Lucyler had spent his life defending the Daegog, but he had hoped to erase some of those mistakes today. It would have made his remaining years so much easier.

"Oh, Richius," he sighed. "I am glad you are not here, my friend."

Richius would have been appalled. For all his blustery talk of revenge, Richius had a conscience. It was what made him special in Lucyler's eyes, and in the eyes of Tharn. A moral Naren, a novelty. Lucyler laughed and leaned back on his elbow. It was cool up here on the hill and he was comfortable. The battle would last through the night perhaps, but by morning they would all be on their way home. Shohar would have a hundred more skulls to add to his collection, and Praxtin-Tar could brag over another massacre. Karlaz would satisfy himself knowing that he had avenged his village. And Nang? Lucyler shrugged. That monster would be sorry he'd missed it.

The only thing that gave Lucyler comfort was the thought of Blackwood Gayle, burning. Even he wouldn't escape the blade this time. He hoped Shohar would be the one to find him. The Skull-Taker could cut his head off, then present the gilded remains to Richius as a gift. Tharn would probably praise him for it.

Lucyler lay down on the earth, picked a blade of grass and wedged it between his teeth, then stared like a child into the sky, imagining shapes in the clouds.

Finally, it was quiet. All the world seemed to have dropped away behind him.

Cassis chanced a look over his shoulder. The city of beggars was gone, swallowed up by the mountains rising on either side of him. He could still see the trails of smoke reaching skyward, but the smell was gone, and the sound of screaming had stopped echoing off the canyon walls. He dared to slow his horse. The beast was lathered and exhausted from galloping. Cassis put his hand to his mouth and found it was trembling.

He'd done it. By God, he had really done it. Marlyle had seen him, but Marlyle was dead now, souring the stomach of one of those cats. Cassis had slipped out of the city while Marlyle and the guards charged the lions. If anyone else had seen his treachery, surely they were dead now, too. As Cassis was dead. He would ride to Talistan, bribe some peasant with the gold in his pockets, and General Barlo Cassis would be gone forever. He would be one of the heroes of Ackle-Nye, gone and soon forgotten. Like the rest of his garrison.

"To hell with you, Arkus," he spat. The curse reverberated up the canyon walls. Here it was very narrow and the rocks amplified every sound. Cassis heard his breathing and the echoing of his horse's hooves, but he heard nothing else and the silence was magnificent. He thrilled at it. He was alive!

"To hell with you, Arkus!" he cried again, lifting his voice higher and laughing. Maybe he would go back to Nar and spit on the old man's grave. But no, Arkus would never die. Others died for him. That's how it was for royalty. Cassis knew he would never be royal himself, but that was all right. He would become a farmer, or maybe a blacksmith. And he would leave Talistan and go to live in Criisia or Gorkney, somewhere far away. Somewhere that his face would never be recognized. He would hide his sword, too, or maybe sell it. Cassis was tired of killing. He had given his last order and murdered a man whom he once considered a friend—if legionnaires had friends. They probably didn't, he supposed, and that made him hate his old life even more.

He rode on, imagining the new life he would make. His horse was first to hear the sound. A scraping, up in the mountains. The horse twitched. So did Cassis. His eyes shifted to the place where the sound had come from. Or was it over there? Cassis mumbled a curse. There were animals in these mountains. He had seen a bear once. He put his hand to his sword pommel and listened.

An arrow came down, then another. Cassis swore. His horse gave a rattling whinny and collapsed, two shafts sticking from its neck. Cassis tumbled from the creature's back, spilling onto the hard ground. The impact knocked the breath from his lungs. Panicked, he made to scramble to his feet as something big and white dropped down out of the mountains before him. Cassis looked up. It was a man and it was not a man. Naked and tattooed, its white head was bald but for a snake of hair pulled back in a tail. Cassis scrambled backward, falling over his dying horse and rolling onto his back. The man-thing stalked him. Others like it fell out of the canyon, surrounding him. Cassis reached for his sword but the big one brought down a foot, stopping his hand. Cassis lay very still.

"All right," he said unsteadily. "Take it easy. Easy. Triin, right? You're Triin?"

The tattooed man smiled, baring teeth filed down to fangs. He hovered over Cassis curiously, inspecting him with his animal eyes. Cassis let him trace a finger over his face, studying his lines. The man laughed savagely, then pointed to himself, poking a finger at his own bare chest.

"Nang!" he barked. "Nang!"

Cassis fought to still his fear. "Just take it easy," he tried, hoping his tone would relax them. "I'm no one. I'm just on my way home. All right? Retreating."

The creature bent over him and studied his features. He ran his hands over Cassis' skull, feeling its shape and studying it with astute eyes.

"Mmmm, Shohar," he commented. "Shohar min taka."

Cassis watched in horror as the fanged Triin took a knife from his belt. He tried to fight his way to his feet, but hands were all over him, holding him down. He screamed and kicked but they ignored him, and the one with the knife inched closer, put the blade to his throat, and carefully began carving off the general's head.

FIFTY-ONE

It took over a week for Richius to make his decision, but in the end it seemed the most natural of choices. He wanted to fight Nar, and Tharn wouldn't let him. But there was a place he could go where Tharn had little sway, and where they might just welcome a man with his outlaw reputation. The Dring Valley was no place for him and he knew it. Besides, since Tharn had returned he was seeing Dyana only at mealtimes. She was back to her sad, respectable self, and Richius thought better than to try and change her. Her husband was alive again, maybe even immortal. It was time to give up.

When the day of his decision finally came, he awoke with a grim smile. There were tasks at hand, preparations to be made. He would have to tell Tharn to make Jarra warlord. Worse, he would have to say farewell to Dyana and Shani. He breakfasted alone that morning, rehearsing his good-bye speech in his chamber while he ate, wondering if they were missing him in the dining chamber. He supposed so. It was the only time Dyana could really speak to him, if only to give him a surreptitious wink while Tharn's back was turned. She would certainly be disappointed in his choice, maybe even beg him to come with them to Falindar. But Falindar was no home for him. There was only one home for a Vantran, and that was Aramoor.

He finished his breakfast and left the plate on the bed, then dressed himself in a clean shirt and a pair of breeches made for him by the women of the keep, who had been treating him with unfamiliar deference since his confounded ascension to lordship. He decided he would see Tharn before speaking to Dyana, asking the cunning-man's permission for a private talk with his wife. The baby would be with her, he hoped, and he could say a proper, if unintelligible, farewell to her. But before Tharn there was one other person he wanted to see, someone he had almost forgotten about since Tharn's return.

As always, he found her reading a book, this time in the garden. She smiled as she saw him coming toward her.

"Kalak!" called the spritely Pris, leaping off the cracked fountain rim she used as a seat. She closed the book and waved at him, bidding him to hurry. Richius smiled at her from across the garden and quickened his pace. He adored Pris. She was the kind of child he hoped Shani would become. The girl's white head bobbed excitedly as he approached.

"You were not at breakfast," she scolded. "Why?"

"Am I to explain everything to you now?" he laughed. "Were you so insolent with your father?"

Pris frowned, and Richius realized she was slowly deciphering his words. "Insolent," he said. "It means rude."

"Father never let me question him," she admitted. "But you are not like Father."

"True," said Richius. He sat down on the edge of the fountain gently, testing its sturdiness. "I was busy this morning, Pris. I have something to tell you, and I don't know what you're going to think of it."

Pris hopped back onto the fountain and looked up at him. "Bad?" she asked.

"Not really," he assured her. "I'm going away. I'm not going to be warlord here anymore."

Pris' eyes widened. "Away? Where away?"

"Have you ever heard of Liss?"

"Yes," said Pris. "Father told me once. They are far away, on an island. Is that where you are leaving for?"

Richius nodded. "Sort of. They have ships around Lucel-Lor, helping us. They fight against Nar. I'm going to help them now."

"No, no," said Pris. "You cannot go. Father made you warlord. Chose you, Kalak. He liked you."

"And I liked him," said Richius sadly. "But it was an accident, Pris. I was the only one around when your father died, and he wanted to make sure someone would look after you and your family. I know he would have chosen Dumaka Jarra if he could have, but there wasn't time. So now I'm just doing what he would have done himself. Tharn's back and he will make it all right. He will make Jarra warlord."

"Will he take care of us?" asked Pris.

"You know he will," said Richius. "He's a good man, and your father trusted him. He will take the best of care of you, I'm sure. And I'm sure it's what your mother would want. I'm not Triin, after all. You should have a leader that's of your own people."

Pris dropped her head. "I am afraid for you," she said. "Bhapo told me you would be safe now, no more fighting for you. If you go to fight you may be killed. Like Father."

"Pris," said Richius gently. He slipped his arm around her tiny shoulders. "This is something I have to do. Your father died defending his home. That's what I'm going to do. If I'm killed doing it then at least my death will have some meaning. But my life won't have meaning if I stay. I have to try. Can you understand that?"

"No." She raised her head and focused her sad eyes on him. "I do not. I do not understand why Father died. Or the others. All the women cry now. Mother cries. Why, Kalak?"

Richius was silent for a long moment. At last he sighed and said, "Because they miss people they love, that's why. But I like to think the dead see us crying, wherever they are, and know we miss them."

Pris looked dazzled by his answer. "I miss Father," she said. "And I will miss you."

"Oh, Pris," said Richius. "I'll miss you, too." He bent forward and placed a delicate kiss on her head. "I'm not leaving for another day or so. I'll see you before I go. Tell your mother for me what's happening. Tell her I'm sorry about everything. She'll know what you mean."

"I will tell her."

"Good," said Richius, rising from his seat. "I'll see you later, when we sup."

Pris said nothing more and he left her, steeling himself as he walked back toward the castle. Next was Tharn. He supposed he would find the cunning-man in the quarters he had selected for himself, habitually huddled over papers and maps. Since Karlaz and his lion riders had left, there had been almost nothing for Tharn to do but rest and occupy his mind with the few books he could wrestle away from Pris. They were so much alike, thought Richius. She was more Tharn's daughter than Voris'. But Pris had taken the news of his departure surprisingly well; he expected Tharn to put up more of a struggle. Not that it mattered. Tharn could easily stop him from fighting in Lucel-Lor, but the seas and the Lissens were under no one's dominion. Richius had made up his mind to be as stubborn as Tharn.

He entered the castle quietly, passing under the iron gates. That's when he heard the scream, like the braying of a lamb. But then it took on volume and definition, and he knew at once it was Pris.

He ran back toward the courtyard, dashing through the hall and passing under the gate. There in the yard was Pris, held aloft in a massive, gauntleted fist. The fist connected to a broad-shouldered body hung with a black cape and capped with a maniacal, masked face.

Blackwood Gayle, grinning like a madman, lifted Pris by the hair and held her up like a prize turkey. Behind him rode a brigade of skull-faced soldiers, sitting like statues upon their giant warhorses. The baron's one eye twinkled as he saw Richius skid into the courtyard.

"Good morning, Vantran," came the devilish voice. "Did you miss me?"

Richius stood stupefied, staring slack-jawed at his nemesis.

"Why so shocked?" asked Blackwood Gayle. "You should have known I'd come back for you. Or did you think I was dead?"

Richius chanced a small step toward Gayle. There were only a few yards separating them. Behind Gayle the Shadow Angels sat in mute abeyance, awaiting word from their master. Richius' eyes darted up to the watchtower.

"Your man up there is dead," said Gayle, reading Richius' mind. "You forget what a Shadow Angel can do. You should have been better prepared for us." Gayle hefted Pris and laughed. "Or was this the best you could do?"

"Let her go," commanded Richius. "Now."

"These gogs always meant so much to you," chuckled Gayle. "I will let her go. *If* you agree to my terms."

"You're a coward, Gayle. Hiding behind a child. A coward, like your father."

Gayle's face did a horrible contortion. The gauntlet opened and Pris dropped to the ground. She scrambled toward Richius.

"I am not a coward," Gayle growled. He folded his arms and watched as Pris wrapped herself around Richius' legs. "One of yours?" he taunted.

Richius pried Pris' arms away. He took her hands and knelt down to face her.

"Go inside," he ordered, "quickly," and shooed her toward the castle. Pris disappeared, crying wildly for help. Richius could hear a commotion brewing inside the castle.

Don't come out here, Tharn, he thought. *Please.*

"Now we talk," said Gayle. He hoisted a thumb toward the soldiers over his shoulder. "Recognize them?"

Richius nodded. "Shadow Angels."

"Compliments of our friend Biagio," said Gayle with a smirk. "You know what they can do. And I know you don't have the means to stop them. So listen to me very carefully. I have a proposition for you."

"I'm listening," said Richius. With only a handful of warriors left in the castle, the Shadow Angels would have no trouble reaching Dyana and Shani. It would be a massacre. "What's your proposition?"

Gayle grinned. "I'll bet there are people in there you care about, eh? People you wouldn't want to see harmed?"

Richius wouldn't reply.

"Where's Voris? I expected to see him here, protecting you."

"He's dead," said Richius. "Like your horsemen. What's your proposition?"

The insult erased Gayle's smile. "Simple. You and me. Here and now."

Richius laughed. "Oh, yes. That's a wonderful idea. Very generous of you, Baron. I'm sure your friends behind you won't help you at all."

Blackwood Gayle began to answer, then saw a small group of warriors rushing out of the castle. "Ah, here come your own friends. Pretty meager, I'd say."

The warriors swarmed into the courtyard with their jiiktars raised. Richius put up a hand to halt them and they obeyed, stopping just short of Blackwood Gayle.

"Call them off," ordered Gayle. He made no move to reach for his own weapon. "You'll be sorry if you don't."

"They don't understand a word I say," said Richius wickedly. "They may cut your throat by accident."

Gayle's face was stone. "If they do, then every one of these Shadow Angels will ride down on your little castle. Those are the orders I've given. Kill me, and all of you die." He laughed. "These Angels are such fanatics, you know."

Richius ordered the warriors back. Dyana came racing out of the castle.

"Richius," she cried, running up to him. She glared at Blackwood Gayle. "What is happening? Who is this?"

I'm glad you don't remember, thought Richius as he pulled her arm away. Gayle leered at her menacingly.

"I am Blackwood Gayle, baron of Talistan. And who are you, woman? The whore Vantran came to save?"

Richius scowled.

"Oh, yes," crooned the baron. "I've heard that story. Biagio told me himself. And guess who told him? Who do you think betrayed you, Vantran?"

"Baron . . ."

Gayle laughed. "You don't know, do you? It was the old man! Your dear Jojustin. Pity, don't you think? You can't trust anyone these days."

It was the news Richius had dreaded, and it ate at him. But it was also part of Gayle's tactics. "Get inside, Dyana," he said.

"No," said Dyana. "I will not leave you!"

"Go!" shouted Richius, grabbing her arm and pushing her roughly toward the gate. "And tell your husband not to come out here."

"Have her bring you a weapon," thundered Gayle. "We have a score to settle, you and I."

Dyana hovered by the gate, waiting for Richius' order. He held up a hand to stop her as he faced Gayle.

"A duel?" he asked. "Why would I fight you?"

"I'm getting impatient," rumbled Gayle. "Your time is running out. Tick tock, tick tock . . ."

"Dyana, bring my sword," Richius called. "And tell everyone to stay inside. Everyone, do you hear?"

She didn't answer but sped into the castle. The warriors kept their eyes trained on Gayle.

"Now," said Richius, "answer my question. Why should I fight you?"

"I'm giving you a choice, Vantran. Fight me, or everyone in this castle dies, including that lovely thing that just left." Gayle licked his lips. "Lovely. Just like your wife."

Richius leapt forward, balling his fingers into a fist and driving it into Gayle's astounded face. Gayle stumbled backward, too slow to avoid the attack, and the fist collided with his mask, driving it into his flesh. The mask buckled and Gayle howled, felled by the blow. The Shadow Angels began to move, but Gayle ordered them back.

"No!" he cried. He put his hand to his bloodied face and rose to his feet, hissing. "No one will have you but me, Jackal. You're mine!"

"Then come and get me, you murdering bastard. I'm ready for you!"

Gayle laughed and took off his mask, flinging it over his shoulder to reveal his hideous visage. Blood dripped down his forehead into his blind eye. "Not yet," he said. "I want to do this right. Man to man, Aramoorian to Talistanian, once and for all!"

"And what assurance do you give me, monster? I'm fighting for the lives in this castle. How do I know you won't deceive me?"

Gayle raised a hand to the soldiers behind him. "Lieutenant," he called. A single Shadow Angel trotted out of the lineup. "This pup and I are going to duel. If I am killed, you will turn around and ride back to the Empire without harming anyone inside this castle. Is that clear?"

"Yes, Baron," answered the soldier.

"Repeat it for me."

"If you are killed we will ride back to the Empire. We will harm no one inside this castle."

"They're Shadow Angels, Vantran," said Gayle. "They follow orders to the letter. You know that."

Richius was stupefied. "Why?" he asked. "What's the point of all this, Gayle? You have the men to take the castle. Why not just do it? You're a bloody bastard, I'm sure you'd enjoy it."

"Indeed I would. But then I might not get the chance to fight you myself, and I do so want that. It's part of my sad tale, you see. My men are all dead. You killed them. And now the Narens are calling me a coward. They think you've beaten me, Vantran. But you never could beat me. I was always your better. Now I'm going to prove it."

"That's a big boast. And if I lose?"

"Fight well," advised Gayle. "Your friends are depending on you. If you lose they will die, quite horribly I assure you. Particularly that pretty one."

Richius swallowed his ire. "I'll fight you. But only if you leave this castle alone, even if I lose."

"No chance," said Gayle. "I want your best, Vantran. You need something more than your own wretched life to fight for. The lives in the castle for your best duel, those are my terms. Consider your situation. I think my offer is quite generous."

Dyana came through the gate then, bearing Jessicane. She had taken it out of its scabbard so that the old blade glimmered in the sunlight. She handed it to Richius.

"What will you do?" she asked.

"I will fight him," said Richius softly.

"No," she gasped, clutching his hand. "Richius, you are still weak. He is too big. He will kill you."

"He will kill us all if I don't fight him," said Richius. Gayle was waiting impatiently, tapping a foot on the grass. Richius ignored him and walked Dyana toward the door. "Get inside," he said. "Order the warriors inside, too. Close the gate and get ready for a fight. And whatever you do, don't let Gayle see Tharn."

"No," begged Dyana. She would not let go of his hand. "Do not do this. Run inside. We can fight them."

"We can't win, Dyana. There are too many. Do as I say. Take Shani and hide somewhere in the castle." He put his arms around her. "I love you," he whispered.

"And I you. Live for me."

"Hurry up, Vantran," said Gayle. "I'm ready."

"Dyana, get inside. Order the others in for me. Tell them it's what I want."

Quickly Dyana told the warriors to follow her inside. Each flashed Richius a pleading look, but Richius waved them to go. They surrounded Dyana and escorted her through the gates. Richius waited until the iron gate closed before turning his attention back to Gayle, holding out his broadsword for the baron to see.

"Do you know this sword?" he asked. "You should. It killed your uncle. And now it's going to kill you."

An insane fire burned in Gayle's lone eye. "I hope your father taught you well, whelp," he said, and drew his own sword, a long, thin blade with a serrated edge and jewel-encrusted hilt. With his other hand he unclasped his cape and let it fall to the ground. "I was always better than you, Vantran. Always."

Richius hefted Jessicane in two hands and stepped forward. "Prove it, murderer."

They began to circle each other, Gayle dancing gleefully in a wide arc while Richius kept his steps short and light. He knew the baron's bulk could easily exhaust him, and without any armor it would take only a single blow to bring him down. But Gayle wore only leather himself, and Jessicane's toothy edge could easily bite through it.

As they squared off, Richius' eyes kept darting back distractedly to the castle. The gate remained closed, but concerned faces stared down at him from the dingy windows. He forced them out of his mind and concentrated on Gayle, who was closing the gap between them.

"Your wife was a tasty bit," he taunted. "She called for you when I killed her."

Richius felt his legs turn to water. *A trick,* he told himself. *Don't listen.* But Sabrina's image flared in his memory, clouding his mind. He fought to suppress it, struggling not to hear her distant screams. He glimpsed Dyana's worried face pressed against a windowpane. She would be next if he didn't win.

Gayle screamed and charged forward, thrusting with his sword. Richius skidded aside, batting the blade away. Jessicane rang out as the two swords collided, driving Richius to a knee. Gayle howled and hammered down again and again, raining blows on Richius, who kept his blade extended like a metal roof against the vicious onslaught.

That's it, he thought. *Tire yourself.*

Blackwood Gayle backed off and Richius sprang, both hands driving his sword at the baron's belly. But Gayle was agile and expected the counter. He twisted and let Richius skid by, then swung his weapon. The flat of the blade smashed against Richius' unprotected back, setting the acid-chewed skin afire with pain. Richius gasped and stumbled away. Gayle simply laughed.

"You are weak," the baron chortled. "No match at all. As I suspected."

A little prayer sprang into Richius' mind. He was panicking. Unbearable pain squeezed his breath into short bursts. Fevered drops of sweat blossomed on his forehead. In the windows he saw Dyana's mouth moving, urging him on desperately. Najjir was beside her, her eyes wide. Mercifully, Tharn was nowhere to be seen. If Gayle knew he was here . . .

"Come along now, boy," jeered the baron. "Your lesson isn't over yet."

Richius lifted his sword again and readied for another bout. He needed an advantage over Gayle, but didn't have one. Already Jessicane had become like lead in his grasp. And Gayle was barely winded.

Gayle charged unexpectedly forward and they clashed again. His sword swung up toward Richius' head. Richius swiped the blade aside and drove his knee into Gayle's hip. The baron's own knees buckled for an instant and he tumbled into the dirt, rolling away from Richius' attack. A handful of dirt sprang into Richius' eyes, forcing him to back away while Gayle regained his footing. The two duelists moved apart and righted themselves. Gayle was gasping at last, dizzied by the attack. Richius blinked away the motes of dirt. The flesh of his back still tingled. He shouted and came at Gayle again, pressing him back with a ferocious series of blows. Gayle parried each of them expertly. Sparks flew from the clashing blades. Exhausted, Richius backed away, readying for the baron's counter. But Gayle was breathing too hard to attack.

"You're tiring, Baron," hissed Richius. "You're getting sloppy."

Gayle spat a wad of saliva at Richius and wiped a hand over his sweaty face. Blood dripped into his eye, blinding him. Richius saw the chance and sprang forward, growling like a wildcat and flinging himself at Gayle. The Talistanian brought up his defense an instant too late. Jessicane glanced off his blade and across his rib cage, cutting open the leather armor and tasting the tender skin beneath. Gayle swore and thrust at Richius, driving him back. Blood sluiced from his side. He doubled over for a moment, then came at Richius again, screaming and unleashing a berserker barrage.

Jessicane blocked the blows, but the attack went on and on. Fatigue tightened the muscles in Richius' arm. The flesh of his back roared with pain. He was panting, fighting off the tide of metal by instinct alone. He glimpsed the gate of the castle moving upward and an animal panic shot through him.

"No!" he cried. His eyes swept back to the castle and caught the image of a cloaked man emerging from the shadows.

It was all Gayle needed.

The thundering pain of a kneed groin ripped Richius in half. Gayle's sword pommel slammed into his temple. The world winked out of view. A nauseating sensation overcame him, and when his eyes opened he was staring at the sky. The looming figure of Blackwood Gayle blotted out the sun. Quickly he tried to snatch up his sword, but Gayle's boot came down on his fingers. Richius cried out in anguish, and all his thoughts were suddenly of Dyana.

We are dead, he thought.

"You have lost," echoed Gayle. He brought the point of his sword to Richius' throat and pressed a foot down on his chest. The baron was wheezing and laughing at the same time, favoring his bleeding side as he pushed the air from Richius' lungs. "I am the best," he declared triumphantly. "The best."

Richius fought to remain conscious. He saw Tharn step out from the darkness of the gateway. A trio of warriors was with him, each with a bow in hand and a jiiktar on his back. Richius cursed. What did it matter now? Gayle had beaten him. The castle was finished anyway. He gritted his teeth and awaited the final blow.

"Do it," he spat into Gayle's face. "Kill me."

"Oh, no," sang Gayle. He leaned a little closer. "Not yet. I want you to see what I'm going to do."

"You are a butcher!"

Gayle seemed to love the insults. "Yes, yes," he agreed. "And so much worse, as you shall see. Who should I take first, Jackal? Your pretty little bitch?"

"You will take no one, monster," declared a ringing voice. Tharn stepped into the courtyard with his trio of bowmen, walking without a cane, as straight and upright as any man. His shoulders were squared and his tufted hair stood in hackles from his scalp, and as he spoke he bared his teeth like a wolf. The voice bespoke nothing of infirmity, but rang in the yard with the might of a trumpet and the defiance of a battered flag. Astonished, Gayle turned toward the castle.

"Who are you?" he asked incredulously.

"I am Tharn," proclaimed the cunning-man. "I am Storm Maker."

The sword in Gayle's grip slackened. "You?" he roared. "You!"

"Back away, savage," commanded Tharn. The veins on his face twisted like snakes. He brought up a glowing fist and his broken body seemed to grow, nourished by the glamour he called down from heaven. Behind the castle, the sky deepened to a violent gray. "Away," he ordered. "Today you are undone!"

"Do not thwart me, sorcerer!" bellowed Gayle. An electrified cloud rose over the castle like a demon's hand. Gayle drove down hard on Richius with his boot. "I will kill him!"

Tharn twitched a finger and his bowmen loosed their arrows. The shafts slammed into the baron's neck, piercing his windpipe. Richius twisted out from under the man, grabbing his sword, barely able to hold it and staggering to his feet. The Shadow Angels snapped their reins. Gayle gurgled an order and watched in horror as Richius brought Jessicane down. His skull cracked, and Blackwood Gayle of Talistan dropped in a heap to the ground.

"Inside!" Tharn commanded. Richius turned to see the cunning-man with his arms outstretched, a monstrous, black aura sparking around him. His crimson eyes pulsed with fire. He was a thing of hell, a devil, mad and possessed of some unholy force. The warriors of Castle Dring came screaming out of the gate, storming toward the Shadow Angels. Richius stumbled forward, dropping Jessicane and struggling toward the gate. His crushed hand drooped uselessly at his wrist and the pain through his body made every step an agony. Behind him the Shadow Angels drew their swords to meet the handful of warriors. He could see Dyana rushing out to help him.

"No!" he moaned. "Go back."

But Dyana dashed out into the yard and grabbed his arm, wrapping it around her neck and dragging him under the gate. The sky outside darkened. Richius turned to glimpse the crazed figure of Tharn raising his hands, and the astonished faces of Shadow Angels as they eyed the raging thing growing over the castle. Tharn's robes blew wildly against his body. A roaring boom detonated in the heavens, shaking the walls of the keep and sending chunks of stone tumbling down from the towers. Dyana fell and put her hands to her ears. Richius dropped down over her as shards of rock shook from the cracked ceiling. Dyana tried to rise but he held her down.

"Stay!" he ordered, shielding her from the rocky rain. Out in the yard, the Shadow Angels fought against the stiffening wind. Branches blew back from tree trunks and snapped away. The horses reared as their masters urged them onward. A purple mist twisted around their hooves. And Tharn endured it all like a mountain, tall and wrathful and remorseless.

"Die!" he shouted.

Another vicious hammerblow detonated in the heavens, an earth-shaking boom that toppled a handful of horses. Richius felt a viselike pressure squeezing his head. Beneath him, Dyana screamed. In the yard, more horses tottered and collapsed, throwing off their riders as they snorted blood and cried in pain. Richius cried out, too. The terrible pressure made his eardrums pop with a sharp snap. He crawled toward the gate, shaking and stretching out his broken hand.

"Tharn!" he called. "Stop!"

Tharn ignored him. The Drol was almost invisible now, cloaked in the lavender mist. Through the haze, Richius could see the writhing figures of the Shadow Angels as they clutched at their heads, trying to keep their skulls from splitting. The enormous pressure of the air grew to a terrible crescendo. The mist rose with the tortured cries of the men. Richius felt himself losing consciousness, drifting away even as he dragged himself toward Tharn.

"Stop," he groaned. He clawed at the dirt, crushed by the furious noise. Tharn was gone, swallowed up in the purple storm. Richius put his cheek to the ground and covered his head with his arms, burying himself in the grass. The pressure bore down on him, suffocating him, until he could stand no more. He was going to die. Dyana, too. But not Shani. Shani would live. Richius closed his eyes and let the pain come, calmed by the serene image of his beautiful daughter. . . .

Then the weight of the storm was gone. Groggily, he raised his head. A dying breeze stirred the dissipating fog. The world was still. He heard a clamor behind him, near the castle gate. He struggled to his feet and heard Dyana's call.

"Richius!" she cried frantically. "Where are you?"

Numb and baffled, Richius rose, tears streaking down his cheeks as he staggered toward the castle. There he saw Dyana calling for him through the fog. She rose when she saw him and ran to him, throwing her arms passionately around him and speaking his name again and again. Richius buried his face in her hair.

"I'm alive," he assured her. "I'm alive."

Slowly the fog lifted around them. Richius embraced Dyana. And then at once the same horrible notion occurred to them. Dyana pulled free of his arms and shrieked.

"Tharn!"

A hedge of purple mist rolled back from the yard, revealing the cunning-man's crumpled body. He lay on his back in a twisted heap, his chest rising and falling with desperate breaths, his fingernails scratching up earth as he tried to drag himself onto his side. Richius and Dyana raced over to him, kneeling down beside him. The glamour had abandoned him. Once again he was a mangled creature, deformed and hacking up blood.

"My wife?" he said in a shaky whisper. "They are dead?"

Dyana lifted his trembling hand and put it to her breast. "They are dead, my husband," she answered. "You have saved us."

Another plume of blood gushed from Tharn's mouth. Beneath it swam a crooked smile. "Saved . . ." he gasped. "Saved . . ."

"Tharn," said Richius desperately. "Don't move. We'll help you. . . ."

"I am dying," croaked the Drol. His body shook as he spoke, enduring every word like torture. "Lorris calls me. Your hand, Richius, your hand . . ."

Richius gave Tharn his good hand, placing it with Dyana's in the cunning-man's gnarled fingers. Tharn looked up at them with his crimson eyes, and there was something of joy in them before the inner light dimmed. The body seized, the fingers fell away, and the Storm Maker of Lucel-Lor drifted into oblivion.

FIFTY-TWO

Like most events in Nar, the funeral for Emperor Arkus was a thing of scale. Count Renato Biagio, resplendent in crimson, addressed a crowd of over ten thousand mourners before sealing the giant mausoleum that would house the bones of the Great One forever. It had rained all that day and the night before, but Biagio endured the storms with grace. He himself was past mourning now, and there were schemes in his mind that preoccupied him.

All the nations closest to Nar City had sent delegations to the funeral, all bearing wishes for Arkus' ascent to heaven. The legionnaires of Nar had been assembled at the order of their supreme commander, General Vorto, who stood beside his good friend Herrith on the ceremonial dais, watching Biagio with his cold blue eyes and stupidly betraying his every treacherous thought. On the dais with Biagio was Admiral Danar Nicabar, Vorto's naval counterpart, who had docked the *Fearless* in the harbor and who, at Biagio's order, had recalled the entire Black Fleet from its war in Lucel-Lor. The crowds marveled at the sight of the proud armada, a hundred gleaming warships choking the watery horizon. As Biagio finished his eulogy, his eyes flicked to Herrith. Among the crowds were a thousand of Vorto's soldiers, religious devotees all. On the sea waited Nicabar's unflinching armada. Biagio grinned at the fat bishop. He ended his speech and surrendered the floor to Herrith.

Under the shadow of the great Cathedral of the Martyrs, Bishop Herrith stretched out his arms, hushing his flock with the power of his

office. He told the throngs of frightened Narens that God was merciful
and that He would guide them with His mighty hand by divinely choosing a worthy successor to the Iron Throne. They were a people of mo-
rality and faith, said the bishop, and they needed a leader whom God
would not shun. Biagio smiled throughout the bishop's speech, already
certain of his nemesis' plans. The count was not fearful. He was the
Roshann, and the Roshann was everywhere. Herrith held no surprises
for him.

When the talks were done and the roses thrown, Biagio and Nicabar
hurried from the dais, disappearing into the crowd. Swallowed up in the
ocean of flesh, Herrith and his lapdog Vorto did not pursue them. A rush
of excitement raced through the count as he made his way through the
Naren streets. As he had suspected, the awesome sight of Nicabar's navy
had stilled the bishop's hand. Even Vorto, a man with an army at his
beckoning, didn't dare challenge the cannons of the Black Fleet. Biagio
and Nicabar boarded a stout rowboat that was waiting for them at the
pier and departed Nar City.

Biagio stood up in the boat as the sailors rowed them toward the fleet,
but his eyes were not on the armada. Rather, they lingered long and bitterly on the crowded Black City, on the rows of soldiers who had been ordered to assassinate him, and on the impossibly tall Cathedral of the
Martyrs, that garish monument to Herrith's merciless God. Biagio waved
theatrically. Over his shoulder, the long-range guns of the *Fearless* were
trained on the city. The count laughed, happy with himself. The *Fearless*
would take them to Crote. For now, Herrith and Vorto would have Nar
City. But power was a fleeting thing.

"There will be a reckoning!" Biagio called, sure that no one on shore
had heard him. Again he laughed, full of vicious glee. Herrith was a
clever man, but he had made some frighteningly stupid oversights. One of
them was a midget with a giant brain.

Nicabar, who had been talking with a sailor, came up behind Biagio
and put a hand on his shoulder. "It's done," said the admiral. "They tell
me Bovadin is already aboard."

Biagio gave a terrible smile. Throughout Nar, there was only one man
who could synthesize the drug that kept them all alive. Now that the Iron
Circle had corroded, it was a fortunate thing indeed that the little scientist had chosen their side.

"Bad luck for you, Herrith," whispered Biagio. Not even Bovadin
knew for sure, but he supposed withdrawal from the drug was fatal.

When Lucyler returned to Dring, he went at once to the dilapidated
residence of the valley's former master. Those in the castle had been waiting for him, for he had been seen approaching with the barrel-chested

Karlaz, and the word spread swiftly from the watchtower that the two heroes of Ackle-Nye were returning.

Richius heard the news of Lucyler's return while fitting his horse with a pair of shoes. He told Dyana he would meet Lucyler at Tharn's gravesite. He was skimming stones off the little stream behind the keep when he saw Dyana and Lucyler emerge from the thickets. Lucyler seemed stricken. His face was creased with lines Richius had never noticed before. Lucyler took three steps before he noticed the marker beside Richius. It was a man-sized gravestone crudely carved by one of the valley's elders, a farmer with an amateurish talent for masonry. Lucyler slowed as he approached the headstone, almost stopping until Richius bid him forward.

"Come, my friend," said Richius. He went to Lucyler and took him by the hand, guiding him toward the grave beside the stream. Lucyler stared at the inscription for a long moment before his gaze dropped to the ground.

"I knew when I saw Dyana," he said grimly. "What happened, Richius? Was it Gayle? I know that scoundrel escaped Ackle-Nye."

"He died saving me," said Richius. He recalled with regard the cunning-man's insistence that he live. In the end, they were so much alike. Tharn had wanted to save a stranger. Richius had wanted to save Dyana.

Lucyler sank to his knees and kissed the gray rock bearing Tharn's name. On the other side of the stream, in a place unmarked and unceremonious, there was another grave, one Lucyler had helped to dig. In the place where Dinadin rested there was no gravestone, only the easy shade of a tree and a handful of poppies Richius had planted when no one was watching. It occurred to him as he watched his broken friend that this bright little refuge had suddenly become a very dim place indeed.

"It was his choice," said Richius. "I swear to you I did not ask it."

"He was a good man," said Lucyler. He looked up at Richius. "You know that now, yes?"

"They were all good men," replied Richius. "They all deserved better than what they got."

Lucyler looked again at the grave marker, grimacing. "This is it for him, then? The end?"

"There is talk in the keep about a proper funeral. Now that all of you are back, we can have a ceremony if you like. Is that what Triin do when a leader dies?"

"I do not know what Tharn would want," replied Lucyler. "He was simple in many ways. Perhaps this is enough for him." He rose to his feet. "I will have to tell Karlaz of his death. He is waiting for me back at the keep. He expected to tell Tharn about our victory."

"Tell *me* about it," pressed Richius. "A messenger told us that you'd won. Is it true? Did you beat them back? All of them?"

Lucyler nodded as if his mind was a thousand miles out to sea. "The lions were unstoppable," he replied. "Just like Tharn said they would be. Karlaz lost only three men."

"And the city? How did the warlords do?"

Lucyler grimaced. "I am a slaughterer now, Richius. A butcher. There were thousands of us, and we were out of control. The Narens in the city never had a chance. Shohar ordered his men to take skulls. They hacked the Narens to pieces, made them eat each others' hearts." Lucyler sighed and bit down hard on his trembling lip. "I will never be clean again," he said. "Tharn would be ashamed of me."

"Then you did win. We're safe."

"Maybe safer than you know," said Lucyler. "I have more news for you, my friend. Your emperor is dead."

"Arkus?" asked Richius, astonished. "When?"

"Before the attack on Ackle-Nye. Nang came across a messenger in the Run, on his way to Ackle-Nye. He tortured the man. He wanted to know if more troops were being sent. But Nar City is mourning the loss of your emperor."

Richius fell back against a tree. "Dead," he whispered. It was too unbelievable, like a dream. With the old man gone, Lucel-Lor truly was safe. It might be months before they sent more troops, or maybe never. Tharn had gotten his wish. Lucel-Lor was free.

"He should have died in Falindar," said Lucyler bitterly, rubbing a hand over the rugged gravestone. "That is where he should rest."

"He'll rest well enough here, next to Voris and the others. It's quiet here. I think he would have liked it. And people can come and see this place and remember. They won't disturb Dinadin. They won't even know he's here."

Lucyler smiled bleakly at his comrade. "What will you do now, Richius? Will you stay here?"

"I've been wondering that myself. I'm not warlord here anymore. Jarra is master of Dring now. Before he died, Tharn told me he would do that for me. No one has questioned it. Jarra has told us we can stay, but it doesn't seem right somehow, and I know there are people in Nar who will come looking for me."

"Then come with me to Falindar. There will be much to do with both Kronin and Tharn dead. You could help me."

Richius chuckled. "I don't know anything about being a warlord. If I did, I might have kept the job here. Besides, my work with Nar isn't done yet."

"Oh?"

"Aramoor, Lucyler. I still have a kingdom to free. If the Lissens go on fighting, I have to help them."

"Richius," said Lucyler evenly. "Aramoor may never be free again. We freed Lucel-Lor. That should be enough for any man. Even you. Do not destroy yourself chasing something that can never be. This is your home now. You must try to forget Aramoor."

Richius smiled. "You know I can't do that."

Lucyler nodded. "You are welcome in Falindar," he said simply. He started back toward the keep then saw Dyana in the trees. Lucyler tossed Richius a grin.

"She is yours now, then?"

"We will marry," replied Richius. "And we will be together. Finally."

Lucyler winked at Richius, then turned toward Dyana. Richius watched him perform a flourishing bow before disappearing into the trees. Dyana came to Richius, looking over her shoulder after Lucyler.

"You told him?" she asked.

Richius nodded. "He took it as well as could be expected. He said he knew about it when he saw your face."

Dyana's brow wrinkled with puzzlement. "He does not seem sad."

Richius took her hands and brought them to his lips. "He is happy for us. I told him we would marry."

"Yes," she said. "Soon. As soon as we can."

"We'll need a cunning-man or some priest. If we go with Lucyler to Falindar we can find one there."

"Yes," agreed Dyana. "Falindar. We will stay with Lucyler and let Shani learn from the wise men there."

Richius stepped out of her embrace. "It might not be for as long as you like, Dyana," he warned. "I've told you that already."

"I know," she said sadly. "But for a little time at least. Time for us to be together."

"Yes," said Richius. "Together."

He brought her close again and kissed her. They would be together until the storms blew them apart and the shouts of his bloodline called him back to war. But for now, Aramoor was a lifetime away, and her kiss was an eternity.

PEACE

From the Journal of Richius Vantran:

The death of Arkus still haunts me. It is like hearing that a god has died. Someday there will be songs about him, the ancient emperor who searched the world for magic so that he might steal another day.

But the real magic of Lucel-Lor is gone now. And I will miss Tharn profoundly. We were not so different, he and I. We both loved Dyana. We both tried to save her. In the end, I think he loved me, too. Not like he loved Dyana, of course, but like he loved Voris and Kronin. He loved the fire in them, the grace. If he saw grace in me, then truly he was a sorcerer. But I have only one life to give, and cannot begin to repay the blood I have made flow. Tharn died saving me, exhausting himself to the point of ruin. Sabrina died for my foolishness, and Dinadin for my blindness. Even Voris and Kronin were swept up in my fate. If there are gods watching me, then I hope they remove this awful curse.

But for now we will have peace. Without the Run, Lucel-Lor will be sealed. Liss continues to prowl our shores, thirsty to sink more Naren ships, and the lions of Karlaz stand guard over us like concerned fathers. Lucyler says they fought bravely and I cannot doubt it, for never have I seen such magnificent beasts as those golden monsters of Chandakkar. Were I Arkus, perhaps I too would have thought them mystical. But like so much of Lucel-Lor they are only flesh and bone. Nothing here is as Arkus believed. I have seen magic and I cannot explain it, but I know it is not the burgeoning thing Arkus thought it to be. There was only one magician here, one man cursed or blessed by nature. Now that he is gone perhaps Nar will leave this land in peace.

But I know there can be no peace for me. Biagio will not suppose me dead. He is the Roshann, and the Roshann is everywhere. There will be assassins coming, and this valley will not be safe for us. Even with Jarra as warlord, Biagio will look here for me. Falindar, too. So we are without a home, my little family, but we will survive. Somewhere in this vast land there is a hiding place for us. Somewhere Shani can grow without Nar's shadow stalking her.

Yet these are worries for another day. We have weeks yet, my family and I, my beautiful "kafife." For now I will let the Lissens worry about Nar. The pull of Liss is strong in me, but I yearn for at least a taste of peace. Biagio will have to find us first, and that will not be easy for him. These Triin have made me crafty. I am Kalak. I am the Jackal of Nar.

ABOUT THE AUTHOR

John Marco is an avid fan of military history and literature, and spends much of his free time in bookstores. Prior to writing his first novel, *The Jackal of Nar,* he worked in various industries including aviation, computer technology, and home security. Now he writes full time from his home on Long Island, where he is currently at work on the second book in the Tyrants and Kings series.